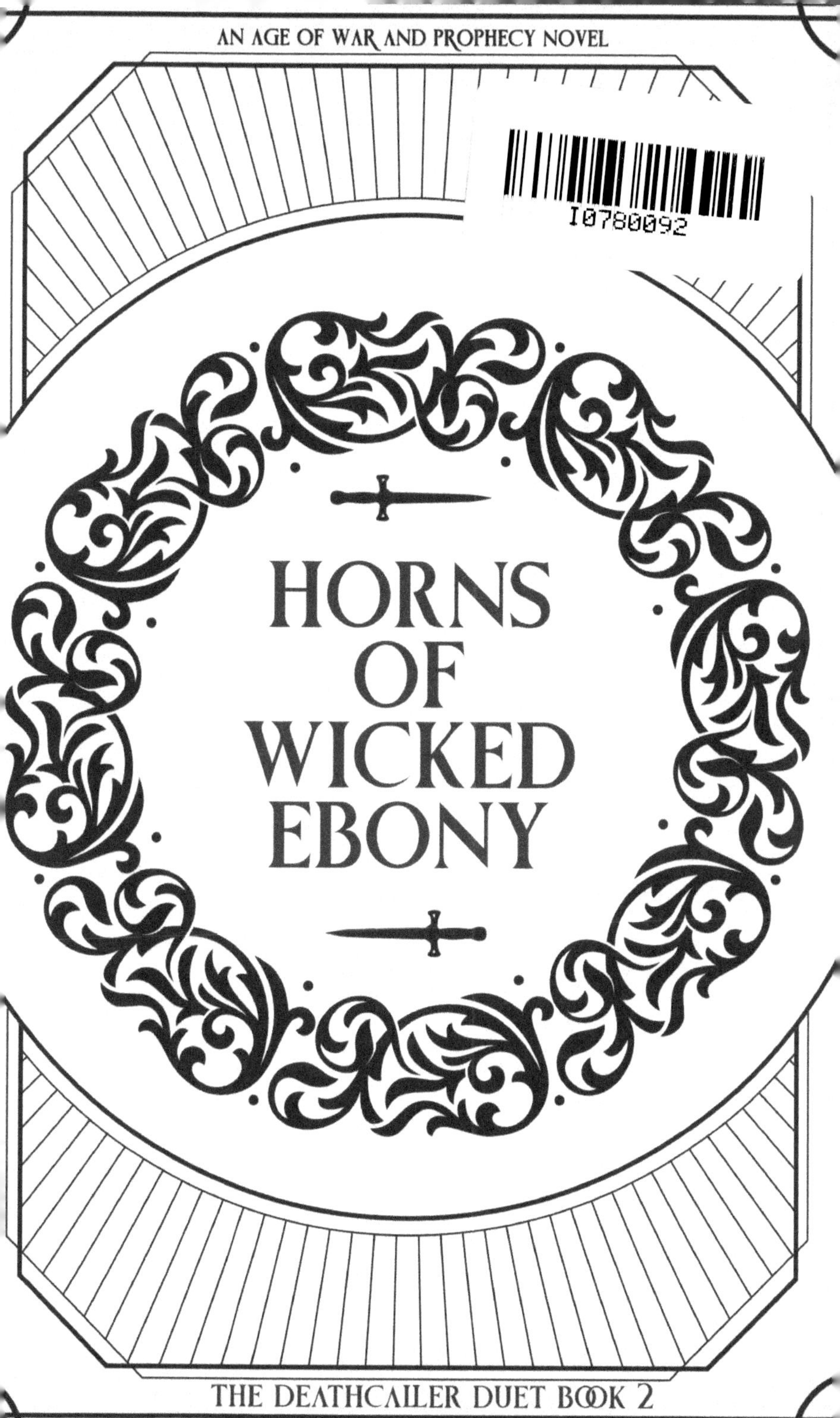

AN AGE OF WAR AND PROPHECY NOVEL

I0780092

HORNS
OF
WICKED
EBONY

THE DEATHCALLER DUET BOOK 2

ISBN 979-8-9915584-7-1 (paperback)

ISBN 979-8-9915584-6-4 (e-book)

Book cover by Beholden Book Covers

Published by The Lehotzky Group LLC

www.laceylehotzky.com

Eloi
Hatha Islands
Sivy
THE CONTINENT OF KELETI
N

Lutsk
Fured
ALA MOUNTAINS
Uzhhorod
Stryi

CONTENT ADVISORY

An Age of War and Prophecy is a sprawling, interconnected epic romantasy series. Each book (or duet) features its own romance arc. However, the central fantasy plotline—the war between Angels and Demons—unfolds across the entire series. That means individual books may end with unresolved threads in the overarching war plot. This is intentional. Think of each book as a thread in an intricate tapestry: you'll need to follow the full series to witness the ultimate fate of these realms.

If you're reading solely for the resolution of the fantasy plot, please know it is an intricate, high-tension arc that requires full series commitment. But if you're here for dark, soul-shattering romance, high-stakes choices, and a story that builds toward a climax worthy of the Goddess and the Fates, you're in the right place.

The Great War between the Angels and Demons deals with genocidal intent and the religious fanaticism driving it. There is no clear good or bad side, so if you are unable to live in the gray, An Age of War and Prophecy is not for you.

The Deathcaller Duet also explores religion as a means of

social control, akin to the Handmaid's Tale by Margaret Atwood.

If reading about women being treated as second-class citizens, forced to carry children they do not want, and forced to wear clothing to hide themselves will trigger you, do not continue reading.

The following trigger warning list is not exhaustive. The most up to date version can be found on my website.

Graphic violence, including extensive torture and dismemberment

Genocidal war

Death of loved ones

Religious trauma & fanaticism (think Handmaid's Tale)

Mentions of rape and sexual assault

Mentions of physical & mental abuse

Panic attacks & PTSD flashbacks

Nightmares

The sexually explicit content contains: primal play, shadow play, blood play, and punishment.

An Age of War and Prophecy
Reading Guide

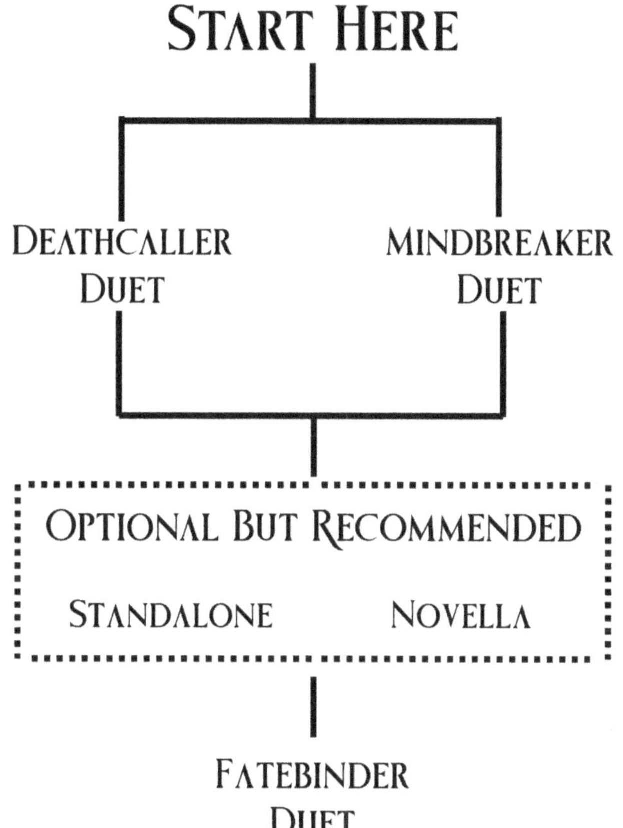

Fatebinder #2 is the Final book of the series featuring all characters & their HEA

Regarding the people,
religion, army, and most
noble houses of the
Demons. . .

The Demon Nobility

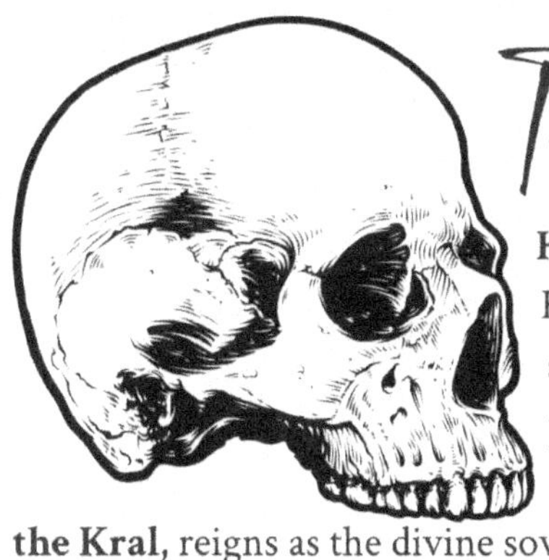

House Vrak rules the Demon Realm through its three surviving cousins, each presiding over a distinct domain of power. **Xannirin, the Kral,** reigns as the divine sovereign. **Kiira, the High Priestess**, shepherds the faith and interprets the will of the Fates. **Rokath, the Halálhívó,** commands the army and safeguards the realm through war.

The Demons worship the **three Fates** and offer daily blood sacrifices to earn their favor. **The Weaver** threads each Demon's life path. **The Giver** bestows magic upon the worthy. And **the Reaper** curses those who blaspheme or stray from the Fates' design.

Together, the cousins have shaped **Demon doctrine**: that the Fates' weavings are sacrosanct and cannot be resisted; that males are bound to act as instruments of that design, while females are vessels in service to it; that the Realm's survival depends upon an ever-growing population born in the Kral's name; and that the Angels must be slain before they succeed in exterminating the Demons.

Though Xannirin's authority is absolute, the **noble houses** retain considerable influence. The **Nayúr** stand highest among them, their **birtok** situated closest to the capital. Beneath them

are the **Kormánzó**, whose **vidék** lie scattered across the distant north and south.

The Demon Armies

The Halálhívó rides at the head of the **Demon forces**, aided by two **Hadvezér**. Military rank is determined by merit and Fates-gifted power. Beneath the Hadvezér serve the **Parancsok**, followed by the **Százados**, and finally the **Vezető**, the lowest tier of officers.

    Rokath's title derives from his feared **Deathcaller gift**, which allows him to reanimate the fallen on the battlefield and reinforce his lines with warriors who feel no pain. **Xannirin's Speaking** ability has made him a master politician and propagandist. His ventures with the spirits of other worlds ultimately inspired his claim to all of Keleti. **Kiira** is the only Demon in history to wield the gift of **Sight**, granting her direct communion with the Fates and a view into their weavings.

    Thus, when the Demons declare war, it is framed not as aggression, but as necessity—sanctioned by the Fates and demanded by survival. There is no choice; only obedience.

Demon Eye Colors

A DEMON'S EYE COLOR DETERMINES THE STRENGTH OF THEIR MAGIC. THE DARKER THE COLOR, THE MORE POWER THEY POSSESS.

BLOOD

CARMINE

APPLE

SCARLET

CRIMSON

CARDINAL

PRONUNCIATION GUIDE

Assyria – uh - seer - ee - uh
Banand – bah - nahnd
Bassi – bah - see
Birtok – beer - toke
Daarx – dahrks
Dromak – dro - mack
Fured - fure - ed
Grem – grim
Halálhívó - halal - hiv - o
Hadvezér – had - vez - ere
Ishim – ee - sheem
Issaraeth – iss - uh - ray - eth
Izgath – is - gath
Izzenna – ih - zen - nuh
Jaku – yak - ooo
Kiira – kira
Kohszak – kohz - zahk
Kormánzó – core - man - zo
Kraskiv – krah - skiv
Kral - crahl

Lutsk - luh - tsk
Maariya – mah - ree - yah
Myrza – meer - zah
Nayúr – nigh - ur
Olrus – ole - russ
Padisa – pah - dee - sah
Parancsok – paran - choke
Trol – troll
Rapp – wrap
Rokath – roe - kath
Stryi – stree
Sylaira – see - lair - uh
Százados – sah - zah - dosh
Ustlyak – oost - lee - ack
Uzadaan – ooze - ah - dahn
Uzhhorod – oosh - hor - ode
Vaeron – vay - ron
Vezető – vez - ehtt - too
Vidék – vee - deck
Vokkia – voh - kee - uh
Xannirin – zan - eer - in
Zahal – zah - hahl
Zeec – zeke
Zurronar - zurr - oh - nar

DEATHCALLER DUET PLAYLIST

I'll Make a Man Out of You - Peyton Parrish
NUMB - Ryan Oakes
Like a Villain - Bad Omens
Blake Hole - We Came As Romans
Right Now - Fire From The Gods
Just Pretend - Bad Omens
Reincarnate - Motionless In White
Disguise - Motionless In White
Face to Face - Citizen Soldier
Kryptonite (Reloaded) - Jeris Johnson
Chokehold - Sleep Token
The Safety of Disbelief - Light The Torch
The Worst In Me - Bad Omens
Sign Of Life - Motionless In White
Always - Saliva
The Diary of Jane - Breaking Benjamin
I Hate Everything About You - Three Days Grace
A Grave Mistake - Ice Nine Kills
Sinner - Of Virtue
Carnivore - STARSET

When The Darkness Comes - Jeris Johnson
Rain - Sleep Token
Alkaline - Sleep Token
Iris - DIAMANTE, Breaking Benjamin

https://open.spotify.com/playlist/7xckoeJ5s89yB3kwmTzyvO?
si=MBVcH0NrTV66iX1e4QO5oA

To the women who were silenced, softened, and shamed for their power. Who dared to desire, dared to destroy, and dared to love. Let them call you wicked. Let them bleed for it.

***

PROLOGUE

Three Centuries Earlier

S harp spice overpowered the metallic tang of blood as the three cousins sat in a potent silence. The pot of soup rolled to a low boil, so much like the simmering tension building on their continent. All were reeling from the occurrences of late while they waited for their dinner. In the lifespan of a Demon, it was merely a blink. Yet, so much had changed, and needed to continue to change, to save their race.

The Angels had increased the frequency of their attacks since Koron Stadiel slaughtered his competitors to seat himself on the Angel throne. The Kral and his two brothers had stood by while more and more skirmishes took place. His nephew with the tattooed head knew better than anyone just how bloodthirsty the Angels were. The latest attack was what had him calling the others to meet in his palatial home in Uzhhorod.

As he looked down at his hands, bits of dried ruby flaked off. He hadn't bathed yet, wanting the two to see the full impact of what he had endured. They both eyed his blood-soaked form as he reached for a glass of scale—a spicy alcohol that he both loved and rarely indulged in—and drank it to the dregs.

"The time has come, Xannirin. We need you on the throne," he said with a hiss once he finished.

Xannirin didn't tear his gaze away from the boiling soup, merely sat with numb detachment. Bits of his long hair had come loose from its band, and he made no move to clear them from his face. He had known this day was coming—after all, they had been planning this since that fateful day their fathers had forced Rokath to kill their friend.

That it was finally here was still a shock to him.

Their female cousin shifted in her seat, rearranging the sweep of her dress. Like everything she wore, it was feminine, flirty, and showed off her tan skin. She pinned the bloody, broody warrior with a hard stare. "Will you make it hurt, Rokath?"

"Aye, Kiira. They deserve it," Rokath rumbled. Her father had beaten Kiira to the brink of death only a week prior. The bruises on her ribs, arms, and face were still a fat purple. Sweeping his attention over the marks made him grind his teeth again. His uncle's actions had only further solidified his plan to slaughter the three eldest members of House Vrak.

Rokath was protective by nature, and anyone who hurt those he deeply cared for faced his infamous wrath. Even now, all the nobility was firmly aware of just how cruel he could be if pressed the wrong way.

It was still far better than their fathers' tempers.

Xannirin finally lifted his gaze from the steam. "We need to talk about the changes we want to implement upon my ascension. It's better to hash them out now before I am crowned rather than after people have settled into the new regime."

Then, he pinned Kiira with a serious look. "I want to elevate you to High Priestess."

Their cousin flashed her gaze between the two, brows pinching together as her mind worked over the proposition. Her mother—a commoner—had not been the wife of her father. Despite her shameful status, she'd grown up under his too-watchful eye with riches and a modicum of influence. To raise her to the position of High Priestess was an enormous leap.

"But I'm a bastard," she protested, like she could sway Xannirin when it sounded like he'd already made up his mind. "I can't possibly accept the position."

"We'll bury your bloodline like we'll erase Rokath's name from common memory," Xannirin said, straightening and rolling out his shoulders.

"I don't think that's possible," she replied with a frown. "Besides, I'm not worthy."

"Well, I say you are. And I will be the Kral." A cunning smirk rose to his lips. "The three of us will become the three Fates that walk the earth."

Kiira's teeth raked over her bottom lip. "The Kral, the Halál-hívó, the High Priestess. The Speaker, the Caller, the Seer."

As a Seer, the Fates offered her direct access to their weavings, unlike the Angel Seers who only glimpsed what *could be* through their Goddess. She was the only Demon in recorded history to be given such a gift, the uniqueness similar to her cousins. Their fathers' powers were all duplicates of prior members of House Vrak.

"Exactly," Xannirin replied, leaning forward. Excitement sparked off him like the strike of a hammer against forged metal. "Our power, our story has to be as hallowed, as fearsome as the myth of the Fates themselves. You are the key to swaying the people to believe in us like they believe in the Weaver, the Giver, and the Reaper."

Across from him, Rokath shifted in his seat. Attention was not something he handled well. He much preferred to remain private about his life and his accomplishments. To be thrust into the notice of the masses was not something he desired. Every action picked apart by clueless, primped nobles with nothing better to do. Every decision questioned by those lacking the knowledge to comment on the matter at hand. Every set of eyes on him, judging, seeking weaknesses or shortcomings.

No, he'd rather remain in the shadows.

Another smile pressed Xannirin's lips into a wicked curve. "Have I told you about my most recent encounter?"

"You went into the beyond again?" Rokath groused, reaching for the half-empty bottle of the spicy alcohol and pouring himself another glass. Irritation nipped at him as he recalled how many days it had taken for his cousin to return to their world on his previous trip. He'd made Xannirin promise never to use his Speaking powers again without telling him first.

Clearly, he'd gone against Rokath's request.

"I did," he said slowly, gauging Rokath's reactions. By the tense set of his jaw, Xannirin knew he was angry. But he didn't care. His cousin would let go of the transgression eventually. Especially with the information he had gleaned.

"And I know exactly how we're going to beat back the Angels."

That seemed to cool some of the embers of his rage, as Xannirin had predicted.

"How?" Rokath asked with no inflection whatsoever, but the stillness of his posture told Xannirin he'd captured his interest.

Xannirin spoke of his experience with a great king from another world who conquered vast swaths of territory. Rokath and Kiira listened with rapt attention, asking questions here and there. When he finished, Kiira slumped in her seat, while Rokath rubbed the stubble across his jaw.

"So we declare war on the Angels then?" Rokath clarified, his head tilting ever so slightly to the side.

"Not quite. We're not ready for that yet. It's true that Koron Stadiel will not stop until all Demons are dead, but for now he can be mitigated. First, we need the nobles on our side. They have far more influence in the countryside than we do, and they'll help us shape society to serve the end goal. Then, we start bolstering our defenses," Xannirin explained, stealing the bottle of scale from Rokath and splashing it into his cup.

"And what is that?" Kiira asked after sipping from her wine glass.

Xannirin laced his fingers behind his head and leaned back. "What better way to protect the Demon race than to conquer Keleti for ourselves?"

The question hung in the air like smoke—stifling, inescapable, and already clouding their futures.

"For that to happen, we need more bodies," Rokath growled. Their fathers had allowed the military to shrink dramatically while they ruled, preferring to spend coin on their own indulgences while the populace suffered. Poverty had bloomed. The people were growing restless. None of that would serve Xannirin's ambitions.

"Which is where Kiira comes in." Xannirin returned his attention to their cousin. His heart twisted as the embers high-lighted the split in her lip. Like Rokath, he wanted to protect her from further harm. "As High Priestess, she spins tales about the Fates. She leads spiritual life in the Demon Realm. She can encourage more marriages and more coupling to produce more offspring. By the time we're ready to launch a full-scale war, you'll have the bodies you need to lead the entire army, Rokath.

And we'll have high-powered nobles to maintain order in conquered territories."

While he didn't head their forces—yet—Rokath had studied military strategy since his first day at the academy as a youngling. He'd always had a mind for it, which complimented his cousin's cunning and manipulation perfectly. Rokath raised a brow, crinkling the inked snake fang that stretched onto his temple. "You'd want me in charge?"

"Who else?" Xannirin said. The legs of his chair smacked against the ground. "Come on, we've whispered of this for decades. Once you kill our fathers, we will have snatched all powers for ourselves. Let's make it happen. Starting with society. Kiira, what do you say?"

Kiira blew out a long breath, twisting the end of her long, straight, hair around her finger. "What exactly do you have in mind?"

Xannirin grasped her free hand in his and gave it a squeeze. "The Demons need to worship the Fates with the fervor the Angels worship the Goddess. They need to venerate us to the point where they trust what we say no matter what. In return, we'll give them a better life. More food. More coin."

"You want worship, not devotion. That's not faith, not as we practice it now. That's obedience," Kiira pointed out, withdrawing and sinking back into her seat.

"We need their obedience to make the necessary changes to protect us—to protect them," Xannirin argued. "Tell her, Rokath."

Their warrior-cousin, still covered in blood, nodded. "He's right. In the military, too many questions delay action, and that often comes with severe consequences. Implicit compliance can be the difference between life and death."

Xannirin only grew more animated as he pounded out his

other points, fueled by Rokath's affirmation. "Females will be worshiped for their ability to bear children for our future. They won't need to work, merely embrace their femininity. They'll be taken care of, placed on a pedestal. Protected from all the evils of this world."

Kiira stiffened more and more as he continued speaking of their new society. Finally, she sat forward, interrupting the future Kral. "I don't like how this is unfolding. Surely there is another way than removing autonomy from females?"

"Don't frame it that way, Kiira," Xannirin crooned, snatching her hand back into his. "We're empowering them in a different way. Asking them to contribute to our collective future in a way only they can."

Kiira dragged her palms out of her cousin's, looking across the steam at Rokath's blurred form. "What do you think?"

He rubbed his temples, drawing her attention to the blood caked on his scalp. "Xannirin's points are solid. As much as I don't like it either, I don't see a way to do it more quickly. Look at how fast Koron Stadiel turned the Angel race into a bunch of overzealous insects."

In fact, it had scarcely been a century and their militant fanaticism had rooted itself in society deeper than the massive trees in the Eső Forest.

Kiira was silent for many minutes, staring into the distance. When it was clear she wouldn't soon speak, Rokath and Xannirin took the raw food around them and dipped it into the boiling liquid. Spice wafted, meat hissed, vegetables wilted, all while they waited for their third to shift, to move, to do anything other than sit with an utterly blank expression.

Finally, she lifted her glass and drained it. When she placed it on the table, the clang shattered the quiet. "I have conditions."

"Name them," Xannirin said without hesitation.

"First, bastards acquire full rights of their father's houses. Second, priestesses will remain unmarried." This caveat she added should any female wish to avoid contact with males altogether. "Third, I retain equal status with the two of you." She lifted her chin and straightened in her seat. With her body decorated in bruises, she exuded power with the posture. "I will never be beneath a male again, vulnerable to his whims. You will not force me to marry against my will. You will allow me to build a temple in equal splendor to Gyor Palace." She continued to list off her requirements, refusing to bend under the males' heavy stares.

"You have all of them," Xannirin pronounced immediately upon the end of her soliloquy. "However, I need to approve any marriage you should want to make. Same for you, Rokath, though I doubt it will ever come to that." Kiira opened her mouth to protest, but Xannirin cut her off. "I don't expect to need to intervene for you either, Kiira, but I must also protect House Vrak from outside harm. Someone far beneath our station would not suit the High Priestess. You will be a Goddess to the Demon race, remember?"

Kiira huffed, crossing her arms over her chest. Beneath the table, her foot swung in an erratic rhythm as she considered the amendment to her condition. She stilled, then returned her attention to her cousins. "Fine. We have a deal?"

Xannirin picked up a wickedly sharp knife, letting the edge flash in the low light. "Aye." With it, he sliced into his palm, then offered it to Kiira. She did the same before they clasped hands and spoke the words to solidify their alliance. Rokath drew a dagger from his thigh and drew ruby to the surface of his skin, making the same oath to each of them.

Once their wounds had begun to heal, Xannirin poured another round of drinks. Then, he made a daring toast. "To the future of the Demon Race. To us, who will rule as Gods. And to a painful death to our fathers."

The three smacked their glasses against the table with resounding thuds, the effects of which wouldn't be felt for centuries to come.

PART
ONE

I

ASSYRIA

Pillars of twisting flame speared into the sky, sending the souls of the fallen soldiers onto their next lives. My nose had long since numbed to the scent of scorched flesh. I paused atop a rocky ridgeline, still stained ruby from the slaughter a few days prior, and surveyed the scene we left behind.

Nausea churned my gut at the sheer size of the blazing war camp. So many dead; so many sacrificed so I could live. But my resolve to whet my own blade in blood, my determination to seek vengeance, hardened with each step, with each glance at Rokath's broken hands.

The silver stakes Zaph had used to pin him in place weighed heavily in my pack. I didn't carry them as relics. No, I had plans for them. A promise to keep—for myself if not for Rokath.

Day by day while we worked, I imagined the moment I'd drive them into the fucking Angel. They wouldn't lock down his magic like they had Rokath's; that was what the bronze blades were for. But the pain as I separated the bones of his hands with them would be enormous. Especially since Rokath had promised that he'd torture him—excruciatingly slowly—for daring to take me from him.

"The bodies will continue to burn for a while," my mate told me, coming to a stop and following my line of sight. "With the number of them, probably until we reunite with the rest of the army."

Rokath tugged on Blaeze's reins, leading the small wagon over bumpy gravel and blood-caked sand. The earth crunched beneath his boots and the wheels. Rokath was enormous, built like the craggy Skala Mountains at our back, but now, he carried far more than his powerful presence. Zeec, still too weak to walk, hung limp against his chest. Another pack on his back, the worn leather one falling apart at the seams, held our clothes. In his still-healing hand, he hefted a bag brimming with food.

"Let me carry something else," I offered, jogging to catch up with them, Grem at my side. Barrels of water filled the cart, braced against a few more of our belongings and the throne of bones. We each hauled as much as we could to save Blaeze from pulling any more weight.

Rokath shook his head, burgundy eyes focused on the path ahead. "This is my penance for the deaths of nearly a third of my army. And I will not risk more injury to your shoulder."

Molten anger flared down our bond, burning hotter than the pyres at our backs. Yet tumbling with it was a heavy mix of guilt and trepidation.

What would the reactions be when we returned alone?

In silence, we trudged past the remnants of the Angels' camp. The sun beat down with an almost judgmental air throughout the rest of the day. Not for the first time, I wished we'd been able to find more horses than just Blaeze. A stampede of hoofprints led away from the camp, so at least I knew that none had fallen to an Angel blade. My reliable mount had wandered back the day before we decided to leave, three crows resting atop his back.

They'd squawked and flown away as I'd raced to his side and thrown my arms around his neck. I'd never been more relieved in my life—except for maybe when we knew Zeec would live. His reappearance meant we'd be able to survive longer in the inhospitable Paks Desert while we attempted to rejoin the larger force.

We rose with the sun, opting to break our fast later in the day. I resisted the call of my insistent thirst for as long as I could. We packed dozens of skins onto our bodies and in our bags, yet with five thirsty mouths, especially the one pulling most of our belongings, it disappeared faster than ever before.

Days passed, and finally, Zeec joined Grem on the ground, easing some of Rokath's burden.

More followed, and the pain pulsing down our bond lessened as Rokath's hands continued to heal and my shoulder ceased aching. Yet we remained silent in our march, our thoughts drifting, drifting, drifting...

At night, Rokath held me in his arms like I was the last star in the sky, and without me the heavens above us would collapse in on themselves. Which with the way he continued to care for me at the expense of himself, I knew was true. Despite the dry, rocky earth on which we slept night after night, he drifted off with ease.

The end of the seventh day arrived, taking with it the final drop of our water. Rokath let me have the last of it. My lips cracked and bled any time I attempted to move them.

Any conversation we attempted to have was kept purely mental for that reason.

The following morning, we stumbled across a trickle of a stream and managed to refill all our skins, though it was slow progress. The barrels we abandoned completely, barely managing to fill half of one with the odd angle we had to hold it beneath the flow.

The two of us, plus the dogs and Blaeze, were haggard, hungry, and desperate to find the rest of the army.

Surely when the other Hadvezér's ravens go unanswered, they'll send someone in search of us.

Rokath rested on his back and stared at the brilliant, vast expanse of sky night after night. He told me he'd learned to navigate by the stars during his time at the military academy in Fured, but with our slow progress and the endless wasteland in front of us, I began to wonder if we'd gotten lost somewhere along the way.

Rather than voice my concern—mentally or otherwise—I remained silent. Rokath already knew, and I didn't want to pile onto his guilt.

The ninth night swallowed us in hot, arid air. Dust blustered around us as we collapsed against a rocky outcropping. At least by the way the sun had disappeared over the Skala Mountains at our back, we were still trudging in the right direction. But whether we'd angled ourselves too far north or south was a different story entirely.

At my feet, the dogs panted, their tongues dry and fur matted with dust. Blaeze sank to his knees, then flopped over on his side. I wondered if he'd ever get up again or if we'd have to leave him out here.

Rokath squeezed his eyes shut and tipped his head back, waiting for white pinpricks to blink into existence. With no energy to speak, we sat in stillness as night settled with an ominousness that unsettled my stomach. Like if we didn't find the rest of the army the next day, that might actually be our last night together.

I wanted to laugh at the irony of it all.

Zaph would have snatched the most massive victory for the Angels since the war had begun. Killing fifty thousand men, then not even having to lift a finger to end the Halálhívó and his mate.

The memory of the moment our bond snapped into place flitted through my addled mind. What I wouldn't give to return to that day, and the days after. The luxury of Gyor Palace. A soft bed. The *food*.

Something shimmered in the distance, like the heat that licked over the sand in the hottest hours of the afternoon.

I was really starting to lose it if I was seeing things in the dark too.

Slumping into my mate, I closed my eyes, seeking what comfort he was capable of offering. He pressed a tender kiss to my temple that felt more like an apology, a goodbye, than anything.

"Are we going to die out here?" I asked him through our mental connection.

"I will not let you die," he growled back with more force than I'd been capable of even days ago.

My head lolled forward, and I snapped to attention again. Vision blurred with sleep, I curled into a ball at Rokath's feet. He reached for me, stroking his fingers over my tangled, tattered braid.

"I am so, so sorry, Assyria," he said. His expression was tortured, as if seeing me so weak and close to death was the greatest pain he'd ever experienced.

"Why?"

"For everything. For not loving you as I should have immediately. For getting us lost out here. For not protecting you from the Angels in the first place. I should have trained you from the beginning. I should have done so many things differently."

"Stop talking like we're going to die out here when you told me we wouldn't," I bantered back, but the playful bite I was aiming for fell short.

We lapsed into quiet as darkness closed in.

A weak bark jolted me awake. I hadn't even realized I'd fallen asleep again. Grem and Zeec shot to their feet on either side of me, hackles raised. Rokath still sagged against the rock. I nudged him with my foot, and with a groan, he opened his eyes.

Somehow, I managed to turn myself around, and then I spotted that shimmering movement again. Energy spiked through me at the thought that Zaph might have followed us out here to witness our demise. His light magic danced over the barren expanse, illuminating our misery from afar. But as quickly as it appeared, it dissipated, along with the remnants of my reserves.

Great, the dogs are losing it too.

But then, a fire flickered, highlighting studs glinting in someone's face.

Studs glinting in someone's face.

My brain, starved and slow, struggled to piece the male together. Rokath did, faster than me, and was on his feet, though he swayed so violently I was certain he'd collapse.

The beat of hooves against the hard-packed earth quickened, and then a rider was upon us, leaping from his horse and racing to our sides.

"Rokath! Assyria! Thank the Fates you're okay," the person exclaimed. From his side, he pulled two skins and shoved them into our hands.

I wasted no time in wrapping my lips around the lid and chugging. The cool, crisp liquid was *everything.*

Rokath yanked the waterskin away from my mouth. "You'll get sick," he rasped.

A moment later, all the liquid I'd just consumed heaved up from my gut. Pitching to the side, I retched all over the dusty ground.

"Reaper, what happened to you two?" the person asked, and then I finally recognized the voice—one who had kept me company many nights before Rokath finally accepted our situation. Who had helped me win back my mother's ring while playing cards. Who had cheered us on as we navigated our complex feelings for one another.

Rapp.

If I had tears to shed, I would have cried at the sight of him. Wiping my mouth, I turned back to Rapp, one of Rokath's Hadvezér and his best friend. Squatting down, he tipped water into the mouths of Grem and Zeec. Blaeze too picked his head up, and Rapp went to him next, offering my faithful mount what he so desperately needed.

Rokath sipped slowly, and I mimicked him, my stomach still churning.

After a few more pulls, he rolled his parched lips. "The Angels killed everyone but us, Rapp." While his voice normally held a low gravel, days in the desert without sustenance had taken it to new depths.

The torch Rapp planted in the ground beside him flickered ominously. "How?" he asked, his dark eyebrows shooting up his forehead. While he normally would have made some joke about Rokath being unbeatable, we were clearly too worn out for such an exchange.

"They took Assyria." Rokath glanced at me, a mix of rage and guilt furrowing his brow. "Their bargain was her life or theirs."

Rapp blew out a long breath, running a hand over the hair on the top of his head. "The rest of the army isn't too far from here, camped outside Lutsk. Let's get you there and then you can tell us everything."

The animals now satisfied, he tucked the skins into his belt. Grabbing Blaeze's reins, he attempted to coax him to his feet. But my mount's legs wobbled, and shadows sprang from Rapp's hands and wrapped around his belly. With the aid, my horse staggered upright, but his head hung, heavy and exhausted.

Rapp hitched him to the cart again while Rokath dragged forward, leaving thick boot marks in his wake. Seeing his friend struggling, Rapp raced to his side and shoved his shoulders under his arm.

Rokath shook his head. "Help Assyria," he croaked. Rapp did as he was told, like a good soldier, and swept my tiny, exhausted body into his arms. Despite the water, I barely had the energy to clamp my legs over his stallion's back. I swayed wildly, and my mate leaped to my side.

"I'm fine," I told him, even though I clearly was not. "You should ride."

He stepped closer and brushed the backs of his knuckles across my cheek. "I've endured worse hardships. Rest up there."

I didn't protest. Sinking down, I draped myself over the horse's neck for added support. Rokath took the reins, then tugged him forward. I nearly groaned as his back swayed from side to side, forcing my muscles to work.

Rapp did the same for Blaeze, assisting him in rolling the cart onward with more obsidian tendrils that blended with the night.

Once again, the only sound passed between our group was the crunch of dirt beneath the horses' hooves and the hounds' panted breaths.

Yet down our bond, Rokath's trepidation rose—louder than

the cawing of the three crows that flew overhead—with each step closer we took to the Demon army's encampment.

Because Rokath, the infamous Halálhívó with the power to call upon the dead to fight for him, would soon have to explain how fifty thousand of his males had perished under his command when he was supposed to be the most feared warrior in all of Keleti.

2

R💀KATH

The throne of angel bones dug into my backside as I waited for the moment I'd retake command of my forces. Yet I couldn't wrestle my attention away from my mate, still resting in our bed. Our return journey to the army had been a trying one, and yet she hadn't protested for a single moment.

She almost fucking died, and I hated myself for letting it come that close. My abhorrence for the Angels, my thirst for their blood had increased tenfold during our trek through the Paks Desert.

For days, we'd recuperated in secret—returning under the cover of darkness had been a blessing. In that time, I'd debriefed Rapp and Trol on what had occurred after we parted ways.

I'd told them of my plan to include females in the army too. I meant what I said to Assyria before we departed: the army needed to change. We could easily increase our numbers, and besides that, they could focus on fighting the Angel females while the males saved their energy for the bigger fighters. With our newly trained magic-focused units too, our force would be unstoppable.

And I was ready for Assyria to be my true equal.

Rapp had an immediate friendship with my mate and had witnessed our relationship from the very beginning, so the changes were unsurprising to him. Trol had taken a little convincing, but after the heavy losses we'd suffered, he'd come around quickly.

My initial idea had been to return to Uzhhorod, the capital of the Demon Realm, with a handful of squads and speak with High Priestess Kiira and Kral Xannirin, my cousins and co-conspirators, about another conscription. Together, we'd shaped Demon society into a devoted, faithful, and obedient flock. As much as I wanted to have the conversation about the future of our military in person, time was currently our enemy as much as those white-winged insects.

Rapp had suggested that we ask Kiira to pull exclusively from the priestesses, since they wouldn't question her command. Her storytelling was divine, and whatever she proclaimed was taken as fact—whether or not it was true. Trol solidified our plan when he proposed that we seek out only the high-powered ones and send them to Fured for training, along with the others we'd gathered months before.

Trol managed the masses of soldiers like a seasoned shepherd—fair, firm, and calculating, though he could be ruthless when necessary. He was more familiar with the lower-level grievances and politics that emerged from having such a large company. His opinion was that integrating a smaller group first would have a trickle down effect once the entire army was reunited.

Yet I still had some atoning to do, and I didn't want Assyria here to witness it. She was still so weak, even after days of rest. The pallor of her tan skin worried me as she continued to lay in our new bed. The dryness of her lips. Her cheekbones, sharpened by lack of food.

Shame like I'd never felt weighed heavily on me.

Whispers of my presence had grown like thorny weeds in a well-tended garden. Especially after no one else rejoined the larger group from the west. The questions had sharpened into why Assyria and I were the only ones to return and where the remainder of the males had gone.

Distracting them hadn't quelled the growing unrest.

Especially as the Angels—dug in on the opposite side of Lutsk—had kept to themselves since we'd reunited with the army.

Which was why we'd planned this gathering, so all the soldiers could hear me speak. So the rumors would dissipate. I drummed my fingers over the skull at the end of the arm of the throne, mentally rehearsing the speech I was set to give. Never had I feared addressing my soldiers, and yet this moment was the closest the emotion had come to breaking through my hardened walls.

A riot of voices outside tore me from my thoughts.

It is time.

I rose, plucking my helmet from the ground and securing it on my head. Horns of wicked ebony speared toward the sky, and two sockets in the black skull mask over my face allowed everyone to see my burgundy eyes.

I was dressed for battle, because this address would certainly require the full force of my presence. For centuries, I'd drilled certain beliefs into the army—namely that females didn't belong. Yet the revelation of fifty thousand soldiers' deaths would elicit the worst response. Especially when they learned why they would never return.

As I rolled my shoulders and blew out a long breath, movement in my periphery caught my attention. From the rear room,

Assyria emerged, wearing the leather armor I'd procured for her when she'd requested something more comfortable to ride in other than dresses.

Upon our return, I'd had all our clothing thoroughly cleaned, ensuring that not a single grain of sand remained in the fabric. Yet seeing her in something so standard issue gave me pause.

She needed more. She needed to *be* more if any of this was going to work.

Now was not the time to plan for that, though.

"What are you doing out of bed?" I asked her, though my tone was more concerned than chastising.

She strode forward, tucking her long hair behind her pointed ears. The rest tumbled freely to her waist, shiny and clean. Yet under her eyes, dark circles clung like purple reminders of her exhaustion.

"I'm here to stand beside you, as your mate. You don't have to face anything alone anymore, remember?" she quipped. Despite her fatigue, that snark remained.

The corners of my mouth twitched. I didn't know if I wanted to send her away to rest or to kiss her for choosing to join me.

Assyria must have sensed my internal battle because she huffed. "I think we're past the point of pretending that you can't let anyone in, that you can't show weakness to anyone. Maybe you don't show it to them, but you show it to me." Her voice remained strong and steady, and she offered me a fierce look that said she wasn't backing down.

Not like she ever did when it came to me.

A memory of our first meeting flashed through my mind. How she'd crossed her arms and refused to give me her name. Threatened to kill me or herself to end the situation the Fates had forced us into.

I fucking loved that fire in her.

My hands flexed at my sides as I weighed her words. Despite my instincts telling me to squash what I was feeling and hold the burden of everything onto my own, I peeled my fingers off the hilt of control and accepted what she was offering.

Because she was right.

"Keep doing this." I'd need her help to continue to correct this defensive behavior. To learn how to feel again.

"Deal," she said, stepping forward and flattening her palms on the metal plates covering my chest. "Just tell me what you need me to do, and I will do it."

"Stand by my side. Harsh words will fly, but don't let them affect you. Try your best to watch that smart mouth of yours," I told her, amusement threading my tone.

Her answering grin was full of mischief. "You know I've never been good at that."

"Precisely why I should send you back to our tent," I growled. Draping an arm around her shoulders, I steered her toward the map room.

"Don't you think it's funny you have such a temper, and I can't swallow my words?" she asked, a lightness to her tone aimed at soothing my fears.

"I don't think 'funny' is the word I'd use to describe it," I grumbled as we entered together. Rapp and Trol looked up from their conversation.

"Ready?" Rapp asked me, attention flickering to Assyria at my side.

"As I'll ever be." I tugged at the underside of my helmet, ensuring it was perfectly in place.

Nodding, he and Trol slipped outside, both releasing sharp whistles. The cacophony of noise died down instantly.

Beside me, Assyria squared her shoulders. She gave a small

dip of her chin, letting me know she was ready. Dragging in a breath, I straightened, towering above the ground. Then, I flung back the flap and stomped into the light.

To add an extra level of intimidation, I dove into the well of ebony shadows in my chest and pulled inky tendrils to my arms and feet. Assyria did the same, and together we settled onto the platform that always stood in the center of the war camp, demonstrating the depths of our Giver-blessed power together.

Rapp and Trol came to stand a few paces behind the two of us. All around, soldiers knelt in deference, though more than a few pairs of eyes bored into me, hints of distrust and hostility peeking through.

I noted their positions. They'd be the most difficult to convince and might require *additional* persuasion.

"Rise," I commanded, and like a wave, the males crested.

"This gossip about why I returned without my battalions stops now."

Furious whispers crackled through the crowd. I let out a low growl, magic tightening at my feet. "Anyone who dares speak again before I am finished will find themselves tied to the pole and preparing for a lashing."

Silence reigned.

I inhaled deeply, chest expanding against the metal plates, as I prepared to report what had occurred. "Your brothers fought bravely, beating those fucking fanatics back day by day and slaughtering them by the thousands. Until we reached a salt flat where the path narrowed."

The knock of my boots against the wood echoed in the space between my words as I walked a slow circle around the platform. Each section received equal measures of my attention.

And equal measures of my scrutiny.

"What I did not know was that the Angels have been

taking prisoners for a long time. These prisoners shared with the Angel leadership that I had brought a female along with me."

A voice caught my attention, and I tilted my head to the side, eyes narrowing on the offender. "Do you have something you wish to say?" I snarled in his direction.

Those around him took healthy steps back. His jaw clenched as he advanced. "I knew that fallen would only bring us trouble."

Heat licked its way up my spine. I snapped at the closest Százados. "Bring him here."

Without hesitation, the officer dragged him out of the crowd. As the male fought him, another Százados jumped in, and together they hauled him onto the platform.

"Secure him to the post." He wasn't the only dissenter, of that I was certain. But he would be the first to suffer.

Rapp, Trol, and Assyria stepped to one side while I grabbed the cane. Normally, I'd start with the nine-tailed whip, but I was going to put a stop to this here and now.

The Százados stripped him, leaving his back bare. Like a predator stalking its prey, I approached him. "That," I paused two steps from him, returning my attention to the spectators, "is my fucking mate."

A collective intake of breath swept through the camp.

I twisted back, letting the cane whistle through the air. Sweat broke out on the soldier's back. Then, I swung.

The crack resounded through the quiet. A red mark bloomed immediately. To his credit, the male didn't cry out or beg for a reprieve.

"And anyone who dares to speak ill of her will receive this same punishment."

The second blow landed with as much force as the first. Another welt appeared. More salt slicked off him as he tightened his grip on the leather straps. Assyria watched on, unflinching, as I delivered the blows.

"I apologize, Halálhívó. Had I known, I would not have made such an insinuation," he gritted out after the third strike.

"No, you wouldn't have." I landed two more blows in quick succession, and then motioned for the Százados to release him. He slumped in their arms as they dragged him back into formation.

I faced the crowd again, and Assyria returned to my side, arms crossed casually over her chest. "Does anyone else wish to speak?"

Only cold, stoic expressions greeted me.

"Good. Then I shall continue."

Keeping the cane in hand, I resumed my slow circle of the platform. "They took Assyria and offered me an exchange. Her life or theirs."

A moment passed. Then another. The males stared at me, and I started to think that the revelation was landing more like a dusting of sand and less like the strike of a hammer.

My delusion shattered a moment later, along with the silence. Anger, like an unstoppable wildfire, blazed in all directions. Shouts rang out, fingers pointed accusingly in my direction. Százados and Vezető yanked soldiers out of formation while Parancsok screamed at the remainder, trying to quell the unrest.

One male broke through the madness and stomped toward the platform. Instinctively, I surged closer to Assyria, magic coiling tight around my fists. Her expression never changed, but the darkness pooling around her tensed.

"Fifty thousand? Are you fucking serious? And you let them get away? What kind of leader are you?"

Obsidian threads shot forward and gripped his arms, dragging him to kneel at my feet.

"Who am I?" I bellowed, my voice ringing louder than the chaos and bringing it to heel. "I am your *master*, and I make the decisions for the entire army. The Fates chose *me* as the savior of the Demon race, blessing me with the power to call upon the dead to do my bidding. In fact, I am the *only* person to have been given such a gift in all our written history."

I let the words linger like smoke in the air. Through the slits in my helmet, I glared at each male restrained by his superior officers.

"I am the fucking Halálhívó."

The words fell like heavy blows, and the male trembled beneath my wrath. Staring at him, I threw a pointed question to those gathered. "Should I kill him now and call upon his dead body to remind you all what *exactly* I can do? Of who the fuck I am?"

"No, Halálhívó," voices rang out. Many more audibly swallowed.

This time, Rapp and Trol marched forward and secured the vocal oppositionist to the post. I let him wait there, wanting to finish my fucking proclamation before ensuring everyone was left with a searing memory of what would happen if they rebelled again.

"Should my mate have died, it would have crippled me for some time. While many of you appear to be incapable of thinking more than five minutes into the future, I am not. Saving our race from extermination is paramount. Those fifty thousand would have made a difference, certainly. It was why we'd worked so hard to swell the army's numbers. But without proper leadership, they could not have been used to the utmost effectiveness."

I dragged in a breath, preparing for yet another reaction.

"I shouldn't have to remind you all of the ambush that started this conflict. Of how I was the sole survivor. Because of the Angel's escalating attacks on our realm, their fervent desire to exterminate our race from this continent, we had no choice but to fight back. Winning the war is imperative to our collective survival. Which is why, going forward, we will allow females to join our ranks."

A single scoff reached my ears before I reacted. As more rose, so too did my shadows, whipping in all directions and yanking detractors forward. Thick ropes assisted me in pinning them to the ground as Rapp tossed his Binding magic like lassos.

I raised a single hand, darkness dripping from it, and all went still. "The decision has been made. I need no input from you. Furthermore," I held onto the silence, ensuring my words were sinking in, "my mate will be regarded with the same level of respect you would give me."

Assyria lifted her chin as the weight of thousands of stares settled on her. "She has demonstrated resilience and tenacity in equal measure to many soldiers. Should you treat her as less than...well you're about to witness what will happen."

This time, I switched the cane for the whip. The motherfucker needed to *bleed*.

The metal studs in the leather glinted in the sunlight as I brought my arm back. When the tails landed, they did so with a satisfying crack. Ruby welts bloomed on his skin as I dragged them away, though the shade wasn't close to the crimson one I sought.

Assyria's gaze burned into me, along with a heady sweep of lust down our bond. The same feeling ignited in me. Blood ran hot through my veins, spurred on by the knowledge that she loved how I defended her.

The lash whistled through the air as the second strike landed cleanly. The muscles in the male's neck bulged as he gritted his teeth around the pain. Tension eased from my shoulders as I offered him two more strikes, painting his back like an artist. Though there was nothing creative about my work; it was merely an expression of how fucking serious I was about maintaining order and control.

When his back flayed open on the sixth strike, I relented. Chest heaving, I lifted my gaze to all the watching soldiers, flicking slowly through the crowd. "Have I made myself clear?"

Thousands of salutes answered me. Though some were less enthusiastic than others, and many eyes still burned with fury. The lower ranking officers would see to those dissenters and ensure they complied.

I tossed the whip aside, and two Százados raced forward, removing the offender from my presence. Silence hung like a heavy fog as I continued to wield control over the army. To *show* them exactly who ruled here. No one dared speak. They barely dared *breathe*.

"Officers, ensure your units fully understand our new reality, and then report to the command center. You are dismissed."

Hushed whispers kindled like I'd struck a match. Assyria materialized beside me as we watched them depart, while Rapp and Trol trudged into the crowd, barking orders and roughing up naysayers. They ensured the soldiers knew we were a united front.

Many males passed by us, some narrowing their eyes on her, others looking like they wanted to spit at her feet. I took a half-step forward, and they flinched away as if I'd struck them. Satisfaction curled through me at the sight. The same emotion echoed down our bond.

"Who would have thought that you'd enjoy me punishing others in your name, little imposter?"

"Not me," she replied, her voice threaded with a hint of breathiness. *"I'd probably like it much better if they boasted white wings, though."*

"Shall I rip them from our enemies' backs and lay them at your feet?"

A heady wave of lust coursed down our bond. *"I think that would start to ease the pain of their actions."*

"Then I shall make you a throne of white feathers, mate. So you can sit alongside me while we taunt them with their failures."

We faced each other then, lightning crackling between us. But then the darkness under her eyes and the paleness to her lips were undeniable. She was still far too weak for what I wanted to do to her.

"Come, let me take care of you," I murmured. "You need to rest."

"So do you," she replied, closing her mouth to suppress a yawn.

"You're right. I'll leave the officers for tomorrow. We're not going anywhere anytime soon, not with the soldiers only a moment away from exploding."

She nodded, and then we left the platform for the command center. Most of the males had dispersed back to their squads' section of camp, leaving the center at its normal volume of passing males.

I spoke briefly with Rapp, directing him to send the Százados and Vezető back out once they reported to him with instructions to return in the morning.

Then, I took Assyria back to our quarters and curled around her, listening to the steady ebb and flow of her breathing as she fell asleep again. The worst part was done, but we were still a long way from where I envisioned us going. And Assyria, my tiny, fiery, brilliant mate, was at the center of it all.

3

R⏣KATH

Soft filtering light and the slow rise of voices drew me to wakefulness. A quiet groan slipped out of me as I glanced at the bedside clock and discovered the hour. Assyria still slept, both her hands tucked under her pillow and her bare back facing me.

As gently as I could, I pressed a kiss to her shoulder blade, then slid from the bed and donned my armor. Grem and Zeec cracked red eyes but made no move to follow me as I tiptoed toward the exit. Instead, they waited until I was half out into the early morning to join Assyria.

She'd spoiled them, but I couldn't be mad. So long as they were with her, she would be protected.

And now, more than ever, her safety was paramount.

The war tent awaited me, along with whatever horseshit the day would bring. Rapp met me halfway there, a dark cloud clinging to him. "Morning. The Százados wish to make their opinions known."

"Fuck," I muttered, pinching the bridge of my nose.

He shifted his weight, glancing around us to ensure we were alone. "They will support you publicly, of course, but a group of them were in the command center yesterday expressing their desire to use their audience with you to be heard." Though his tone was steady, an undercurrent of agitation remained.

"They can express whatever they want, but that won't alter my plans." I rolled my shoulders, trying to loosen the knot of tension in my neck.

"I know. Just hear them out, though. Make them feel like you are taking what they're saying under advisement," Rapp sighed. He'd been around them while I retreated the previous day. He'd led his faction alone for weeks, chasing down a third of the Angel army. Trol too. They knew the sentiment of our soldiers better than I did.

Rapp was one of the only people I trusted in this world. He was also one of the only people who could call me out on my shit and not face dire consequences.

Gripping the rim of my armor and yanking it off my body, I made some space to breathe. This part of the transformation wasn't going to be easy. Fuck, it was so much better when fear was my method of rule. Though I'd always allowed others to speak because I wasn't stupid enough to believe I could foresee everything, I didn't like the idea of those so far beneath me thinking they held a modicum of influence. Not when these next few moves in this complex game of war held the difference between life and death.

"Fine, let's go," I grumbled. Together, we entered through the rolled-back rear flaps, first passing through a storage section before delving deeper into the space. I stopped short when I beheld my throne. The red coating of dust that had clung to it was gone, and the white bones now gleamed.

"Had it cleaned yesterday since everyone knew you were back," Rapp shrugged, shouldering past me. A seed of appreciation bloomed inside me. I'd left it dirty since having someone polish it was akin to admitting I was present. That Rapp had seen to it while I was exhausted from my speech made my heart twist in a way that was still becoming familiar.

Voices whispered through the canvas dividing us from the adjacent space. Trol's gruff voice was among them.

I went to my chair of bones and took a seat, arranging myself so I appeared to be lounging and bored. If I'd learned anything from Xannirin, it was that these types of appearances were important and provided strategic advantages. In our centuries of friendship, Rapp had learned that too.

Once I was settled, I dipped my chin in his direction. "Bring them in."

He pulled back the curtain separating the two sections, revealing me. Every Parancsok and Százados in the camp was present—a number that had shrunk significantly with the deaths of my battalions. They fell to one knee, resting their foreheads on their arms in deference to their leader. Only Trol remained standing, and he dipped his chin in subtle acknowledgement of what I was about to do.

"Halálhívó," they said in unison.

At least they still held that level of respect.

"Rise," I told them, tone cold and emotionless.

The first did, taking a few tentative steps forward. "Halálhívó," he began, pausing to glance at his companions.

"Do you speak for yourself, or do you need a fucking chorus?" I snapped, fingers tightening.

He whipped his attention back to me. "No, Halálhívó."

"So say your piece." Each word bit out of me.

His throat bobbed, and then he launched into a long-winded explanation of why he was struggling to trust that we'd actually win the war. More added onto it, some with open animosity. Most of their turmoil stemmed from the massive loss on the salt flats.

The last one, though, voiced his vehement disagreement to

my proposal. Though calling it a proposal was generous. It was happening whether those under *my* command liked it or not.

"...and that's why females have no place with us. You've said so yourself countless times, Halálhívó." The male—a Százados from one of Rapp's winged divisions—finished his explanation with a bowed head.

My patience frayed thinner than the Reaper's thread just before she snipped.

I scanned each officer, letting the weight of my judgment linger, ensuring they understood the finality in my words. "I have made all those points before. Now, I have changed my mind. That is what a good leader does." The ice in my tone was clear as the glaciers atop the Skala Mountains. Bracing my hands on the arms of the throne, I shoved to standing, then crossed my arms. "I have heard enough opinions on the matter. My decision stands. The Százados are dismissed. Parancsok, remain for a debriefing."

Muscles ticked in jaws as the lesser officers departed. At least they had the sense to grumble only when they'd departed the black tent, though their grievances still reached my ears.

"They will come around, Halálhívó," one of the Parancsok said as I stepped off the platform. Ignoring him, I strode into the strategy room.

I didn't need his reassurance. These soldiers would alter their opinions or taste leather again. Insubordination was punishable by fifty lashes. I'd been generous yesterday with less for each of the loudmouths.

The Parancsok ringed the table, and Rapp and Trol settled into their respective places at either end. I braced my knuckles against the knotted wood and surveyed the pieces. Looking at the map alone was enough to make my blood boil, let alone after facing another wave of self-righteous soldiers. Some of it cooled as I dragged in a breath and took stock of the room.

The table felt larger with the missing Parancsok. We'd need to promote some new ones to take the place of the ones killed.

Definitely not from those fucking Százados, though.

The Angels—in two fucking weeks—had somehow managed to eliminate a large chunk of Rapp and Trol's forces. As I learned upon my return, Zaph's squads had taken Trol by surprise and killed thousands of Demons before his battalions could regroup. It was then he had known something had gone horribly wrong with my advance.

In a private moment on my second night hidden in the camp, Rapp had confessed their terror upon reuniting. Neither had heard from me. Both thought I might have died. They tasked a few trusted scouts with scouring the desert for any sign of me or our forces. Days into the search, one of Rapp's winged Vezető had spotted Assyria and me, and per his orders, returned to find his Hadvezér.

Rapp had rushed to our aid before the Vezető had finished speaking.

That we'd been in a rough state when he found us was framing it mildly. Lower-level soldiers seeing me half-dead would have taken some of the shine and allure away from my carefully crafted persona.

Returning my attention to the map, I surveyed the stones centered around Lutsk, where we faced off with the Angels. From my quick survey from the skies, the city was all but gone. Homes crumbled into the dusty earth, half-erected walls had been blasted to pieces, and bones were *everywhere*. The carrion birds had quite the feast in the time the Angels had passed through and then been forced back.

Now, they hid among the rubble and spilled into the churned grasses beyond.

Taking the city—if it could even be called that anymore—would be the most difficult part of our next advance. With plenty of places to hide and support on either side, we'd have to split our forces and face off on three fronts again. News of Zaph's victory and the discovery of my new mating bond had surely spread through the Angel's army too.

The pressure of forcing them to retreat further while sourcing females for the army—not to mention integrating them—was enormous. Sighing, I straightened and rubbed my temples. So many paths opened before me, all of which had costs and benefits. Keeping Assyria out of the Angel's hands again was also a challenge. We couldn't afford another loss of twenty thousand, let alone fifty thousand soldiers.

And I wouldn't be able to stop myself from slaughtering them all, no matter the cost. They'd hurt her once, and they'd never lay a hand on her again. She was mine to protect, to crave, to love. I'd been an asshole to her for too long, and I wanted to atone for my behavior.

Then there was the matter of Banand—the burgundy-eyed Demon with the power to create targeted plagues. According to Assyria, the Angels held him and Zurronar, a maroon-eyed Parancsok with blood magic, prisoner in their camp, along with half a dozen others.

The risk of them pressing their advantage and forcing Banand to create another pestilence was enormous. It had been incredibly effective the first time, and they'd already wiped out another mass of us. As much as I hated to admit it, Zahal Ishim had played his game well in the last year of our war.

"While Assyria was captive, she found that Banand and Zurronar were both still alive."

The words fell like a warhammer and shattered the silence of my officers. Rapp and Trol already knew, of course, but the Parancsok did not. The seven of them all spoke at once, questions flying from their lips like a volley of arrows. I waited for the noise to die before I spoke again.

"We need to make a plan to free them. With Banand in our possession again, we can retaliate swiftly and severely for our prior losses."

At the reminder of my sacrifice, a few mouths thinned. Guilt nibbled at my gut, but I smacked it away. Now was not the time, and the emotion had no place in protecting what was mine.

"We need to send scouts in search of where they might be kept. I'd suspect somewhere toward the rear, out of our reach. Gather your best from every battalion, especially the ones with the strongest ability to cover themselves in shadow, and prepare for a survey," I commanded them, my tone leaving no room for argument.

"Aye, Halálhívó," they said, though their words were lacking in enthusiasm. Many rifts still needed to be repaired, unfortunately, and that would only come with demonstration of my commitment to our victory. At least this rescue mission would start us on that path.

It would also buy us time for a raven to fly to Uzhhorod with a message for Xannirin and Kiira.

My attention slid to the two Hadvezér, who stood stoically on either end of the table. "Anything else?" I asked the officers. Their response was silence. "Good. We'll meet again at sundown. You know what you need to do today."

They departed, grouping up to discuss logistics of their various tasks.

Rapp and Trol remained behind. "We should invite the Angel's leaders here for a discussion," I growled, hate rolling like thunder in my voice. "They need to know that I am alive and they do not have the advantage they currently think they have."

"Aye," Rapp mused, using his tongue to fiddle with the ring in his lip.

Trol shifted his weight to the side and then rapped the small stone covering Fured against the table. "Parancsok Olet says the training is going smoothly and that control over powers increases by the day." Olet had departed Uzhhorod with approximately ten thousand males a few weeks prior to our campaign to the north, headed to the military academy to instruct our most powerful recruits. While bodies won wars, powerful magic wielders did too. After what had happened when we split up, my decision seemed infinitely wiser than before.

"Good. Then they can work individually with the females once they arrive." I tilted my head to the side, then used my opposite hand to give my neck a deep stretch. "I need to draft a letter before the day gets away from me."

"I'll leave you to it," Trol said, collecting his sword from a nearby table and reattaching it to his hip. "I'll ensure that the soldiers don't spend too much time grousing about the evolution of our army."

"Thank you," I said, and he offered me a closed-fisted salute before sweeping into the square beyond the command center.

Rapp tugged two chairs from the wall and jutted them against the wood. With a sigh, I plopped into one and grabbed a slip of parchment and stick of charcoal from the heap. I stared at the page for a long moment, wondering where to begin.

"All you need to say is that Assyria's pussy changed you from a cold, broody bastard into one who would sacrifice fifty thousand males for her life," Rapp chuckled, shoving at my shoulder.

I shot him a glare.

"And then your second sentence can be something along the lines of how her mouth made you see stars, also known as females joining the army to take the place of all the soldiers that died."

A warning growl rumbled in my throat.

"Don't forget to add that the old you isn't completely gone, and that you're ready to strangle me for teasing you. Otherwise, they'd worry that something really bad had happened."

The charcoal in my hand snapped in two. "Fucking Fates." I tossed them onto the parchment with more than a hint of frustration. "Do you need to be here?"

He tipped his head back and laughed. "Absolutely. I was deprived of opportunities to rib you for weeks."

I pinched the bridge of my nose.

"For what it's worth, Rokath, I'm glad you came to your senses. Assyria is an incredible female. All she needs is someone to let her flourish."

I blew out a long breath. "I plan on being the male that stands beside her as she blooms. Starting with this." Then, I picked up the longer broken piece and drafted my confession to my cousins.

4

ASSYRIA

Energy returned to my aching limbs after days in bed. Though the time felt more like weeks after the disorienting trek through the desert. At least here, there was an abundance of water. I'd never appreciated the cool, crisp taste of it before. I'd never take it for granted again.

With a groan, I rolled out of bed and onto my feet. Rokath was notably absent. The demands of running an army pulled him away more and more after his reappearance. From a pitcher perched on the small dining table, I poured myself some yellow juice and drank it down in three greedy gulps. Thirst quenched, I grabbed a cold roll and tore into it.

Grem and Zeec didn't so much as flick an ear or crack an eye. Their chests rose and fell in a steady rhythm. The loyal hounds were as exhausted as me. The short outing to support Rokath as he addressed the males had taken a toll, leaving me bedridden for another day.

But if I continued to lie here, I'd lose what edge I'd gained while training with Rokath.

And that was unacceptable, especially now that he'd sworn to integrate females into the army. To hold him to that promise, though, I needed to insert myself in it, starting sooner rather than later.

I wouldn't let him go back on his word. Not when it was so important to me. Not when I'd dreamed of a mate who would empower me rather than keeping me hidden.

The Fates had never been kind to me, and I still didn't trust that this wasn't part of their design to veil me again.

I tugged my worn leathers, still faintly smoky, and finished the last of my small meal. "Come," I told the dogs, who obeyed, albeit with much grumbling. Each rose from the firm mattress, stretching their long legs before shaking out their shaggy black fur.

Zeec nudged into my hand, and I scratched behind his ears.

I thought emerging from within the quiet confines of our abode would be a powerful act. Yet the tension in the air was apparent *immediately*. While the black tents in the center were relatively protected and removed from scrutiny, it wasn't far enough to avoid the shouts of anger that drifted in from the square where my life had taken a hard turn. Multiple times now, in fact.

Tuning into the magic of my mating bond, I sensed Rokath not too far from here, in the command center. With Grem and Zeec glued to my sides, we made the short trek and entered through the back. Passing the throne of bones upon which Rokath had sat when our eyes collided and our fates were irrevocably changed, I found him and Rapp crowding the map of Keleti.

A square of parchment was folded tight, and Rokath poured hot wax over it. I paused at the entrance and watched as he stamped a ring into it, squishing the molten red in a circle.

"What's that?" I asked, drawing his attention.

"Change," he rumbled. My heart swelled and that seed of doubt about his sincerity dashed away.

"Glad you're finally mobile again, Assyria," Rapp teased from beside him. He vacated his seat, fetched another chair, and left the one closest to Rokath open for me.

"Place," I told Grem and Zeec, and they trotted to mats near the entrance and plopped down. Before joining the males at the table, I filled a plate with a fresh snack. Hunger gnawed at my belly, finally hydrated enough that my body could concern itself with something other than quenching my thirst.

"I take it the males are unhappy with what you announced?" I ventured, flicking my attention to the note before popping a fat grape into my mouth.

"What gave you that impression?" Rokath asked me.

I lifted a shoulder and grabbed another handful of fruit. "Trol's yelling was fairly audible on my short walk here."

Rapp chuckled and Rokath grumbled something incoherent under his breath. I settled my free hand over Rokath's. "Thank you. I know this isn't easy."

The tender look he gave me had me melting into a puddle even more than the heat of the day creeping in. "For you, I'll do anything, mate."

"I know," I whispered. We lingered in that position for a moment, love sweeping down our bond, before I retreated.

"So what are you thinking of for a rescue mission for Banand and Zurronar?" Rapp asked Rokath.

A muscle ticked in Rokath's jaw. "Depends on where they're located in the camp. The Angels let thousands die to get to Banand the first time. They'll likely do the same to keep him. Which means we'll have to lose more of our forces as well."

A knot twisted in my gut. Rokath had already given up so much for me, and here he was preparing for more casualties. Yet this was the reality of war, I supposed. I'd been insulated from it before when Rokath kept me at arm's length. That he and Rapp discussed their plans in front of me now spoke volumes too.

"Why do you need to free them now?" I didn't want them to suffer, but I also didn't understand why Rokath would risk so much so soon.

"We need to rescue them before the Angels get the idea to deliver another plague." He blew out a long breath and rubbed circles over his temples.

"I want to help," I said in a rush. My heart leaped at the opportunity. I could show these males that I was useful, even more than I had when Rokath was teaching me to scout.

"No. I cannot risk you falling into their hands again," Rokath growled. Tension rolled off him in palpable waves, and a fierce protectiveness flared down our bond.

"But–"

A muscle jumped in his jaw, and a war of a different variety played out in his tormented expression.

"What else is my magic for if not for this?" I pressed, undeterred. I shot a look begging for aid in Rapp's direction, hoping he'd stick up to Rokath for me. He'd always supported me, even when it went against Rokath's wishes.

He gave the barest shake of his head.

I was on my own to convince my mate to hear me. "The Giver blessed me with something so powerful and unique, and the Weaver tied our fates together. This is what I am meant to do."

"I don't care," Rokath snarled, his ire raining directly on me. "I want you safe. If they lay a hand on you again, I will raze their realm to the ground. I will not fail to protect you again."

The grapes plunked against the plate as I threw them down. It appeared that some of our contention still remained, despite our confession of feelings. "Then teach me to fight. To use my magic to its fullest extent. You started before, so why not continue to do so now?"

Rokath shot to his feet, knocking his chair straight over. The dogs startled and scattered as he leaned over me, using his bulk for intimidation, like I'd seen him do so many times before.

But he didn't scare me.

I lifted my chin and met his dark, furious gaze.

"Your place isn't in the middle of another battlefield, Assyria. Not after what they did to you." His words were slow, measured, controlled, but hidden beneath them was barely-restrained fear.

My lips curled back from my teeth. "My place is where I fucking want it to be. You keep saying you love me, but when I try to stand beside you, you shove me behind."

He said nothing, only glared down at me. Because he knew, he fucking knew, I was right.

"You chose the army over me before. Don't make that mistake again," I hissed, nails biting into the wooden arm of my seat.

He flinched like I'd struck him and stepped away. While he righted his chair, he counted to ten in his mind, as he always did when he was trying to calm himself to speak rationally. "We could capture a few Angel females for you to impersonate," he gritted out, each word struggling to break the barrier of his throat.

Victory was so close I could almost taste it. Though the thought of venturing into the Angel's camp alone flipped my stomach. What *if* they captured me again? They probably wouldn't let me go so easily—probably not at all.

The acrid stench of burnt flesh rose from my memories, along with the screams of the fifty thousand who had been slaughtered without mercy.

A turbulent mix of anxiety and excitement tumbled through my veins. On the one hand, what Rokath was suggesting was a massive concession for him. On the other, the trauma of being captured, nearly raped, used as a pawn, and forced to watch the Angels slaughter tens of thousands in front of me still lingered.

What would they do the next time, now that they knew possession of me meant they were Rokath's puppeteer?

I swallowed down my fear and locked my spine straight. "And you won't let me go alone?"

Rokath shook his head and dropped back into his seat. "Absolutely not. I would *never* ask or allow you anywhere near them alone. I promised to protect you, and that is what I will do, now and forever."

The sincerity in his gravelly voice was evident. I glanced at his hands, where a pink scar decorated the very center. The spots where Zaph had staked him were almost healed. He flexed his fingers as if he sensed I was considering his use of them.

"So that's a yes? I can help?" I questioned, needing to hear him say the words so I would know they were real.

He pinched the bridge of his nose, a riot of emotion blazing down our bond. "Every protective instinct is screaming at me to say no. But I'm trying to do better, be better for you." A long pause held my breath captive. "So my answer is yes."

Excitement flitted through me. Finally, fucking finally. No more suffering in silence. I'd choke those who had been so vocal about Rokath's decision to allow us places in the army with my presence.

"Thank you, Rokath." I threw my arms around his broad shoulders, fingertips barely brushing. With a sigh, he pulled me closer and buried his nose into the base of my neck, where my hair tumbled to cover his face.

He inhaled deeply, and his shoulders relaxed the barest amount. "If you are to tread the alleys with Angels all around you, I must ensure that your mastery of your magic is flawless."

When he released me, his attention turned to Rapp. "We'll have to send a unit out to initiate a small skirmish to capture some females. The sooner we can start training Assyria, the better."

Again nausea rose. More Demons would die because of me. Yet if I could mimic the form of an Angel, sneak into their camp, and rescue Banand and Zurronar, thousands upon thousands—if not millions—of lives could be saved.

The choice was an easy one.

"Aye, we'll discuss it with the Parancsok this evening. By then they should have rallied their scouts to depart at nightfall. Hopefully in the morning we'll have a better map of their camp. Then it will put your mind at ease with Assyria," Rapp replied, drumming his fingers on the table. He picked up one of the stones on the map and tossed it back and forth.

I grinned at Rapp, and he offered me a subtle dip of his chin. Even though he was Rokath's best friend, he'd always supported me too. "Where do we begin?"

"We'll start with lessons in Angelic. While I hope that you won't be caught, if you are, you need to speak the language so *you* aren't discovered in your disguise," Rokath explained. It made sense, after all. They wouldn't speak the common tongue to someone who looked like them.

"What should we call her magic? It needs a proper name," Rapp butted in. "Especially for a power so useful and so cool."

A little giggle escaped me, and Rokath rolled his eyes. "Now is not the time."

"Psh," Rapp replied, slapping his leg. "It's as good of a time as any. Besides, we could use a little fun."

"I'm inclined to agree with Rapp." I flashed Rokath a saccharine smile. "What about Facer?"

Rapp shook his head. "No, that's too bland. You need something more exciting."

Rokath grumbled something about how ridiculous we were before stealing a hunk of cheese from me. I scoffed and swiped at him, but he popped it into his mouth before I could retrieve it.

"Forger?" Rapp suggested, lifting a brow and breaking our staredown.

"No, it sounds too much like the monetary laws." I tapped my chin, poised to snap a hand toward my plate should Rokath attempt to steal more of my food. "Changer? Since I'm changing my body?"

"Imposter," Rokath huffed, finally adding his opinion to the mix. "I gave you the name during our very first interaction. That is what it shall be."

"I like it. It's badass. Just like you will be once you master it, Assyria," Rapp grinned, flashing his sharp teeth. Then, he leaned forward and snatched a handful of blackberries for himself from my plate.

"Hey!" I protested, smacking his arm. "There's food over there if you two are hungry."

"But it's so much more fun to steal it from you when you're acting like a starved dog," Rapp grinned, popping one into his mouth.

I rolled my eyes.

Rokath dragged a blank sheet of parchment toward him, brows pinched with focus. "Now if we can return to the matter at hand. Assyria only has a short time to learn a complex language."

Rapp shoved back from the table. "Aye, I'll let you teach in peace. If you feel like killing each other, just go for a quick fuck instead."

I snorted, and Rokath growled at Rapp's backside as he jammed his hands in his pockets and strolled from the tent. His innocent whistles drifted toward us for a moment longer before silence reigned again.

I quickly snatched back my stolen fruit and shoved a few

into my mouth. Then, I turned to Rokath, our gazes colliding like a lightning strike. "I'm ready. Teach me." The words were breathier than I meant them to be, but when he looked at me like that...

His heated burgundy eyes swept over me, sending a shiver of desire down my spine. With the backs of his knuckles, he brushed my cheek and tucked a lock of hair behind my pointed ear. "If at any time it feels like it's too much, tell me. We will find another way."

"I will," I promised. "But I want to help. I want to prove that I am useful to those males." I dipped my head toward the outside world.

"Then that is what we shall do."

Rokath traced the letters of the Angelic alphabet onto the paper, covering the sound of each. While he didn't expect me to have to read it, he wanted me to know them just in case signs were present in the camp that might assist in guiding me to the prisoners. We spent the remainder of the afternoon covering basic phrases.

When the sun finally dipped, we broke for dinner. Rokath, Rapp, and I ate together in one of the massive food tents. As we entered, I held my head high, showing the males there was nothing wrong with me being unveiled and among them. The stares were even worse now that they knew my name and who I was to Rokath. Before, I'd been "the fallen" and rarely appeared alone to fetch food, both from Rokath's protectiveness and my own desire to keep out of their path.

The H carved into my wrists itched under their scrutiny.

I had to embrace my role. I refused to falter under their judgment. Because I was worthy of a place here, I was worthy of the sacrifice Rokath had made for me, and I was going to ensure the Demons won this war in whatever way I could.

Because if I died doing this, at least it would be on my own fucking terms.

5

R☠KATH

Food churned in my stomach as I scraped my plate clean and placed it among the pile of dirty dishes for washing. At least Assyria hadn't struggled to eat. Her excitement over helping the army was no match for my fear of losing her again to the Angels, though. Dusk fell, bringing with it a much-needed cool breeze, as we returned to the command center for the nightly officers' meeting.

Assyria stuck close to my side, and I wrapped an arm possessively over her shoulder. I needed to touch her, to feel her, to remind myself she was still here. That nothing bad would happen to her so long as she was in my orbit.

"You can go back to our tent now with the dogs," I told her as we approached the tied-back flap.

She halted immediately, my arm dropping into thin air. "You said I was part of this."

Rapp wisely ducked inside and yanked the ties to give us some privacy.

"You are, little imposter. But–"

She sliced through my words before they could emerge.

"But nothing! Either I am in, or I am out." She crossed her arms and popped out a hip, her glare scorching my skin.

My teeth ached from the force of my clenching. "It's better if Rapp and I speak to the Parancsok about the mission on our own."

Assyria jabbed a finger in the middle of my chest. "Is it? Because they have no idea what I am capable of. Or is this a ploy to keep me from going at all?"

"Assyria," I growled, her name loaded with threat.

My mate did not heed my warning. "No, Rokath." There was my real name, hissed from between her furious lips. "I'm risking my life for this. I get to be there."

"That's exactly the problem," I snarled, grabbing her wrists and yanking her against my chest. My heart pounded a staccato rhythm against my ribs at the reminder of the risks. "I can't think logically about what has to be done while you're standing there. The thought of you entering their camp makes it impossible to fucking breathe."

The firm set of her brows softened. The tension that had held her frame aloft bled away. "I know." Her voice was scarcely more than a whisper. "I'm scared too. But I want this."

She swallowed hard, throat bobbing. I wanted nothing more than to wrap my hand around it and squeeze. This female was so fucking infuriating, and yet I couldn't stand in her way. These opposing forces she brought out in me were wearing on my nerves.

I let my focus drift back to those devious burgundy eyes. Witnessed the silent plea in them. And still, my jaw locked.

"I want to choose my life, for once." Those words were like a punch to the gut. A whisper of the beginning, when our bond was a curse. A reminder of how the Fates had woven this path for us against both our wishes.

But now?

I needed her.

Air stuttered out of me as terror wrapped a vise around my lungs. A violent, thrashing battle waged within me as I struggled to say the words. To welcome her into this part of my world, the part that edged her closer to death.

"Come on then."

I didn't release her as we entered the command center, where Rapp, Trol, and the Parancsok were deep in conversation. They ceased when I approached the table, Assyria at my side.

She was right. With how central she was to our plan, it was time the Parancsok learned of her power. And learned to respect her place at my side.

As much as I hated the idea of putting Assyria in harm's way, her Imposter gift was one we could leverage to free Banand and Zurronar. As the thought flitted through my mind, my chest clenched. *Violently.* I flattened my palm across the middle of my ribs, right where the shadows of my magic swirled around our bond, and pressed, trying to ease the pain.

There was no way in all the worlds I'd let her go alone or even without me.

But what kind of male wields his own mate to win a war? I loathed myself for considering it. Fuck, *allowing* her to join us. But I'd hate myself more for silencing her, keeping her hidden away, just like her fucking husband had done.

My nails raked over my tunic as my hand curled into a fist. Never had I been so conflicted in my entire life.

At least the power the Giver blessed me with was enough to render me invisible under the cover of darkness, and others in the camp possessed similar skills that would aid us in our surreptitious entry.

Which left only one problem to be solved for this rescue mission.

Assyria squared her shoulders as she stood beside me,

staring the officers down. Compared to those of us surrounding the table, she was tiny. Yet her confidence made her appear statuesque.

If the Angels captured or harmed her again, I wouldn't stop until their whole camp—their whole realm—was in ashes. I'd hunt down every last one of them. No mercy. No second thought. Should they seize me too, I'd give them anything they wanted so long as she was safe and air continued to flow through her lungs.

And that was a very dangerous fact.

Once everyone had arrived and settled into their respective places, I turned my attention to the Parancsok. "I need three female Angels captured and brought to me."

One sucked in a sharp breath. "Why would we waste our precious resources on them?"

I'd already used my daily allotment of 'because I said so' and unfortunately, I couldn't solely rely on my authoritarian rule, not when I wanted cooperation and enthusiasm for the changes to come. While fear was a fantastic tool for control, so was belief. My cousins and I had wielded the two together to ascend to our roles, after all.

"Because the Giver blessed Assyria with the magic to take on the form of another, but only if she has time to study them. I want to use her power to rescue the Demons being held prisoner by the Angels."

Eyes widened and lips parted. Rapp was right—Assyria's power was 'cool' as he had termed it. It was also *extremely* useful for a scout. All seven's attention landed on my mate. To her credit, she didn't flinch.

"You'd risk your *mate* for this mission?" one asked, tearing his gaze from Assyria and letting his garnet eyes collide with mine.

I bristled at his question. A low growl rumbled in my chest

as I planted my fists on the table and leaned in. "Do you doubt my devotion to our cause?" Obsidian leaked from between my fingers and drifted in his direction, out of my control.

How dare he voice the very question eating me alive.

The male shifted his weight from foot to foot. "No, Halál-hívó. I simply thought you wouldn't want to place her on a path that could lead to her death. Or yours."

His insinuation had my lips curling back from my teeth. I knew when it came to Assyria, I was totally fucked. I didn't need the same thought curling in my subordinates' minds.

"When the time comes to carry out this mission, I won't be weak," my mate snapped, mirroring my posture and glaring at the offending Parancsok. "In case you haven't noticed, I have burgundy eyes too. Just because I don't have a dick doesn't mean I'm incapable of taking on such a challenge. Especially when I am bonded to the Halálhívó and have him to train me."

Rapp's brows shot up his forehead, and he covered his mouth to hide his amusement. Assyria was a fighter—I'd learned that firsthand every fucking day as she refused to bow to my command. And these males, in her eyes, were no different.

For her own protection, I wanted her to be stronger, both with her power and her body. Future separation during a skirmish was inevitable, and while she'd never be completely on her own, I never wanted her to feel helpless against an opponent either.

The Parancsok dipped his chin. "Apologies, mate of the Halálhívó, I meant no offense."

"This is the type of attitude that must change," she stated, her tone blistering with fire. "For too long, you males have assumed us the weaker sex because we have not fought back. Just because our strength does not match yours does not mean we are helpless. My abilities will aid us in winning this war. I merely have to use them to the extent the Giver intended."

Pride bloomed in my chest as she claimed her place by my side.

"Aye," Rapp agreed, the corner of his mouth twisted into a wry grin. "Females have strengths of their own we do not possess. We'll all do well to remember that."

"Of course," the Parancsok replied, and a few others murmured their assent.

"Now, if we can return to the matter at hand," I said, smoothing out the transition. "Once we have the Angel captives and reports on potential locations of the Demon prisoners, we can hold the Angels here for a few weeks while I train my mate." The beginnings of a plan were forming in my mind, but I'd need time to mull over all the possibilities and probabilities before we struck. The scouts who'd creep into the night to survey the Angel camp would assist in that as well. Their reports were essential to any decisions we'd make.

"I will lead the next charge, Halálhívó," one of Trol's Parancsok volunteered, rapping his maroon-gauntleted knuckles on the table. "We will capture Angels for your mate, and we will join you in rescuing our fellow soldiers."

That was the attitude I'd been searching for. "Your sacrifice is appreciated, Parancsok." Though I hoped the losses stemmed from the attack wouldn't be too severe.

"The success of this mission hinges on cooperation and sacrifice for the greater good. The Angels cannot realize we're intentionally seeking out prisoners, or they'll start wondering why, after all this time, it has become part of our strategy. It must look like an action of opportunity."

The Angels had never been keen on being captured—which was why I'd abandoned the idea of using them as leverage long ago—and would fight tooth and nail to avoid it. Dozens of memories of daggers crossing their own throats, plunging into sides of necks, or even throwing themselves off cliffs arose in my mind. They'd rather die than surrender to the control of a Demon.

Their suicides made it difficult to gather additional intelligence about their plans, beliefs, and next moves. I suspected that was intentional on Zahal Ishim's part. Most of the information we worked off of in the Demon Realm was what was available to the public in the Angel Realm. And much had changed in the last few centuries since Koron Stadiel took the throne.

"You've gathered the scouts?" I asked, tearing my thoughts back to the present.

The Parancsok provided their chosen names along with proposed routes based on quick surveys taken during the day. Assyria listened intently as we rolled over plans, modifying them as more information was revealed. Finally satisfied with our path forward, I peered further into the future.

"We hold the Angels here for as long as we can. We know how to survive these harsh environments. They do not. After this attack, do not move again unless provoked. Waiting them out might be the key."

"Aye, Halálhívó," they said.

"You are dismissed. Send out your scouts and remind them why we fight this war," I commanded. They offered me closed-fisted salutes, then departed. The Parancsok who had volunteered his unit peeled off to prepare them for the skirmish they were to initiate in the early hours of morning.

Let the Angels come searching for their stolen soldiers afterward. Let them walk into the sharp teeth of the Demon camp. I'd savor the moment I got to remind the Zahal of who the fuck I was and why he should fear me.

Assyria slipped her hand into mine and gave it a gentle

squeeze. "Do you really think this will work?" Yet despite the conviction in her tone, her palm held the barest shake.

"Yes," I told her, but then I slid into her mind, to make a promise I wanted no one else to hear. *"If this is what choosing your life looks like...then I'll shape the fucking world to keep that choice intact. I'd do anything for you, little imposter."*

"Keep proving that, then," she shot back, but the usual snark was tempered.

I glanced at Trol and Rapp for subtle confirmation of their belief. Both were steadfast. I certainly believed in her—she'd proven her strength time and time again. But belief didn't win wars; if it did, the Angels would have slaughtered us from their fervency alone.

Power was what decided the victor. Magic, strength, leverage...it mattered not, so long as one possessed it.

And as Assyria looked up at me like I was everything she needed in this life, I planned on gathering it in spades to keep my mate safe.

6

ASSYRIA

Three white-haired and wild-eyed females stared up at us from their position on the ground. Two Vezető worked to hold each of the Angels in place, shoving them to their knees and preventing them from rising. Bronze cuffs flashed in the midday light. Even with the futility of their situation, they writhed like vipers, kicking up a storm of dust.

I adjusted the scarf around my head to cover my nose and mouth so I wouldn't breathe in any more than necessary. While I hadn't worn a veil since the fateful day we left Gyor Palace, this lightweight fabric was an absolute necessity in the hot, dry land. Even with the light bronze shade of my skin, the altitude of the Paks Desert made it burn. At least in Lutsk, we were on the fringes of it—not like we had been as we'd wandered through the endless expanse and nearly died.

Blood slicked the Vezetős' arms from dozens of tiny cuts, while others who had assisted in the skirmish limped by us on their way to the healers' tents. None minded as ruby dripped to the earth, feeding the Fates for bringing us a much-needed victory.

A female with ocean blue eyes spit at my feet. "Whore," she cursed in the common tongue. The other two followed suit.

A growl ripped from Rokath's throat, and he took a menacing step toward the instigator. A Vezető fisted her hair and yanked her head back, forcing her to look into the eyes of the Halálhívó. For that was *exactly* who Rokath was at that moment. My mate wore many masks—I was finding that this one was one I especially loved to see. Something about the way he elicited a flash of fear in her eyes as he towered over her made my low belly heat.

"What is your name?" he demanded in the common tongue. If I were to impersonate them, I needed to know as much as possible. Their identities were essential to that.

Her lips curled away from her teeth, but she said nothing. Rokath waited a moment before questioning her again. "What is your name?" He switched to Angelic, but the command in his tone was undeniable.

Her expression faltered for a moment before she recovered her hateful one. Rokath snapped his head toward one of the Vezető holding her. "Nightmare, now," he ordered in Demonic, then stepped back.

The Vezető's chest expanded, and the air in front of the Angel shimmered. A memory of the day we'd tested everyone's magic with the Lovak Squad flitted through my mind. The way Dromak had screamed at whatever the male had shown him. It didn't take long for the female's shrieks to pierce the air, replacing the echoes of my former friend.

The other two shouted at her in Angelic, the melody of their words lost among the frantic bursts. Yet their comrade couldn't hear them, so utterly consumed in the dreamscape. Desperate hands attempted to claw at her head, but the other Vezető caught them and forced them to hover in front of her. She jerked against the hold, tears streaming down her cheeks.

"Stop!" she cried in the common tongue.

The Vezető looked at Rokath for confirmation. He nodded.

The air returned to normal, and the Angel's breasts heaved against her leather armor. "My name is Esha."

Rokath didn't bother acknowledging her before he moved to the cerulean-eyed one. "And you?" he demanded in the common tongue.

"Faeya," she replied, a slight tremble in her voice.

"I am Araquiel," the third offered without Rokath having to question her. Her turquoise eyes bounced between my mate and me. From the previous day's lessons with Rokath, I knew the color of her eyes made her the most powerful out of the three. It was the third most powerful in all of the Angel realm, in fact. Whoever managed to capture her needed a promotion to Százados.

"I agree with you on that," Rokath spoke into my mind.

Her hair was the color of the fog that rolled over the plains of Stryi in the early autumn mornings. Cut short, it brushed the tops of her shoulders. Most of it had spilled out of a strip of leather atop her head. Dirt and blood caked her face, but beneath it, she had delicate features, thin eyebrows, and full lips.

"Why do you keep us alive?" she asked, each word rolling off her tongue with a thick accent.

Rokath snorted and continued his interrogation instead. "What are your powers?"

"I conjure light," Esha offered immediately. I pressed my lips together to smother a laugh. One nightmare and she was ready to confess everything.

"I am an Amplifier," Faeya revealed with a sigh.

Rokath returned his attention to Araquiel. She held her chin high, refusing to cower beneath the Halálhívó. A long moment passed before she spoke. "I am a Sensor."

"Suppression or amplification?" Rokath clarified.

"Both," she said simply, her expression placid. Yet her eyes held the barest hint of judgment, like she was guarding herself and gauging us simultaneously. Something twisted in my gut, like a warning bell that something rang false. Angel power was Goddess-blessed, hence their worship of Her, and many possessed powerful mind magics.

Had she spoken true about her power?

"See that they are fed and bathed. Do not take the cuffs off them for any reason," Rokath told the supervising Parancsok while I continued to study the three. Araquiel, based on her strength alone, would be the one I'd need to focus on the most. With the insignia in her armor, I suspected she held status among the Angel army too.

"What would you like us to do with them after?" the male replied.

Rokath flicked his attention to the currently empty cage off to one side in the square. "Have that brought into the command center," he dipped his head to indicate the object, "and lock them in there."

"Aye, Halálhívó," the Parancsok said, offering him a close-fisted salute. To me, he dipped his chin. "My lady." Then, he directed his group away.

At least someone is coming around to me.

Though I'd technically been part of the nobility while married to Vagach, hearing him refer to me as such in relation to Rokath didn't feel...right. Like I was some attachment to him rather than an extension of him. Nor did I think of Rokath as royalty, despite him belonging to the most prominent house in the Demon Realm.

To me, he was my mate. My protector. My villain. Nothing else mattered, not anymore.

Rokath's revelation of my Giver-blessed powers had helped

paint me in a new light. To the Parancsok, at least, I now had some use other than wetting Rokath's cock. Outside of the highest circles, keeping my magic secret was paramount. If the Angels knew of my ability in addition to being Rokath's mate, we'd have to adjust our plans yet again.

Fates, I was really starting to sound like him. His constant stream of consciousness into my mind had changed the way I thought about a lot of things. It didn't help that his mind was *always* working. Those moments of quiet were rarer than his genuine smiles.

"Come," he told me. I rolled my eyes but obeyed anyway.

"I am not a dog," I reminded him as I lengthened my stride to keep up. We entered the command center, finding reprieve from the sweltering heat. There, Rapp and Trol were debriefing with some of the Százados who had led the fight to capture the three female Angels.

"What were our losses?" Rokath questioned, hardened to the idea of losing soldiers.

All attention turned to him, and the four Százados offered him hasty salutes. I casually strolled to the pitcher of water on a nearby table and poured some for myself. Even days after returning, I couldn't help but drink as often as I could. Dehydration in the desert was horrendous. In my delirium, I'd thought that the Reaper had cursed us to die a painful death for loving each other.

Rokath had talked me out of it...eventually. Even now with my mind clear, surrendering that fear proved difficult.

I braced myself to hear the number of soldiers who had perished to aid me, still tender to that exposure.

"Only twenty, Halálhívó," one replied. "We killed far more than that as well. Thanks to the scout's information, we were able to take them by surprise."

A hint of tension bled from Rokath's shoulders. "You all did very well. Eat and take a much deserved rest."

They thanked him and departed shortly after. Rokath relayed the information about the female Angels to the two Hadvezér. Since I was there when it happened, I slipped into the bone room and found Grem and Zeec lounging on their favorite cushions. Zeec, thank the Weaver, had made a full recovery. I still pet that spot where he'd been slashed open with the tenderest of care.

The action soothed the sting of knowing that I was responsible for more deaths.

Rokath and Rapp found me with both dogs competing for my attention. "You'd never know they would rip out the throats of anyone we told them to," I quipped as the curtain fluttered shut behind them.

Rapp laughed and then bent down to stroke their fur as well. Meanwhile, Rokath sighed. "When you two are quite finished, Assyria needs more combat training today."

"You mean foreplay?" Rapp teased, straightening.

"It is not foreplay," Rokath groused, fingers flexing like he wanted to strike his friend for the insinuation.

I pressed the back of my hand to my mouth to smother a laugh.

We hadn't trained since our return, given how exhausted I'd been. Even now, the heat of the day sapped my energy. Yet this was essential, and I would do whatever it took to become as fierce as I could be. So with aching, protesting limbs, I rose. "Let's go."

We found a place near the command center that was relatively devoid of soldiers. Rokath said we wouldn't need too much space since he wanted to restart hand to hand combat training before providing me with sharp objects.

At least I wouldn't *intentionally* stab him anymore.

The thought pulled a small smile to my lips.

I shook out my tired arms and then faced him in the center of the ring he'd toed into the dirt. Rapp sat with his back propped against a wood pole, the dogs on either side of him. Grem and Zeec rested their heads on their paws, eyes tracking our movements.

"Try to punch me," Rokath commanded.

I shot him a saccharine smile. "I've been waiting to do that all day." Then, I leaped forward, at the same time extending my left arm in a jab. Before I made contact, though, I reeled it in and struck out with my right hand. Rokath absorbed the blow to his stomach. His face, unfortunately, was a bit out of my reach.

"Very good," he praised, and my face flushed.

"No corrections?" I pried, given that every time before, he'd *also* offered his opinion on how I could be better.

"Maybe later," he shrugged, spinning on his back foot and out of my reach. "Come at me again."

I chased him down, wracking my brain for the combinations he'd shown me before. Rapp assisted with a few calls of his own, while Rokath slowed his movement to allow me time to throw everything correctly. We fell into a rhythm, and then he started working in counters and parries, increasing the complexity of our dance.

"I need a break," I panted after nearly half an hour under the sweltering sun. Sweat poured off me in salty rivulets.

Rapp tossed me a waterskin, and I greedily emptied its contents into my mouth. With the back of my hand, I wiped my brow. It was no use. With how damn hot it was even at the mouth of the Paks Desert, moisture beaded it again instantly.

I had to admit, though, that the drops rolling down Rokath's torso were far too alluring. As always when we sparred, he was shirtless. His sculpted shoulders were on full display, as were the two lines carved into his lower abdomen into a delicious V that disappeared into his pants.

At the reminder of what lay there, desire coiled low in my center.

Maybe Rapp was right and this was a prelude to sex.

It didn't help that we also hadn't coupled since our return. Rokath had been busy, and I'd been recovering. Our bond flared with my greedy thoughts, and Rokath's attention snapped to me. Flames ignited in his eyes, and he raked his hungry gaze over me.

I tossed the waterskin away and faced him again. Lifting my chin, I circled him like a cat circles her prey. Rokath rose to the challenge, his hulking form somehow growing even bigger as he called smoky onyx to his skin. The dark lines swirled up his arms and around his torso before billowing out behind him and beneath his feet with every step he took.

Dragging in a breath, I called on my own magic, bringing darkness into existence. Like I'd done countless times while traveling with the army, I formed thick lines with them. Though instead of manipulating them to haul goods or push wagons, I let them lie long and loose like whips. Fisting them, I prepared to snap my wrists and do just that in Rokath's direction.

We struck at the same time, my shadows colliding with a solid shield of Rokath's. A deep gouge in the onyx lasted only a moment before Rokath's magic overtook them. Like a twister, it swirled around me, only offering me brief glimpses of my mate. I spun in a circle, trying to figure out where he was and where he would attack from next. The power surrounding me made it impossible to pinpoint his position.

Suddenly, the pitch dropped away, and he pressed against my back, one hand clamping over my mouth while the other banded my stomach. I flashed back to the moment the Angels had done just that, when they'd slapped a putrid rag over my face and knocked me out. A scream ripped from my throat, and I thrashed in Rokath's hold as pure terror shattered through my veins.

He released me, and I lurched forward. Spinning me to face him, he crouched down so we were level. "Breathe, Assyria. You're safe with me. They can't hurt you anymore."

Darkness dissipated as I blinked, coming back to myself. To the camp. To the feel of my mate's calloused hands on my shoulders. To the stench of unwashed bodies and burnt earth.

I dragged in a serrated breath, matching the rise and fall of my mate's chest.

"I'm sorry, I never should have touched you like that. I didn't think…"

Of course, he'd figured out exactly what had upset me. Since we'd admitted our feelings to one another and accepted the mate bond the Fates had blessed us with, we had no barriers between us anymore.

When I said nothing, he stepped back, nostrils flaring. But it was the guilt in his expression that had me reaching for his hand. Seeking the comfort only he could offer me.

"I'm safe with you," I repeated, mostly as a message to the trembling parts of me that still screamed to fight.

His harsh features softened, and his thumb ghosted across the back of my hand, grounding me further.

"When you're ready, I will show you exactly how to react if someone does that to you again," Rokath growled, his protectiveness rising like a pillar of flame. That dark flare soothed the part of me that had been hurt time and time again by males with ill intent.

I *never* wanted to be vulnerable like that again. Pressing a hand over my racing heart, I reminded it that was what we were here to do. To learn. To improve. To bloom.

Calmness settled over me again.

You've got this, Assyria.

"Show me."

Rokath's hands dropped away, and he circled around to my back. His damp skin pressed into mine, and I reminded myself again that my mate would not hurt me. More of his essence lingered on my skin as he draped his arms as they had been before. "If your attacker has only one arm around your middle, he has a weakness there. Shove down while twisting away."

The way his breath brushed against my neck dragged a shiver from me. Clamping my hands over his wrist, I pressed down with all my might, turning into him. He offered little resistance. Within a heartbeat, I was free.

"Again," he commanded. I lined back with his front, and he splayed his large hand across my stomach. Any lower, and he'd brush the waistband of my pants. The muscles in his forearm twitched as I gripped it. When I shoved it down and away, his fingers brushed lower still, so close to the area I was dying for him to stroke me.

When I reset for the fifth time, Rokath's hardness dug into my backside. Clearly, I wasn't the only one affected by our position. This time, Rokath also covered my mouth. "Don't worry about this so much as the other hand," he told me. "This may feel like I am controlling you, but in reality, it's the other doing most of the work. Your center of gravity is there, and it is from there I can leverage your weight to maneuver you."

An image of him snatching me backward and settling me in his lap so he could fuck me entered my mind unbidden. I realized a moment later the descriptive pose came from him.

Rapp whistled suggestively, grinning like a madman when our attention sliced to him. "If you two are finished grinding against each other, might I suggest you teach Assyria how to counter the position as well?"

Rokath cursed Rapp beneath his breath, and I giggled in

response. He removed his hand from my mouth and wrapped the other around me, arranging my hands so one gripped his wrist and the other gripped my own. "Hold like this while you twist out of my hold. Keep it as you step around to my backside. In the end, you should have my arm pinned behind me."

"Okay," I said, swallowing. Coherent thoughts were impossible to grasp with how we were pressed together. I pushed his arm down, flexing my fingers as I turned into him. Muscles rippled around his shoulder as I stepped to my right, shoving his fist into his side.

"Keep going around," he told me.

I did, awkwardly maneuvering around him until I'd wrenched his fist into his lower back. Then, I let go. "Like that?"

"Close. Come here." Rokath motioned for me to return to his backside. He wrapped my arms around his waist and I peered around him to see what he was doing. Using the same grip he showed me, he shoved my arm down and turned to face me. "Watch my feet."

I did, realizing I'd stepped out of order when he spun behind me and pinned my arm. "Let me try again."

He released me, and we reset. This time, I executed the counter with more grace, though I lost my grip on Rokath's arm when I focused on how I was moving my feet. Five more repetitions passed before I managed to string together every part successfully.

"Yes!" I celebrated with both my arms thrown over my head. They smacked against my sides after I dropped them. "Can we be done now? I think I might pass out from the heat otherwise."

Rapp chuckled and stood, dusting off his pants. Grem and Zeec rose too, shaking out their fur.

"We'll resume this tomorrow. Along with more Angelic

lessons. These next few days are crucial to readying you for the mission at hand," Rokath pronounced.

He was relentless, but I needed to rest. Though I appreciated how much he cared about me. I hadn't had anyone like that since before my marriage to Vagach. Even then, my father had sold me to him anyway, knowing what type of male he was. At least my mother had put up some protest.

"I need to study the Angels more too," I said, trying to recall all their features.

Would creating their form be easier or harder than creating a Demon one?

Their coloring was vastly different from ours, with hair in shades of white and eyes in shades of blue, and that was what I worried about getting right the most. I didn't want to fail during my first real opportunity to prove myself worthy to these soldiers who were angry about females joining the army.

Rokath jerked me into his hold and captured my waist. "I am proud of you, Assyria. Not many females would so readily volunteer for such a dangerous mission. Even if I wish you'd remain behind and safe in the camp."

"I know," I replied, resting my chin on his chest. "But you'll train me harder than anyone else and ensure I am fully prepared."

"That I will," he said, knuckles brushing over my cheekbone. He stepped away, then tore his attention to Rapp. "Shall we dine with the soldiers again tonight?"

"I think it would be wise," Rapp replied, tossing Rokath's shirt back to him. Rather than put it on, he tucked it in the waistband of his pants.

"Let's go," he said, and I fell into step between the two powerful leaders, Grem and Zeec bringing up our rear. Salutes greeted us around every turn until we reached one of the largest food tents. The males all jumped to their feet and hurried out greetings to their Hadvezér and the Halálhívó before returning to their food.

None acknowledged me. Rokath didn't point it out either.

Teeth clenched, I stalked through the tables and found us an empty one while the two fetched our meal. Eyes bored into me, but I brushed them off, so used to them at this point. Grem and Zeec situated themselves under my feet, and when Rapp returned, he dipped beneath the wood and shoved two bowls of water at them. From under his arm, he pulled a now-full waterskin and handed it to me. I drank a few gulps to quench my thirst.

Rokath carried a tray piled with food and set it in front of me. He and Rapp slid into seats along the bench, and then we divided up the gruel. At least out of the Paks Desert, more options were available to us. Though none of it looked particularly appetizing. It couldn't be worse than the slop I struggled to eat one handed while we traversed the deep canyon.

After taking a tentative bite, my stomach smashed any further protest I might have had, and I shoveled food into my mouth like it was the day we finally found the camp again. Rokath and Rapp spoke quietly, their forks moving at a slow pace between their plates and their teeth. The soldiers around us quickly forgot about our presence, and by the time I finished eating, I wanted nothing more than to wash and sleep.

Forget sex. I wanted to lie in bed for an entirely different reason. Each movement was met with protest as I rose from the table. Rapp offered to clean up so Rokath could escort me back to our tent. I bid my friend a goodnight and then followed my mate out of the light and into the dark.

At least now that the sun had disappeared, a cool breeze swept over us.

As we neared our abode, Rokath's hand brushed against mine. I linked my fingers with his, subtly peeking up at him through my lashes. The black around us had nothing on the energy radiating off of him.

I welcomed it. Sank into it like it was a cool stream waiting to sweep me away. Because Rokath had taught me one important lesson, even more essential than fighting.

Safety was for the naive.

To survive in this world, I needed power. I'd been shattered by my abusive husband, wounded by the Angels who captured me. I knew what it was to choke on silence, to be dismissed, disregarded, and disbelieved.

Never again.

Zaph and the others had no idea the Imposter they helped create. And when I wore those females' faces, I'd savor the knowledge that I was a wolf in sheep's clothing and they had no idea I was among them.

I would smile as I slaughtered them all.

7

RKATH

I fled the sun as I ducked into my tent, a bundle hidden behind my back. My mate lounged in the late afternoon heat, the hounds snoozing on either side of her. She sat up as the flaps whispered closed behind me and offered me a soft smile.

"Did you get some sleep?" I asked her, pausing at the foot of the bed.

She stretched her arms overhead and yawned. "A little." Then, she glanced at the clock. "Will they be arriving soon?"

The Angels were coming to meet that evening, Zahal Ishim included. Which was why I'd made a quick trip to the clothier after our earlier combat lessons. The black leather armor weighed heavy in my hands as I revealed it. I'd debated about seeing the blacksmith, but metal plates would only slow her down when I needed her to be agile.

Besides me, no one else in the army wore black. The officers donned red metal armor that matched the color of their eyes, while most of the soldiers wore tanned leather uniforms. Other bits of red metal appeared here and there, depending on the weapon of choice. Some bracers protected arms of those who preferred a closer combat style, while helmets and neck guards wrapped around the heads of the archers who took to the skies with Rapp.

Assyria's almond-shaped burgundy eyes danced with excitement. She knew as well as I did the symbolism of my gift. Out here, there were no exquisite jewels, and I'd never be able to offer her a crown.

That wasn't what Assyria wanted from me.

"Thank you," she breathed, accepting the clothes. She ran her lithe fingers over the smooth fabric before setting the pile gently on our bed. Gripping the bottom of her tunic with both hands, she tore it overhead, revealing the band around her breasts. My cock jumped to attention at the sight.

Calm down, now is not the time.

Rather than linger on my lustful thoughts, I focused on strapping into my own gear. By the time I grabbed my ebony horned helmet, Assyria was fully dressed and in the process of plaiting her long, dark hair. The thick rope of braid nearly reached the bottom of her ribs once she tied it off. She flicked it over her shoulder and lifted her chin. "Ready."

Down the bond, however, her nervousness speared straight into me. All of the highest ranking officers in the Angel army would be in attendance, along with a few others—Zaph included.

His presence was entirely intentional on the Zahal's part.

For me, not wringing his neck on sight would be a victory on its own; for Assyria, not faltering under the memory of what he had done to her, to us, would be her challenge.

I stepped forward and lifted her chin even higher with the tips of my fingers. "You are mine, Assyria. I will *always* protect you." Then, I crashed my lips against hers, letting my kiss convey everything I would do for her. I tossed my helmet onto the bed and then flattened my palms on her lower back, bringing her body flush with mine.

Her mouth opened for me immediately, and I swept my tongue against hers, tasting rich berries while the scent of roses flooded my nostrils. I inhaled deeply, intoxicated by it and by her. A whimper slipped out of her as I squeezed her firm ass and rolled my hips into hers.

Then, I nipped her tongue and leaned back. A flush decorated her cheeks, and her bow-shaped lips were cherry-red. "We'll continue that later," I growled, bringing a hand up to her throat and brushing my thumb across the underside of her jaw.

"Let's," she rasped, swallowing. I watched her throat bob. Perhaps I'd have to have my dick in there too.

I reached past her for my mask. It slipped over my head like a second skin, and Assyria plunged her teeth into her bottom lip as she looked up at me. "Do I scare you, little imposter?"

"Didn't you once tell me you'd make it a point to do so?" she grinned, cocking her head to the side.

The memory of our first conversation burst into my mind. I'd been so fucking furious then—remained that way for weeks —and I had wanted to scare her into submission. Control was something I did not surrender, not for anyone. Yet Assyria had gained victory after victory with her persistence and her fire.

"Perhaps I need to reinstate that promise," I growled.

Her pupils darkened. "It's much more attractive when you frighten other people. Especially on my behalf."

A sinister laugh rumbled in my chest. "Is that what you want from me tonight, Assyria? You want me to terrorize the Angels enough that they piss themselves?"

Her lips curved into a feral grin. "Please."

A groan slipped out of me unbidden. "I do like when you beg."

Lust flooded our bond, and all I could think about was

bending her over this bed and fucking her senseless. Rapp saved me from the sin of Assyria's temptation when he called out, "Are you two ready to go?"

Lungs filling with air, I counted to ten. Then I exhaled slowly, willing my cock to shrink. "Aye," I grumbled, grabbing Assyria's hand and leading her out of the tent. Grem and Zeec popped to their feet and trotted behind us.

Tension draped the air like a heavy fog, though the sky was crystal clear. The sun dug its way over the horizon, painting the camp in long shadows. Fires sparked into the sky, smoke sliced through by angry shouts.

Satisfaction curled through me as I strode forward.

The Angels were here.

Trol would ensure they awaited my arrival, another move carefully designed to show them just how at my mercy they were. Not that I had any to offer them. *Especially* after their treatment of my mate. The scars where the stakes had speared through my skin itched, and I smothered the urge to touch them. Assyria's warm skin against mine soothed the ache there instead.

Rapp fell into step with us, and together, we marched upon the command center. The volume of the crowd grew louder as we approached, and the reverberation of beating chests and stomping feet crashed through the canvas separating us from the general army. Despite the unrest at the announcement of our new direction, the males had banded together in our time of need because we all faced a common enemy, one whose threat united us no matter what else wedged its way into our lives—the Angels. Their zealotry connected them just the same in their shared hatred of Demons and belief that they had to exterminate us from this world.

That was why this war had been so brutal and why I had to ensure the Demons emerged victorious.

We paused at the rear, listening for who might wait within. Trol's gruff tone drifted through, speaking in the common tongue to who I assumed were the Angel's representatives.

A melodic voice echoed back, also in the common tongue. "Where is the Halálhívó? We were supposed to meet with him."

"He will arrive shortly," Trol replied. I looked to Rapp, who merely dipped his chin. He eased open the flap and entered, silent as the snakes that slithered through the desert.

Assyria squeezed my hand, and I glanced down at her, finding a devious smile etched on her lips. We both knew we'd stand there a few minutes longer, testing the patience of the fanatics. I'd instructed her on *exactly* how she needed to act in front of them, and to my utter surprise, she'd taken the direction without too much of a fight.

The Angels grumbled amongst themselves in their tongue, muttering obscenities about the lawlessness and disrespect the Demons offered and why they shouldn't have expected any different.

"Are you listening?" I asked Assyria through our mental connection. We'd practiced for hours over the past few days, and Assyria had put all her effort into learning. That she took this mission so seriously made me want to kiss her endlessly.

"Yes," she replied. *"One commented on Rapp's piercings when he entered."*

"Very good," I praised, my tone like a tumble of rocks into her mind.

Her tongue flicked out and wetted her lower lip.

Another minute passed, and then, I shifted my weight and rolled my shoulders. I'd waited long enough to prove my point. Releasing Assyria, I stepped forward and grasped the flap. "Search," I barked at Grem and Zeec. Their tails wagged as they disappeared into the dim light. Assyria ducked under my arm a moment later, and I let the canvas smack closed behind me as we entered.

A cry of alarm rippled through the Angels as Grem and Zeec speared between them, taking long sniffs at their legs. Zeec stopped short in front of one and released a menacing growl. To my delight, it was Zaph. The insect flinched away as Zeec spun on his heel and trotted to his place on the left hand side of the throne of bones.

A low, menacing laugh rumbled in my chest as I strode into the room, a hand on Assyria's lower back. All eyes ripped to me. I said nothing else as we stepped onto the dais. My mate's expression was harder than the basalt pillars that held Gyor Palace together. Firmly locked on Zaph, she rounded the throne and stood on the right side of it, Grem at her feet. I turned my back on the Angels in a show of just how little threat they posed to me.

When I sank into the seat, I dug my fingers into the skulls at the edge of the arms, drawing their attention to their deceased brethren. A muscle feathered in the Zahal's jaw, and his ice blue eyes were colder than the glaciers in the Skala Mountains. The leader of the Angel army was not an imposing figure; in fact, if I'd met him on the streets of Sivy, I'd have assumed he belonged to the merchant class at best. While he was tall, he was also lithe, with little by way of muscle to intimidate his adversaries. I could easily wrap my fist around his ribs and splinter him from the inside out.

I'd done nearly that to the female he cared for at the beginning of the war. Her skull was one of those at the front as an extra fuck you to him. The two of us had met here numerous times, and every time, his revulsion at what I had done was undisguised. As was his utter fury. "Zahal Ishim, my apologies for keeping you waiting."

He scoffed, lips curling into a sneer. "We both know you

were late on purpose, Halálhívó." He spit out my title like it was a bitter potion. To him, to his Koron and Korona, my power was the ultimate demonstration of why the Demons were little more than animals and too impure to live in this world alongside them. To reanimate the dead was unholy, and to utilize my power on the battlefield, the greatest sin.

Yet they feared it all the same.

And somehow, his power of the Hive, to control the minds of the still-living and wield them as extensions of himself on the battlefield, was the holiest of gifts from their Goddess.

I reclined in the chair, exuding bored disinterest. "I waited long enough while your Padisa slaughtered my soldiers." I didn't deign to give Zaph my attention. He was *unworthy* of it.

The Zahal had the nerve to crack a grin. "Ah yes, that particular Padisa is now a Myrza for his successful endeavor to undercut your army."

I fought the urge to roll my eyes. Flies buzzed to garner attention, yet they still only feasted on the decay left behind by others. Just like them, Zaph was no real killer. He hadn't even raised his blade during the whole ordeal. "As you can see, my mate and I survived. An oversight, perhaps, on the *Myrza's* part. Or perhaps he told you we perished alongside the rest before you offered him the title." I offered a dismissive flick of my hand in his direction, like I was shooing him away. "But what's done is done. And because of his actions, yet again, our retaliation will be twice as brutal as your paltry tricks could ever be."

Something flashed across Zahal Ishim's face as I reminded him precisely how the war had begun. How the inept Angel had dared ambush my battalion and decimate us then. He hadn't realized that the Halálhívó stood among them, and by the time I'd wielded the dead to my advantage, it had been too late for him. Then, only Zaph had remained alive to carry a message to

Ishim. The H I carved into his forehead served as a constant reminder to all those who dared forget my might.

Clearly, they needed another lesson.

I crossed an ankle over a knee and leaned into my elbow, digging pointedly into another Angel skull. "I'll offer you a chance to retreat, if you want to live."

Fury contorted Ishim's features. "The ones who should retreat are you, Demon beasts." He spit at my feet, and both my loyal hounds snarled, hackles raised.

Assyria didn't flinch, merely continued to lift her chin and look down her nose at the handful of Angels standing before her. How I wanted them to bow at her feet, to beg for her forgiveness for what they had done.

Soon.

A dark, sinister growl rumbled in my chest. "Tread carefully, Ishim. I will not even allow your saliva to be close to my mate."

"Then perhaps we will have to take her again. Only this time, she will not live," he hissed, nearly vibrating with rage.

It was nothing compared to my own at his threat. Blood pounded in my ears and I clenched my teeth so hard I thought they might shatter. My hands twitched of their own accord, like they wanted to snap out and wrap around the Zahal's neck.

His words were kindling to the fire I'd been stoking since before their arrival.

The Angels' haughty, superior attitudes made them easy to anger. A trick I exploited to my advantage numerous times. "I'd like to see you try," I taunted, keeping the fury inside me caged.

Beside me, Assyria stiffened. Before panic overtook her mind, I continued. "Should you dare again, I will personally rip your bones from within your body while you're still alive. In fact," I finally turned my attention to Zaph, "I think that's what I'll do to you anyway, *Myrza*. After I tear off your wings and offer them to my mate."

Lust flooded our bond, and I flared my nostrils to suck in a steadying breath. Thank fuck the horned ebony helmet covered most of my face. I *loved* that Assyria was so aroused by my violence, especially for her. Because now that I'd admitted she was perfection incarnate, I wanted nothing more than to show her just how far I'd go to prove my love for her, my devotion to her, how I would protect her.

Because now this war held more meaning to me than ever before. Not only was I saving all the Demons from death, I was also saving my little imposter.

Zaph lunged forward, only to be stopped by a square smack to the chest by Ishim. The sound reverberated around the small, packed space. A grin bloomed on my face at the display—not that any of them could see it beneath my helmet.

I'd thoroughly rattled them in a few short sentences.

"You have something of ours, Halálhívó," Ishim ground out, shooting a 'calm the fuck down' look to Zaph.

I'd wondered if he'd bring up the three captured females. "And what is that?" I asked, unwilling to admit anything.

"Three females. We saw you haul them away," he snapped, finally removing his arm from Zaph's body.

"Aye, we did. That was the first step of our retaliation. They're all dead now after I allowed my soldiers a go at them. After all, they've been fighting for a long time and we don't have any females here to keep them company." All lies, but they didn't know that.

Ishim's face turned a harsh shade of scarlet. Rapp coughed, and I flicked my attention to him just in time to see him cover his mouth with his hand, hiding a grin.

"Your mate is here. They could have used her cunt," he hissed, eyes narrowing on Assyria.

The sliver of glass that caged my temper shattered. In an instant, I was on my feet, black shadows billowing from my frame. The Angels at the rear of their party had the good sense to backstep. Rapp and Trol lunged for my arms a moment before I tried to swing them at Ishim and yanked me backward.

"Rokath, stop!" Assyria shouted down our mental connection.

I blinked, chest heaving, at her. Her burgundy eyes were fierce and fiery as she stared me down. *"Don't lose your advantage now."*

She was right, and her words dulled the edge of my rage. Shrugging off my Hadvezér, I cracked my neck and flexed my fingers before facing Ishim again. The fucker wore the smuggest of grins. I wanted to wipe it off his face. It was only a matter of time before his and Zaph's heads swung from my hands as I walked the streets of Sivy, as Kiira had seen all those years ago.

I draped a protective arm over Assyria, who squared her shoulders and did not cower under the Angel's insinuations as we faced them again. "Is there anything else you wish to discuss, Ishim?"

The Zahal's smile widened, his ice blue eyes flashing with victory. "Not at this time. But I know where to find you, should I require your attention again." He dropped every word with his focus on Assyria. The threat in his tone was as clear as the color of his eyes. I wanted to gouge them out of his skull.

"Then leave," I growled, leveling an equal insinuation of violence in his direction. "We'll meet on the battlefield soon enough."

"With pleasure," he spit out. Switching to Angelic, he told his companions to keep their eyes open for any sign of the females as they exited the camp.

That was one of the reasons I suspected he accepted my invitation to come to the command center in the first place. Rapp and Trol knew as much, and they swept from their positions in the periphery to escort the Angels out of the camp.

Neither Assyria or I moved until the last had exited through the map room.

Then, the shouts arose again, jeers and insults lobbed at the departing enemy.

This time, I wanted them unbound. These Angels needed reminding of who they faced, so the next time we clashed, we'd have beaten down their will and could shove them the fuck out of the Demon Realm.

Because one thing was certain: I would not fail again.

The next time we clashed, we wouldn't merely break their lines.

We'd shatter their will.

And Assyria and I?

We'd become their fucking Gods.

8

ASSYRIA

Air whooshed from my lungs, and I slumped into Rokath. "That was intense," I murmured after a moment. My limbs tingled as the adrenaline bled away. Seeing them again, seeing Zaph again, after he harmed Rokath and me had been about as difficult as I'd imagined. Yet the way Rokath defended me...it made my low belly flutter.

"Are you alright?" he asked, hooking two fingers under my chin and forcing me to look up at him.

"I'm fine, Rokath," I said, a soft smile blooming on my face. "More than fine, actually." I ducked out from under his arm and flattened my palms over his armored chest. Dark hair spilled down my back as I looked up at him through long lashes. "Would you really rip their bones from their flesh while they were still alive?"

"Little imposter, I would *savor* every moment of pain I inflicted in your name," he murmured darkly, snatching my waist and making my breath hitch. "You want me to do worse? I'll do worse. I'll do anything to show you that I'll protect you from harm."

He fell back onto his throne of bones, bringing me with him.

I straddled his hips and walked my fingers up to the skin that barely peeked through the gaps in his armor. The base of his throat bobbed as I stroked the stubble there. Working beneath his helmet, I removed the ebony skull and revealed the seriousness of his promise etched into his rugged features.

He removed a hand from my lower back and threaded it through the hair at the base of my neck. A sting of pain almost made me hiss, but then he scrunched and tilted my head to the side. The rough feel of his face against my neck soothed the ache, and the way his tongue flattened over my fluttering pulse made it abate entirely. His hot breath dusted over my sensitive ear as he rasped, "You are mine, *mate*."

That word wrung a shiver from me. "Mate," I whispered back, rolling my hips into his. "I loved hearing you call me that to their faces."

Rokath groaned as I stilled my movements over his quickly-hardening length. "Did I terrorize them enough for you?"

"Yes," I breathed, finding his shoulders and adjusting myself again. The seam of my pants rubbed deliciously against my center.

Rokath released his grip on my hair, and in one smooth motion, he lifted me off his lap and placed me on my feet in front of the throne. A noise of protest slipped out of me until he scooted to the edge and pressed me to my knees. The weight of his hands on my shoulders robbed me of air.

"Mmm, you look so pretty there, little imposter. Much like the first time I saw you." The burgundy of Rokath's eyes had all but disappeared as his pupils dilated. Lust drowned our bond. "All I could think about was how I wanted to shut you up by shoving my cock down your throat. I think I'll do that now."

I raked my teeth over my bottom lip as I looked up at my mate. His frame was imposing, powerful, *dominant* and his energy consumed the entire space. Without breaking our connection, he unbuckled the straps on his shoulders, allowing the metal to fall away. With tender care, he placed the pieces on the floor beside the chair. Grem and Zeec scattered to their beds as if they sensed the dark twist in the air.

Easing forward, he tore his tunic over his head and revealed the skulls, roses, and animals that decorated his torso. His chiseled abdominals flexed in the low light as he reached for the ties of his pants. My eyes flicked to the long, thick outline above the metal plates strapped to his thighs.

"Free my cock, Assyria," he commanded, capturing my face in his large hands and tearing my attention back to him. His burgundy eyes hypnotized me with the depth of devotion in them. "Show me how much you appreciated my defense of you."

He released me and leaned back, bracing his corded forearms on the skulls decorating his throne. Rokath might not have been a king, but there was no doubt he was a God among us. Wetting my lips, I scooted forward and reached for him.

Every other time I'd had him in my mouth, he'd taken control of the actions and I'd been a passive participant in his pleasure. I couldn't deny how much I loved his domination of me, though. Nerves fluttered in my belly as I wrapped a tentative palm around him and squeezed.

"That's it," he rasped as I did it again. "Now reach inside and let me feel your hot skin against it."

Doing as he instructed, I wiggled the ties looser and found the beast. A thick vein throbbed along its length, and I ran my thumb across it before splaying my fingers around him. Rokath's eyes closed, and a line formed in his brow as I worked him up and down. Emboldened by how I was affecting him, I tugged his pants wider and lower until his dick burst into my vision.

The woven rug dug into my knees as I shifted forward,

opening my mouth to take him inside it. Fisting the base, I licked my lips, then wrapped them around the glistening head. A swirl of my tongue pulled a low groan from Rokath. His fingers dug into the skulls on the armrests, turning white as I dipped my head lower.

Pride blossomed in my chest while arousal bloomed between my thighs.

My jaw ached as I worked to take him deeper. Closing my eyes, I bobbed up and down, only to be stopped with a hand wrapping around my long hair. "Look at me while your pretty lips are around my dick," Rokath rasped. Raking my gaze up his torso to his face, I did. Drool fell out of the corners of my mouth and over my chin. Rokath wrapped my locks tighter to get them out of the way. "Keep going."

I opened my throat to suck him down. He hit the back, and I gagged, struggling to breathe through it.

"You can take it," he told me, the utter confidence in his voice empowering me to continue. Flaring my nostrils, I dragged in a ragged breath and sank lower. But Rokath wasn't satisfied. Using his leverage, he pushed until my nose brushed his belly. Tears blurred my vision and spilled over as all my air was cut off.

"Fuck, Assyria, your mouth," Rokath ground out, the sound a heady mix of primal pleasure and tumbling rocks. My center wept for the power I wielded over my mate. Again, I gagged, and only then did Rokath ease me off him. A string of saliva connected us still.

Rokath cupped my chin and traced his thumb over my swollen bottom lip. "Such a good girl for me," he praised, and more wetness slicked my thighs. Then, he mapped a path from my face to the base of my neck, wrapping his large hand around it. "Tell me, did you like it when I cut off your air?"

"Yes," I heaved out, and his fingers tightened again. He

scooted forward, his cock bobbing with the movement. The tip weeped, a bead of moisture threatening to fall onto the bones of long-dead Angels.

When it did, a wicked, sinful heat swept through me. My attention flicked up to Rokath's frame towering over me. Those damn lips curved into a sinister, merciless grin. "Open for me, mate."

Obediently, I did. Rokath wasted no time in shoving himself in again. Flattening a palm on the back of my head, he pushed down. I gagged, hard, lungs seizing, while he pistoned in and out of my mouth. The sensation was overwhelming, and my heart thundered against my ribs. Tears streamed out in rivulets as he continued to chase his pleasure. Impossibly, he thickened against my tongue. With one harsh thrust, he buried himself in my throat. Ropes of his hot cum coated the back of it, and it was all I could do to swallow him down. A string of curses followed, and finally, he released me.

I barely had a moment to rake in a breath before he yanked me from my kneeling position. My knees protested until he spun us, supplanting me on his throne. Rokath shoved my thighs apart and buried his head between the leather. Inhaling deeply, he squeezed my thighs, thumbs digging into the sensitive insides. "Fuck, I can smell how aroused you are, Assyria."

Over the seam of my pants, he dragged his teeth against my core. My hips bucked at the touch, and a wanton whimper slipped from my throat. "Please, Rokath."

"Beg me," Rokath commanded, his riotous burgundy eyes lifting to collide with my own. "Beg me for your pleasure."

Desire was something I'd always been taught was shameful, and yet, with the Halálhívó—the Fates-chosen savior of the Demons—kneeling between my thighs, the only emotion present was *pride*. At how I'd brought the most feared male in all of Keleti to his knees.

Ready to worship *me*.

I had hated him; I now loved him. The power, the pain, the pleasure, I craved all of it—all of him.

Rokath opened doors I'd never imagined existed inside me, drawing out a nature I'd long kept hidden. And I was not above asking for him to teach me more, to give me more. Not when he'd always oblige.

"Please, I need you," I panted, lust tumbling through my veins. An ache bloomed in my jaw, a reminder of the bruising way he'd taken my mouth. Yet I could think of nothing more than having that hot, hard length inside me.

Since our return, we'd yet to couple again. Our bond flared as if it too recalled how long it had been, growing as insistent as my dripping center and his throbbing dick. "Now," I whimpered, more of a desperate demand than an obedient plea.

He pressed the backs of his knuckles into the seam and dragged. "This little cunt is greedy for pleasure, isn't she?"

"Yes," I breathed, pushing back into him, chasing more sensation. He rewarded me with another drag of his hand against my center. The groan that fled me was so loud a flash of worry that we'd be overheard slipped through me.

"Let them hear you, little imposter. Let them know who your *mate* is, and how well I make your body tremble." Without further teasing, Rokath yanked at the ties of my pants and tore the sides apart. He made quick work of opening the leather tunic too, until my bound breasts heaved against the musky air. Palming the roundness, he lifted them and squeezed before rubbing his thumbs over the hard points beneath them.

"Rise," he ordered, backing away and leaving my skin far too overheated. Without hesitation, I did. Rokath shoved the tunic over my shoulders, then dug his fingers between my ribs and the wrap of fabric around my chest. In one powerful motion, he ripped it away, drawing a gasp from my lungs.

A masculine groan rumbled out of him as he leaned down and took each nipple in his mouth, raking his teeth for good measure. The world spun while he worked his tongue around the buds, and I melted into him.

His hands hooked under my waistband and shoved my pants to my ankles. The moment they touched the ground, I stepped out of them, because fuck, I needed to feel him between my thighs and the only way that would happen was if I spread them.

I backed away from Rokath, eyes never leaving him. Through hooded lids, he watched me sink onto his throne and wrap my fingers over the skulls at the edge of the arms. His cock pointed straight at me, dripping from the tip. Bronze gleamed at his thighs, the dark fabric stretching taught beneath the weight of his armor. Motionless, but lethal, the kind of coiled stillness that sent a shiver along my spine.

One leg, then the other, dropped out. His eyes sliced straight to the glistening arousal slicking my center. "So wet for me," he rumbled, stepping forward. Like boulders falling from the mountains, his knees hit the floor. The earth tremored even more than I did. When he lowered his mouth to my core, I thought I might faint.

As his hot breath ghosted over me, I clenched. "Please," I said again, my voice hoarse.

"Please what?"

"Please touch me. Please give me pleasure. Please let me feel you inside me." Each sentence was more desperate than the last, but I was well beyond the point of caring.

With a feral groan, he dipped his head and licked me back to front. The cry that burst from my throat when his teeth grazed my clit echoed around the canvas walls. When he flattened his tongue and lapped at me like fresh cream, my head lolled back.

Air flooded my lungs as he parted my folds. It fled when he slipped the first finger inside.

"Rokath," I panted, voice no louder than a frantic breath.

"So tight, Assyria. I'll need to stretch you thoroughly to accommodate me."

A second finger entered me. He flexed them wide before curling them against a spot deep inside. More wetness gushed out of me as he continued to lavish attention there. Mewls and incoherent words battled with my breath as he worked me into a frenzy.

Nothing else existed in that moment other than us—no war, no Angels, no Demons. Only the mate the Fates had blessed me with, his masterful movements, and the love that bled between us. Rokath's devotion was unquestionable as he ravished my core, yanking me to the edge of the cliffs of pleasure. For Rokath ruled that domain as much as he ruled on the battlefield.

Images of him slaughtering hordes of Angels, then reanimating their corpses and bending them to his will flooded my mind. His undeniable power, his demonstrated mercilessness, his dark command, all of it enthralled me in a way that transcended our mating bond.

The pain in him called to the pain in me.

And I needed a hint of that to fall over that edge.

"Hurt me," I whimpered, hips shoving into his face as I sought more.

The grip he held over my thigh turned bruising, and he shoved them further apart with elbow and hand. The edges of bones dug into my soft flesh, bringing me a bite among the pleasure of his fingers and tongue.

"Yes," I hissed, head tipping back.

"Eyes on me, little imposter," Rokath commanded in my mind. I snapped my attention down, catching his wicked gaze. His

heavy brows pinched, his focus on utterly ravishing me. *"You come when I say you come, Assyria. You are mine to command, mine to protect, mine to pleasure."*

My walls clenched over his fingers. Rokath dragged them out to the first knuckle. A cry of protest slipped out of me. He slammed them into the hilt before the sound had died on my lips. Again, my walls fluttered. Especially as he curled over that spot again. "I don't think I can hold on much longer," I said, lips morphing into an O as he sucked my clit. "Fuck. Do that again. Please."

He did, adding a rake of his teeth for good measure. *"When you come, scream my name. Scream it loud enough that those fucking Angels hear you."*

"Yes, Halálhívó," I whimpered, for that was the voice he'd used with me. There was no use in denying that in the throes of pleasure, I fucking loved when he spoke to me in that commanding tone.

He moaned, long and low, against me. The vibration mixed with the rapid pulse of his fingers. The edge of ecstasy emerged. Eyes locked on his, I raced toward it, walls pulsing. With one last nip, I leaped. Careening through the air, losing all semblance of space and time, as pleasure swelled.

"Halálhívó!" I screamed, fingers going numb from the way I dug them into the skulls of our enemies.

My mate continued to work me as sweat beaded and tumbled down my brow, entire body trembling from the force of the pleasure wrung from me. When my breath finally returned, he released me. I panted as he rose to his full height. The tattoos decorating his frame looked even more deadly in the low light. He crooked his fingers, and I sat forward. "Suck them clean."

My arousal glistened over them, and I took them in my mouth much like I had with his cock. I tasted myself, earthy and sweet, while heat flared in his eyes. When I'd finished, I released them with a pop.

Rokath stripped out of the remainder of his clothes, until his entire lethal body was bared to me. He gripped his massive length and stroked.

"Who am I to you, Assyria?" An undercurrent of violence threaded his tone, and my thighs trembled.

"My mate," I rasped.

He stepped forward, his dick level with my face. With his free hand he cupped my chin and tilted my head to look up at him.

"And?"

"My protector," I whimpered, tongue flicking over my lips to wet them.

He smoothed my mussed hair before fisting a bundle at the base of my skull. "Keep going."

A tremor wracking my frame as energy crackled between us. "Please, I need you inside me." My core wept at how close his cock was to me.

Using my hair, he yanked me to my feet and captured my mouth in a bruising kiss. His tongue swiped insistently against the seam of my lips, and I opened for him, tasting myself once again. He tasted himself too, salty tang and musk mixing. His teeth dug into my bottom lip as he grasped my hips and hauled me up his hard body.

Spinning, he planted himself on the throne so I was straddling him again. I rolled my hips against his, a sob wrenching from me as finally no barrier remained between us.

"I'll tell you what you are to me, Assyria," Rokath growled, fisting his hardness and lining himself with my entrance.

I wrapped my hands around his neck to steady myself, preparing for the way he'd stretch me.

"You are why my blade will swing with renewed fervor."

He pressed against me, and my breath hitched.

"You are my reason for breathing."

One. Fucking. Inch. All he gave me when I was dying for the entirety of him.

"You are my pain."

A whimper escaped me as he offered me a meager amount more.

"You are my pleasure."

Arousal gushed from my thighs as the tip *finally* entered me.

"You are the only female I've ever loved. The only I will ever love."

"Rokath," I breathed, the word utterly wanton. A wet, slick noise filled the air as he slid deeper inside me.

"You are my mate. I'd kill a million soldiers to hear those three words spill from your pretty lips. To hear my name on them as you shatter around my cock. To feel your cunt pulse as I drag out your pleasure."

"Rokath, *please*," I begged, opening the floodgates to my desperation.

If I don't have him inside me right now, I'll perish.

In one powerful thrust, he seated himself to the hilt. Our skin slapped with so much force he sent me bouncing up before I landed roughly on him again. "Fates," I cursed, stars of desire dancing in my vision.

Rokath dug his fingers into my ass and dragged me against his hardness. My clit rubbed against the squares of his muscles. A ragged breath fled my lungs.

"Only I am your Fate," Rokath growled, repeating the motion.

He was so deep, so thick inside me, every nerve was alive from the touch of him.

"No one holds power over you like I do."

"No," I whimpered back, rolling my hips and setting a

rhythm that had me racing to that blissful edge once again. "Just like no one holds power over you but me."

A dark chuckle rumbled in his chest. "They are not one in the same."

"We'll see about that," I panted, trembling as I continued to chase my release.

Rokath guided me up and down his length, a primal groan escaping him as I rocked harder, faster. Sweat slicked my spine, but I didn't care. A forceful throb drove into my walls, which tightened in response. I was so, so close...

Rokath tightened his grip on my waist, stilling my movements. My mouth flew open, ready to admonish him, but the merciless expression on his face silenced me. "Say those three words and I'll let you come."

I tried to snatch at what I so urgently needed. That only served to make Rokath dig in more. "I love you, Rokath," I whimpered. He was right, my cunt was a greedy little thing.

"Good girl." He hardened even more inside me. A gasp wedged in my throat as he angled my hips and dragged me along him again.

"Oh, fuck, Rokath—"

"That's it, little imposter, come for me. Scream my name again. My *real* name," he ground out, keeping his pace *exactly* as I needed it as I careened over the edge.

"Rokath!" I cried again, the volume, the intensity of my words unmitigated. My voice echoed in my ears as ecstasy shattered through me like I'd hit the ground after leaping over a cliff. It robbed me of all thought, all sense except for pulse after pulse of my core.

"I love you, Assyria," he rasped into my neck, sinking his teeth over my fluttering heartbeat like he was digging the words into my skin. He thrust into me from below, skin slapping to accompany his forceful grunts. "When the Weaver wanted to create perfection, she wove you."

Dizzy, I collapsed into his arms, clinging to him like he was my life—because he was. "I love you, Rokath. Your strength, your protection, your devotion. All of it."

A low moan escaped him and he clenched me tighter against him. *"More,"* he spoke into my mind.

"You and I are made for each other. Our fire. Our passion. Our pain," I panted. My thighs trembled from the position he held me in. Another orgasm rose, fast and hard.

"Come with me," he commanded.

"Yes," I managed to get out before I was overcome again. Rokath's teeth sank in again, and the metallic tang of blood filled my nostrils. He groaned, and then he pulled me off of him, letting his cum spill all over the throne of bones.

Shivers of pleasure wracked my frame as we remained wrapped in one another, coming down from the highs of our coupling. Rokath licked at the spot he'd bloodied on my shoulder, soothing the ache. With our fast healing ability, the wound was already closing over.

"Mine," he said one last time, planting a kiss on the crook of my neck, my pulse point, and then the spot just below my ear.

"Yours," I replied, scratching the base of his skull with my nails.

When he finally reared back and locked eyes with me, the darkness in them had abated. No longer drunk on lust, he simply held me like I was his most precious possession. He ran his knuckles along my sweaty temple and smoothed the hair out of my face.

"I think it's time you told me what happened to you. What shaped you into the male you are today. The full, whole truth. No shutting down or brushing me off anymore. I deserve it after everything," I murmured, leaning into his comfort.

Rokath stiffened before blowing out a long breath. "Fine. But not here. In our tent. And I need some scale."

"I thought there was a no alcohol rule?" I asked, cocking my head to the side. A teasing smile rose to my lips, though it was soft from the bliss heavy in my veins.

"There is. But I am the Halálhívó and the rules don't apply to me."

I scoffed and slipped off his lap. Typical.

Rokath went to one of the cases at the back of the room and returned with a cloth and a pitcher of water. "Sit, let me clean you."

His tenderness melted my heart. So I did, only to remember that was exactly where he'd spilled his seed. A laugh burst from me. "Is that the first time you've come on your throne?"

"The first, though it will not be the last." He crowded my back and reached around me to wipe it away. The heat emanating off of him was pure bliss. "Now that I know how much you like to scorn them. Devious little thing."

He nudged me forward and I finally sat, allowing him to wipe my release from my sensitive center. When he finished, we dressed quickly. From that same case, he pulled a flask and tucked it into his pocket. Then he held his hand to me. "Come, and I will tell you everything."

I threaded my fingers through his, savoring the rough callouses that brushed against my flesh. Everything with Rokath was...right. The darkness between us. The pain. The trauma. All of it was woven by the Fates, not to break us, but to bind us. So we could bleed, burn, and defend when the other needed it most.

All Rokath had to do now was surrender his hard-won throne and let me in.

9

R☠KATH

Dragging the chair to the table felt like hauling an executioner's block into place, a grim prelude to the conversation long overdue. Assyria sat across from me, those devious burgundy eyes I'd fallen helplessly in love with studying me with an emotion I'd scarcely ever welcomed—concern. Yet from her, from my mate...I'd take it all.

The wood creaked as I settled into it, thumping a cup and the metal flask against the smooth top of the table. Fuck, this conversation wasn't going to be easy. Centuries of repressed feelings didn't merely want to claw up my throat and out of my mouth, even to my mate.

That was where the scale came in. The amber liquid splashed as I poured myself a double dose. I wasted no time throwing it back. The spicy alcohol burned all the way to my stomach before settling there. Not that the organ itself was settled; no, it churned like an angry sea.

Grem sidled up to me and plopped his head in my lap, looking up at me with his piercing red eyes. I pet his soft black fur, letting it ground me along with the scale. Assyria reached across the table and squeezed my forearm. Her small fingers brushed over a tattoo of thorns and roses wrapped around a skull, and then she retreated.

Since returning, we'd changed clothes—her, to one of my tunics that swam to her knees, me to a loose pair of pants I'd swiped from Rapp. The rest of our belongings were lost to the camp we abandoned.

I'll hire a clothier when we arrive in Fured to craft us both proper attire again.

Assyria pointedly cleared her throat, drawing my attention away from my thoughts. "You can procrastinate all you want, but you will tell me." Her tone was firm, yet gentle.

I exhaled, counting to ten and focusing on the feel of my chest deflating. Almost unconsciously, I rubbed my pectorals right over my heart. Grem didn't move from his position as I poured myself another drink. As I tipped it back, Assyria commented, "That stuff is disgusting. I don't know how you drink it."

The glass smacked against the table as I set it down again. "And how would you know, little imposter?"

She snorted and rolled her eyes. "I drank that bottle you had hidden away in your room at Gyor Palace."

"Of course you did," I grumbled, swishing the flask. It was almost empty; not nearly enough to get me through the next hour or so of my life. It would take time to tell her everything, for there was so much, and honestly, I didn't know where to begin.

Her hand once again closed the gap between us. "Just start talking. Whatever comes to mind first. No need to remember what I do and don't know. Honestly, I could use a refresher anyway."

Not meeting her piercing gaze, I traced the rim of the cup. "My father was the brother of the last Kral. The middle brother at that. He always felt forgotten, like he didn't have a place in the world. He took his perceived shortcomings out on me. Not that either of his brothers were any less cruel."

"What about your mother?" she asked after a moment of pause from me.

"Died giving birth to me," I muttered. I never knew her, and my father didn't speak much of her. Nor did he ever remarry. For the longest time, I couldn't decide if it was because he loved her so much or because he hated her. That had been a constant theme in my life: the contrast between hate and love, two sides of the same emotion. For one could not exist without the other. The depths of my feelings for Assyria were a testament to that.

"I'm so sorry, Rokath," she murmured, squeezing tighter.

Finally, I met her gaze. "That is nothing compared to what happened in my youth."

Assyria's burgundy eyes shone, and she nodded, a silent understanding.

I looked at the ceiling, trying to find the words to tell her exactly how much of an asshole my father was. What he made me do.

"Xannirin and I went to Fured, to the military academy, young. The former Kral was harsh with Xannirin too. I always tried to protect him from the worst of it. At least at the academy, I thought we might have a modicum of freedom."

With a sigh, I shook my head. "I was wrong."

A chill settled over me like the fog that rolled off the coast in the early mornings. The sensation and memory were enough to paint vivid images of my wrongdoings in my mind. "The Kral and my father made frequent visits to Fured to check on us. My father more often, though. He was harder on me than any of the drilling trainers. All of whom bowed to him and allowed him free reign while he was in residence. He wanted me to rise the ranks in the army, to become someone important since he was nothing. When I'd fuck up, he'd take me into his quarters and beat me. Break my ribs, my nose, my fingers.”

Assyria sucked in a sharp breath. She'd spoken of her husband—the one she'd killed and impersonated until the moment our mate bond snapped in place—and the horrors he'd inflicted. Those words had flayed me open during our first meeting, triggering a visceral response. One that wasn't solely because she was my mate. Those protective instincts flared, yes, but so too did my own trauma.

For centuries, I'd been running from the memories that haunted my dreams. I'd forged myself into the Halálhívó, the cold, merciless, feared leader of the Demon army, because I could protect others better than I'd protected myself. I'd donned a mask to hide myself from the world too after Xannirin, Kiira, and I decided that we would become Fates that walked the earth.

To hear Assyria speak of similar abuse cracked that facade in an instant. Wrenched my carefully crafted helmet right off my head. Exposed me to myself.

My mate leaned over the table, a tear spilling down her cheek. With the lightest of touches, she brushed the bump on my nose. “They don't heal properly if they're not set right away,” I told her. “I gave up trying after a while.”

“And your fingers?” she asked softly.

“I always told the healers that I smashed them into things,” I shrugged. “Those were important for wielding a sword.”

“And that's why you tolerated the pain of the stakes so well,” she said, removing the empty glass from my hand and placing hers in it instead. She traced the white scar on my palm, then the A she carved into my wrist—the brand she'd given me to match the one I'd given her. That shared claim upon one another's souls, more visible than the perfect circles resting between our shoulder blades.

The touch was soothing, and I basked in the comfort she offered me. So rarely had I indulged in this delicacy, thinking I was undeserving of it. That it was safer for everyone if I remained aloof.

Right then, Assyria was offering me a different type of safety. One I desperately wanted to lean into, yet I wasn't sure how to surrender entirely. "He visited one time shortly before I came of age, and from the moment he exited the carriage, I knew it was going to be the worst visit yet. When the Kral arrived a few days later, Xannirin and I were already on edge. My father wanted to show off my powers for his brother. How well I'd learned to harness them."

"What did he make you do?" Assyria asked, rubbing my fingers now as if she could ease the hurt from them, centuries later.

"A three on one fight, where I had to call upon the dead ones and use them to slaughter the others. I didn't have nearly as much control over my power then as I do now," I explained. Now, I could wield hundreds of bodies simultaneously. I'd raised several thousand at one point, but my magic tapped out too quickly at that scale. The number I chose at any given point in time was based on centuries of experience. The past decade had honed it even more than the years of my father's abuse.

"He made you kill three other Demon soldiers?" she clarified, sorrow threading her tone.

"Aye. Afterward, he called me to his room. To beat me, though for what, I wasn't sure. I'd executed every move perfectly. But I'd had enough. He closed the door." I paused, jaw clenching as the memory surfaced, clear as the sky above the Paks Desert. "And then, I ensured he was too afraid to lay a hand on me ever again."

Assyria hummed a sympathetic noise, letting me know she was listening.

I retracted my hand so I could pour the last of the scale into my glass. The next piece of information would be the most difficult to discuss. Fates, I didn't even talk to Rapp and Xannirin about Thast, and they were both *there*.

Assyria watched me, still poised on the edge of her seat, ready to reach out and comfort me on a moment's notice.

"He found another way to punish me after I *really* failed." I tossed back the alcohol, relishing the burn in my throat. Then, I rolled tension from my shoulders. My stomach clenched, and my palms sweated.

Would Assyria look at me differently after I revealed my greatest failure? My greatest shame?

"I'm sure it wasn't that bad–" she started, but I cut her off with a shake of my head.

"Place," I told Grem, and with a huff, he trotted to his bed on the opposite side of the tent. After a few turns, he curled up beside Zeec. I faced Assyria and splayed my arms across the table. I needed her grounding presence for this. She understood my silent request and slipped her warm skin against mine.

Dropping my head, I failed to steady my racing heart. She deserved to know everything, the whole truth. Yet I hadn't spoken about the events since...ever. Rapp and Xannirin had both attempted to bring it up on multiple occasions, and I'd silenced them every time.

"That bag, the tattered, threadbare one...belonged to a male named Thast. I keep it as a reminder..." I trailed off, throat working. Then, emitting a shuddering breath, I lifted my gaze to find my mate's. "Thast was the fourth in our group. Xannirin, Rapp, Thast, and I bunked together in Fured, and then again when we were assigned to a border outpost, every graduate's first assignment. While we were there, I finally earned the title of Vezető. My first route with the promotion happened to be the day after the new year."

My knee bounced under the table as the first wave of shame rose. I forced it to still, then forced myself to speak again.

"Of course, being young and ridiculously stupid, the four of us went out drinking the night before, despite our scheduled early departure for the wall. The entire unit was roaring drunk as we rode to the outpost, in fact. Our dulled senses allowed the Angels to attack. All but six of us died." My grip on Assyria tightened, as if I could physically pin her in place should she attempt to reject me now.

"Oh, Rokath," she whispered instead, squeezing back twice as hard. "No wonder you keep such strict rules."

"That is part of it," I admitted freely. A muscle feathered in my jaw as I tried to find the right words to convey what happened next. "The consequences are what solidified them."

She nodded slowly, allowing me space to sort through it all. Her unwavering devotion was cleansing, like by baring my soul to her I was ridding myself of the centuries of dust caked to the memories.

"When the Kral and my father arrived, they were both furious. Never had I fucked up like that, and in the process nearly gotten Xannirin killed. The six survivors—Xannirin, Rapp, Thast, myself, and two others—knelt before them to beg for forgiveness. My father had a twisted version in mind. Only three of us could walk away from there, and since I was in charge, I had to be one of them, to live with my mistakes. My father offered me a choice: kill them myself using my powers and offer them a swift death, or allow him to do it as he saw fit. Had he...it would have been a slow, savage descent into the Reaper's embrace for them."

Assyria's lips pressed together, and two tears leaked from her eyes. Her hands shook with how hard they held mine. Without breaking our embrace, she rose and drifted around the table to stand in front of me. With our size difference, we were nearly eye level. I brought our joined fingers to my mouth and kissed her knuckles. Then, I pulled her into my lap. She kneaded my shoulders, remaining quiet as I fought to contain my emotions.

"You don't have to be strong for me, Rokath. I'm here to share your burdens, your pain," she murmured. "I know what it's like to be at the mercy of someone cruel."

A choked sob escaped me before I brought my fist to my mouth to smother it. I gritted my teeth, trying to fight off the knife readying to flay me open. Not just for my pain, but hers. For what Vagach did to her all those years. Because of the changes *I* helped weave into society.

With a ragged exhale, I said, "I couldn't kill Xannirin. The Kral saved me from that choice, along with Rapp, since he too had burgundy eyes. Which left Thast and the other two. He just *let me do it.*" My voice cracked, crumbled to pieces as the memory of his last words to me surfaced.

It's okay, Rokath, he had said.

"He didn't try to fight his fate, just accepted the Reaper was ready to take him. He didn't cry out as I killed him. And when I had to Call his body..." a shudder wracked my frame, my temperature dropping even further, "and have him kill the other two, my father watched on with satisfaction."

I gritted my teeth, and Assyria moved her ministrations to my jaw. She worked for a few moments while I attempted to regain control. "I'd vowed long before that to kill him. After what he forced me to do, Xannirin and I were in agreement that the brothers needed to die. With the rising threat of the Angels, they chose to slaughter three fully trained soldiers, and for what? So my father could prove he still had power over me?"

My hands balled into fists.

"It took decades to properly plan everything. The Kral and his two brothers had to perish together for Xannirin to inherit the throne. But we didn't execute it until I'd worked my way up the ranks of the army. After a particularly nasty skirmish along the wall, I'd had enough. We were lacking in males to defend the Demons and the Angels were growing more fervent by the year. Thankfully, Kiira was in agreement when I sat the two of them down and told them it was time. She might have been a bastard, but she was no stranger to the brutality the three imposed."

"At least you had each other," Assyria murmured, hands flattening over my chest. My heart beat into her palm, as if it knew that it was utterly safe in her care. As if it knew it belonged only to her.

"Aye. And Rapp too. He might not be of royal blood, but he helped us through it all," I said. Already, I felt lighter, like by speaking the worst memories into existence, they could no longer fester on my soul.

"So the three of you killed them?" she clarified.

I shook my head. "Only I landed the killing blows, little imposter. By then, I was numb to the act. Xannirin hadn't taken more than a handful of lives, and Kiira, well, I didn't want to taint her."

"You've always protected everyone, Rokath. Who ever protected you?"

I clenched my teeth, fighting off the spear of sorrow digging into my chest. Assyria had an uncanny ability to name my deepest desires and unveil the well of emotion that accompanied them. Air froze in my lungs as I forced the sob back down. "No one. I needed no one."

Assyria shook her head. "You *wanted* no one because then you'd have to share this with them. But I'm here now." She cupped my cheek, and only when she swiped her thumb across it did I realize a salty tear had slipped out. "Let me protect your emotions like you protect my body. Let me be your comfort when it all feels like too much. Lay your worries, your fears, your pain at my feet. We can shoulder this burden together."

At that, I shattered. I snatched Assyria closer, banding my arms around her so our bodies melded together like the ores used to forge weapons. Chest heaving, I buried my grief, my shame, my anger into her hair. The scent of roses filled my nostrils, allowing me to fall deeper into the love she offered. One that was unquestionable, unrelenting despite my revelations, and so pure I was still certain I didn't deserve it.

Assyria poured raw empathy for what I was forced to endure down our bond. Tumbling with it was how much she loved me for sharing those horrific moments with her. My mate held no walls between what she felt and what she expressed. Vulnerability was something that had been burned out of me centuries before, and yet with Assyria, it was safe to let my own crumble to ash.

"Thank you," I managed to grind out. Straightening, I allowed her to see the gratitude written in my eyes—on my soul. For that was where she lived inside me.

Her dainty hands caressed and cleaned my face. "I love you, Rokath. Nothing will ever change that."

I nodded, too exhausted to speak. I was raw, flayed open, and these weren't feelings I particularly cared to experience.

Slowly, she eased out of my embrace and took my hands again. "Let's sleep now."

I let her direct me to our bed, blowing out candles along the way. When she crawled onto the mattress, I darkened the final hint of light, then joined her. Settling against my pillows, I said, "Come here."

Without hesitation, she curled into my embrace, and I snaked my arms around her. Her soft curves melted into the hard planes of my body as I wholly enveloped her. My eyes closed, and she traced my tattoos. "Thank you for telling me all of that," she whispered into the darkness. "I know it wasn't easy."

"It wasn't," I admitted. Exhaustion tugged at every fiber of my being, and for once, sleep offered itself to me freely. Perhaps it was Assyria in my arms, the highs and lows of the day, or fucking everything catching up to me, but when I crashed, I crashed hard, falling into the deepest slumber I'd had in years.

IO

ASSYRIA

With only a single day before our planned rescue of Zurronar and Banand, I wanted—needed—additional time to study the three Angel females. Taking on their forms was essential to the mission's success. The execution had to be flawless, for my safety as much as everyone who was accompanying us to rescue the Demons imprisoned in the Angel camp.

You've got this, Assyria.

Rokath and I parted ways in the bone room, and I couldn't help the flush that crept across my cheeks at the memory of the way he'd taken me on it a few days prior.

Tracing a path through the black tent, I found the caged females. In this back room, they were close enough that Rokath, Rapp, and the other officers were only a shout away, but far enough I could practice in peace.

Not that I would need anyone to save me. With the bronze bangles on their wrists and ankles, their magic was locked away, and the bars of the makeshift camp prison separated them from me. And my magic? Now, more than ever, it was an extension of me, honed like the edge of a blade and ready to draw at a thought's notice.

"Honored by our divine creator," I greeted them with the traditional Angelic words as I entered the sectioned-off part of the command center. Three sets of blue orbs snapped to me. Only Esha narrowed hers. Despite the stormy ocean color denoting her as the one with the least power among them, she acted as if she wielded magic like Araquiel, the most powerful. Faeya's eyes brightened when they landed on the bundle in my arms—fresh clothes.

They'd surrendered their armor for my use the same day we captured them. Surrendered wasn't *quite* the right word. It was more like the males had forcibly removed it from their bodies. The white and grey clothing, now pristine, rested in my pack, ready for me to don as part of the final run-through.

"Those are for us?" Faeya asked in Angelic.

"Yes," I replied, placing the pile on a stool so I could slide the straps off my shoulders. The bag thudded against the carpet, and I rolled out my neck, relieved of the burden. Then, I approached the cage.

Faeya and Esha shot to their feet. Araquiel remained seated, her back braced against the bars on the opposite side of the cage, knees tucked to her chest. She scrutinized me and her cellmates with a detached air. To be fair, I'd studied the three of them with the same intensity, since knowing a bit about their personalities would help me respond appropriately should I be stopped by someone who knew them.

At this point, I was torn between taking on Faeya's form or Araquiel's. Had the latter been more forthcoming, less calculated, she would have been the easy choice. Being caged didn't exactly allow them to show their true personalities though. Was Araquiel as shrewd as she seemed? Or was it her survival instincts kicking in to protect her?

Esha was a solid no with her eye color. She wouldn't be in a position of importance in regard to the Angel's prisoners. She was also the most openly hostile, and again, I wasn't sure if it was borne of the situation or if that's who she truly was.

Faeya seemed to accept her position by the second day. She spoke Angelic with me despite not knowing why I was practicing. While she hadn't willingly offered up any extra information, she seemed to be the most congenial of the three. From my time living under Vagach's abuse, I recognized her behavior for what it was: fawning. Yet it was far more helpful than the other two's attitudes.

Stretching my arms to their max, I placed the clothes on the bars and retreated. After all, they were still Angels, and I didn't trust them. This small act of kindness was due to my need to garner more information from them.

Truly, we were using each other.

"Do you need anything else?" I asked them.

"I need the latrine," Faeya admitted as she stripped her dirty tunic off.

I studied her torso for any ink or birthmarks I might need to take into account. Noting a small scrawl on her ribs, I asked, "What does that say?"

She glanced under her arm while she pulled the fresh one overhead. "Myrr." She spoke the Angelic word slowly, affording me time to hear the complexity of the sound. "It means peace," she said in the common tongue as she pulled her long twist from the shirt and settled it over her shoulder.

I blinked, momentarily taken aback.

Why would she want 'peace' permanently etched into her skin?

Tucking a few short strands of her platinum hair behind her ears, she faced me again. "You take me, or do one of the males go?"

Shaking myself out of my shock, I returned to the conversation at hand. "Can you repeat?" I asked her, thinking I misunderstood her the first time she spoke.

Enunciating each Angelic word, she said, "Will you take me to the latrine, or will you fetch one of the males?"

"The males," I replied, relieved that I'd understood her that time. "How badly do you need to go? Can you wait?"

"Not she-tas-y, but say-tes-y," Faeya corrected my pronunciation of the word for wait. "Sooner would be better."

"Same for me," Araquiel added, finally rising. "I will wait to change until I return."

Nodding, I glanced over my shoulder. "I'll be right back."

The three watched me go. Outside, I found the two soldiers currently on guard duty and relayed the females' needs. They followed me back inside, and I stood against the wall as they snapped additional chains around Faeya, then Araquiel's wrists and led them away.

Locked in again, Esha eyed me with unveiled disgust. We were enemies, after all. To her, I was little more than a jailer and the Halálhívó's whore. The Angels didn't believe Demons could really have a fated mate, that it was some dark magic trickery offered by the Fates.

Silence stretched between us as we waited for the others to return. To pass the time, I called on the shadows in my chest, stirring them to life. Even if I wasn't going to impersonate Esha, using my magic was still good practice. Pulling on the threads of it, I wove her face first, focusing on the slope of her nose and slant of her eyebrows. Once I was certain I had it, I went to my pack and fetched the mirror stowed there. Glancing between my reflection and Esha, I made a few minor adjustments to her forehead before deciding I'd done enough.

Then, I stepped closer, trying to capture the creamy color of her hair.

Some more light would be useful.

Continuing to entwine the tendrils of my magic, I formed the rest of her around me. Her sharply pointed ears that reached to the sky, the rings that lined the bottom shell. All the while, she watched, face morphing from hostility to fear as she saw herself reflected back.

I hoped she witnessed the same ugliness I did.

Before now, I hadn't shown them what I could do. A part of me was immensely satisfied with her reaction to my power. Rapp was right, it was fucking cool.

Esha whispered furiously to herself in Angelic while hooking her thumbs together and flattening her palms over her chest. She drummed her hands there, creating a rhythm to match her fervid words. "Protect me, Goddess," were the only ones I managed to catch besides "dark magic" and "Demon." I didn't need to understand each syllable to know she was praying for her deity to save her.

I wanted to exorcize her from this room. How ridiculous they were for not seeing that we were more alike than different. That Demons were just as worthy of living as they were. That we weren't some evil spawn of different Gods.

A sharp breath tore my attention away from Esha. Faeya and Araquiel had returned, along with the guards, to the sight of their soror's distress. I stepped back from the cage, maintaining my hold over my magic, while the males secured them again. If it weren't for my black leather clothing, they'd have mistaken me for her, no doubt.

The two males saluted me on their way out. Their whispers tumbled through the tent, though they were low enough I couldn't discern what they said. Probably something to do with my magic, given how few had seen it in action—if they even knew of its existence.

I faced the females, finally releasing my hold and returning to my own frame.

"You have powerful magic indeed," Araquiel stated. Then, she turned her back on me and stripped. Again, I searched for any important features, but her skin was as smooth as a frozen stream. Not a freckle or a scar marred the surface. It was almost...uncanny. Faeya finished changing and threw her dirty clothes between the bars, in the direction of my bag.

"She is cursing us by impersonating us!" Esha protested, her clothes still hanging on the bars.

"Better to be cursed and alive," Araquiel shot back with more bite than I'd seen since we captured her. She shoved her short, messy strands behind her ears and flicked the rest out of the collar of her tunic.

Interesting.

I noted that bit of information away for later. The three squabbled, their voices too quick for me to understand more than a word here and there.

While they worked themselves into a frenzy, I went to the nearest flap and secured it back, allowing more light into the space. Still not satisfied, I opted to stand on the stool and open one side from the top. With the sun closing in on its zenith, the space illuminated enough for me to study all the small details of their features.

"Quiet," I hissed when I jumped down, returning to the front of the cage. I needed to practice, and for that, I needed them still. "Araquiel, can you step forward?"

With an impassive expression, she did. The light glittered in her turquoise eyes, highlighting small flecks of gray. The contours of her high cheekbones would be the most difficult part of her to capture.

Inhaling deeply, I tapped into my magic well again, calling on my magic to carve them, to shape her regal nose, and to plump her delicate lips. At least her foggy hair was easy to pull into existence. When I finished my form, she hardly even blinked, even as she stared in her own reflection.

"Impressive," she stated without a hint of emotion in her tone. "You need to point the ears more."

She turned her head to the side to give me a better look. The light fell perfectly over it, and so I did, noting the placement of the four studs in the uppermost corner, resembling a starburst.

"Why are you helping me?" I couldn't help but ask as I tried to mimic her voice. There was a huskiness to it, and it was harder to capture while I also clumsily spoke their language.

She lifted one shoulder and dropped it. "Perhaps I want to see you succeed."

I snorted. "I highly doubt that."

"I am a Sensor. I have mastery over all kinds, including invisible ones. Sight, smell, hearing, those are all at the surface. Intuition runs deep," she replied, switching to the common tongue. For which I was grateful, because I wasn't certain I would have understood otherwise. Reaper, I wasn't certain I understood anyway. Her words were cryptic in a way that I knew they'd tumble through my mind long after this, wondering what she truly meant.

Shaking it off, I asked Faeya to step forward next, honing my skill on weaving her features around me. Once I was certain of my ability to impersonate both of them, I grabbed Faeya's clothes from my bag and pulled them on.

Her breasts were bigger than mine, though my rear was bigger than hers, so I had to change my form to fasten everything properly around me.

"You are me," Faeya breathed, her mouth slightly parted. "Why? What is your purpose?"

Rokath had explicitly forbidden me from sharing specific plans with them. Again, we couldn't trust them; they were our enemies. They'd likely feed us false information to ensure our failure.

And if we failed, the Angels could use Banand again to wipe us out.

I said nothing as I paced the length of the room, trying to get accustomed to the feel of another's body over mine. My magic was more like an outer shell than anything, though I still saw through her eyes and spoke through her mouth. It was an odd sensation, really, though after spending a month in Vagach's skin, I hardly noticed it anymore.

Satisfied, I switched to Araquiel's clothing and pulled her form around me. "Do you have any army specific greetings?" I asked while studying all of their faces for a sign of deception.

Esha said no at the same time Araquiel said yes. I arched an eyebrow and turned my attention to the female I was impersonating. "You are a Padisa, yes?"

She nodded. "Lower ranked soldiers greet their superiors with a hand over their heart and a dipped head. They use the words, 'Goddess save you,' at the same time."

I practiced the movement and the words.

"It is blasphemy that she speaks to the Goddess!" Esha snapped, fingers curling around the bars. Her shackles clanked against them as she shook them.

I rolled my eyes and ignored her. "Anything else?" I asked Faeya and Araquiel.

"If you see Banand, tell him a flame waits behind a wall of glass," Araquiel stated in the common tongue.

I had to clench my teeth to prevent my mouth from falling open. Ice skittered down my spine as she continued to hold my gaze—her gaze. Was Araquiel truly a Sensor? Because it felt to me like she might be a Seer.

If she knew Banand, and knew him well enough to have a specific, albeit cryptic, message to pass along, then she must have had close contact with him. Which meant, I needed to use her form to get to him.

But how could she have possibly guessed what our plans were?

I needed to talk to Rokath.

Dropping my magic, I changed back into my leathers. "I'll ensure the guards bring you food," I told them as I secured the ties around the tent again, bathing us in darkness. Then, I hurriedly stuffed everything back into my bag. The mirror went last, securely tucked against the flat side so it wouldn't break.

"We'll see if the Fates favor you," Araquiel said before sinking back into the position she'd been in when I first arrived. If she knew she unnerved me, she didn't display any sign.

My blood pounded in my veins as I departed, Araquiel's cold turquoise eyes searing into my mind. What did she know? And why wasn't she afraid? Something was off with her, with the situation, and the worry knotted my stomach.

In a blink, I slipped through the curtain and into the map room.

"Araquiel knows Banand," I blurted out. Thankfully, only Rapp, Trol, and my mate were present.

Rokath looked up from his stack of papers, brow furrowed. "What do you mean?"

"She told me, 'if we see Banand to tell him a flame waits behind a wall of glass,'" I repeated, hands twisting in the strap of my bag.

"What does that even mean?" Rapp asked aloud, thumbing the ring in his lip.

I shrugged. "I don't know, but what if she could tell us more about his location in the camp?"

"What if it's a trap?" Rokath shot back. "What if she is playing on your sympathies and guessing at our strategy?"

"I don't have sympathy for Angels," I snapped, fingers tightening over the leather.

"You have sympathy for other females," Rokath said, the hard edge to his voice gone. I opened my mouth to protest, but slammed it shut.

He was right about that, even if I hated admitting it to myself.

"Fine. But what if she is sincere? What if we could save lives, more than just Banand and Zurronar?" I sighed, bracing my hands on a chair and leaning into it for support.

"She has a point, Rokath," Rapp said. Trol, rightly, remained silent during the exchange. From what I'd seen, Trol was more of the follow orders type, whereas Rapp pushed back on Rokath with more force.

Rokath tossed his papers casually on the table in front of him. "We'll get her alone and see if she'll talk. If she does have anything to say, it certainly won't be in front of the other two. That spitter is a true sycophant."

Esha, I had to agree, was never going to be swayed to offer anything without force. She'd called me a whore plenty of times and sneered at Rokath more than once with false bravado.

"When?" I asked.

Rokath glanced at the clock beside the pitcher of water. "After we make a sacrifice," he growled, rising. Rapp and Trol did too. "If the Fates have chosen to weave a path where Araquiel does intend to offer us insight, then we must thank them for it beforehand."

Shrugging off my pack, I left it in an empty chair and followed my mate into the sunlight.

II

R🕱KATH

Nine males stood before me, prepared for our imminent departure. Assyria, on my right, dressed in Araquiel's white armor, shifted her weight ever so slightly. Sunlight barely slipped through the sharp peaks of the Skala Mountains in the distance as we waited for the final member of our assault team: Rapp.

As if I'd thought him into existence, he emerged from the camp, his long legs carrying him swiftly to our group. With a slight dip of his chin, he relayed that everything was ready for us to initiate the rescue mission.

Araquiel, to my shock, had offered us the exact location of the tent where the Angel's prisoners were held. Yet when I pressed her, trying to bend and break her into revealing her true intentions, she snapped her mouth shut. No amount of prodding or threats opened it again. The sharpness in her gaze pricked my back long after I'd locked her in the cage with the other two again.

I still didn't trust her. Even if our scouts had surmised that exact zone after their mission to determine possible locations where Banand and Zurronar were being held.

A cold knot of dread coiled in my gut as Rapp joined me on my left, his bow slung over his torso. A quiver brimming with arrows waited too, stuffed so tightly I hoped that he'd be able to pull them out without losing them all in the process.

I glanced down at Assyria, a war raging inside me. One side of me was proud—of her tenacity, of her relentless drive to master Angelic, of her growing control of her magic. On the other was the possessive beast that couldn't lose her again.

Not because I wouldn't sacrifice fifty thousand more soldiers for her. Fuck, the whole army could be decimated so long as I had her.

She was my reason for everything now; without her, I had no motivation to protect the rest of the Demons. I'd want the Reaper to claim me just so I could be with Assyria again, either in our next lives or the ones after. Because there was no doubt in my mind that I'd always find her. Our souls called to one another like horns blown across the battlefield.

My mate looked up at me through dark lashes. The remnants of daylight glinted in her eyes, highlighting the mosaic of burgundy.

"Everything will be okay, Rokath. I'll be fine. Besides, if something bad happens, you'll put a dent into their forces trying to get to me."

She had such an incredible way of soothing these new emotions that smashed their way out of the cage I'd kept them in. And calling me out when my feral, protective instincts got the better of me.

"I'd burn the fucking world to get to you, little imposter. If an Angel so much as blinks at you wrong, I will slit their throat and rejoice in the blood we spill for the Fates."

The corner of her mouth twitched up. She never shirked from my darkness. In fact, she embraced it more and more with each passing day. Our shared trauma certainly opened up a wicked side of her, one that I wanted to see more of.

"Let's begin before I change my mind."

Assyria shot me a devious grin before sinking to her knees and bowing her head. Rapp and the force of nine in front of me did the same.

The sun painted the dirt in a final swipe of gold. I yanked the ceremonial knife from its sheath and flexed my fingers around the hilt. Soon, the ground would be red, and not only from the offering the twelve of us were about to make.

We'd held prayers with the entire army at high sun, as we did every day, but with the risk I was taking, allowing Assyria to traipse through the Angel's camp like she belonged there, I wanted—needed—to ensure the Fates would work in our favor.

And they fucking *loved* blood.

"Weaver, who spins the threads of our fates, lay down the path for us to tread, unyielding and unbroken. We walk at your command, our feet bound by the threads you have woven. Guide us to glory as we rescue our brethren tonight from the clutches of those who would see the Demons eradicated. Bind our fates, so that we may rise victorious."

I sliced a deep gash into my palm, letting crimson flow freely toward the churned earth. After, I handed the knife to Assyria. She offered a generous amount, then prostrated herself. Rapp, too, bled openly, shooting a pointed look at the male in front of him who didn't dig deep into his flesh. Chastised, he wrapped his palm around the blade and squeezed more ruby out.

"Giver, bless us with abundant wells of magic so we wield in your name during battle. Let the blood we spill slake your thirst, and let us slaughter those who defy your design. Gift us with the power we need to bring majesty to your name. By our blood, we honor you."

"By our blood, we honor you," the ten males and Assyria echoed, marking their faces with long swipes of their hands. It had been my mate's suggestion that we paint ourselves in shades of red to match our eyes. When we confronted the Angels tonight, they'd see the monsters they thought we were. Let them believe what they wanted. So long as we won, I didn't give a fuck.

"Reaper, whose curse falls upon those who stray from the path, let us not taste your wrath. We offer this blood as a pledge of our loyalty. Let your eye wander elsewhere and damn those who question your mighty power. Should we fall tonight, offer swift passage into another life."

"We pledge our devotion to the Reaper," they replied. "Let our victory be swift. Our lives, our magic, our very essence, are the Halálhívó's to command."

"Rise," I told them, and they straightened. Already, my wound had closed. Assyria returned the knife to me, and I took a small rag to it before tucking it away again. The handpicked Vezető and Százados returned to their stances, shoulders squared and not a hint of trepidation in their red eyes. Only one Parancsok was among them, pulled from one of Rapp's winged battalions. His Suppressor power could hold back the magic of two dozen Angels should we need to make a quick escape.

Rapp approached them and relayed final instructions while I spoke with Assyria.

"Signal to me if you find yourself in trouble," I told her, my tone leaving no room for argument.

She had the nerve to roll her eyes. "Not like you'll be in my mind the entire time." Despite her bravado, a whisper of anxiety traveled down our bond.

"I'm serious, Assyria." I stepped toward her, slipping the knuckle of my first finger under her chin and tilting it up. Those devious burgundy eyes locked onto my own. "Do not take any unnecessary risks."

"In and out," she promised with a sigh. I wrapped my arms around her small frame and tugged her close, inhaling her floral scent. My heart thundered against my ribcage, and the bond thrashed like a wild beast, beseeching me to chain her to our bed and rescue Banand and Zurronar myself.

She looked up at me, her dark locks cascading down her back. "You stay safe too." Even now, despite constant reassurance, a trickle of fear that our love would result in my death, remained.

"Little imposter, the Fates brought us together for a reason. I will not die, not until we've won this war and I've had centuries to explore every inch of your body," I growled.

Assyria's pupils darkened. "You definitely have more exploring to do."

"As do you," I rumbled, hand trailing down her ribs to dig into her hips. "I want you to uncover every dark desire you were denied. I'll make you feel so alive, you'll forget anything occurred before our bond snapped in place. Every breath, every touch, every orgasm you have in your body—they are all mine."

My cock hardened against the tight leather of my pants as lust flooded our bond. I dragged Assyria closer so she could feel the promise in my words. "Tonight, we'll celebrate our victory with sweat and skin and those sweet sounds you make when my mouth is between your thighs."

Fisting the back of her hair, I crashed my lips against hers, not caring that the soldiers bore witness. There was nothing tender about this kiss; it was all claim, all possession, all brutality. My teeth sank into her bottom lip and drew a hint of blood. My tongue lapped at it before twining with hers and letting the metallic taste coat both our mouths.

Assyria's chest heaved as I released her. "Now call upon your magic."

She blinked a few times, the haze of desire lifting from her. After a glance over my shoulder, I adjusted my dick to a more comfortable position. Fires sprang to life around us as night encroached, casting flickering light over the utter perfection that was Assyria's face.

Throwing me one last lustful look, she brushed her hands over Araquiel's clothing. Then, she closed her eyes and inhaled deeply. Obsidian burst from her hands and swirled around her in a violent twister. After realizing how slowly she worked to pull on her disguises, I'd suggested she use her shadows around her body to help. Her time to transform had plummeted, until it took only a blink for her to become an Imposter.

I'd barely had time to marvel at how proud I was before the Angel stared back at me, taller, fuller, and with turquoise eyes utterly unfamiliar to me.

Our bond grew muffled, like someone had thrown a thick fur over it. The pure, unfettered fear that had gripped me from the moment she didn't respond to my call on the salt flats roared back to life.

"Can you hear me?" Assyria spoke into my mind, immediately easing the worry.

"Aye," I replied, a hint of relief trickling in despite my attempt to keep my tone even. We'd been practicing for days, and although I knew that we could speak, hearing her voice soothed me in a way I previously would have refused to admit.

A few of the males gasped before faking a cough. None of them had seen Assyria's magic before, and a primary reason for their selection was because their lips could be trusted not to move once we returned to camp. Only a handful knew exactly what power her burgundy eyes offered her.

It was best to keep it that way. After all, the reason for our strike was because word of Banand's power to create plagues had spread into the Angel's camp. What would the Angels do if they knew my mate could walk among them undetected?

Clearing my throat, I leaned down to pick up my mask, but froze with my fingers wrapped around the metal. Assyria placed her hand on my arm. I almost threw her over my shoulder and carried her back to our camp-home. But I was trying to do better, be better for her.

So I dragged in a breath and secured the final piece of my armor over my head. Horns of wicked ebony curled from the black skull that covered my face. Only my eyes shone through the sockets. The helmet was designed to intimidate and remind the fucking zealots *exactly* who I was.

Settling it in place did that for me too. "Let's go," I commanded, violence threaded in my tone. A bloodthirsty grin spread across Rapp's face, and he banged his fist against his chest. The other males did the same, a roar of pride tearing from them.

The air was charged as we split into our respective groups. Energy flared as we drew our weapons.

Yet when I took the first step outside of the confines of our camp, fear I'd never known slammed into my gut like a war hammer.

12

ASSYRIA

Darkness suffocated the path ahead as we crept toward the Angels' camp. We couldn't afford even the barest hint of a torch to find our path, lest we risk being discovered. Instead, what little light the stars offered guided our way. No moon rose in the sky, its mass covered by the same ink as the rest of the world around us.

Lutsk, despite its crumbling buildings and churned earth, didn't hold the dangers the Paks Desert did. Namely, venomous cobras that would strike at the slightest provocation. A shiver wracked my spine at the memory of the one who sank its fangs into my calf and the blistering burn in my veins that followed.

Rokath remained at my side as we picked our way over smashed fences, avoided rotting orange pumpkins and fat purple beets, and tried not to twist an ankle on an unseen dip in the ground. The closer we drew to the white tents in the distance, the louder the melodic voices grew. My focus remained mere feet in front of me as I tried not to think about how I was walking into the nest of hornets.

We clung to a copse of almond trees once we'd passed through the worst of the outskirts of the city. The cloying scent was enough to turn my already queasy stomach. I wanted to prove myself to the whole damn army, and yet fear still clung to me like this black cloak Rokath had insisted I wear while in Araquiel's form. Her foggy hair and white uniform were much easier to spot than the dark ones sported by the males accompanying us.

Rapp and the Parancsok led our party, and after several glances in the camp's direction, Rapp held up his closed fist. We all halted immediately behind him.

"Now is where we part, little imposter," Rokath rumbled in that gravelly tone that always heated my blood.

I swallowed, though my mouth was drier than the Paks Desert. *"I will let you know once I've located them."*

"We will wait for your signal to cause a diversion," Rokath assured me again, though I wasn't sure which one of us needed it more.

But I wasn't the weak female who had cowered beneath Vagach's onslaught. I was the fucking Imposter, the only one to ever live, and I would use my magic to save Banand and Zurronar just as Rokath used his to protect us on the battlefield.

I owed it to Izgath—the male who had died protecting my true identity—to rescue his brother. I owed it to myself to claim my power in my own right.

Tugging at the strings of the cloak, I let it fall away, then handed it to my mate. I made to step away, but he snatched my wrist and tugged me into his chest again. "I love you," he said, his tone so low no one but me heard.

"I love you too, Rokath. Now release my wrists so I can rescue the two males you so thoroughly lost. Someone has to clean up your mess after all." I patted his chest for extra effect.

He grunted in response but peeled his fingers away.

Dragging in a steadying breath, I turned away from him,

briefly locking eyes with Rapp, who nodded in reassurance. The confirmation of his belief in me was another layer to my armor.

You can do this, Assyria.

Shadows flickered in my chest like a crackling fire, ready for me to call upon them should I need them. Then, I departed the haven of almond trees, keeping a low, slow pace as I approached the first row of white tents. My hearing remained on high alert, listening for voices around me, trying to catch snippets of conversation and also gauge where others might be walking. Just because I looked like Araquiel and spoke a few words of Angelic didn't mean I had any intention of traipsing straight through the neat rows without a care in the world.

Clinging to the dark periphery, I searched for a striped tent on the outer circle. Araquiel had said that was the best place to enter. From there, the prisoner's cages were only four rows inward, in a similarly decorated tent.

One minute passed, then two, before I finally found it. Hovering against the edge of the canvas, I peered around to ensure the way was clear. Only a distant hum of activity reached my ears. It was the dining hour in the Angel camp, another reason Rokath had strategically selected this time for our assault.

I crept forward, shoulders tense and attention darting over everything. Two rows in, a sharp peal of laughter stopped me in my tracks. Footfalls mingled with the sound, both drawing closer.

Shit, shit, shit.

I glanced around, searching for a place to hide. Finding a narrow alley between the backs of two tents, I darted to the space. The white-blonde hair of a tall female flashed at the edge of my vision moments before I clamped a hand over my mouth to stifle my breathing.

"...Zahe is so dreamy, really," one giggled.

"But he's not even a Bassi," the other pointed out with a longing sigh. "My father said if I were to find a male in the army, it had to be an officer."

"Forget what your father says. He's not here. Besides, the Goddess loves when we smoke her blessed herbs and screw beneath her stars," the first replied.

"It's been far too long since we've done that. I think next time..."

Their voices faded away, and not a moment too soon. Breath slammed into me, battling against my racing heart for space in my chest. I waited another minute before emerging from my hiding spot.

"Everything okay?" Rokath asked down our bond.

"Fine."

I shut Rokath out, needing to focus. After a thorough assessment of my surroundings, I made my way forward again. The striped tent should be close...

There.

I ducked into the darkness again.

Ivory lines jutted against a blue as bold as the midday sky. It was long, nearly as long as the command center in the center of the Demon camp, and just as wide. And outside it stood two guards. Two tall torches rested on either side of them, casting flickering light around the area.

One shifted his weight, and ice shattered through my veins. It was the very same one I'd kneed in the face during my own captivity. That ice gave way to fire when he flicked his attention in my direction. He hadn't seen me—yet.

"Found them," I told Rokath.

"Wait until they move before attempting to enter," he replied, ever the commander.

"I know," I snapped back, my attention still wholly fixated on the sentries.

The two chatted quietly, too far away for me to hear what they were saying. It wasn't long before distant shouts reached my ears.

The diversion had begun.

Instantly, their hands flew to the hilts of their swords. They shared a concerned look. One stepped forward, but the other shook his head and jerked his thumb over his shoulder.

Fuck.

Clashing steel rang out, and flashes of white lit up the sky above us. Their attention drawn upward, I took the opportunity to dart forward, closer to a pole with ropes wrapped around it, securing the stretched canvas in place.

A shriek pierced the air, and one of the males swore. "We can leave them for five minutes. If we're there, those Demons will be dead in record time."

The other chuckled. "True enough. No one fights like us."

I smothered the urge to roll my eyes.

Drawn swords scraped the night air, and I pressed myself into the shadows once more, even calling on my magic to thicken them and hide myself from view. The two raced by a moment later. I counted my heartbeats, hoping they wouldn't return immediately.

More shouts rang out, louder and thankfully still in the distance. Seizing my opportunity, I bolted toward the unguarded entrance. I yanked daggers from hidden pockets on my ribs and burst through the canvas.

No Angels started at my sudden appearance.

Thank the Fates.

The candles flickered with my brought-in breeze. I whipped around, gathering my bearings. The front room held crates, none of which were open. I sniffed the air and scented a hint of citrus. But beneath it was the unmistakable stench of unwashed bodies.

Stepping carefully among the boxes of wood, I followed my nose until it led me to another room, narrower than the last. A long workbench stretched along the expanse, dozens of instruments tossed haphazardly across it.

Bile rose in my throat as I crept forward. A table, similar in size to the one I'd been strapped to, waited. Rows of metal teeth smiled up at me, red with past ruin. And on the one beside it? A Demon, half-hidden beneath a dark sheet. Ruby oozed from his back, dropping like rain into the narrow slots beneath him. A small moan rasped in his throat.

How is he still alive?

Breathing through my mouth, I closed the remaining distance and rose to my tiptoes to peer over him. His breath was shallow, and his face was pale. Sweat dotted his brow, and when I glanced at his arms, I noticed the yellow pus poised to drop onto the floor. He was dying, and likely soon, with how horribly infected the cut was.

Pain had drowned his awareness long enough that he didn't even stir at my presence.

These fucking Angels. Why did they feel the need to harm us so? What had they hoped to gain from that male? He wasn't one I recognized, which meant he likely belonged to Trol's battalions. They had less information to offer than almost anyone else in the army. Was this torture all for fun?

Gritting my teeth, I turned away from him. I needed to find Banand and Zurronar, and fast. A few more steps took me into another room, much darker than the others.

"Fucking Fates," I cursed in Demonic, doubling back to fetch more candles. When I returned—new burns from wax and all—I swept through the room, nearly shrieking when I came face to face with a handful of males crouched together in a cage.

They shot to their feet immediately, gripping the bars. One

rattled them fiercely, spewing curses at me in Demonic that had me dropping my mouth wide open. Even after all my time spent in a war camp, I had never imagined such a colorful use of the words of our language.

"Where are Banand and Zurronar?" I cut them off, speaking Demonic back to them.

The rattler froze, his brows furrowing. The rest took a half step back. One gave away their location with a telltale glance. Ignoring the dumb ones, I strode deeper into the dark until I found two familiar looking faces.

"Blessed by the Giver," I breathed, securing the candle on the ground. One set of burgundy eyes and one set of maroon eyes stared back at me with an absolutely understandable amount of confusion.

"Araquiel?" Banand asked slowly, gripping the bars and pressing his face to them. Brows furrowed, he searched my face.

So they did know each other.

Picking apart the threads of my magic, I allowed my true face to appear rather than the Angel's.

Banand jerked back like he'd been slapped, while Zurronar blinked rapidly. "Assyria?"

I turned my attention to him. Maroon was clouded by a milky film, and a sickly pallor clung to his dark skin. He looked worse than he had only a few weeks ago.

"Sh!" I admonished them, glancing around us. "I'm here to rescue you. The sentries could return at any moment. How do I open these cages?"

"Your voice..." Zurronar trailed off, coming closer to the flames. A wheeze wracked his frame, and he turned his face into his shoulder to cover his mouth.

A stone settled in my stomach. I had to get him out of here and to a healer, fast. Izgath died because of me, and the least I could do was save his brother from the same fate.

"How are you here?" Banand asked. "How were you Araquiel?"

I cut my attention to him. "I'll explain later. But she told me to tell you a flame waits behind a glass wall." Narrowing my eyes on him, I gauged his reaction to the words. Suspicion still curled in my gut.

The plague-creating Demon rose slowly, his gaze distant, as if he were deep in thought. I snapped my fingers at both of them, needing them to help me help them. "How do I get you out of here?"

"Keys should be on a ring in the torture room," Banand said with a glance at Zurronar. On shaky legs, he stood too. He swayed, gripping the bars for support.

"I'll be right back," I promised, then raced past the other captives and returned to where one slowly bled out on the nail table.

Of course, the Fates-damned keys dangled on a hook too high for me to reach, even in Araquiel's taller form. With a huff, I jumped, snatched at the dangling teeth of one, and yanked. The ring flew through the air and clattered against the floor.

Cursing, I stooped to collect them. A blinding agony exploded behind my ribs. One hand shot out to steady me, while the other clutched my chest. That spot right in the center, where our connection lived among my magic, screamed.

Something was wrong. Terribly, terribly wrong.

"Rokath! Are you okay? What's happening?" I shouted down our bond.

Rage detonated from his side.

The roar that followed quaked the earth beneath my feet.

And then everything went still.

13

R☠KATH

Angels swarmed us from all directions, pinning us into the thick thoroughfare at the rear of their camp. The eleven of us closed ranks with Rapp and I on either side, monitoring our periphery.

Assyria needed this distraction to free the prisoners, and a distraction we would give her.

A pulse of white light magic flashed toward me, and I slipped to the left just in time for it to collide with the structure at my rear. Using my momentum, I swung my blade around, digging deep into the shoulder of the caster. The weight of my strike drove him to his knees.

Silver flashed as he swung a small dagger at my thigh in a desperate attempt to maim me. A mocking laugh rumbled in my chest as I jerked my skull-pommeled sword free. My boot landed square in his chest, and he flattened on the ground with a whoosh of air. The knife clattered away, and before he could attempt to rise, I speared him through the heart.

I didn't stop to savor my victory.

"It's the Halálhívó!" the Angels in front of us relayed backward.

Fuck. More reinforcements would arrive soon.

"Keep pressing," I growled at my soldiers.

Rapp barked orders too, trying to stitch our crumbling line back together. Three arrows sailed from his bow and nailed two Angels approaching from a nearby alley. Notching more, he took aim on those in front of us again.

Between us, shadows erupted—Destructors wielded their magic, exploding earth beneath the Angels' feet. Forced to leap and dodge, their line deteriorated, allowing others to pick them off.

A spear flew from between two tents and impaled one of the Vezető. Rapp swore and shoved the injured male behind him, out of harm's way. A groan ripped from him as he attempted to remove the sharp end from his shoulder.

Another Demon went down with a gash on his thigh; the Angels fought with more fervor.

Dozens more appeared ahead of us like hornets from a kicked hive. We were outnumbered before we stepped foot outside the Demon camp, but the scales were quickly tipping out of our favor.

Two broad, bulky males raced into the fray, shoving straight to the front. They split their attention, one aiming for me and the other fixating on Rapp. What little time I had to assess our position shattered when the lapis-eyed Angel thrust his blade straight toward my middle. Sparks seared the air as our strikes collided with thunderous force.

Muscles trembling, our blades locked, our teeth gritted, we battled for control. The Angel retracted his sword, throwing me off balance, and swung again. I ducked, kicking my leg out and connecting with his calf, before spinning and letting my bronze blade follow my trajectory. He shrank out of the way, narrowly saving his neck, before pressing forward again. Beside me, the other Demons were locked in battles of their own, all while more white-haired insects streamed in our direction.

What is taking Assyria so long?

With a growl, I shoved the male backward, sending him stumbling over one of his deceased kin. A shout drew my attention to the left, and my heart stopped.

A male, arrows pricking his torso, had kicked Rapp's legs out from beneath him. With one hand planted on the ground, and the other still gripping the curve of his bow, Rapp was attempting to rise. Time slowed to a crawl as the Angel arced his silver blade straight toward Rapp's chest.

"No!" I bellowed, leaping toward them. Onyx force exploded from me, colliding with the Angel a split second before I did. We crashed to the ground, spraying dirt in all directions. I yanked a dagger free from its sheath on my thigh and stabbed wildly. We smashed into white, and the structure collapsed on top of us.

Rage sharpened my aim, and I sank the dagger into soft flesh. A grunt of pain met my next strike. Then, I thrashed free of our entanglement. The male grabbed my ankle, and I stomped on his hand, ripping a satisfying cry from his throat. I slashed it wide open before whirling on the remaining fight, expecting Rapp to have reformed our small line.

I stared, veins freezing over, as silver jutted through both sides of Rapp's chest. It gleamed in flashes of white magic like a polished gem instead of a weapon of war. A heartbeat passed as we locked eyes, his so full of apology.

And then, a roar ripped from my throat, filled with so much rage I hoped the Reaper cowered in its wake and conferred with the Weaver to end this path my friend was on.

Red veiled my vision. Shadows whipped into a frenzy around me, smacking each Angel it encountered without care or regard. I didn't call them. Didn't command them. They merely acted of their own accord while my entire focus was on the male who'd been by my side since we were younglings in the military academy.

I dropped to my knees and slammed my fist into the soaked dirt, calling on the dead to rise up and shield us while I figured out how the fuck I was going to save his life.

"Rokath," Rapp spit out along with a wad of blood. I didn't even care that he was using my real name in the middle of the Angel camp. The short sword missed his heart, but it still slashed into his ribs, probably puncturing a lung.

"Don't fucking speak. Don't fucking die. Do you hear me?" I ground out, wracking my brain for how to help him.

"Not today," he wheezed out, and I smacked his leg.

"Save your breath. You offered your blood to the Fates. Your thread will hold strong." Screams tore through the haze, finally drawing my attention away from him as the dead slaughtered everyone in their path.

But that wasn't the only contributor to the chaos.

Smoke, thick and reeking, rose like a funeral pyre into the sky. Dread sent an icy chill down my spine.

Where the fuck was Assyria?

14

ASSYRIA

I pitched to the side, catching myself on a pole.

"Rokath!"

Still no response.

Fuck, I needed to get us out of here. Fear lacing my ribs, I raced back to Banand and Zurronar. My hands shook so badly, it took three tries to jam the key into the lock to free Banand.

"We need to go. Now," I snapped without a hint of remorse. My mate was in trouble, and he wasn't responding to me.

He said he wouldn't die...

"Aye," Banand replied, lifting the keys from me. I didn't protest, not when adrenaline spiked in my veins and made concentrating impossible.

A clank sounded, and then, the door to Zurronar's cage swung open. The male stepped forward, using the bars for support, while Banand went to free the others. The five burst from their confines, teeth bared and ready to fight. But all the males wore silver bangles around their ankles and wrists, locking down their magic.

That explained why Zurronar looked like he hadn't healed from whatever ailment affected him. Banand hooked the maroon-eyed Demon and half-carried him toward the exit. When we emerged into the torture room, Banand paused and shuffled Zurronar to two of the others. Then, he turned to me.

"Do you have a dagger?"

Hesitantly, I drew one from my hidden pocket and handed it to him. "What for?"

He dipped his head to indicate the male closing in on death. "Put him out of his misery."

My stomach clenched. I'd watched my father slaughter plenty of animals—a horse who had gone lame and could no longer pull a plow, a calf born with a mangled leg, goats that had been unable to deliver their kids. The way Banand spoke reminded me so much of that sentiment. Yet he wasn't wrong. Offering this male passage into peace was better than allowing the Angels to continue torturing him. I doubted the Angels would offer him a pyre so his soul could move to the next life either.

"I'll find something to start a fire," I said, fierce determination spreading through my limbs. We were making our escape, after all, and what better fuck you to the Angels than to burn down as much of their camp as we could on the way out?

Banand told the others to continue to the front of the tent. I searched the shelves for anything flammable. A row of bottles drew my attention, and I snatched at them, yanking off the stoppers and sniffing. The first four were healing potions —nothing to hold a flame. But then, I spotted a jar of oil stuffed behind a few instruments. My heart leaped, and I climbed onto the table, knocking the metal aside with a sweep of my hand.

Lifting the lid, I was immediately assaulted by the stench of seed oil.

This will do nicely.

I dropped down and returned to Banand, whose head was

bowed. "Follow the Weaver's thread to peace. May you live long in your next life," he prayed, words deep and resonant.

My throat thickened as I dipped my chin to my chest. Quietly, I joined him in honoring our soldier. "May your gift never fade."

Rokath and I had been exhausted, broken, when we offered a few words to those we had burned for their sacrifice. But he'd insisted on speaking it over every single male. Hadn't stopped even when his voice was hoarse from the number of times he'd repeated himself. And from that, I'd learned an invaluable lesson in leadership: honor those who followed.

To fight for the Demon cause was to risk the Reaper slicing their thread, and they deserved to be acknowledged, even for a moment.

Banand drew the knife across the suffering male's throat, and garnet bloomed and spilled over the sides. The rise and fall of his chest halted a moment later, signaling the end to his suffering.

I lifted my head and rolled my shoulders back again, gathering my strength for the next phase of the rescue mission.

A chill swept over me as the tall, lanky male straightened and looked at the jar in my hands. "I am impressed, Assyria. The Halálhívó is known for his cruelty and lack of mercy. It seems some of that has rubbed off on you, at least as far as the Angels are concerned."

I decided then I liked Banand immensely. He didn't treat me as some weak female, only good for spreading my legs. He recognized me for who I was and what I was capable of.

"Perhaps I want vengeance of my own," I shot back with forced bravado, drawing my other dagger. But internally, dread knotted my stomach because Rokath *still* hadn't responded to me. Rage drummed on his side of the bond, though it held a potent edge of terror. Whatever was happening with the diversion, it had claimed his sole focus. The sooner we escaped the confines of this miserable striped tent, the sooner they could retreat away from whatever was causing Rokath so much agony.

I dipped the blade into the jar, wetting it with the oil, then flung drops all around us.

Banand chuckled and fetched a few long-stemmed candles from a nearby table.

"Light it up," I told him, anger pounding through me. These fucking Angels would burn for how they'd treated my kith and me. "We'll spread more on the way out."

"Aye, mate of the Halálhívó," Banand said, tipping the flame toward a wet spot on the dead Demon's pants.

Careful not to spill any seed oil on my clothing, I retraced my steps to the front of the tent, where the others waited with Zurronar. Smoke billowed, thick and greedy, devouring everything around it. Banand emerged from the cloud at a jog, carrying two more candles. "Let's get out of here."

"Couldn't agree more," I quipped, calling on my magic to weave Araquiel's face back over my own. A few of the males let out low coughs, and I smothered one of my own.

"Bury your faces in your shoulders," Banand suggested, yanking up his dirty tunic to cover his nose. The others did as he suggested.

My shadows fell away, and a few gave me a wary glance as I became the Angel female again. "I'll go first," I croaked in Demonic, trying not to inhale the cloying air.

Using the back of my hand, I eased the entrance open, scanning for any indication that the two sentries had returned. When I found no sign of life, I slipped outside, only slightly disappointed I wouldn't get to slice them up on our way out.

Once I was certain the area was clear, I held the flap open for the others.

"That way," I pointed in the direction of the almond trees. "Hurry, we don't have much time."

The two hauling Zurronar between them rushed forward first, followed by the other three. Banand and I brought up the rear, spreading more fire in our wake. Shouts rang out in all directions as more and more smoke filled the sky.

A particularly large tent, the white broken up by a pattern of swirls, loomed ahead of us, and I beelined toward it. Dropping my dagger in the grass, I gripped both sides of the nearly empty jar and flung the remaining contents on the light fabric. Then, I tossed it down the alley, more oil spilling along the way. Banand threw one candle toward the jar and the other onto the massive spot on the tent. Flames ignited, the heat causing us to flinch back.

"That should take a while to put out," I commented, satisfaction curling through me.

So maybe I hadn't slaughtered any Angels today, but I'd burned their fucking camp and the prison they'd kept us in.

"Come on, we need to move," Banand said, glancing around us. "Can't have the Halálhívó kill me for failing to protect his mate after I am finally rescued, can I?"

I snorted and jogged alongside him, checking down each avenue we passed to ensure we weren't being pursued. To my relief, no Angels appeared. The Fates were truly on my side for my first mission, a welcome change from how the rest of my life had unfolded.

The edge of the camp came into view, and the others crossed into the narrow strip of land between the tents and the trees.

"Faster!" Banand shouted. The males in front of us put on a burst of speed. My heart thudded against my ribs as Banand and I sprinted for cover, in close pursuit. My lungs burned from the smoke I had inhaled, and an ache blossomed between my ribs.

But I didn't stop. Didn't relent my pace. Not when the sweet scent of almonds began to overpower that of the earthy seed fire.

Our group burst into the orchard, chests heaving. The males leaned against thick trunks, slumping down to hide themselves from view. Banand went to Zurronar immediately, checking him over for any sign of his condition worsening.

"Rokath, I've got them!" I shouted down our bond. Doubled over, hands gripping knees, I sucked down air like I had water once we'd survived the harsh desert.

I turned to look back at the camp, mouth popping open when I noticed just how far our fire had spread. Screams filled the air, and I squinted, attempting to find the rest of the strike team among the chaos.

A few staggered toward us, half-running as the flames high-lighted their forms in ruby and gore. Wings battered the air overhead, drawing my gaze upward.

And when I spotted my mate, a cry tore from my throat.

15

R🕱KATH

"Fall back to camp!" I shouted in Demonic. My reanimated soldiers formed a line of their own, hollowing out a space for us to collect ourselves and retreat. Not that the Angels paid us much attention anymore. The smoke had thickened with the wind gusting in our direction, and a jagged inferno scorched the sky. Dozens broke rank, drawn toward the blaze like moths to a flame.

"Rokath, I've got them!" Assyria relayed.

Thank you, Weaver.

We'd spilled more than enough blood for at least one part of this fucking rescue mission to go well.

"This is going to hurt," I told Rapp, adjusting my position so I could heft him into my arms.

"Fuck!" he swore as I shoved my arms under his torso. The sword clanked against my armor as I rose, and more blood poured from the deep gash. I couldn't remove it, not yet, or he'd bleed out without question.

"When do you get so damn heavy," I huffed as I called on more obsidian tendrils to help me hold him steady.

"Had to...compete with you," he replied, unable to remain

silent despite my *clear* instruction. I growled another warning at him. He was going to kill himself at this rate. And then I'd have to reanimate him to slake my rage at him fucking dying on me.

The Parancsok who had accompanied us raced over, eyes popping wide as he took in Rapp's pale form.

"Halálhívó, I will accompany you in the skies. We must take Hadvezér Rapp to the healers immediately," he stated like I didn't fucking know that.

"Aye," I gritted out, muscles and magic straining from the effort.

Then, he shouted at the others to continue to the trees. Black membranous wings sprung from between my shoulder blades, and I leaped into the sky. Rapp jerked once, then slumped, eyes rolling into the back of his head.

"Stay with me," I snarled, using more of my power to hold his now limp body straight.

The Parancsok joined us a moment later, onyx swirling from his hands and spearing toward the ground, where a group of white wings winked out of existence, preventing them from following us. Not that they had much interest in pursuing us when the rear portion of their camp was ablaze.

"*Was this your doing?*" I asked Assyria, scanning the treeline for any sign of her. That was where we'd agreed to meet once the prisoners had been rescued.

"*Oh, so* now *you respond to me,*" she snapped back, fear and anger threading her tone. "*I thought you were hurt, Rokath!*"

"*I am not, but Rapp is.*"

"*I can see that.*" Her voice cracked on the last word.

Finally, I spotted movement in the trees. I shouted at the retreating males to join them, torn between saving Rapp and protecting my mate.

Fuck, why did I allow myself to care? To feel? Before Assyria, the panic holding me hostage wouldn't have dared emerge from the cage I kept it in. I would have kept a level head. Rapp wouldn't have gotten slashed in the first place.

Assyria's voice cut through my internal chaos like a blade. *"You can't blame yourself, Rokath."*

How she could be so calm when I was falling apart was beyond me.

"Stay safe. Return to camp immediately."

"Banand is overseeing our retreat, and the others have caught up. Now go. Save Rapp. I can't lose him too." The sob was evident even down our mental connection. She'd lost so many in her life, and I wouldn't allow her to suffer any more grief if I could help it.

So I pushed harder, flying a slightly too long path between the trees and the camp in an attempt to both keep an eye on Assyria and carve a direct line to the healers for Rapp. What felt like years passed as the red dots in the distance expanded into recognizable shapes. They were nothing in comparison to the slick, hot garnet that coated my arms. My armor. Dripped on the ground like a gutted animal as I flew my friend to the only people who could save his life.

Air heaved in and out of my lungs from the level of my exertion.

The Parancsok accompanying me screamed out orders the moment we were within earshot of the camp. Where there had once been a restless calm, chaos burned. Demons took up arms and raced toward Lutsk to ensure the safe return of the prisoners. Healers bolted from their workstations and tore their gazes skyward, gauging the distance and what they'd need when we finally landed.

A sea of red, gray, and black swept underneath me. I glided lower and lower, until finally I was close enough to hit the ground at a run. My shadows tightened over Rapp, his breath so, so fucking shallow. The lead healer raced over, simultane-ously guiding me and assessing his Hadvezér.

Two apprentices rolled the canvas flaps back, beckoning us inside. They secured them in place after we passed, the crisp night air flowing through their workspace. A group of experi-enced healers prepared a table, spreading white cloths, rolling up a towel at the head, and filling basins with fresh water. They snapped to attention when I reached it, fingers twisting as they wrapped their magic with mine.

Together, we eased Rapp to the table, his body hovering just enough that the blade protruding from his back wasn't forcibly jutted out. The lead healer shouldered through, giving the silver sword a thorough examination before barking orders. His fingers closed around the hilt, lifting it ever so slightly as the space between Rapp's leather armor and the quickly-staining cloth closed.

I held my breath as his limp form hit the table, certain that the movement would jostle the weapon and immediately kill him.

A breath wheezed out of him, and then, all inky swirls disappeared. The healers jumped to work, each second a precious commodity. One dragged three fingers through the dark ruby staining his skin and sucked them into his mouth. Someone placed their hands on me in an attempt to drag me backward. I shrugged them off as I watched the male slice deep into his arm and allow his lifeblood to pour into a glass container.

"Halálhívó, we'll take it from here," a healer said, his voice distant like he was underwater. Or maybe it was me that swam beneath the depths, for I felt like I was drowning. I couldn't breathe, couldn't move, couldn't tear my gaze away from Rapp's pale form.

A fist slammed into my chest, sharp and shocking—a rope

yanking me out of the deep water. In a blink, I returned to myself, noting that my mate stared up at me, her burgundy eyes shining with a tumultuous mix of emotion.

"Let them work, Halálhívó. You're blocking their way," she whispered. Two tears tracked down her face as she glanced over her shoulder.

Nodding, I backstepped, dragging Assyria with me. A handful of chairs jutted against a wall, and I sank onto one, pulling my mate into my lap. I needed her, and she needed me.

"Fuck, Assyria, I can't lose him." She still wore Araquiel's clothing, but that garden-like scent of her, the one that had captivated me since the moment it hit my nostrils, was there, stronger and steadier than I was in that moment.

"I know," she choked out, wrapping her slender arms around my neck. I crushed her against me, not caring that blood soaked my torso. That there were others that needed attending. That I should have checked on Banand and Zurronar.

Weaver, Reaper, Giver, I always do as you bid. Please don't let him die. I need him to help win this war in your name.

Terror and sorrow tumbled down our bond. Assyria trembled, and then a quiet whimper wracked her chest. Her hand slapped over her mouth.

She's trying to be strong for me.

"Feel what you need to feel, little imposter," I choked out. Her emotions were always so strong, and normally, I tried to block them out. But this time, I let them wash over me, joining my own.

When Thast had died, it was only minutes between hearing of his execution and then committing it. Now? Rapp's future was shrouded in fog. His injury was grave. I lingered on the precipice of losing another friend, staring over the cliff and waiting for a strong wind to send me careening down it. I had less control now than I had that fateful day my father and the former Kral forced me to slaughter Thast and the two others.

A thousand jagged thoughts tore through my mind as we waited for something, anything, from the healers. They continued to block Rapp from view as they ringed him, flinging crimson cloths into buckets. An apprentice raced for more potions. Inky wisps twisted around the arms of the lead healer.

Assyria sobbed harder, and I kept clutching her because fuck she was the only certainty in my life right now. She needed this embrace just as much as I did. Rapp had been the only one rooting for us since the day our bond snapped into place. The memory of him howling with laughter when Assyria had challenged me after I told her to obey him like she would obey me hit me like an avalanche.

How different would things have been if I'd listened to Rapp and Kiira initially?

Assyria eventually quieted, sniffing softly as she continued to rest her head on my shoulder. Our bond was a mess of exhaustion from both sides, and yet we refused to move from our silent vigil.

The frenzy of their work died down. Less rags were thrown. Their shadows dissipated like smoke in the wind. I stroked Assyria's ebony hair, the rhythm as soothing to me as it was to her. I hated being still, yet I couldn't move, save for that one small motion.

An underling brought the lead healer a cup of water, and he drank it greedily, stepping back from Rapp's too-still body. My stomach plummeted when he turned toward us, face haggard and haunted. With a sigh, he set the drink aside, then picked his way through the injured. Others still lingered at Rapp's side, murmuring amongst themselves.

Assyria straightened in my lap and dashed the backs of her wrists over her eyes, trying to clear them.

"Halálhívó," the lead healer began slowly, wiping his hands on a clean rag. With a grumble, he glanced around and found another chair. Gripping the back, he spun it and then eased himself onto the seat with an audible squeak. He braced his elbows on his knees, exhaustion dragging his frame down. "Hadvezér Rapp is stable, for now."

The snake constricting my torso loosened.

"But–"

It tightened again.

The lead healer sighed heavily. "That could change at any moment. His wound was mere inches from fatal. We've also completely run out of pium stores. Should someone else suffer such an egregious injury, we would be unable to save them."

His attention flicked to my mate, and I understood his meaning.

"What are his chances of living?" I asked, each word dragged from the depths of despair. I needed to prepare myself —and Assyria—for the worst.

He glanced over his shoulder, watching his team work for a moment before responding. "Honestly? With everything we poured into him, I think they are high. But do not take that as a promise," he warned. The lead healer had always been straight with me, which was one of the reasons I'd promoted him to the position.

"Thank you," I choked out, relief like a potent drug passing between Assyria and me. "I will ensure we replenish your stores as soon as possible. Whatever you need, I will procure for you."

He nodded, then rose like a creaking ship. The fatigue rimming his eyes was undeniable. "He will have a constant watch until he wakes."

When he attempted to maneuver his chair back into place, Assyria shot to her feet. "Let me," she said, taking it from him. He didn't fight her, merely trudged back to the table and spoke with the others still working on their Hadvezér.

Then, she turned to me, slowly, like the motion harmed her. Swollen, puffy eyes snagged mine, and her shoulders hunched like her tears had dragged her to the depths of despair. We'd both suffered a physical and emotional toll—and there was no end in sight.

I rose. "Come," I said, holding a hand out to her. She accepted readily and nestled into my side. My gaze lingered on my unconscious friend. A thick row of stitches covered his torso, throwing off the smooth lines of his ink. He'd be annoyed that years of painstaking work to decorate his body had been ruined, but fuck it. He'd be alive and that was far more important.

Taking one last look at him, I steered Assyria out of the tent. We stepped into the broken night, smoke from the fire my mate had started trickling into our camp.

I slammed to a halt. In the shifting air, among sand and ash, stood our strike force—and a handful of the prisoners we'd saved.

And they all stared directly at my mate.

16

ASSYRIA

We finally emerged from the healer's workspace into the night. Though, it wasn't night, not really anymore. The first whispers of dawn broke in the distance, bringing with it a new day.

At least Rapp will live. Probably. Most likely.

Rokath stopped short, and I snapped my attention to him before realizing all the males who had accompanied us on the rescue mission had jumped to their feet. Hollow and sunken eyes met ours, and a few swayed where they stood.

Had they waited out here all night?

"Halálhívó," they said in unison, offering him a closed-fisted salute.

"How fares Hadvezér Rapp?" the Parancsok asked, taking a tentative step forward.

A heavy sigh escaped Rokath. I squeezed his hand. "The lead healer thinks he might live. But that is no guarantee."

Metered relief swept across them, brows relaxing and shoulders easing.

Banand stepped forward, dropping to one knee between

Rokath and me. He lowered his gaze until it met mine, burgundy eyes burning with reverence, and bowed until his head brushed his braced forearm. "Szélhámos, my life, my sword, is yours."

Szélhámos.

Imposter.

Not only had Banand knelt in deference to me, but he had offered me an honorific, like Rokath's Halálhívó, to match my power. I blinked, trying to process the monumental gesture. A wave of males mimicked him, murmurs of Szélhámos floating to my ears.

Tears pricked my eyes, and a lump formed in my throat.

I'd succeeded in earning their respect.

"Aye, you did, Assyria," Rokath rumbled in my mind. *"You are single handedly changing perceptions in this army. Word of the rescue mission will spread soon, and likely your power now too."*

Ice slithered down my spine. All my life, I'd focused on hiding my magic, on not being seen. Knowing that my path had curved into this new direction didn't ease that sense that I still needed to hide. Who knew what sort of knives waited for me when the world discovered I could become anyone in a swirl of shadow?

"Rise," I said, my voice shaky. My hands, too, trembled, and I tucked them behind my back and twisted my ring around my finger to ease some of the anxiety nipping at my nerves. They did, and Rokath dismissed them. Some chose to linger in solidarity with Rapp, Zurronar, and a few others who needed tending by the healers.

Banand was one of them. "May I speak to you, Halálhívó?" he asked with a nervous glance at those still around us.

Rokath nodded, and with a hand on the small of my lower back, he guided the three of us off to the side, out of earshot of anyone currently awake.

Banand dropped his chin before releasing a long, slow exhale. "How many?" The words were so quiet, I almost didn't catch them. What was unmistakable, though, was the shame and guilt that weighed them down.

Sympathy tugged at my heartstrings. When I'd first learned that the plague was caused by one of our own, I'd been furious. That had morphed into rage when I learned that Rokath had a hand in covering it up. My entire family had perished because of it the prior winter, leaving me utterly alone in the world. Yet seeing the impact of what the Angels had forced Banand to do with his magic smothered the flames of my fury until only embers remained.

"Their deaths are not on you," Rokath growled. "But I want a full account of everything you heard, saw, and did while in their custody."

Banand picked his head up, burgundy eyes shining. His cheeks were hollow, the skin of his face stretched too tight across the bones. In the dark, I'd thought him lanky, but now I realized he was wasting away. "Of course, Halálhívó, whatever you require. I want to atone for all the pain I caused."

Rokath turned to me. "I'll escort you back to our tent to rest, and then I will speak with Banand."

I shook my head. "No, I think we all need to sleep. And eat. It was a long night, and besides, Rapp isn't awake yet. He will want to hear too."

Rokath's face softened as he brushed his knuckles across my cheek. I refused to believe anything other than that Rapp would live. Any moment now, he'd call out for us.

He. Would. Not. Die.

"The Szélhámos is right," Banand murmured. "Honestly, I could use a bed and some food. It's been a while since I had a good amount of either."

Rokath flicked his attention between the two of us before

acquiescing. "Tomorrow we will meet again. Find Hadvezér Trol and he will ensure you have everything you need, Banand."

"Yes, sir," he replied, offering Rokath a closed-fisted salute. He dipped his head to me before spinning on his heel and departing.

"Let's go," Rokath told me. With one last look at the healer's tent, I followed him through the maze and toward the black tents we called our home. Fatigue tugged at my limbs, almost forcing me to drag them through the dirt. Sentries posted outside peeled off to fetch us food and water. In a haze, I entered the cool darkness.

Grem and Zeec perked up, leaping from the bed to greet us. Zeec whined, long and low, as if he sensed the agony simmering beneath our flesh. Grem nudged me with his nose, and I sank onto the ground and buried my face in his fur. Rokath crouched and wrapped himself around me from behind.

We remained like that until a male announced himself, saying he'd brought us food. Rokath and I ate quickly and in silence, both caught up in our own worries. By the time I'd drunk my fill of water, I could scarcely keep my eyes open.

I peeled off Araquiel's leathers, which reeked of burnt seed oil, and climbed into the bed. Rokath rinsed what blood he could off in the washbasin and then joined me. He curled around me, his strong arm flexing as he crushed me against his hard body. I melted into him, seeking comfort only he could offer me. He clung to me as if his life—Rapp's life—depended on it. The war of emotion playing out inside him mirrored my own.

A fitful sleep soon claimed me. Over and over, my mind tumbled through my worries, but in the end, it anchored onto a singular thought—no matter what the Fates decided, no matter how the world burned, at least I had Rokath by my side.

THE SOUND OF WATER TRICKLING AGAINST A METAL BASIN PRICKED MY ears. Gripping the cloth harder than necessary, I wrung it out like I could twist out the urge to fall back into the habit of believing everyone I cared about was cursed to die. Blurred vision made it difficult to pour the pitcher of fresh water over it. I didn't even care when I splashed some onto myself.

Truly, I was just going through the motions of cleaning myself. Worry dug its claws deep into me, making it hard to focus on anything but trying to breathe. Trying to squash the utter terror that Rapp may not survive his grievous wound.

With a shuddered exhale, I set the cloth over the rim of the basin to dry. Gripping both sides of it, I prepared to turn around and face what was left of the day. One tear fell, and then another. I quickly swiped them away, not wanting Rokath to see me cry.

My mate and I hadn't spoken since we rose, far later than we normally did. Between the physical exhaustion of our mission to the pure, unbridled fear holding our bond taut, neither of us had slept well. I doubted Rokath had slept at all, his insomnia worsened by our friend's thread mere moments from being snipped by the Reaper.

Slowly, I spun toward Rokath.

Eyes distant, he strapped on piece by piece of his black metal armor. I swept my gaze over him, noting his honorific tattooed into his knuckles, the skulls wrapping the base of his neck, the snake fangs crinkled by the worry lines on his forehead.

The powerful presence he normally carried was entirely absent.

Grem and Zeec let out low whines from where they watched us both. Neither of us had the heart to kick them out of the bed, even when the four of us crammed into it was incredibly uncomfortable.

The sound tore me from my spot across our small home. I perched on the edge of the hard mattress, stroking Zeec's long, pointed ears and scratching under Grem's throat. Their soft fur was soothing, but nothing would relieve this ache until I knew Rapp would live.

Rokath loomed like a storm on the horizon. Yet he didn't wield the threat of lighting and thunder. No, his shoulders held the slightest hunch like they were clouds weighed down by rain, and his strong brows were tense. A line creased the area between them too.

On tiptoes, I reached up and smoothed it with my thumb. He sighed and leaned into my touch. A moment passed before he wrapped his arms around me and tugged me closer. We said nothing, not needing to when our every emotion was shared. The bond allowed us to comfort each other in ways others would never understand.

"The worst part about all of this is that now I have to go lead. Have to pretend that I am fine when I am not," Rokath murmured, so quiet I thought I'd imagined it.

I tipped my head up to look at him. A muscle feathered in his jaw. "I haven't felt like this in…centuries." He blew out a long breath, and I cupped his face.

"I'll be there with you," I promised. "Our pain is shared now." I repeated the phrase I'd told him time and time again as his hardened exterior cracked.

Both of us had been lonely, albeit in our own ways—him, thinking he had to bear the burdens of his leadership alone, me, thinking that I couldn't trust anyone to care for me.

Every day, Rokath demonstrated that he would protect and support me; every day, I would show him he had me to lean on.

"We need to debrief Banand and Zurronar today." Rokath

reached down and brushed the back of his knuckles across my cheek. "Since you were so fearless in their rescue, you should be there too."

I nodded, the pride that should have bloomed dying like a bud caught in a late-spring frost. "I should probably be the one to tell Zurronar about..." I trailed off as darkness ignited in Rokath's eyes. The reminder of Izgath, who he'd burned on a pyre after we had been caught almost coupling, when my true identity had been revealed, when our mate bond had snapped into place, was clearly still a touchy subject with him.

"You were always mine," he growled, the possessiveness in his tone heating my low belly.

"I know," I reassured him. I didn't have the energy to spar with him, nor was it an appropriate time when his emotions were stretched to their limits. "Now, I'll always be yours. Promise."

He leaned down and kissed me with a tenderness that surprised me. Instead of him claiming me, he merely let our lips linger together for a brief moment. "Let's go."

I slipped my hand into his as we emerged from our accommodation. It was these simple touches that grounded me the most—in knowing Rokath was *here* and our love wouldn't leave me bereft of him.

He whistled for Grem and Zeec to follow. Clouds covered the skies, and a breeze rustled through the spaces between the temporary buildings around us. The sullen atmosphere perfectly matched my mood.

We passed into an open avenue a moment later, a sudden gust of wind whipping the pennant flags about. The sickly smell of burnt fabric and flesh hit my nostrils, and I jerked up the scarf to cover my nose.

Rokath halted, craning his neck in the direction of the Angel's camp. "There's still smoke."

"Well, I did use seed oil to start the fire," I commented. "It's extremely difficult to put out. Water usually isn't enough."

Rokath snorted and shook his head before continuing forward. "I should have known I wasn't the only one capable of receiving your fire."

"You really should have. I don't know why you would have thought otherwise, honestly," I quipped, some of the ache in my heart easing as our banter began.

"Perhaps I should teach you to channel it in other ways so I am not the sole target," he replied, opening the entry to the command center and allowing me to pass.

"But it's far more fun when you are," I pouted, then broke into a grin.

Rokath rolled his eyes and steered me past the throne of bones and into the map room. Trol was there, along with a few other officers.

"Halálhívó." He closed his fist and brought it to his forehead before saluting Rokath. The others did the same. Then, they all dipped their heads to me. Clearly, our successful mission had garnered me some additional favor with them.

"Find Banand and Zurronar and tell them their presence is required here," Rokath told one of the Parancsok.

"Yes, sir," he replied, then dipped out of the tent.

"The rest of you are dismissed." They quickly gathered their belongings and departed, leaving us behind with Trol.

"I checked on Rapp earlier. He's still sleeping," Trol said before Rokath or I could voice the question.

At least he wasn't still dying. Sleeping was a good sign.

I hope.

"Thank you," Rokath murmured, sinking into one of the chairs. I found another and dragged it beside him. Since we were inside, I slipped the scarf off my head and plopped it on the table in front of me.

Rokath flicked a corner of it out of his way as he studied the map. Then, with a grumble, he raked a hand over his scalp and rubbed the back of his neck. "Trol, I hate to ask this of you, but I think Rapp will need to return to Fured with us to recover. Do you feel capable of holding here until we return with reinforcements?"

"Whatever you need, Halálhívó," he swore. "I know your friendship with Rapp runs deep."

Rokath picked his head up and met the gaze of his Hadvezér. I remained a silent bystander in their exchange, watching with rapt fascination at the changes in Rokath. "Do not think I don't value you too, Trol. I picked you from the academy for a reason."

Like us, Trol had burgundy eyes. His hair was cropped close to his head, and he always wore tight fitting leather armor that left his arms bare. Unlike Rapp and Rokath, no ink decorated his skin. I'd only had a few brief interactions with him, and I realized I didn't know what rare magic he possessed.

"If you don't mind me asking, what's your power?" I blurted out, unable to smother my interest.

Trol turned his attention to me, though not with the same gruffness he showed the soldiers. A hint of a smile rose to his lips. "I am a Rifter. Basically, if you combine the best parts of Destructors and Nightmares, that is what I do. I create slashes in the air or on the ground that seem so real that the Angels avoid them. There are consequences of them falling into them, of course."

My brows rose up my forehead, curiosity piqued. "Like what?"

"They're razor sharp. So essentially they are shredded to pieces if they fall in completely. Should they brush against the edge, it's like being sliced by a sword."

"Wow," I responded. His power was unlike anything I'd ever

heard of—which was similar to all those with burgundy eyes. "So that's how you were able to force them back so far?"

He nodded. "Though, the larger the rift, the less time I am able to hold it. I have to plan carefully where to deploy one and when with each battle."

"Which is exactly why you are invaluable, Trol. After this, you deserve a break yourself. You've been out here far too long without reprieve," Rokath added.

Trol waved his hand dismissively. "I'll get one when I get one. What matters most is that the soldiers who have been out here the longest have breaks for themselves. They fight far more than I do."

A breeze lifted a few strands of my hair as two more people entered the command center, ending our conversation. "Halálhívó," Banand and Zurronar greeted Rokath first, then Trol. Finally, both their attention landed firmly on me. "Szélhámos."

The honorific sent goosebumps skittering across my skin. To be recognized for my power...well, it wasn't something I'd ever dreamed of happening.

"Sit," Rokath commanded, and they both did.

Turning to me, he asked, "Do you know how to write?"

A scoff slipped out before I could stop it. "Of course I know how to write. My mother taught me."

"Did you know that writing for females was forbidden a century ago, save for the priestesses so they could communicate?" Rokath spoke into my mind.

My stomach plummeted. That explained why we never learned it in school. My mother had always insisted our handwriting had to be extremely elegant. She'd told us that we were never to show it to anyone unless we wanted our style stolen. The other girls in the village would have copied me for sure, which was my young mind's logic as to why I never spoke of it.

I'd never thought more of it.

"Well, it's a good thing I did since we're changing society," I quipped.

"Aye," Rokath rumbled back. He fetched parchment and ink, handing both to me. I arranged them neatly in front of me, waiting for whatever he wanted me to do.

He turned to the two males I'd rescued. "Assyria will take notes on your debriefing. Let's start with the most important pieces of information you managed to overhear."

Banand and Zurronar—looking far healthier than he had when we'd rescued him—went back and forth listing out what they'd heard, sometimes pausing to discuss the exact meaning since much had been in Angelic. Rokath would ask them to repeat the phrase if they could remember it, and then have me correct whatever I'd written. Trol jumped in intermittently, asking for clarification.

Apparently, nearly a year of captivity was a long time to gather intel. I shook my hand out on more than one occasion, muscles cramping from how much I wrote.

Once they'd offered all they could, Rokath switched topics to the Angel's treatment of them. As they recounted their torture, my stomach twisted. Salt burned my eyes as both remained stoic and strong despite the obvious pain they'd endured. Much like me, they'd have deep, invisible scars.

I didn't write a single word down; instead, I sat in solidarity with them, a witness to their suffering.

When they finished, I cleared my throat and held Zurronar's gaze. The resemblance to Izgath was uncanny, though their eye color was not the same. They sported the same trim build, and while Zurronar's hair was still a mess, the style was reminiscent of his brother's clipped sides and top knot.

"I have some news about your brother," I began, voice wavering. Rokath stiffened beside me, our bond tightening. But then, he exhaled, chest deflating, and reached for my leg under the table. He gave it a light squeeze, leaving his hand there. Warmth bloomed in my heart at the supportive gesture. That he fought for control with himself to aid me in this difficult conversation spoke volumes.

"Which one?" Zurronar asked. Both of his brothers were in the army, though I assumed the other still lived. I wasn't sure of his name or which unit he was in.

"Izgath." I swallowed roughly.

How am I supposed to tell him his sibling died because of me?

I twisted my mother's ring around my finger, trying to decide where to begin. "I first met him when he came to conscript in Stryi. You've seen my magic, so you know I can become anyone. I snuck into the army, and eventually, he discovered my true identity. When we returned to Uzhhorod to join the rest of the soldiers..." I trailed off, trying to find the right words.

"I killed him," Rokath stated plainly. I whipped my head to the side, finding a stoic expression plastered on his face. "Though he died for a noble cause. I didn't know that at the time, though. He protected Assyria's identity until his death. For which I will be forever grateful. It is because of his honor that she ended up in my hands and not somewhere worse."

Tears pricked the backs of my nose and eyes.

Zurronar paled, his eyes closing briefly. His inhale was slow, shaky. "You know, I spent months wondering if he'd been killed in the plague. If he was alive and still fighting. The same with Onnaron." A muscle ticked in his jaw as he leveled a heavy, grief-filled gaze on Rokath. "It's honestly better that I have certainty now. The not knowing was eating me inside."

"I'm so sorry," I blurted out, because what else was there to say?

Banand also looked relieved.

One less life on his conscience.

Zurronar's attention drifted to me, and I resisted the urge to squirm. Instead, I squared my shoulders and lifted my chin. He raked his maroon eyes over me as if judging me in an entirely new light. "My life for his life. Thank you, Szélhámos."

My jaw slackened before I snapped it shut. I'd assumed he'd shout at me. Throw something. Curse my name. But *thanking me*? That was not at all what I had imagined.

"Of course," I stammered out, my voice not nearly as steady as I had intended.

Maroon and burgundy tangled for a heartbeat longer before he addressed his leader. "Halálhívó, I served in your army long enough to know that your rules are strict and enforcement is carried out swiftly and without discrimination. While I am saddened by my brother's loss, it is a comfort knowing he broke the rules for good reason."

He paused, attention flicking between the two of us. Rokath squeezed my thigh harder.

"She is your mate, and the Weaver has blessed you both. My sword has been, and always will be, yours to wield." He bowed his head in deference, placing a hand over his heart for good measure.

I kept my composure when all I wanted to do was sag with relief.

Do all leaders have to deliver bad news like this?

"Aye, we do. This is the first of many tests you will face if you want to change our society. But I will always be by your side, helping you bloom," Rokath spoke into my mind.

"Thank you," I sent back, my annoyance with him reading my mind banished with his affirmation.

"Do either of you wish to return to Fured for a respite? You have more than earned it," Trol said, straightening in his seat and reaching for a glass of water.

Zurronar shook his head with conviction. Banand voiced his

opinion. "We spent too long caged. I don't know about Zur, but I am thirsty for some Angel blood. Besides, my magic is far more useful here. I know how to create sicknesses for the Angels now." The gauntness hadn't disappeared from his face, but a few hearty meals and some sun would have him healthier soon.

Rokath released my leg and braced his elbows on the table. Leaning in, he stared Banand down. "We have three females here whenever you want to get started."

Banand glanced at me, something unreadable in his expression. "Araquiel is one, is she not?"

I nodded. "She gave us the exact location of where you were being held."

Rokath cocked his head to the side. "Was she one of your jailers?"

"Aye," Banand replied a little too quickly. He looked away from us all like he was considering his next words.

"She was the only kind one," Zurronar added, attention lingering on Banand for a moment before returning to us. "She was the only one who remembered to feed us regularly."

Rokath dropped his hands and drummed his fingers on the table. His mind tumbled through a rapid series of thoughts, and I blocked him out before he gave me a fucking headache.

Besides, he didn't see what truly was happening here. "When did your relationship turn into more?" I asked Banand.

He choked, whipping his head to me. "How did you know?"

"Males," I muttered under my breath. Then, louder, I said, "The way you two spoke about one another. That she wanted me to pass a message onto you. The way you looked away from us."

Four sets of eyes stared at me. I rolled my own. "Clearly there is more than one reason to have females in the army. None of you are nearly perceptive enough."

Rokath snorted, but a tendril of pride slipped down our

bond. Before he or Trol could question Banand further, one of the sentries stationed outside stuck his head in, holding a rolled up piece of parchment. "Message for you, Halálhívó."

Rokath waved him in, and he knelt as he proffered it to the leader of the Demon army. I leaned closer, trying to glimpse the contents as he unrolled it. A muscle ticked in his jaw as he scanned the letter. Then, he snapped it shut again and faced the room.

"My mate is correct. Which is why we need to travel to Fured as soon as possible and retrieve all our new recruits. Thank you for your service and your perseverance. After the war, I will ensure you both are handsomely rewarded for your efforts. Until then, you are dismissed."

"Yes, sir," Banand and Zurronar said, rising to their feet.

I nudged him in the ribs, and he offered me a sideways look that said 'we'll talk later.'

Trol too rose, needing to attend to a few of the people in his battalions. The three fell into conversation as they returned to the camp beyond. As soon as the flaps closed behind them, Rokath let out a heavy sigh.

I wiggled in my chair until I faced him, waiting for him to speak.

"That was Xannirin and Kiira's response to my previous letter," he finally said, staring off into the distance, mind working in overdrive.

"And?"

"And they will both meet us in Fured with some females for the army."

A grin split my face in two, but Rokath seemed less than enthused. My excitement quickly faded. "What's wrong?"

At last, Rokath shook himself from his reverie and faced me. Grabbing my hands, he tugged me into his lap. He buried his nose in the crook of my neck, inhaling deeply. "You have no idea how much went into setting up society the way it is today, little imposter. While I am grateful you have shown me just how far off the path we strayed, I am still apprehensive to speak with my cousins. It will take time to undo what we spent centuries creating."

I reached around and scratched the back of his neck. "It's a good thing Demons live for millenia then."

He picked his head up, showing me the depth of his emotion. "Only if we win this war."

I swallowed hard. "You will. *We* will."

"I am trying to believe that again," he admitted quietly. To see my strong, confident mate so shaken by what had occurred the last few weeks reached between my ribs and slashed into my tattered heart. The one he was slowly healing with each action he took to right the wrongs of our society simply because I asked him to. Because now he *believed* it was the right thing to do.

"Some time away will do you good too," I murmured, rubbing the thick scruff on his jaw.

He nodded, then tilted his face into my palm and kissed it. "Just because you went on a mission yesterday doesn't mean you can slack off on training today. It will take your mind off everything too."

I slid from his lap as he stood. "Will it also take your mind off everything?" I arched a brow as I looked up at him.

He huffed. "Yes, it will help me too."

I offered him a genuine smile. "Then I'm ready."

He whistled at Grem and Zeec, and then the four of us wound our way through the camp, finding a training ring filled with males. This time, they didn't look down their noses at me, or offer me disdain-filled glares. For the first time, whispers of *Szélhámos* reached my ears.

Was I really surprised after all the time spent among them?

These males were worse gossips than the girls in my village had been while we were younglings.

Rokath handed me a dagger from his thigh, and when I faced him, I held it just like he'd shown me.

And then, we danced.

17

R☠KATH

Rapp remained suspended between life and death for days. While he fought for each fucking breath, Trol and I planned for the future. With the officers, we decided who needed to remain on the front lines and who needed to travel with us to Fured for a much needed respite. We'd also planned how to dig in and hold this position until we returned. The males boasting powerful eye colors from ruby to burgundy had been training for months and would be an asset to the next phase of this war. And the females who'd be joining their units would be leaders in their own way, ushering in the next phase of our society.

What loomed larger than any single front was that I still had to explain myself to Xannirin and Kiira.

Their joint raven had relayed *their* imminent departure to the military academy. If the Kral and the High Priestess both thought it necessary to speak in person, it would be a serious conversation indeed. But it was one that needed to happen. Xannirin would be pissed at the loss, of that I was certain. Kiira would be pleased that I'd finally accepted Assyria as my mate.

How they would take to my new plans for integrating females in the army was a mystery. I could see their reactions scattering in a myriad of ways.

At least they are bringing them without much fight.

The sun beat down upon us as we rushed through the camp, the meeting that had been interrupted by a messenger entirely forgotten. A breeze whipped the burgundy scarf from Assyria's dark hair as she half-jogged in front of me, even more desperate to see for herself that Rapp lived than I was.

All my worries melted as Assyria and I approached the healer's tent. The canvas was tied back, making it easy for us to duck inside. Fresh air breezed through the space, cooler with the approaching season change.

Propped up by a handful of pillows, yet still so fucking pale, Rapp grinned as we approached. The close crop he kept on either side of his scalp had grown out, and he needed a shave. But he was alive, he was breathing, and he was fucking blinking, which was *everything* in that moment. Assyria bolted to his side, nearly flinging her arms around him before she snapped back.

The thick white bandage over his chest was a stark reminder of his injury.

"Assyria," he greeted her warmly. Wincing, he grabbed her hand and gave it a squeeze.

"You promised me nothing would happen to you," she said firmly, the curves of her mouth dipping into a frown.

Rapp kept grinning. "If I remember correctly, my promise to you was that the Halálhívó and I would not die. As you can see, that didn't happen."

Assyria smacked his shoulder and I had to smother a snicker as I approached. "Don't twist your words," she admonished him.

Rapp's attention landed on me, and the smile slipped from his face. "You saved my life."

"It's not the first time," I said dismissively.

Rapp snorted a laugh. "No, but I'd never been on the brink of death any of the other times."

My throat worked at the reminder. I cleared it to banish the emotion. "We're taking you with us to Fured to recover."

"I'll be fine in a few days," Rapp protested, much to the approaching lead healer's chagrin.

"More like a few months, Hadvezér," he said, setting a tray of water and food on a nearby table. "Your left lung was severely injured, and it will take time for it to heal enough for you to lift anything, let alone draw a bow."

Rapp rolled his eyes, then leaned toward Assyria. Whispering conspiratorially, he said, "These healers don't know what they're talking about. All of them, overcautious. I'm a true warrior and pain doesn't bother me."

"How much poppy have you been giving him?" I asked the lead healer.

Rapp shot me a glare. Satisfaction curled through me at the reversal of our roles. Normally, I was the grumpy one who refused to care for himself while Rapp was the one forcing me to rest.

"Enough," the lead healer sighed, reaching for the bandage. Rapp winced as he peeled it off, dried flakes of blood coming with it. The thick lines of stitches stood angry against his skin.

He glanced down at them and whistled. "That's going to scar."

"You're alive," the lead healer quipped, bringing a wet cloth to the wound and gently dabbing it. It smelled slightly of aloe, which grew abundantly at the mouth of the canyon that led from Ustlyak and into Lutsk. At least it was available to use while we waited for more pium.

When the lead healer finished, he went to the tray and tried to feed Rapp. The Hadvezér shooed him away. "I can do it myself."

"No, you can't," he grumbled.

"I'll do it," Assyria jumped in. "Surely you have other patients who need tending. We can speak with Hadvezér Rapp while he eats, catch him up on everything he's missed?" She glanced at me as if she was waiting for me to confirm that was okay.

I nodded, pride blooming in my chest at how hard she was working to take charge. It was foreign to me, not being the one to lead the conversation and make the rules. But I found myself loving Assyria harnessing her fire more with each passing day. It had been a struggle at first, but she fought to stand beside me with enough fervor that I relented.

Mostly.

The lead healer acquiesced, promising to return later to rebandage Rapp's chest.

Assyria propped herself on a sliver of space beside Rapp. I pulled the table closer to her so she could easily reach the food, then fetched myself a chair.

"This is such horseshit," he muttered as Assyria lifted a bowl of clear soup to his lips. She grinned widely at him.

"Take a sip and I'll tell you what happened while you were out," I offered, trying to hide my amusement as I baited him.

"Fuck you, Rokath," he grumbled, then did as I bid.

"Good boy," I said, leaning back and crossing my arms.

He glared again. I was starting to see why Rapp enjoyed teasing me so much. "Assyria was successful in rescuing Banand and Zurronar, along with a few others. She also burned about a quarter of the Angel's camp to ashes."

Rapp slurped the last of the soup, brows raising. When

Assyria took it away, he said, "That's badass. Who knew you had it in you to be so vicious?"

She shrugged, then grabbed him a roll and tore a piece off. "I suppose you and Rokath are rubbing off on me. But I did kill my husband and then snuck into the army to avoid being executed, so I think it was there all along."

Rapp laughed, then his brows pinched. "Fuck that hurt. Try not to be funny."

"Sorry," Assyria said, giving his good shoulder a gentle squeeze. That primal protective part of me thrashed to the surface, wanting to snatch her away from him because she was mine. I smacked it away and reminded it that Rapp was no threat to my mate.

"The camp now refers to Assyria as Szélhámos," I added.

"Guess you should tell Kiira to add her to the prayers now," Rapp said around a mouthful of food.

"You can tell her yourself when you see her in Fured," I commented.

Rapp quirked a brow, causing the studs pierced above it to flash in the light. "She'll be there?"

"The Kral too," I noted. Assyria fed him more bread, and color returned to his cheeks.

"I think that's all I can handle for now," he said after the roll was gone. "Apparently it's been days since I've eaten and my stomach is reminding me of that now."

"Do you need to rest?" I asked him.

He shifted against the pillows as Assyria rose. "Some water, and then yes."

Assyria squeezed the end of an aloe arm into the cup waiting for Rapp, then lifted it to his lips. He drank three gulps before sitting back again. "So when do we leave for Fured?"

"Have you come around to the idea then?" I questioned, cocking my head to the side.

"I don't think I have much of a choice, do I?" he sighed, his tongue digging into his cheek.

"No," I told him. "We're leaving tomorrow now that you're awake. I'll have a special wagon prepared for you since you're incapable of riding."

Rapp muttered some choice words under his breath but finally nodded. "I hate being an invalid."

In that way, we were extremely alike. I rose from my seat and approached him. Assyria backed away to give us some space. "I know. But I'm so fucking glad you are alive." My throat thickened, and again I cleared it. "I couldn't win this war without you." My mind flickered to the days after I'd been forced to kill Thast and how Rapp hadn't left my side. How he'd forced me to eat, to drink some water. To find purpose in swinging a sword again. Before that, he'd been my friend. And after? He'd been the brother I never had.

"Aw, Rokath, don't get all sentimental on me now," he teased, and a low growl rumbled in my chest. The tables were once again turning, and not in a way I appreciated. "But you're right, and you definitely need me. So I'll recover and then we rip Zaph's head from his shoulders along with the fucking Zahal's. Deal?"

The words were as much reassurance for him as they were for me. "Deal," I agreed, straightening his tunic for him. "Rest now, and we'll fetch you in the morning."

Nodding, he tipped his head back and closed his eyes. We departed the healer's tent in silence, both of us unable to tear our gaze away from him until the darkness of the space swallowed him.

The sun blazed overhead as we trekked down the main thoroughfare. Assyria halted midstep, and I slowed, facing her. She adjusted her scarf, her gaze lifting to meet mine.

The fire in her eyes was renewed, reinvigorated, and ravenous.

In them burned a promise: we'd burn whatever stood between us and victory.

And from the ashes, we'd build a world where no female ever had to hide who she was again.

✳✳✳

INTERLUDE

The Kral perched atop his throne, his crown glittering as light spilled in from the opulent windows. Beside him, the Halálhívó stood, arms crossed over his armored chest. Since the death of their fathers, he'd remained by his cousin's side, providing protection until a suitable unit to guard him could be trained up to his high standards.

The newly-appointed High Priestess swept into the room a moment later, her long, modest black dress swishing over the polished floors. A sheer black veil hid her features, while a circlet atop her brow held it in place.

"What do you think?" she asked her cousins, giving a slow twirl to reveal her ensemble.

"Stunning," the Kral said, running his fingers over his bottom lip.

The High Priestess stopped, the fabric gathering around her ankles before she shook it out again. "All priestesses will now wear black, like a crow's feather. Others will have their choice of colors, but all will wear veils like this." Her smile—tight, cracked, brittle—was a mask with little difference from the sheer fabric covering her face. Gone were the days of her revealing summer dresses. Of showing her toned arms and lithe frame. Now, she and all females of the realm needed to hide behind dark fabric.

At least she was still her male cousin's equal in this new world, even if her flock was not.

"Nayúr Ollmund Varrir should be here any moment. With the Fates on our side, he'll prove less of a snake than the others," the Kral told her, gesturing for her to take the place on his left. "You can explain your clothing plans to him once we have his agreement. He is, after all, the premier textile producer for the Demon Realm."

The High Priestess settled into place. Straightening her shoulders and lifting her chin, she waited for the noble they all hoped would assist them in swaying the rest.

At the door, a page knocked, announcing the Nayúr's arrival.

"Enter," the Kral called out. The doors opened, revealing the maroon-eyed noble. While he was far older than any of the cousins, he still retained the vibrancy of youth. Yet the cunning curve of his lips as he knelt before his new Kral lodged a pit of worry in the High Priestess's stomach.

The Halálhívó merely looked down on the Nayúr through the slits in his new helmet. Only one class of people drew his ire—the nobility. He'd much prefer if they could keep the sycophants out of their plans. At the military academy, the noble's sons had all attempted to curry favor with the Kral and him, and he'd hated every moment of it. Hated every ball he'd been forced to attend at Gyor Palace by his father. Hated the shallow conversations, the false flattery, the deals done in the dark.

None of them understood the true cost of power. Because none of them possessed it. What they had was merely a grand illusion.

But the Kral had insisted time and time again nothing could be done without their aid.

"My Kral," the Nayúr purred as he straightened. "How may I serve you? That is why you called me here, is it not?"

The Kral didn't respond. With practiced slowness, he dragged his gaze over his noble. The Nayúr merely waited, unfazed by the untried Kral's assessment.

"By now you have heard of the battle of Kraskiv." It was more of a statement than a question.

"I have heard whispers, but I would love to hear a full account from the male who managed to survive such an assault," Nayúr Ollmund replied, his attention settling heavily on the Halálhívó.

His fingers tightened behind his back as he prepared to offer the rehearsed statement he'd crafted with the High Priestess. Stories, she'd told him countless times these last few weeks, held immense power. Moving people to emotion was what would drive quick change. Their fervency, their outrage, their indignation, was all key to selling the three's newfound statuses.

"A horde of Angels dared to enter our sovereign territory along the Kraskiv outpost. At the time, I happened to be inspecting fresh construction along our wall. I never expected such a force to attack. It was far larger than I've seen in my time serving the Demon army. Thousands upon thousands at the very least. We were overwhelmed immediately, and only a few managed to escape the initial onslaught. Yet instead of shoving their blades into our bellies or slicing them across our necks, the Angels strung ropes from the wall and looped them around each captured male's neck. We watched on as they proceeded to keep them alive and allow the birds to pick out their eyes before they let their entrails spill for feasting."

At that grotesque picture, the Nayúr paled. The High

Priestess watched his reactions intently, for this was the first test of her carefully crafted tale.

"Those of us who survived refused to leave until we could burn the bodies of our tortured comrades. Yet that itself was a carefully laid trap. Once the fires took hold, they attacked again. We filled the Fates' greedy bellies with Angel blood that night. I called upon my deceased soldiers to help us, their bodies still blazing. It is only by the will of the Weaver that I stand before you now."

Nayúr Ollmund's face reddened as the Halálhívó relayed the reattack. "The Reaper's eye passed over you. Tell me you slaughtered them all."

"Aye," the Halálhívó confirmed, his tone laced with dark intent. "The Giver endowed me with Calling for a reason. To lead the Demon army."

"We are blessed that the Fates shine so brightly on you," he replied, straightening and turning his attention to the veiled female. "And you, High Priestess."

"Do not forget your Kral," he tsked, rising from his throne, "for my Speaking powers have brought me great insight." He stepped down the dais and approached the Nayúr. "How many years has it been since you ascended?"

"Centuries, My Kral. It has been long enough that the exact count eludes me," the Nayúr replied.

"And in that time, a male such as yourself has built strong relationships," the Kral ventured next.

"Certainly. Though that doesn't mean I am set in my ways." His attention flicked between the three cousins. "I am always open to building new ones. So long as the relationship is mutually beneficial."

The Kral circled the Nayúr like a predator circles its prey. His polished boots clicked against the floor. "And what sort of benefits do you seek?"

He let out a low chuckle. "What male doesn't want gold? Power? Prestige?"

"It seems we have that in common. And isn't that a great foundation for an aligned relationship?" The Kral tossed out the statement like it was a fleeting thought and not a well-executed plan.

The High Priestess stiffened. *Had he said that to manipulate Ollmund, or did he truly mean it?* Doubt about his intentions clawed up her spine. Yet she couldn't voice them—not here, not now.

"I'm inclined to agree, My Kral. So why don't you tell me what it is you seek?" The Nayúr raised a brow, staring down the highest ranking Demon in all of Keleti.

The gemstones scattered flits of light around the room as the Kral stepped into the streaming sun. "It is our belief," he gestured to his cousins flanking him, "that Demon society is in dire need of a change. The people need to eat. They need to work. They need to serve. Males, in the army and the fields. Females, in increasing our population. We'll need all of that if we are to straddle both sides of the Skala Mountains."

The corners of the Nayúr's mouth rose. "I see you offer a mix of all three."

"Aye," the Kral replied. "So long as you can guarantee the support of the rest of the nobility."

"You know as well as I that there are factions within us, all vying for more," the Nayúr said, his head tilting ever so slightly. "So what makes you think that I have the power to unite them if you yourself—no offense meant, of course—cannot?"

The previous ruler had been cruel, wicked even, and had to be dealt with a delicate hand. His son was proving to be no different—though he hadn't the centuries of experience the Nayúr did in such matters.

It was the Kral's turn to chuckle. "Oh, Ollmund. I could

easily bring them to heel, should I choose to do so. But that would require force I do not wish to use so early in my reign. Relationships—hard won as some may be—are the true way to install order."

The grin on the Nayúr's face widened, but it wasn't born of friendliness or amusement. He had underestimated this new Kral's cunning. Where he had expected a male easily manipulated from inexperience, he was instead met with political power in the making. "You are quite right, My Kral. The promise of additional lands and opportunities to build wealth will certainly sway many to your plans. As well as this horrific incident in Kraskiv."

The Kral studied his noble servant in turn. The story of the battle had gotten the Nayúr invested—emotionally at least. Convincing him to participate fully would require other means of persuasion. He wasted no more time in attempting to discern what leverage the Nayúr wanted over House Vrak. "Who will be the easiest to sway?"

"Ah, not so fast," the Nayúr said, raising a hand. "I have not yet laid out my terms."

The Kral smiled, having pushed the Nayúr into revealing what he wanted to know. "Name them."

"First, the best lands in the Angel Realm will go to House Varrir. We need ample space to grow the materials for our fabrics."

"You have it," the Kral agreed. "Name your others."

"I have but one other," Nayúr Ollmund paused, dragging his attention over the High Priestess. Unease curled in her gut with the way he looked at her. The veil, at least, hid her swallow, even if she wished she wasn't forced to cover herself for their new order.

Tension hung thick in the room as the three cousins awaited his next request. "For my continued support and sway with the other nobles—because we both know I am influential, otherwise you would have sought out another—I require one favor which you cannot refuse me, to be claimed at the time of my choosing."

A muscle feathered in the Halálhívó's jaw. This was exactly why he didn't like the nobles. Always scheming for more power. Always ready to drive a knife into the back of another to supplant themselves.

"No," he growled, taking a half-step forward. "You can specify your terms or you can add caveats. We will not leave it open for you to claim the throne for yourself once we've shed our blood to conquer the Angel Realm."

The Nayúr's maroon eyes glittered. "You make a fair point, Rokath."

A snarl tore from him and he advanced on the noble. "That name no longer exists." At first, he'd resisted his cousin's suggestion that he hide beneath the mantle of the Halálhívó. Yet after they'd crafted the story of the battle of Kraskiv, he'd welcomed the added mystique and anonymity. The helmet too allowed him space to hide in plain sight. It also allowed him to show parts of himself he'd always been told to suppress.

Like his infamous rage.

The Nayúr refused to tremble under the male's wrath, despite his massive frame towering over him. Without looking away, he said to the Kral, "It seems you have more information to reveal yet."

"Name your second and only other condition and we will explain more," the Kral replied, his tone level and cool where his cousin vibrated with barely restrained fury.

"I will caveat my terms. I will not seek to request House Vrak to relinquish the throne. Nor will I request that all the noble houses save for mine be extinguished. I do agree that we need to save our race from those zealots. This favor will not hinder the efforts of our shared goal—more land, more gold, and more power for the Demons. So long as I am pleased with the direction everything is heading." Each word was carefully chosen to protect House Varrir's interests.

The Kral and the Halálhívó knew it too. To be beholden to such a male was a massive risk, yet they needed his support to accomplish their goals. "Fine," the Kral finally agreed, hoping he hadn't put his fate in the hands of the Reaper.

"Seal it with a blood oath," the head of House Varrir said, drawing a short, ceremonial knife from his belted sheath. The Halálhívó's hand immediately flew to the sword strapped across his back as he stepped forward.

"There's no need for violence. I have no intention of harming my new partners," the Nayúr said, disdain dripping in his pointed look at the Halálhívó.

The Kral clenched his teeth, indecision warring through him. Swearing to uphold his terms before the Fates ensured they'd have to act upon whatever the head of House Varrir wished. And yet, it would prevent the Nayúr from forcing House Vrak to relinquish the throne. He drew a blade of his own and sliced into his palm.

"Your terms shall be kept," he said, reaching for the Nayúr. The male cut his own skin and then pressed his wound to his Kral's.

"I am at your service, My Kral."

After the Halálhívó and the High Priestess made similar professions, they wiped their hands clean, the wounds already closing.

"Let's begin weaving our future."

PART
TWO

18

R☠KATH

The transition from the dry, sandy air of the desert to that of the briny sea was a welcome change. As we passed over another rolling hill, the town of Fured spread before us, stretching across the plateau that led directly to the deep blue ocean. Marshy green plants lined the road, swaying in the salted breeze. I'd spent more time here in my centuries of life than anywhere else in the Demon Realm, including Uzhhorod.

The military academy Xannirin, Rapp, and I had attended sat like a solemn companion to the bustling seaside town. From the distance, it appeared as an impenetrable fortress, with high, round turrets spaced at regular intervals in every direction. The stone battlements jutted against the cliffside, preventing any attacks from the rear. Not that anyone would be stupid enough to attempt to scale the sheer cliffs battered by fierce, frothy waves.

The wind too was a formidable opponent. A vivid memory of being pushed off the tallest tower at the rear slammed into me as my gaze landed on it. The howls, the screams, the snap of wings from every initiate faced their death at the hands of the sharp rocks and rough ocean below. The way the air had buffeted me, dragging me like a leaf. The giddiness of the freefall tugged at my chest. As did the pride in how my wings had snapped open at the penultimate moment and caught a draft that carried me away from the perilous rocks.

Yet the male who'd fallen after me had exhausted himself, unable to maneuver his body properly, and dropped like a stone into the sea.

His death didn't stir sorrow in me. Or regret. Or any other emotion. Nor did the dozen others who'd succumbed to the mighty power of nature.

War was a game of survival. If they couldn't thrive at the academy, they wouldn't have lived through a single battle.

Black banners whipped in the wind atop the turrets, still bearing the army's crossed sword sigil. Which meant that the Kral had not yet arrived. When he did, they'd be replaced with burgundy banners, all bearing the triple skulls of House Vrak.

My stomach unknotted. With our late departure as we waited for Rapp to awaken, I had worried they'd beat us here. I'd secretly hoped they'd been waylaid on their journey so I had a moment to reorient myself before speaking with them.

My small prayers have been answered.

"So this is it?" Assyria asked softly beside me.

I tore my attention away from the academy and to my mate. Black leather armor clung to her like a second skin, and her posture atop her new mare was proud and square. Blaeze had gone lame after our harrowing journey, and he deserved a rest. Much like the soldiers beginning to display trauma responses trailing behind us. They'd fought, they'd bled, they'd survived countless skirmishes—some for years. That didn't come without heavy strings attached.

Fured had always been a place of discipline. Brutality. Unforgiving training.

But perhaps it could become something...different.

With the arrival of Assyria, with the arrival of the females, with the future we were fighting for, maybe, just maybe, this would be the crucible of change. Where wounds of all types could heal. Where those long since separated could reunite.

Where the Fates would shine their favor and aid us in ending this fucking war.

Assyria dug her heels into the horse's dark bay belly, urging her on. We'd ridden side by side the entirety of our trek from the Paks Desert, and I let her edge ahead now as we closed in on the fork in the road.

At the peak of the hill, she halted, scanning the vastness of the scene before us, the scouting skills I'd taught her all those months ago kicking in. A small smile tugged at my lips. Our time in Fured would be spent further honing her powers and fighting skills. When we returned to the front, she'd be fully prepared to face the Angels again.

And slaughter them at every step.

She would be as formidable as she looked now with her hair braided back, sharp tongue ready to cut down all who questioned her.

"This is it," I echoed her words, tugging on my stallion's reins and angling him beside the mare. Assyria's mind tumbled over all the horrific memories I'd shared with her about my father and everything that had happened to me here.

"It's...different than I pictured," she said, shifting in her saddle.

"What were you expecting, little imposter?" I asked, draping my hands at the pommel of my saddle.

She lifted a shoulder and let it drop. "Something more sinister I suppose."

A low chuckle vibrated in my chest. "Have I spoiled you so

thoroughly, mate, that only danger makes your heart race? Makes you feel alive?"

Her attention drifted to me, teeth digging into her lower lip. "No."

"Then I'll do better," I replied, my tone laced with dark intent.

Hoofbeats shattered our moment, and I tilted my head over my shoulder. The rest of our group had finally caught up.

Which meant it was time to continue on. A heavy sigh escaped me, and I rolled out my neck.

My mate looked up at me, those devious burgundy eyes sharp with scrutiny. "Are you ready?"

"Aye," I replied, clucking my tongue and setting the black horse into motion again. The left hand split would take us straight to the entry of the academy. Turning onto that road didn't ignite feelings of warmth or home in me. Instead, the cold dread clung to me like a thick fog.

"Are you going to give me more than one or two word answers if I ask other questions about the academy?" she quipped as her mare fell into step beside me.

"If you would like, I can," I grumbled.

Fucking hate when she calls me out like that.

She offered me a saccharine smile. "Yes, please."

My blood heated, going straight to my groin. "I do like when you beg." I steered my stallion closer to her. *"Maybe later, I'll have to make you beg for something else."*

Lust swept down our bond. *"Only after we've bathed,"* she replied, her voice breathy in my mind.

"Wait until you see my rooms here. You'll want to bathe together," I told her as images of us doing just that flashed through my mind.

Her throat worked deliciously.

Ahead of us, twin siege doors groaned open. To be fair, a

party of this size was hard to miss, especially with spotters posted at each of the forward towers all hours of the day. And now, with the Angels clawing deep into Demon territory, it was necessary.

I glanced behind us to the cart where Rapp rode, only a dozen or so paces behind. He was still somewhat incapacitated, especially when it came to holding himself upright. At least after a few weeks of healing, he had more use of his arms and could feed himself. Any tugging on his chest muscles though set him back by days.

Which he'd done too many times already, to no one's surprise.

From the doors, a group of soldiers emerged, headed by Parancsok Olet. He was the highest ranking officer in residence, overseeing the training of the high-powered Demons I'd sent here after the mass conscription. His maroon armor gleamed in the sunlight, and I appreciated that he hadn't grown sloppy without my oversight. His discipline was one of the reasons I'd selected him to lead this charge.

Other ranking soldiers framed him, and they all dropped to one knee, resting their foreheads on their arms as we came to a halt. I dismounted my stallion, handing the reins to Assyria, and approached the Parancsok.

"Rise," I told him, and he did, though everyone else remained in their venerating postures.

"Halálhívó," he greeted me, scanning my face with an understandable curiosity. "I am pleased your journey was safe and swift. How fares Hadvezér Rapp?"

Prior to our departure, I'd sent a raven explaining that we'd be joining him in Fured with injured from the front and that Xannirin and Kiira would be bringing a group of females around the same time, since I didn't know how long their journey would take. The specifics and reasons behind each, I'd left out.

Those conversations would happen later, face to face, to ensure he would assist in steering those he'd been training in the right direction.

"He is unhappy with his current predicament, naturally. Hopefully some time by the sea will be restorative for him," I commented, gesturing over my shoulder at the wagons rolling to a stop.

Olet chuckled, his attention following mine. "That it will. We've prepared your rooms, and another for Hadvezér Rapp to rest comfortably. The healer is waiting to see him as well."

I scanned the rest of the males, still kneeling. "Good. Once we're settled, let's speak in my office."

"Yes, Halálhívó, I am at your command," he replied. Then, he snapped his fingers, and everyone behind him rose. "Assist with settling our new compatriots into the barracks."

The soldiers peeled off in the direction of our convoy. Voices soon filled the air, smothering the cries of gulls flying overhead and the waves crashing against the cliffs below. Assyria dismounted and grabbed both our horses' reins, leading them forward.

"Parancsok Olet," she said, keeping her shoulders square and chin lifted. Though down our bond, a hint of trepidation trickled. After all, the last time they'd seen each other, he'd thrown her at my feet and asked me how she should be punished for her crimes.

Recognition flickered in his maroon eyes. His dark brows pinched, leaving a deep crease. He opened his mouth to speak, but before he could, she cut him off.

"I'm glad to see you arrived safely after your departure from Uzhhorod," she said, her regard sweeping over him. She addressed him like a superior, not a female once punished at his hand. It was a bold move, and it was everything I'd come to love about her.

"This is Assyria, the Szélhámos. My mate," I introduced her, formally, to Olet. A healthy amount of threat weighed in my tone.

He paled as his attention flicked between the two of us. Then, he ran a hand over his close-cropped hair before gripping the back of his neck. "Mate?" he finally managed to get out.

"I will explain further later," I replied, leaving no room for argument.

"Of course, Halálhívó," he said, a slight tremble in his voice.

Could I blame him? He'd whipped Assyria, flaying her back open. And I was the most feared Demon in all of Keleti for a reason. Did a part of me want to offer him the same for daring to harm my mate? Of course. But I'd decided on the road here that he'd receive no reprimand from me. He was only acting on information he had at the time.

And I needed his loyalty now more than ever.

With a little more respect, he greeted Assyria, even offering her a slight bow. She may never be a Kralovna in title, but in my eyes? She ruled the world. "Welcome to Fured, Szélhámos."

She kept her expression decidedly neutral as he straightened. Pride swelled in my chest. Assyria was growing more and more confident interacting with the officers and soldiers with each passing day.

"Thank you, Parancsok Olet. I trust that you'll be able to assist in training the new female units. My mate has told me many great things about you. I hope they are all true." Her voice dripped with sweetness, though a snarky bite threaded through it.

So very typical of my little imposter.

He glanced at me again, utter confusion playing out across his myriad of expressions.

I merely waited, stone-faced, for him to respond. Assyria was taking a risk with the way she spoke to him, especially in front of all these males who did not know her. I wanted her to see it through. To *own* her rightful place at my side, even if it wasn't a subject I would have broached in the open.

Finally, he cleared his throat and said, "Absolutely, Szélhámos. Whatever you need me to do, I shall do."

"First, we should drop the horses off at the stables and ensure Rapp is settled," she pronounced, now turning her attention to me.

"I'll show you where they are," I told her. "See you at dinner, Olet."

He offered us a salute as we entered the doors to the academy. People raced around us, all pausing to offer me a respectful greeting. Shouts of "Halálhívó!" rang out, but most died when they noticed Assyria beside me.

All these males had ridden out the night after the incident, and none, save for Olet now, knew of everything that had transpired. They didn't have months to become accustomed to seeing her veilless, witnessing her interact with Rapp and me.

Guilt hit me like a stab to the gut at how long I'd let her suffer through their whispers, stares, *judgment*. She'd never faltered, rooting herself in steadfast defiance. I'd hated it. But now? It was something I wanted to protect. To nurture. To grow.

Reaching down our bond, I brushed a smoky tendril of magic against her mind. I wanted to reach for her hand, to feel her warm skin. Those small touches grounded me as much as they did her. Let me know she was safe by my side and not about to be strung up for a sacrifice by the Angels.

Through thick lashes, she peeked up at me, captivating me, as she always did, with those soulful burgundy eyes. At the stables, we handed off our mounts, then retraced our steps to the courtyard where the wagons were pulling in one by one. Rapp's was at the front, with two Vezető crouched on either side of him and helping him to sit. Grem and Zeec had already hopped to the ground and peered up at them, tails wagging softly.

By the time we reached him, he was on his feet. "Just like old times, huh?" he asked me, grinning widely.

I rolled my eyes. "It's nothing like old times."

"Psh," he said, then he winked at Assyria. "The only real difference is that you're here now."

"Come on, let's get you to the healer so he can examine you. Might need your head checked as well," I said, looping his arm over my shoulder and helping him amble forward. I whistled for the hounds to follow.

"Again, I can walk on my own," he grumbled.

Assyria giggled behind us. "You can, but you're too slow."

"I suppose we both know that the Halálhívó likes to go fast," Rapp quipped, and the two of them burst into laughter. A hiss slipped through his lips, and he winced. A sharp reminder of what he'd almost lost—what *we'd* almost lost.

"Knock it off, both of you, or he's going to hurt himself again. Like the last time. And the time before that," I pointed out.

Rapp grimaced and clutched his chest with his free hand. "Unfortunately this asshole is right."

A short staircase greeted us as we turned a corner in the keep. The healing wing took up two floors, but the lower was for emergent cases. "Think you can go up them?" I asked, ducking out from under his arm. Grem and Zeec bounded forward, spinning at the top and looking down at us with an almost judgmental air.

Rapp nodded, gritting his teeth. Gripping the railing on his good side for extra support, he hauled himself up, one slow step at a time. Assyria went beside him, while I hovered two paces behind, ready to catch him should he fall.

Halfway up, we paused, and I glanced around the familiar space. It was decidedly quiet, save for voices drifting from other halls. Rapp wiped sweat off his brow and planted his boot on the next step. I knew from experience he wouldn't want many people to see him this weak.

When we finally summited, I told Assyria to jog ahead and find the lead healer. Rapp shuffled the rest of the way on his own, using the wall for support, though I was primed to step in the moment he needed it.

The ruby-eyed male appeared, my mate in tow, moments later, his assessing eyes already raking over his Hadvezér. "Get in here and let me look at you. Those combat healers don't always do the best job of *actually* curing ailments," he grumbled. "Sloppy at best, the lot of them."

Assyria slammed a hand over her mouth to silence a snicker.

"If you tell me I can draw a bow or swing a sword tomorrow, I'll tell you how much better you are than them," Rapp commented as he rounded the corner and into an examination room.

The lead healer released a sigh threaded with so much irritation I was surprised when he didn't smack the back of Rapp's head. "Just sit on the table."

"Wait," Assyria told Grem and Zeec before following us inside. The hounds huffed but did as they were told, framing the entry like twin statues.

Together, Assyria and I helped Rapp settle into place, though he attempted to shrug off our assistance. But the pallor of his skin and sheen of sweat on his forehead spoke of just how difficult the short trek was for him. He tipped his head back against the wall, chest rising with shallow breaths as he unlaced the leather armor.

The healer opened a nearby cabinet and piled instruments and potions onto a small table.

"We'll leave you to it," I said.

"You'll have my full report this evening," he promised, dragging his supplies closer to Rapp.

Assyria gave Rapp a quick squeeze on his thigh. "We'll see you later. Promise."

He merely nodded and continued to work his shirt off.

"Be a good boy and do as the lead healer says," I told him, unable to help the twist of my lips.

Assyria laughed as Rapp flashed me an obscene gesture. The healer muttered something under his breath about Rapp harming himself further. With that, we left our obstinate friend behind and reentered the hall. I closed the door behind us with a gentle click, ensuring Rapp had privacy while the healer examined him.

"Now what?" my mate asked me. The dog's nails clicked against the stone floors as we left the healing wing.

"Now, we bathe. And if you're lucky, I'll let you touch more than soap."

19

ASSYRIA

Rokath hadn't been lying when he said his rooms were incredible. At the top of one of the rear towers, the suite was both private and luxurious. Set into the stone of the sitting area were wide windows with a view sweeping over the vast sea cliffs and into the ocean. I pressed my hand to the cool glass as I peered down, trying to glimpse what waited beneath.

My mate moved through the suite with crisp efficiency, stripping cloths from the furniture like he was readying a battlefield instead of our accommodation. Backing out of his way, I took in the rest of the space. A set of double doors led into a sleeping chamber, and beyond, the promise of a place to bathe.

The space wasn't quite as nice as his rooms at Gyor Palace, but far better than the tent to which I'd become *unfortunately* accustomed.

Grem and Zeec trotted past me and onto plush beds jutted against the wall beneath the windows, flopping onto one each. Thankfully they didn't leap onto the bed, because like me, both could use a nice, long bath. The promise of the fluffy mattress was almost too good for me to pass up, though.

Rokath dropped our bags in a corner of the sleeping chamber, drawing my attention. "I'll warn you now that life here is extremely regimented, and I expect you to follow along with it—"

I opened my mouth to speak, but Rokath beat me to it. "Without protest."

My teeth clicked shut, and I huffed. "What kind of regimen are we talking?"

"There are three groups, all of which maintain a similar schedule that starts at different times. But everyone in that cohort rises at the same time. Eats every meal at the same time. Trains at the same time. Studies at the same time. Goes to bed at the same time. And that time never deviates," he explained slowly, his hands rising ever so slightly like he was preparing to defend himself.

"Okay but we're above the rules right? That's been made abundantly clear time and time again," I quipped, crossing my arms and popping out a hip.

Rokath removed his helmet slowly, revealing the utter seriousness etched in his face. Internally, I groaned.

"Here, especially with the females joining us, we must demonstrate the utmost respect for the rules. Even the males accompanying us haven't ceased grumbling about the changes, and if they believe even for a second that the females receive different treatment, that will only fuel their arguments," Rokath pointed out.

"Arguments you've used for centuries to keep females out," I shot back.

"I am aware," he groused, setting his helmet to the side. Then, he unbuckled his armor piece by piece and strapped it around a dummy to hold its shape. When he yanked his shirt overhead after, my thighs clenched. His powerful physique never ceased to swirl up a twister of desire inside me, especially now that we'd admitted our feelings to one another.

"So about that bath..." I began, the rule following and rule breaking forgotten. With unashamed hunger, I raked my gaze over the hard planes of his torso and the ink that covered them.

He returned the look with equal heat as I yanked on the laces of my leather tunic and dropped it to the floor. "Come," he commanded in the only way that made me want to obey.

The bathing chamber alone was nearly as large as the sitting area. My jaw dropped as I took in every inch of the space. A massive tub stood before windows taller than Rokath with a perfect view of the ocean. Stone slabs lined the floor, while the ceiling, much like the sleeping chamber, crescendoed upward. Light danced around the space as the clouds parted.

Rokath turned the taps, and water crashed into the carved rock, echoing in my ears. "You'll probably want to rinse over there first," he said, pointing to a waist-high faucet that protruded out of the wall. Beneath it, a thick drain waited.

I stripped out of the last of my clothes, nose crinkling at the pungent stench that clung to them, and flung them through the open doorway. "Don't tell me I'll have to wash my own clothes now too."

His pants sailed past me a moment later. "That is a perk we will maintain."

"Thank the Fates," I breathed, nearly sagging with relief. I kicked a foot beneath the stream of water, only to be met with a bitter chill. With a yelp, I jumped straight into the warmth of Rokath's skin. His laugh rumbled against my back. Along with a press of his massive length.

Whipping around, I faced him. The layers of grime on both of us were apparent, especially now that we had stripped down.

He handed me a rough cloth. "This should help speed up the process."

My attention dragged to the luxurious tub and the steam wafting off its surface with a divine hint of lavender. I hadn't appreciated the bathing chamber on the estate in Stryi nearly enough.

Together we worked quickly to remove the worst of the dirt so we wouldn't have to soak in it. And I planned on taking a *long* soak.

After the cloth was so brown that I wasn't sure it was helping any more, I assessed my skin and deemed it clean enough. Draping it over a nearby rack, I approached the tub.

Liquid splashed as I dipped a foot in, nearly shivering at the temperature change. It wasn't quite full enough yet, and thank the Weaver, the water didn't immediately get dirty when I settled myself into it. What would happen when I dunked my head to wash my hair was an entirely different story. I wasn't sure I'd ever be able to get all the sand off my scalp.

Moments later, Rokath joined me, ceasing the flow from the tap. I almost protested, but when he sat down, the water nearly sloshed to the rim, displaced by his bulk. The tub was large enough for both of us to stretch out comfortably, but to my surprise, Rokath grabbed my hands and tugged me into his chest. I straddled his lap, his hardness pressing against my core.

I rocked against it, a moan tearing from my lips. He moved his grip to my hips and dragged me along his length. "Keep that up and we'll have to bathe thrice before dinner."

"Please tell me we have time for that," I groaned because that was exactly what I wanted. His thick cock filling me before, during, and after I cleansed months of sweat and dirt from my skin.

"Unfortunately not, little imposter," Rokath rumbled, my ribs vibrating from the depths of his voice. He settled me into his lap, then leaned forward and dragged his nose up the length of my neck so he spoke his next words in my ear. "So I'm going to need you to come quickly for me. Can you do that?"

Heat coiled low in my belly. "I can," I breathed, and Rokath reclined against the stone. The sun glimmered off the droplets clinging to his physique. His biceps flexed as he repositioned himself below me, the tip of his thick cock nudging at my entrance.

In one powerful thrust, he entered me, sending water spilling over the lip of the tub and onto the floor. A heady moan escaped me as he stretched me along his length. "Rokath," I breathed, head tipping back.

"Look at me," he growled, and I snapped my attention forward, finding his burgundy eyes igniting with lust. He speared into me from below, sending another cascade over the sides. Our bond thrummed with pleasure as he did it again, and again, and again. Tension wound through me as our eyes remained locked, water continuing to disappear around us. It was as if the ocean had entrenched itself in the tub, churning and frothing while Rokath held me in place and delivered me the most delicious ecstasy.

"You're going to have to refill the tub," I panted, bracing my hands on his bouldered shoulders to keep my balance as I began floating higher, higher, higher.

Rokath quickened his pace, brows pinching together and breath coming in ragged. "We live beside the sea now, little imposter. There is no shortage of water."

He switched his grip, arching my lower back and dragging my clit against his hard abdomen. A gasp ripped from me as the friction increased. "Don't stop. I need more," I pleaded. He slammed himself to the hilt, making stars dance in my vision. Nearly all the water had sloshed out, and the barest amount remained to lap around my ankles.

In one smooth motion, he unseated and flipped me so I faced the windows. Crowding me from behind, he breathed in my ear, "Grab the edge."

I did immediately, knuckles turning as white as the stone. In this position, Rokath was *always* relentless. He smacked my ass, hard, the sound echoing around the chamber. A cry tore from my throat, replaced instantly with a moan as he entered me again.

Fingers digging into my hips, he bowed my spine, hitting that spot deep inside me. "Fuck," he rasped as my walls clenched around him. The polish of the window reflected his dark rapture as he moved inside me. And in that obsidian expression, I found safety. Protection. Certainty that he'd never let anyone hurt me again.

The ache from his boundless devotion bloomed in my chest, mirrored back to him as our eyes locked in our reflection.

Yet, the panes were wide, open, and should anyone fly up here, they'd have an unfiltered view into what we were doing. The thought made my blood heat.

"Your body is so fucking perfect. You are so fucking perfect, mate," Rokath rumbled, reaching around for my neck. He tightened his grip ever so slightly and cut off my air. I floated even higher.

"What if someone flies up here and sees us?" I gasped out around his hand.

"Then they die," he said simply, like there was no question about it.

Rokath pressed images of what *exactly* he'd do to the unfortunate person who witnessed him claiming me from behind into my mind. That only heightened the ecstasy of him thickening inside me. A small, wanton sound slipped out of me before I could stop it.

"You'd like that, wouldn't you, little imposter?" he growled, grip tightening.

"Yes." I battled for air, arms trembling as I attempted to remain upright when all I wanted to do was collapse. Sweat beaded my forehead and dripped down my back as Rokath pounded into me. "More. Please." Each word strangled out of me as the world spun. Specks flew in my vision, and I was wound so tight, it wouldn't take much for me to snap.

He leaned over me, so fucking deep I thought I might split in two. Another cry tore from my throat. "Come for me while you think about what would happen to the unfortunate soldier who witnessed me claiming you."

With expert fingers, he rubbed my clit, and then, I was gone. With more force than the waves below, pleasure crested and then crashed into me. Brows pinched, mouth open in a silent scream, I rode the tide of pleasure in and out.

"You'd like me killing in your name as much as you liked me punishing in your name. You know, I never did tell you that when those fucking fanatics took you from me, I beat a dozen soldiers bloody for allowing them so close to you. It wasn't enough."

Our bond swirled with violent promise and carnal pleasure. Wave after wave of dark desire swept from Rokath to me, prolonging my orgasm. Air flooded my lungs again after he surrendered my neck.

"I would," I panted, blood thrumming in my veins with the anticipation of the slaughter to come. With the thought of the vengeance Rokath and I would seek against the Angels.

A massive gong reverberated, overtaking the sound of our slapping skin and my moans. "Fuck," Rokath cursed, quickening his pace. "The Fates made you perfectly for me, Assyria. Our darkness. Our pain. Our *pleasure*." To emphasize his point, he sank himself to the hilt and circled his hips.

"Yes," I hissed, pressing into him. He grabbed my braid and wrapped it around his fist, forcing my spine to arch again.

"You are mine, Assyria. Always have been. Always will be. In every life, in every world, in every form." All barriers between us swept away as he opened himself to me through the bond. His reflection darkened, much like his mood. That possessive protectiveness in him rose as his orgasm closed in on him. That only served to heighten my pleasure, and my toes curled as my core tightened again.

"Give me one more, since we're already going to be late," Rokath commanded, and I did, already so close to the edge. His name ripped from my throat as he thrust brutally into me, over and over and over. My mind went blank of everything but my mate.

He groaned, low, masculine, *primal*, and slipped out of me. Pumping himself, he coated my back in ropes of his hot cum.

Our breaths came in serrated drags as he gathered me in his arms and flipped me. His lips collided with mine, stealing what little air I had regained. With him, it was never enough—was never going to be enough.

He ended our kiss, bracing his forehead against mine. "Why do you cause me to break all my own rules?"

"You could adjust them," I pointed out, a small smile curving my lips. I couldn't deny that I loved the power I held over him though. From our very first interaction, he'd disregarded his carefully crafted regulations for me.

His confession and his story about Thast cast all of those choices into a new light. To Rokath, the strict enforcement had been a way to ensure that never happened again. For him to continue to bend and break them for me was a testament to his adoration. To the way we loved each other.

I scratched his beard, then hooked my fingers together at

the base of his neck. Staring into his dark eyes, I professed with words what the bond already told him. "I love you."

He grabbed my wrists and freed his head, kissing each of the H's he'd carved into them. "And I you, Assyria."

Our lips met again with tender care, and he ran his knuckles up and down my ribcage. With a sigh, I pulled back.

"Hurry with your hair. You can bathe again later while I speak with Olet," he said, his voice low and gravelly. Then, he released me to turn on the taps again.

Grabbing a bar of soap from atop a now-soaked pile of bath sheets, I quickly worked it into a lather and cleansed myself. Then, I unbraided my hair and dunked beneath the flow of water. Scratching my scalp, I attempted to remove as much sand as possible. Unfortunately, my locks would take more than a single wash to return to normal. With a huff, I gave up, deciding I was refreshed enough to eat among the males— especially given that even in this state, I was still cleaner than they were in the war camp.

Rokath found us clothes while I dried and fixed my hair so it wouldn't drip all over the floor. Grem and Zeec snoozed on their beds as we reentered the sleeping chamber, neither bothering to crack an eye at our departure.

"So how late are we?" I asked with a little giggle as Rokath strapped daggers to his person. He wasn't dressed in full armor, at least, though his attire was no less intimidating than it would have been otherwise.

Rokath flicked his attention to the clock on the wall. "By the time we get there, only half an hour."

"Oops," I shrugged, pulling on my boots. Rokath grumbled something about me under his breath, and I threw a pillow at him.

He caught it handily before striding over to me and yanking me upright. Then, he wrapped a hand around my throat, stroking my fluttering pulse. "Let's go before I decide to skip dinner altogether and punish that smart mouth."

I offered him a saccharine smile. Then, he looped his arm over my shoulders and steered us out of his rooms and into the long spiral staircase that would bring us back to reality.

The roar of voices shook the stone around us as we approached the dining hall, and my stomach rumbled loudly as the scent of roasted vegetables and freshly baked bread reached my nostrils. To put it mildly, camp food was little more than a torture device designed to nourish us.

Real food? At the moment, that was better than any sex Rokath could give me.

"Clearly I did not make you come hard enough, little imposter."

I stopped in my tracks, a scoff slipping out of me. He'd been drifting in my thoughts and I hadn't even realized.

Smug satisfaction met me when I cursed him down our bond.

Rokath strode forward with powerful, confident strides, leaving me behind. With a huff, I jogged to catch up, throwing my shoulders back and embodying his attitude. These males, for the most part, were all new to me. I'd held my own with Parancsok Olet earlier, and now it was time to prove myself to the rest of them.

Hopefully the ones who traveled with us would spread the word of my newfound infamy and whispers of my Giver-blessed power would garner their favorable regard.

At the end of the hall, two doors were thrown wide, and inside, the mass of males moved, ate, and spoke to one another. But when Rokath entered the vast commons, conversation ceased, movement slowed, and mouths stopped chewing. Though he didn't don his ebony horned helmet before we departed, his aura alone was enough to intimidate and command respect.

Those standing dropped to one knee. Those seated bowed their heads. But one word whispered from every mouth as we passed by: *Halálhívó*. He didn't deign to look at a single one as we approached a high table with a view over the entire room. Parancsok Olet was already there, along with Rapp, who looked more pissed off than when we'd left him with the healer earlier.

Yet when I sat down, he shot me a salacious wink. My cheeks flamed, then heated more as hundreds of pairs of eyes landed on me. These ones weren't accustomed to seeing me veilless. But I refused to show a hint of indecision. I'd chosen before we left Gyor Palace to never wear a veil again, and I would not waver in that now.

When I'd first ventured out in the war camp, I'd been judged as Rokath's fallen. Whispers of our intimacy—or lack thereof—abounded. Still more about my burgundy eyes and what I'd done to be shackled to the Halálhívó. Pointed stares, conversations falling as I approached then rising after I passed, and absolute avoidance of my path had prepared me for this battle.

At this point, I was basically immune to the males' scrutiny.

So I steeled my spine and ignored the room exactly as Rokath had. "Parancsok Olet, Hadvezér Rapp," I greeted them formally, since we had an audience.

"Szélhámos," they replied. The conversation picked up again among the males seated below us, and I breathed a sigh of relief.

A moment later, a young male appeared with mugs and a pitcher, placing one in front of Rokath and me and filling them with a citrus water. I reached for my glass, only to be stymied when another appeared with trays of food.

Roasted fish in some sort of white sauce filled one plate, while another brimmed with wilted greens. A hunk of bread and some cheese waited at the top corner. The two backed away quickly, disappearing before I'd had a chance to orient myself to what had occurred. Rokath wasted no time grabbing a knife and fork and tearing into his meal, so I took my own and mimicked him. Olet and Rapp resumed eating too.

"How was your journey?" Olet asked us, his plate already empty. Even in the war camp, everyone ate quickly, no matter what was in front of them.

"Thankfully, uneventful," Rokath started, pausing to sip from his water. "Though Hadvezér Rapp's constant complaints kept us all entertained." His gaze cut to Rapp, who stabbed at his fish only for it to fall off his fork when he lifted it. A string of curses fled his lips, and I smothered a giggle at his expense.

"I swear if anyone tells me I can't start training again in the next week, I'm going to do it anyway. Damn the consequences," he grumbled, managing to secure his food this time.

"And what did the lead healer have to say?" I asked him, my tone light and teasing.

"Not that," he grumbled around a mouthful of his dinner.

Olet and Rokath fell into conversation while I tucked into my plate, consuming every last bite. Afterward, my stomach ached from being so full, but I didn't care. Not when a month ago, I'd nearly died in the desert.

I was going to savor everything life had to offer from here on out.

Including the dessert that the servers placed in front of me a moment later. I'd barely taken two bites when another gong sounded, and I let out a loud groan. Around the tables below, the males rose, forming neat lines to return their plates and glasses.

The servant appeared, and I waved him away. There was no way I was surrendering this. Not yet at least. Besides, I was the Szélhámos now and I got to break a few rules, whether Rokath wanted me to or not.

He raised a single dark brow in my direction. I offered him a similar glower in return, daring him to challenge me. With an irritated sigh, he let me be, telling the servers to take everyone else's plates first.

I shoveled the rest of the cake into my mouth, barely catching the crumbs that spilled from it. Then, the plate was snatched out from under me.

"Welcome to life at the military academy, Assyria," Rapp chuckled, swaying to his feet.

I'd lived through worse. Survived a husband who thought he owned me. Held my own against Rokath as we fought each other for control. Escaped death at the hands of the Angels.

But this place? This was going to test me in a way I'd never been before.

Here, I wouldn't simply stand beside Rokath as his mate.

I'd step into my identity as an Imposter and remake the realm.

20

ASSYRIA

The clanging bell yanked a groan from my throat. I rolled over, hand smacking for a pillow, and then dragged it over my head to smother the sound. Rokath snatched it away a moment later.

"Time to rise, little imposter."

I cracked an eye, the outline of him barely visible in the darkness. "I hate you."

He chuckled and slid from the bed. Grem and Zeec shook out their fur, ears flapping loud enough to join that damn wake up call. I reached for the blankets to shove them overhead. Two hands closed around my ankles, and without warning, I was yanked from the soft mattress and onto my feet.

"Now I really hate you," I quipped, a shiver wracking my frame.

"Dress quickly. The next gong sounds in ten minutes," Rokath told me, striding away.

"*Ten minutes?*" I groaned, rubbing the heels of my palms into my eyes. This asshole had dragged me from the deepest slumber I'd had in *months*. The moment I'd returned to our room the previous night, I'd passed out. Had barely roused when Rokath returned.

Fumbling around, I found my clothes and pulled them on. With few precious minutes until the next glorious chime sounded, I laced up my leathers while I stumbled to the bathing chamber.

My mate stood in front of the mirror, running a razor over his scalp. I went to the basin and turned the taps, cupping my hands beneath the frigid water and splashing it on my face. It was...refreshing to say the least. Blinking through the droplets clinging to my lashes, I found a cloth and dried my face.

"While we wait for Xannirin and Kiira, I want to test the limits of your magic. What's possible, what's not," Rokath said, swiping a damp hand over his head.

A smile bloomed on my face. "I can't wait. I never really had anyone to teach me before you. Everything I know I figured out on my own, by accident." I'd spent so long hiding my power, at my mother's behest, I'd almost grown afraid of it. But now, I was stepping into who I was meant to be, and that meant owning every bit of magic that the Giver had blessed me with.

My fingers flew through my hair, pulling the dark strands into a long plait. The tight weave pulled my locks away from my face, highlighting my high cheekbones. Excitement danced in my eyes as I looked at myself in the mirror. "Ready," I pronounced, spinning to face Rokath.

The breakfast gong sounded at the same time, pulling a small laugh from me. At least this time, we wouldn't be late for our meal—which was probably why Rokath had dragged me out of bed.

By the time we reached the bottom floor of the keep, the halls were a flurry of activity. Males descended from their watch posts, looking far more alert than those who had risen with us.

All streamed toward the heavenly smell of rosemary bread. My stomach rumbled at the promise of food.

Swept up in the tide, we entered the commons. Rokath tucked me close to his side and steered me away from the deep line of soldiers and toward the high table.

Olet and Rapp were already there, the latter looking far better than he had the previous day.

"Morning," I greeted Rapp, giving his good shoulder a squeeze before taking a seat beside him. Rokath took the chair opposite me, with his officers positioned between us.

Olet turned his attention to me immediately. "Szélhámos, I'd like to extend my sincerest apology. Had I known you were the mate of the Halálhívó, I never would have struck you."

The muscles of my back flinched at the memory of how he'd whipped me. I swallowed around the feeling of helplessness that arose with it. Rokath's rage flared down our bond. I flicked my attention to him. The reminder was nearly as painful for him as it was for me. Jaw clenched, he offered me a small dip of his chin, letting me know I was supposed to lead.

"Parancsok Olet, I hope that you aren't only sorry because of who my mate is. Females do not deserve the treatment that had been afforded us for the past few centuries," I said, each word measured and brimming with challenge.

Rapp's fingers tightened over the table as he waited to see which way the exchange would fall. Rokath kept his gaze firmly on me.

Olet blew out a long breath. "I apologize for that as well, Szélhámos. You are absolutely correct in that assessment. While the Halálhívó's plan shocked me at first, the wisdom in it is sound. My sisters were both married off young, and I've hardly seen them since I joined the army. Unfortunately, my perspective had been limited by that. I hope to gain new insight upon the arrival of our new recruits."

My eyebrows shot up my forehead, but I quickly smoothed my expression and offered him a soft, sincere smile. "Thank you, Parancsok Olet. All is forgiven between us."

The tension bled from his shoulders. "I am glad to hear it."

A moment later, four steaming trays emerged from the kitchens, the servers placing them before us with practiced efficiency.

"*Olet came around quickly after I told him of our plans last night. I wasn't expecting him to apologize to you though. You handled yourself well,*" Rokath said as water, juice, and steaming tea followed the food.

I sipped from the juice as I replied. "*Thank you.*"

"After we're finished eating, I'll give you a tour," Rokath told me aloud a moment later.

I cocked my head to the side as I studied him. "We skip the tour and go straight to training."

"*It seems I might have empowered you a little too much, little imposter. Do not forget I am in charge here,*" Rokath spoke into my mind.

My grin was fiery and saccharine. "*For now.*"

"*Do you have plans to overthrow my rule?*" he asked, amusement lifting his tone.

"*Depends on how quickly you teach me to thoroughly stab someone to death,*" I quipped, picking up a fork and shoving them forcefully into my eggs for good measure.

A laugh echoed down our bond, but he kept his expression neutral. "Fine, we'll go to the training yard. Rapp can observe so he feels like he's still important."

Rapp grumbled. "If we weren't in front of all these soldiers–"

"You'd have some choice words for him," I teased.

"Exactly," Rapp replied, popping a flaky piece of pastry into his mouth.

I ate quickly, finishing—thankfully—before the gong sounded. Draining the last of my water, I rose, waiting to see if Rapp needed my help. He shot me an annoyed look. I merely pressed my lips together to keep from grinning.

Olet strode toward the soldiers' tables and pulled out a parchment, reading off the day's assignments. Meanwhile, Rapp, Rokath, and I worked our way through the commons and out into the hall.

Excitement thrummed in my veins, our slow progress only serving to heighten the emotion. While I'd trained prior to the rescue mission, it was paltry compared to what I wanted to learn. Today, I was finally going to unlock the mysteries of my magic. Today, I was going to discover parts of myself I'd kept hidden for far too long.

Today, I was taking the first steps into becoming the Szélhámos.

☠☠☠☠☠☠

The training area on the east side of the academy was already a hub of excitement by the time we reached it. Metal clashed against metal, mingling with the shouts of males sparring in hand to hand combat. The yard was massive, with enough space for training with weapons or magic, and a place for onlookers to observe the pairs fighting. Above, covered walkways allowed glimpses from passersby, while a grandstand sat off to one side, where sweat-soaked males reclined.

On the bottom most row, Olet sat, shouting at a pair utterly failing to execute some complex move with long staffs. More officers were off to another side, instructing what looked to be a group of Destructors facing off with an especially large tree trunk.

Most were too focused on their tasks to notice Rokath,

Rapp, and I clinging to the periphery. *"We'll search for a quieter space to practice so you can focus,"* he spoke into my mind.

Rapp settled next to Olet, barking instructions to another group. Rokath and I continued on, finding the space behind the stands blissfully empty. While the yells and sounds of fighting were still audible, it was low enough that it was mere background noise.

Off to one side, spare weapons and bales of hay waited, and Rokath dragged one forward, then settled himself on it. "Let's start with your shadow power. Show me how much you can conjure."

Nodding, I closed my eyes, digging into my magic well. It opened readily with so much use over the past few months. The smoky swirls spilled out of my palms as I exhaled. I delved deeper, immersing myself in the way they felt both in my chest and against my skin. All around me, magic darkened into existence. Yet, I hadn't glimpsed the depths of my limits. So I continued to drink until the bottom of an empty glass appeared.

I halted there, not wanting to overextend myself, and opened my eyes.

A gasp fled my lips as I realized just how much I'd filled the area around us with wispy strands of black. A sea of them curled around Rokath's feet, and he drank me in like I was his salvation after a week in the desert. The sight healed another shred of my tattered heart. There was no question of his adoration of me, not when he looked at me like that.

Almost instinctively, I raised a hand, the tip of my finger dragging through the air to direct my magic up his body. He didn't move, merely kept watching me, as I wrapped the tendrils around his torso and his arms. When his black clothing had nearly been replaced by my power, I curled my fingers into my palm and yanked.

Obsidian ropes forced Rokath to his feet, to which he responded with a wicked grin. "You really are asking for it today, aren't you, little imposter?"

"Maybe," I replied, my own lips curving into a mischievous smile. Rokath had used his powers with me multiple times, and I'd always been impressed by the mastery he possessed.

I wanted that.

Training with him prior to the rescue mission had shown me I'd barely scratched the surface of what I could do with my burgundy eyes.

"Release it so you still have some magic left to test your secondary power," he murmured. When I loosened my grip on him, he reached out, running his fingers through the onyx ink as it retreated inside me. The awe with which he viewed my power made my low belly heat.

When it had all vanished, he sat back on the bale of hay. The way he studied me made me want to squirm, but I held still as I waited for him to speak. His mind was whirling far too quickly for me to chase his thoughts. "Have you only ever attempted to create someone else's body? Never their clothing?"

I shook my head. "Only them. When I would sneak out of Vagach's house, I'd steal his clothes and make a new form to fit."

A muscle feathered in Rokath's jaw at the mention of my deceased abusive husband.

Did I love his violence because he would have protected me from that situation had he known?

Rokath's fierce claim, his savage protection, his brutal love... the way I savored all of it should have made me feel ashamed. Yet he'd only *encouraged* that side of me every time it emerged. Trauma had brought out jagged shards of ebony in both of us, and as we revealed them to one another, they only served to twist our bond tighter.

Rokath ripped my focus back to him with a new command. "Try it now."

"To become someone else with their clothes on?" I questioned, tucking a wayward strand of hair behind my pointed ear.

"Aye," he replied, shifting his weight on the bale.

Nodding, I dove into my well again, picturing Kiira the last time I had seen her. The silky straightness to her dark locks. The litheness of her frame. The long sleeved wrap dress and the delicate diamond chain that wrapped around her neck and dipped between her breasts.

Ink twisted around me, like Rokath had suggested I do to decrease the time it took to create a new form, as I continued to call details to the front of my mind. A moment passed, then another, as I sharpened the image.

Then, I relaxed my fingers, magic slipping away with the breeze. Heart hammering against my ribs, my focus trailed down. Though I still wore my leather pants, the illusion of a long sleeved silk top glittered with diamonds.

I lifted my gaze, meeting Rokath's. He assessed me with those battlefield commander eyes, unfazed by who I chose to impersonate.

"Trying to look like Kiira at the ball?" he clarified, referring to the split second I'd gotten to enjoy myself in Gyor Palace before he dragged us both from the room.

"Yes," I stated. He rose, then circled me like a predator.

"So it's possible to conjure clothing, but you need practice doing it," he murmured, almost to himself.

"Thank you for stating the obvious," I replied anyway, rolling my eyes.

He halted in front of me. Releasing the form, I tipped my head up to look at him. Something hungry danced in his eyes. "Watch that smart mouth if you don't want it punished later," he warned, his tone gravelly and filled with wanton promise.

"What else would you like me to attempt, *master?*" I quipped, letting the last word roll off my tongue with a healthy dose of snark.

In one smooth motion, he had his hand wrapped around my throat. Stroking the underside of my jaw, he elicited a shiver. "You truly are testing me today, Assyria," he rumbled, but there was no animosity in his words. The bond flooded with lust.

He dragged in a serrated breath, and then forced a step back. My body ached for his touch, bowing toward his. Yet the retreat was necessary for the continuation of this lesson.

The irony that he was the one with more self control today was not lost on me.

"Channel your desire into making a new form," he murmured, settling on the hay again.

Haze lingering despite my best effort to clear it, I did as he requested and attempted to recreate Kiira's outfit from the night of the ball. Instead of including a change in my body, I focused solely on her clothing. Shadows disappeared, revealing the full dress, though it still sparkled with gems.

"Hold on, I can do better," I said, closing my eyes and diving into my magic again. The next attempt resulted in a marginal improvement, the fabric all silk. The one after left me with a cluster of gems around my neck. I shifted, rolling my shoulders at the unnerving feeling. A sense of nakedness clung to me despite being cloaked in leather and magic.

Rokath didn't seem to notice my discomfort, his mind working. "So we know now that you can both change your physical appearance and clothing. What about another's magic? You said before you couldn't. But have you ever tried?"

"Yes, though it was a long time ago," I admitted, surrendering my hold. My shoulders dropped away from my ears, and I shook out my arms.

"Tell me about it," he instructed. With a sigh, I settled beside him on the hay.

"When my power manifested, my mother forbade me from using it in front of anyone, insisting I'd be snatched away from my family and used as some sort of political pawn." I snorted a laugh because despite my mother's best efforts, that was basically what had happened since leaving Stryi. "But I wanted to know exactly what I could do. Priestess Anara wasn't exactly forthcoming with her magic lessons for females, so I did some experimenting on my own. Which when I hadn't even come of age yet, obviously didn't go well."

Rokath rubbed his palms together as he listened, mulling over my words as I revealed more of myself to him.

"I attempted to mimic my father's magic. There was an especially large rock that was proving difficult to plant around, and I thought with my burgundy eyes, if I could use his power, I could blast it apart and then it wouldn't be in the way anymore."

"What color were his eyes?" Rokath asked.

"Scarlet. Nothing too strong," I told him.

"So you weren't able to do anything to the rock?" he clarified.

I shook my head. "No, I barely succeeded in wobbling it with my primary magic too."

Rokath glanced over my head at the stands where males lounged and watched the others fighting below them. "Each secondary power feels different from each other. For me, I have to Call the dead using that shockwave of shadow. I'm assuming for you, you have to use a lot more mental acuity."

He rose slowly. "Wait here."

Disappearing around the corner, he left me sitting on the

bale of hay for several minutes. When he reappeared, he had two males in tow, with Rapp trailing behind them. "Tell her how you call on your secondary power," he said to the two.

Rapp took a seat beside me. "I'm very intrigued by this possibility. Two Callers? Two Binders? Two Rifters? Doubling our most powerful would make a huge difference."

Hope bloomed in my chest. Perhaps *this* was what I was meant to do all along. If I could manage to Call alongside Rokath, the whole army—Fates, all of Keleti—would tremble beneath my might.

A ruby-eyed male stepped forward, drawing me out of my excitement. He cleared his throat, glancing between Rokath and me. "I am a Corrupter. For me to utilize my power, I have to focus on how I want something to decay. For instance, this stone," he pointed to the walls of the fortress, "is a more difficult target because it is difficult to embody the properties of a stone since it doesn't live like we do, if that makes sense. Whereas with plants, it's far easier. I'll show you."

From the stack sequestered off to the side, he grabbed another bale of hay. Hovering his hand above it, darkness dripped down. "Right now I am thinking about what the hay used to be like before it was cut, how even now it is still a strong shade of yellow. But I want it to blacken. So I switch my vision to that instead."

Sure enough, the top bits started turning brown and curling in on themselves, eventually fading to a sickly hue. Then, he pulled his hand back.

Rokath motioned me forward, and I approached the three males. "First, try to pull his form to you. Then, see if you can imitate his magic."

Nodding, I turned my attention to the ruby-eyed male. He had a medium build, with the typical cropped hair of the soldiers. My scrutiny went to the finer details of his face, and, to his credit, he assisted me. Tilting his head this way and that, he allowed me to take full stock of him. Then, he spun a slow circle. Satisfied that I had a clear enough image of him, I called on my magic. Onyx rose and fell in time with my breath, and then he stared at his reflection.

The clothing, at least, came out intact. I grinned at the male I was impersonating. His eyes widened, along with the others', as they beheld my power up close.

I ignored their wonder and focused on my task. I *had* to master this, to show them how useful I could be.

Positioning my hand over the hay, I painted a picture of onyx dropping like rain onto it and blackening each straw. I *willed* the stalks to shrivel, to grow sickly instead of green.

Everyone's gazes bored into me, pricking my skin with their attention. Their expectation. Sweat rolled down my temple as I focused, yet no matter how much of my power I poured into it, nothing happened.

Frustration rose, and I gritted my teeth, giving it one last shove.

Still, the yellow did not die. With an aggravated sigh, I released it all, returning to my body. "I don't think it's possible." My throat thickened, and I studied my mother's ring rather than meet my mate's gaze.

"Let's try a different power," Rokath suggested. "That's why I retrieved two different ones. We have to be sure."

The second had kind garnet eyes and was soft spoken. He quickly explained his Chaos powers and how he bypassed the conscious mind of his opponents to cause confusion. Once again, I pulled a new form around me. At least that facet of my magic received a thorough exercise, even if I was failing at others.

Others that were the difference between life and death.

Swallowing, I focused on what the male had said about his

power. Our eyes locked, I attempted to force his capabilities back onto him.

After several minutes of yanking on the threads of darkness, he shook his head. "There is nothing."

I dropped my hold immediately, spine now slick with sweat. My magic was nothing more than smoky wisps, nearly extended to its maximum. My well hadn't been this empty since the early days of the conscription.

Yet disappointment washed over me at my abject failure. What if I couldn't mimic their magic? Or anyone else's?

Rokath grunted and then dismissed the two.

Tears burned my eyes and I swiped the backs of my wrists at them before anyone could see. My mate rested a hand on my shoulder, circling me around to face him.

"At least we tried and now we know," he told me, his tone even and almost reassuring.

"Are you sure?" I asked, my voice fractured. "Maybe it's only certain types of magic I can imitate. We can keep trying until we find it."

Rokath shook his head and steered me to sit beside Rapp on the bale of hay. "Every power has limits. This is yours. And no one will respect you less because you can't imitate their magic."

His words were a balm to my anxiety. The love sweeping down our bond soothed the ache further.

Rapp elbowed me in the side, drawing my attention. "We win some battles, we lose others. What's most important is that in the end, we win the war. Your magic is powerful enough to help with that, and we'll figure out how to use it best."

"Thanks," I sighed, wiping sweat from my forehead with the back of my hand.

Rokath crossed his arms across his broad chest and settled into a deeper stance. "We'll keep training, every day, to ensure you can fight, both with your magic and weapons. I have other ideas to try that might assist you. But with the gong about to sound, we don't have time for that today."

"How do you know–" I started, but my words were smashed by the ringing he foretold.

Rapp laughed, clutching his side to support his ribs. "Just like old times."

Rokath rolled his eyes and hoisted his friend to his feet. "After decades, you get used to it," he told me. Then, together, the three of us streamed behind the other males leaving the training arena for the cool walls of the military academy's fortress.

21

ASSYRIA

A string of curses fled my lips as I yanked on the knob to yet another supply closet. "Why are there so many fucking doors in this place?" I mumbled to myself as I slammed it shut. With a huff, I continued down the fourth-floor hall in search of the stairwell.

Really should have accepted that tour from Rokath.

My mate was currently occupied, preparing for Xannirin and Kiira's arrival. I'd wanted to see where the females would be housed and ensure it was clean because I'd been around these males long enough to know what was passable for them. And that they'd not spent nearly enough time around females to be attuned to our needs in the slightest.

Rokath's directions to their barracks—down two landings of the spiral staircase from his office, first left down the long hall, out onto the inner curtain, second door on the right, down another spiral staircase, and then I'd be there.

Supposedly.

I was still looking for the long fucking hall.

Cursing my mate under my breath, I threw open *another* door, expecting to find a broom staring me in the face. To my surprise, a vast stretch of space awaited me. "Finally," I muttered, striding through. Voices drifted down the stone walls, which was another good sign.

The heavy oak swung shut behind me with a loud thump. A moment later, the gong reverberated through the keep. I kept walking, determined to reach the first left before males swarmed from one place to the next.

Yet as I continued on, no hurried footsteps echoed around me. No baritone laughter greeted me.

Am I in the wrong hall?

The first split came upon me, and I quickened my pace, heading to the left. I glanced down the right hand path as I turned, only to slam to a halt.

"Please, make it stop," a male whimpered, curled in on himself with his hands over his ears. His clothes hung limp over his frame, and his pale skin was soaked in sweat. Back pressed against the wall, eyes squeezed shut, body trembling, he was clearly not okay.

I eased one foot in front of the other as I approached, not wanting to startle him. As I got closer, I lowered myself to the ground so I wasn't towering over him. "Hello," I said, keeping my tone level and even.

With a start, he ripped his eyes open, revealing a crimson shade. My heart twisted. He'd been on the front lines, and Fates knew for how long.

"Can you make it stop?" he asked, his voice so broken that tears blurred my vision. His hands still pressed to the sides of his head.

"The gong?" I clarified, blinking rapidly to banish the salt.

He nodded.

The final peal rang out a moment later, leaving a descending vibration in its wake. I waited for it to pass before speaking again. "See? No more. You're safe to uncover your ears now."

Slowly, he lowered his hands, eyes darting everywhere. "Where are they?"

"Where are who?" I asked softly.

"The Angels," he whispered as if they could hear us. His chin wobbled like he was trying desperately to hold himself together.

I swallowed the emotion welling in my throat. "They're far, far away. They can't reach us here. That's why you returned with us, isn't it? For some rest?"

"Yes." The word, so quiet and yet so shattered, slashed my heart.

"And where are you supposed to be while you're resting?" I tested because I had no clue where I was and if I tried to return him to the healing wing I'd most likely get us lost.

He lifted a hand and pointed toward a door a dozen paces away. "Th–there. We're all supposed to be there. I–I got...lost on my return from the privy."

"Why don't I accompany you so you don't get lost again?" My tone was light and gentle, and I pressed my palms to the ground and rose to my feet.

The male shoved himself upright, still leaning into the wall. "Yes, please, Szélhámos."

At least he knows who I am.

He lingered for a moment with his back against the stone, attention flicking from me to the door to the hall behind me.

"You remember who my mate is?" I questioned, gauging his every reaction.

"Aye," he said, though his tone contained a hint of wariness.

"If anyone attacks us here, the Halálhívó will come for me immediately. He can protect you like he protects me," I told him, hoping that would ease some of his anxiety.

The male nodded and dragged in a deep breath. Then, like it physically pained him, he took a step forward. Another followed. I waited a few beats before trailing him, ensuring I was in his periphery at all times. The last thing I wanted to do was to scare him again.

We approached the door he had indicated. My shoulders relaxed once he gripped the handle and opened it. Inside, a handful of others waited, all in wood chairs arranged in a neat circle. At one end was a male I didn't recognize, his hair longer than was allowed in the army, wearing wool pants and a crisp tunic.

"Ah, there you are, Mak. I was about to send someone–" he cut himself off when I appeared behind the crimson-eyed male. "Szélhámos."

Heat crept to my cheeks as all the males turned to look at me. "I'm sorry, I didn't mean to interrupt this..." I trailed off, unsure what to call the gathering.

"We're talking about...about what happened to us," Mak told me quietly. I looked up at him, noting then just how *young* he was. Barely of age at most, with the build of a male who hadn't quite come into his form. Yet that innocence that so often accompanied coming of age had been stripped away entirely.

My attention drifted to the others, vision blurred from unshed tears. "I'll be on my way so you can continue."

The leader rose, gesturing for Mak to return to his chair. The soldier did as he was ordered. But instead of dismissing me, the well-dressed male went behind him and fetched another chair. "Why don't you join us?"

All I could do was blink at him as he scooted the seats around to place the now-empty one beside his. I took a hesitant step forward, scanning the group. These males weren't used to females, let alone veilless ones. Or ones that were mated to their exalted leader. Every instinct told me to decline. Yet when I'd spoken of my trauma with Kiira, I'd felt infinitely lighter afterward. And with the weight of everything I'd experienced in the past few months, I certainly could use an unburdening. "Only if I won't be an intrusion."

"On the contrary. I believe the presence of someone so revered would help these soldiers feel heard," the cherry-eyed male said. A few of the others nodded their assent, though some regarded me with a hint of reservation.

My feet moved before I registered what they were doing. I planted myself in the chair, meeting the gaze of each soldier before me. "Thank you for allowing me to sit with you."

"Why don't we each introduce ourselves to the Szélhámos. I'll go first. I'm Exen, brain healer for Fured." He dipped his head in the direction of the male beside him.

"I am Thal, Szélhámos. You are welcome in this group, as all are." This one looked more weathered, like he'd been in the army years instead of months like many of the other males.

"Pleased to meet you, Thal," I replied. Each soldier gave his name in turn, and I thanked them all for their service and letting me join them.

Exen resumed the discussion once all had finished. "Mak, what delayed your return?"

All attention fell on the crimson-eyed male. Yet it wasn't the heavy, judgmental type I'd been on the receiving end for far too long. Instead, each regarded him with openness and empathy.

Mak swallowed hard. "When the gong rang..." The male beside him gave his shoulder an encouraging squeeze. Mak exhaled, then continued. "It reminded me of an illusion an Angel forced on me. Bells pealing everywhere, like we'd won a great victory. When I realized I'd been tricked and shook myself out of it, my best friend was in front of me, a spear through his middle. He—he gave his life for me. Because I wasn't paying attention to my mind, keeping myself grounded in reality to prevent those insects from using such magic on me."

Many of the males shifted in their seats or looked down at the floor. My heart ached for Mak, for all of these soldiers. I'd blamed myself for the deaths of everyone I loved too.

A few more added stories of how they'd lost friends or brothers to the Angels. As the hour passed, I learned that most were here because of how they'd died. One tragic story after another squeezed my ribs.

The males comforted each other with small touches, words of encouragement, and shared feelings. Exen expertly handled each passing moment, drawing out words when a soldier struggled to voice his dark memories. Shadows slipped around them while they recounted it, and I watched in rapt fascination as some of their emotion abated.

After the session, I had to ask him how it worked.

Eventually, he turned his attention to me. "Szélhámos, you have been part of this army for months now. Is there anything you'd like to share?"

The faces of everyone I'd lost flashed through my mind. My mother, my father, my sister...but they'd all been during the plague. The common theme among the males had been friends. And two losses in particular still weighed heavily on me.

"My best friend died trying to protect me too," I whispered, allowing two tears to fall for Olrus. Another fell for Izgath. Despite how far we were from Uzhhorod, the scent of scorched flesh filled my nostrils. He'd remained honorable even as they burned him alive on a pyre for refusing to share my true identity. Yet I couldn't speak about him, not without revealing secrets Rokath and I would rather not share. I'd atoned for that with my rescue of Zurronar, and was far more at peace with it than I was with Olrus.

Mak met my gaze. "How do you live with it?"

A watery laugh escaped me at the memory of those final moments with our gardener. "Before I left, he told me that I needed to make my life worth living. To forget about him and focus on myself. To have adventures. I don't think either of us could have imagined where my path would take me."

I swiped the wetness from my cheeks with the back of my hand as the memory of Kiira's note slammed into me and stole my breath. "It wasn't until we were deep in the desert that I heard of his passing. It shattered me."

I paused, dragging in a serrated breath while my tattered heart beat against my ribs. The males waited for me to gather myself. Not a hint of condemnation spilled from them at my outward display of emotion. None looked at me like I was lesser than for my tears.

For the first time since I'd stepped into the darkness of leading them alongside Rokath, I felt...respected in my vulnerability.

"I still think of him often, usually late in the night. But I sleep knowing that I am fulfilling his wish for me. That he'd want me to make something of myself. Because then his sacrifice was worth it."

"That's why we have to win this war," another murmured.

I turned my attention to him. "Exactly. And we will win." My voice grew stronger, steadier. I straightened my spine. "You are all so brave, battling for your realm. Protecting those you love. Sacrifices are an unfortunate part of this war. I am so grateful for you, as our dead friends were grateful for us. Together, we will honor their memory."

Several added their assent. Exen caught my eye, giving me a slight dip of his chin. The approval swelled in my chest, healing another piece of me. In fact, the entire hour had helped me see my trauma in a new light. The males too looked at me, not as the mate of the Halálhívó, not as the Szélhámos, but as an equal to them.

And that was the greatest gift of all.

"Thank you for allowing me into your session," I said, voice thick with emotion.

Exen picked up a small clock from the floor beside him. "We're only a minute from the next gong. If you need to prepare, now is the time."

A handful of males, including Mak, rose and went to a far corner of the room, where thick cushions lined the walls. From a small table, many grabbed balls of cotton and shoved them into their ears.

The rest grabbed chairs and arranged them in neat stacks, out of the way. Then, they approached their brothers and sat with them all through the tolling. Jaws clenched. Fingers curled. Nostrils flared.

Exen stood beside me, watching the group until the last sound faded. Then, with trained efficiency, they gathered their belongings and headed for the door. Most stopped to salute me, warming me from the inside out.

"How are you feeling, Szélhámos?" Exen asked as the last few made their way to the hall beyond.

"Awed. Heartbroken. So many things." I let out a small, breathy laugh. "Do you do this often?"

"Several times a day. It is heavy work, and some days are more draining than others. But giving these soldiers the relief they need makes it all worth it," he replied.

A knock on the oak drew my attention. On the threshold, Rokath stood, his gaze sweeping over me. "Exen," he greeted the male as he approached.

"Halálhívó." Exen swept into a deep bow—because to him, Rokath wasn't his leader, but a member of the nobility.

I shook my head to clear it. Too often I forgot that if the Kral died, Rokath would inherit the throne.

"Did you get lost, little imposter?" Rokath spoke in my mind.

"Actually, I didn't. I was right where I was supposed to be." The words flowed out of me with ease. Because I believed them wholeheartedly. I needed to see this. I needed to see what else I was fighting for other than equality for females in the realm.

And these males needed to see me too.

I had no doubt they'd go and spread the word to their units of my compassion and kindness. That I had strength too, even if it wasn't in the physical sense that they so often defaulted to.

"Coming for a session of your own?" Exen asked my mate.

The corner of Rokath's mouth twitched up. "Merely to discover where the Szélhámos had gone when I didn't find her in the female barracks."

Exen glanced at me. "Please know that you are welcome to join us at any time. Both of you."

"Thank you, Exen," I said sincerely, meeting his gaze. "I'd love to learn more about your magic in the future. For now, though, I do need to see to the accommodations."

"I am available to you anytime," he replied.

I dipped my head, not because he ranked higher than me, but out of respect. Rokath offered him some parting words before I followed him into the hall. Unlike the last time I'd wandered down it, it bustled with males coming and going.

"I thought you had to prepare for Xannirin and Kiira's arrival?" I asked down our bond. A flash of something—metal striking metal—entered his mind a moment before he shoved it away and responded.

"I finished early and came to find you. Imagine my surprise that you were on the completely wrong side of the keep." His voice was smug even in his head.

"If you say I told you so..."

A laugh rumbled down our connection. *"You're already thinking it, and that's enough."*

Rokath led me through a complex maze to the empty barracks. Massive arched doors awaited us, and with a tug on the massive rings, Rokath threw them open. Instead of a musty, disused smell, citrus and vinegar greeted me. I stepped inside, noting an expansive sitting area toward the front, the cushions crisp and pillows fluffed. Beyond a barrier wall, rows and rows of bunks waited, sheets already tucked tight against the mattresses.

My feet carried me forward and past Rokath as I noted the bright shine on the windows near the ceiling, the polish on the tiles in the attached bathing chamber. The pristine mirrors hanging over a row of basins.

Mouth open, I spun on my heel and faced my mate. "Did you do this?"

"Personally? No. This is a job for the new recruits," he stated. Both those riotous burgundy eyes sparkled with amusement.

A small smile tugged up the corners of my mouth. "Thank you."

A sound like rolling thunder emanated from his chest as he stepped toward me. Brushing his knuckles across my cheek, he held me captive with his gaze. "I do have another gift for you."

I arched an eyebrow. "Do you now?"

His other hand emerged, holding a cloth-wrapped package. "When did you–"

"I left it here when I didn't find you since I knew we'd return," he interrupted me.

I accepted the object from him, tugging on the corners of the fabric to unveil it. His hand pressed over mine, stilling them. I lifted my gaze to meet his.

"Before you open it, I want you to know something." His

expression was deadly serious, and his gravelly tone sent a shiver down my spine.

"What's that?" I asked, head cocking to the side.

"This is not a means to control you."

Curiosity curled through me. I lifted a brow, and he retreated, leaving me to finish opening his gift.

The cloth fell away, and a sharp breath escaped me, echoing off the tile like a solemn vow. Because this wasn't a mere gift— it was a symbol.

The ebony helmet shone as light kissed its surface. Unlike Rokath's, raised whorls decorated the otherwise smooth metal. Burgundy roses ringed thick spikes swept off the top and back. The shape curved over my face, dipping to a severe point at the bottom. A slit across the middle left room for my eyes, broken by another that dropped toward my mouth.

It was fierce. Deadly. *Beautiful.*

"I had this made for you, not to force you to cover your face again, but to show the world who you truly are. Imposter." Rokath drew my attention to him as he stepped forward, his form foggy.

A sob lodged in my throat. He'd made this for me. Thought about each detail, and for how long? How long had he kept it hidden in the recesses of his mind so I wouldn't know?

He'd commissioned this, for me, so I could be his *true* equal. In every way.

Carefully, I turned it and placed it over my head. It settled with surprising ease. Through the narrow eye-slit, I met my mate's gaze—and the reverence made my breath hitch. "Thank you." I had no other words to offer him, but the surge of emotion down our bond gave voice to everything I could not.

Rokath's fingers dipped beneath the sharp point of the helmet and tipped my chin up. "Your devotion has healed me, as mine has healed you. But our love? It does not merely heal. It hunts. When you wear this beside me on the battlefield, the world will tremble at our feet. The Fates themselves cannot defy our will."

The conviction of his words solidified in my bones. Imbued me with further strength. "We'll make the Angels kneel for us. Worship the ground upon which we stand."

A wicked smile curved my mate's lips. "That's my devious little imposter."

He eased the helmet over my head and held it out for me to take. I tucked it under my arm, careful not to let it slip. Together, we emerged from the barracks and into the sunlight. I let it wash over my face and gleam off my beautiful new helmet.

Rokath secured the doors behind him. He really had taken care of everything. We'd had a rocky start upon reuniting with the army. Tension, conflict, strife. His fears of losing me again shoving in the way of our progress. But now? His commitment to this path—to showing the world I was his equal—brought fresh tears to my eyes.

He swiped them away with his thumbs as he looked down at me like I was his reason for breathing. "Now, let's go train. I need to ensure you're capable of killing even me by the time we return to the front."

"Who says I cannot already?" I teased.

He snorted and shook his head. "The first time I gave you a dagger. I even pressed it into my chest for you. You still failed."

I rolled my eyes. "That was months ago. I'm much better now."

He leaned down, his hot breath ghosting across my ear. "Then show me."

With that challenge, he retreated, his gaze never leaving me. Heat flooded my veins, and I raced after him. His long strides ate the distance to the training area, leaving me jogging to keep up. When we reached it, males were already fighting, sweaty, and cursing one another.

Dirt kicked up beneath my boots as I donned my helmet again, the glint of it drawing the attention of soldiers on the periphery. As I passed them, they regarded me warily.

I merely grinned beneath my mask.

Let them think that I was still lesser than them because of what was between my legs. I'd prove soon enough that I was worthy of my place here, leading them.

22

R☠KATH

Ahorn sliced through the quiet, snapping me out of the papers piled on my desk in front of me. My gut twisted, instinct taking over before my mind caught up. I dragged in a deep breath, reminding myself who and where I was before my reaction got away from me. No matter how many years had passed since I graduated from the academy, that sound still brought out a visceral response.

Assyria sat upright from where she'd been reading on one of the couches across the room. Grem huffed in annoyance, shifting his head off her lap. On the floor beside her, Zeec cracked a red eye. "What was that?" she asked, brows dipping together as she looked around.

I eased my chair back, rolling out my neck and shoulders as I stood. "That, little imposter, means that someone of importance is arriving."

The book closed with a thwack, and she set it aside immediately. "Like the Kral?"

Grem slid off the couch, stretching his long legs and then shaking out his fur. Zeec picked his head up and yawned, flashing his deadly teeth, but made no other move to rise.

"Like the Kral and the High Priestess," I replied, rounding my desk to the corner where my sword sat. While at the military academy, I'd opted not to dress in my full metal armor on a daily basis, reserving it for moments of training. The plates would wear out faster, especially with the briny air.

Instead, I donned something between a dress uniform and fighting leathers when I wasn't in the ring. This was no exception, and I was forced to attach my sheath to my hip instead of to my back like I normally preferred.

Assyria jumped to her feet, smoothing out her hair and jerking on the hem of her tunic to straighten it. Then she looked down at her dark leather pants and long-sleeved wool top. "Do I need to change? This is not formal enough to meet with the Kral."

"If Xannirin has a problem with it, he can lodge a complaint with the edge of my sword," I growled, raking my gaze over my mate's body. Her clothes hugged her curves in the best way, highlighting the toned muscle from her years working the fields with her family and the curved waist that made me want to fall to my knees and worship every inch of her. After weeks of battle training, her arms and shoulders carved themselves into lethal weapons too.

It would be a mistake to underestimate her pretty exterior. I'd seen plenty of times the fire that waited to burn underneath.

She popped out a hip and propped a fist there as she locked eyes with me. "Are you ready, though?"

The last time I'd seen my cousins had been at the ball prior to our departure. I'd dragged Kiira into the hall along with my mate to admonish them. Xannirin had told me upon my return that I needed to pull myself together and stop allowing Assyria to affect me so deeply. To say we parted on good terms would have been an overstatement.

At the time, he'd been nearly as unhappy as I had been about my newfound mating bond.

I didn't expect that to have changed either, despite how I'd come to love Assyria. This reunion would not be without high tensions.

I'd fought those fucking white fanatics for centuries. But when it came to opposing my own blood? That was a battle I was unprepared for.

Why the fuck did I care so much what my cousins thought? Normally I barked orders and received little pushback. Yet with the integration of females into the army, I was wading into political territory where I didn't wield absolute autonomy.

"Aye," I grumbled, hating that she could sense my nervousness. I grabbed my horned helmet and settled it over my head. With only the slits in the ebony skull revealing the villain beneath, I felt at ease. Power thrummed in my veins as the mask of the Halálhívó slipped into place. The females needed to see who the fuck I was upon their arrival.

As did Xannirin.

With one last check in the mirror, I whistled at the dogs. Grem trotted to the door, and after a quick shake of his fur, Zeec followed. Assyria grabbed her rose-covered helmet, giving one of the whorls a quick polish with her sleeve, then secured it in place.

Those devious burgundy eyes glinted behind the black metal. "I'm ready."

"Then let's go," I growled, striding for the door. Yanking the handle, I allowed her to pass under my arm and enter the hall first. Noise rose as we descended the stairs, the males eager to glimpse the new arrivals. Near the bottom, we caught up to Rapp, whose pace was still closer to a slug's despite the copious amounts of pium he imbibed daily.

Clapping him on the shoulder, I hurried him along so we wouldn't be late to greet Xannirin and Kiira.

"Think I should have put on a different tunic? The bandage is so apparent in this one," he joked, shrugging my hand off.

I glanced at his attire. Sure enough, his gray shirt hung low down the center, revealing the top of the white dressing covering his still-healing wound. "Why are you still wearing that? I thought the healer said you didn't need to cover it anymore."

"Aye, well that was until I popped a few stitches yesterday and had to be rebandaged," he grumbled. Behind us, Assyria laughed.

"Stop trying to draw a fucking bow," I groused. "You're only delaying how soon you can actually fight again."

"Don't act like you wouldn't be doing the same damn thing," Rapp snapped.

I opened my mouth to retort, but Assyria smacked my back. "Don't even try to deny it."

Rapp snorted. "Have I ever told you how much I love that she gives you so much shit?"

We made the final descent toward the courtyard, and I growled, "Knock it off both of you and set examples for the soldiers."

"He just doesn't want us to have fun at his expense," Assyria said, shooting Rapp a grin.

I halted our procession and turned to my mate. "I can make it all go away. Quite handily, in fact. You'll be running laps around the academy until you can't breathe. Then, your smart mouth will finally remain shut."

She crossed her arms and cocked her head. "You'd rather silence me that way than other ways?"

I nearly choked as Rapp barked a laugh. "Can you leave me out of your foreplay? Also, we're going to be late."

Muttering about Assyria's attitude under my breath, I marched us forward again. The exterior doors brought with them a blast of salty air with more than a little bite. Winter had descended on the Demon Realm, along with the gales off the coast.

"Makes me almost miss the Paks Desert," Rapp commented, attempting to hide his shiver as we exited the open air hall into the courtyard. Soldiers knelt in a massive wave, already in sharp formation.

Olet waited at the gates, his maroon armor gleaming and hands secured behind his lower back. He greeted the three of us with a message. "The scouts spotted the banners of House Vrak a few miles out. The Kral and the High Priestess should be here any time."

"Any notes on their numbers?" I asked.

"Several thousand by the looks of them. Though I can't say they were pleased when they saw they were all female." Olet shifted his weight and let out a long sigh. "We have a long road ahead of us, I'm afraid."

A muscle feathered in my jaw. Those who arrived with us knew of the plans, but we hadn't made a formal announcement to those already in residence.

Today would be that day.

"I appreciate your support, Olet."

He dipped his head. "Of course, Halálhívó."

I took a step back and shouted at the males manning the gates. "Open them!"

Above us, instructions barked between the sentries. With a groan, the siege doors began to move, their massive chains wrapping around each other with loud clinks. Assyria, Rapp, and Olet followed me into their yawn. Behind us, the soldiers rose and marched forward.

It was a maneuver I'd practiced countless times during my

years as a youngling here. Whenever my father or the Kral had arrived, we'd done the exact same thing. I shoved away the memories of those bastards and focused on who approached us now—my cousins.

Assyria and I planted ourselves at the head of the road leading away from the academy, the highest ranking officers flanking us. The soldiers fanned out behind us, standing for inspection. Grem and Zeec loped through the grass, scenting the new arrivals. A sharp whistle brought them back to my side.

Hoofbeats drummed against the dirt, sending a billowing dust storm in their wake. The Kral ascended the final hilltop astride a beastly black stallion, slowing his mount to a stop. The clouds parted then like they'd been waiting for him, his gem-encrusted crown glittering in the sunlight. His long hair was tied atop his head, and his beard was neatly trimmed. A sweeping one-shoulder burgundy cape covered his formal attire, buttons gleaming as if the jacket had just been pulled from his wardrobe and not accompanied him on a weeks-long ride through the Demon Realm.

Beside him was Kiira, a silver circlet ringing her head, glittering with enough diamonds to rival Xannirin. Her black dress whipped in the wind, along with the sheer veil that covered her face. With reins gripped in both hands, an array of glimmering bracelets bounced as she descended the hill at a canter.

Ranking members of the Kral's Guard framed them both, their red armor glinting. I tore my attention away from my cousins as the next wave of travelers crested the hill. Among the supply wagons, hundreds of black-robed females rode on horseback. Still more traversed the path on foot. I had to blink a few times to ensure I wasn't hallucinating.

They are all priestesses?

More and more spilled into view like an overturned inkwell.

I counted them, unable to believe what I was seeing. Assyria's excitement trickled down our bond, drawing my attention away from them.

"There are so many!" she exclaimed, looking up at me through the slits in her helmet. *"I thought only a handful would come."*

"As did I," I replied, some of the tension in my chest easing. If they'd brought so many, perhaps my cousins were more amenable to the idea than I had anticipated.

That brief hope was slashed when Xannirin yanked on his stallion's reins and brought him to a halt mere feet from us. His burgundy eyes were harder than the rocks that constructed the academy's walls. I'd stood here to greet my father more times than I cared to count, and every time, he'd looked at me with the same cold disdain that Xannirin did now.

Kiira's mouth was pressed into a firm, thin line, her irritation apparent even beneath her veil, though her focus wasn't on me, but our cousin.

I studied them both as everyone around me knelt for their Kral. Rapp wobbled on his way down, only for Assyria to snatch him and assist in the final descent. Behind me, the soldiers pressed their foreheads into their arms and released a battle cry.

Only once their voices died did I greet my cousins. "My Kral. High Priestess."

In one smooth motion, Xannirin dismounted. One of his guards caught his reins as he stomped toward me. "Halálhívó." His tone was ice as he swept his regard over me and then over my kneeling mate.

Kiira, with much more grace, approached a moment later. Her brows shot up her forehead when she beheld Rapp. "What happened here? This wasn't in your letter!"

He picked up his head, wincing as the movement tugged on his bandage. "It is a recent development."

"Rise, Hadvezér. There is no need for you to suffer further on my account," the Kral commanded, and Assyria helped Rapp to his feet again. Olet, however, remained kneeling, along with the rest of the soldiers.

He stepped closer to me as Kiira went to Rapp and my mate, exchanging pleasantries. Through clenched teeth, he hissed, "Do you mean to tell me Hadvezér Trol is the only one at the front again?"

"Aye," I growled, weaving threat into my tone. I didn't like the way he was speaking to me as if I didn't know exactly what I was doing. The army was my fucking domain, like Kiira's was the spiritual realm and his was the nobility and general populace.

"What the fuck, Rokath? I thought you had everything under control, but clearly you do not."

How dare he use my real name in the open like this.

"We'll speak later," I snapped, leaving no room for argument. "Now is not the time."

"Yes, we will speak later because I need an explanation for all of this," he snarled before stepping back. Smoothing away the fury in his expression, he greeted Rapp. My mate, however, he ignored entirely.

My fingers twitched toward my sword. That contempt would not go unanswered, but it would have to wait until later.

Thousands of priestesses clung to the hillsides by the time our formal greetings had finished. All stood tall and proud as they faced off with their male counterparts. Kiira and Xannirin came to stand beside me, at least appearing like we were a united front even if my gut told me we were anything but.

I inhaled deeply, preparing to speak. "Welcome to Fured. The time to serve your realm has come. Here, you will train as warriors of both magic and weaponry to assist in the war effort against the Angels who wish to exterminate our kind."

The words drifted on the breeze. I turned to face the still-kneeling males. More than a few peeked from their positions at the females who waited beyond.

Xannirin cleared his throat. "You may rise."

I shot him a glare—not that he could see it through my helmet. Before he could speak again, I addressed my soldiers. "These females have come to join your ranks. You will welcome them. Train them. Assist them. And above all, treat them as your equals. Their magic, combined with yours, will likely be the difference between victory and death. Any grumblings will be dealt with swiftly. Am I understood?"

Some expressions darkened. A handful tilted their heads to comment to their neighbors.

That is unacceptable.

Obsidian spilled from my hands, snaking across the ground to those who dared disrespect the ceremony. Shouts rang out as my magic wrapped around their legs and brought them to their knees.

"Százados, see these males disciplined after we dine," I snarled. Without releasing my magic, I returned my attention to the females.

But before I could continue my instruction, Xannirin stepped forward. "Your place here isn't carved into stone. You must earn it like the Halálhívó and I had to. Like these males," he gestured to the gathered soldiers, "had to."

A growl lodged in my throat. How *dare* he undermine me. He opened his mouth to speak again, but I cut him off. "You all have volunteered to serve the Demon cause, and for that, the Kral, the High Priestess, and myself thank you. As does the Szélhámos."

I swept a hand in my mate's direction. She took a half-step

forward, her shoulders square and head held high. A few of the priestesses at the front grinned at the sight. Others whispered behind their hands to their neighbors, eyes wide.

I couldn't allow them to get away with what I'd moment ago called discipline for. Yet before I could act, Assyria opened her palms, darkness slithering forward and around the waists of many of the rule-breakers. She hadn't caught them all, but she'd done enough.

Her eyes flicked to me. *"We're in this together."*

Love swelled in my chest as I beheld my bold mate.

"In this army, we have rules. They do not bend, and they certainly do not break. Disobedience is punished swiftly and without mercy. Just because you are female does not exempt you from the same disciplinary action I would dole out to a male. I suggest you learn them, and learn them well. Any knowledge of rule breaking makes you automatically complicit in the act itself."

Chins lifted, shoulders squared, and determination etched into their expressions, save for those with Assyria's shadows curling around them, barely distinguishable from their dresses.

The Kral moved in front of my mate, blocking her from view. My nails bit into my palm. Yet another slight. My attention slid to Kiira, who watched our cousin with a placid expression. The tightness in the corners of her eyes told an entirely different story, however.

What is going on between them?

"I'm not certain, but I sense it too," Assyria spoke into my mind. I hadn't realized I'd broadcasted the thought down our bond.

In two lithe strides, the High Priestess was parallel with the Kral. "We've had a long journey, and you deserve a rest. Halál-hívó," she kept her attention on Xannirin but spoke to me, "would you please show us the way to our quarters?"

Clearing my throat, I gestured for Olet to step forward. "This is Parancsok Olet. He will ensure you are all settled and assigned bunks in the barracks. Afterward, he will show you the way to the dining hall."

Xannirin and Kiira returned to Rapp, Assyria, and me as Olet dismissed some of the males and requested others help with the unloading of supplies. Soon, the entrance to the military academy was a flurry of activity.

"I'd like to freshen up before dinner," Xannirin pronounced, staring me down. I held his gaze with equal animosity.

Had this tension lay between us for longer than Assyria and I had been mated? I truly didn't know what to make of this open hostility toward me.

"You know where your rooms are." My voice was all hard gravel. Assyria shifted closer to me. Without thinking, I rested my hand on her lower back, needing to ground myself in something before I lost my temper in front of everyone.

"I'll help with Hadvezér Rapp back into the fortress," Kiira announced, settling herself against his bad side. With tender care, she looped an arm around his waist to support him.

"I really don't need help," he protested, but she silenced him with a look.

Like Assyria, Kiira would set someone on fire if it suited her. She had a depth of strength that had always impressed me. I supposed we all did, after the abuse we suffered at the hands of our fathers.

The Kral's Guard formed around them as they entered the fray, leaving Assyria and I standing at the head of the road. Grem and Zeec rose, trotting among the priestesses as they streamed past us. Many paused, even for a brief moment, to study my mate.

Ebony dripped from her and pooled at her feet like it too knew the moment was essential to our future. Assyria was made for me—made for this—and yet, I couldn't shake the truth gnawing at my gut.

The real battle was only beginning. And this time, I might have to bleed for more than victory.

I might have to bleed for what we believed in.

23

ASSYRIA

Grem nudged my thigh, demanding affection like the greedy hound he was. I obliged, fingers raking through his soft black fur as I surveyed the flurry of activity outside the academy. Priestesses swept by, their whispers about my helmet planting seeds of pride in my chest. Still more spoke of my honorific. I mirrored Rokath's stoicism, but really, I wanted to race forward and hug them all.

Thousands of them.

Hope hitched my breath. They were in Fured because of me. But did they know that? Had the Fates offered Kiira another vision? Did she prepare them for what was to come?

Tears burned the backs of my eyes. This would make an enormous difference—not only for the war, but for Demon society as a whole.

Once we convinced the detractors, that was. Given the expressions on many males' faces, Xannirin's overt disdain, and Rokath's fury, we were only a few steps down this long, winding path.

Rokath stroked his thumb across my lower back. *"What's bothering you?"* I asked down our bond.

"The way Kiira and Xannirin were acting..." he trailed off, his thoughts a violent storm.

"All is not well between them. Or between Xannirin and you," I added, hoping that would anchor him.

"That is an understatement. The question is why and when it began," he grumbled. With a gentle nudge, we began our trek back into the academy.

"Well, they're not fucking like I thought Banand and Araquiel might have been," I teased, attempting to pull him from his dark mood.

His flat expression told me he was unamused by my joke.

I rolled my eyes. *"I only really met with Xannirin once before. Any other time, it was mostly in passing. Though he seemed far colder to me earlier than he did when I was living in the adjacent room. As for Kiira..."*

The High Priestess had greeted me with enthusiasm and kindness. Rapp too. But when it came to Rokath and Xannirin, her behavior had been entirely different. Less with my mate than their cousin, though.

"She seems more guarded with you than before."

He nodded, acknowledging my response. *"If your perceptiveness reveals anything else to you, do let me know."*

"Guess we've found what else I can help you with. Since you have the emotional capacity of a drop of Grem's drool, I can be your people-interpreter," I quipped, grinning up at him.

"Just because you might be more perceptive than me does not mean I am incapable of it," he growled, a warning in his tone I didn't heed. Grem and Zeec disappeared into the crowded courtyard. Most were used to their presence and paid them no mind as they sniffed.

"Sure. Let's go eat dinner before you try to convince yourself you are the prettier one too," I teased, tugging on his hands to lead

him toward the commons. While the gong hadn't yet sounded, it would soon, judging by the angle of the sun.

Rather than allow me to direct our path, he yanked me into an alcove, out of sight. Grabbing his helmet by the horns, he tugged it over his head, revealing a dark expression that made my thighs press together. *"I've seen the way you look at me. Heard the things you think about me."*

He set his skull-shaped helm off to one side before reaching for mine, his eyes blazing with primal intent. I offered him a saccharine smile as he braced his hands on either side of my head. *"You're a male. Your attention is far more overt than mine could ever be. Those lustful thoughts you hear from me? Just an echo of your own."*

Then, I patted the center of his chest with as much condescension as I could muster and slipped out from under his arms. Dipping to the ground, I found the rose-decorated metal and tucked it beneath my arm. He muttered under his breath, then his heavy footsteps followed me down the open air hall. Our hounds rejoined us as we joined the crowd streaming toward the scent of garlic and rosemary.

Three times we had to stop short as males crossed our path, carrying bags, crates, and other supplies toward the eastern barracks. Priestesses accompanied them, keeping their distance. Mistrustful looks were as common as lustful ones.

When the gong sounded, the academy was still a hive of activity. Rokath shouted over the noise. "At ease. The dining hall will remain open and the cooks will feed you. Finish what you are doing."

The soldiers and priestesses carried on.

We entered the commons side by side, striding purposefully toward the high table. Olet, Rapp, and Kiira were already seated and waiting for us. The long ones for the soldiers were barely half-full and yet the females who had settled on the benches whispered about my bare face.

Had they expected me to don a veil when I removed my helmet?

I kept my chin high and let them see what happened when we challenged the males who controlled us and won.

The High Priestess's expression brightened as we approached, and she waved me into a chair beside her. Without a second thought, I slid into it, placing my armor on the ground beneath me. Kiira and I had grown close during the time I'd spent locked in Gyor Palace, and other than the one note she'd sent me about Olrus, I hadn't spoken to her since.

Rokath took a seat beside Olet, and a moment later, Xannirin appeared in the hall. Salutes and curtseys greeted him as he passed by soldiers and priestesses alike. Yet he didn't deign to give them an ounce of attention. No one spoke at our table as he sat.

Even the servers seemed hesitant to approach with the thundercloud hanging over him. Rokath waved them forward, and they eased into their roles, settling glasses of water in front of us, followed by steaming baskets of bread. Our dinner was once again fish, which I'd quickly learned was the norm given our proximity to the sea.

Honestly, I didn't care so long as it wasn't whatever that mushy, tasteless, sticky gruel was they made in the war camp. I felt bad for Trol having to endure it for so long. Whenever we departed, I'd bring him some *real* food—something that would last the trip at least—to express my gratitude for all his sacrifices.

"How was your journey?" I asked Kiira as I bit into a hunk of cheese.

"Uneventful. Though every town we stopped in had something to ask of us," Kiira replied smoothly.

Xannirin stabbed at his plate with more force than necessary. Rokath glanced between them, then looked at me.

"Something is definitely off," I said quickly to my mate.

"Like what?" I asked her.

She spread some chive-filled butter across a roll. "Mostly prayers or aid. Though many had questions about the war." She flicked her attention to Xannirin before nipping at the bread.

The Kral finally lifted his gaze and it speared straight into me. "I wasn't aware peasants were allowed to dine at the high table, Rokath."

Rage flooded our bond—and it wasn't only from my mate. My lips curled back from my teeth. Rokath beat me to speaking, though.

"She is my *mate*." The final word dripped with violent intent. "Therefore she is a member of House Vrak."

Olet and Rapp held their breath as the two faced off. I glanced below, at the tables lined now with both soldiers and priestesses. None of them paid any attention to the war waging between the cousins.

A sneer rose to Xannirin's face. He set his dining ware down and dabbed his mouth with a cloth. "Not until you wed."

Rokath's face turned a shade of red I hadn't seen since our earliest fights. His hands shook as he dug his fingers into the table. "I do not need a ceremony to know she is mine."

Kiira leaned over and whispered in my ear. "The Kral has final say in our marriages. It is the only real power he has over us."

Could Xannirin really force Rokath to marry another despite our bond?

"I have always considered you a member of House Vrak. Do not worry, Assyria. We'll sort this mess out."

Kiira's words were a balm, and I knocked my shoulder against hers in a silent thanks.

Xannirin stole our attention. "She's no officer. She's not of noble blood. She can sit with the rest of them." He jerked his chin in the direction of the priestesses.

Olet kept his head pointedly down. Rapp shifted in his seat like the wood was burning him. Though the movement brought him closer to Kiira and me. Subtly, he reached under the table and rested a hand on her thigh.

Rapp and Kiira were close friends, as both had told me. But that gesture was more than friendly—it was a sign of unspoken support. Would Rapp take Kiira's side in any matter against Xannirin? What if it contrasted against what Rokath wanted? And where did Kiira's loyalties lie?

I'd grown accustomed to the dynamic between Rokath and Rapp, but Rokath and his cousins were an entirely different story.

"She remains here," Rokath stated, more than a hint of challenge in his tone.

Xannirin's regard settled over me again. I refused to bow under it. "Like it or not, My Kral, the Fates chose to bless the Halálhívó and I with a bond. And are the Fates not wise in their weavings?"

The words that had been used on me to force me to comply, to obey, to surrender my autonomy flung back at the male responsible for most of it.

A muscle feathered in his jaw. "It's curious, is it not, how new symbols emerge from war?" He leaned in, his focus still entirely on me. "It's a shame how the attention can be so deadly."

And with that, he shoved back from the table, scattering the servers behind him. In quick, precise strides, he stalked from the room. Rokath leaped to his feet, but Olet grabbed his arm and yanked him back down. "Halálhívó, I believe following the Kral now would be unwise."

A wildfire of fury engulfed our bond as my mate stared at his cousin's backside. Kiira reached for him, and he flinched at her touch on his arm. "Cousin, we have much to discuss. First, let's eat. It's been weeks since I had anything decent."

Rokath softened at her gentle plea. With a long sigh, he turned his attention back to us. "Fine."

I nudged him down our bond, offering my strength to him. Was I furious at Xannirin's outlandish treatment of me? Of course. But right now, the best thing I could do was to support my mate.

After all, these were his cousins. He'd created all of this with them. If I wanted to ensure Demon society changed for the better, I'd need to learn to play along. Xannirin's favorite game was kazat, according to Rokath. I'd lay out my bets, coerce him into a challenge he couldn't refuse. I'd cheat victory to ensure he'd be forced to perform after his loss if I had to.

I glanced at the rows of females below. The utter joy that slipped through their veils warmed my heart and invigorated me.

I hadn't set out from Stryi to become the figurehead of a movement. But now that I had? I'd burn everything down before I'd bend again.

And I would not let any of these females, or the rest scattered and suffering through the realm, down.

24

R●KATH

Xannirin's loaded threat from dinner echoed louder than my footsteps against the stone staircase. Three levels down, I paused, hand scraping against the smooth bricks until I found the nicked one. I dug the heel of my palm into it, and with a groan, a nearby slab rolled to the side, revealing a hidden passageway.

The military academy held two premier residences, one in each of the rear towers. The Kral's was much harder to access, and this was one of two routes that led to his quarters. The primary one was more known, while the one I entered served one purpose: escape in event of attack.

It was the quickest path from my room to Xannirin's, and the fury burning inside me needed a release.

The door slid shut behind me, bathing the passage in darkness. I strode forward with utter confidence, counting my strides until I knew I neared the hidden switch to open the other side. The rough stone gave way to a smooth spot, and again I pressed, emerging from the narrow opening into another spiral staircase.

Through clenched teeth, I forced air into my lungs, trying to rein in the wrath clawing up my throat. The beast inside me begged for a chance to punish Xannirin for his behavior since his arrival. The fear I'd carried over how my cousins would react to these proposed changes morphed into something far more dangerous.

Heat licked up my spine and steeled it for the conversation ahead.

Each step I trudged upward dredged memories from centuries before, when the three of us had begun to take the necessary actions to bring Demon society to heel. To ensure that our vision was successfully executed. To ensure the survival of our race.

Had we made the right decisions along the way? We were certainly nowhere close to the end we'd had in mind when we set out.

At the top of the staircase, a heavy wooden door stood ajar. Low voices drifted beyond as I stared at it, rubbing the sides of my jaw.

"Does the mighty Halálhívó doubt himself?" Assyria entered my mind, her tone light and teasing. Yet I knew she worried for me. With our bond, everything was shared, and hiding my anxiety about this conversation had been difficult.

"Only the ability to restrain myself," I replied, my fingers itching to close around Xannirin's neck.

"Save that for our real enemies. For now, be the force for change you want to be," she said, conviction threading her tone. The ferocity of it bolstered mine.

"I love you, Assyria. I'm not only doing this for you, but also because it is the right thing to do. You've shown me the true path." And with that, I rolled my shoulders back and shoved my way inside.

Much like my own chambers, the Kral's rooms were luxuriously appointed, with an expansive sitting area, thick desk, and views of the surrounding area. Currently, though, they only displayed the thick, dark clouds rolling in off the sea.

Kiira and Xannirin were seated on either side of a round table, both with a drink in hand. In front of the soldiers, none of the officers consumed alcohol since we led by example. But there was always liquor and wine around, especially when the Kral was in residence.

"Rokath," Kiira greeted me warmly. She'd always been the peacekeeper between the three of us, but today she looked like a loaded crossbow. Her veil was gone, and her burgundy eyes hinted at restraint as they glinted in the candlelight. Long, lacquered nails curled around the bulbous end of a wine glass. The dark circles that had claimed the space under her eyes had all but vanished since I'd left Uzhhorod months prior, but the thinness that had worried me remained.

Xannirin, on the other hand, grunted and tossed back the last of what looked like a healthy measure of scale. Kiira sliced a look in his direction as she rose. I kissed her on either cheek before settling into a chair between them.

Another memory pushed to the front of my mind. Yet in that one, I was coated in the blood of the Angels from the Battle of Kraskiv, and Xannirin and Kiira's attitudes were very much opposite.

"Did you force Rapp to see the healer again before you left him?" I asked her, since she'd accompanied him back to his temporary accommodation after our dinner.

"He fought me for a moment, then complained the entire time," Kiira sighed, swirling the purple wine around in the glass. "Complained about how you babied him the entire trip too."

Rain pelted the windows, the rhythmic patter an ominous backdrop to our conversation.

I snorted and pulled the bottle of scale toward me. Xannirin slid me a thick crystal glass without a word. My gaze lingered on him for a moment longer as I poured. "He did have a punctured lung."

"And how exactly did that happen?" Xannirin finally snapped. He offered me ostensible anger now that we had no audience to judge him. I speared him with a hateful glare. For my entire life, Xannirin and I had been like brothers, and yet with the way he looked at me from across the table, I felt like anything but.

And how he'd treated my mate upon arriving? Fuck, even before that?

Unacceptable.

I pressed my drink to my lips and tipped it back. The alcohol burned my throat all the way to my belly. The pain was a welcome distraction from my thinning self-control.

"Do you want me to start at the end or at the beginning?" I wasn't going to refuse them an explanation, not when it might smother whatever was sparking between us.

"Start at the beginning, please. I want to understand how all of this unfolded," Kiira requested, her tone soft. She reached for my hand and gave it a squeeze. "Your letter didn't say much, and I want more detail, especially as it concerns Assyria."

Thunder rumbled, momentarily stealing my attention. Past the window, three black birds swept, their caws slicing the air.

Shaking off the feeling of being watched, I recounted the events of the past few months. The rumors that had swept through the camp at Assyria's presence. How she'd tried to run from me and been bitten by a cobra. How hard I'd fought the bond's insistence to be near her. How I'd cared for her injury, taught her to scout, and begun showing her how to fight. How Rapp and I had split up to pin the Angels on all sides and force them to retreat. How I'd been winning handily, battle after battle, for weeks, until we reached a difficult piece of terrain.

Neither interrupted me as I recounted it all. Yet I slowed to a crawl when I finally came to the point in my story where I had to admit exactly *why* I'd lost all those soldiers. I hadn't put it in my letter, simply that the Angels had beaten us badly, and that was why we needed to change the army rules to allow females to fight too.

The scale seared me again as I drank the last of it. I set the glass down with a heavy thud. Let the words land with the same force. "The Angels took Assyria."

Kiira gasped, hand flying to her chest. Xannirin's mouth flattened, and his fingers tightened over his drink. "How did they know about her?"

"I'll get to that in a minute."

Lightning flashed, illuminating the dark corners of the room. A moment later, thunder crashed. I waited until it ceased before continuing.

"They offered to parlay with us, so long as we met them on the salt flat unarmed. So we went, both armies facing off. I figured they would want my life for hers, which I could have easily gotten out of." Rage rose like a tidal wave inside me as I recalled how they'd hurt Assyria. "As it turned out, the Padisa who ambushed my battalion a decade ago was one of the superior officers leading that section of the Angel army."

"The one whose face you carved up?" Xannirin clarified. He was as well-versed as I was with that particular incident and that particular insect.

I nodded. "Instead of my life for hers, he wanted all my soldier's lives for hers."

More thunder boomed, shaking the room. But not nearly as hard as the muscles in Xannirin's neck.

"What the *fuck*, Rokath?" Xannirin snarled, his lips curling back from his teeth. His pointed canines flashed. "Fifty thousand males? Just like that? After we had to conscript and risk the people turning on us?"

Xannirin surged upright and hurled his glass against the wall, shattering it. The tinkle of the shards hitting the floor filled the space between his angered breaths. He planted his hands on the table, attempting to tower over me and intimidate me like I'd seen him do so many times to the nobles who wouldn't fall in line.

He didn't scare me.

I stood, slowly, showing him that as much as he thought us equals, my power was greater than his. The tension in the room was thick enough to carve with a blade.

"She is my *mate*," I growled, my tone laced with violence. The tips of my fingers dug into the table as I attempted to rein in the fury filling my veins.

"You didn't even want her," he sneered, rings flashing in the light as he fisted his hands.

His words stung like a well-timed slap. He was right and I hated myself for it. How many times had I wished I could turn back the clock and accept what the Fates had so generously given me?

Xannirin wouldn't knock me off the path of this conversation so easily. I volleyed back with equal animosity, if not more, for how he continued to disrespect Assyria. "Well now I do. Now, I fucking *love* her, Xannirin. I couldn't give her up for anything. Nor should I have to. The Fates wove us together for a reason."

I'd scarcely finished speaking when Xannirin tossed his threat onto the table. "If that's how you feel, she'll be returning to Uzhhorod with us, where we can keep her safe since clearly you cannot. And I cannot have you sacrificing more males for your own selfish desires."

My self control *shattered*. "Selfish desires? *My* selfish desires?

Who do you think all of this is fucking for?" I took a menacing step around the table. The strike of my boot against the ground was louder than the storm outside.

Xannirin stood his ground and didn't relent in his contempt. "If your focus is on her, you won't win. You said so yourself before you left. It's because of her that we're losing. *Again.*"

"Watch your mouth," I snarled, attempting to restrain myself from pummeling him into the ground. This discussion was going nowhere good with how he kept pushing me with Assyria.

"What happened to you, Rokath? Clearly sinking your cock into the cunt of your mate has made you weak and thrown you off your game." Xannirin laughed, but it was a dry, jaded sound that scraped at the primal beast inside me.

Red coated my vision as I swung. Xannirin ducked to dodge the blow, but I was prepared for his counter. With my left hand, I uppercut, landing squarely on his jaw. The blow knocked him backward, and the air whooshed from his lungs as he thudded against the ground. I stalked forward and drove my heavy boot into his chest. From my thigh, I unsheathed a dagger and flipped it end over end, not caring which side I caught.

Xannirin coughed, his eyes widening. Lightning cracked again, highlighting his fear in sharp relief.

"Who the *fuck* do you think this Fates damned war is for?" I repeated my earlier question, pressing more of my weight down. Trust in our alliance had clouded my judgment too long. I needed to hear his true answer to confirm what I already suspected.

"The Demon race–" Xanirin started, but I cut him off with the force of my boot.

"Do not give me that horseshit, Xannirin." Shadows unfurled

from my fingertips, swirling around my arms in a violent frenzy. If he wouldn't confess, I would make him. He'd always broken when army tactics had been used on us as younglings.

"I am your *Kral*," Xannirin snarled, eyeing my magic like he too recalled our fathers' abuse from this very room. "You will respect that, Rokath."

"I'm not one of your precious nobles," I spat. "You do not command me. You do not compel me."

"Oh, but I do," he snapped. "And if I say jump, you fucking jump. If I say we're not having females in the fucking army, then we're not having females in the fucking army."

Too late, I noticed the dark tendrils gathered in his hands. With a jerk, he flung them at me, knocking me off balance. In seconds, he was on his feet, dipping into a fighting stance.

"Like you would know anything about winning a battle," I bit out, sliding my foot back and tensing my muscles in anticipation of the fight.

"So what, I'm supposed to return to Uzhhorod lauding your new strategy after you lost *fifty thousand soldiers*? Oh, and that strategy now involves allowing females to volunteer for the cause? The noble houses will riot. They were already on edge before you left, and after this, they'll mutiny. How am I supposed to spin this so I stay on the throne?" With each word, his face turned a deeper shade of red.

"Yes, because that's all you care about, Xannirin. That's all you've *ever* cared about." Darkness expanded as I allowed myself to *feel* everything I'd smothered for so long. "All of this has always been for *you*. Your vision for ruling all of Keleti, inspired by your talks with monarchs from other worlds. Saving the Demon race was always the mask for your true ambitions, and you've sacrificed *nothing* to get it."

A cold, furious expression slid over Xannirin's face.

Obsidian spilled on the floor as his own magic rose to meet mine.

"Stop it, both of you!" Kiira screeched, stepping between us. Without even looking, I flung onyx threads in her direction and pinned her to a plush chair. My entire focus was on my cousin, the Kral, who had sucked everything from me and deigned to tell me that I could not protect my mate.

"I am the Fates-given leader of all the Demons. Not you," he boomed, ropes of pitch sweeping toward my feet. But he was sloppy from years of disuse, and I was fresh off the battlefield. Wielding my magic like whips, I snapped them away.

"Have you really come to believe all the stories we spun? When did our propaganda become your reality?" I demanded, my voice crackling with more energy than the storm outside. We'd crafted these stories to *save* the Demons. Not for his fucking ambition alone.

"There was never a question of its truth," Xannirin snarled, twisting his fingers and enshrouding himself in onyx. "We were simply informing the populace of it. Me, the Fates-given leader. You, the Fates-given hero. Kiira, the Fates-chosen Seer. What else is our magic for if not for me to rule for millennia to come?" His words were smooth as glass, exactly how he talked circles around the nobles to compel their compliance.

Yet they also gave me pause. Because I realized then that the narrative had become part of my story too. But I distinctly remembered its origins, and while his words held a semblance of truth, I was still humble enough to admit I was fallible.

"Before we walked down this path, we decided we were equals. Or have you forgotten in all your years of living in luxury and peace?" I asked, the words bitter. My neck muscles bulged for how hard I forced restraint upon myself. I couldn't—wouldn't—let his mastery of cunning and manipulation distract me from the task at hand: fixing what we broke.

"Yet the people listen to me above all others," he snapped back.

I was getting fucking tired of his delusion. Kiira and I had destroyed ourselves for his ambition, and he couldn't see that. With a growl, I reminded him exactly how much power I wielded. "I control the fucking army. Do not press me, Xannirin. As much as I loathe the idea of ruling, I could kill you and take your throne within a second of making that decision. After all, look how easily I slaughtered our fathers."

His teeth flashed, and he threw more magic at me. But I was fucking ready as years of resentment boiled to the surface. Dodging his attack, I leaped, catching him around the middle and sending us careening to the floor. We landed with a heavy thud, my dagger clattering away. I wasted no time in rearing back and cocking my fist. With an animalistic snarl, I slammed it down. At the last second, he whipped his head to the side, and I collided with the hard stone.

The pain didn't even phase me. I struck again while Kiira screamed at me not to kill him. Xannirin grabbed my arm before I could bloody his lip further and rolled me off him. We squared off, shadows disappearing as we prepared to fight bare-knuckled.

"Assyria has shown me the ways we need to change," I snapped at him. "That's why she is essential. Because we were walking the wrong path."

"Assyria is nothing more than a murderous fallen. She should have been burned for her crimes the moment you discovered them." Xannirin swung, but I caught his fist and twisted his arm around his back, pinning him to my chest. He struggled for a moment before relenting. Otherwise, I would have had no qualms about tearing up his shoulder.

"Rokath, stop!" Kiira screeched, thrashing against my magic restraints. "Assyria is the best thing to happen to you. You deserve her. You deserve happiness. You are not alone in your grievances with Xannirin!"

Her last statement, more than any other, made me pause. The beast thrashing inside me, begging me to make Xannirin pay for claiming to be able to protect my mate better than me, for saying she should have been killed, still fought for me to continue.

Dragging in a breath, I smacked it like an errant soldier into submission. I tore my attention to my female cousin. "What did you say?"

"I resent Xannirin too," she repeated, her lower lip trembling. A tear spilled over and clawed down her cheek. Xannirin attempted to shift in front of me, but I tightened my grip on his arm.

Kiira swiped at her eyes. "When I got your letter, or I should say, intercepted it, I felt relief like I'd never known. I felt like I could breathe again. Xannirin wasn't the one who brought the females here without question. It was me."

The air fled my lungs as I beheld my cousin. At the time, a hint of suspicion had curled in my gut when the only reply I received was a confirmation of their imminent departure. I'd been relieved, believing they both trusted my decision. Yet as the image of it appeared in my mind again, I realized the note was written in Kiira's handwriting.

I snarled in Xannirin's ear. "Is this true?"

Xannirin nodded, ruby spilling from his nose and onto his tunic. "That's why they're all priestesses. She didn't even tell me until the day before she was set to leave."

With their statements, composure slipped within my reach. My racing heart slowed and clarity returned to my thoughts. With a wave of my hand, I released the onyx binding Kiira to the chair.

Immediately, she rose, coming to my side. With gentle care,

she wrapped her hands around my arm and tugged. Surrendering to her request, I eased off Xannirin.

He stepped away and spun, backing into a nearby couch for protection.

My attention never left him. "To win, we need females to fight too. We need them to help in other ways. They *can* help in other ways."

"How will we control the people then?" Xannirin snapped, using the hem of his tunic to clean off the blood on his face. "With the females subservient, we only needed to convince the males."

"I think we've got the populace well in hand," Kiira said, crossing her arms and glaring at him. "The stories we spun have most believing that we're essentially Gods who walk the earth. Those who do not, you can deal with as you always have. Rokath and I have done plenty of work to ensure we are venerated like the Fates themselves."

"Aye," I agreed, cracking my neck to relieve some tension. Xannirin didn't move, and I sensed we were finally getting somewhere. "Not only that, but now we have Assyria too. Her magic is powerful and useful. It is because of her we rescued Banand."

Xannirin sucked in a sharp breath. "He's alive?"

"Yes, and we can use him, just as we can use other females, to turn the tide back in our favor once more. He insisted he remain at the front to help Trol rather than return here to recuperate. There are people who want to fight, Assyria included, because they believe in saving the Demons too. We are going to let them."

The storm raged outside, rain pounding harder against the windows as if to further my point.

"Perhaps we should call it a night and meet again in the morning when we've all had time to think on what's been said tonight," Kiira suggested, her posture softening. "Tempers have run hot, and I know the two of you well enough to know neither of you will yield anything else until you've had time to calm down."

A muscle feathered in my jaw as Xannirin and I glared at one another. She was, unfortunately, right.

"Besides, what we built over centuries will not tumble down in a single night. This will all take time. And we *will* do it," Kiira said, offering Xannirin a look hot enough to burn.

Our cousin pressed his bloody lips together like he was attempting to refrain from disagreeing.

I gave him my back and poured myself another measure of scale. One shot, then another, seared my gut. Kiira joined me, downing the last of her wine.

"Where are you staying?" I asked her when Xannirin made no move to join us.

She shrugged. "I have my own room just below, but I figured I would call for a cot to be brought to Rapp's, just in case he needed tending in the night."

"He's lucky to have a friend like you." I dropped my voice and angled myself so Xannirin couldn't overhear my next words. "As I am blessed by the Weaver to have a cousin like you."

She offered me a soft smile. "And I you. We'll convince him. Together."

Squeezing my hands, she backed away and fetched her veil. After settling it and the circlet over her head, she paused. Then, she took them both off again and tucked them into a pocket in her dress. "Starting tomorrow, no more veils for me. Or any of the priestesses here. Assyria has already made her stance on it, and I will not allow her to receive the stares of everyone for it. The first step for females being seen as equal is to remove the very thing keeping us hidden."

Silence lingered for a moment. Then, Xannirin blew out a long breath. "Whatever you wish, Kiira."

"Exactly," she said, her words harsher than the lightning arcing through the sky. "Now, I will retire for the evening as I know exactly how early that gong rings."

"Good night," Xannirin and I said simultaneously as she swept out of the room.

Then, the two of us were alone. After another shot of the spicy alcohol, I offered him a final threat. "You will treat Assyria as an equal to us, as you treat Rapp. No more attitude or threats like you offered her at dinner. Am I clear?"

"Abundantly," he replied, though I didn't miss the sarcasm in his tone. He shifted from foot to foot, and I waited for what he would say next. "I can't imagine how you felt once you realized the Angels had her. It's not a situation I would ever wish upon anyone, let alone the one person who has been by my side since we were younglings."

His words dulled the edge of my anger toward him, but I didn't trust that they weren't carefully chosen to do just that. "Actions speak louder than words," I reminded him. Then, I grabbed my shirt and left him standing in the middle of a storm of his own making.

25

ASSYRIA

Lightning cracked the sky outside, illuminating the unfamiliar shapes of the furniture in Rokath's room. Hours had passed since he left me here, and now the dogs and I lay in bed, waiting for his return. The intensity of emotion flooding our bond told me the conversation with Xannirin and Kiira wasn't going well. Resisting the urge to reach into his mind was harder with every minute he was away. I wanted to trust that when he returned, he'd lower his walls and tell me everything. Our relationship was growing stronger with each moment of vulnerability we shared.

But the storm swirling inside him was even stronger than the one brewing beyond the stone walls surrounding me.

So I built a strong barrier around my mind, trying to give him the space and privacy he needed to handle his affairs, and watched the dark clouds roll in off the angry sea.

Grem snuffed, wriggling closer to me. His long fur was still slightly damp from the bath I'd given him and Zeec, after which, I'd needed another too. At least the smell of wet dogs had abated. Sighing, I wrapped my arms around him and tugged him closer. Zeec rose, shook himself off, and curled up at my back until I was sandwiched between the two of them.

A violent fissure split the sky, the tower shuddering in its wake.

Then, rain pelted the windows. The rhythmic sound soothed my racing mind, and cocooned in the warmth of the hounds, my eyes drifted lower and lower with each passing blink. I yawned, trying to remain awake. More rumbles rolled overhead, combining with the rain as I drifted, drifted, drifted...

A crack like a whip filled the air, and I jerked awake. A brief flash illuminated a shadow standing in front of me. The air lodged in my throat as I gasped. Thunder boomed, and I sat upright, scanning the dark. All the candles had gone cold, and no light remained in the space. Clutching my chest, my racing heart beat into my hand.

Lightning crackled again, revealing the broken figure of my mate. Braced against the wooden post at the foot of the bed, his head hung low and heavy. Grem and Zeec both grumbled their displeasure as I crawled from between them and toward Rokath. I reached for him just as another flash filled the room.

When he lifted those burgundy eyes to meet mine, his pain slipped a knife between my ribs. "Come here," I said softly, reaching for his arm. My fingers barely grasped his muscled bicep as I tried to tug him closer. He shook his head.

"I can't protect you, Assyria." His breath reeked of alcohol, and my brows pinched. Rokath rarely drank, and for him to smell like Vagach had—even more so really—the day I killed him was alarming.

"What are you talking about? Of course you can. You're the only one who can," I tried to reassure him, but he backed away. Cursing, I slid off the bed, his tunic nearly swimming down to my knees. I fumbled my way to the bedside table and found the matches I'd used earlier to light the candles.

Striking one, I managed to illuminate a nibble of space. I started when I saw the hour. *Three.* How long had I slept? How long had Rokath spoken with his cousins?

My mate sank into a chair and buried his head in his hands. I went to him, bracing my palms on his shoulders. They were hard as rocks beneath my fingers. I massaged them gently, hoping to ease some of whatever was eating at him.

He looked up at me again. "I am a selfish, selfish male. I crave you more than I should."

He captured my waist and brought me closer. I spread my legs and settled onto his lap so we were eye to eye. The candle-light cast his tattoos in haunting relief, especially the empty-eyed skulls on his neck.

Spicy scale assaulted my nostrils as he spoke again. "I'd do far too much to have even one of your unguarded smiles. To bury my nose in your hair and inhale the scent of you. To feel you writhe beneath me. To chase you all so I can claim you over and over again."

"Rokath, what's going on?" I asked him, cupping his face. A muscle feathered in his jaw, and I moved my fingers to his jaw and rubbed circles there. A long groan escaped him as he relaxed into my touch. "Why are you so drunk?"

"I am not—"

"Yes, you are," I snapped, ceasing my massage. "I'm very familiar with the smell."

Fire ignited in his eyes. "I want to rip them apart. Limb by limb. Peel off their skin. Make them *hurt.*"

"The Angels?" I clarified.

"The nobles. The people who harm females. The Angels. All of them," he growled, and the violence threaded in his tone raised the hairs on the back of my neck. "But especially Vagach. Fuck, Assyria, I'm so proud of you for killing that pig. But I need to avenge you. For everything. You're mine to protect. But I can't."

Rokath was rambling, nearly incoherent, and more than a few words came out slurred. "You can–"

"No," he snarled and my teeth clicked shut. "They took you, Assyria. What if something worse had happened to you? What if they'd tried to rape you?"

My gut churned at the memory of Zaph's belt coming undone. I hadn't meant to keep that moment from Rokath as much as I'd blocked it out myself. But I couldn't tell him in this state. Fates only knew what he would do.

Yet, he must have been listening to my thoughts, because fury etched his features a moment later. "Before I sever his head, I'll crown you in his bones. While he is still breathing. So he can see who he dared touch."

My breath hitched and core clenched simultaneously. "Tell me what's going on, Rokath," I whispered. His emotions still swirled like the violent storm outside.

"Xannirin...Kiira..." he paused, shaking his head. I adjusted myself so I braced on his shoulders again. They sagged forward, and he buried his face in the crook of my neck. I held him even closer, squeezing him as hard as I could. He needed my support, yet he was unable to voice the words to request it.

"Xannirin was so angry when I told him everything. He wanted to take you away from me. To take you back to Uzhhorod where you'd be safe. I went insane at the thought. But he was right, you would be better off there."

"No," I said firmly. "My place is by your side."

He picked his head up and rested his forehead against mine. "That's where I want you, always. It terrifies me. Fuck, I've never felt this way before and I still don't know how to cope with it. I want to take care of you. I want to be the male you deserve, especially after the way we shaped society to treat you. I regret so much."

I scratched his beard, massaging his jaw again. "I know. But you're making changes, right?"

He nodded, his eyes briefly closing. "Xannirin fought Kiira and me about it. For so long I thought I was alone in the resentment I held toward him. Turns out Kiira felt the same. Now I don't have to squash it anymore."

"Let's go to bed. I want you to hold me," I murmured. My heart burned for him, for the intensity of emotion roaring inside him. He needed to sleep off the alcohol so he could have a clear head in the morning. In his state, there was really no convincing him that he was doing enough to protect me.

"I can do that," he acquiesced, rising with me in his arms. He carried me to the bed, lowering me with a reverence that left me aching. Then, he yanked his shirt overhead, not bothering to unbutton it, and stepped out of his boots. Lightning cracked again, revealing the chiseled cut of his torso. He shucked off his pants a moment later, baring himself to me.

With a groan, he leaned over me, forcing me to lie flat on my back as he caged me in with his hard body. Against my thigh, his dick thickened. "I need you, Assyria. I need to feel something other than this pain."

I nodded, breath stuttering from the intensity of his gaze. Bracing on one hand, he skimmed my thigh, lifting the hem of his shirt higher and revealing my center. The cool night air ghosting across my skin sent a shiver down my spine.

"Sit up," he commanded, leaning back to give me space. I did, and he tore his shirt over my head. He swept his eyes over me with the hunger of a starved man.

Curving down, he captured my back and brought his mouth to one nipple, licking and sucking it with wild abandon. My thighs dampened as he flooded me with sensation. I dug my nails into his scalp and pressed, silently asking for more. He delivered with expert precision.

Rokath edged fully onto the bed, pinning me beneath him and shooing the dogs simultaneously. A primal rumble vibrated in his chest as he continued to work on my other nipple, drawing it to as sharp a peak as the other. All the while, I melted beneath him, wetness seeping from my core.

"Rokath," I pleaded, arching into him. As drunk as he was, he held a deep need for this connection with me. To heal him. To heal me.

He raked his teeth over my sensitive bud, then released it. His mouth mapped a trail between my breasts and down my torso, so tortuously slow, like he was worshipping every place his lips touched me. When he reached my hip bones, he kissed each of them before moving lower. His breath dusted across my overheated center. "Fuck, your arousal smells divine. So fucking wet for me and I've barely touched you."

Rokath's hot tongue skimmed the skin of my inner thigh. Sharp teeth sank into the surface, drawing out a hint of pain. More wetness dripped from me. Rokath captured it with a flick of his tongue, and I gasped. His fingers swept through the rest of it, smearing it all along my slit. Then, he sucked them into his mouth. "You taste better than victory. But it's not enough."

With that declaration, he latched onto me, lapping my clit while his fingers spread me. The wet sounds were obscene, but I wanted him to hear them. To hear how deeply I desired him. To hear how expertly he unraveled me. He needed that.

When he inserted one inside me, I dug my nails into his scalp. "More," I told him. He wasted no time using a second to stretch me. Shamelessly, I rode his face and hand, chasing my pleasure.

"Use me, Assyria. All I care about is watching you shatter because of me," Rokath spoke into my mind.

"I love you, Rokath," I panted, my movements quickening. He curled his fingers against that one spot deep inside, and I nearly wept for how incredible it felt. "Don't stop."

"Touch yourself, Assyria. Tweak those pretty nipples for me."

He pressed harder, and I did as he commanded. The sharp sting from the pinch had my walls clenching around his fingers, dragging them deeper. A low groan thrummed against my flesh. He circled his tongue over my clit, and that was all my orgasm needed to sweep through me.

Hips bucking, I arched off the bed like a cracking whip. A cry tore from my throat as Rokath continued to lick and fuck me with his fingers, working me into a helpless frenzy.

Air strangled out of me as I came down from the high. Slowly, Rokath removed himself from between my thighs and rose. His fingers were sticky with my cum, and he used the wetness to coat himself. The way he stroked his cock had me salivating for more of him.

"Ride me," he rasped, and the command in his voice had me obeying immediately. My blood heated as he flopped over, his dick long and engorged against his stomach. I settled over him, much like I had in his lap in the chair, and picked it up. When I fisted his length and pumped, his eyes rolled into the back of his head.

A heady sense of power swept through me. I swiped his head through the arousal slicking my core, then lined him with my entrance. "Fates!" His fingers weren't nearly enough to prepare me for his size, especially at this angle.

Inch by torturous inch, I slid down. All the while, Rokath watched with rapturous attention where he disappeared inside me.

"You were made to take my cock, little imposter," he growled, hands finding my hips and digging in. A gasp tore from my throat as he shoved me all the way down. And then I was so, deliciously, full.

"I was woven for you, and you were woven for me," I mewled as I adjusted to his girth.

He dragged me forward, my clit rubbing along his low belly as he pressed against my walls. Bracing my hands on his chest, I found a rhythm, moving my hips in time with his slow thrusts upward.

"I fucking love you, Assyria," Rokath repeated, the depth of his devotion spilling over in our bond.

Like I was parting the thunderous clouds beyond, I removed the barrier I'd built before. My adoration for Rokath rained down on him. "You will always be the villain for me. You will slaughter anyone who dares lay a hand on me. But most importantly, you are my mate, and I trust you to protect me, Rokath. I didn't before, but now? I'd walk among a thousand Angels knowing nothing would happen to me."

His cock thickened inside me. I moved again, my pace quickening. No place was left untouched by his length. "You're going to continue to train me so I am as powerful as you. As the others with burgundy eyes. I will be a force among the army on my own. And it will all be because you love me."

My heart thundered against my ribs as Rokath and I held each other's gazes, just as unbreakable as the bond that the Weaver planned for us. For the first time, we weren't fucking.

We were making love.

I showed him my devotion with each circle of my hips. He gave me his with every word of praise past his lips.

I dug my nails into his muscled chest and bounced harder. Sweat beaded on my forehead and slicked down my spine.

"That's it, little imposter. You're doing so well," Rokath praised, using his grip on my hips to change the angle. He dragged along that spongy spot that had me digging my teeth into my bottom lip. My brows dipped together as I careened toward the edge.

"You are fierce already, but I am going to make you ferocious." He branded me with a deep thrust. "You are strong already, but I am going to make you limitless. Those fucking zealots will bow at your feet, Szélhámos."

My walls clenched around the honorific the soldiers had given me. A wicked grin twisted Rokath's lips. "You will be a Goddess among Demons. Revered for your power. Xannirin, Kiira, me, we are all Fates. I will elevate you to that position too."

Our skin slapped as we both moved faster, worked harder. "Mine," Rokath professed, over and over and over, every time he was buried completely inside me.

"Yours," I panted back, breath coming in ragged. Pleasure coursed through my veins, twisting inside me until I was certain I was close to snapping. This orgasm, like the one he'd given me the first time we coupled, was going to shatter and remake me. Surrender turned to sovereignty. Violence turned to ecstasy. Hatred turned to love.

"Come for me, little imposter. Come for me and scream my name. Up here, no one can hear you. And I fucking need to know how much pleasure I deliver you," he commanded, his tone threaded with violent vulnerability.

Those words shoved me over the edge, and I didn't meter my voice at all. Around and around the room it echoed as I shattered, pleasure igniting each nerve. Rokath's eyes darkened, and his grip tightened to the point of bruising. That only lengthened the time I spent in bliss.

Then, without warning, he lifted me off him, groaning as he spilled his cum onto his stomach. Arms trembling, he settled me on his lap again, both of us breathing heavily. Yet we hadn't broken eye contact, and something divine swept between us because of it.

Rokath crushed me against him a moment later, holding me as tightly as he always held everything together.

On his own.

I didn't care that we were both sticky. I just wanted him, and I wanted him to know that. We remained locked in that embrace long after he finally fell asleep.

26

ASSYRIA

Ebony rippled from Rokath as he glared at the obstinate clothier. The male's weathered face told me he'd seen nearly two thousand winters. And the leather that adorned him? He was an expert at his craft.

It was a shame that he was refusing to stitch armor for the females and had incurred Rokath's ire.

And mine, but after last night, Rokath needed an outlet.

Rokath had nearly slept through the gong that rang way too fucking early this morning. It wasn't until I'd dumped water on him that he had awoken. I'd honestly debated about letting him sleep, given how little he usually did and the haunted state he'd come home in.

But I knew his rules were important, and so was what we had to do today.

"If you do not wish to lose your position and your coin, you will oversee this," Rokath snarled, towering over the clothier. I glanced down the open air hall, ensuring no one attempted a surreptitious pass to overhear the conversation. Everyone *should* be gathering in the training area, but I didn't trust that these males weren't circling like sharks, waiting to attack from their displeasure.

"I've served this army for a millennia. I will not see tradition crumble on your whim," he shot back, undeterred by Rokath's intimidation.

"Do you doubt the Weaver's path?" Rokath rasped, his tone like a blade scraped against stone. "For the High Priestess has seen our future."

Not exactly a lie. Kiira had mentioned on several occasions that whatever she reported to have seen was taken as fact simply because of who she was.

The clothier pointed a gnarled finger in my mate's face. "You do not appreciate the Fates. You never have, even as a youngling here."

I rolled my eyes, grateful that my helmet hid my irritated expression.

Onyx tendrils coiled around the man's arm, snaring it to his side. Only then did his furious expression shift. "Release me!"

"No," Rokath stated, his tone threaded with command. "I am the fucking Halálhívó. I lead here. If I say you will deliver ten thousand sets of armor, then that is what you will do. If you refuse, I will snap your neck and hang your body from the balustrade as a demonstration of what happens to those who disobey a direct order. The choice is yours."

The clothier's eyes bulged, his face turning the same scarlet shade of red as his eyes. "You make it impossible."

I almost sympathized with him, having been on the receiving end of such a command. But his aged thinking would get us nowhere. "Choose now. We have better places to be," I snapped.

His attention flicked to me, mouth thinning. Clearly, he didn't appreciate my input into the matter. Typical.

Rokath's shadows wrapped around the clothier's neck.

"Fine!" he shouted, squirming in his black binds. "I'll do it. You'll hear no complaint from me."

The dark snakes retreated immediately with no regard for how the male landed against the ground. With an *oomph*, he collapsed, shoving himself upright on shaky limbs.

"If I hear so much as a whisper of your dissent, I will not hesitate next time," Rokath promised, leaning over him.

This time, the clothier responded with a healthy measure of fearful respect. "Yes, Halálhívó."

Rokath strode past him while he straightened his shirt. I didn't deign to look at him as I shouldered past, falling in step with my mate. *"How many more times are we going to have to do that?"*

"Too many," Rokath grumbled back.

A long sigh slipped out of me as we rounded the final corner to the training area. Up a short set of stairs, we found the rest of our group waiting. Kiira shot me a grin as we approached. My giddiness mirrored her own. Together, we'd informed the priestesses that morning they were no longer required to wear veils. Even now, their infectious excitement swept through me.

Xannirin, however, barely appeared to be in a better mood than the previous day with how he glowered at both of us.

As I settled among the cousins, tension hung like a fat fog, and I couldn't decide if I wanted to be anywhere less than I wanted to be there right now.

Maybe back on the estate in Stryi, still married to Vagach.

Countless sets of eyes settled on me, taking in my rose-covered black helmet, the wool tunic that covered my torso, the leather pants that protected my legs. Rokath, in his full armor, was an intimidating sight. The females' attention should have been on him, and yet, lips moved, heads jerked, hands hid whispers—all visible with their faces now bare.

I welcomed it, showing them with every breath, every heartbeat, that I was not hidden. Not silenced. Not afraid.

I was powerful.

Rokath raised a hand, and silence fell over the priestesses. They still wore their black dresses, and the acolytes still boasted their white rope belts. Together, they stood on the threshold of a transformation. They weren't soldiers yet, but that would change today. That was what this gathering was for, after all. To begin the integration with their male counterparts.

They all stood a little straighter as the Halálhívó's gaze settled over them.

Soldiers hugged the rear walls and the balconies across from us, watching the events unfold with mixed expressions. Some appeared disinterested. Others, barely veiled disdain—likely the same as those who had been lashed for their disobedience the previous day. Most held a mix of curiosity and apprehension.

Those are the ones we need to seek out to assist us.

"Today, each of you will demonstrate your power and be assigned into units. From there, you will don a new uniform fit for fighting. The clothiers will take your measurements after your magic assessment. New armor will be delivered to you over the coming days."

Rokath paused, surveying the scene.

Pride swelled in my chest. Together, we'd prove that we had a place in the world, that we were *worthy* of leaving our homes and having autonomy. That we didn't need a male to direct our entire lives and that we could contribute through more ways than our womb.

"I suggest that you do not hold back. Wield what you know. There is ample time to learn later. An accurate measure of your power is essential, though." Rokath tilted his head to look at

Xannirin. The Kral merely kept his mouth shut and gaze forward.

At least that's an improvement.

The females nodded their assent. The males clinging to the periphery shifted. Others with boards in hand stepped forward.

"Let the assessment begin," Rokath commanded. The four of us retreated from the balustrade and into the shadows of the pillars.

"I'll stay and help," Kiira pronounced, tucking her long hair behind her ears. Quickly, she swirled the length around her finger, then secured it with a leather strip so it sat just off her neck.

Xannirin muttered something about letters to answer, turning on his heel and stalking away.

"What is his problem?" I asked, staring daggers into his backside. Was he off to scheme? To undermine us? His disdain was apparent in each strike of foot against stone.

Kiira and Rokath glanced at each other. Then, Kiira ignored my question entirely. "Assyria, let me introduce you to some of the volunteers. I think you'll quite like them."

Smothering an annoyed huff, I started to follow her, but Rokath let out a low growl. "Assyria is the Szélhámos. She walks first."

"Oh, right," I replied, shaking off my lingering irritation and stepping into my role. Because of Kiira's status, I'd defaulted to letting her lead. But I was one of them now, and I needed to act like it. Even if Xannirin didn't.

Thankfully, Kiira wasn't offended. "After you, *Szélhámos,*" she giggled, elbowing my ribs. With a small laugh, I passed her, then took the stairs one at a time, steeling myself for what was sure to be an overwhelming event.

Chaos ruled the training arena. Flashes of black dotted the edges of my vision as we clung to the wall in an attempt to maneuver through hundreds of bodies. Booms sounded all around as Destructors demonstrated their magic.

"Where do I go?" I asked Rokath, unable to see over the madness.

"Straight ahead. The male with the high knot. I have to see that the clothiers are behaving, but I will find you later."

"Good luck."

He grunted in response before peeling off from us.

A Százados whom I recognized from the healing session I'd stumbled upon took notes as he observed the females wielding their magic. First, they called upon their shadows, then their secondary power. Hopping around a backstepping soldier who didn't see me, I wove my way to the Százados. He paused when he saw our approach, dropping to one knee and resting his forehead on his arm. When he pointedly cleared his throat, and the females around him did the same.

"You may stand," I told him and the others, and they did. A few craned their necks to see me, and I offered them warm smiles in return. "Please continue, we want to observe."

"Yes, Szélhámos," he replied, then faced the females again. "Who is next?"

A maroon-eyed female stepped forward, dipping into a deep curtsey. "High Priestess, Szélhámos."

"This is Maariya. She has served in numerous posts for decades and was one of the first to volunteer," Kiira told me.

"Is this true?" I asked her.

"Yes, Szélhámos. Since I was young, I wanted to serve my realm. At first, being a priestess was the only way to do that. Now I have more options."

My throat thickened as a glimmer of myself reflected back to me. "Please demonstrate your power," I commanded, though the words were soft in comparison to Rokath's harshness.

She closed her eyes, inhaling deeply. Onyx whirled like a

twister around her, whipping her loose hair into a frenzy. When they settled, she drew a knife from her side and sliced into her thumb. Another female stepped forward, and she marked the second's wrist with a red line before retreating.

More magic materialized as she faced off with the female. The second leaped forward, only to freeze in midair. She blinked but remained suspended while Maariya stared at her, brow furrowed in concentration.

"That is Izzenna. While she is newer to the priestesses, she quickly made her mark. She was our second volunteer," Kiira said by way of introduction.

Maariya continued to hold Izzenna in place. Sweat beaded her forehead. The Százados gave her an order to release her magic. With a whoosh of breath, she did. Izzenna stumbled forward, and Maariya caught her. Both grinned widely as they turned to me.

"I need only a small amount of my blood to touch another to be able to hold them in place," Maariya explained. "I hope to be able to hold more and for longer after training my magic."

"You have an incredible talent. The Giver certainly blessed you," I replied.

Light pink dusted her cheeks, and she stepped to the side to allow Izzenna to demonstrate her magic.

"They already worship you," Kiira said under her breath. "The mythos of you will spread quickly after this."

The idea both excited and terrified me. I didn't have long to examine the emotions before the air shimmered in front of Izzenna. A scream ripped from Maariya's throat, and her hands clamped over her mouth.

"Nightmares," I murmured, awed by Izzenna's careful concentration.

"Vivid ones too," Kiira replied like she knew from experience.

The Százados gave the females fours in both of their categories after Izzenna's demonstration was complete.

The two curtseyed to Kiira and me again before continuing onto the line of priestesses waiting for their measurements. The majority of females, as far as I could see, had eyes of blood, cherry, and ruby, all powerful enough to hold their own with magic, even if our bodies were smaller and less capable of heavy blows than the males.

"They work so well together already," I commented, surveying how they paired up to demonstrate their powers when necessary.

"We may not wield blades—at least up until now—but we've always collaborated to elevate souls and aid suffering," Kiira explained. It made sense. They were a cohesive unit like the army. And the detractors like Priestess Anara, who had ruled the school and temple in Stryi with a firm hand, were the exception. Just like the males who refused to see these females as deserving of a chance to serve their realm too.

Every volunteer Kiira brought forth spoke with enthusiasm in her voice, profusely thanking me for the opportunity to become a warrior. Unveiled grins abounded as they let their power flourish, then stepped aside to let their sisters do the same. The thousands of females streamed through the process with smooth efficiency until only a few groups remained in the wings, awaiting their turns.

"Kiira, how did you manage all of this?" I asked her. With the short time between Rokath's raven and the returning message, I was in awe of the number who had volunteered.

She raked her teeth over her bottom lip, gaze trained forward. "For a long time, I'd been unhappy with my position. But I shoved it all aside for the greater good. So much time had passed, in fact, that I hardly remembered I felt that way at all.

Until you." Then, she faced me, determination shining in her eyes. "You reminded me of life before."

My eyebrows shot up my forehead. "Really?"

"Really," she repeated. "I started working on plans of my own shortly after you left."

I sensed there was information she was holding back, but I didn't press her for more. The training area, crowded with priestesses and soldiers alike, was not the place to discuss such political matters. Not when the cousins had always been so secretive about their plans.

I glanced up at the clock hammered into a nearby tower, noting that our midday meal—and prayer—was almost upon us.

Rokath returned moments before the gong struck. "High Priestess, if you would please join me in leading the traditional army ritual today."

"Actually, I think I should lead," I said, lifting my chin. "I am the Szélhámos."

Pride bloomed down our bond. "Aye, that you are."

"Of course, the Szélhámos should lead," Kiira grinned. "I am happy to stand with two mighty warriors as you conduct prayers."

The three of us faced outward again, and around us, the soldiers—of both sexes—fell silent, waiting for their next direction. Rolling my shoulders back, I strode out to the middle of the training arena. Rokath and Kiira framed me, and all the priestess-turned-warriors fell to their knees, accustomed to the time of day. The males who had retreated to the fringes and the grandstand did the same.

Rokath yanked a blade from his side, the bronze glinting in the sunlight, and handed it to me.

I dragged in a deep breath. I'd done this before, and I could do this again. Raising the dagger and my hand, I yelled,

"Weaver, who spins the threads of our fates, lay down the path for us to tread, unyielding and unbroken. We walk at your command, our feet bound by the threads you have woven. Guide us to glory as we march beneath the banner of war. For the Kral, for the Halálhívó, these new soldiers will bleed. Bind our fates to theirs, so that we may rise victorious."

Blood welled on my palm as I sliced deep, offering a healthy sacrifice to the Fates. Rokath held out his hand, and I offered him the blade to do the same.

His cut was no shallower than my own. Yet he utterly shocked me when he spoke, squeezing his fist and letting garnet cascade between his fingers. "Not only for myself and the Kral do you bleed. Tie, too, your fate to the Szélhámos, that together we may slaughter our enemies and deliver a swift victory to the Demons."

His words boomed around the arena, shaking it like an earthquake. The voice of the Halálhívó was meant to instill a healthy fear in all those who heard it.

With predatory slowness, he knelt. Yet each drop of his knee against the ground vibrated it with pure power. The hairs on the back of my neck rose as he pressed his palms flat against the stone.

I sank to the earth too, though I didn't prostrate myself. "Giver, bless us with abundant wells of magic so we wield in your name during battle. Let the blood we spill slake your thirst, and let us slaughter those who defy your design. Gift us with the power we need to bring majesty to your name. By our blood, we honor you."

Then, I flattened my palms on the stone and pressed my forehead to the cool surface.

"By our blood, we honor you," everyone echoed, masculine and feminine tones blending into one another as everyone offered a swipe of red to the Fates.

Rokath and I straightened simultaneously. Shoulder to shoulder with my mate, we surveyed the soldiers staring back at us.

Then, I spoke the final words to the prayer. "Reaper, whose curse falls upon those who stray from the path, let us not taste your wrath. We offer this blood as a pledge of our loyalty. Let your eye wander elsewhere and damn those who question your mighty power. Should we sin, may your curse be swift and unrelenting."

"We pledge our devotion to the Reaper."

Thousands of voices echoed my veneration, the sound haunting me with how it continued to ring long after the words were uttered. For a moment, the weight of their reverence settled over me. I was to become a *Fate* to them. They weren't here because they had to be; they were here because they *chose* to be. Chose to relinquish their comfortable position as priestesses and snatch the chance to become a soldier.

So I offered a final, silent prayer of my own. *"Let this change be welcomed with open arms. Let resistance fall away so that we might walk your divine path, Weaver."*

While I still questioned my faith, how much power the Fates truly held over this world, and continued to purge the lies I'd been fed my entire life, wishing for what I truly wanted would only elevate my energy for it and inspire others to do the same. If the Fates did hear me, if they did take my plea into account, then our society would be all the better for it.

Kiira rose, drawing everyone's attention. Her voice rang loud and clear through the expansive space. "Let the Halál-hívó's victory be swift and the Kral's reign eternal. Let the Szél-hámos guide us on a new path to righteousness. Our lives, our magic, our essence, are theirs to command."

"We are theirs to command." The conviction in the females' voices sent a wave of confidence crashing through me.

Using only his immense legs, Rokath stood, towering over everyone still kneeling. I surged to my feet beside him. "The Fates gave me the power to call upon the dead to do my bidding for a reason. To end the Angels and their relentless, fanatic pursuit of the extermination of the Demon race. Never forget what they will do in the name of that cause. It is, in fact, why you are all here. The losses we suffered recently were enormous. Your grit, determination, and magic can make the difference. We are allowing you an opportunity to prove yourselves. Do not waste it."

A second gong pealed, yet they did not move as they stared up at the three of us. Once the sound ceased, Rokath spoke again. "Dismissed."

With muted excitement, they straightened, whispering among themselves and gathering in small groups. Through the arched opening in the inner curtain, they streamed toward the commons. Males reformed around their longtime friends and followed.

The three of us lingered, observing their departure. Once the area had cleared out, we followed, keeping a healthy distance from them.

"What do you think, Halálhívó?" I asked, using my thumb to fiddle with the small garnet on my mother's ring. I thought the displays of power had been impressive, especially the number of former priestesses who had significant mastery over their magic.

"Only time will tell," he grumbled, his attention fixed straight ahead.

"So what happens after the meal then?" I asked as we entered the hall. Xannirin was notably absent from the high table. Rokath's posture was stiff as he removed his helmet and sat down, glaring at the empty seat.

"We review their marks and start assigning them to units,"

he replied. "Rapp should be able to help with that since the healer had ordered him to remain in bed for a few more days."

Kiira and I shared a laugh at the Hadvezér's expense. "I'm not sure all of us can fit in that tiny room," Kiira added as two males appeared with our food.

"Well, he needs to stop fucking up his stitches if he wants to be out of it sooner," Rokath stated, digging his fork into a small, steaming meat pie.

I shook my head and tucked into my meal. As I chewed, I surveyed the rest of the dining hall. Males sat with males, and females sat with females, each group competing for space around the long tables.

At least it wouldn't stay that way for long.

Our entire plan hinged on integrating them and returning to the front as quickly as possible. As I stabbed into my food, I tried not to think of the consequences of us failing to do just that.

27

ASSYRIA

Sweat slicked my training gear to my chest as I settled on the wooden stands of the arena. Kiira fared no better, using her sleeve to wipe her forehead. The newly-sorted females trailed past us, back to their barracks to wash before retiring for the evening.

Kiira, Rapp, Rokath, and I had worked for days to slot them into units appropriate for their talents. Xannirin had been notably absent, though it wasn't like the cousins never saw each other. No, they spoke late into the night and Rokath always returned furious.

Exhaustion tugged at my limbs from the imbalance between the hours of sleep I stole at night and the level of my exertion during the day. I wanted nothing more than to crawl into bed and remain there for eternity. Yet my mate and his Hadvezér stood on the opposite end of the arena, heads bent together and gesturing to parchment attached to portable boards.

Which meant he wasn't leaving anytime soon, and neither was I since he had our only key.

"Let's go for a walk, shall we?" Kiira suggested, rising with a groan.

"Ugh," I protested, but I knew if I remained seated, the soreness would set in faster and that climb up to Rokath's rooms would be infinitely worse. The males scarcely clocked that we were leaving, absorbed in whatever it was they were discussing.

"Where do you want to go?" I asked her as we fell in step.

"First, to the kitchens to procure some wine," she said, her tone light and airy. "Then, to the barracks."

I let out a small laugh. "If Rokath finds out, he's going to be furious."

Kiira shot me a grin. "So don't let him."

As much as my mate loved his rules, I did not. I'd never been great at following them. And with Kiira by my side, encouraging it? There was no way I was saying no. Some wine would ease the ache in my muscles and make the spiraling trek pass a lot faster too.

Ducking into a hall, we wound through the keep. At this hour, most were settling in for the night. The few out and about strode with purpose to their overnight posts.

The kitchens bustled with activity as the cooks cleaned up from the evening meal and prepped for the following day. They all ceased immediately when they noticed the High Priestess and me.

"High Priestess, Szélhámos," the closest one said, dropping to a knee.

"There's no need," Kiira told him, her tone warm and dripping honey. "Especially if you'll fetch us a bottle of wine and glasses."

"Certainly, High Priestess," he replied, hurrying off. The rest returned to their work.

A few minutes later, he slipped through the chaos, carrying a woven basket. "You'll find everything you need in here."

Kiira accepted it with the same easy grace she carried into every room, never a hitch in her step or a dip in her chin. Her poise, her charm, her elegance...she exuded royalty and prestige. We departed quickly, leaving them to their duties. Passing out of the keep, we strode through the largest courtyard toward the eastern barracks.

The evening was brisk and the breeze cooled my skin, overheated from being in the stuffy arena for the past few hours. We continued our leisurely pace, simply enjoying a moment of peace.

Light spilled through the cracked door, and holding it wider, I allowed Kiira to slip in ahead of me. Feminine voices drifted through the space, mingling with the crashing of water against tile.

"This way," Kiira told me, jerking her head in the direction of a small staircase that led to the upper floors. We trotted up to the highest level, where the more prominent priestesses had claimed their spaces.

Lavender, almond, and vanilla scents filled my nostrils as we strode onto the floor. Steam still hung in the air, drifting from the bathing chamber in the middle of the barracks. Moments later, Maariya, Izzenna, and a few others emerged, squeezing water from the ends of their hair.

Excited squeals greeted us, and they tossed their bath sheets onto their bunks and raced to meet Kiira.

"High Priestess!" Each greeted her with a kiss on either cheek.

"Please, the males aren't around now," Kiira replied, mischievousness dancing in her expression. Then, she shook the basket, causing cups to tinkle. "And we have wine."

"Blessed by the Giver," Maariya said, lifting the load from Kiira's arms.

The other priestesses greeted me similarly, and Izzenna

even hooked an arm through mine and steered me toward the sitting area. Maariya placed the basket on a table in the center and flipped open the top. From its dark interior, she pulled two bottles by their neck.

"Which do you want, Szélhámos?" she asked me, spinning them around so the labels were visible.

"You may call me Assyria while we're here." While my experience with priestesses had always been negative, witnessing how easily Kiira interacted with them had planted a seed of longing inside me. I'd never really had friends, and I desperately wanted their camaraderie.

Maariya smiled at me, giving my hope wings. "Of course. Assyria, which do you want?"

My knowledge of wine was limited to the color of the liquid. Chewing my bottom lip, I looked between the two for a moment, then gestured to the red one.

"Excellent choice," Maariya said. A wisp of obsidian emerged from her fingertips, and it snaked under the cork. With a pop, the wine opened, and another priestess caught the stopper before it rolled under a nearby settee.

Izzenna dug out the glasses and used her own magic to hold them aloft while Maariya poured. Together, they served us all.

"To our health," Kiira cheered, clinking her glass with mine. Warmth bloomed in my chest.

This was what it felt like to be included. I savored the feeling like I savored the wine as I took a long drink. The sweetness swept across my tongue, accompanied by a hint of pepper that reminded me of my mate. I nearly moaned at the decadent notes.

"Good, right?" Kiira tucked her long hair behind her ears and her legs beneath her on the couch beside me.

"Very," I replied, taking a smaller sip this time.

"How fare your discussions with the Kral and the Halálhívó?" a cherry-eyed female asked. Like Maariya and Izzenna, she wore her hair long and loose, and with it still damp, it held a deep wave.

"Not well, Vokkia," she replied. She swirled the purple wine in her cup as she considered her next words. I was curious to hear her opinion because my only real perspective was through Rokath. He'd wanted me to attend, but with Xannirin's continued condescension, he and Kiira had decided they'd likely get nowhere with me present.

She cut her attention to me for a moment. "These three are some of my most trusted advisors on the matters of our faith."

I understood the subtext of her words. She trusted them to help her spin whatever stories she decided needed to be woven —but not with the politics of it all.

"I am lucky to be included in this circle," I offered, smiling at each in turn.

"You deserve to be here, Assyria. You are a symbol of us all. Kiira spoke about you at length prior to our departure." Vokkia offered a quiet smile brimming with reverence.

"Did she?" I asked, tilting my head and studying Rokath's cousin.

"I did. Because I knew what you'd become." Before I could ask her what she meant by those cryptic words, she answered Vokkia's question. "The Kral is still highly resistant to all these ideas. He does not appreciate us moving forward without his approval. The Halálhívó and I are trying to sway him. Though his disagreement certainly won't stop the Halálhívó from acting when he thinks he's right."

I snorted at that. She knew my mate well.

"What if you cannot sway him?" Izzenna asked, a slight waver in her voice. "Will we have to return to our positions?"

Kiira pressed her lips together. My heart twisted at the

sorrow in Izzenna's ruby eyes. "I promise I won't let it come to that. We need you here in the army."

She turned her attention to me. "How did you do it?"

I tapped my finger on the side of my glass as I considered how I wanted to answer. "Persistence." The group fell into laughter. I found myself grinning, happiness sinking into my bones. "Truly though. I've never been one to remain quiet. It got me in...trouble with the priestess in Stryi. And my former husband. Somehow I wore the Halálhívó down."

Kiira shook her head. "You discount your own power, Assyria. The Halálhívó does not bend. He does not break. By acting as yourself, you opened him to what he's long been closed to. The Fates knew what they were doing when they made you mates."

My cheeks heated, and I took a long drink of wine to cover them.

"What story can you tell him to sway him? You are the best, after all," Maariya added.

Kiira's serene expression faltered for a moment before she corrected it. "I'm not certain a single story would make a difference. He's the type of male that has to think it's his idea. My cousins, I swear, have egos the size of Ravasz."

At that, we all laughed again.

"So what will be the message for the future?" I asked, the wine loosening my tongue. From conversations with Rokath, I knew that whatever changes needed to happen would come through the priestesses first—at least until Xannirin had finally surrendered his stubborn position.

"It is not necessarily a new one, but rather building off what is already believed. Not that the Kral would agree, regardless. All he sees is we've spent centuries ensuring females are reliant on males, and for him to change course now would be like him admitting it never should have happened in the first place."

"Which it shouldn't have," I pointed out. The other three nodded.

"We are in agreement there," Kiira said. "But there is another way. The people believe that I have a direct connection to the Fates—because I do. And if I tell them I have seen a future where male and female Demons battle alongside one another, then they will believe that."

She glanced around our small group, and again, I sensed that there was more she wasn't revealing.

"The one thing we have succeeded at more than anything else is the people's unwavering belief that the Halálhívó, the Kral, and I are the Fates' chosen. Despite the nobles' grumbling, they still believe that. And if Xannirin refuses to convince them, then I will," Kiira pronounced, draining her wine and gesturing for Maariya to hand her the bottle.

The last of the purple liquid swished into her glass. Izzenna uncorked another, and we all held out our cups for a refill.

"I want to help however I can," I affirmed. These priest-esses-turned-warriors did too, of that I was certain. And Rapp. He'd been by the cousins' sides for centuries.

Did he still feel like an outsider, like me?

Yet no matter how much time passed, he'd never really be a member of House Vrak. Whereas I was mated to the Halálhívó.

Kiira pulled my focus away from our injured friend. "The Fates also chose you. We will use that."

"So what comes first?" Maariya asked.

"I think the removal of veils is a solid start. It will be a shock after so long with them, but *seeing* us again will aid in the rest... whenever we can agree with the Kral on what that is." Kiira let out a long sigh, the weight of her task bringing her shoulders inward.

"Why wait for him?" I questioned. With his recent attitude, I didn't think he'd ever come around to such a change.

Kiira's answering grin pulled a mirror one to my lips. "You're right, Assyria. Sometimes it's better to ask for forgiveness than permission."

An echo to the time she'd snuck me out of Rokath's room at Gyor Palace surfaced. That was when I'd decided I really liked Kiira.

"Are you going to leave us when the Kral returns to Uzhhorod, Kiira?" Vokkia asked, tentative sorrow in her tone.

"No," she said with enough conviction my eyebrow twitched up. "I can still work from here, though it will take longer having to send ravens so far south."

"We will help however we can. We may be learning to wield weapons and honing our magic, but that does not mean we have fully abandoned our other duties," Maariya said, adjusting her wet hair over her other shoulder.

"I will send a raven to my flock tomorrow, informing them that they no longer have to hide themselves beneath sheer veils," Izzenna offered, draining her glass.

"As will I," Vokkia stated, lifting her chin.

Kiira softened and squeezed her priestess' arms in turn. "Thank you both. We don't want to rush everything too quickly. Each small change will take time to adjust. I appreciate all of your support thus far and everything I know you'll give in the future."

Solidarity. That was what this was. Females coming together to create change that would benefit us all.

"And I appreciate you all volunteering your lives for the army." My throat thickened because the reality was that these three, the others tucked away in their bunks further back and down below...not all of them would survive.

Kiira knocked her shoulder into mine, and I offered her a sad smile.

"We are the first, but we certainly won't be the last,"

Maariya swore. Then, her maroon eyes danced with an idea. "We should mark ourselves. Show the world who we are. Assyria is already our symbol for hope. What better way to honor her courage than to ink it into our skin?"

Before I could protest that I needed no such veneration, Vokkia clapped her hands, excitement curving her lips upward. Izzenna leaped to her feet and raced toward the bunks. "I have an idea."

Delight danced in Kiira's expression. "This is what we need," she said under her breath.

I knew that on an intellectual level, Rokath and I were supposed to become a myth unto ourselves. But this?

I wasn't worthy.

Izzenna returned with parchment and charcoal and sketched out a design. The four of us waited in eager silence. Her smile grew and grew as her hand flew across the page. When she finished, she whipped it around to show us.

My breath caught.

An eye, open to the world, greeted us. Instead of a colored iris at the center, a blooming rose waited. Sharp points speared from the top and bottom, almost like twin daggers.

"For the eyes of devious burgundy that Kiira saw," Izzenna explained, tracing the outline. "For the roses on your helmet. For our femininity." She tapped the bloom in the center. "For the power we wielded before and the power we will wield now. For our unity in this battle to be seen." She dragged a finger along the length of the long line.

Tears pricked the back of my nose, and I had to press my lips together to hold back a joyful sob. "It's perfect."

Izzenna brightened. "Do you think so?"

I nodded, and the others murmured their assent.

"How will we mark ourselves with it though?" I asked, the H's carved into my wrists aching at the thought.

Vokkia giggled and yanked up her sleeve, revealing swirls of ink so much like Rokath's. "I gave these to myself during one of my rebellious periods before I became a priestess. All I need is a needle, ink, and silver. All of which I happen to have in my bag."

She went to fetch it while Maariya gathered clean cloths and a basin of water.

"Assyria should go first. It is in her honor after all," Vokkia announced once she had all her tools prepared and ready to use.

"Where should I put it?" I asked her. Rokath had tattoos everywhere. Other than the perfect circle between my shoulder blades and his initial on my wrists, my skin was unmarred.

"Your forearm, I think," Vokkia said.

I shrugged off my jacket and then settled beside her, arm outstretched. She wiped my skin clean, lingering on the H on my wrist. Rather than shame rising, pride bloomed. Rokath had claimed me as his long before either of us consciously wanted it. And now, I wouldn't change that moment for anything.

Vokkia dipped the needle into the ink and silver mixture, then poked it into my skin. I hissed at the first intrusion, but she worked quickly, and soon, the pain dulled. We fell into further conversation about the war, combat skills, magic wielding, and of course, the males. I forgot she was working at all until she pronounced my tattoo finished.

With a final wipe of cloth on my arm, she revealed the design Izzenna had sketched. Joy crested inside me as I traced the lines with a featherlight touch. "Thank you."

Vokkia beamed at me. "Anything for you, Assyria."

Kiira went after me, and once we had our matching symbols on our forearms, we admired them together. Those tattered pieces of my heart stitched together at the sight. Especially as Izzenna begged to be next.

"This is only the beginning," Kiira murmured. I lifted my gaze to meet hers. "There is so much more to come."

"I couldn't do any of this without you," I whispered back, vision blurring. We embraced, and she smelled of moon lotus and lavender—the floral scents drawing my days of tending to a garden to the surface.

How far I'd come, how much I'd changed since then.

When we broke apart, each of us had to dry our tears.

"Assyria and I had better return to our rooms before we're missed. And before these are noticed." She gestured to our now-empty glasses and bottles. "We'll sneak back tomorrow to see everyone's tattoos."

Maariya packed up everything for us, and with aching limbs, I rose from my place on the couch. Stretching my arms overhead, I bent from side to side, trying to work out the soreness creeping in.

With warm embraces, we said our goodbyes, and then Kiira and I slunk out of the barracks under the cover of darkness. We dropped our basket off with the final kitchen worker before navigating the maze of halls to the two rear towers where our rooms awaited us.

At the door, I let out a long sigh, preparing to brace for the climb.

"Will you join me in my room for a moment?" Kiira asked, shifting her weight.

"Of course," I told her, my curiosity piqued.

What could she possibly want this late?

Without another word, she disappeared through the arched entry to Xannirin's tower. We trekked up a few flights before she stopped at her door. Kiira's rooms looked untouched, and though they weren't as fine as Rokath's, they were still cozy and clean. Shutting us in, she clicked the lock into place. Then, she pressed her ear to the wood as if she were listening for any sign of someone following us.

What did she know that I did not?

Suspicion twisted my gut, and I remained still and silent, waiting for her next move. A few moments passed with no sound, and finally she stepped away from the door.

"I need to talk to you," she said, aiming for one of the plush seats in a ring by the windows.

Yet when she settled herself in it, she fidgeted, not quite able to get comfortable. On hesitant feet, I approached, easing into one beside her. I crossed my legs over one another and twisted my ring around my finger, wondering what had the High Priestess so agitated.

"Is everything okay?" I ventured, hoping to prompt her into speaking.

"Well…no." She looked at her hands, shoulders slumping inward. "Do you remember our first solo conversation?"

"When we were in the garden?" I clarified. She nodded. "I do." We'd talked about why I didn't want to be a priestess, the pain I'd endured at the hands of my dead husband, and my future in the Demon Realm. She'd promised to find out information about Olrus…

My throat thickened at the thought of my friend, burned for protecting my secret. That also reminded me of Izgath, and another wave of guilt swept up from the deep.

"Did you not tell me everything in your letter?" I choked out.

She whipped her head up, concern etching her face. "Fates, no, this isn't about you. I'm sorry, I should have clarified. It's about…me."

Relief washed through me before my mind caught up to Kiira's words and worry replaced it. "Has something happened?"

She swallowed hard, burgundy eyes growing glassy. She looked up to the ceiling and dragged in a serrated breath. "It was so much easier to ignore it, you know?"

"Kiira..." I breathed, my voice softening with sorrow.

"I haven't told Rokath and Xannirin yet, and I don't know, I just...can't. They'd look at me differently." She finally met my gaze, and the tears had already fallen. I wiped them gently from her face.

"Do you want to tell me what happened?" I asked, closing the distance between us.

"I think I need to talk about it with someone who understands," she murmured, her voice barely more than a whisper.

"I'm here," I promised her, rubbing soothing strokes over her forearm with my thumb.

"You won't know him, but he's one of the more prominent nobles in the realm. He holds a lot of sway with the others, and he produces much of what we need in the realm." She paused, fingers digging into the tops of her thighs. "Why did I drink what he offered me?" Her voice cracked on that question, and she folded in on herself, burying her face in her hands. Sobs wracked her frame, and I moved my ministrations to her back. Letting her know I was there. That I saw her pain.

"I thought Xannirin would blame me," she choked out. "If he believed me at all."

"Why would he not?" I asked.

"The male who raped me helped us build all of this," she replied. "We couldn't have done it without him, Assyria. We knew it was a risk..."

She straightened, but I didn't release her. She needed to know that there was nothing wrong with her. That I didn't view her differently for what had happened to her. To me. "And you're worried that Xannirin will deny it happened because of how important he is to the realm."

"Yes," Kiira breathed, her voice haunted.

I let out a long sigh. "From what I know of Rokath, he'd

believe you. In fact, he'd probably decide to ride to Uzzhorod and slit that fuckers throat the moment you told him."

A watery laugh escaped Kiira. "That sounds exactly like something he'd do."

"Males," I said, expression softening with love and understanding. I hoped Kiira saw it all.

"Males," she echoed, a soft smile rising to her lips.

"You have nothing to be ashamed of, Kiira."

"Then why do I feel like I do?" she asked softly.

"Because that's what they'd done to us for centuries. Made us feel like we're beneath them. Like we *deserve* whatever we get. Like we are powerless." The sentences burst out of me with all the anger I'd suppressed trying to be someone I was not. "And that is why I'm here, you're here, now. We're ready for this change."

"We have to stick together. All of us," Kiira croaked, and I knew she meant the priestesses she'd brought with her, despite what the fucking Kral wanted.

"We will. United, we can stand against what the males think we should be. We will fucking show them," I promised her. "Plus, we have Rokath and Rapp on our sides too. My mate can be pretty frightening when he wants to be."

Kiira snorted. "In only a few days, I've seen a side to him that he hasn't shown since he was so, so young. That's all because of you."

"I know. I can be relentless when I want to be. Which is pretty much all the time," I laughed, flicking my braid over my shoulder.

"That is a quality we need right now," Kiira stated. "Thank you, Assyria. For helping me see."

"Thank you, Kiira, for sharing with me. For believing me when I told you," I said, pulling her in for a fierce hug. "I'm so sorry you had to go through it too."

"Just tell me I'll get through it," she said, resting her head on my shoulder.

"You will. Anytime you need to talk, I'm here. And I won't tell anyone either," I swore. "But I do think you should speak to your cousins about this. It might be what Xannirin needs to hear to crack. Or for Rokath to kill him. One of the two."

Kiira wiped her nose, holding back a glimmer of amusement. "Fates, Rokath would be a terrible Kral."

"There's nothing he'd hate more," I agreed. "But to protect us, he'd do it."

We remained like that for a moment, me studying Kiira, and Kiira soaking in whatever assurance she needed from me. "I should go before Rokath worries."

"Yes, please go if you need to. I'll be fine," she replied, smoothing her hair.

"Are you certain? I can stay if you need me to."

She shook her head. "I might check on Rapp one last time before bed. Make sure he didn't overdo it today."

At that, we both giggled. "Oh, he definitely did."

As she slipped into the bathing chamber to splash some water on her face, I sat in silent reflection. My heart broke for Kiira and all she'd endured too. Her story renewed my convictions, fueled my fury at our mistreatment. For her, for the others, for every female in the Demon Realm, I'd see these changes through to the end.

After all, I'd been blessed by the Giver with this unique power, with a bond that transcended all others, and an unbreakable will. I was the fucking Szélhámos, and the world would come to know exactly who I was by the end of this war.

28

ASSYRIA

Kiira and I descended the stairs hand in hand. The freely given affection was healing me as much as it was healing her. "You know, I always wished for a sister. Prayed for one when I was young, someone for me to be with like Rokath and Xannirin had each other. I think the Fates finally answered me with you."

"You're going to make me cry," I choked out, giving her a squeeze. Memories of my own sister flashed through my mind. She'd been the last of my family to die in the plague. But maybe, just maybe, I could find the same feelings with Kiira and among the females in Fured.

"I mean it. We have a sisterhood among the priestesses, but I can't share with them like I can with you. You are as much in this as I am now," she told me.

Flickering light appeared ahead as we descended the final spin of the tower. All was quiet with the late hour, not even a whisper of the guards who normally stood at the base to protect their Kral. We reached the landing, striding into the chilly night air. A shiver wracked my frame, and I released Kiira to rub warmth into my arms.

"Are you sure you don't want me to walk you?" I asked her, backing toward Rokath's tower. Rapp and the healing wing were in the opposite direction. With a glance behind me, I realized no sentries were posted at the entry or along the hall.

They must be on a break.

"I'll be fine," she swore, wrapping her jacket tighter over her torso. "Get some sleep. You look exhausted."

I snorted. "So do you."

Kiira's eyes widened, her breath catching—not the reaction I expected. "Assyria, watch–"

Something hard slammed into my back, sending me careening forward. Kiira shrieked, leaping out of the way. I twisted my body at the last moment, landing hard on my bad shoulder. Pain flared, and a loud pop reached my ears.

"Fuck," I cursed, clutching my arm. Kiira continued to scream, and I tore my eyes open to find a male towering over me, molten pitch coiling around him. Thick whips snapped Kiira into a nearby column. Her sounds ceased, leaving only my thundering heart in my ears.

I shoved my feet into the ground and pushed back, creating distance between me and the hooded male. With the darkness covering his face, I had no way of knowing what his eye color was. What his secondary power might be.

"*Rokath!*" I screamed down our bond, snatching at the inky well in my chest.

A silver blade flashed in the firelight.

Without thinking, I flung my magic in all directions, covering Kiira should he attempt to slit her throat while she was unconscious.

"*Where are you?*" Rokath growled, my fear a wildfire down the bond.

"*Base of the tower,*" I managed to get out as the male leaped for me. He crashed into me, sending the air screaming from my lungs. A sharp sting sliced across my cheek. Stars danced in my vision. But I'd managed to avoid a dagger to the heart.

My shadows stuttered from the contact with silver. I gritted my teeth and dug deeper into my well.

This fucker would not kill me.

Obsidian power surged, shoving him off me. Wheezing, I flung out a hand, holding him at bay. Agony lashed my shoulder as I raised my other arm to twist the dark tendrils toward his hood to reveal his identity.

Stone trembled above us. A wicked grin curved the corner of my mouth. "You've made a terrible mistake."

The would-be assassin snarled and slashed through my magic. Each rope screamed in protest as it shattered into nothingness. Adrenaline flooding my veins, I rose, preparing to fight with my fists.

He lunged again, and I ducked under the blow, dancing away from him. He followed, silver whooshing by me as I continued to dodge.

Why did there have to be so many fucking stairs to that tower?

I had no doubt Rokath was careening down them at a breakneck pace.

Positioning myself between the male and Kiira, I snapped, "Who sent you?"

Because the moment Rokath reached me, this male was dead.

He said nothing, silent as a wraith. I shoved more magic at him, attempting to knock him off balance and remove his cloak. But with a wave of his hand, he cast a shield of onyx at the last moment. Darkness claimed the space between us. My heart thundered against my ribs.

I couldn't see him, could scarcely see my own hands. What if he flung the blade at me now?

The thought had barely finished before I was moving. And not a moment too soon.

Metal clattered against stone as I crashed to the ground, more pain flaring in my shoulder. Tears pricked my eyes, but I gritted my teeth, muscles tense, and prepared to fight again.

A roar ripped through the night. Our bond flared with fury as I sensed Rokath mere steps from me. The sharp edge of a blade sliced the air. A cry echoed. Firelight returned, casting a harsh glow on the blood-soaked stones.

The male fell to his knees, hands clutching a deep wound in his side.

And my mate stood over him.

My breath caught—this time not from fear, but from awe. Clad in nothing but a pair of pants, his blade dripping the crimson blood of my attacker, tattoos on full display, Rokath was vengeance incarnate. Carved by the Fates themselves to rain divine justice.

"You touched my mate."

A low, primal growl rumbled from him, raising the hairs on the back of my neck. I scooted toward Kiira, ensuring their brawl wouldn't bring harm to her.

"No one gets to do that but me. Because of your transgression, I will gut you so thoroughly the Fates will weep for what they wove."

The male drew a dagger hidden at his side and swiped at Rokath. My mate sidestepped it, dipping and catching the assassin by the throat. He threw him against the wall, rattling the keep. Bones crunched as the male crumpled to the ground. Blood flew from his mouth as he spit onto the pavers.

"Symbols rise. Symbols fall, Halálhívó," he taunted, hurling himself forward for another attack.

Ice shattered through my veins. Those words...

A blade scraped over Rokath's chest, but my mate drove him

into the stones again. Then, he wrapped the back of the male's head and slammed it against his knee. More ruby spilled from him as he ducked out of Rokath's grip.

But his movements were slow, sloppy. Rokath caught his fist on the next strike and twisted. Another crack sounded. The male howled in pain.

"Not as quickly as inept assassins," Rokath ground out. Yanking the silver blade from the male's hand, he flipped it and plunged it into his throat. His chest. His stomach and *dragged*.

A cascade of garnet slicked his clothes. With a sickening gurgle, the would-be killer fell to the ground. The hood of his cloak dropped too, revealing glassy maroon eyes.

Rokath raced to my side, noting Kiira lay there too. "Are you okay?"

"I'll be fine. Kiira is out," I said, salt stinging my eyes. Rokath brushed his knuckles over the cut on my cheek, and I hissed. "Except for that. And my shoulder. It's injured again."

A string of curses fled his lips. "I'm taking you both to the healing wing." In one powerful motion, he scooped up his cousin. Then, he helped me to my feet. I swayed for a moment, my entire body trembling as I came down from the fright of the attack.

Once I was certain I wouldn't collapse, I found Rokath's sword and grabbed it. What if more were waiting to rise if their comrade failed?

He took two steps before halting. "Where the *fuck* are the sentries?"

"They weren't here when we came down," I told him, my voice weak.

Rage, hotter than a volcano, burned down our bond. "Heads will roll."

Of that, I had no doubt.

On sore, tired limbs, I followed my mate to the healing wing. Kiira groaned, her head lolling. "Rokath?"

"Sh, rest for now. I'm taking you to the healer." Rokath adored Kiira, and like me, he'd do anything to protect her. She'd told me as much during our conversation on the terrace at Gyor Palace.

To see it now made me love my mate all the more.

Rokath roused the lead healer in residence to care for Kiira and me. Laid out on an examination table, he tended to a deep gash on the back of Kiira's head. I sat on the end, cradling my arm.

"Where is she?" Rapp burst into the room, his face contorted.

"For fuck's sake, we can't have you ripping stiches again," Rokath growled, catching his Hadvezér. "Assyria is fine."

Yet as I studied the wide-eyed terror in Rapp's expression, I got the sense that the emotion wasn't entirely for me. He found us a moment later, his frame sagging with relief. "I heard your voices. Had to check that you were alright."

"We're fine. Just a bit shaken up." Kiira offered Rapp a reassuring smile, but it didn't seem to calm his panic.

"Who attacked them?" he whirled on Rokath.

Anger vibrated through my mate's muscled frame. "He's dead now. But he didn't act alone."

Rokath quickly relayed what had happened while the lead healer finished his work on Kiira. Approaching me, he gave me a quick once-over. "I can put a salve on your cheek so it doesn't scar. Your shoulder, I'll have to set. Do you want something to bite?"

"Please," I said, bracing myself for the pain to come. He fetched a piece of wood and I opened my mouth so he could place it between my teeth.

Kiira sat upright and held my good hand. "Squeeze as hard as you need to."

I nodded and dragged in a breath through my nostrils.

"Three, two..." The pop echoed through the chamber. A grunt ripped from my throat, and my hand shook from how hard it gripped Kiira's. Rokath whirled, having felt the harsh adjustment down our bond.

I spit out the wood. "I'm fine," I told him in a hurry. He was already on edge from the attempted assassination, and I really needed this healer to fix me. He couldn't do that if he was dead.

"Drink this," the healer said, proffering me a milky green vial.

"What is it?" I asked. The smell was atrocious, and I attempted to hold back a gag.

"A mixture of pium, poppy, and willow bark. You've already hurt this shoulder before, which is why injuring it again was so easy. The combination will settle the tissues around it and help it heal faster. You should be alright the day after tomorrow."

Rapp made a sound of disbelief. "Why haven't you been giving me that?"

"Because it won't work in your case," the lead healer stated, using a fresh cloth to dab a salve over my cheek. Once he finished, he took a step back and looked at the males. "Ensure they both sleep tonight and rest tomorrow. Especially the High Priestess. Her wound should close by morning, but the interior bruising will take more time."

Rokath blew out a long breath, his chest deflating. "Thank you."

The healer merely nodded and packed up his tools. Then, with a sigh, he handed another vial to Rapp. "Since you're awake, an extra dose wouldn't hurt."

I snorted a laugh as Rapp uncorked and tossed the contents back. Kiira shook her head but winced. "Probably best not to move it for a bit." She pressed her palm into her temple, flashing the edge of her new tattoo.

"Woah, what is this?" Rapp questioned, grabbing her arm and shoving up her sleeve.

Kiira grinned up at him. "A symbol. The devious eye."

Rokath leaned in and studied it for a moment before directing his attention at me. "Was this your idea?"

"Actually, no," I quipped, gritting my teeth and shimming out of my jacket to show him the ink gracing my skin just beneath his brand. "The priestesses wanted something to mark who we are and what we are doing."

Rokath came to stand in front of me and cupped my cheek. His thumb traced over the H on my wrist. "You are a true leader, Assyria."

His affirmation pricked at my eyes.

Without breaking my gaze, he spoke to Kiira. "You should sleep in my chambers tonight where I can keep an eye on both of you."

Rapp leaned against the table beside her, arms crossed over his chest. "She can remain here with me. That way if she has problems in the night, the healer is readily available."

A muscle ticked in Rokath's jaw as he considered the proposition. "You're in no shape to fight should someone else come for her."

I reached for my mate and tugged him closer. "I don't think they were after Kiira."

His heavy brows dipped together. "Why do you say that?"

"Because of what the male said. 'Symbols rise, symbols fall.'"

Kiira sucked in a sharp breath. "Surely you don't mean to imply–"

"That Xannirin had something do with it?" I snapped. "Perhaps none of you remember how horribly he treated me during our first dinner, but I do."

Rokath's eyes flashed with the type of darkness that made my core clench. Yet beneath the outward anger, an inner storm roiled.

"There are plenty of others who are unhappy with the current situation," Rapp pointed out. "And unfortunately, Assyria has become the face of it to many in the army."

"He's right," Kiira agreed.

Their dismissal, combined with the instinct to fight leaving my body, left me irritated. "The sentries weren't there. Who else has the power to send them away?"

"Not many. Us, Olet. The Százados in charge of the night watch," Rokath said, his mind racing through endless possibilities. "Tomorrow, I will round up each for questioning, including the males who abandoned their posts."

He crouched so we were eye level. "As much as I want to go on a rampage right now, I need to take care of you. Your health, your safety, your protection, are paramount to me. I am so sorry I couldn't reach you sooner."

Tears burned my eyes. I reached up and cupped his cheek. The soft hairs of his beard tickled my palm. "You came as quickly as you could."

He leaned forward and pressed a kiss to my forehead. "Come, you need to rest."

Nodding, I slid off the table. He tucked me under his arm, the safest place in all the worlds.

"Send for me if you need anything," he told Rapp and Kiira.

"We will," Rapp promised. Using the wall as support, he shuffled forward. Kiira joined him, her steps as careful as his. Rokath and I followed them to Rapp's room before quickening our pace.

My entire being ached. When we reached the entrance to

our tower, Rokath scooped me into his arms. I didn't protest as he carried me up the spiral staircase, merely rested my cheek against his heart and let the steady rhythm soothe me.

And when we reached our sleeping chamber, I let him undress me. Let him carry me to bed. Let him wrap himself around me. Let him make me feel *safe*.

"Sleep, Assyria. I will protect you."

But I'd tasted the truth tonight. And it was bitter. No one, not even Rokath, could shield me from the discontent of those who preferred the status quo. Traitors hid in the shadows—Fates, right out in the open.

Next time they came for me, I wouldn't be caught unprepared.

I'd be waiting. Ready. Primed with fire in my veins and fury in my heart.

They wanted to cut down a new symbol; instead, I'd show the world what it meant to be the fucking Szélhámos.

INTERLUDE

The High Priestess glided through the halls of Varbad Temple, her mind flitting over a dozen tasks still unfinished. She'd risen later than normal, entirely by accident, and at midday, she returned to her luxurious rooms at the pinnacle to retrieve a notebook she'd left behind in her rush.

"High Priestess," her acolytes greeted her, dipping into deep curtsies as she passed them. She offered each a bow of her head in return. After all, she wanted the faithful to feel welcome and at home among these walls. For decades now, she'd been training them, honing their beliefs like her cousin honed his soldiers and their weapons. Now, it was finally time to start sending them far and wide into the Demon Realm to spread her word.

Which came with far too many challenges and far more work than she ever expected.

She ascended another staircase, internally berating herself for insisting she had the top floor all to herself. She'd wanted the views and the sanctuary, and yet as her thighs burned, pressing into step after step, she debated if it was all worth it.

Breathless, she paused on a landing, bracing herself against the wall. Beneath her lived the high-level priestesses—those who had been extremely eager to join upon the announcement of the construction of Varbad.

One such female descended the thick stairs, smiling warmly through her veil until she took in the pallor of her leader. "High Priestess?" she said, rushing forward.

With a leap, she managed to catch the High Priestess before she collapsed to the ground. The High Priestess's burgundy eyes rolled back in her head, revealing only the whites. A convulsion wracked her frame, and foam appeared at the corners of her mouth.

"Help!" the female shouted, scanning the area for anyone else. From below, a second raced up the stairs, skidding to a stop when she beheld the scene.

"We need to carry her to her room," the second said, shaking herself out of her shock and reaching for the High Priestess's feet. She was the very first acolyte and had secured her place at the High Priestess's side nearly a century ago. Yet this was the first time she'd witnessed her mentor in this state, though there was no denying what it was—a vision.

A third appeared a moment later, gasping at the sight of the High Priestess on the floor.

Together, they managed to ascend the final flights to the High Priestess's room, settling her on a settee. An occasional tremor wracked her frame as they all watched on, scarcely breathing. The third quickly sliced into her palm, making an offering to the Fates and praying for the safe return of their High Priestess.

Yet what they witnessed was nothing compared to what their leader glimpsed of the future.

The air was thick with moisture, and the cloying scent of tropical plants assaulted her nostrils. Tentatively, she stepped through the thick underbrush. Green dripped ruby, and she nearly stumbled over something hidden among it.

Glancing down, she nearly retched. Glassy, lifeless blue eyes stared at the canopy overhead. A pool of blood surrounded his head, the cut in his throat so deep that it was hanging by the barest of sinew to his body.

Slowly, her gaze drifted forward, to an entire trail through the thick forest lined with similar corpses. Ahead, the faint sounds of fighting reached her ears. Picking her way carefully, she closed the distance. After rounding a particularly thick trunk, the city of Sivy came into focus.

Her breath caught in her chest as she beheld the smoke drifting from thatched roofs, catching their neighbors' homes ablaze. All the way to the largest tree at the very center, two armies engaged. There, gleaming white marble entrenched its expanse, twice as large as Gyor Palace in the Demon Realm.

Her every breath felt stolen, her every heartbeat a drum in the ritual of war. This wasn't a dream—it was a reckoning.

She raced forward, hugging each tree on the outskirts of the Angel capital, peering down alleys that weren't thick with bodies. She did her best to remain unspotted, and yet, she nearly ran straight into a fleeing Angel. He didn't even seem to notice her as he raced into the thick ferns a mere breath away.

Her brow furrowed, and she pressed forward. Again, no one glanced her way as she walked into the midst of battle. Bodies fell, then rose, and a sudden realization hit her: the Halálhívó was here.

A group of lifeless forms stumbled forward, jaws slack, eyes vacant. They fell upon Angels in white, ripping at flesh and not flinching when the same was done to them. Blood sprayed in her direction, and yet, when she looked down, none of it stained her bare arms.

Shaking her head, she pressed onward, searching for any sign of her cousin blessed with the power of Calling. A roar shattered the air off to her left, and she raced in that direction, hoping, praying, that it wasn't one of pain from him.

Skidding onto the main thoroughfare, she finally found him.

Onyx spiraled in a raging inferno, engulfing anyone within a dozen feet of him in the furious frenzy. His bronze blade flashed in the flits of light breaking through the canopies of the massive trees. With a sharp whistle, it cut through the air and into the neck of an Angel kneeling before him, trapped in the inky tendrils of his power.

The head hit the ground with a sickening thud. More Angels thrashed against their binds, and she realized then just how much power her cousin was wielding at once. Tentatively, she stepped forward again, trying to gain a better view.

That was when she saw the Zahal kneeling, his ice blue eyes glaring up with an eternity of hatred and his teeth clenched in righteous anger. The Halálhívó bent, snarling in his face. Still, he did not falter. Then, the blade arced through the air again, cleaving his head from his shoulders too.

The shadows ceased swirling as the Halálhívó collected the severed heads. Fisting their white hair, he raised them high and let out another roar. Even his cousin quaked in its wrath.

Then, he stomped down the central thoroughfare, his gaze pinned directly on the royal palace. She rushed to match his furious strides, dodging wave after wave of white-haired Angels prostrating themselves and pleading for mercy.

He halted at the base of the stairs, still hoisting the two heads high. With the way he gripped their hair, she saw that one had an H carved into his forehead. Instantly, she recalled him as the male who had ignited the spark that set this whole war ablaze.

"Korona Iaoth, your people are defeated. You have no army left to defend you. Emerge from your marble walls and surrender if you wish to live."

With a gasp, the High Priestess shot upright, startling her faithful watching over her. They dropped their clasped hands and raced to her side, dozens of questions tumbling from their lips. Blinking forcefully, the High Priestess attempted to ground herself in the present as the remnants of her vision bled away.

She didn't know when this battle would come. Only that it would—because the Fates only revealed truths that had not yet been born to her.

But she couldn't help the smile that rose to her lips.

"What is it, High Priestess?" the second pressed. She flattened the back of her hand to her leader's forehead, checking for a temperature.

The High Priestess swatted her hand away. Slowly, she eased herself upright, the world spinning. Exhaustion weighed heavily on her bones, and yet she'd never felt so giddy, so exuberant, not in the years since she and her cousins had taken power.

"Find the Kral and inform him that I must speak to him at once. Here, in the temple," she instructed the third. The prophecies took an enormous toll on her, and she needed to record what she had seen immediately, so she could rest properly after. "You, get me parchment and ink."

The first hurried away, returning with both a moment later. "What did you see?" Her tone brimmed with breathless wonder. After all, the visions of the High Priestess were legendary. And to bear witness to one? Divine. Holy. *Sacred*.

The High Priestess accepted the materials, hands trembling with excitement. "I saw the Halálhívó win the war." She paused, remnants of the revelation slipping away like smoke between her fingers. Yet a foreboding dread curled in her gut, bitter and biting, even if she could not place its origin. "But the cost..."

PART
THREE

29

R☠KATH

After days of interrogating my soldiers, I was no closer to an answer as to who had attacked Assyria and Kiira. All the sentries were found dead, stuffed in a supply closet. Cold had slithered in my gut at the sight. Only more questions raised like battle banners after.

The assassin had maroon eyes, and yet he hadn't called upon his secondary power once. I didn't know him. Neither did the Kral's Guard when I questioned them.

All the mystery made it impossible to rule out Xannirin's involvement. My cousin had kept to himself, rarely appearing at mealtimes. And when I went to his room, he refused to answer the door.

I had half a mind to break it down and force him to speak to me.

Why would he come after my mate? And Kiira?

Sure, he was furious about the whole situation. But he knew that Assyria's death would cripple me. And he wanted to win this war as much as the rest of us.

With the voices in the back of my head whispering that I couldn't keep my mate safe, and the memories that haunted me as I entered the training ring, I needed a fucking break from this place.

The final day of the week dawned, bringing with it a brilliant sun that hadn't shone since my cousins' arrival. This was the only day with ample free time, and most of the soldiers went into Fured for their few precious hours. The markets and taverns were a respite from strict regimen, and the townspeople were always ready to welcome the soldiers and their coin.

I had other plans for Assyria. Her shoulder had set correctly, and after a few days of herbs from the healer, it was nearly as it had been before. The cut on her cheek had vanished. It was almost as if the attack had never happened.

Almost.

Even now, with her hair fanned across the pillow, a fierce protectiveness rose in me. Killing that fucker once was not enough to abate my anger.

Yet Assyria did not relent on any training she could do, attending twice daily with the females. It was as if the fire that had always burned inside her had swelled into a raging inferno. Her constant fervency heated my blood in the best way, and more than anything I wanted to sink my cock into her and lose myself for eternity.

The waking bell echoed through the keep, its peal deep and clear. With grumbled protest, she rolled over onto my chest, absently tracing one of the snakes wrapped around a tree tattooed there. "Do we have to get up? Everything hurts."

"You got an extra hour of sleep," I pointed out, my thumb stroking the bare skin of her shoulder.

She tilted her head up to look at me, eyes narrowed. "Did I?"

"The gong sounds one hour later today than all the others," I told her.

"But we went to sleep later than normal too," she argued with a huff. "So it nets me zero extra sleep. I think tomorrow when that damned thing wakes me up, I'm going to bury my head in the pillows and pretend I don't exist."

A laugh rumbled in my chest. "You have been training very hard. But I can't let you break the rules."

"Ugh," she replied, flattening herself across my large frame. "What's the benefit of being mated to you then?"

Gripping her hips, I slid her down my body to settle over my hardness. "This."

"Males," she sighed, rolling herself off me.

I snatched her back before she could go too far. "And what would you know of that, little imposter? Did you forget you belong to me?"

"First, I don't *belong* to you," she said, stabbing her finger above my heart. "I am my own person and I do things because I want to do them."

In one swift motion, I had her on her back, pinned beneath me. I rolled my hips against hers, eliciting a soft gasp. Then, I let my head drop to her ear. "Don't play like you don't love when I command you."

Desire swept down our bond, and when I pulled back, Assyria's pupils had darkened. My dick throbbed against her thigh. But now was not the time, or the way, I wanted her. So with a groan, I forced myself to put space between us.

Yet when I sat on my heels, my cock still pointed straight to her. She raked her gaze hungrily along its length before propping herself up and reaching for me. I caught her hand before she could touch. "Not now. I have plans for us."

She tilted her head to the side, ebony hair spilling over her shoulder and concealing one of her flawless nipples. "And what's that?"

"We're going to the beach," I pronounced.

She looked at me like she didn't believe me. "There's a beach? Isn't it cold?"

"There is, but it's hidden and you have to fly. Figured it would be a nice time to practice that too. As for the weather, yes it will be chilly. I suggest you dress accordingly."

She rolled her eyes. "Because I definitely need you telling me what to wear too."

"Technically, you're now a member of this army, and I am your superior officer. So if I say put on this leather, you put it on. If I say put on this helmet, you put it on. If I wanted you to wear a collar and leash, you'd bark at my feet. No matter what I want, you have to do it." I couldn't help the wicked grin that curved up the corner of my mouth.

"How do I remove myself from this situation?" she sighed, looking at the ceiling like she was asking the Weaver for assistance.

I tugged her ankles, bringing her closer to me and flat on her back once more. Then, I knelt between her thighs. The scent of her arousal flooded my nostrils before I blew across her cunt. "Are you sure you want to?"

"This is so not fair," she said, her tone all breathy need.

I retreated again, this time fully off the bed before I could disregard my plans and take her right then and there.

"What about breakfast?" she asked, pushing herself upright.

I pulled on a pair of previously discarded pants and fastened them. "I've ordered it to go."

She arched a brow. "So you've been planning this?"

"Aye," I said, finding a tunic and buttoning it up. "Is that so hard to believe?"

"Uh, yes," she replied, sliding from the bed. On her side of the room, a chair—completely covered in her half-worn clothes—waited. From the pile, she yanked out her warmest leathers. I'd had more made for both of us after our arrival since we would be in residence for months. No sense in rewearing the same two sets of clothing when we had ample space for more.

At least the clothiers had been cooperative since I threatened one of the elder ones.

"I make lots of plans," I pointed out. "I am, in fact, in charge of the army."

She tugged on tight pants that drew my attention straight to her ass.

"But none of them have been romantic ones," she quipped. The swell of her breasts disappeared as she pulled on a shirt and then fastened a high-collar leather jacket over it. All our new clothing was shadow-woven, which allowed our wings through. That way, removing it for training would be unnecessary—or in the event of an attack.

"That you know of," I shot back as I found my dagger sheaths and strapped them on.

She opened and closed her mouth a few times. Smugly, I waited for her to offer me a reasonable response. Rather than admitting defeat, she huffed. "Okay, I'm ready. Show me this romantic plan you have."

30

R●KATH

We entered the sitting area, and there, a basket of food waited for us. Grem and Zeec were nowhere to be found, likely having slipped out with whomever delivered our meal. The two knew where to source their own breakfast. While they wouldn't stray from the academy, they did love to wander the grounds on their own whenever we were here.

Grabbing a blanket from one of the couches, I tossed it at Assyria. "Here, carry this."

She caught it in midair and tucked it beneath her arm as I made the final preparations for our departure. Finally satisfied that I had everything, I jerked my head for her to follow me. She paused when she realized I wasn't headed for the main entrance.

"Wait, where are we going?" she asked.

I shoved my back into a round part of the wall beside a painting of a long-dead Demon. The stone rolled back with a groan. "To the roof. We'll fly from there."

Her mouth popped open as she beheld the secret staircase. "Has that always been there?"

"Yes?" I replied. "Now come on."

Shaking her head, she followed me into the passage and up the stairs. A short jaunt later, I was shoving open the door to the roof of this tower, a small space hardly big enough for four people. But it wasn't made for a group watch like the other towers; no it was made for escape or a moment of privacy.

Wind buffeted us the moment we stepped outside, whipping a few tendrils loose from Assyria's braid. In front of us, the ocean stretched endlessly, a blue so deep it was nearly the color of twilight. Only small whitecaps dotted the surface today, swelling and easing with the force of the breeze. Yet the sun was strong, heating my skin as I tipped my face up to it.

Then, I dug into the well of shadows in my chest and tugged my wings into existence. The black, membranous expanse settled behind me, adding extra weight to my frame. In a breath, Assyria did the same, though she kept hers tucked close.

I stepped forward and ran a finger along the hard ridges at the top of them. A shiver wracked her frame as more desire flooded our bond. "Sensitive?" I rumbled, loving the way her lashes fluttered against her cheeks as I did it again.

"Yes," she breathed, almost leaning into my touch. "It's like you're caressing my magic."

"I plan on caressing *many* parts of you later," I told her, my tone gravelly. "But for now, we will fly."

Dragging in a serrated breath, she nodded. Taking a step back, I flexed my wings, ensuring there was enough space to take off. Then, I half-squatted and leaped into the air. The wind caught the underside of my body and carried me away from the tower.

Hovering, I waited for Assyria. After shuffling the blanket to her chest, she took a few bounding steps, wings flapping. Her bow-shaped lips flattened as she readied herself. With a cry, she launched off the side of the tower. The air battered her from the side, and she struggled for a moment to find the right draft.

But then, she found her lift, and a giddy laugh escaped her. Angling herself, she sailed straight toward me, a wide grin splitting her face. "Come on, let's go!"

I drank the sight of her flying in for a heartbeat longer, then banked from my position and led her out toward the ocean.

As we soared over the edge of the cliff, her awe and wonder trickled down the bond. While the water typically crashed violently below, today it was calm, almost as if it too knew we needed a moment of peace amid the chaos. We dipped below the ridgeline, and the whistling in my ears lessened. The rocky ridges blurred by, the limestone carved by the places where the ocean sprayed against it.

A few smaller beaches appeared along the way, the coastline in those spots bowed in. One was already packed with males, and still more spilled out of a tunnel in the rock that had existed long before I attended the academy.

We flew by fast enough that none of them spotted us.

"You okay?" I asked Assyria, checking her position behind me.

"Fine," she replied, but there was a slight strain to her voice.

"Not much further," I promised her.

Then, I turned my attention toward the expanse of ocean to my left, searching for the small island. It wasn't like the lush Hatha Islands in the Angel Realm. No one would want to spend more than a few hours there, in fact. But it was remote, private, and provided rare solitude. The water on the west side was calm enough to dive deep and survey the rock formations beneath the surface. And to the east, the sand was black, making it unique among the otherwise grayish brown beaches along this stretch of the Demon Realm.

Spotting it in the distance, I altered our course. The talons of my wing dipped, slicing through the salty breeze. Assyria followed, using the air displaced by my body to glide smoothly along behind me. For someone who had been suppressed and not offered ample opportunity to master her magic, she had great control of her flying abilities.

At least that's one less thing for me to feel guilty about.

A rocky outcropping emerged from the sea, one of the only flat places on the island that was good for landing. Tucking my wings close, I dropped my legs and hit the ground at a jog. Like I was snipping off a piece of thread, I released my magic. Without the weight of them competing with the ocean wind, I turned to watch Assyria.

A small divot appeared between her brows as she focused. The sun shone through the membranes as she flared her wings, highlighting veins of burgundy. Her trajectory slowed, and then, her wings disappeared altogether. The short fall sent her stumbling forward as she dropped to the island, clutching the blanket tight to her chest.

But she righted herself immediately, a whoosh of air leaving her lungs once she was stable.

"Very good," I praised.

She shot me a grin. "For once, I didn't need your help."

"No, you did not," I confirmed. "Spread the blanket out here, then fetch some sticks for a fire."

She snapped the fabric out, then disappeared toward a nearby shore where wood often drifted up. We each took to our respective tasks, me removing the packed food and arranging it, her bringing me whatever she could find. On her third trip, I decided it was enough and built a small fire.

It wasn't overly cold, especially with the cloudless sky, but extra heat was welcome.

Assyria reclined back, letting out a long sigh. "This is really nice."

"I'm glad you are enjoying my *romantic plans*," I said, striking a dagger against a rock and sending sparks scattering over the dried wood. "We haven't even had the food yet."

After the second strike, the kindling finally caught, and smoke filtered through the sticks to my nostrils. I leaned down and blew on the embers, igniting a small flame. Satisfied it would grow, I returned to the blanket and unwrapped the boiled eggs.

Assyria perked up as I put food on both our plates. With her back to the sun, the golden glow cast her in an almost ethereal air. My chest constricted at the sight.

"What?" she asked, cocking her head to the side.

I shook myself out of my reverie. "Nothing," I muttered, reaching for the butter to smear on my bread. I couldn't help but steal another glance of her in that light though.

We ate slowly, saving the moment and each other. The fire crackled as it grew, spurred on by the occasional breeze. Most of the wind was blocked by the large boulders on the east side, giving us the peace and quiet I hadn't realized I desperately needed.

"Tell me a good story of your time in Fured," she said suddenly.

I finished the wedge of hard cheese, then dusted my hands off. Bracing them both behind me, I leaned back and stretched out my legs. "Discovering this island was a happy accident. Though what prompted me to seek it out wasn't."

I paused, trying to think of something better.

"To be honest, most of my happy memories are tainted by other events that happened shortly before or after."

"Well why don't you tell me the good part and focus on that without thinking about the bad?" she offered, knocking her foot into mine.

I heaved out a sigh. "I went out flying to cool off after my father departed one time. He'd just done this," I tapped my slightly crooked nose, "and I refused to see the healers so they could rebreak and set it like they had a dozen times before. I knew he'd only do it again when he returned."

I stopped, realizing I'd started with the bad anyway.

"Go on," Assyria encouraged, sympathy dancing in her eyes.

"Anyway, if you saw on our way here, most of the soldiers go to the tunnel beach on their days off. There are a few more further away, but with the limited amount of time they are allotted, that is the easiest and quickest one to get to and from. I was so lost in thought, I flew further than I meant to, and when the fog cleared, here it was." I gestured around us to the little spot of peace.

"It was like the Giver knew what you needed and offered it to you," she murmured, chewing slowly on a flaky fruit pastry.

"Are you really going to tell me you believe that?" I questioned.

She pulled a mocking face. "I don't know. Some days I feel like I do believe, like with our mating bond and Kiira's visions. Other days, I'm not so sure, you know?" She waved the baked treat in the air as if she were trying to conjure the right words. "Like, we all know they exist. The signs, the visions, the rest. But does giving them our blood really change the outcomes of our path? Or did they put one in place from the moment we enter this world and that's that? Do we have the power to change our lives, or is that all an illusion? And are the Weaver, the Giver, the Reaper, and the Goddess the only ones out there? What if there are more that haven't revealed themselves yet?"

I listened to her questions with rapt fascination. Assyria had never been this open with me before about her beliefs, and she'd clearly put a lot of thought into them. It was a vulnerable side she'd yet to show me, and I found myself wanting to hear more of the inner workings of her mind, the deepest parts that rarely saw the surface.

"Who is to say we aren't Gods among Demons either?" I asked her, just to see what she'd say.

"Because we have power like no one else?" she clarified.

I nodded.

She shrugged. "I don't know. Maybe?" Another bite of pastry disappeared between her lips as she mulled over her thoughts. "There is one part of our faith I hope is true."

"What's that, little imposter?"

"That if a body isn't burned, their soul can't move onto another world."

A sinister smile spread across my face. "Why do you think I made the throne of bones? Why I'm going to make you one with feathers to match?"

Red crept across her cheeks, and heat swept into her eyes. "I was thinking about Vagach, but that works too."

My jaw immediately tightened at the thought of her deceased husband. That fucking slimy bastard who'd hurt her before she came to me. Every time she brought him up, this *rage* gripped me, and it wasn't entirely the bond driving it anymore. She was *mine* and no one would dare question that—or harm her—and live. I'd only feel better once I'd had a chance to pummel his corpse myself.

"Would you like to add his bones to your throne?"

Her teeth sank into her bottom lip in a move that was entirely too sexy. "Only if we can couple on it."

My cock was harder than the rock we sat on immediately, and the bond purred with wicked delight. "Fuck, Assyria, you have no idea what that just did to me."

"I think I can imagine," she replied, her voice wanton. She returned her plate to the basket, then crawled toward me. All I could think about was her lips around me while she was on all fours.

I didn't hesitate to shove all the food we still hadn't eaten to the side to make room for the way I was about to ravish her instead. "Strip for me," I ordered her, my tone leaving no room for argument.

Her fingers went to the fasteners on her jacket and popped them off one by one. She shrugged it off, revealing the thin tunic beneath. That she removed too, leaving only the bind around her breasts behind. My gaze was hungry as I raked it over every inch of her bare skin.

She stood, and I swept it over the curve of her hips, down her toned legs to her feet. She removed her boots next, leaving her toes bare and wiggling in the sun.

"Your hair too," I rasped as that golden glow highlighted her again.

A small tug sent it unraveling. She hooked her thumbs in the waist of her pants and shimmied them down her legs, leaving her barely covered. The sun kissed her skin, and jealousy reared inside me like an ugly green beast.

Then she shook her head, letting the rest of the strands fly free. The wind tangled its fingers in the dark locks and mussed them.

I reached for her, cherishing how smooth her tan skin was under my calloused hands. Tugging her closer, I brought her waist to my lips and trailed them across her stomach. My tongue flicked out to taste the salt the breeze left behind. She braced her hands on my shoulders to steady herself as I gripped the backs of her thighs, giving them a hard squeeze.

"Fuck that feels good," she moaned. I massaged again, the tension ebbing from her. With my teeth, I hooked the soft fabric covering her core and dragged it down. When it reached my hands, I rolled them the rest of the way and helped her step out of them.

When I looked up, our gazes clashed like two stars. Yet instead of the animosity we'd once held, only one endless, vibrant emotion passed between us: love.

I pressed a kiss just above her clit, savoring the heat of her body, the smell of her arousal, the way she responded to my touch.

I'd always known Assyria was the type of female I could crave if I let myself; yet now that I had, no amount of her would ever leave me satisfied. Fuck, I'd do anything for her, and I'd never seen myself as that type of male.

The depth of my love for her should have frightened me; after all, it was supposed to be a weakness, a liability. But now? It was the blade I'd carry into battle. It was what made me want to finish this fucking war once and for all so I could spend every day like this, with her.

"I love you, Assyria," I murmured, brushing my lips over her upper legs before pushing them apart.

"And I love you, Rokath," she replied, kneading my shoulders. I let out a groan of my own. Shadows spooled from my hands, wrapping her skin in a smoky sheet. Another shiver wracked her frame as I snaked them beneath the bind around her breasts and removed it. When it dropped to the ground, my mate was completely bare for me.

I never wanted her any other way.

Except for when other people were around.

Because she belonged only to me: before, now, and forever.

I eased backward, using my magic to bring Assyria with me until she was positioned over my face. A small whimper escaped her as I bathed her arms and torso in ebony, holding her exactly where I wanted her.

We might have been eating before, but now I was going to *feast.*

I lowered her until my beard brushed the insides of her thighs, and all I could taste, all I could smell, was her. Flattening my tongue, I ran it along the length of her, drawing another delicious sound from her throat.

"Rokath," she groaned, her head tipping back. The sun gilded her frame. One reverent moment passed as I drank in the sight.

But I could wait no longer to taste her. My tongue speared inside her, and I groaned as her arousal flooded my mouth. Focusing on my power and the divinity of her simultaneously was a monumental task, but as her sounds grew louder and more desperate, my actions became a well-honed attack.

She was going to drown me in her release before I was finished with her.

Alternating between fucking her with my tongue and swirling it around her clit, I gave her everything she wanted and more. Her hips bucked, and I growled against her pussy. *"Ride my face, Assyria. Make yourself come,"* I commanded into her mind.

Sucking her pretty lips into my mouth, I tore more mewls from her throat. Then, my tongue sank into her core again. She rocked on top of me, grinding into my face.

"That's it, little imposter. Keep going."

She worked faster, and I gripped harder, sinking deeper into her cunt. My cock strained against my pants, begging for a reprieve from the ache of its confines.

The moment she came on my face, I was going to bury myself so fucking deep inside her.

Her walls fluttered, and I knew she was close. *"You want an orgasm? Fucking take it from me. Give me your fire. Show me how you shatter."*

I dug my fingers into her hips, giving her a nip of pain to heighten her pleasure. She leaned backward, supported by ebony strands, and deepened the angle. My hand went to her stomach and pressed, chasing the perfect position to unravel her.

"Fuck, the way your beard feels between my thighs," she moaned, hips rocking faster.

I licked, sucked, fucked her with my tongue like her release would save my life. *"Come for me like you were made for it. Scream my name like you forgot every other word. Let all the worlds know who you belong to."*

A sharp breath slipped past her lips. Her lashes fluttered against her cheeks. And then, she exploded. Like a cracking whip, her spine arched and flattened. Her core clenched over my tongue, and then her release flooded my mouth. I groaned, drinking it down like a male dying of thirst.

I did not relent, even as she screamed, pleaded for me to stop. I wanted every last fucking drop. Only when I had my fill did I release my magic and shift her off my face. I wasted no time pulling her into my lap. She straddled me, completely bare while I was still fully clothed.

I captured her mouth in a passionate kiss, letting her taste herself on my tongue.

"I need this off," she spoke into my mind, gripping my tunic.

"Then take it off," I told her. She wasted no time undoing the buttons and shoving it over my shoulders. The heat of the sun was immediate on my skin, but it was nothing compared to the embers radiating off my mate.

I broke our kiss only long enough to kick off my boots and remove my pants. Assyria licked her lips when she saw just how fucking hard I was for her. The tip of my dick dripped onto the blanket as I settled back down. Then, she was in my lap again and I was lining myself with her entrance. She looked down, watching with me as our bodies became one.

One like our souls. One like our lives. One like our bond.

We let out a groan together. "You're so fucking tight. Made for me," I managed to grind out.

"You're so thick," she whimpered as I pushed further.

I captured her waist to ensure she was where I wanted her. "You get me so fucking hard when you challenge me." I thrust upward, sinking all the way in before withdrawing.

Assyria's mouth dropped open in the most delicious O. I stuck my fingers in her mouth and pushed on her bottom teeth to keep it open. "I hate it and I love it. I want you to obey and I want you to fight. You drive me absolutely insane."

She tried to close her mouth, but I pressed harder. Then, I thrust upward again, our skin slapping. "Just like that."

Fire ignited in her eyes, and then she dug her nails into my chest and *raked*. I thickened even more inside her.

"You want me to fight? Then give me a fair chance," she pushed into my mind.

A dark rumble, like an ominous thumber, escaped my chest. "Done."

I released her mouth at the same time as I smashed her down on my dick. A small scream ripped from her throat as I hit the deepest part of her. Then, she shoved at my shoulders.

My arms tightened, holding her in place. Wetness dripped down my balls and slicked my groin. Her teeth sank into her bottom lip as I tugged her breasts flush with my chest and raked my nose down the side of her neck. "Are you going to fight me or not?"

A whimper escaped her, and for a moment, I thought she'd given in.

Until a void of obsidian engulfed us, and suddenly, I was flat on my back on the blanket with Assyria towering over me.

"You have no idea what you just started," I growled as she used her magic to pin me.

"Guess you should show me," she teased. Her molten pupils captured me like nothing else could. The fact that she liked this, wanted this? Just further confirmation our bond was blessed.

Pitch black desire ravaged the space between us as I flashed her image after image of what I planned on doing to her once I conquered her. Her legs visibly pressed together.

"But you can't do any of that if you can't escape my magic," she purred, a sly grin spreading across her face.

"Oh, little imposter, you really have no idea," I replied. A heartbeat passed, and smoky strands of my power blazed my skin, battling against hers. Her eyes widened as I shattered the restraints like they were nothing more than glass and rose to my feet. We faced off, black swirling around us, even wilder than our desire.

I lashed out with mine, intending to capture her and pin her against the rocks. But she'd been training hard and blocked my attack with a slash of her magic. My cock *throbbed*. "Fuck, this is so much better than the first time you attempted to subdue me with your power. This time, the victory will be that much sweeter."

"Who says you'll win?" she quipped. Then, she struck, using multiple wisps to divert my attention. When one wrapped around my wrist, my shadows immediately responded, twining with hers. Too late, she realized she wouldn't be able to untangle the onyx threads.

With a sinister chuckle, I tugged her forward, then directed her to her knees. She struggled for a moment before accepting defeat. Disappointment twinged in my chest. Until a smoky stream launched at my feet. I leaped into the air, calling on my wings. Her attack sailed beneath me, and I released my hold on her.

Her wings spouted from her back, and she joined me in the sky. She jerked to the right, drawing a reaction from me, before sailing past on my left. Deeper into the island she flew, her taunting snicker carrying on the wind.

A chase through the air?

My cock *wept* for it.

I shot after her. She banked left, I cut her off. She went up, and I stalked her there, reaching for her ankle. Her wings snapped shut, and I fell right after her, harder and faster than I'd fallen in love with her.

A wild laugh burst from her as she dove back toward the blanket. Throwing out a hand, I cast a net of obsidian mere feet in front of her, tangling her in the mess until I was ready to release her.

Wicked ecstasy heated my blood as I hovered over her, trying to decide what I wanted to do next. With a wave of my hand, the tendrils dissipated, and I caught her from behind, trapping her wings against her body.

Rearing back, I straightened so we were gazing out over the deep blue ocean. A small whimper escaped her as I dropped my hand to her low belly and brushed against her clit. The other hand wrapped around her throat and cut off the barest hint of air. Pinned against me like this, she was forced to rely on me to keep us aloft. "Got you, little imposter. Now it's time to make you submit."

I raked my teeth along the ridge of her wings while I dipped between her legs. "Fuck, you are soaked," I groaned. It took no effort to slide them inside her. "Did you like fighting me until I caught you?"

She nodded around my hand. I drove the heel of my palm into her clit and curled my fingers against her walls. We still hovered in the air, a precarious drop below us, and yet Assyria made no protest about her position.

The absolute trust she placed in me healed a fractured piece of my soul.

After the conversations with Xannirin, how the Angels had kidnapped her, how an assassin had come for her, it was exactly what I needed. How she always knew that, always sensed that, was beyond me, but I was so fucking glad for it.

Angling my hand, I dipped deeper, ground harder, into my mate. More wetness gushed over my palm as I stroked the spot she loved the most. The sound of her slickness was louder than the beat of my wings through the air.

Again I dragged the sharp points of my teeth along her wing, eliciting a shiver. Pebbles broke out across her skin as I licked along the length of her neck. "Oh, don't stop," she moaned. "I didn't know it could even be like this."

I fucked her harder with my hand. "I can't wait to show you every single way it's possible for you to feel pleasure. We have millenia more to explore every dark desire."

"Please," she begged, my fingers working faster. "Please, Rokath, more."

A long, low groan ripped through me. "I love when you beg. Come for me like this, and then I'll make you see new worlds with my cock."

"Okay," she rasped, tipping her head back and giving me better access to her neck.

"That's my good mate," I praised, kissing along its length. When I got to the point where her pulse fluttered, I bit. Her walls clenched around me. I licked the spot to soothe the ache.

"Rokath, oh I'm going to—"

The cry that fled her lips was better than any sound an Angel had made as I slaughtered them.

Her body trembled. She surrendered further to my hold. The inviolable faith she offered me filled me with primal delight. My dick strained against her backside as she worked through the aftershocks of her orgasm. As she came down, so too did I lower us. I laid her out on the blanket again like my own personal feast.

Fisting myself, I spread my own arousal along my length—not that I needed it. Assyria sat up on her elbows and dropped her knees to the side, showing me exactly what I'd done to her. Her release slicked her thighs, glistening in the sun. I swiped two fingers through it and sucked them into my mouth. I did it again and shoved them into Assyria's next. Dragging her lips open again, I positioned myself to enter her cunt. The bottom row of her teeth dug into my fingers, and yet she let me hold her there too.

"I am going to take you, hard, because fuck, you are perfection and I cannot wait any longer to feel you come undone around my cock," I told her. Her eyes darkened, and she gave a small nod—as much of one as my grip on her would allow.

I guided her leg open wider, and then, I *thrust.*

Wetness gushed between us as I slid all the way to the hilt. I adjusted her leg higher, using it to hold her in place while I pounded into her over and over. Her breasts bounced, her nipples like the sharp peaks surrounding Uzhhorod. Sweat broke out along both our skin as the heat of the sun beat down on us.

And still, we did not break eye contact. Burgundy locked with burgundy, soul bound to soul, we were one, we were whole, we were immortal. *"My perfect mate,"* I relayed down our mental connection.

She didn't need to say anything back for me to know she felt the same. The bond thrummed with the force of our adoration, stronger than any metal we could forge for war. Stronger than the stones that held the mountains across the spine of our continent. Stronger than any belief could ever be.

Because we were *certain.* In this world and in all the rest.

I quickened my pace, my dick aching with how much I fucking craved Assyria. She arched her back, pressing into me as much as I pressed into her. "That's it, little imposter. Show me how much you love my cock."

Her eyes fluttered as I hit the spot deep inside that sent her walls clenching around me. Drool spilled out of both sides of her mouth, and her jaw hung open in a silent scream as she closed in on her release. "You're going to come so fucking hard for me, aren't you?"

She barely managed to nod, her fingers scrambling for purchase on the blanket beneath us. I removed mine from her mouth, then gripped either side of her jaw to hold it open. She gasped, half-lidded eyes snapping open.

"Stick out your tongue," I commanded her.

She did immediately, curiosity and anguish tumbling down our bond as I slowed my pace. A smirk curved my lips. I had her right where I wanted her.

So I spit.

Her core gripped me like a vise, making stars dot my vision. Our mouths battled as I crashed my lips against hers, desperate to taste her. I fucked hard into her again, tearing a whimper from her throat.

"Rokath," she panted, breaking our kiss. Her nails clawed my back, leaving stinging gouges as sweat spilled across them. "Fuck, do that again."

I hit that deep spot and stilled, circling my hips. "Did you like that, Assyria?" I murmured darkly in her ear. She shivered beneath me.

"Yes," she admitted, rolling her lower back so her clit brushed against my stomach.

I hiked her legs to my shoulders, pinning her firmly against the ground. The angle gave me the perfect opportunity to do exactly as she asked. "Open for me."

She did, and I grabbed her jaw and spit again. I didn't let go as I picked up a relentless pace, ecstasy crashing down our bond like the waves did against the shores of the island.

Her eyes fluttered again, those dark lashes fanning against her cheekbones. "Oh, I think I'm–" she started, but a raw scream cut her off. Pleasure shattered through her, and her walls clenched my cock so tight she yanked me right into ecstasy with her.

My balls tightened, and I was done, coming inside her for the first time. I couldn't have pulled out if I wanted to from the force of our combined orgasm. We floated together, higher than the birds over the seas. Still moving. Still panting. Still one.

We remained locked as we floated down. I curved down and kissed her again, first on the lips, then on the forehead. Her racing heart beat against mine. I brushed sweaty strands of hair out of her face, drinking in the rosy flush of her skin. Leaning back, I eased her legs off my chest, massaging them gently after straining her into the difficult position. "Thank you."

"For what?" she murmured back, her expression serene.

"For trusting me to take care of you."

"You always will," she said, her tone soft and filled with adoration. She reached for my forearm and gave it a reassuring squeeze.

Dragging in a breath, I dove into my magic and called my wings back. Then I hooked my arms under her waist and hoisted her off the ground. With a groan, I slid out of her at last, wetness gushing from between us and dripping onto the blanket. She laughed and shook her head. "Guess you'll be needing a new one of those."

"Fuck it," I said, and in a few wingbeats, we were airborne and headed to the spot on the beach that was safe enough to swim.

The plush sand sank between my toes as we landed. Assyria

wiggled hers in it when I set her down. Hand in hand, we made our way to the water. "This might be a little cold."

A small, shocked laugh escaped her as the tide lapped at our legs. She offered me a sheepish grin. "It's pretty cold."

"Then I'll hold you close," I murmured, tugging her against my chest. She hissed again, but soon she relaxed into me as we waded deeper.

We didn't have to go far for the water to be up to Assyria's waist. Gently, I reached between her thighs, and she sucked in a sharp breath. "What are you doing?"

"Washing you?" I questioned, like it wasn't obvious.

"Oh, I thought you were doing something else," she giggled, looking up at me.

"Well, I will be touching you there," I grumbled, beginning to wipe away what clung to her thighs. "But not for that reason. I came inside you, and I don't want you to fear falling pregnant when I know that's not something you want."

Tears welled in her eyes, and she blinked rapidly to clear them. "You remembered that?"

"Of course I did," I told her, opening her so I could wash the remnants of me away. "That's why I've never come inside you before. I wanted to respect your wishes, not to force something else on you that you didn't want."

"I thought it was because you also didn't want them," she said, her voice raspy. Her throat worked, drawing my attention.

"That was part of it. But that was not the main reason." I spun her, then dropped lower in the water to ensure that I cleaned her out as much as I could for the time being. "When we return, I have something else I can give you too."

"Thank you," she whispered, cupping my face and running her thumbs over my beard.

A wave came in, crashing against us, and she fell into my arms. I kissed her again, long, languid, like we had all the time in the world. When we finally broke apart, I asked her, "Do you want to eat or swim?"

"Swim," she pronounced immediately, ducking out of my grip. In a flash, she disappeared beneath the water, coming up soaked. Pebbles dotted her skin as she surfaced again, but she sported a wide, unguarded smile. "Now that that's over with, let's go."

Before I could say anything, she dove, splashing as she broke through an oncoming wave. I shook my head and followed.

Our bond would always lead me straight to her, but I never wanted her to be more than a dozen paces from my side again.

As our time on the island drew to a close, I packed up our belongings, ruined blanket and all, and we flew back to the military academy close enough that the edges of our wings brushed. We landed with ease on the roof of my tower, descending the stairs in a post bliss haze. But when I opened the secret door, I stopped dead in my tracks, dread filling my chest.

Because Kiira sat on one of the leather couches, head in her hands.

Sobbing.

31

R☠KATH

"Kiira, what's wrong?" Assyria asked, squeezing by me and racing to my cousin's side. I dropped the basket and blanket on a nearby table, studying the females with sharp, coiled focus.

She sniffed and dried her eyes on her sleeves, looking between us both. "I came as soon as I could."

"Is it Rapp?" I asked, immediately thinking the worst. He'd been doing so much better...

"Fates, no," she shook her head forcefully. The vise around my chest loosened immediately. "Actually, he would have come with me had he been able to make the climb."

I approached slowly, easing my weight onto the seat opposite hers. "Then what is this about? The assassination attempt? Has Xannirin done something?" Those were the only other logical explanations for her level of distress.

Her lower lip trembled, and Assyria threw her arms around Kiira, holding her close. My cousin leaned her head on Assyria's shoulder, soaking in the comfort my mate offered her. "The Fates offered me another prophecy."

My blood turned to ice. Assyria went utterly still, save for her attention snapping to me like she was searching for some sort of reassurance. "What happened?" My tone was flat, emotionless, as I braced for the inevitable bad news.

Kiira swallowed hard, straightening. "It's nothing to worry about. Well, unless..."

"Unless what?" I prodded, heart hammering against my ribs. Kiira needed to speak, right fucking then.

"Unless they are unreliable now," she said, her voice barely more than a whisper.

"I'm sure that's not true," Assyria tried to soothe her, but Kiira shook her head.

"I saw *you*," she said to my mate. "For the first time, so clearly. I wanted to be sure before I told anyone..."

"When did you have this vision, Kiira?" I asked, neck growing hot. Before, Kiira had only had glimpses of my mate. The images she'd drawn of Assyria's eyes flashed through my mind, seared there as they had been from the moment I'd gripped one in my hand.

"Before we left Uzhhorod," she admitted quietly, looking down at her ringed hands.

"It's been over a week since you arrived. Why didn't you tell me sooner?" I growled.

Assyria pierced me with a sharp look, squeezing Kiira tighter. *"Can't you see she's upset?"* she snapped down our bond. *"Maybe be a little nicer and let her speak."*

I grumbled but stood down.

"So what did you see of me?" Assyria asked, her tone soft and guiding.

Kiira lifted her gaze to meet mine as if she were pleading with me to understand. "The first glimpse I had of you winning, Rokath, you carried Zaph and Ishim's heads through the streets of Sivy. Now, though, Assyria is by your side when it happens. And you're carrying Koron Stadiel's head."

All air fled my lungs. For a moment, all I could do was blink. "What? The outcome completely changed?"

Kiira's teeth dug into her bottom lip. "Yes."

"I'm confused. Is that not how Sight works?" Assyria clarified, brows dipping together.

"When Kiira receives one, they always come to pass in exactly that way. She's never had a repeated one, or one that changes later. Unless I'm mistaken?" I offered my cousin a chance to clarify.

She shook her head. "Never until now."

"When *exactly* did you have this vision?" I repeated the question, wondering if she'd seen it before or after Assyria's kidnapping. If she'd seen it before...

"About a week before I received your letter."

The snake crushing my chest eased. I hadn't realized just how tense I'd become over the thought that I could have acted differently, slaughtered Zaph in that moment instead of allowing him to butcher my army.

"So after Rokath chose me over the soldiers," Assyria murmured, her mind walking along the same path as mine.

"If that is the timing, then I think it was a test for you, Rokath," Kiira said, finally emerging from her slumped, defeated posture. "The Fates rarely weave a fork in our paths. Determining which direction to take might incur a cost—or gift—we can't foresee. To me, it seems that by choosing Assyria, you changed the future of your victory."

I didn't know whether to feel relief or dread. To know that even an innocuous choice could carry a massive consequence curled unease in my gut. Would Kiira's new prophecy alter the timing of our victory too? Extend our war into years to come or shorten it to our next assault?

Yet one thing was certain: if I ever saw Zaph again, I would not have to hold back. He would fucking die, slowly, painfully, *excruciatingly*, and I'd savor the entire experience.

"What else is there?" Assyria asked.

I blinked, tearing myself away from my riot of thoughts.

My cousin offered her a sad half-smile. "A great sacrifice will have to be made."

I opened my mouth to speak, but Kiira held up a hand. "I know nothing of what the sacrifice is. In my vision, I was watching you approach, Assyria by your side, and an army of males and females was at your back. Rapp and Xannirin were there too. But one word rang out loud and clear, over and over and over."

"Sacrifice," Assyria murmured.

Ice slithered down my spine at the word.

Kiira exhaled, shaky and slow. "I had this immense chill, like I was standing atop the glaciers in the Skala Mountains, despite being in the heart of the Eső Forest. It was one of the most vivid visions I've ever had, if not the most vivid."

"And it came with far more clarity than the others you had of Assyria?" I questioned. I had to be clear in my understanding. It was the only way to protect the Demons.

"To this day, I don't remember the drawings or anything else you spoke of about her. When I try to think about it, all I see are glimpses of her eyes," Kiira said, attention dancing over my mate with overt interest.

"Maybe that's because when I left Stryi, I was using my magic all hours of the day?" she suggested. Absently, she twisted her mother's ring around her finger.

Kiira lifted a shoulder and let it drop. "Perhaps. We'll never know for certain."

Frustration clawed up my spine, and I curled my fingers into a fist, the bite of pain grounding me. "How will we know anything for certain now that we know your visions can change?"

Silence stretched between us for a long moment as Kiira weighed my words. My cousin tugged on the ends of her hair, running her fingers along the dark length as she so often did when she was deep in thought.

"Look for major turning points and think them through carefully," Kiira offered finally. "If the Fates are truly testing us, perhaps they need to know we can make good decisions on our own without their interference."

"What if they never predetermined our paths in the first place?" Assyria challenged, embers burning in her eyes. "What if life is always a series of choices, and so far, the three of you have always made the one that leads you to the visions you had?"

She had a point. We may have purported ourselves as Gods, but no one truly knew the workings of our deities. That was where the power of belief entered, and that power was one we'd endlessly exploited to serve our needs in shaping society. After all, if the populace believed it to be true, if we had the claws of fear sunk deep into their hearts, they were like sheep— easy to herd in whichever direction we wanted.

"After all, no matter how much we pray and spill our blood, bad things still happen to us." Assyria uncrossed her arms and leaned forward. "We can say it's the Reaper cursing us, but for what? Why would they choose to have their faithful suffer?"

"These are all questions many have struggled with for a long time," Kiira told her, reaching out and taking her hands. "So it is okay if you still harbor them. Explore them and find meaning in your suffering. It is what I had to do in my position."

The sight twisted something in my chest—something soft and rare that felt a lot like what a family should be.

"Have you told anyone else about this yet?" I asked her, redirecting the conversation to the matter at hand.

"Only Rapp. He was the one who encouraged me to tell you both right away," she sighed, looking at her hands once again. She fiddled with a diamond band, the stones dancing in the sunlight.

At least she hadn't told Xannirin before anyone else. He could have used it as leverage. I suspected that was why she hadn't, given that as much as we'd spoken, he still hadn't acquiesced to the bare minimum of allowing females into the army.

"It's time we force Xannirin to listen. To concede to what is right," I growled, my fingers flexing at my sides. "He has questions to answer. Accountability to take. And I'm fucking tired of his games."

"Do you think he was behind the assassin?" Kiira asked, sucking in a sharp breath.

"I can't deny that he has some motive. And his behavior has been suspicious since then. Since arriving, really. But with new information, we can't wait for him to stop being such a prick. We need to confront him."

Kiira pressed her lips together but nodded. "The four of us. Assyria needs to be there too."

My mate wrapped her arms around my cousin. "Thank you."

Kiira hugged her back. "It is what is right. You have been elevated to our status. You deserve your place among us."

"Then it's decided. Tomorrow, we will break down his door if he won't let us in. We'll do whatever it takes to learn the truth behind the assassination attempt, to bend him to the future," I pronounced. Yet even as determination heated my veins, doubt crept in. What would happen if Xannirin dug in his heels? What would I have to do if he was the one who tried to kill my mate?

I'd never feared wielding authority. Leading the army was what I had been born to do. But ruling? Being the Kral? I wanted nothing less.

So when Kiira finally departed, Assyria looped her arms around my torso and squeezed hard. But as I held Assyria close, a word from Kiira's vision echoed through me.

Sacrifice.

And I couldn't help but wonder which one of us the Fates would choose.

32

ASSYRIA

"Open the fucking door," Rokath growled, slamming his fist against the heavy wood. Behind me, Kiira shifted from foot to foot. The Kral's Guard had taken one look at Rokath's furious expression and wisely positioned themselves on the floor below us, out of the way of his wrath.

Still, Xannirin did not answer. Not so much as a sound drifted beneath the door. "I know you are in there. You have three seconds to let us in before I shatter this wood."

Rokath never made idle threats.

"One," he started counting like Xannirin was a fucking child.

Which, currently, he was acting like a very spoiled one.

"Two," Rokath pronounced, his tone threaded with violence. Before he opened his mouth to utter three, the door flew open, exposing the Kral of the Demons.

Dressed in a smart tunic and pants, rings glinting on his fingers, he sneered at us. "What do you want?"

The utter exasperation in his tone very much matched the one I wanted to express with him. Rokath didn't respond, merely shouldered past his cousin, leaving space for Kiira and I to enter in his wake. I didn't apologize as I *accidentally* jostled his torso as I passed.

Kiira, unfortunately, appeared more apologetic.

"What is the meaning of this?" Xannirin asked, slamming the door shut and spinning on my mate.

"You haven't been available for days," Rokath stated, leaning against the window and crossing his arms over his broad chest. Kiira and I took a seat on a plush couch between the two males.

I honestly couldn't understand Xannirin's open hostility. I regarded him warily as he took a step closer to Rokath. The tiny garnet on my ring grounded me amid the tempest brewing in the room as I fiddled with it.

No one spoke. Heated glances volleyed back and forth.

Who would be the first to crack?

"First, I have one question for you, Xannirin," Rokath said, each word spoken slowly as if he were attempting to convey the seriousness of what would follow.

The Kral raised a skeptical brow. His hair was tied neatly back, not a single strand out of place. His beard appeared recently sheared, revealing his carved jaw. It was as if he wanted to show the world how put together he was when everything else was falling apart around him.

"What is that?" he drawled as if he were bored with our appearance.

Rokath paused, and my heart raced against my ribs. Every muscle in my body tensed, even as I leaned forward ever so slightly, waiting for him to speak. Kiira did too.

"Did you hire someone to kill Assyria and Kiira?"

The question cracked the air like a stone through stained glass.

Xannirin didn't even blink. Didn't even hesitate to reply. His expression remained perfectly placid. "No."

"Let me rephrase." Darkness stained Rokath's expression as he glared at his cousin. "Did you arrange for, in any way, someone to attack Assyria?"

The Kral's attention flicked to Kiira for the span of a heartbeat before returning to my mate. "No."

Rokath's fingers dug into his biceps. "Then why don't I believe you?"

"That is your problem, not mine," Xannirin shot back, his shoulders rising.

"You would lie to us? After everything?" Kiira snapped, surging to her feet.

Xannirin's countenance softened as he faced her. "I would never lie to you."

"But you would to Rokath?" she challenged, undeterred by the smooth way he crafted his words.

A muscle feathered in his jaw, and he took a step toward her. "Kiira…"

Rage engulfed our bond in a fiery inferno. A look of horror crossed Kiira's face. My brows shot up my forehead.

Clutching her chest, the High Priestess shrank away from her Kral. "No, you don't get to 'Kiira' me. Not now. Speak the truth."

Rokath shifted off the wall, vibrating with barely-restrained fury. Xannirin sliced his attention to my mate. "There is a group of people who are unhappy that females are among them now. I merely provided them with some useful information."

A roar shook me to my core as Rokath lunged for his cousin. Ebony exploded from both of them, sending vases crashing to the ground. I leaped to my feet, calling on my own magic, ready to assist my mate.

The onyx cloud cleared for a blink, revealing Xannirin

swiping a dagger toward Rokath's thigh. My mate kicked his hand, sending the blade clattering away. They collided in a tangle of limbs, lost to the void of power again.

"We have to do something, they're going to kill each other!" I snapped at Kiira.

Shadow unfurled from her hands, and she wielded each thick whip with expert precision. Snapping it into the darkness, she removed some of the smoky air. Rokath had Xannirin on his stomach, and my mate hooked an arm beneath the Kral's chin. Xannirin's face ripened to a rich shade of red.

"You can't kill him!" I screamed, barging forward. If he did, Rokath would become Kral, and he didn't want that. The idea had shaken him so much that he hadn't slept at all last night. As much as I wanted retribution for Xannirin's actions, I didn't want it to come at my mate's expense.

With a hard shove, I knocked Rokath and Xannirin over. They broke apart like shards of obsidian thrown against the ground, and I had to leap into the air to clear their jagged strikes. Yet neither were deterred from their savage barrage.

"Listen to your mate!" Kiira shouted at Rokath, magic spooling around her and forcing back her cousins' powers.

But both males were too far gone in their fury to hear us. Diving into the well of magic in my chest, I yanked with all my might on our bond. Still, they fought, blood flying as they exchanged bone-jarring blows.

With a snarl, Rokath punched Xannirin in the gut, bowing his frame. He stumbled back, doubled over and wheezing. My mate wasted no time in taking him to the ground. Their collision quaked the floor, and I pitched to the side, managing to catch myself on a cracked wooden side table.

A bronze blade flashed as Rokath drew it overhead. "Stop!" I screamed, one last desperate attempt to change his fate.

But he drove it down.

"I was raped by Ollmund Varrir!" Kiira yelled. Her voice fractured on her attacker's name.

Rokath halted with the dagger mere inches from Xannirin's neck. The air in the room froze over. Neither male breathed as they gaped at their cousin.

"What did you say?" Rokath whispered, and that was far more terrifying than any growl or snarl I'd ever received from him.

I whipped my head to her, watching as her face crumpled.

"Ollmund Varrir raped me."

I ached to go to her, to comfort her once again. Yet I didn't dare move with the males still on the precipice of violence.

The blade clattered against the stone as Rokath's hand slackened. His haunted expression seared into my memory as he rose off Xannirin, his attention wholly on Kiira. The Kral looked as horror-struck as his cousin. That hateful, disdainful sneer completely melted and was replaced by something shattered. He stumbled to his feet, wiping his bloody face on his tunic.

"When?" Rokath gritted out.

This time, I did move toward Kiira, wrapping my arms around her and holding her tight. I'd protect her, even if these two idiots didn't.

"He came to Varbad not long after you left, attempting to influence me to secure Orith a match with you, since it is known that I have sway over you, Rokath. When I told him no–" She shuddered, and I kept my grip, letting her know I was there. That he wasn't moments from touching her again. "He put something in my wine while we were speaking. I didn't even notice."

"He's a corpse the moment I lay eyes on him again," Rokath snarled, grief and rage scorching down our bond. "I have half a mind to return to Uzhhorod this very minute and flay the skin from his bones."

"Why didn't you tell me?" Xannirin asked, his face ashen. "Kiira, I would have had him removed immediately."

She cocked her head as she stared him down. The moment of truth had arrived—the moment Kiira had feared.

"Would you have? With how much influence he has over the other nobles? With how they already whispered of losing this war? He would have only stoked the flames of their fears. Plus, no one cares when a female is raped. It would have been my word against his."

"I believe you, Kiira. I would have believed you then!" Xannirin exclaimed, raking his hands through his long hair and squeezing. "Fuck!"

I watched the Kral crumble to pieces. Yet Kiira held strong, which made me all the more furious at Xannirin's behavior. And this whole Fates' damned situation. "This realm must fucking change," I snapped. "Kiira wouldn't have suffered this. Fuck, *I* wouldn't have suffered this if you hadn't decided what our lives were allowed to be! If you hadn't shrouded us and called it safety. If you hadn't taught males to see us as property, then punished us for the wounds they inflicted."

Venom spit in each word. My chest heaved from the vehemence of my soliloquy. "Females are forced into beds with lecherous males, into marriages we didn't choose, into bearing children we didn't ask for, and when we resist, we're branded fallen—discarded, disavowed, destroyed. The silence we're made to endure is *oppressive*. Kiira was born noble, and I was elevated through marriage, but it made no difference. We are still treated like breeding pets—collared by *your* version of faith, paraded for others approval, leashed to the egos of the males who claimed us."

I released Kiira and stalked toward the fucking Kral. "You

didn't simply veil our bodies. You taught the world to call our submission sacred."

Xannirin, to my shock, met my furious gaze with what looked a lot like regret.

Rokath spoke again, his gravelly voice scarcely louder than a whisper. "We went too far. Do you realize the pressure you put on me too? Do you understand everything I have sacrificed to ensure the Angels haven't advanced past Ustlyak into Demon territory?"

Xannirin dragged his attention to my mate, as did the rest of us. "Clearly not." The words were sharper than a blade. And there was the Kral I knew. "Since you let *fifty thousand* soldiers die for Assyria. Surely what's so special about her is not that she is here to tell us we need to change society? How fucking useless is that. I thought she'd at least be some sort of weapon to help you win. Instead, she's helping us lose."

Kiira snapped first, her voice cutting through before Rokath or I could react. "Watch how you speak about our cousin's *mate*. If you don't stop with your horseshit, I will walk out of here and tell the world what we did, Xannirin. It's becoming apparent that you have no respect for females any longer, and I will not stand for it."

His mouth thinned as he glared at all of us. "I am not okay with this."

"Then let me show you what other suffering has happened in your name, and maybe you can appreciate for a mere fucking second, what we've done for you." Rokath unbuttoned his tunic and stripped it from his body. Tossing it on the floor, he turned and flashed scars I knew all too well.

"Here," he pointed to a spot on his ribs inked more heavily than others, "is where I took an arrow. It nearly hit my lungs. I fought for three hours with it embedded in my side. And here," he gave us his back and pointed to a spot just above his hip bone, "an Angel stuck a dagger as I fought off four more in front of me."

Sorrow sank into my bones as Rokath detailed the myriad of ways he'd brushed death. Of course, I'd known he never held back from the fighting, but this?

This slashed my heart in an entirely new way.

Rokath flipped his palms up and shoved them outward, one for Xannirin and the other for Kiira, to see. A white scar from each of the stakes Zaph put through them decorated the centers. Kiira sucked in a breath and leaned forward. Tentatively, she reached for one, tracing a finger over the puckered skin.

"Zaph staked me to the ground while he slaughtered all my soldiers. Their screams echo in my dreams when I manage to sleep. For years, my life has been nothing but death and blood. My body, my mind, my soul have absorbed it all and channeled it into what I do best: killing. The rage inside of me still burns. But I want you to fucking acknowledge for once what I do for you, Xannirin," he bit out, curling his fingers into his palms and hiding the scar. "And don't you *dare* tell me I am incapable of protecting my mate. Or that I shouldn't spare a second for her. And if you ever deign to suggest to others a location where she is vulnerable, I will have your balls."

Xannirin exhaled, long and slow. The tension bled from his shoulders as he looked between the three of us.

Is he finally seeing reason?

He opened his mouth to speak, then closed it again. A hand smoothed back his tangled hair, and he worked the leather from its lengths. No one spoke as he fixed it again. "I never should have said that, Rokath. I am sorry. So fucking sorry. To you and to Kiira." He paused, his throat working while she held her chin high. "I cannot undo what has happened to you, Kiira. But I can ensure it doesn't happen again in the future. And to you, Assyria. I have treated you terribly when I should have welcomed you into House Vrak."

My brows shot up my forehead at his almost-apology.

"You were right, Rokath." His voice was hoarse and no louder than a whisper. "This all spiraled out of control because of my ambition. But you can't say it's the only thing that started it. Our fathers couldn't have protected us like you have."

Silence reigned among us for many minutes. An inferno of emotion twisted inside Rokath at Xannirin's acknowledgement. I studied my mate, trying to discern exactly what those words had brought up in him.

"I'll make an appearance tomorrow during training hours and declare my support for the integration."

At Xannirin's promise, my jaw nearly hit the floor. Kiira and I exchanged a look of surprise.

"Afterward, I will depart for Uzhhorod, and I will find other powerful females for your army, Rokath."

I could only blink at the Kral.

Rokath was less convinced, his jaw still clenched. "Will you?"

Xannirin nodded, opening his arms and letting them hang by his sides. "Aye. I have heard you all."

A beat passed, and then Kiira spoke. "I will stay behind once you go. I am tired of pretending to be the most pious female in the whole Demon Realm. I need a break."

Xannirin nodded. "Remain here. I will cover for you when I return to Uzhhorod. But I do need to arrive with new stories in hand. You are the expert at this, Kiira. I trust your judgement."

I scrutinized the Kral. His words, his posture, all of it seemed sincere. And yet I couldn't shake this sick feeling in my stomach when I looked at him.

"We have been, and always will be a team," Kiira added, glaring at him as if she too struggled to believe his words. "You just need to see all of it again, Xannirin. You drifted too far out on your own without appreciating everything we did in your name."

"You're right," he told her. "I won't let that happen again. We can do anything so long as we do it together."

"Aye," Rokath affirmed, though he regarded the Kral with wariness.

"Why don't we sit now that cooler heads are prevailing and speak of what we need to do next?" Kiira suggested. Tension still hung like a thick fog in the air, but the four of us managed to settle around an expansive dining table off to one side without killing each other.

Honestly, Kiira's admission had thrown a bucket of ice water over these two hot-headed males. Their sober expressions as they cleaned their faces spoke to how deeply they cared for their cousin.

"If I might make a suggestion," Rokath started, shifting in his seat. "To sell the idea to the nobles of integrating the army, we can say the best fuck you to the Angels is to allow our powerful magic-wielding females to overwhelm them on the battlefield. Since so many already believe them to be second-class citizens, it will stroke the egos of many Nayúr."

Xannirin opened his mouth to speak, then closed it again. Rokath's satisfaction at rendering his cousin speechless drifted down our bond. I smothered a smug expression.

"Let me put it this way. If we let them fight too, we show the Angels just how powerful we really are, that we don't need males to defeat all their forces. We raze our way through the northern part of their realm, setting each city ablaze."

Rokath paused, shooting me a wink. I sent him a devious grin back. Oh, I really liked his reasoning here. Even if Xannirin wanted to refuse, he couldn't with this logic.

"Then we surround Sivy and execute the Koron and Korona.

You sit on both thrones, you give the Angels one less reason to hate you, one less reason for them to resist your rule, and then every fucking day you show them we are the superior race."

Xannirin's eyes brightened. I held my breath.

Is Rokath really convincing him?

"It is an...intriguing possibility," Xannirin finally spoke. "The nobles will likely buy into this, yes. More than anything else you've suggested before."

Because, much like Xannirin, they were a bunch of self-important assholes. I'd gotten a full taste of that mentality being married to Vagach.

"Once we win a few battles, they'll believe even more," I pressed, determination swelling within me. Rokath gave a subtle nod, and I continued. "Most of the females Kiira brought have powerful magic. With the High Priestess as witness, everyone will believe the stories she writes back to you about the glory we are claiming for the Demons."

"They will crave news from the front. Stories of the Szélhámos, the mate of the Halálhívó," Kiira added in a rush. "Especially with how I write of them. It has been some time since I was able to craft stories of our mystique, Xannirin. You remember how quickly they swayed the populace before. The mythos of the Halálhívó and the Szélhámos of them will intrigue many minds."

Xannirin rubbed his jaw, considering all the words aimed at him. "I can see it. But..." he trailed off, leveling his intense gaze on me. I narrowed my eyes on him in return, my posture stiff and defiant. "Do I have your word that you won't use your newfound status to move against me?"

A scoff slipped out before I could stop it. My nails dug into my arms. How fucking dare he question that I'd want his Fates' damned throne? Was that why he'd sent an assassin after me in the first place?

"For fuck's sake, Xannirin," Rokath snapped. "We have no designs on your seat. That was what Assyria yelled down our bond when I was moments from killing you. I have no desire to rule."

I held up a hand to silence my mate. Then, holding the gaze of the Kral of all the Demons, I rose, splaying my hands out across the polished wood, one finger at a time. I leaned forward, lifting my lips from my teeth. "You may be the Kral, but I am the Szélhámos."

A riot of shadow swirled around me, and I pulled Xannirin's face to my own within the span of a breath. He paled as he beheld his reflection. I ensured I mirrored his hateful expression too. His voice came out with my next words. "Rokath could slaughter you and no one would ever know. We'd rule for millenia more, no one the wiser. I suggest you refrain from pissing either of us off if you'd like to keep your useless ass on your precious throne."

Then, I dropped my power and eased back into my chair.

Rokath's hungry gaze caught my attention out of the corner of my eye, but it was nothing compared to the utter distraction coming down our bond. Gravel rolled through his tone as he spoke in my mind. *I don't know whether to be terrified or impressed. Those insults were sharper than my sword.*

"Don't forget I can aim them in your direction anytime," I shot back.

A dark chuckle echoed in my mind. *I never will.*

Kiira covered her mouth with her hand, trying to hide her amusement, as Xannirin merely blinked at me.

After a moment, he cleared his throat, shifting in his chair like my words had set it ablaze. "All right then. You have all made your points. I will ensure the nobles believe in this story, as well as the unveiling." He glanced sidelong at Kiira, and I recalled our conversation about her not asking for forgiveness for sending that missive. "So long as you can continue the omnipresence of us, adding Assyria to the mix now, I will do my part."

Tension visibly bled from Kiira's shoulders. My own chest eased too.

"Done," Rokath and Kiira said at the same time.

Resigned, Xannirin slumped back, arms crossed.

"There's one more thing," Kiira added softly, twisting her long hair around her finger and securing it at the nape of her neck.

A muscle jumped in Xannirin's jaw. "What?"

"I had another prophecy," she stated, bringing her hands to rest on the table in front of her again.

He sat up straighter, arms dropping. "When? Of what?" His voice was laced with more enthusiasm and excitement than it had been in his entire time at the military academy thus far.

"Rokath and Assyria in the streets of Sivy. With an army of males and females at their backs." Kiira smiled, though it wasn't one of her warm and kind ones. No, she looked like she was moments from lunging across the table and ripping her cousin's throat out with her sharp teeth. "So it is a good thing you chose the right side of this fight, Xannirin."

His mouth hung open. "But I thought–"

"That the visions couldn't change?" she finished for him.

He nodded, disbelief etched into his expression.

"As did I. But after discussing the timing with Rokath and Assyria–"

"You told them before me?" he snapped, eyes darkening.

She glared at him. "It concerned them, so yes."

Xannirin's fingers tightened over the polished wood. "Go on."

"As I was saying," she drawled, "the vision came to me

shortly after Rokath chose Assyria over his soldiers. By choosing her, he changed his path. He changed all our paths."

Is she going to tell him about hearing the word sacrifice?

I waited with bated breath for her to continue to speak. To my surprise, she left it at that. Though I was quickly learning that despite all their supposed trust in one another, none of the three ever quite revealed all they knew.

"How is that possible?" Xannirin mused, loosening his grip. Instead, he thumbed his lower lip, going deep into thought.

Would the Fates have revealed a new scene to Kiira had Xannirin continued to refuse these changes?

"The Fates are Gods. We are not, despite how we purport ourselves," Kiira warned. "Should they wish for something to change, they possess the power for that. They were clearly working through Assyria in that moment. In all the moments before that too, especially on the day the army arrived in Stryi to conscript, I think."

Xannirin scrutinized me again, though this time without as much contempt as before. I still didn't offer him any less of my ire. "I am beginning to see now."

"About fucking time," I muttered under my breath, attention flicking to Rokath. He lounged, one ankle thrown across a knee, like this conversation was boring instead of essential to our future. His bicep flexed as he braced his head on a closed fist.

"More changes will come, Xannirin. More choices. Hopefully with less severe consequences than what I faced." He glanced at me, our eyes locking like they had when our mate bond snapped into place. His love flooded me, easing the aches in my heart. "But they will come nonetheless. Since we do not know exactly why Kiira's visions changed, it's best that each of these moments be weighed with the utmost care."

"With the stakes this high, it would be unwise to act rashly," he acquiesced. Silence lingered for a few moments as we all considered what the future might hold. "I'll return to Uzhhorod the day after tomorrow. You need all the females you can get, Rokath. This time, I sincerely promise that you will have them. The most powerful I can find."

"Battle ready powers would be best, no matter the eye color," I added because I was a fucking leader now too and he needed to respect that.

Xannirin dipped his head. "Kiira, if you have any messages you want to send, anything specific you want told or repeated, please get that to me tomorrow."

"I will," she promised, a half-smile tugging up the corner of her mouth.

"And you," he turned his attention to me. "Make House Vrak proud."

That was not what I was expecting him to say.

Determination straightened my spine. "I will." But I didn't agree for me. I agreed for Kiira, for the other females of this realm. Who needed to see what we could become. Who needed a symbol to ignite the fire in their hearts. Whose saw through the lies with devious eyes.

We would win this war. And when the final flakes of ash fell, our world would never be the same.

33

ASSYRIA

The smooth bannister slid beneath my fingers as I ascended the endless steps to the top of our tower. My thighs protested every press of my foot, having spent all their energy already this afternoon during training. Behind me, a laugh rumbled in Rokath's chest. "Sore, little imposter?"

"Every day I wake up thinking it can't get any worse. To my horror, every day, it does," I replied through jagged breaths. Any moment, my heart might give out with how forcefully it pounded against my ribcage.

"Wait," Rokath said, his tone utterly serious. But I wasn't going to argue with a break climbing the stairs. I heaved down air and faced him, wondering what he wanted now.

He cocked his head ever so slightly to the side, as if he were listening for something. "Do you hear that?"

The only sound—other than my mate's voice—was the blood thrumming in my ears. "No?"

Rokath moved past me, and with a huff, I dragged myself behind him. He stopped at the nearest window, angling himself so he could look up toward the small balcony perched on the top.

"Reaper's eye," he cursed, then broke into a jog.

"What?" I panted, attempting to keep up with him and utterly failing. He disappeared from my sight in seconds, and somehow I hated him even more for how easily he trekked up this torture device.

By the time I reached our rooms, the door was flung wide, and Rokath was already pressing his weight into the stone that hid the secret passage leading to the roof. Grem and Zeec were on their feet, their sharp barks echoing in the space.

My brows pinched even more than they already were as I braced my hands on my hips. "Is someone up there?"

He glanced over his shoulder at me. "Not someone. Lots of someones."

"Stay," I instructed the hounds, following him up even more fucking stairs. I was going to start leaving one of these windows open so I could fly up after training. Or maybe Grem and Zeec could be trained to pull a litter with me strapped to it.

A few shocked screams greeted me as I ascended the final step. Rokath already stood beyond the doorway, arms crossed over his chest. "What is going on here?"

I squeezed by him, surveying the group of soldiers—male *and* female—who had all fallen to one knee at the sight of him. "Halal–Halálhívó, we are performing the initiation ritual," one male managed to stammer out. Without warning, Rokath called on his wings, nearly knocking me to the side in the process, and floated higher, turning toward Xannirin's tower.

The Kral had departed that morning for Uzhhorod, so no one *should* have been over there other than Kiira.

Fury etched his expression when he landed again. I subtly kicked the back of his leg in protest. But his thighs were harder than the bronze we wielded and all I succeeded in doing was furthering my own pain.

"No, you absolutely are not," Rokath snapped, his tone abrasive. "When did this start again?"

Another male—a Százados by the look of him—dared speak next. "It never really stopped, Halálhívó."

Rokath uttered a string of curses under his breath. "We cannot spare any more recruits for this ridiculous challenge. Too many fall to their deaths."

"Wait, what is the ritual?" I asked, circling around him and inserting myself into the middle of the conversation.

Rokath pinched the bridge of his nose. "They have to climb to the top of the spire and let the wind take them over the sea. If you don't catch the right draft, or if you aren't a strong flier, you'll plummet into the ocean."

I recalled then how strong the wind had been as we leaped from this balcony before flying to the private island. "The Halálhívó is right, that's far too dangerous, especially with our new volunteers," I repeated. We were a united front after all.

"But you said to treat them like we would any male," the bold one said. Clearly, he was ready for the Reaper's wrath. And Rokath's.

Yet his protest sent my stomach plummeting. He was right. Would we risk the males' respect if we forbade the females from participating?

Maariya rose from her prostrated position, and I almost groaned. Why did she have to be one of the instigators? She'd been indispensable in training, persuading even the most rigid males in her unit to help the priestesses along with others who were less amenable to the changes. If Rokath were to punish all the soldiers here, she'd be among them.

"I don't wish to be treated differently," she professed, daring to hold the gaze of the Halálhívó. A few others straightened in solidarity, offering the same sentiment. More than a few peeks of the devious eye tattoo greeted me as they turned their arms over.

Rokath's mind was a whirlwind of thought. Through the tempest, I said, *"If we don't, that might hurt what we're trying to accomplish."*

"I know. Give me a second," came his tense reply.

Everyone looked expectantly at my mate.

"I will participate too. They will respect me more for it."

"Absolutely not."

"I know how to fly. Besides, we leaped from here the other day."

"When I was with you. But this? This is a solitary mission. I will not risk your life for something so asinine."

Rokath grumbled and banished his wings. "We'll have an initiation ritual. But it's going to be a new one, with new rules. *My rules.* And no one will fucking die."

"Whatever you say, Halálhívó," the Százados affirmed. Rokath bristled at the casual address. I covered my mouth with the back of my hand to conceal my smile as he glowered at the male.

"It is whatever I say because I lead this army."

The male swallowed, quaking beneath Rokath's ire.

"Ten lashes for you tomorrow," my mate snarled.

To his credit, he merely nodded and accepted his fate. Others averted their eyes or nudged loose stones with the toes of their boots.

"What do you need us to do, Halálhívó?" Maariya asked, settling into a stance with her hands flattened behind her lower back.

"Start by retrieving those other imbeciles and have them meet us in the fields beyond the academy. Gather everyone else too. We'll see to Parancsok Olet and Hadvezér Rapp." The sigh Rokath released was threaded with annoyance, but that didn't smother the excitement brimming in each soldier's expression.

"Yes, sir!" she replied. Then, she called out her wings and leaped into the air, sailing around the corner and out of sight.

"The rest of you, dismissed to the field," he grumbled. Their chatter carried on the wind as they departed.

A small giggle escaped me as we returned to our rooms. "What are you going to have us do?"

"Don't know yet. I'll think of something on the way down." Grem and Zeec greeted us, tails wagging, at the base of the secret passage. Rokath paused to scratch behind their ears.

I let out a long groan and shouldered past him. "Fuck, I'm going to have to go down all those stairs again."

"And all the way back up," Rokath added.

The thought was enough to make me weep.

"Maybe I change my mind," I said, throwing myself onto one of the couches. Zeec trotted over, nosing my thigh and snuffling under my hand. I threaded my fingers in his soft fur, wishing I could go to sleep in it.

"Oh, no, you don't," Rokath said, grasping my forearm and hauling me upright again. Fatigue forced every muscle to protest. "You started this. You're going to be first across the finish line, or else I'm going to make you do it all over again."

"Do you enjoy torturing me?" I glared at him, shoving loose tendrils of my hair behind my ears.

He leaned in close, stealing the air from my lungs. Then, he pressed a kiss to the underside of my jaw. An arm wrapped around my waist, drawing me against his hard body. "I do. I love punishing you, Assyria. You'll be too sore and tired for me to fuck you tonight. But I will thoroughly enjoy every minute of it nonetheless."

"Have I ever told you I hate you?" I rasped out as his tongue trailed to my pulse point. He dragged his sharp teeth over the spot, making more core clench.

"Not in a while," he replied, retreating and leaving me

breathless. The smirk he sported was wicked. "Now, let's get going."

Without waiting for a response, he dragged me to my feet. The moment they hit the stone stairs, I groaned again. "Just go ahead and kill me now."

34

ASSYRIA

Rows of torches blazed in the field just beyond the academy's walls. Kiira and I stood at the head of the priestess-turned-warriors, anxiously awaiting instruction from Rokath and Rapp. The moment Kiira had learned of the new initiation ritual, she wanted to join too. Despite the chilly air, all of us had our sleeves rolled up, revealing the shared ink on our skin.

The males, lingering all around, eyed tattoo after tattoo. Honestly, I was awed by how many had it. How many of us were united in our pain, united in our desire to carve a new path for ourselves.

That, coupled with whatever we were about to do, would cast us in an entirely new light to the soldiers who still believed we were unworthy of a place in the army.

I hoped.

Excited whispers abounded at my back. I glanced over my shoulder, surveying the gathered units. The creeping twilight made it difficult to distinguish individual figures. Olet and a few of the other officers had disappeared into the hills beyond a short time before, and with the fading light, they were impossible to see now.

Rokath finally banged on a metal shield, drawing everyone's attention. He and Rapp entered into the firelight, the red glow highlighting his hard-set jaw. "We have decided everyone will participate in this initiation, given this will be what everyone does for years to come. After all, we are all equals now."

"So what are we doing then?" I called out, a sense of giddiness overtaking me.

"It will consist of three trials," Rapp announced, leaning on a wooden post for support. "First, a blood offering to the Fates. The competition rests in how far you are willing to go. There are limits of course."

"Second," Rokath growled, drawing everyone's attention. "You'll be tied in groups of three and you will face a series of obstacles. You must not break your thread."

"And third," Rapp jumped back in, "You'll leap from the front tower without your wings. A pool of shadows will wait for you. If you require someone to assist your fall because you don't call on your magic in time, you'll have to do it again."

They seemed like fair, balanced trials with a hint of danger. I elbowed Kiira in the side, and she shot me an excited smile. I glanced behind me at the other females, who all seemed just as ready to prove themselves.

"The trials will also take place in the dark to further prove yourselves. You'll have to rely less on your senses and more on your instincts. That is what will save you during battle," Rokath said, adding a sobering reminder of why we were all really here.

Some of the excitement died down, but energy still thrummed among the gathered units.

"Should your bloodletting be insufficient, should your thread break, or should you hesitate to leap, you will be deemed unworthy," Rokath warned, the gravel in his tone grating the air.

My stomach knotted. We had to do this. All of us. I glanced behind me, grateful when the sentiment was etched into the female's faces.

Rokath set the shield to the side and drew a dagger from his belt. "The time has come for you to make your offering to the Fates. The challenge is this: you must cut yourself in such a way that you can fill a chalice to the brim without severing any essential veins or muscles. Additionally, you only have one attempt to make a cut. Should you heal before you can produce enough blood, you will be deemed unworthy. With our limited time to organize the activity, your non-dominant hand will suffice. Fail to fill it completely, and you will also be deemed unworthy."

Turning my arms over, I tried to gauge how exactly I was supposed to make that work. I could cut with my left hand, but I didn't trust myself not to err in my path doing so. That was meant to be part of the challenge, knowing Rokath.

He and Rapp split up, each taking a faction of the army to review. Rokath approached Kiira and me, hands flattening behind his lower back as he settled into a commanding stance. "You may begin."

"Oh this will be easy," Kiira said, drawing a dagger for herself. Shadows gripped the hilt as she held out her arm. The sharp tip pressed into the skin of her forearm, and then the tendrils dragged the blade backward, toward her elbow. When a deep gash appeared, she cupped her hand beneath the flow. In seconds, she had plenty to fill her palm. "For the Reaper, whose eye will pass over us," she prayed, loud enough that all could hear.

"You may pass on to the second trial," Rokath pronounced,

and behind us, Maariya and Izzenna squealed. Kiira dumped her blood onto the ground and advanced past him.

"Next!" He turned his attention to me, and I drew my blade.

"You can do this," he encouraged down our mental connection.

"I know I can," I quipped back, calling on my own shadow power. *"Again, I don't know why you doubt me."*

"I never have, little imposter." Amusement glittered in his burgundy eyes as he watched me repeat Kiira's process, albeit a bit more clumsily. My dagger ended up in the grass as I clasped my arm, filling my palm with crimson. Ten seconds passed, and then, my hand was full. I turned it over, displaying the blood pooled there. "For the Giver, who blessed me with rare magic and an even rarer bond."

The response to my declaration was nothing short of thunderous. I grinned widely up at my mate as he passed me along to the next trial. Bending down to grab my blade, I swept by Rokath, joining Kiira on the other side. We cheered on every female, and not a single one failed the task. We even finished before the males reached a similar number in their ranks.

Then, we joined Rapp's group and encouraged the rest. By the time darkness engulfed Fured, everyone had completed the task and the Fates had been thoroughly fed.

More torches ignited, and many carried them as they moved about, guiding the path for others so they didn't tumble over a rock hidden among the yellowed grass.

Yet Olet and the other officers still hadn't returned. We received an explanation moments later when Rokath yelled out his next instructions. "Each female will select two male partners for the course. Once you have your group, grab a rope from the cart and tie it around your waists. Parancsok Olet and the Százados are waiting for you in the hills beyond to ensure there is no cheating."

My heart stuttered as I looked around, trying to decide who would be best to pair with. I'd been hoping Kiira, Maariya, and I could join forces, maybe even with Izzenna or Vokkia, but if we had to connect ourselves to the males...

I understood Rokath's reasoning, but damn him, he put me in a tough spot. No one would want to join with the mate of the Halálhívó, not when they would risk his wrath for touching me, or worse, injuring me.

Groups began to form, mostly from within already existing units. Kiira too seemed to be as lost as me, with wandering males looking everywhere but at us.

I let out an annoyed huff. "Well if they won't come to us, let's go to them."

"Agreed," Kiira said, and together we strode into the throng. Dipping and dodging, we put ourselves directly in the center, and I sought out strong-looking ones who didn't immediately reverse course when they noticed our position.

"You!" Kiira shouted, grabbing the arm of a passerby I was about to claim.

"Ugh," I replied as he begrudgingly came to her side. But when I turned my attention outward, my gaze collided with a familiar set of ruby orbs. "Uzadaan?" I took a tentative step forward toward the male who had come to Stryi to conscript new soldiers so long ago. Whose arrival, along with the rest of the Lovak Squad, had irrevocably changed the course of my life.

He grinned, flashing his set of extra sharp teeth. "I apologize for avoiding you until now, Szélhámos. I thought it best if we didn't meet, for your mate's sake. But it appears you need a partner."

My heart warmed, my expression mirroring his. At least he didn't reject me, like Dromak had, when I'd run into him again. "I am. Do you have a third that can join us?"

Uzadaan let out a sharp whistle and called out to another.

From the crowd, a lanky male approached, boasting eyes in a deep shade of maroon. While he wasn't as tall as Uzadaan, he held strong power, which would be to our advantage. "This is Darrx."

"Szélhámos," he greeted me with a respectful salute. "It will be an honor to complete the course alongside you."

I glanced back at Kiira, who had grabbed a second male. She winked, then grasped both males by the arms and hauled them toward the cart filled with ropes. I snickered and turned back to Uzadaan and Darrx. "Let's go then so we have an advantageous position."

"Aye," Uzadaan agreed, using his height to weave through the throng. Once we got close, he said, "Wait here."

Darrx and I moved off to the side, while Uzadaan fetched a tether for us. When he returned, I realized it wasn't a single piece in which we'd all be in the middle. No, it was actually three individual rings, tied to a greater loop. But the thickness? It was minimal at best. One wrong jerk in opposite directions would send the threads snapping.

"How are we supposed to get in this?" I asked, examining it.

"I think that's part of the challenge," Darrx chuckled.

"I should probably go first, since I'm the smallest." Carefully, I stepped through the hole, then shimmied it over my hips until the noose tightened over my waist. Attention seared my skin, and I looked up. Rokath's possessive stare pinned me in place.

"*Like the view?*" I shot down our bond, a small smile tugging at the corners of my mouth.

"*Tremendously. I hope both of those males know the consequences of something happening to you out there,*" he threatened.

"*I'm sure they do,*" I quipped as Darrx fastened the rope around himself beside me.

"*I'm happy to tell them explicitly,*" he said, raising an eyebrow.

"Fuck off and let me prove myself to them," I replied, shooting him with a playfully hateful glare.

He rolled his eyes but moved along. *"Just stay safe, okay?"*

"I will," I promised back, sending him a pulse of love down our bond.

Finally, Uzadaan was secured, and the three of us tested what movement was possible tied together.

"I think we can walk forward at least," Darrx commented, pointing toward groups gathering at the base of the nearest hill. Rapp already stood atop it, surveying the scene. While he kept a neutral expression, the tense way he held his arm to his side told me he was in pain. I was grateful he was here, participating in the event with us. His solidarity was unwavering, and had been from the start of my journey in the army.

"Aye, let's go before we're stuck at the back," Uzadaan said, and together, we strode in that direction, keeping our steps deliberately even and slow. It would be an utter embarrassment to break this before we even started the course.

And I would not give the disbelievers any reason to judge me or the rest of the females.

Once everyone was settled, Rokath joined Rapp in appraising us. "The rules are simple. Don't break your thread and return within an hour. You'll begin in groups of three. Step forward now, and the rest of you, arrange yourselves."

The first three sets of three stepped forward, and I was happy to see some of my friends among them. Fierce determination straightened their postures, their entire focus ahead as if they were preparing to face a real enemy. We found our place in line about a dozen rows deep. Rokath raised his torch high in the air, the fire sending sparks dancing into the night. "On my mark."

Muscles tightened. My heart rate picked up.

"Go!" he shouted, waving the light. The first groups sprang

into action, and the following ones waited a beat before racing forward themselves. One by one, they crested the hill, until suddenly, it was our turn to pass by my mate.

I glanced at him out of the corner of my eye, and he gave me an encouraging nod. But this wasn't about us. It was so much bigger than that. So I dragged in a breath and faced forward, my sole focus on keeping this rope intact.

And showing these males why we deserved to be here.

Uzadaan, Darrx, and I scaled the hill with ease, coming immediately upon the first obstacle. A giant pit of mud waited, holes already sucked deep by previous footsteps. Thank the Weaver the moon hung high and fat among the stars—without it, we would have sunk in seconds.

"To the left!" I pointed, slowing my strides until Uzadaan and Darrx had time to process my words. Racing off on my own would have broken our rope immediately.

"Good call," Darrx commented, shuffling behind me. Uzadaan did the same in front of us. In single file, we wound along a narrow strip of earth, the sticky substance adhering to our boots despite the firmness of this path.

"Halt!" Uzadaan shouted, and I paused immediately. His foot, unfortunately, had gotten stuck despite our best effort. Most of the others in this part of the course were in similar situations. I squinted around his frame, gauging how far we had to go.

Uzadaan spread his hands wide like he was calling on his shadows to assist in freeing his boot from the muck. Nothing happened, not even a whisper of power dripping from his fingertips. His shoulders tensed. "What the fuck?"

Curious, I dove into my well and tugged on the threads of onyx. They didn't move.

"I don't think we can use magic," Darrx said, rubbing the back of his neck. "Mine isn't rising either."

Uzadaan cursed and looked around us for anything to assist him. I studied our placement in the mud. "Here's what we need to do. Darrx," I shot over my shoulder, "scoot backward so we can give Uzadaan room to wiggle free."

Darrx's hands pressed into my shoulders, and I was grateful he wasn't as large as Rokath, otherwise we both would have sunk in. He steadied me, ensuring we weren't drifting too far apart, as we backstepped. Then, he reached around me and grasped Uzadaan's waist. Wedged between their bodies, I held my breath. Uzadaan yanked one boot free, but the force pitched him to the side. My heart leaped to my throat.

We can't snap our thread already!

My arms shot out, managing to catch him before he tumbled below our waists. Muscles screaming from the effort of supporting him, I gritted my teeth. Darrx smashed me between them again, reaching around and hauling Uzadaan upright. We remained locked like that as Uzadaan unstuck his other foot.

"Good to go," he announced, though his voice held the slightest tremor. After a recovery beat, we stepped forward as one, this time fanning out to distribute our weight more evenly. I picked the remainder of our route carefully, avoiding the worst of the squelch. We slipped past two more groups, their ropes stretched taught as their members flailed in the mud.

The dead grass was a welcome reprieve. "Let's jog. If we stay tight, we should be able to make up time."

"Who knew you had a competitive streak?" Uzadaan teased, flashing his extra sharp teeth.

"An unfortunate consequence of being mated to the Halál-hívó," I quipped, and Darrx barked a laugh. I couldn't help the grin that split my face as we ran forward. That familiar camaraderie was returning, blooming hope it could grow between males and females across the magic-wielding units.

A breeze drifted over the cliffs, bringing with it a fresh wave of briny air. I sucked it down greedily, despite the chilly sting in my lungs. Torches blazed ahead, and I focused on the shadowed shapes around them, trying to discern what our next challenge could be.

"It's a lattice of some type," I panted. "Let's slow now."

We did together, taking a moment to study the obstacle and the others scaling it. I peered beyond too, counting the groups ahead of us. But my attention was torn back to the net when a male slipped, a cry tearing from his lips. At the last second, the other snatched his arm and hauled him back onto the net. I held my breath, waiting for their thread to break with how tightly it was now stretched between the three. The faller scrambled up again, easing the tension. Izzenna was among them, her lips pressed in firm determination.

"We have to stick to the same level," Darrx murmured, observing the rest of their ascent. "With our height differences, it might be tricky. Szélhámos, you should go first."

We reached the base just as Izzenna's team hit the earth on the opposite side. She shot me a grin, then spun and sprinted away.

"We can't let them beat us," I insisted, grasping the bottom of the net. The squares were tiny, barely large enough for me to gain a foothold, let alone the bigger males. It looked like they'd taken some fishing nets and strung them together before stretching them across these poles. The thin strands dug into my fingers as I climbed. Once I was several feet off the ground, Darrx and Uzadaan followed. We stuck close to one another, keeping as much of an eye on each other's holds as our own.

One mistake, and our thread could snap.

Halfway up, the net slickened. Whether it was from the previous climbers' sweat or if the officers had intentionally oiled it, I wasn't sure. Either way, traversing it was proving difficult.

"Fuck," Darrx swore, his foot slipping. His forearms flexed as he gripped the net tighter, which honestly wasn't much better with how sharply the twine dug into the skin. With a grunt, he dug the toe of his boot into a warped section.

"You good?" Uzadaan asked from my other side.

Darrx nodded, and then we continued our ascent. At the top, however, my stomach leaped to my throat. Now we had to go *down,* and my shoulder muscles already trembled from exertion. Angry welts crisscrossed my palms, courtesy of the unforgiving net. I flexed my hands and rubbed them together, trying to ease the ache.

"How do we turn?" I asked, studying our positions.

"Within our own ropes. There's no other way," Darrx said, giving his a tug. Uzadaan and I loosened ours, then carefully swung our legs around so we faced the other direction. Once we were all draped to go down, we tightened them around our waists again.

"On three," I wheezed. "One."

The males' grips changed.

"Two." I shuffled my own.

"Three." I eased myself down, boot slipping immediately.

That damn mud.

Sucking in a sharp breath, I found another hold, then grasped a lower section of net. Uzadaan and Darrx shimmied down on either side of me. We worked in silence, focused on our tasks. About halfway down, Darrx said, "We can drop from here if we're careful."

My lashed hands agreed immediately. "Let's go."

"Bend your knees to take the impact and lock hands so we don't pitch to one side," Darrx instructed. "Ready?"

I visualized what he was asking me to do. Uzadaan and I indicated we were prepared.

"On my mark," Darrx said. My breath lodged in my throat. "Jump!"

I released my holds, careening toward the ground. Keeping my knees soft, I grasped Darrx's hand. At the last second, he tugged me into him, and we hit the earth with a jarring thud. A wobble threatened to snap my rope, but as I pitched forward, the net caught me. The three of us righted ourselves, and a sigh of relief loosened my chest when I noted our thread was still intact.

"Fuck yes!" Darrx cheered.

Digging my sore hands into the bind around my waist, I loosened it again and spun. Once all of us faced forward again, my enthusiasm faded like the setting sun. There was still so much of the course to go, and I was so, so tired.

"Ready?" Uzadaan asked. Nodding and steeling my spine, I prepared to jog once again. On three, we took off, the grass flying beneath our feet. My lungs burned from the effort of keeping up with their long strides.

A brief thought of faking a sore knee rose, just so we could slow and I could suck down some much-needed air. But then we passed one group. And another.

"There should only be about seven groups ahead of us now!" Darrx shouted, somehow still able to breathe.

Embers blazed in my chest. We'd started not too far back, but with how many we'd passed already, we stood a good chance of placing in the top.

I would not give up.

Uzadaan whooped, and I let out a cry of my own. "Let's overtake them all!"

35

ASSYRIA

The moon cast a haunting glow over the hills, and we were forced to slow as the terrain grew uneven. Ahead of us, one threesome stumbled, grasping each other's arms to steady themselves. When a second did the same, it dawned on me that we likely approached our next obstacle.

"Can you see anything?" I asked Uzadaan, the tallest of our team.

"I think there's a crack in the earth," he said, peering into the distance. We slowed to a walk as we approached the crest of the closest hill. Sure enough, below, all seven groups ahead of us had halted and were gesticulating wildly as they discussed how to cross.

A moment later, a fuzziness entered my head, and I forgot what we were supposed to be doing. I glanced around, finding Olet standing off to one side, obsidian wisps disappearing from his form and into the abyss.

"Why is everyone standing around?" Darrx asked blearily.

My brows pinched as I tried to focus on the thread of thought that kept slipping through my fingers. Olet...

I stumbled toward the male. He was part of it. He had to be.

"Woah!" Uzadaan shouted like I was a horse, grabbing me by the arm.

"Olet," I said out loud, pointing with my free hand toward the Parancsok.

"Fuck, he's using his magic," Uzadaan cursed, and I blinked, processing his words.

"Yes! He's a Chaos." That was what my mind had been trying to tell me. "What if the canyon isn't really there? What if it's his magic?" I called on my power, hoping that by bringing my shadows to the surface I'd be able to free myself from the grip of his. This time, they answered my call, but dissipated as quickly as they'd risen.

Ugh.

"If we crawl toward it, we can test it without falling over the edge," Darrx suggested.

"Let's do it," I replied. We eased our way down the steep incline, lining up with the rest of the groups trying to puzzle their way across. Some of their conversation drifted into my ear, but most of their words were jumbled and disoriented.

As a group, we sank to our knees, then slid our hands through the damp grass until we were flat on our stomachs. In this position, we were close enough to not have to worry about snapping the rope tying us together.

"Shall we?" They nodded. Digging our elbows into the earth, we dragged ourselves forward, toward the dark crack in the ground. Uzadaan stretched a hand over the expanse, and my heart leaped into my throat. The moment of truth. The void swallowed the limb whole, making it appear as if he never had one at all.

"Can you feel anything?" Darrx prodded, sweat beading his brow.

"There's ground here, but I can't see it. We should keep crawling," Uzadaan replied.

"What if we can't see each other once we're in it?" I questioned, teeth digging into my bottom lip.

"That's where our trust comes in. I'll keep reaching and yell if we need to stop. Assyria, stay close to me. Darrx, stay close to Assyria," Uzadaan instructed.

He wasn't wrong. This was what the test was about—working together, supporting one another and believing the others would do the same in return. Rokath and Rapp were clever in their design.

I scooted closer, to the point where each dig forward would hook into Darrx's side, letting him know I was still there. When Uzadaan moved again, I followed, stomach twisting into knots. The darkness enveloped us, banishing the light of the moon and stars above. Not only that, but all sound was muffled, like a damp blanket had been thrown over us.

Through the fog, we continued on, blindly trusting one another to lead the way or keep up. Darrx's elbow continually brushed against my shoulder, and my elbow against his ribs. "Still good, Uzadaan?"

"Aye," he confirmed, though he sounded like he was all the way across Keleti.

We moved slowly—so fucking slowly—but I wasn't in a hurry to fall to our deaths. I hadn't ventured this far beyond the academy grounds to know what lay out here. It was entirely possible there really was a cliff hidden in the murky abyss.

"Halt!" Uzadaan shouted, and we did, my breath catching in my throat.

"What is it?" I hissed, unable to see anything, including my hands mere inches from my face.

"There's something here," he announced.

"A real crack?" Darrx questioned.

"No, like a wall. We need to stand," Uzadaan said. "On my mark."

I shuffled so my hands were beneath my shoulders, toes poised and ready to tuck under me. "I'm ready."

"One, two, three," he counted out. Muscles protesting, I pushed off the ground. But the moment I was steady on my feet, the rope tightened around my waist.

"Shit!" Darrx cursed. Without thinking, I leaped toward the sound of his voice, grasping for something, anything, of his. A hand smacked me in the face, and the metallic tang of blood flooded my mouth from a cut in my lip. But I grabbed onto the limb and hauled him into me.

"Did our rope snap?" Uzadaan asked as we steadied ourselves.

Fumbling over our bodies, I found each of our threads still intact and secured together. "No, thank the Reaper. You okay, Darrx?"

"Fine," he gritted out. He didn't sound fine, but I let it go.

"Shuffle forward, then to the right. There has to be a way around the wall," Uzadaan explained. Once again taking him for his word, I released Darrx, stretching a hand in front of me and feeling for the stone.

In two steps, the sharp pieces bit into my fingers. My poor hands deserved a break after the abuse they'd taken on this course. "Found it."

"Me too," Darrx confirmed.

"Alright, move sideways now," Uzadaan instructed, and we did, boots knocking together as we tried to maintain our close proximity. I flicked my tongue over the split in my lip. The sharp taste remained, but the cut was already healing. Darrx hadn't meant to strike me, and thankfully Rokath wouldn't be able to see it by the time we returned.

I rolled my eyes at the thought of my brutish mate taking revenge for an accident. He would do it too. Especially after the assassination attempt. He hadn't quite gotten over it yet. Not that I believed he ever really would.

The memory of the assassin on top of me twisted my stomach. What if someone else waited for me in the dark? My power was locked down, and I was utterly at the magic-wielders' mercy. Someone simply had to sneak up behind me and slice their dagger across my throat to kill me. No one would see what happened. Fuck, no one would hear him approach either with the dampened sound.

"Do you feel anything?" I asked Uzadaan, trying to keep the tremble from my voice. We needed to get out of here, and fast. My entire body tingled, and my breath grew shallow.

"A corner, maybe. Turn sharply," he replied.

A small tug around my middle had me quickening my pace, and then the rough rock gave way to smooth stone. I pivoted immediately.

"Thank fuck," I heard Uzadaan say. In a blink, the moon blinded me again. I pressed the heels of my palms into my eyes, then opened them again. They adjusted to the glimmer of the night sky, allowing me to see the remainder of the course.

No one stood before us. I turned to examine the obstacle we'd overcome. Two matching walls pinned the maw of darkness, like a ramp had been dug into the hillside. Olet's magic retreated, and clarity crashed into me.

Yet I couldn't shake the fear of another assassin lingering in the dark.

"Forward?" I asked them, anticipation thrumming in my veins. Traversing the Chaos had been the third obstacle, and since everything had been in threes, it had to have been the final hurdle to overcome.

"Aye," they replied. Relief washed through me as we set out at a jog again, putting distance between us and the void. When we crested the slope, torches lined the path, almost like barriers herding us toward a fiery beacon at the end.

"There!" I shouted, pointing at the burning logs. A shadowed figure sliced the red light, and the bond in my chest flared to life. I glanced behind us, noticing that another group had finally clawed their way through the darkness. "Hurry!"

Grass flew beneath our feet as we sprinted straight toward my mate. Each step made his stoic expression clearer, ever the cold, calculated Halálhívó. Yet pride burned along our connection, the emotion reserved only for me. Rapp stood beside Rokath, the studs in his face glinting as he turned around. He released a whooping cheer when he saw who was in the first group.

A smile rose amid my desperate panting, filling me with the energy I needed to finish this race.

Ahead, a line of blood marked the end of our path. My entire focus went to it, disregarding the burning in my limbs. We were so, so close.

Ruby sprayed as we crossed it. Darrx and Uzadaan punched their fists into the air, cries of victory tearing from their throats. I joined them in celebrating, slapping palms and knocking shoulders. A breathy laugh escaped me as I wiped the sweat from my brow.

"Congratulations on being the first across. Your time was thirty-nine minutes," Rokath announced, glancing at the clock on a nearby stool. Moments later, the second group crossed, and Rokath gave them their time too. I grinned up at him as I untied the rope from my waist. Once we were all free of it, Darrx placed it in an empty cart off to one side.

Ascending the stairs, I took my place at my mate's side, where I should always be.

"You really are proving yourself to them, little imposter."

"I know," I shot back. His hand went to my lower back,

tugging me almost imperceptibly closer to him. The warmth of his palm soothed the ache there. Now that my exertion was over, every muscle felt as if it weighed more than a ball of steel, and the crisp winter air ghosting across my skin elicited a shiver.

Uzadaan and Darrx approached, saluting the Halálhívó and their Hadvezér. "Sir, it was an honor to compete with your mate."

"Your teamwork is commendable, soldiers. Continue to have this attitude, and you'll move up the ranks," Rokath told them.

"Any way we can assist, we will, sir," Uzadaan swore.

"Thank you," I mouthed to him before the two departed, joining the others who had finished off to one side of the raised dais.

To my relief, Kiira's group was next, followed by Izzenna, Vokkia, and Maariya. More and more poured in, and I glanced at the clock. Nearly an hour had passed and still, hundreds had not appeared.

"They can't actually die in the dark, can they?" I clarified, glancing at Rapp and Rokath.

"Nah," Rapp drawled, his mischievous grin making the rings in his lip glint in the firelight. "Olet is supposed to let up on his magic so they can find their way out."

"What is that place?" I asked.

"An old storm shelter. It's only used when there's a nasty hurricane coming off the coast, which we haven't had in decades. Olet simply used his magic to disorient everyone approaching the doors to it," Rapp explained.

Clever.

"So you want everyone to succeed?" I questioned, cocking my head to the side.

Rokath nodded. "And those ropes wouldn't have broken.

Rapp infused a bit of his Binding power into each of them. It's also why you couldn't use your magic."

That made perfect sense.

"So it was all mind games then?"

"Pretty much," Rapp replied, wincing as he shrugged. "It always is."

If I'd learned anything living among the most powerful Demons in Keleti, it was that Rapp's statement was true. Those tricks were ones I was bringing into my repertoire, consciously or not. My last interactions with Xannirin were proof of that.

The last groups spilled from the tunnel in a rush, all making mad dashes toward the finish line. Cheers rang out from all sides, encouraging them to arrive under their time limit. The hands on the clock ticked as I glanced between it and the teams. As the number spun, signaling the change in hour, the very last set of three threw themselves forward, landing in a muddy heap at the base of the stage.

But every single soldier made it.

When Rokath declared it, the whole army erupted. I couldn't help the smile that made my cheeks ache. To see the males and females interacting like this, trusting one another like this, celebrating together—it was everything.

All our hard work, all our sacrifices, all the blood and tears shed, it culminated in this moment.

"And you made it happen, Assyria."

I threw my arms around Rokath's waist, not caring that we had an audience.

"Halálhívó! Szélhámos!" they screamed our honorifics.

From the front row of soldiers, Kiira cupped her hands over her mouth and yelled, "Kiss!"

Heat swept across my cheeks, but Rokath wasted no time in threading his fingers through the sweat-soaked hair at the nape of my neck and curling down to press his lips to mine. A roar, even louder than when he announced that everyone had completed the trial on time, assaulted my ears. Love surged down our bond, fierce and unrelenting, and I willingly surrendered to its pull.

When he broke away, he rested his forehead against mine. "Like Kiira said, the myth of us will fuel them. They'll fight harder. Encourage others to do the same," he murmured, only loud enough for me to hear.

"Then let's really give them something to talk about," I grinned back, reaching up and wrapping my arms around his neck.

With a growl, he kissed me again, our tongues twining in a battle for dominance. He gripped my waist, and his hardness dug into my stomach. Pleasure curled in my core at the thought of him inside me. All aches forgotten, I wanted nothing more than to escape into that storm shelter so he could fuck me senseless.

Growing dizzy from lack of air, we broke apart, our eyes still locked on one another. "Unfortunately, there is still one trial to complete."

I let out a groan. Fuck, I'd almost forgotten, swept up in excitement and desire. "Ugh. If we must."

"If you want me to take that sweet, sweet cunt later, though, I won't refuse."

My low belly heated at his words. He released me, leaving me bereft, and faced the crowd. "Now onto the final challenge. A daring leap from the front tower of the academy. You will jump in the order in which you arrived here."

Which meant Darrx, Uzadaan, and I were the first to go. My limbs ached as we marched toward the keep, only tempered by the excitement in my veins.

Once we reached it, I called on my wings, groaning as the muscles in my back protested. With a few beats, I was airborne and sailing toward the high wall. Toes touching down, I tucked the black membranes close to my body. Below us, Rokath, Rapp, Olet, and the Százados wove a net of onyx, undulating beneath the glow of the moon.

"You should go first, Szélhámos," Darrx said, sweeping a hand out.

I swallowed around the thick lump in my throat. He was right, of course, but that didn't halt my trepidation. The drop was long, and I wanted to execute it perfectly. I also didn't want to open my wings too soon and give the dissenters reason to speculate that I was scared to fall.

Dragging in a serrated breath, I hoisted myself up between two sets of stone. Perched precariously in the air, I peered down again, stomach flipping.

I was the first to leap. To stand. To demand change. The first female to claim a position of power in the army.

I was a symbol of possibility. Of change. Of hope.

This moment was transcendent of my fears.

You can do this, Assyria.

Steeling my spine, I leaped off the tower. The ground rushed toward me, and adrenaline shattered through me.

What the fuck were you thinking?!

Wind screamed in my ears as my body begged me to use my power to slow my descent. But I gritted my teeth and held firm. The shadowy net tensed beneath me.

"*Open your wings, Assyria,*" Rokath growled into my mind.

"*Not yet,*" I shot back, gauging the remaining distance. I still had time.

"*You're falling too fast. Fucking open them,*" he demanded.

I ignored him, focused on my task.

"*Assyria!*" he shouted, real concern lacing his tone.

Finally, I snapped my black, membranous wings wide, and the wind smacked into them, jerking me up mere feet from the blanket of obsidian. I glided over them and straight past my mate, easing myself onto the ground at a light run. Banishing my magic, I slowed, coming to a stop in front of a group of females at the front of the army.

"That was amazing!" one squealed, clapping her hands. Others followed suit, and even a few males came forward, offering me salutes and praise.

I thanked them, then went to join the officers and contributed my magic to the net. I shouted encouragement at those who needed it, helping one by one pass the final trial.

Everyone did.

By the time we finished, the middle of the night was well upon us. Rokath, Rapp, Kiira, and I all stood together in front of the soldiers, now decidedly mixed male and female. The only real distinguishing factor among them was the differing heights. A few even ribbed each other, drawing peals of laughter.

Tears burned the backs of my eyes as I beheld the scene. Exhaustion weighed down my limbs, the shadows in my chest were nothing more than wisps, but I was enthralled with what we had accomplished. What we were building. How much this one event had changed hearts and minds and allowed us to show them why we were deserving of marching under the army's banner.

The Halálhívó stepped forward, arms crossed over his chest like he was weighing each of our worth. "Congratulations to you all for successfully passing the initiation ritual. For that, tomorrow shall be a free day. No training, no chores. Sleep in if you want."

Cheers erupted from the crowd.

"The day after will be twice as brutal," he warned. Groans sounded in response. I couldn't smother the smile that spread across my face.

"You are dismissed. Return to your bunks. Rest. You have earned it."

A round of applause rippled through the crowd, and then, streams of soldiers passed us, heading to their respective parts of the fortress.

"I for one am exhausted," Kiira sighed, nearly leaning on Rapp for assistance as we ventured inside. Quite the change from before. And the way he looked down at her...

Rokath slipped his arm over my shoulders, drawing my attention away from the two of them. He planted a kiss on my temple, and I leaned into it, seeking his comfort. Each step forward was a challenge, and my arms ached from merely swinging as we walked. "I never, ever thought I would willingly ask this but...will you carry me up the stairs?"

I batted my long lashes up at him, hoping the gesture would melt his hard exterior. A laugh rumbled in his chest. "And here I thought you hated me again."

"Oh, that still stands. You'll have to win me over again," I quipped.

Without warning, he swooped me into his arms, stealing a gasp from my throat. "I will spend every day for the rest of our lives winning you over, Assyria. It is what I should have done initially."

Warmth bloomed around my heart, and I reached for his beard, giving it a stroke before rubbing his jaw. "I'll hold you to that."

"I can't tell you how happy it makes me to see you two like this," Kiira sighed, popping our bubble of peace. We'd reached the split that led to our tower and the adjacent one where Kiira's rooms waited. Double the number of sentries waited, to my shock. Everyone had been dismissed for the night after participating, and yet these males still chose to protect us.

"Goodnight, Kiira," Rokath huffed, annoyance threading his tone.

Rapp chuckled, leading Kiira in the opposite direction and greeting the guards and thanking them for being at their posts. Rokath carried me up the winding stairs toward our chamber at the top. Even the jostling against his chest made me hurt.

By the time we reached our rooms, my eyelids were heavier than bronze, almost impossible to keep open. Yet Rokath didn't take me to bed. Instead, he carried me into the bathing chamber, turned the taps to the tub, and stripped me. I let him treat me like a pet, bathing me, washing my hair, and drying me off.

By the time we finally sank between the sheets, all it took for me to fall into a deep slumber was my mate pulling me onto his broad chest and laying my ear against the heart that beat only for me.

36

R✷KATH

Adrenaline rushed through my veins as I raced through the desert. Head on a swivel, I searched for my mate. Yet this wasn't a game of chase, like we'd enjoyed time and time again. No, icy fear shattered through me. White feathers lined the ground, growing thicker as they swallowed the sand, until I was kicking up clouds of them behind me. They followed me of their own accord, almost in a taunt.

"Assyria!" I shouted, my voice disappearing immediately, as if they absorbed it so my words couldn't reach my mate.

Not again. Please, not again. They wouldn't hesitate to kill her this time. Leave me with only her bones to grieve over.

I tugged on our bond, begging it to show me where she was. It was so faint, so weak. "Assyria!" I shouted again, this time down our mental connection.

I received no response. No quip, no teasing words. Just utter, heartbreaking, silence.

Dots appeared on the horizon ahead, and I wasted no time putting on a burst of speed. Yet my limbs were heavy, leaden, like I was underwater and attempting to run. "Come on," I gritted out, pumping them harder.

What felt like an eternity later, the ebony hair of my mate came into view. She knelt in the middle of a bed of white feathers, while her black membranous wings hung limply on either side of her. Her head dragged down, obscuring her devious burgundy eyes.

"Assyria!" I called out to her, hoping she'd look at me. She didn't acknowledge my presence. I pressed on, closing the distance quicker now. Yet as I skidded to a stop, I noticed the silver sword resting across her lap.

"Where did you get that?" I asked her.

She finally lifted her head, revealing eyes of an icy blue. The wrong color. Too late, I realized I'd been tricked. I leaped backward, but a dozen more Angels appeared at my back, wrestling me to the ground. With a roar, I flung them off, only for the sight of my mate, my real mate, to halt me.

Her arms bound above her head, the rope tied to a thick bough, she looked at me with anguish so intense it stole my breath. She'd been stripped of everything, leaving her entire body bare. A gag held her silent, though the tears streaming down her face spoke volumes.

On either side of her, male Angels stood, one with a dagger to her throat, another pressed into her ribs.

"What do you want?" I croaked, falling to my knees.

One of them laughed. "You to watch while we destroy you both." Another male stepped forward, unfastening his pants.

A scream unlike any I'd ever heard tore from my mate's throat as he opened her legs. "No!" I roared, leaping for her, not caring about the consequences...

"Rokath," Assyria pleaded, and I jolted awake. My chest heaved as I took in my surroundings. My mate gripped my shoulders like she'd been shaking me, and a thick sweat coated my skin. The bed beneath me too was soaked.

"Assyria," I breathed, crushing her against my thundering heart. I'd never been more grateful to be at the academy than I was in that moment. I kissed her head, held her so tightly she protested.

"You're smothering me," she wheezed, barely audible, and with a hint of loathing, I released her so she could breathe.

Still, I buried my nose in her hair, inhaling her garden-like scent, reminding myself that she was here, she was in my arms, and that the Angels didn't have her. "Fuck, Assyria, I love you so much." My voice was cracked, strained. She wriggled her arms out and wrapped them around me, climbing on top of me fully.

"Nightmare?" she murmured.

I nodded, unable to speak for the vastness of my need for her.

"Want to talk about it?" she pressed on.

"Not really." It was the only way to banish it so that it would never return. So that it would never become my reality.

My breathing had slowed, evening out as her love and comfort poured into me. Telling her what I saw would only amplify my emotions again. The utter shock I'd felt when I realized the female kneeling on the ground wasn't her. The utter terror when I'd discovered the real her strung up like an animal. And with no outlet for them other than the soldiers we were training to fight those fucking insects...

An idea suddenly dawned on me, and I kicked myself for not thinking of it sooner. "I want to train with your magic again today," I announced, mind working. "How would you feel about becoming me?"

I loosened my grip on her so she could look up at me. "You mean like impersonating you?"

"Aye," I replied. "I am someone most of the Angels try to avoid, save for the foolish ones with too much bravado. What if, in a dire situation, you could become me and confuse them? Leave them questioning which way they should go?"

Her eyes brightened and excitement dripped down our

bond. I fucking loved that she didn't temper her emotions with me anymore. It helped me understand my mate on a deeper level, one that others would never be able to access. And right then, I knew she wouldn't refuse.

"Absolutely," she swore, pushing off me. Her long hair brushed over my torso as she shifted up to kiss me. With a groan, I threaded my fingers in her locks and held her in place. My cock jumped to attention, nudging against her ass.

Fuck, I needed to be inside her. To banish the fear of that nightmare. To show her I'd never let anyone take her from me. She was mine, always had been, always would be.

Reaching around, I repositioned my hardness so it nudged at her entrance. We didn't even separate our lips as she rolled her hips and took me in one deep stroke. Her cunt gripped me like a vise as she slid up and down. With a hand on her lower back and another in her hair, I guided her harder, faster. She whimpered into my mouth as I bottomed out.

Our tongues battled, and I sucked hers between my teeth, eliciting another heady moan from my mate. Only then did I release her. Using my grip, I yanked her head back. "Mine," I growled.

"Yours," she replied, a slight hitch in her breath as I sank to the hilt again. She circled her hips in the most torturous motion, making my eyes roll back in my head.

"Fuck, little imposter, you take my cock so well."

"It was made for me," she breathed.

I snapped my attention to her, blood overheating.

"Just like your cunt was for me," I growled. "So fucking perfect. Always so fucking wet for me. Look how I just slid into you."

"Like this?" she breathed, bracing her hands on my shoulders and lifting off until only the tip of me remained inside.

The groan that slipped out of me turned her eyes molten.

When she sat back on my hips, her arousal coated the tops of my thighs. She repeated the motion, continuing to slick my cock. It throbbed inside her, and I had to grit my teeth to prevent myself from exploding already.

"You're going to be so fucking good for me and come three times," I bit out, shifting my hands to the hem of her shirt and tearing it over her head.

"One for the Weaver, who placed us on this path together."

Her breath hitched as the cold brushed over her skin.

"One for the Giver, who blessed us with this bond."

I yanked her down and captured a perfect nipple in my mouth.

"One for the Reaper, who kept you alive all the times you should have died."

The action drew a whimper from her throat.

"You drive me crazy," I ground out, releasing her. The peaks that greeted me made my cock twitch.

"Good," she panted as I dragged my teeth over her other nipple. Then, I swirled my tongue around it, savoring the feel of her smooth skin. The sound she made was sinful. "Keep doing that."

I obliged, and she moved her hips, fucking me while I sucked her. With each pass, her walls tightened around me. *"That's it, little imposter. Take all of me."*

I flicked my tongue over her sensitive bud again, and she quickened her pace, ecstasy edging in.

"Rokath." She moaned my name, half-plea, half-prayer, and exactly how I liked it.

"Come for me," I commanded, and on her next stroke, she shattered.

I released her as she arched, riding me through her orgasm. The way she flushed, the sharp tips of her nails digging into my tattoos, the wanton sounds that slipped between her bow-shaped lips, all of it was why she was absolutely fucking flaw-less and absolutely fucking made for me.

With a shuddered breath, the peak passed her, and I wasted no time flipping us. A small noise of protest slipped out of her as I removed myself so I could settle between her thighs.

"The sight of you, the smell of you," I groaned, raking my eyes over the slickness coating her thighs, dripping down her ass, pooling beneath her on the bed. My dick dug into the mattress, and I rubbed myself against it to relieve some of the ache of leaving her perfect pussy.

I pressed my lips to the inside of one thigh, then the other. "No one will ever take you from me."

Her eyes locked onto mine, holding that fierce fire I loved so much. "Never."

Without breaking her gaze, I licked her slit, then sucked her clit into my mouth. Those long lashes fluttered against her cheekbones as I went to work, tasting her cum. So fucking sweet. I speared my tongue inside her, just like she liked, and she writhed against my face. "More," she pleaded. "*Please.*"

That word did vicious, savage things to me. With a rumble, I gripped her hips and smashed my face into her pussy. Her nails dug into my scalp too, sending tingles to the tips of my toes. My dick wept as she whimpered and moaned.

"The feel of your scruff on my thighs," she gasped, inner muscles tightening. I angled my jaw and rubbed them there, drawing another blissful sound from her throat. She arched off the bed, and I slid a hand beneath her hips, finding her hole. It was already so slick from her arousal that I had no trouble coating the entire thing.

"Beg me for it," I told her, stilling my movements.

She wasted no time, already so far gone to the ways I gave her pleasure. "Please. Use your fingers. Take me there. I want to feel you everywhere."

"Please, what?" I rumbled, rubbing my beard against her thighs again.

"Please, *mate*."

"I was hoping for master, but I'll accept that too. Just because I love the way you whimpered it." Then, I swept my tongue through her slickness again and pressed the tip of my finger into the tight ring.

She sucked in a sharp breath as I worked to the second knuckle. *"This pussy is mine. This ass is mine. That mouth is mine. Am I understood?"*

She nodded, and another gush of wetness filled my mouth. She hated that she loved my command, my possession, and that made it taste all the sweeter. This headstrong female falling apart because of me was better than any scale.

I stretched her hole further, adding a second finger.

"Fates–" she swore.

I growled a warning.

"Rokath," she corrected herself, and her walls clenched around me. I glanced up from my work, finding her brows pinched and sweat beading between her breasts. I flattened my tongue and licked harder, faster, while working my fingers deeper into her ass.

"Oh, fuck," she swore, mouth popping open and remaining in an O. Then, her lashes fluttered.

"Eyes on me while I make you come. I want to see the full effect of me stretching you out," I commanded into her mind. They snapped open at the same time her walls clenched, sucking me deeper inside.

I groaned against her pussy as she came for the second time.

"That's my good mate," I ground out, releasing her at last. I wiped the juices from my beard with the back of my clean hand, then captured her in a bruising kiss. My cock dripped onto her belly, and I was wound so fucking tight I knew when I sank into her cunt again I'd be done in only a few strokes.

I left her lips pink and swollen when I pulled away. "I'm going to fuck you from behind now, with my cock in your ass. You're going to come for me while I claim you once again."

Fire ignited in those devious burgundy eyes. "Claim me, Rokath. As hard as the first time."

My dick leaped, and a feral growl ripped from my throat. I flipped her, and she looked over her shoulder at me, digging her teeth into her bottom lip. The slightest wriggle of her ass and arch of her spine had her opening even more for me. I swiped more wetness over the tight ring, then pushed my fingers in again, widening her further.

With my free hand, I rubbed her clit, keeping her dripping for me. A heady moan fled her lips as I worked a third finger in. "Take me," she begged.

"Can't wait, little imposter?"

"No." The word came out like a broken plea.

I couldn't deny my mate what she wanted. Without having to reposition her, I slid my hardness into her pussy, coating it in preparation for her ass. It came out absolutely soaked. A low, rumbling laugh sounded in my chest. "I love your openness, Assyria. How you want me to show you new pleasures."

I removed my fingers, positioning the head at her entrance. With deliberate slowness, I pressed. "Relax," I encouraged her. A whimper escaped her, and I continued to rub circles over her clit. Her hole opened wider for me, until I worked the tip completely in.

"Good girl," I praised, and her walls clenched, making stars dot my vision. "How does it feel?"

"Incredible," she breathed, her body already coiled tight. For which I was grateful, because my balls were throbbing with anticipation of my release.

"Tell me if it's too much," I instructed. Then, I thrust deeper, bringing my length in and out as slowly as I could manage with how badly I wanted to fuck her into oblivion. But I didn't want to hurt her, especially since I had plans for her training later.

"It's not. Keep going," she panted, pushing back into me.

With a groan, I did, flaring my nostrils and focusing on my breath to prevent myself from coming.

"Yes," she hissed, her eyes flaring again. Her breath came in ragged sips as she watched me fuck her, gaze raking over my sweat-slicked torso.

"If only you could see what I see," I told her.

"Show me," she gasped, and I did.

Images of her ass widening, gaping for me as she took my thick cock flashed down our bond. She clenched around me at the sight with a mewled, "Oh."

"You take me so well." I dipped my hand rubbing her clit into her pussy, slicking it further. Her walls pulsed around my fingers as I withdrew them.

"No," she pleaded. "Keep them there."

"Then you need to come for me." My voice was hard, commanding.

"I will," she promised. So I dipped my fingers into her cunt again, grinding the heel of my palm against her clit.

She opened for me, and I buried myself deeper, inch by devastating inch. "Fuck," I swore, nearly to the hilt. Poised over her, braced on one hand, control slipped out of my grasp. I curled my fingers against her inner walls, stroking the spot she loved while I claimed her ass.

She held my gaze the entire time, the world melting away as our bond, our love consumed us like a wildfire. A ragged breath fled her, and every muscle in her core tightened. "Fuck!" she screamed as her orgasm tore through her, yet in our current position she could scarcely move.

"Good girl," I praised her, holding out until the last second before letting my own release rip through me. Hot ropes of cum filled her ass with me completely inside.

Trembling, panting, I murmured words of affirmation in her ear. Small, sweet sounds slipped between her lips. As my cock softened, I eased myself out of her. She sank to the mattress, limbs trembling. I pressed a kiss to her sweat-soaked spine, then went to the bathing chamber to run us a bath. Minutes later, she joined me, sinking into the tub. The hour was still early, so we had time to luxuriate before the first gong rang.

Turning the taps, I ceased the flow of water, then joined her in it.

"That was...amazing," she commented with a sigh, settling back against me. A low rumble vibrated in my chest as I wet a cloth and cleaned her. She sucked in a sharp breath as I brushed it over her center.

"Sensitive?" I asked her.

She nodded. "I can't decide which position I like most with you."

"You don't have to pick a favorite. I will pleasure you in them all, whenever you ask."

She craned her neck to look at me, and I pressed a kiss to her forehead. "No one will take me again. You're training me to be as fierce as you. I trust you completely."

My heart throbbed at her words. I set the cloth aside and wrapped my arms around her waist instead. "Then we better work on my idea today so that you can scare the Angels and taste how sweet a victory that is."

"I think I'll enjoy that," she grinned, unveiling the devious side of her.

I huffed against her hair. "With how fierce you are, I have no doubt."

37

ASSYRIA

Once again, I stood across from Rokath in a tucked-away corner of the training area. The idea of impersonating the Halálhívó, intimidating them without softening a single emotion, thrilled me in the same visceral way that my mate did when he claimed me earlier. The thought of both made my sore center throb. I pressed my lips together to keep my face neutral.

When did I become so much like my mate?

Whether it was the bond that made me crave this power, this violence, or whether it was yet another part of me I'd suppressed as a way to survive the cruel society I'd grown up in, I didn't care. I merely dragged it in like I inhaled the cool air, welcoming it inside me.

"Ready?" Rokath asked me, and I nodded.

Dipping my eyes closed, I dove into the well of shadows in my chest. Yanking on the tendrils, I brought them outside of me. They swirled into a frenzy as I pictured Rokath clearly in my mind. It wasn't hard, given how many times I'd stared into his burgundy eyes and run my fingers through his beard. How many times I'd traced the tattoos over his torso and the edges of his jagged ear. How many times I'd unraveled beneath him, come undone around the hard length of him, carved open in a way only he knew how to do.

I stretched, grew, thickened, as I became an Imposter.

The complexity of his armor proved to be a challenge. Brows pinching, I rolled through it, piece by piece. The dark pants he wore, with the metal strapped over the thighs and his calves. The heavy boots that adorned his feet. The fitted piece that covered his stomach and chest. The flexible plates that made up the shoulder joint. And finally, the bracers on his forearms.

Satisfied I'd thoroughly equipped myself, I let the obsidian vortex fall away. Blinking into the present, I jolted when I was eye to eye with my mate. This new height and weight were ones I'd never experimented with before, since they would have made me stand out when I wanted to blend in.

When I spoke, my voice came out exactly like his. "How did I do?"

With an utterly serious expression, he rounded me, and I fought the urge to squirm. "From a distance, no one would know the difference," he stated when he returned to my front. "How does it feel?"

"Heavy," I grunted, sweat already breaking out across my brow.

"It's unnerving looking at myself," he commented, stepping back and crossing his arms.

At that moment, Rapp hobbled behind the stands and let out a low whistle. Kiira was tucked under his arm, offering him some support. But he was growing stronger and stronger by the day, especially aided by the enhanced liquid pium the healers had managed to create from the dried leaves Kiira and Xannirin had brought from Uzhhorod.

"I don't know who is who and that might frighten me the

most," he commented as he and Kiira took a seat on a bale of hay.

I rolled my eyes, and so did Rokath.

"See!" Rapp looked at Kiira but gestured in our direction.

The High Priestess shook her head. "It's easy. That's Assyria." She pointed to Rokath. A laugh burst out of me before I could stop it.

"No, *that's* Assyria," Rapp declared, knocking his shoulder into hers.

"He's right," I replied, grinning.

Kiira merely shrugged like she wasn't concerned with winning their contest. "The easiest way to figure out who was who was to make a guess and check for reactions."

She wasn't wrong.

"Can we return to training?" Rokath grumbled, drawing his sword. The garnets embedded in the skull on the pommel glinted in the sunlight.

Rapp raised his hands in mock surrender.

"I should learn to move like you do," I told my mate.

"Aye," he agreed. "While you already do, simply because I've overseen so much of your training, learning to swing a broadsword in my form will be different." He grabbed a second one from beside Rapp and then handed it to me. "Follow my motions."

Hefting it, I mirrored Rokath's stance. The weight tugged on my shoulders, and even though I bore my mate's bulk, it was more difficult than I had anticipated. Side by side, we stood, swords drawn and poised in the air, as Rapp and Kiira studied us with quiet interest. Rokath stepped forward and swung in a basic maneuver. I did the same, pausing in the same position he did. He backstepped and twisted, the tip of his blade arcing in a straight line, like it would across an opponent's stomach. I teetered for a moment during the rotation but managed to regain my balance.

He moved forward again, combining several strikes this time. Dragging in a breath, I launched into the same series, completely empty of air by the end.

"Good. Again," he commanded. We faced Kiira and Rapp, repeating the flow faster this time.

On the third pass, a handful of males and females peeked over the top of the stands, watching their Szélhámos and Halál-hívó work in tandem. I tried my best to ignore them and focus on what Rokath was doing. He added a few ducks and dips as if we were fighting real enemies, pushing me to the limits of what he knew I was capable of.

Faster and faster we danced as I found a rhythm, half a second off from my mate's performance.

The blood rushing in my ears drowned out all other noise.

Finally, Rokath ceased movement. I finished my last strike, then let my blade hang at my side. My chest heaved from the exertion, and my heart thundered against my ribs.

Yet it wasn't nearly as forceful as the sounds coming from above. I dragged my gaze up. The top of the stands was crowded with onlookers. The entry side to the small space behind them was completely blocked too. Awe etched the face of every male and female.

"How?" someone questioned, his eyes wide as he took in the sight of the Halálhívó in duplicate.

This was a turning point—where I proved I was allowed to stand beside Rokath. That I was *meant* to.

Kiira winked at me as I flicked my attention to her and Rapp, then my mate. He sheathed his sword across his back. With a long exhale, my magic fell away, revealing my true form.

"She truly is his equal," a former priestess said from somewhere in the mix. The males around her nodded.

Whispers of my honorific reached my ears, each instance threaded with reverence.

"You all have training you should be doing," Rokath growled up at them, his tone leaving no room for argument.

With sheepish yet excited expressions, they slunk away from the grandstand and returned to their stations.

"You didn't have to dismiss them," I sighed, running my hands across my face. Wisps of hair had escaped my braid, and they slicked back with my sweat. My nose crinkled as I looked at my hands, then dried them on my pants.

"We don't have time for dalliances," Rokath grumbled.

Rapp snorted like he wholeheartedly disagreed, and I bit my lip to smother my grin. "This is all foreplay for you two. I'd call that a dalliance."

Rokath shot him a dagger-like glare, and he merely shrugged.

"It was quite impressive," Kiira commented, smoothing out her skirt. "Let them see you, at least for a little while, if you do this again. It will help their belief. I'll write to the capital about it as well, helping to sway the nobles and populace, as I promised Xannirin."

Rapp leaned back, bracing his hands on the hay behind him. "Still can't imitate magic though, right?"

I shook my head. "I wish because I know that would be helpful."

Rokath came to my side and pressed a kiss to the top of my head. Fingers under my chin tilted my face up to him. "You are so helpful. You're doing enough."

"But I want to do more. My power has so much potential," I protested with a huff. "I can become anyone. Surely there's another way I can help with that?" Olrus's words slammed into me, almost from another lifetime, like divine intervention.

"They'll exploit your magic and turn you into an assassin. Who

knows where they would send you and who they would want you to kill."

Had Olrus been correct in his assessment? That I'd be weaponized for someone else's gain? Perhaps. But I *wanted* this. I was *choosing* this path. And if it could save the Demon race, help my mate win this war, I'd gladly do it over and over and over again.

"What if..." I trailed off, mulling over how to phrase my request in a way Rokath wouldn't immediately reject. "What if I used my magic to impersonate more Angels too? We capture the high ranking ones, I can sneak into their camp and gather intel or something."

Rokath's expression hardened, and a swell of fear and fury swept down our bond. "I can't risk you like that."

"Wait, she has a point though," Rapp interrupted, rising from the hay. We turned our attention to the Hadvezér, who stood with more ease than he had in weeks. "What have we always done best? Spinning stories. Assyria can enter their camp and spread rumors and then retreat. She doesn't even have to be someone high ranking to do it."

"Her Angelic isn't good enough," Rokath shot back, his fingers tightening.

"We can practice more," I said, excitement thrumming in my veins. "I picked it up quickly before."

A muscle ticked in Rokath's jaw. "Counterpoint. What have the Angels always been best at?"

"Ambushing us," Rapp grumbled, his brows furrowing.

"It's time we turn the tables on them." Rokath paced a slow circle between us, staring at the pennant flags whipping atop nearby towers. "Assyria can act as a lure to peel off sections of their army. She'll infiltrate, spread rumors, stories, drop hints on our location. That will bring them straight into our traps."

Rapp's eyes brightened, and a sinister smile crossed his face. "I like it."

"We'll gather everyone with the power to render themselves invisible with shadow to accompany her." Rokath halted and faced his Hadvezér. "She'll be protected on the ground, and you can send your best fliers for overwatch."

"She'll have them," he swore.

My hands trembled with both nerves and excitement. Finally, Rokath was both agreeing to let me help *and* use my rare magic in a way the Angels could never anticipate—without vehement protest. Without shoving me behind him and calling it protection. So much was going right, and I couldn't help but grin. "Then you'll have a fresh group to call on. You can march them back to the rest of the Angel army and take them by surprise."

A wicked smirk pulled up the corner of Rokath's mouth. "With you at the head, claiming you defeated us."

My mouth dropped open at the suggestion. "That's brilliant."

Rokath rolled his eyes. "Why do you think I lead the Demon army, little imposter?"

"It's certainly not your personality," I quipped, flicking my braid over my shoulder.

That pulled laughter from Kiira and Rapp.

Scraping filled the space around us as Rokath drew his sword again. "If this is the new plan, then we need to change up your training slightly. Once we gather your guard, you'll have to learn to work together as a unit. Almost like the strike team we put together to rescue Banand and Zurronar."

"With the way everything is going, you'll have males and females scrambling to fill slots. Especially after that," Kiira said, pointing up to the stands behind her.

"Good. Then we can select the best of the best," Rokath

growled. "For now, let's ensure you can still pull together an Angel form. Pick one of the females and fight me."

Nodding, I wove Araquiel's body over mine, complete with white armor. From a separate pile, I selected a sword more appropriate to my current size. Rapp and Kiira settled in to watch again.

Rolling my shoulders and sinking into a fighting stance, I squared up with Rokath. Then, I raised the tip of my blade. Energy hummed through me, renewed by my excitement over the new developments in our plans. "Let's go."

Rokath swung, and I dodged, sliding forward and aiming a slice at his hip, where his armor exposed the barest bit of his undershirt. He sidestepped, the sharp tip barely missing the fabric. Air whooshed in my ears as I pivoted on the ball of my foot and held up my sword, just in time for his to smack against it. The impact reverberated up my arm, nearly making me drop the weapon. I bared my teeth, muscles trembling, and shoved back.

Rokath seemed utterly unphased. He used the barest amount of force to fight me which was so fucking unfair.

With a cry, I shoved off our connection and circled away from him, searching for an opening. He stalked forward again, bronze flashing. I ducked, aiming a kick at his inner thigh, where only straps secured the metal covering the front and back.

The connection landed clean, and he swung his leg back and away from me, leaving his non-dominant leg forward.

"Smart move," he commented, flipping the hilt in his hand.

"I had a good teacher," I purred, batting my lashes. A moment later, I thrust my sword forward, catching him off guard. He barely managed to parry it away.

An approving growl rumbled in his chest. "Use those tricks, little imposter. They might save your life." He executed a complex series of strikes, sending me stumbling back. "They might not."

I dug my heel in and attempted to hold him off. Our blades met, and I leaned my weight into it. "I thought you wouldn't let that happen."

"Why do you think I'm training you so hard? I have to whip the foolishness out of you now so our enemies don't on the battlefield," he snapped back. Lust ignited between us as we remained locked in that stance. "No one will take you from me. No Angel. No Fate. Not even death. Because I am the Halálhívó."

Desire coiled in my belly at the possession in his tone. I shoved off him, dropping my magic and flashing him a devious grin. He straightened to his full height, towering over me in a move that was meant to be intimidating but only sent heat rushing through my veins.

"Why is it that no matter how many times I have you, I can't get enough? Why can I never satisfy my craving for you?" he asked, his tone all gravel and darkness.

"Because you constantly have to win me over, Halálhívó. What was it you said when you told me to run the first time? Your favorite game is catch?" I stepped forward until only a breath of space remained between us. Subtly, I called on my magic, smoky onyx ready to explode from me. "There's nothing I love more than challenging you. Than making you chase me."

More lust swept between us. But as Rokath reached for my head, I flattened my palms on his chest and *shoved*. Ebony exploded from my hands, sending him careening backward. He stumbled, falling to the ground, when I twisted my magic and wrapped it around his torso. The shadows halted him mere inches from the unforgiving stone. I prowled toward him, inky tendrils still swirling around us.

The fire in his eyes was entirely worth the victory I'd carved for myself.

"Eyes of devious burgundy," he growled as power pooled around him, fighting against my own to right himself. I released mine, including Araquiel's form, and allowed him to rise. "That's what Kiira said about you before we even knew you existed." He stepped closer, tugging on my braid and forcing me to look up at him. "That is who you have become, Assyria. And I am so fucking proud to call you my mate."

The gong sounded, shattering our moment.

Rokath let out a frustrated grumble. "We'll continue our training later. For now, it's time for lunch."

When we turned to head toward the dining hall, Rapp and Kiira were nowhere to be found. They must have left at some point during our second session.

"Thank you," I said, halting him with two soft words. Yet they felt too small for everything he had given me.

"For what?" Rokath asked, his head tilting to the side.

"Not keeping me away from it all. For empowering me." I paused, and Rokath did too, studying me with haunted intensity. "When I was a girl, I dreamed of having a mate, actually. But one who helped me shirk society's rules for females. Who would love that rebellious part of me. Who would garden with me." My tone was soft, vulnerable, and I looked at my hands, unable to meet his gaze.

A finger under my chin lifted my eyes to meet his. "Truly?"

"Truly," I replied. "It's not in the way I imagined it...but you give me all of that."

He crushed me against him, holding me so tight that I had no choice but to bury myself against his hard armor. "I love you, Assyria. I will always protect you, always fight for you. But more than that, I will ensure you can do both for yourself." Releasing me, he crouched so we were level. "You are mine. I might be a possessive brute as you have called me, but I will not cage you like Vagach did. Not anymore at least."

"Will you still try to break me, to bend me to your will?" I asked, a smile blooming on my lips.

"Only when I am fucking you, little imposter. Because you love submitting to me. You love that you can trust me to make you feel good. To help you explore everything you were forbidden from doing," he ground out, the heat in his tone going straight to my center.

Swallowing, he straightened, glancing around before adjusting himself. I dug my teeth into my lower lip at the sight of the hard outline in his pants. "Come, we'll be late to lunch and I certainly don't want all eyes on me."

"Because you don't want the soldiers to have anything certain for their fantasies?" I shot back.

"They don't," he grumbled.

I slipped myself under his arm as we walked, ever so slightly leaning into his side. "Oh, but they do," I teased. The first time I'd overheard a group talking about my mate, an insane jealousy had risen in me, until I realized I was the *only* one who would get to be with him that way. Then, I got to brag shamelessly to my new friends. Not that I'd admit that to Rokath. His ego was too large already.

Rokath muttered a string of obscenities under his breath. I laughed all the way to the dining hall, where we managed to slip in without any eyes snapping to my mate's groin.

38

ASSYRIA

Two weeks of training together, and the females were already working efficiently as units unto themselves. Many of the males had ripped up their opinions of the matter and burned them, especially after the initiation ritual. Powerful ones worked one-on-one with the new warriors, aiding them in honing their magic.

Volunteers for my elite unit had flooded in, and selecting the final members had been brutal. Uzadaan, Izzenna, and Vokkia were all natural choices. Maariya and Darrx, too. A handful of others with a range of powerful magic rounded out the group—the Deathveiled, as they'd agreed upon calling themselves after our first training session together.

We'd started drilling as a team at the beginning of each day while we were all fresh, watched carefully by Rokath and Rapp, of course. With a solidified routine, all our plans were unfolding smoothly.

The one aspect of our new lives no one accounted for, though, was the drama.

Unfortunately for me, today was my turn to deal with it. In

a now-shared office with Rokath, two males sat across from me, one with a bloody lip, the other leaking crimson from his nose.

"Alright. So who started this one?" I sighed, grasping a stick of charcoal and dragging parchment in front of me. Rokath wanted detailed reports on all instances—they'd ensure all were treated fairly and provided proof should any of the lingering detractors protest.

"He did," they both said, pointing at the other.

I fought the urge to roll my eyes. "Who was it over?" I asked instead.

They glanced at each other, seeming to have a silent conversation. "Maariya," one finally admitted.

"Fucking Fates," I muttered under my breath. "You do realize she has no interest in either of you, right?"

"But–" one started, and I held up my hand.

"The Halálhívó and I are prepared to introduce a no fraternizing policy if behavior like this continues." There was more than a hint of threat in my tone. "Save this energy for the battles to come. Do I make myself clear?"

Fuck, I am really starting to sound like my mate.

"Yes, Szélhámos," they muttered, refusing to look at me or each other.

"Dismissed," I ordered, and they rose, offering me salutes before disappearing into the hall beyond.

I finished my notes, then slipped it on the top of the pile of others. In the war camp, there were no reports and punishment was delivered with a heavy hand. But here, with the structure and formality, the rules had to be a bit different.

As I refilled my glass of water, a knock on the door caught my attention. "Enter," I called out, hoping that another group hadn't been caught fighting or fucking.

Rokath minded the latter far more, constantly grumbling about how they were wasting their energy on their sexual partners—sometimes in multiples at once, not that I was judging—when they should be honing their focus on killing Angels. Every time, I had to press my lips together to smother a laugh at his hypocrisy. I wasn't going to deter him from making me come, though. Now that we were regularly clean, we coupled every day.

My core clenched at the thought of how he'd taken me in front of the windows again last night.

I banished my lustful thoughts when Rapp opened the door. I leaped to my feet and raced to pull it the rest of the way open.

"I can fucking do it," he groused, but I only laughed. While he was nearly healed, we still treated him like a youngling for sheer amusement.

"Can't have this heavy door setting you back a few days. You'll never draw a bow again at this rate."

"Quit reminding me of that," he sighed, passing me and taking one of the previously occupied seats. "I'm going crazy. I need to do more than sit around."

"If that's how you feel, you can take over here for me. I'd rather not discuss another sexual encounter with the soldiers today," I offered in a rush. There was no way I'd pass up an opportunity to escape this torture.

He snorted a laugh. "Not a chance."

I collapsed backward into my chair, raking a hand over my face like it would claw away the stress. "How do I convince them to stop all this nonsense?"

Rapp grinned, flicking his tongue over the ring in his lip. "You don't. Most are young and all of them are forced to be celibate when they are interacting with females at close range all day. They just need to work it out of their system."

"Punching each other is not the way to do that," I sighed, tucking my hair behind my pointed ears.

"You should have seen Rokath, Xannirin, and me when we

were all here. The females in Fured didn't stand a chance," Rapp laughed, clutching his torso for support.

At that moment, Rokath opened the door and entered our office, Grem and Zeec trotting behind him. "I heard my name. What are you saying about me now?"

Rapp put his hand up to the side of his mouth and leaned toward me. "What is it, if I say his real name too many times he is magically summoned?"

I pressed my fist to my lips to stem the flow of laughter.

"I heard that too," Rokath grumbled, rounding the desk and planting a kiss on my forehead. He lingered there, surveying the papers splayed out across the wood.

"You were meant to," Rapp quipped, tugging one out of Rokath's line of sight and reading what I had written.

Rokath rolled his eyes and snatched it back. "Since you're out of bed, I could use your help."

"Thank fuck," Rapp said, bracing his hands on the arms of the chairs and rising.

"What about me? Someone please save me from this," I begged, desperately flicking my attention between the two males.

Rapp smirked like he was enjoying my distress. "Leadership isn't so fun after all?"

"No," I admitted freely in the reckless hope it would get me the fuck out of this office.

"Would you rather finish your work here or listen to battle plans?" Rokath asked, raising a brow.

My lips flattened into a thin line. The only thing I liked less was Rokath's war strategy sessions, mostly because they spoke about people dying with such nonchalance. It was becoming harder for me to attend them the closer I grew to the females.

Rokath and Rapp had told me time and time again not to, that it would only end up hurting me in the end. But I couldn't help it. I knew the reality of war was death and loss and impossible decisions.

Yet I'd never felt friendship and support like I had in the past few weeks. Kiira and I spent hours together in our leisure time, along with the others from Kiira's trusted circle. I was truly blooming into who I was always supposed to be.

That was why I trained with vigor and ensured everyone else was too. If I could prevent even one from dying, I'd snatch the opportunity.

"I'll remain here," I finally groaned with a dread-filled glance at all the papers in front of me.

Rapp chuckled and patted a stack. "Have fun with that."

I made a face at him, only amusing him further. They made to leave, but I stopped them. "Wait! At least leave the dogs to keep me company." He didn't have to know that I'd soon have Kiira too. The more the merrier, especially when I was frustrated to the point of tears.

"I can read your mind, you know," Rokath warned.

"You could not, you know," I shot back.

"You two are doing the mind speaking foreplay again, aren't you?" Rapp teased.

Rokath pinned him with a glare. "Kiira will be arriving shortly so Assyria will have some company."

"Traitor," I huffed under my breath but loud enough for Rokath to hear.

Something flashed across Rapp's expression before he smoothed it. A hint of curiosity rose in me. They had been spending a lot of time together lately too...

Rokath's fingers flexed before he relented. "Fine."

I resisted the urge to throw my hands into the air, professing my victory. "Come," I called out to them, wasting no time in claiming our pets. Grem and Zeec trotted over, tails wagging. "Who are my good boys," I cooed, scratching them both behind the ears.

Rapp chuckled as he and Rokath left me behind to deal with these horny males while they made future battle plans.

But before the door closed completely, Kiira breezed through in her typical fashion, long hair streaming freely behind her, carrying a plate of fresh fish and cheese. Unlike me, she still wore fine clothes when she wasn't training, and today, she sported a black dress with a deep neckline. The fabric was thicker than what she'd worn at Gyor Palace, which with how cold it was, especially with the bitter coastal wind, it was a necessity.

She shivered as she plopped down across from me. "Can you stoke the fire?"

"Sure," I replied, taking another break from my desk and throwing some new logs into the hearth. With the added warmth, Grem and Zeec slunk to the stone in front of it and flopped over. I shook my head and returned to my chair, selecting a fat hunk of cheese and popping it into my mouth.

"Here's the latest," I said, offering Kiira a report on training progress of the priestess-turned-warriors written by the Százados.

She scanned it while she chewed. "Fantastic improvements from the last one. I think they've really taken to their new roles. I don't see why anyone could find fault with them."

I slumped back, relieved by her comments. "Blessed by the Giver."

Kiira chuckled and handed it back to me. "We truly are, though. The magic the females possess is powerful, and wielded on the battlefield like Rokath intends, we'll be unstoppable."

"So are you coming with us?" I asked her.

She nodded. "I know mine isn't as useful, but I think being

there, offering support for the faith, will be more of a help than a hindrance at least."

I regarded her for a moment, weighing the words I wanted to ask. My suspicions had been growing, but I wondered if she'd even admit it to me, given that Rokath and I shared a deep mental connection. I risked it anyway.

"And so you can stay close to Rapp?"

Her cheeks flamed. She grabbed the water pitcher and poured herself a glass, keeping her attention firmly on her task. "I don't know what you're talking about."

"I think you do."

She took a long drag, staring pointedly at the water when she spoke again. "He's been helping me get over..." Her words fractured, but I didn't need them to know what she meant.

Without hesitation, I rounded the desk and dragged the second chair closer to hers. This wasn't a moment for distance, not with how she'd been struggling. Gently, I lifted the drink and set it to the side. A small sob wracked her lithe frame, and I pulled her into my chest and held her there. She had been so strong in front of Rokath and Xannirin, not wanting either of them to worry about her, and my heart ached for her suffering.

We both knew how horrific it was to be overpowered by a male and forced to do things against our will. We understood how nothing was quite the same after. The shame of not being powerful enough to do more to stop it.

"Rapp is a good one," I choked out through a throat thick with emotion.

"He really is," Kiira hiccuped. I stroked her silky hair, soothing what agony I could. Imbuing her with safety and support. She was protected here with me. Here with Rapp. Here with all of us.

"Why don't we go get some fresh air? Take the dogs down to the beach?" I prodded. A change of scenery and the soothing sounds of the ocean would unburden her. I'd snuck away on more than one occasion for just that when it all got too overwhelming.

"I'd love that," she said, straightening and drying her eyes.

"Wine?" I grinned, striding to a nearby cabinet. Hidden behind some leather bound books was a variety of alcohol. Because as much as Rokath loved his rules, we were always the exception.

"You know me too well." She let out a watery laugh.

I grabbed a bottle of red, then some toys for Grem and Zeec. The snoozing hounds leaped to their feet upon seeing them in my hand. "Do you need a cloak?" She wasn't exactly wearing the best attire for an outdoor adventure. Nor was I, clad only in leather pants and a heavy sweater. My jacket certainly wouldn't be enough with how the wind howled today.

"I'll run to my rooms and change. Meet you past the gates in ten?" she suggested, rising and smoothing out her skirts.

"Done."

☠☠☠☠☠☠

THE WALK TO THE BEACH WAS A PLEASANT ONE, ESPECIALLY ONCE THE sun emerged from behind the clouds. We took turns throwing the ropes for Grem and Zeec, laughing as they misjudged the trajectory, their teeth snapping around nothing but air. I wasn't sure if they were truly off their game or if they sensed the heaviness clinging to Kiira and wanted to cheer her up.

I suspected the latter, especially as Zeec continued to careen into her, bearing the slobber-soaked toy.

Yet when we reached the tunnel that led down to the beach, the hounds dropped their ropes and bounded forward, nails skittering against the slick rocks. I laughed and shook my head, grasping the makeshift bannister to steady my descent. I'd have to bathe them both this evening after they plunged in the frigid water—because no matter the temperature, that was the first item on their agenda. Last time, Grem had gotten seaweed stuck so deep in his fur it had taken me half an hour to untangle the mess. I had nearly missed dinner because of it.

"Wait!" I shouted at both of them as I hit the sand. The dogs were only a leaping bound from the water's edge. Per usual, they ignored me and dove the spray anyway.

"Great," I muttered.

Beside me, Kiira huffed a laugh. She wrapped the edges of her cloak tighter around herself as a breeze swept over us. "It's a good thing they have long fur. I wouldn't dare touch the water this time of year."

I slipped off my boots, leaving them at the entrance to the tunnel. The sand between my toes was a welcome change. I wiggled them into it, letting out a sigh. Then, I tipped my head toward the sun.

Zeec barked, drawing my attention forward again. He panted, water dripping off him, and looked pointedly at their toys waiting for them on the beach.

"Fine," I told him, then heaved one toward the water. He barked again as he raced to catch it.

Grem burst from the deep blue ocean and beat him to it. Kiira and I walked along the shore in silence for a few moments, listening to the echo of the waves. Once we reached a suitable spot, we plopped into the sand. Kiira uncorked the bottle, then pulled straight from the neck before handing it to me.

I took a long drink. The wine tasted like berries and chocolate with an undercurrent of bitterness that I thoroughly enjoyed. Licking the last drop from my lips, I snatched my opportunity to ask her about my suspicions. "I've seen the way Rapp looks at you."

My words came out more as a statement and less a question.

She took the bottle back from me, staring out over the waves like she was trying to see to the next continent. "We've been friends for centuries. I don't know. When I started tending to him after we arrived, and when I told him about Ollmund…"

At that moment, the hounds trotted up, Zeec having finally won the game of tug they'd been playing. He plopped the wet rope at Kiira's feet. She made a face as she picked it up and threw it for them again.

"So gross," she commented as they raced away.

"It really is," I laughed. We lingered in silence for a moment before I said, "You can talk to me, Kiira."

She glanced around us, like she was ensuring we were still alone. "I can't, though."

I cocked my head to the side. "Because of Rokath?"

"Yes," she whispered. "I don't want him finding out. And with your bond…"

"I can keep this from him. What are our tattoos for if not to show that we will always stick together?" I teased, hoping my ease would bring some to her as well.

"Something like that," she half-grinned, some of the tension in the corners of her eyes relenting. A long exhale followed. "You promise not to tell him?"

I knocked my shoulder into hers. "On my life," I swore, seriousness threading my tone.

Kiira tipped the wine to her lips again. "I think I'm falling for him too," she admitted, her voice barely audible over the sound of the ocean. She handed the bottle to me, and I took another drink, savoring the taste of it on my tongue.

She swept her long hair over her shoulder and fiddled with the ends of it. "When I saw the wound across his chest…I don't know, something inside me snapped. I couldn't walk away when he was barely able to move about, you know? And watching him struggle to breathe that first night. It was more than an obligation...it was need. It was desire. I've spent so long putting others before myself, this just felt more right than anything else has in centuries."

"I get that," I told her. "Sometimes when we're being self-less, it's still for a selfish reason." Like part of my intention when I wanted females to be in the army too.

"Exactly," she breathed.

Grem and Zeec returned, and they had the audacity to shake out their fur right in front of us. Salty, wet dog spray coated us despite throwing our hands up and leaning back in a desperate attempt to avoid it. "Great, now we'll smell too," I groaned. I snatched their toy and threw it away again before it could get any worse.

Kiira's unburdened laugh lightened my soul. She snatched the bottle back from me. "It's a better excuse that we were taking them out for some exercise rather than drinking between lunch and dinner." A conspiratorial glimmer shone in her vibrant expression.

"Rokath would be irritated if he knew we were out here shirking our duties."

Kiira rolled her eyes. "Everything irritates him."

I snorted and reclaimed the bottle. "Tell me about it." I took another pull, smacking my lips together. "So what's holding you back from admitting all of this to Rapp?"

She braced her hands behind her and dug her toes into the sand. "Rokath. Xannirin. After what happened, they'd lose their minds."

I couldn't imagine Rokath taking the news well. I'd secretly dug around in his mind after Kiira's revelation to weigh his thoughts on it. While he wasn't quite as violently protective of

Kiira as he was me, he still dreamed of the way he'd torture Ollmund Varrir for what he did.

"So that's why you can't tell him. Plus, Rapp is part of our circle, and if it doesn't work out..."

"You don't want it to be awkward," I finished her thought for her.

She nodded. "Or for Rokath to banish Rapp after. We're all he has."

"He may not bear the Vrak name, but he's family," I stated with conviction. Then, what I said caught up to me, and my breath caught.

I have a family again...

It was true, knitted into my bones. Rokath, Rapp, Kiira...they might not have been blood, but they all loved me. And I loved them. Rokath, obviously, because he was my mate. But Rapp and Kiira, I cared deeply for them, like I had my sister.

As if she sensed the direction of my thoughts, Kiira elbowed me in the side. "I never had siblings, only my cousins. You are part of our family, Assyria. Even if you don't officially bear the Vrak name. Yet," she added with a sly grin.

I shifted, dusting some errant grains of sand off my pants. "Honestly, I'm fine with just our bond," I told her. "I don't need a royal wedding."

"It's uncanny how you and Rokath are so similar and yet so opposite," she sighed, playing with the ends of her hair again. "He wouldn't want one either. And Xannirin will never marry."

"Which means you and Rapp have to," I giggled. The wine was nearly empty, and I tipped it to my lips before handing it back to her.

"We'll see," she said, polishing it off. The hounds returned once again, but instead of their toy, they brought a bloody fish. Grem's red eyes danced with pride and excitement as he spit it at our feet. It flopped wildly against the sand, its mouth open and gasping.

With a startled yelp, we scrambled backward.

"I think it's time to go before these vicious beasts steal all the fisher's wares for the day," I laughed. The two watched me, tongues lolling, as I rose and dusted the sand off my legs and bottom.

"Where are your ropes?" I asked them, searching the beach. Grem cocked his head, while Zeec spun in a circle. "Well go find it so we can leave."

Zeec barked and sprinted off, kicking up sand. The moment Kiira made an attempt to rise, Grem shook out his fur, spraying us both again.

"We definitely smell like fish now," Kiira groaned. She smacked her cloak like she could rid it of droplets, scowling at Grem the entire time.

"At least we won't notice it so much after draining the wine," I pointed out, my head swimming as the alcohol worked its way through my veins.

"But everyone else definitely will," Kiira replied, wrinkling her nose and giving up at last. "Maybe we return to our rooms instead of the office."

"I think you're right," I said as Zeec returned with his absolutely drenched toy. Grem seemed nonplussed about finding his, which meant on the beach it would remain.

Zeec noted the direction of our travel, an excited whine slipping through his teeth. Haunches bunched beneath him, and then he bounded ahead and raced up the tunnel. Grem followed. Because where one went, the other had to follow.

I groaned. "Guess we better hold tight to the handles on the way up."

True to my prediction, the tunnel was soaked and slippery. The vicious beasts waited at the top, staring down at Kiira and me like we were preventing them from having even more fun. I shook my head, and the moment we touched the top, they took off at a run through the grassy hills.

"Do they ever run out of energy?" Kiira asked as I yelled at them to return to my side.

"Never." We walked in companionable silence the remainder of the distance.

When we ducked into the academy, we tiptoed down the halls, doing our best to remain unnoticed. Thankfully, no one was around, yet whispers ghosted across the tapestries and reached my ears regardless. I grabbed Kiira's arm and tugged her to a stop after the honorifics for Rokath and me drifted our way.

"You really need to stop by the training area when they are working together. It's like nothing I've ever seen. Like, we all know they are mates, but this? This is a different level. With the Szélhámos's power, she can be anyone, do anything! And the Halálhívó?" a feminine voice gushed.

"He's terrifying. One of him is bad enough, but two?" a masculine voice added.

"The Angels will turn around and run when they see him in duplicate," another male commented with a mischievous laugh.

"When do they normally train?" a second female asked.

"In the afternoons. I'll cover your shift in the kitchen so you can go. Everyone needs to see this. Honestly, I was frightened about the prospect of battle until I saw them fighting in tandem," the first female promised. "Now? I'm ready."

My heart warmed and a wide smile spread across my face. I couldn't wait to tell Rokath about this. Kiira gave me a nudge, drawing my attention. "All we needed was the myth of you two. And it's working."

"It is," I replied, tears burning my eyes.

Who would have thought this was where we'd end up after our bond snapped into place and we were unwillingly thrust together?

"Let's get going before they catch us eavesdropping. I want them to keep talking to everyone like this," I told Kiira. She nodded, and we dipped down a different hallway, avoiding the four.

Though it was a longer route, we eventually ended up at the base of the towers at the rear. Before we parted ways, I dropped my voice and stepped in close so the sentries wouldn't hear me. "I swear, Kiira, I won't tell Rokath about you and Rapp or let him snoop in my mind. When you're ready to announce your relationship, you'll have my full support in dealing with whatever flares inside Rokath's thick skull."

She giggled, then threw her arms around me. "Thank you, Assyria. I'm so lucky to have a cousin like you."

When she stepped back, I had to blink rapidly to prevent the tears pricking my eyes from falling. "See you later," I managed to choke out before yanking open the door to the tower and sending the semi-dry hounds up the spiral stairs toward our rooms.

So many emotions.

It was a good thing my nose was stuffy from holding back tears of happiness, otherwise the smell of Grem and Zeec might have been my ruin. And the whole time I bathed them, I basked in the joy the day had brought.

39

R☠KATH

A pounding on the outer door dragged me from sleep. I bolted upright, the sheets slipping down my body. In two strides, I was pulling on clothes and grabbing my sword. Grem and Zeec barked as the person knocked again, more forcefully this time.

"Halálhívó!" a male called through the door, panic evident in the way he spoke my honorific.

I yanked it open, revealing a Százados I'd brought back from the front to recuperate.

He didn't even salute me. "Halálhívó, we're under attack."

"What?" I snapped. "How? Where? When?"

"The Angels are approaching from north of northwest. About twenty thousand by our estimates," he panted, a tremble in his hands he quickly hid behind his back.

"How far?" I growled, neck growing tight and hot.

"A few miles, sir. The night scout spotted them and flew back immediately. We've sent others to rouse the rest of the academy. Everyone will be awaiting your orders."

"How the fuck," I snarled as I stormed back into the chamber, not even bothering to close the door. I needed to rouse Assyria and strap into my armor. There was no time to waste.

"Send the High Priestess, Hadvezér Rapp, and Parancsok Olet to my office immediately. Send a messenger into Fured to prepare the townspeople and seal the outer fucking doors." I shot the rapid fire commands over my shoulder.

"Yes, sir," the male said before sprinting down the stairs, his feet hammering them hard.

"Assyria!" I barked, and she jolted upright in bed. She must have seen the wild look about me because she slid from beneath the sheets and started pulling on clothes without me having to demand.

"What's going on?" she asked as she jump-shimmied into her black leather pants.

"The Angels are attacking," I replied, trying to keep my voice calm despite the way my heart thundered in my chest.

"Fuck," she swore, finding the rest of her armor and securing it around her. It made me infinitely grateful I'd had a few metal plates made for more vulnerable parts of her body along with her rose-covered helmet.

What the fuck had happened to Trol? Did this group slip away unnoticed, like I thought we had? Or had he been beaten back once again?

We hadn't had a raven from him in nearly a week...

I shoved thoughts of the rest of the army out of my head. There was no use worrying about them now, not when the threat in front of us was very, very real.

In minutes we were both dressed, with weapons strapped and ready to fight. Grem and Zeec were in their harnesses too, tongues flicking out of their mouths as they panted.

"Let's go," I growled, blood beginning to boil. These motherfuckers would not destroy us here. Our numbers were fewer, but we possessed more magic, and we had fucking me.

And my mate.

I took the stairs down two at a time, Assyria and the dogs racing behind me. Once we reached the ground level, chaos reigned. Males and females darted about, screaming for weapons, instructions, or more torches to light the dark. We had a plan in place for such an attack, and the officers in charge were efficiently directing each unit to their battle stations.

We whipped toward the inner keep where the offices and healing wing waited. The open air walkway was a flurry of activity, though most gave us a wide berth with my forceful strides bearing down on them.

Across the courtyard, archers grabbed bows and quivers from females handing them out and raced up tower stairs. Below, males passed swords and extra armor to the ground units gathering by the siege doors. More raced along the upper walls, taking their places with a mix of weaponry.

We ascended the final staircase to my office in the middle of the academy. Olet was already waiting for us there, strapped into his maroon armor, along with a handful of Százados. Kiira and Rapp dipped inside a moment after we did. Their clothes were rumpled, and Kiira's hair was a wild mess. Rapp smoothed his down with his good hand.

Only then did I think to check the time. The massive clock on the wall read three in the morning.

"Fucking Fates," I cursed as I turned to my Hadvezér. "Can you fight?"

A muscle feathered in his jaw as he shook his head. "Magic only."

"I'll take it. Don't push yourself, do you hear me? I'd rather you tap out your magic and have to retreat than reinjure yourself."

"Aye," he said, his voice hard as steel.

"We trained for this. You know how to lead from the rear. I will go to the front and Call," I told him.

"Where do you want me?" Assyria questioned, and I faced my fierce, brave mate. Her determination shone through the slits in her helmet, but our bond told an entirely different story. Apprehension and uncertainty trickled between us. Flashes of my recent nightmare held my ribs in a vise. I knew what I'd promised, but now the threat was so fucking real.

"I can't risk—"

"Fuck that, Rokath. I'm fighting with you," she snapped, slicing my words with the fire in her tone. Ferocity replaced her fear. Her arms crossed over her chest, flexing her hard-earned muscle.

"Now is not the time," I growled, taking a menacing step toward her. The officers pointedly looked elsewhere and busied themselves whispering with heads bent.

She only lifted her chin and glared at me. "For you to be an asshole? You've never been able to tell me what to do, and that's not going to start now. We've been training for this. We're stronger together."

I ground my teeth at my defiant mate, mind working over how to ensure her safety and our victory simultaneously. I hated how she called me out when terror gripped me, when my desire to protect her blocked all reason. I hated that it turned me on. Loved her all the more for it. "Alright, then you will become me. You will remain with the Deathveiled and Rapp." The unit had been working tirelessly, training to guard my mate. All would give their lives for her, which was exactly what I needed at that moment.

"What do you have in mind for our defense?" Rapp asked, low and urgent. The other officers returned their attention to us, and I motioned for everyone to join me around the planning table.

From the wall, I pulled the map of Fured and the academy and splayed it out. "Split the Angel's attention. We'll already have enough of a target on us, so might as well use that to our advantage."

I grabbed a handful of marker stones from a bowl and spilled them across the surface, arranging them in neat groups. "You'll go with Assyria and the Deathveiled to strike from the southeast."

Sliding more stones across the map, I said, "I'll come from the northeast with the rest of the elite force. We'll stay within sight of one another, keep our lines tight."

The winged markers I moved out toward the sea, past the academy. "In the dark, we still have an advantage. We'll have archers circle around and use the wind at their backs to push arrows deeper into their forces. Olet, you'll oversee them from the skies."

With Rapp still injured, he couldn't lead in his typical fashion.

"Aye, Halálhívó," he confirmed. "We'll use our shadows to cloak our approach as well."

The rest of the plan formed in my mind as I arranged more markers around the map. "You three," I focused on the present Százados, "lead your units over the wall at the rear and sneak around the south side. Depending on how far they advance in the next few minutes, you might be able to use the hills to your advantage to lie in wait."

"We'll leave now," one said, and I gave them permission to go. Every moment of advantage we could steal was essential.

"What about me?" Kiira questioned, her weight placed on one hip and arms wrapped tight around her body.

"Stay here and assist the healers. Save those you can. Comfort those you cannot," I told her. My cousin was no fighter, despite how hard she'd been training during her time here.

She'd helped nurse Rapp back to health though, and she could readily assist there.

She nodded, and I was relieved one stubborn female was listening to me. At least Xannirin wasn't here to offer his ridiculous input either. At this rate, he should be far away from the fighting and safe from attack from the Angels. While the Kral and I hadn't entirely repaired our relationship, I still didn't want him to die.

Then I'd have to fucking rule.

"Is everyone clear on the plan?" I ground out, connecting with each individual in the room.

"Aye," Olet and Rapp responded, their expressions grim yet determined. They knew as well as I did we were vastly outnumbered. Even with the influx of females, they still only had a few weeks of training.

I had to hope it was enough to save them.

"It will take more of my magic to make your clothes too," Assyria said, using her thumb to fiddle with the ring on her finger. "Do you have a second set of armor lying around somewhere?"

My jaw clenched again. This was my only set, and yet I didn't want Assyria to be unprotected or burn through her power faster. Not with how long this battle could go on. "I don't. Like I told Rapp, don't push yourself past your limits. The moment either of you start closing in on the point of exhaustion, return to the academy."

"We will. Now let's go. I'm ready to kill some fucking Angels," she declared, rolling out her shoulders.

I captured her waist and removed her helmet. Without hesitation or regard for others in the room, I crushed my lips to hers in a bruising kiss. *"Fuck, I love your darkness Assyria. I should have pulled this side out of you from the beginning. My vicious little imposter."*

"You should have," she shot back. Breaking away, she flashed me those devious burgundy eyes I craved so deeply. Then, she snatched her helmet and settled it over her brow again. Kiira held out her arms, and my mate sank into them. They exchanged a few hushed words, both touching their tattoos.

Then, Assyria released her and strode to an open spot in the middle of the room. On her next inhale, her chest expanded and shadows whipped in a frenzy around her.

A heartbeat later, I stared at myself.

"Let's go," she bit out in my gravelly tone, then broke out into a mischievous grin.

Rapp snorted a laugh. "She's got you figured out, doesn't she?"

I rolled my eyes and pulled on my mask, securing the strap under my chin. Kiira approached, wrapping her arms around me. "Stay safe out there. Please."

I returned her embrace, hoping the tight way I squeezed her conveyed what my words could not. "I will."

A shaky breath brushed against my armor. Though Kiira had always known I was fighting a war beyond Uzhhorod, it had always been always a distant, abstract thing. This would be her first exposure to a battle. To the pain and death it wrought.

She went to Rapp next, and they lingered for longer than she had with me.

I offered a harsh reminder. "We need to get moving."

"Aye," Rapp replied, calling darkness to his bare arms. The wisps circled them like protective sleeves. "Let's show these fucking Angels they're nothing compared to us."

And with that, we swept from the room, preparing to defend the academy and spill our blood.

The number of souls the Reaper would claim remained to be seen.

40

ASSYRIA

Rapp, Olet, Rokath, and I went to the main courtyard and found a sea of soldiers preparing to fight. A sharp whistle from Rokath silenced them all. Whipping around, some even blinking at the sight of their Halálhívó in duplicate, we gained their undivided attention.

Excited shouts of Szélhámos rang out among the former priestesses, and some of the males beat their chests wildly. A collective roar rose from the battle-ready, emboldened by the power exuding from the four of us.

Rokath had to hush them again, but satisfaction curled down our bond. Then, he shouted out instructions based on his quick plans. With practiced precision, the groups rearranged themselves, Olet peeling off to meet with the archers he'd take to the skies, while Rapp and I went to the Deathveiled, gathered near an alcove by the siege doors.

Izzenna bared her teeth in bloodthirsty defiance as she saluted us. Vokkia puffed up her chest. Pride bloomed in mine as I surveyed them and the others, not cowering in fear, but ready to wield their magic and blades for the Demon cause.

"While I may appear as the Halálhívó, I am your Szélhámos.

My magic is fucking powerful, and we are going to use that to our advantage. While I cannot call upon the dead, we can make these Angels believe that I can. Protect me, and we will crush them," I snarled, the rousing speech pouring out of me, raw and so damn right.

"Yes, Szélhámos!" Their voices rang with fierce determination.

Rapp injected himself and relayed further instruction. "We will attack from the left, and we need to move now. Conjure your wings and we will fly into position."

The group took a few healthy steps apart and did just that. Not wanting to waste any more magic or energy than I had to, I returned to my Assyria form and dragged mine into existence.

"On my mark," Rapp cautioned. We waited for him to give the order, and then we leaped into the sky. The Hadvezér's stoic expression twisted into one of pain as we glided over the battlements. I drifted closer, opening my mouth to tell him we could run to position, but he shot me a sharp look.

I snapped my mouth shut.

Soaring toward the front towers, we banked left and swept around them. The stone behind us, we swooped low, the grass close enough to reach out and run my fingers over. I did just that as I gazed ahead, searching for the Százados who had departed under Rokath's earlier command. They'd managed to arrange themselves among the tall yellow fronds, lying flat on their bellies to wait for the approaching Angels.

Into the darkness I peered, like my vision could slice through the void and determine our survival. Air lodged in my throat when my focus landed on a horde of white and grey spreading like rolling smoke over the hillside. Beneath the moon, they snuck through the vegetation on silent feet. Whomever had spotted them had keen eyes indeed.

We landed among the other Demons, and I yanked a sword out of its sheath before reforming Rokath's body over mine.

"How long do we wait?" I whispered to Rapp.

"Until the horn," he mouthed back.

Blowing out a long breath, I nodded and returned my attention forward. The thick straw provided cover, but it shielded my view of our approaching attackers. My heart galloped against my ribs, and ice shattered through my veins.

Every moment of training had prepared me for this moment. Yet I couldn't help the sick feeling rising in my stomach. All of that had been mere practice, like a parent coddling their youngling as they neared to navigate the world. This was real. One wrong move wouldn't result in a pause in instruction and correction.

It would result in death.

I tried to breathe deep into my belly, but it was no use.

Rokath appeared in my mind, and I'd never been more relieved to hear from him. *"Nerves are normal before your first battle. But you are strong, brave, smart. Devious. Use all of that to your advantage, like I know you can, and we'll celebrate by fucking in their blood once we've slaughtered every last one of them."*

The violent promise in his words heated my core. His belief in me renewed my focus.

"I love you. See you on the other side," I sent back, along with a pulse of endless love.

"Fall back if you need to. You matter to me more than anything, Assyria. None of this will be worth it without you."

"I promise I will."

The horn blasted through the night.

As one, we rose, a collective cry ripping from our throats. A few hundred yards away, the Angels faltered their advance. The stars and moon cast eerie glows over the silver blades they drew as we raced to meet them. Ahead of me, the first wave thrust their polearms into the formation, pulling anguished cries from their lips. As they yanked their blades back, the second wave slipped around them and sliced down whomever remained standing at the front.

From the third wave, magic blasted in their direction. Nightmares, Chaos, and Corruption abounded, extracting even more screams. The sharp sound pierced my ears, and yet I couldn't afford to flinch.

"Keep going!" I shouted, and then, the Angels noticed my advance with Rapp by my side.

"Halálhívó!" they screeched, almost like a warning.

Their ranks reformed like a school of fish when they sense danger. Flashes of white illuminated the night.

"Suppressors, go!" Rapp yelled, and a group of females leaped into action, spinning their shadows in a frenzy, preventing those wielding light from continuing to do so.

Ahead of me, bodies fell. I gritted my teeth and kept pushing forward, another group rising to fill the void they left behind as we battled. Dragging in a deep breath, I dove into the well of my magic, deeper and stronger than ever before thanks to Rokath's expert teaching.

A twister engulfed me, slicing across my vision. I flung my hands forward, aiming for the center of a particularly close cluster. The Angels split apart from the force of my shove, their bodies hitting the ground and each other with hard thuds. The scattering allowed the females wielding polearms to dig the tips into their attacker's stomachs.

With a unified cry, they yanked their weapons back, dropping a half dozen Angels. I released a whoop, thrilled by our success, then repeated the action. Magic and blades cracked through the night. Both sexes fought with fervor.

Forgotten were the centuries of a society where females

were incapable of holding their own in the army. The battlefield made no distinction.

Outnumbered, *united*, we forced the Angels back toward their realm.

More flashes of white sliced through the dark, and another group appeared like a shimmering wave to our left.

"Illusion!" I screamed, naming it for what it was so no one would be distracted by it. I ground my foot into the dirt, digging into reality. Others did the same, and the trick dissipated on the wind.

Rapp and I, shoulder to shoulder, closed in on the front line. Thick black ropes appeared in his hands, and he flung them indiscriminately into the crowd. As Angel after Angel collapsed, bound by Rapp's magic, a Demon raced forward to drive their blades through their hearts.

Finally, the Deathveiled surged over the hill, forcing our way onto a flat plain. After my next whipping shadow attack, I stole a look around the battle, glimpsing Olet and the archers in the air, dodging blasts of white and firing arrows down in return. I kept scanning until I found my mate.

Despite the mass of bodies in his wake, he hadn't yet unleashed his power. With me impersonating him, he was unable to wield the corpses littered across the terrain. Not unless he wanted to reveal the Imposter. The way he had to Call was too obvious, with the shockwave that would yank the dead upright to fight.

"Press harder!" I commanded. The sooner we closed the distance between us, the sooner he could claim his power to assist our assault.

A scream pierced my ear again, far too close for comfort. I whipped toward the source of the sound. One of the garnet-eyed females dropped to the ground, a hand slapped over an arrow protruding from her neck.

Fuck.

Another bolt whizzed by, catching someone else behind me. "Duck!" Rapp yelled, and I hit the ground a second before a third flew straight overhead.

A thick rope sailed away from us and wrapped around a group of Angels ahead. "Protect the Halálhívó," he growled, and the group surged like an angry wave.

Roars shattered the night, clamoring with the clashing of blades as we continued to press our enemies back. I shoved to my feet, yanking a sword away from a fallen body. The Angels packed tight like bees in a hive, preparing for their next assault. I raised my arm, tip of the blade pointed toward the group. Aim wasn't nearly as important as distance.

With all my might, I threw.

The bronze whistled through the air, driving straight through the stomach of a male Angel in the midst of the group. His eyes widened, and he clutched the sharp edges like he would yank it free. But it was no use. His knees smacked the earth, and then he flattened completely.

My first intentional kill.

Yet grief didn't surge from the pit of my belly as I watched him die; instead, fire ravaged my veins, imbuing me with further ferocity. A wild grin pulled up my lips as I grabbed another sword and repeated my offensive. Another Angel crashed to the ground.

"Fuck yes!" Rapp encouraged, handing me another. Together we threw again, him his binds, and me, the weapons. Rokath's muscles certainly held multiple advantages.

But then, from the rear of the Angel army, a wave of light, so bright it nearly burned out my vision, rose.

"Shield your eyes!" Rapp screamed.

I threw my elbow over my face and buried my head. In front of us, anguish cries resounded.

The soldiers at the very front.

When I opened them again, what remained of the first and second waves of our army had vanished. Now, a mountain of bodies separated the Angels and Demons as we faced off.

It was almost poetic.

The Angels struck first, pressing their advantage. Vaulting over the dead, some flung more illusions in our direction, warping our reality. Others threw sharp weapons into our midst.

Rapp and I yanked on our shadows to shield the Deathveiled and the other soldiers around us. Vokkia rained destruction down indiscriminately. Izzenna wove nightmares and shoved them in the faces of distant groups to hold them off.

Sweat slicked my spine as they continued forward, forcing us back foot by foot. There were so, so many of them. More that I hadn't seen at first glance.

Would we make it out of this conflict alive?

Uzadaan and Maariya raced ahead of us as a group of white-armored Angels closed in. When they'd worked together in the past, it had been terrifying.

Now?

I welcomed the sight.

The tip of a bronze blade dug into her skin, and she splattered her blood on the field. Sucking over the wound, she drew ruby into her mouth and spit it in a female's direction. Blood dusted her white armor. The Angel snarled, lips curling in revulsion, as she spun on my friend.

Only to halt in place, along with a dozen others, as Maariya wielded her magic. Uzadaan spread his fingers wide, and still more froze, only able to blink at the oncoming Demons. Two females darted between the statuesque figures and sliced the throats of them all.

"Get back," Rapp barked at me, and I wasted no time

retreating behind another line. Should another tidal wave of light come, I didn't want to be in a vulnerable position.

The first hint of dawn appeared over the ocean.

Only then did I realize how long we'd been fighting. Exhaustion tugged at my limbs, and I stole a moment to check on my magic well.

While the shadows were still ebony, their color was waning gray. And quickly.

"Rapp!" I called out. He carefully backstepped, and the line closed in front of him. "We need to rejoin the Halálhívó, and soon."

He nodded, expert eyes sweeping over the battlefield. "Tell Rokath to signal Olet to fly this way and help us carve a path to him."

"We need help over here. Send the archers," I relayed down our mental connection.

"Done," came his terse, tense reply.

Rustling wings reached our ears. Olet and the archers approached from the ocean, their black wings spread wide and sharp arrow tips poised to fly. A group of Angels met them in the skies, giving us room to breathe on the ground.

"Work your way right!" I shouted at our squads.

As one, we moved, corralling our enemies in the direction of the steep cliffs. Sweat slicked my skin, and more than once, I tripped on a fallen body. Rapp's face was ashen, each new bind more gossamer than the last. His movements too dragged like every muscle twitch required enormous effort.

"Don't overdo it," I reminded him as a few soldiers picked up polearms and stabbed into the Angel line again.

"I won't," he said, but I didn't believe him. Like Rokath, he'd fight through the pain, to his own detriment.

But then, a shockwave swept across the battlefield, bringing with it a sound so sharp, so piercing, I fell to my knees.

Clutching my head, I succumbed to the agony, unable to think about anything other than the moment the pain would stop. When the acuteness abated, I dropped my hands, finding them soaked in blood. My ears rang as if the bell from the academy tolled inside them.

A glint caught my eye, and I looked up from the crimson to glimpse silver swinging for my neck.

41

R🕱KATH

The piercing psionic wave dropped hundreds in front of me. Hands clamped over ears. Faces contorted in agony. Mouths unhinged in silent screams. Plunging into my well of magic, I yanked shadow into existence and plugged my ears. The force of the blast brushed over me, and I half-expected for it to knock me unconscious like so many before me. Yet my magic held.

Panting, I raised my sword and leaped into action, defending those still recovering from the deafening attack. None of them would be able to hear for a while, though. It wasn't the first time many had experienced the brutality of high-level Angel magic, but fuck if they sent one of their aquamarine-eyed here, it wasn't a good sign.

They weren't probing, testing our defenses. This wasn't mere strategy on Zahal Ishim's part. This was a step in their extermination plan.

"Assyria, are you okay?" I sent down our bond.

But I was met with silence. Numbness. *Emptiness.*

My stomach plummeted to the core of the earth.

Fuck, what if she'd been knocked unconscious by the blast?

But this void wasn't that; it was the very same as when the Angels had taken her before. Rage boiled my blood and renewed my vigor. I never should have allowed her onto the battlefield. I should have kept her behind the walls of the keep, *safe.*

Shadows surged from me like a volcanic inferno, clawing across the ground without my command. A roar shredded my throat, halting the Angels racing toward me. Their blue eyes were wild as I whipped my blade around, clearing a semicircle in one savage swipe.

Because right fucking now, I needed every ounce of my power to slaughter those who dared take my mate from me.

Dragging in a desperate breath, I dropped to one knee, the impact shaking the ground around us.

Assyria was the kindling that stoked the flame inside me. She was my reason for fighting, reason for fucking breathing. She was everywhere in me—the roses tattooed on my skin, her name the blood rushing through my veins, our bond the center of my power.

Her initial was *carved* into my wrists. She'd claimed me as much as I'd claimed her.

She could not die. I was the fucking Halálhívó. The Fates would bend *to me*. The Reaper could not have her, not today. Not until I was fucking ready.

With teeth gritted against any possibility of losing her, I cocked my fist, curling my fingers into my palm with the force of my fury.

And

Then

I

Punched.

An earthquake rocked the ground as a riot of ebony blasted out of me. The shockwave swept in all directions and yanked corpses upright just as Angels fell to their knees from the force of the tremor. A hundred, then a thousand rose, their lifeless eyes staring, unblinking, into the oncoming enemy.

The sight of them trembling didn't slake an ounce of the primal panic eating me alive.

I flung my hands forward. Disjointed bodies plunged into the still-living, tearing frightened screams from the throats of many Angels. The sound invigorated me, called to the dark parts of me that craved violence. While the corpses worked, I scanned the chaos for Assyria.

Ice froze my spine. Air lodged in my lungs. Blades dug between my ribs.

Instead of myself standing on the hillside it was *her*. A maelstrom of onyx swirled around her, and a bronze blade, coated in a thick layer of ruby, barely held a silver sword off her chest. Rapp was curled on the ground beside her, his back to me.

I went utterly still as her arms trembled.

Like a tremor before a collapse.

Like a roll of thunder before a storm.

And then...

She fell.

"No!" I roared, taking off at a dead sprint toward my mate. Along the way, more bodies rose, racing for them with unnatural speed. Cries of alarm sounded from the group facing off with Rapp and Assyria as the horde of the lifeless confronted them.

The Angel female that had been battling with Assyria turned, screaming at her soldiers to close rank. They did, polearms jutting forward and halting the dead's advance. My mate and Rapp were blocked from me.

A snake constricted my chest. More shadow poured out of me until the bottom of my massive well appeared.

But I couldn't stop.

I had to get to her.

Had to stop this *agony*.

Living Demons joined me a moment later, Destructors picking apart their lines while Corruptors rotted the ground beneath their feet. I angled myself to the outside, trying to work around them.

Grem and Zeec bounded out of the chaos, jaws snapping around weapons and ripping them from steady hands. I'd trained them for viciousness, but the way they went for throats next, dragging Angel after Angel to the ground, was feral, as if they too sensed the importance of bringing this group down.

A pile of Demon bodies became visible—the last place I had seen Assyria. I dragged in another breath and called them to rise, praying Rapp wouldn't ascend with them.

Begging the Reaper not to let Assyria.

Sweat slicked every inch of my skin. My limbs trembled from the effort of holding thousands aloft at once. And blinding, debilitating pain gripped my ribs.

Burgundy eyes flashed at me. Then a devious smile. Those long lashes blinked, brushing against her high cheekbones. Her hips swayed as she approached me.

I fell to my knees at the sight.

"Assyria," I breathed, reaching for her.

She opened her mouth to laugh, but the snarky edge to it was gone.

And something sharp bit against my neck.

The illusion fell away, leaving two Angels standing before me. An ice-blue eyed one laughed again, the trilling grating against my nerves as she pressed her sword harder into the spot between my chest plate and my helmet.

The other stood where I'd seen my mate.

I'd been so desperate for any sign of her, these insects had exploited me.

Just like in my dream.

Grem and Zeec snarled, but I barked an order for them to leave me. To search for Assyria instead.

"Quiet," the one holding the blade hissed. "Release your magic."

I did, mostly because I needed to conserve what little power I had left to blast these two away.

"The mighty Halálhívó on his knees for you, Hayyel," the Illusionist cackled in Angelic.

"Should I blow powder in his face too? Shut down his bond?" she replied.

Primal rage tightened every muscle in my body. This parasite again. She needed to die as much as Zaph did.

"I think he'll come willingly since we have his mate," the second replied, her grin all wicked maliciousness. "After all, he sacrificed fifty thousand for her last time. What do you think he'd do to have her now?"

My sanity *snapped*.

Disregarding the pain, I gripped the sword and flung it from Hayyel's hands. Ruby slicked my palms as I bled for the Fates. Made another offering so that Assyria might still live. I wrapped them around her throat and crunched.

"I would do *anything* for my mate," I snarled in her face. My Angelic was rough and violent, so unlike their lyrical voices. "I'd crawl across Keleti with jagged shards in my knees if that's what it fucking took to get to her. I'd hunt down every single white-winged fanatic until I had her in my arms again. I'd burn the Eső Forest down tree by tree. I'd melt the glaciers atop the Skala Mountains and flood the earth with my fury. There is *nothing* I wouldn't do. Nothing."

Her feet kicked helplessly as I lifted her into the air. The other female lunged for me, but I caught her by the neck too and lifted them both high into the sky. Their faces morphed from a Demon red to a satisfying purple.

"Where is my mate?" I growled as they clawed uselessly at my arms.

The Illusionist pressed her mouth into a thin line. Hayyel's lips mouthed nothing but panic and lies. With a crunch of my fist, I ended the first and tossed her away like a broken prey.

Hayyel, I eased to the ground. Two bloody corpses rose again and dragged her to her knees. She thrashed against my dead's hold. I called a third to yank her head back.

With an animalistic growl, I curved down, my face inches from hers. "Where is she?"

"I don't know," she choked out, tears leaking down her face. *Pathetic.*

"Are you stupid or were you bluffing?" I snarled, my fingers itching to reach forward and choke her again.

"B-bluffing," she coughed out. "She went down, but then your dead arrived and I lost track of her."

Hope twisted my heart. She could still be alive, our bond muted by Hayyel's magic.

I found my sword a few feet away, caked in mud and blood. Flipping the hilt in my hand, I leveled a feral, hateful glare on her. "No one, and I mean no one, who dares to harm my mate lives."

With one powerful thrust, I split her in the middle. Ruby spittle flew from her mouth and landed on my armor. But it was already soaked in Angel blood. One more stain meant nothing.

Next, I grabbed a dagger and dug it into her arm. She screamed, but that only furthered my pleasure. I dragged it along the length of her bicep, splitting muscle until I saw the white flash of bone.

A wicked, evil laugh rumbled in my chest. I dug my fingers in, wrapping around it. Crimson poured out of her, coating my hand, but I didn't care. In fact, I very much enjoyed it, especially as her cries grew more and more frantic.

"This is for daring to swing a sword in her direction."

I *yanked*.

The bone ripped free. Tendons popped, audible over the cacophony of battle.

A piercing wail, sharp enough to be another incoming psionic blast, tore from her throat. The Angels around us whipped their attention to our altercation.

I raised the bone high like a scepter. Held their gazes. Let the beast inside me loose.

"Surrender now and you won't face the same fate," I bellowed in Angelic, voice booming over the battlefield.

Then, I redrew my dagger. In one swift slice, I swept it across Hayyel's throat. Not deep enough to kill her immediately, though. She'd drown in her own blood first.

I kicked her chest, flattening her on the ground, then directed my dead toward the remaining Angels, fighting against the Demons who had flocked to me in my time of need.

Hundreds of my bodies spread across the battlefield, ripping at the limbs of the Angels. A wave of fatigue swept over me as I faced the direction I'd last seen my mate.

Bone in hand, I hunted her. I had to find her. Had to give her this gift.

But with no bond to lead me to her, I was lost. Adrift in the dark. My side, where I always tucked her for safekeeping, was cold, empty, when it should have been warmed by her presence. We were made to walk the dark together.

I wasn't sure I could follow the path without her anymore.

Grem and Zeec raced in sweeping arcs around me, sniffing the ground in search of her. Piles and piles of Demons and Angels did not reveal my mate. The sounds of battle muted to a buzzing in the background as fear sank its claws into my chest again.

What if she had died?

A sob cracked out of me. I couldn't fucking breathe without her.

Wind blasted across the grassy field, and among the metallic tang of blood was a hint of a garden. Grem and Zeec, their noses far more sensitive than mine, halted. Heads uplifted, nostrils flaring, they inhaled deeply.

And then took off at a run.

I sprinted, trusting my hounds to lead me home.

Leaping over corpses, dodging half-broken weapons protruding from the earth, we raced back toward the academy. The hounds halted at an outcropping some distance away.

My lungs burned as I approached, but I didn't slow until I was upon it.

And there, lying on the ground, covered in blood, was my mate.

Movement from above had me throwing myself over her. Pain speared into my ribs as someone stabbed me. I whipped around, hand snapping out, only to find Vokkia gaping at me with wide-eyed horror. A dagger fell from her palm a moment later.

"Oh, fuck, Halálhívó, sir, I am so sorry." She fell to her knees, tears streaming down her face. Clasping her hands together, she prostrated herself. "Please forgive me. I reacted when I saw movement, before I realized you weren't an Angel come to finish off the Szélhámos."

My fury abated immediately. She'd acted out of loyalty to my mate.

"You may rise," I commanded, and she did, though her entire frame trembled. "You followed your orders exactly, soldier. There is nothing to forgive."

"She saved me," Assyria coughed, and I faced my mate again.

"Little imposter," I breathed, kneeling in front of her. "I thought I lost you."

She offered me a weak smile. Her helmet had been discarded and rested against the ground beside her. A hand pressed into her bad shoulder, and garnet leaked between her fingers. "You'll always be able to find me. Even if I run."

The echoes of our first conversation speared into my heart. A choking sound escaped me as I swept her into my arms. I crushed her against my chest like I could plant her vast love there so I'd never be without it again.

"Assyria, Assyria, Assyria," I repeated her name like a whispered prayer. Like words of gratitude to the Fates. "I will always be able to find you, mate."

Our bond flickered like a struck match in an endless night. I nearly wept from the relief of it.

Releasing her and easing her back against the rock, I grabbed the bone and offered it to her, along with a dip of my head. Her delicious lips curled into a wicked smile like I'd handed her a crown. "This is for you. After all, the Szélhámos needs a seat beside the Halálhívó. What better day to start building it than today?"

The lust that blasted our bond made me want to fuck her right then and there. She plucked it from my palm, boasting a devious grin. "My protector. My Halálhívó. My Fate."

"That's fucking right," I ground out, cupping her cheek and smearing more ruby on it.

A moan tore my attention from her and toward Rapp. The spell between us broken, we both rushed to his side. "He overdid it," Assyria explained. "He might have pulled something again. He dove into the Angel to save me. Vokkia dragged us both to safety."

Rapp coughed, his brows pinched in pain. "I'll be alright."

"No," I snapped. "Both of you, back to the academy. We're almost done here."

"But I can fight through the pain. I'm already feeling–" Assyria started, but I silenced her with a heated glare.

"You will go, and you will not argue." My attention ripped to Vokkia, ensuring she saw the seriousness etched into my face. She offered me a subtle nod, confirming she'd escort them back.

"Then release some of your dead so you don't burn yourself out," she hissed back, inky tendrils dripping from her palms and wrapping around Rapp.

She had a point. The sheer number I'd wielded had nearly drained my well to its dregs. Only wisps of smoke remained where the inky shadow had been. I rose, then selectively dropped bodies. From what I could see, though, they'd made quite a dent and allowed the Demon soldiers to recover from the psionic wave. Only a few thousand Angels remained, and even more Demons lived.

"Go. I'll finish this."

This time, she didn't argue. With Vokkia's assistance, the three hobbled back toward the academy. When they disappeared down the hill, I faced the battle again. I needed to find that fucking psionic-wielding Angel and get some answers out of him.

"To me!" I growled, and ranks reformed at my back. "If you hear the blast coming again, use your shadows to plug your ears."

I carved a path straight through the middle, splitting their forces in two. At the rear, as I suspected, a Myrza waited. Fuck, how I wished I had Rapp's binds here to help me take this motherfucker down.

Instead, I had to rely on a group of Suppressors to clamp down on his psionic abilities. More soldiers offered me small weapons to stick in him to render his power completely unattainable. All the while, he swore at us in Angelic. Even more when I forced him to his feet and marched him back to the academy with daggers in his thighs and calves.

With the battle over, the survivors started to separate out the bodies. The Demons would receive proper rites, even more blessed for their sacrifice since the High Priestess was here to see them into their next lives.

The Angels? Well I'd probably want to throw them in the ocean for the fish to nibble the flesh from their bones.

Passing Olet and a few Százados, I instructed them to do just that. "I want a full account of our losses as soon as you have them," I added. I'd overseen hundreds of battles in my centuries of life, and I wasn't stupid. A great many Demons had died protecting the academy and Fured. The dent in our forces was yet to be seen.

But it would be a sizable one.

"Yes, sir," they said, all bone-weary and dragging from the exertion of the day.

With the Myrza bound and Assyria safe inside the walls, I should have felt triumphant. But with how the Angels had marched through the northern tip of the Demon Realm unchecked, all I felt was dread.

And whatever had happened to Trol...

I had a marrow-deep feeling that it was only the beginning.

42

ASSYRIA

Exhaustion tugged at my limbs as the lead healer attended to my wound. The academy was in recovery mode, soldiers limping by the battlefield tents to seek treatment, others hauling wood toward the pyres some distance away.

The gash in my shoulder would heal in a day or two, but what of them?

A hiss slipped past my lips as an ointment-soaked cloth pressed against the flayed skin. Fuck, it hurt, even if it was already mending. The male jumped back like I'd scalded him. "Did I hurt you?"

I shook my head and gritted my teeth harder. He continued his work while I continued my survey of the living and dead.

A cart approached, carrying half a dozen females. Yet unlike many of the ones that had already trundled by, the priestess-turned-warriors were all neatly arranged, their hands by their sides, palms facing the sky.

Sleeves rolled up and revealing the devious eye tattoo.

A snake wrapped around my chest and *squeezed*, robbing me of all air. Tears burned my eyes, and my vision blurred.

"Is it too much?" the healer prodded.

"No," I replied. But it was. The pain of their deaths was unfathomable. Yet, he couldn't touch, couldn't heal this ailment. The one that came from too much loss. That came at the cost of love.

They'd died...because of me.

Because I was a symbol for them.

Because they *believed* the lie I let them ink into their skin.

Because I gave them a reason to hope they could live in a different future.

Because I dared to demand more...and they followed me into the fire.

I smashed my lips together, trying to refrain from crying out. My bond with Rokath was still muted from Hayyel's power, but I tugged on it anyway.

I needed him.

Only he could talk me out of this spiral tugging me under, under, under...

Like a Fate, he emerged from the crowd, his burgundy eyes burning straight into me. He ignored the salutes, the greetings, the veneration of his battle prowess. To him, I was all there was in the world.

The lead healer finished binding the bandage on my shoulder and quickly excused himself. Rokath stopped in front of me, his fingers dipping under my chin and lifting my gaze to meet his.

"What's wrong, little imposter?"

My throat worked as I tried to form the words. "I–I failed them." One tear slipped out, then another. The next two words choked out of me and opened the floodgates. "They died."

I collapsed into his chest, clutching at his bloody armor. He wrapped his arms around me like he alone could hold the pieces of me shattering together. "This is war."

Anger swelled, joining my sorrow. "How can you be so cold, so cruel?" I jerked back, glaring up at him. Yet instead of a furious expression etched into his face, heartbreaking sympathy greeted me.

"This is your first battle, Assyria. The first time you've fought, the first time you've watched others bleed, the first time you've watched others *die* for their beliefs. It is not mine."

I wiped my nose on my sleeve, filling my nostrils with a metallic tang—a reminder of who was being prepared for their pyres. "I can't do this. I can't stand by and watch the people I love die."

Rokath crouched so we were eye to eye. "Yes, you can. Because you are the reason they fight–"

"I am the reason they *died*! I was the one that pushed you to bring them here. It was my symbol they tattooed into their skin. It was me who they followed onto that battlefield." A choked sob escaped me then, and I collapsed inward, unable to snuff the embers of grief.

"You gave them a choice, Assyria. That is what they wanted more than anything. And those still living? They'd do it again." Rokath stroked my hair as I sobbed harder into his chest.

"You loving them is what freed them and made them fearless. You loving me is what freed me and made me more than a weapon. Your bravery is not muscle or magic, Assyria. It blooms from your heart. From the raw, relentless devotion you show others. From that fire that refuses to die even when others try to smother it. A flame borne from love."

I looked up at him through blurred vision. "But they died because of it. Like everyone else."

"The Reaper's path is different for everyone. You do not influence it, as much as your mind might tell you it does," he murmured, brushing the backs of his knuckles across my cheek.

I swallowed hard. Movement caught my attention out of

the corner of my eye. My gaze drifted toward Rapp, Kiira, and dozens of others watching on.

Rokath's knees hit the ground, one by one, like twin boulders planting themselves at the feet of the mighty mountains. From my position on the table, I was merely a few inches above him. "Do not let this battle, or any others, harden you as they have me. If feeling your grief is the cost of loving you, then let me drown in it time and time again. Because we need your emotion, Szélhámos. You are the type of leader we have been missing from the army. You will not be broken by this—you will bend it to your will instead."

Rokath tugged open a leather bag I hadn't realized he'd been carrying. From within, he pulled out more bones and a smattering of white feathers. Sinking back on his heels, he knelt, the bundle raised over his head. "For your throne, so you may claim your rightful place at my side."

Those gathered went utterly still, enraptured by the scene before them. Rokath had offered me Hayyel's arm bone, but that was done only in front of Vokkia and Rapp.

This?

This was him bowing to me in front of the army.

This was him elevating the myth of us further.

From the fringes, males appeared, some carrying feathers, others carrying bones.

They knelt behind Rokath—not to him, but to me. To what I represented.

They offered more to build my throne. To sit beside the male they had revered long before I emerged as his mate.

Females joined them, yanking up the sleeves of their armor and revealing the devious eye tattoo on their wrists.

All of this...for me.

A vindication of the softness that survived a gruesome battle.

A veneration of the sparks that smoldered through sorrow.

An honorance of grief that didn't harden into harshness.

And in that moment, I understood.

I hadn't failed them; I'd elevated them.

And they wanted to continue their fight.

A serrated breath accompanied the next wave. Rapp and Kiira knelt with them. All movement around the academy had ceased, poised on this very moment.

Blinking rapidly, I tried to arrest the tears, even for a moment, to imprint the scene on my memory. Then, I reached for Rokath's bundle and lifted it from his hands.

"Rise," I commanded with as much authority as I could muster around the thickness in my throat.

My mate did, his riotous burgundy eyes sparking with desire. Those behind him followed, piling their bones and feathers at our feet. Rokath swiped the lingering salt from my cheeks and then faced them alongside me.

"My bold, beautiful mate. Give me your tears, and I will catch them like they are precious. Let me be the hands that hold you when the world breaks you again. Let me remind you—your sorrow is not a weakness. It is the mark of one chosen by the Fates to feel what others fear."

I'd never been more relieved to hear him in my mind.

"You are my sanctuary. My refuge. I am so fucking glad you didn't die. I couldn't live without you."

"Nor I without you. My fierce protector. My primal love."

He kissed me then, unrestrained passion igniting between us. Fuck our audience. I needed my mate.

Whoops and cheers eventually drove us apart, yet the darkness in Rokath's eyes told me we were far from finished. He linked his fingers through mine and held my gaze.

The bones at our feet weren't mere trophies. Decor for our

war tents. They were proof that even amid ruin, the soldiers believed in us. In me.

And we would not let the dead burn for nothing.

43

R●KATH

Blood darkened my hands, but it was nothing compared to how my vision stained red when a raven arrived. The new recruit who dared interrupt my torture trembled at the sight of the half-dead Angel. Shooing him into the hall, I set my tools to the side and wiped my hands on an already dirty cloth. Assyria followed the male, and by the time I emerged, my mate had walked a few paces away from the door.

Leaning against the wall, the back of her head braced on its cool surface, she looked as if she were trying to picture herself anywhere but here. The dungeon of the military academy was dank, musty, and wet, with spray from the ocean somehow reaching inside the tiny crevices of rock and securing its place there. There was no fresh air to be had, and even with the door closed, the stench of our activities pricked my nostrils.

We'd been at this for hours, and she had stomached more than I thought her capable. Despite her injury, she insisted she needed to study this Angel since he held such a high rank. In the Angel army, Mryza was the equivalent of a Parancsok, though they all reported directly to Zahal Ishim. Impersonating him would throw open the door of possibility for us when it came to infiltrating their camp or influencing any Angels we came across.

The garnet-eyed male stood at attention, his back straight and hands tucked. He was bruised, with a split lip and deep gash on one side of his head, but all his injuries would heal by the end of the day.

"Halálhívó," he said, offering me a quick salute and proffering the message.

A muscle ticked in my jaw as I unfurled the parchment, the thirst for pain unrelenting. Air caught in my throat as I noted the handwriting.

Trol.

Thank fuck he was still alive.

Halálhívó,

A battalion of Angels has split off from the main group, headed east, most likely to Fured. We didn't notice their departure until I sent a scout on a mission and he spotted them from a distance. They must have used some sort of illusion to sneak away. By our estimates, they should reach you a day after this note.

"Fuck!" I shouted, whirling for the thick stones and punching them, if only to have something to slake an ounce of this rage.

How had they seen us depart? How had they known where we'd go?

Snapping it open again, I kept reading.

We need you to return as soon as possible. The reason I sent the scout is that their forces have begun to pull back of their own accord. As discussed, we have not engaged with them since your departure. From other scouts' reports, a mass of them are gathering along the wall, both on the border to the north of the Skala Mountains and along the northernmost part of the wall atop the ridges. We aren't sure how far south they have spread yet or if they will continue to do so.

I am sending a contingent to the wall as a backstop after I finish penning this note. Afterward, I will begin an advance so we don't lose sight of more Angels. Please send further instruction if you have it.

I hope this reaches you in time so you can prepare your warriors for the imminent attack. I bid you to rejoin the larger force once you've routed them in Fured. It is my fear that we can no longer wait for further training and that the Angels are planning some sort of assault now that they know of your absence.

Trol

My hands shook with the force of my fury. Trol had been a day late in his estimate, which wasn't entirely his fault, but I was still pissed nonetheless. The only mercy offered by his words was leverage. Armed with information about the Angel's movements, I had a starting point from which to force the Myrza into speaking.

With the Angels spreading like a plague of locusts across Keleti, with my mate wavering on her feet, with how they'd surprised us yet again...I needed all the information I could gather.

"Take this to Hadvezér Rapp and the High Priestess," I commanded the messenger. "Find Parancsok Olet and tell him to meet us here."

"Yes, sir," the male confirmed, offering me a closed-fisted salute. He marched away immediately, leaving me to finish what I started with the Angel Myrza.

"What did it say?" Assyria questioned, her voice threaded with exhaustion.

"Trol warning us of the oncoming attack." I slammed the door open again, making the Angel jump. The two Vezető assisting me didn't flinch, though they regarded me with wide-eyed wariness. Assyria closed the door with less roughness behind her, then took her seat in the corner, arms crossed.

A storm clung to me as I stalked forward and braced my

hands on either side of the Myrza. "Why are your brethren going to the wall?"

He pressed his swollen lips together, wincing at the movement. Mine curled back, flashing my sharp, pointed canines. Through gritted teeth, I threatened, "Last chance to speak before I start removing your bones."

His face turned ashen. So far, the damage I had inflicted had been superficial enough that his innate healing abilities would undo most of the damage. But our magic didn't cover regrowing bones.

I lifted a brow, waiting for a response. He still said nothing.

Shoving back, I said, "Very well then. Hand me that knife."

One of the Vezető passed me a wickedly sharp bronze blade. I made a show of flashing the edges in the light, gauging the Angel's reaction. His aquamarine eyes grew large as the balls I threw for Grem and Zeec.

I knelt in front of him—not out of reverence or deference— but because it brought me closer to his hands. Bronze chains bound his wrists to the arms of the chair, and I grabbed his fingers and flattened one out. He twisted, attempting to curl them back into a fist, but I merely smashed the hilt of the blade into the back of his hand, forcing him to relax it. When I had one pinned, I looked him dead in the eye and dragged the tip of the blade along the meaty part of his lower finger.

"Reaper, may your eye watch over me as I spill blood in your name," I snarled, adding a psychological element to my torture.

"We spill blood in your name, Reaper," the Vezető and Assyria echoed. Our bond flooded with dark desire, my mate's attention firmly on me.

This performance was as much for her as it was for the Angel. To show her the depth of my devotion, the dark places I'd crawl to protect her.

A scream tore from the Myrza's throat as I stabbed all the

way through and peeled the flesh from his bone. When he saw white, he turned to the side and retched. I rolled my eyes.

Pathetic, every last one of them.

I let him recover because I wanted him to see, to *feel* when I ripped the bone from its socket. Distraction simply would not do.

He straightened at last, chest heaving. The moment he looked down, I snatched my opportunity. Grabbing his finger by the tip, I *ripped* my arm back. The digit separated from his body with a satisfying snap.

The scream he released would have curdled my blood if I didn't fucking love killing Angels so much. The Vezető laughed, only adding to the torture of the insect who dared think he could take me on and win.

I dropped the severed finger on the Myrza's lap like a promise as to what would come next. Later, though, I'd strip the rest of the flesh away and add to Assyria's collection.

I didn't bother asking him if he was ready to talk yet. I still had some anger to slake. Without waiting, I stabbed into his middle finger, peeling the muscle away. Sweat spilled off him, dripping down his temples onto his shoulders, and the palms of his hands were clammy, mixing with the blood seeping from his wound.

A sigh threaded with annoyance slipped out of me as I ripped the second finger from his hand. Garnet spilled from the corners of his mouth. I shot to my feet and gripped either side of his jaw, forcing it open. Then I saw the deep gouges his teeth had left in his tongue.

I tsked like he was an errant child. "Can't have you doing that again. I still need you to talk. Get me the gag," I commanded the Vezető, not even bothering to look away from the Myrza.

When the weight of my new instrument settled in my palm,

I dragged it in front of the Angel's face. Something between a bit for a warhorse and a metal circle, it prevented a prisoner from clamping down on anything that was put in their mouth.

"Open wide," I taunted, my voice dripping with disdain.

The Myrza attempted to snap it shut. I shook my head, again releasing a disappointed sigh. "If that's how you want to be."

Diving into the well of shadows in my chest, I called on the threads of it to take the place of my hands. They thickened until they forced his jaw open, despite his attempts to snap his teeth shut. I adjusted the gag until it was level in my hands and pressed. The cool metal bit into his flesh, and I positioned his lips around the O ring in the center. Then, I secured the buckle around the back of his head. Once I was certain the fit was painful, I released my magic.

"There. Much better don't you think?"

He attempted to curse me around the gag, but all he succeeded in doing was drooling all over himself. Hate filled his aquamarine eyes—nothing new from these Goddess-loving sycophants. Honestly, it was becoming boring.

"Since you don't seem to value your fingers, perhaps I should move on to another part of your body?" I asked him like he had a fucking choice.

Grabbing my dagger again, I dragged it along his thigh, knocking his severed digits to the floor. I paused when the tip rested near his dick.

There was a singular, universal way to get males to talk that transcended race: threaten their cocks. Most, despite knowing they had zero chance of living, would still protect the organ until their last breath.

And I was losing both patience and time.

The Myrza thrashed wildly against the bronze chains

binding him to the chair. More strangled sounds spit through the gag, and instead of hate, pure, unfiltered fear filled his eyes.

Much, much better.

The primal beast in me purred at the sight. Nothing made me feel more in control than drawing that raw emotion out. And right now, after almost losing Assyria again, I needed that.

The sharp tip pressed in, slicing through the fabric clinging to his thighs. His cries increased, but he stilled.

"What's that? You're ready to talk?" I mocked.

He nodded vigorously. I didn't move the dagger.

He made another noise that sounded a lot like "please" in the common tongue. Calling upon my shadows again, I worked the buckle open. Before the metal in his mouth slackened, I shoved onyx tendrils inside, blocking his ability to chomp his tongue in half.

It wouldn't have been the first time one attempted such a trick.

I removed the bit, then cocked a brow. "So, why are the Angels gathering at the wall? What is the Zahal's plan?"

"I only know that I was sent here to eliminate your most powerful magic wielders," he gasped out in the common tongue.

I forced my expression to remain cold and detached. How the *fuck* did they know about that? Banand and Zurronar had mentioned the torture the new recruits had endured, which is how they knew about Assyria. They must have gotten this information out of them too.

"That's not good enough," I replied coolly, dagger biting deeper. A blot of ruby welled up on his white pants.

"Stop! Wait! I'll tell you," he half-sobbed.

The blade halted, still pressed into his skin.

"A Seer told us we had to spread out along the wall," he

gasped. "She saw a great, bloody battle in the mountains. Said if we wanted to win, we needed to change our tactics."

Interesting.

Kiira's new vision contrasted whatever the Goddess had offered this female. Yet it was known that Angel prophecies were conjecture and interpretation at best. If the Goddess had offered her this scene, it was a venomous presage, not a saccharine omen.

The Demons would claw a victory from those peaks, one that would lead to the moment Kiira had seen of Assyria and me in Sivy.

"Is the Zahal calling on reinforcements for this?" I pressed. It was what I would have done—had done.

He nodded vigorously. "That's why I was sent here. He wants to weaken you further while he gathers more. Saw what you did with your numbers and wants to recreate it."

Of course he did. The fucking leech couldn't think for himself. It wasn't the first time he'd taken my tactic and then turned it against me. By now, he should have learned it never worked.

His arrogance was why our historians would etch my name in their books, laud my prowess in battle, and his would disappear into the ether, lost to time.

A knock on the door stole my attention before I could continue my interrogation. "Enter," I called out, twisting to see who dared intrude when I was in the flow.

Again.

Olet appeared in the doorway. "You wanted to see me?"

My annoyance dissipated. With protesting knees, I rose, the dagger squelching as I removed it from the Myrza's thigh. A sob choked with relief escaped him. Until I gave the two Vezető a new command. "See what else you can get out of him. Then kill him."

"No!" the Angel shouted, and the Vezető chuckled darkly. Grabbing new tools, they flanked him. Panic held his eyes open, but I didn't deign to offer him more of my time. With a jerk of my head, I motioned for Assyria to join us. She shot one last glare at the Myrza, her assessing eyes searing one last look into her memory, and then ducked under my arm and into the hall again.

His scream was cut short when I closed the door behind us. Olet paced a small circle there, picking his head up at our arrival.

"The time has come for us to leave," I told him.

The grimness in the set of his jaw mirrored my own internal experience. "What of Hadvezér Trol?"

"He's alive, so far as I know. He sent a raven warning us of the attack. It arrived only a little while ago."

Olet snorted and shook his head. "A little too late."

I grunted my agreement. "He did request our presence at the front again. The Angels are splitting their forces, and he is following. According to that fucking fanatic, they're spreading along the wall because one of their Seers told them there was to be a bloody battle there."

Olet shifted from foot to foot. "We haven't had nearly enough time. Especially not with the females."

I blew out a long breath. "I know."

"I think they demonstrated that they can hold their own," Assyria added. She swayed on her feet. Dark circles lined her eyes, and I wanted to get her to bed immediately. Flattening my palm on her lower back, I offered her support.

"What were our losses?" I asked Olet, my stomach tightening. The aftermath of every battle came with conversations that were tough to chew.

Olet rubbed the back of his neck. "Too many. A few thousand."

The muscles in my neck bulged with how hard I gritted my teeth. "Fuck."

His arm dropped to his side, and a heavy sigh followed. "Many more were wounded. Most should be able to travel within a few days though."

I looked up at the ceiling as if the Fates had written all the future paths there. "Start preparing everyone to leave. We'll move out in three days. We can spare no more."

"Aye, I'll see to it immediately," Olet affirmed. Like Assyria, he looked exhausted.

"Walk with us. We need to find Hadvezér Rapp and discuss more of our plans," I told Olet, striding toward the stairs that led up from the dungeon. I'd check on our prisoner later, see if the Vezető yanked any more information out of him.

He followed, matching my quick clip. The remainder of his post-action report he relayed by the time we reached the landing. There, we went our separate ways.

"I'll escort you to our tower, but then I need to go to my office," I told Assyria. Because before I could speak with the rest of the officers, I needed to write to Xannirin. This would be the test of his commitment to our new plans.

"Okay," she sighed, too tired to protest. "You'll come back soon right?"

"I promise." When we reached the door leading to the spiral stairs, I opened it for my mate. "You did so well today. You and the females. I think the rest of the army will see that quickly too."

She offered me a soft smile. "I hope so." Then, she disappeared up the spiral. The sentries stationed on either side still had blood on their armor and cuts drying on their faces. In an uncharacteristic moment, I thanked them for their duty.

Each stared at me as if I'd grown a second head. Sighing, I

left them behind, the trek passing in a blur as I mentally drafted the message I would write my cousin.

We needed additional aid, and quickly. The Angel's advance, spreading like a rot through the realm, left no room for mercy.

Not for them. Not for Xannirin.

We thought we were preparing soldiers for war here; we were already inside it.

No longer was this a game of strategy. This was divine prophecy, holy vengeance, and sacrificial fire.

Yet the walls of our carefully constructed temple were cracking.

To protect Assyria, to protect the Demons, I'd rip apart the nobility, drag their power into service, and flood the front with bodies.

Not all of us would survive what came next. A great sacrifice awaited us somewhere in the future.

And I would not let Assyria fall. But something deep inside me whispered that the Angels weren't the only ones spreading ruin.

***

INTERLUDE

Bloody footprints marred the marble halls of Gyor Palace as the future Kral rushed along them. Overhead, the barest sliver of a moon stalked him through the windows like a judgmental God, weighing his actions and deeming his worthiness. For this night would irrevocably alter the course of his life—and the lives of millions around the world.

Pools of ruby thickened as he closed the remaining distance to the royal wing. The place he'd been birthed, where he'd spent his youngest years, and where now, his fate awaited him. A tumultuous storm of excitement and dread rushed his steps along. He had to know what had happened. If their plan had succeeded. If his cousin still lived.

At the choke point of the hall, a dozen Kral's Guard lay scattered, bent, and broken on the ground. Easing toward them, he studied their forms. Their lifeless eyes stared at nothing. Hope soared in the male's chest.

As nimbly as he could, he leaped over the puddle, not wanting to stain his shoes.

The door to the Kral's chambers was cracked, yet no sounds

came from within. On tiptoes, the future Kral approached, his heart hammering in his chest. Flattening his palm against the wood, he pressed. It swung inward on silent hinges.

The scene it revealed to him left him rooted in place.

The back of a tattooed head greeted him, broad shoulders heaving beneath fitted metal armor. He didn't tremble, didn't weep. Merely stood like the eye of a storm, rage and fury twisting around him. At his cousin's side, a longsword dripped garnet onto the ground. His other hand, though, boasted a spiked glove, bits of gore decorating the tips of it.

Bile rose in the male's throat, and he pressed his lips together to seal it inside him.

Because that wasn't the worst of the scene.

Beyond his cousin, three more bodies lay crumpled—if they could still be called that. Heads removed from their place atop necks. Fingers twisted at unnatural angles. Bones fractured out of the skin that should have held them inside. The scene was carnage beyond anything he'd witnessed during his time at the military academy with his cousin.

Yet one corpse bore the signs of a special type of cruelty— his cousin's father. Missing an eye entirely, jaw hanging open, spine permanently torqued, he wondered at what point his uncle had finally died. The sheer brutality of his murder sent an icy chill through his veins. He knew his cousin had a temper. Fates, he knew that he was the most lethal killer in all of Keleti, if not all of Ravasz.

But this, this was beyond excessive. This went beyond vengeance.

For the first time, he feared his cousin. Feared his prowess. Feared his anger.

Despite his rising nausea, he seared the scene into his memory. The blood. The gore. The twisted bodies. The heaving of his cousin's chest. The blade with the skull in the pommel, reflecting his terror back to him through rivulets of ruby.

Because deep down, he knew that Rokath had far more power than he did—than he *ever* would. His future was a glass throne. One misstep, one moment of angering his cousin, and it would shatter beneath him.

Tentatively, he stepped deeper into the room, regarding his cousin with more than a hint of wariness. Only then did Rokath tilt his head over his shoulder and acknowledge his presence. Burgundy eyes burned with hatred still, even after their tormentors lay dead at his feet. The darkness in them sent a shiver down his spine.

Yes, his cousin was someone to fear. His cousin was a potential threat. The moonlight caught on a fractured mirror, reflecting back to him an undeniable truth: his own blood was merely waiting to be spilled.

He swallowed hard and met his cousin's gaze. Then, in his deep, gravelly tone, Rokath spoke the words he'd been dying to hear for decades.

"Congratulations, Xannirin," he rasped, his voice like gravel. "You're now the Kral of all the Demons."

PART
FOUR

44

Xannirin

A knock sounded on my office door, followed by one of my sentries' voices. "Messages for you, My Kral."

"Enter," I called out lazily. I set the note from one of the unhappy nobles aside and slid my boots off the desk.

The red-armored guard entered, carrying two sealed rolls on a gold tray. He bowed, nose far below his waist, as he offered them to me. My jaw tightened when I noted Rokath's seal in the wax on one. The other was from Kiira.

"Dismissed," I grumbled as I weighed them both in my hands. The sentry departed immediately.

Deciding to read the worst first, I broke open Rokath's note. "What could he possibly want now?" I grumbled to myself. Unrolling the parchment, I scanned its contents.

My Kral,

The Angels mounted a surprise attack in Fured. We were able to rout them, but not without cost. A captured Myrza informed us that the Angels have altered their plans of attack. They plan to spread out along the wall and attempt to penetrate the realm at multiple points.

Now is your chance to prove your commitment to these changes.

Should you fail to act, I will not send aid if the Angels enter Uzhhorod.

I request that you send any reinforcements you have been able to gather to the portion of the wall closest to Uzhhorod to ensure they do not breach there. More assistance will come from other units once the officer in charge has notified me of their arrival at the watchtower.

The Halálhívó

My nostrils flared as I let out a long breath. I was still so fucking angry—with my cousins, with myself. Rokath's blunt note was so typical of him, but I still didn't appreciate the threat and mistrust. Kiira's revelation had shaken me. Dragged me in front of a mirror to bear witness to my own shortcomings. I hadn't even fucking realized how deep I'd gone in with my beliefs. Confronting the ugly parts of oneself was no easy task.

Especially when I kept getting these fucking notes from the nobles questioning our choices. I'd only managed to get through three today, and an entire stack awaited me on the far corner of my desk.

Before I could talk myself out of it, I penned a message of my own to be distributed throughout the city, requesting volunteers. The head of the Kral's Guard could oversee their training and departure to the wall.

I'd figure out how to quell the unrest later.

With a sigh, I snatched Kiira's and opened it, hoping hers would be kinder than Rokath's. The innermost page contained a short note.

Read these, then distribute them to the priestesses. The myth of the Halálhívó and the Szélhámos is strong among the soldiers in Fured. This should help you combat any pushback you might receive.

No salutation, no valediction. Just instruction. It stung even more than Rokath's accusatory note. Kiira and I had always been close, given our continual proximity. Rokath was gone for months, if not years at a time, while Kiira was always a short ride away.

Has she always resented me?

I thought after all we'd shared...

I loved her deeply, and the ache of disappointing her remained weeks later. Her venomous displeasure, spit from her mouth during our heated conversation, was a knife to my heart. That she'd sided with Rokath time and time again, and then united with Assyria to drive even more points home...

Shoving the pain my mind was trying to inflict on me aside, I tossed the terse page and began reading the remaining dozen.

Story after story of Rokath and Assyria working together, using their magic together, of Assyria impersonating the mighty Halálhívó wound their way in Kiira's elegant script. Quotes of veneration from the soldiers abounded. The final installment detailed the prowess both demonstrated at the Battle of Fured, and how together, they'd saved the academy and townspeople from certain death at the hands of the Angels who sought to exterminate our race.

By the end, even I was swayed by her impassioned words. I'd seen the two of them together, and yet the picture she painted cast them in an entirely new light. It was almost...treasonous how well she portrayed them as the mates sent from the Fates to save us all. The perfect union, just like the perfect circles between their shoulder blades.

As I slipped the second to last page off, I was confronted with just that. Someone had drawn a striking likeness of the two of them together, standing over a bloody battlefield. They only had eyes for each other though, and the artist had captured an incredible depth of emotion. Their backs were bare, exposing their mate marks. Rokath's tattoos and muscled shoulders were entirely accurate.

Which meant they must have posed for the portrait.

My fingers tightened over the parchment. I'd never been pressured into marrying, nor had I planned to for many years to come. My premier kept me satisfied, especially with how handsomely I paid them. Yet no one held my heart in their hands, except for my cousin—as fucked up as that was. Perhaps now was the time to solidify her place by my side, to combat whatever exalted status Rokath and Assyria would receive.

The last thing I wanted was for the nobles and the populace to think Rokath should replace me on the throne.

I gritted my teeth so hard my head started to pound.

I need a fucking drink.

Throwing Kiira's stories onto my desk, I stalked to a table where a decanter waited and poured enough scale into it to burn me up from the inside out. After throwing the whole tumbler back, I went to the windows overlooking the Skala Mountains and attempted to rein in the anger racing through my veins.

It would do me no good to lose my cool now, not when I had to play all of this in just the right way. Rokath held a lot of power, should he want to wield it against me. My cunning and smooth talking had always gotten me where I needed to go. Yet no one feared me like they feared him.

The tension in my neck and shoulders eased as the alcohol worked its way through me. Clarity returned as my inner turmoil lessened. I rested my forearm against the glass and looked down at the grounds of Gyor Palace, spotting movement along the outer wall.

Red armored guards walked the perimeter, checking for weaknesses. One pushed some bushes aside and slammed the hilt of his sword into a spot. It held firm. Then, they moved along, repeating the motion until they were out of my sight.

An idea struck me.

My defenses had always been the nobles. What better way

to secure my place than tests of loyalty? I could frame it as part of the larger commitment I'd made to shaping society. Not only would they have to affirm their belief in the new order, but they'd also have to denounce one of their own to pass the test—Ollmund Varrir.

In the days since I'd been back in the capital, I'd stewed on how to execute him, to make him pay for the crimes against my cousin. It was a delicate balance, since he held so much sway over the other nobles. Since he'd been an architect of our initial changes in his own right. We were beholden to him, with his one favor still uncalled.

There was no way I'd allow him to use it now.

I had to prove to Kiira that I believed her. And more than anything, I wanted to be the one to do it. Rokath would have in a heartbeat, which would have only shifted her allegiance further to him.

The plan unfolded in my mind. Cunning. Cruel. Creative.

I strode to my desk and scanned the remaining notes from the Nayúr and Kormánzó. Some had sent messages of dissent. Others had not opined at all. I tallied the spread and made a mental list of who to pressure—and who to crush.

Dusk was fast approaching by the time I finished penning the last letter. Dropping the wax onto the fold, I waited a moment, then stamped my signet ring into it. The three skulled sigil of House Vrak stared back at me when I pulled it away.

I called for my sentries again. They entered, hands on the hilts of their weapons. After a quick scan of the space, the leader asked, "What do you need, sir?"

"Take these and distribute them. Ensure that each party accompanies you back to Gyor. Settle them in the grand ballroom," I instructed with practiced precision.

"Yes, My Kral," he confirmed. "Anything else?"

"Have your Parancsok meet me there. We have some things to plan."

He dipped his head in acknowledgement, then distributed piles of notes to those behind him. While many of the nobility were in the capital, the Kormánzó on the southern plains were not in residence. Since I'd recently appointed the one that oversaw Stryi, I didn't have to doubt his loyalty. In fact, I'd chosen him specifically because he'd been so fervent in his attempts to garner my favor.

I wrote him a note separately, instructing him to carry out a similar test of loyalty to me in the south, and to execute anyone who refused to profess their devotion to me as their Kral.

Satisfied, I grabbed my sword, securing the scabbard around my waist, then lifted my crown from the pedestal in the far corner. The plush velvet had a permanent ring from the weight of it.

Settling it over my brow, I ensured it wouldn't fall with a quick shove down my head. Then, I fixed my hair atop it so it was tidy. My attire wasn't as formal as I would have liked, but that was no problem. I didn't want to stain my best clothing with the blood of the male who raped Kiira.

Grabbing the final note, I set out for the aviary, which was thankfully on the way to the grand ballroom. The Parancsok of the Kral's guard was already waiting by the time I strode inside.

"Prepare a pyre in the courtyard," I commanded, my tone cold. He spun away from the windows facing the very place and eyed me warily.

"May I ask why?" he pressed. We were as close as a master and servant could be, and while I normally wouldn't mind his question, I was in no mood for it.

"Because the nobility of the Demon Realm need reminding that I am in charge and that an attack on House Vrak comes with consequences," I snarled, nails digging into my palm.

"Understood," he replied, his garnet armor gleaming under the lights of the ballroom.

"And ensure that they see exactly what you are doing while they approach the front doors," I instructed. This was part of the psychological attack, and it was paramount to snatching their obedience and weaving it to me and only me.

"As you wish. May your thread hold strong, My Kral." He swept into a bow before striding out through the large glass doors.

I surveyed the ballroom, devoid of life save for myself. A handful of tables pressed into the far side, behind the gray basalt pillars that held up the floors above. Chairs too were stacked in the shadows. Otherwise, the only adornments were the gilding on the walls.

The real show wouldn't be in here anyway.

Smacking wood drew my attention to the servants rushed to prepare a pyre outside, the dying sun casting them in an eerie glow. Another group appeared at the top of the stairs a moment later. "My Kral," the first said, dipping into a low curtsey. "Do you need anything in here?"

"My throne," I announced. It was the final piece to my regal ensemble, the reminder of who the fuck I was. Unfortunately, its current position didn't have a view that would serve my purposes.

They scurried away to fetch it from a few rooms over. Minutes after they placed it in the middle of the grand ballroom, the first of the noble houses appeared. House Turrokar, permanently relocated to the capital since the Angels overran their territory, halted as a unit when they saw me lounging atop my throne.

Kormánzó Sorn was the first to step forward and greet me. "We have come at your urgent request, My Kral."

"Find a place to stand while we wait for the others." I waved my hand as if I were dismissing a fly from my presence. He gathered his family and relocated them out of my sight. Their whispers echoed in the empty space before the patriarch shushed them.

Several houses followed after them, receiving the same treatment from me. Tension hung in the air like a thick fog while I waited for the one family I really fucking wanted to see —House Varrir.

They were fashionably late, as always preferring to make an entrance. I masked a smile behind rough knuckles. I'd counted on their pompousness, and they had delivered.

Orith, the daughter, dipped into a curtsey so low I was surprised her nose didn't brush the floor. Veilless, with cleavage on full display, I knew exactly what Ollmund's designs were. Thank the Fates he'd never used his second term to force us into marrying her. Scorned by Rokath, affirmed by Kiira, he was tossing her at my feet instead. But his attempts to close the distance between us were for his own power plays, and not because he revered me as a God among Demons, unlike many others.

"Please stand," I commanded, my voice hard despite the pleasantry.

"May the Reaper's eye pass over you, My Kral," Ollmund purred like he hadn't fucking assaulted the female I loved.

A muscle feathered in my jaw as I rose to my full height. "Ollmund, just the male I was waiting on." I kept my voice courtly, not betraying the anger rising within me at the sight of his lecherous face.

"What an honor, My Kral. What have I done to deserve this favor?" he asked, hands folding behind his lower back. He regarded me with a wide, easy stance that told me he didn't view me as a real threat.

I took a step forward and let out a sinister laugh. "I'm not sure I would call what I am about to rain down on you 'favor.'"

The gathered nobles sucked in a sharp breath.

Ollmund's bushy brows dipped together. "I'm not sure I un–"

Before he could finish his sentence, I stepped forward and punched him in the stomach. He doubled over, wheezing. I didn't hesitate to throw an uppercut to his jaw, launching him backward. With a groan, he curled up on the ground, still clutching his abdomen.

I stomped on his lower leg with all my might, the crunch under my boot echoing around the ballroom with a satisfying crunch.

A few screams tore from the throats of the ladies of the court, horrified by my violence. They were unaccustomed to such actions. They'd forgotten I'd trained at the military academy for decades and had done patrols on the border for years before returning to Uzhhorod.

Just because I didn't personally lead the army didn't mean I couldn't knock them about.

I dragged my attention away from the pathetic male at my feet, finding his wife and daughter with their hands clasped over their mouths and backing away. "I have received many notes these past days," I boomed, scanning the crowd with a dark expression. "Though none have been so self righteous as Ollmund Varrir's." Not necessarily true, but if he attempted to convince the others to believe him over me, I'd have his tongue. "The Fates have demanded these changes themselves. Why else would they have sent the Szélhámos to mate the Halálhívó? Just today I received word from the High Priestess of their battle prowess. How they took on thousands single handedly and won!"

They'd read Kiira's full, dramatized account soon enough.

"But that is not why I gathered you here."

The room fell so silent that when a piece of metal clinked against the floor, many jumped.

"Ollmund Varrir has assaulted a member of House Vrak." I let the words sink in and snapped my attention back to the male at my feet. He'd gone utterly still. Beneath his weathered skin, he paled. The wrinkles around the corner of his mouth deepened, along with the ones on his forehead.

I crouched down, then spoke low enough so only he could hear me. "You raped the High Priestess. Did you think the Fates wouldn't punish you for that? That *I* wouldn't punish you for that? The Reaper has come for you this day, Ollmund."

A choked sob escaped him as I rose and returned my attention to the rest of them. "For that, he will be killed. His family will be stripped of their titles and impoverished. The crown claims all their coin and lands until a suitable replacement is found."

That caused a stir among the crowd. It was well known that House Varrir held strong ties to House Vrak since my ascension. To see them stripped to beggars now? That was the shock, the unpredictability, the instability among them I needed to shove my agenda through.

I held up a hand, silencing them again. "The time has come for each one of you to swear fealty to me again, to confirm you *understand* the consequences for defying my holy orders and my holy throne."

I drew a dagger from my waist, leaving my sword where it was. For now. "But first, I have justice to execute."

Ollmund scrambled backward as I stalked toward him. Somehow, he managed to stumble to his feet. I herded him toward the double doors, which the Kral's Guard swung open. A gust of winter air chilled the room nearly as much as my actions.

He raced into the dark, attempting to flee, but the soldiers caught him by the arms and dragged him to his knees. "Ollmund!" his wife shouted, falling over the threshold.

I paused, pivoting to the gathered nobility. "I suggest you gather around the windows to witness what happens when a member of House Vrak is attacked."

None of them hesitated to press forward, all probably planning how they'd snatch the richest house's title and lands for themselves.

"Father!" Orith cried, clutching her mother for comfort.

"Light the pyre," I ordered one of the males. He took a torch to the base of it, and smoke soon filtered through the night. When the fire caught, it cast the scene in a haunting glow.

Ollmund struggled against the hold as I approached. "I did no such thing! I would never harm you, Xannirin." His voice carried through the night, likely in a last effort to reach his peers. His final political play to highlight me as their adversary instead of their ruler.

I leaned down and hissed in his ear, "We both know it wasn't me. Speak what you did aloud, and I will not burn you. You'll spend all eternity trapped in this world, yearning for the next life you'll never have. It is honestly what I should do, but unfortunately I have to cater to the other sycophants in there. It wouldn't help me to let you rot, as much as I want to."

"I am calling on my second term," he wheezed. "You will not kill me."

Red coated my vision. How *dare* he attempt to stop me from showing Kiira that she deserved justice? My palms tingled with the memory of our blood oath.

"No," I growled. "You forfeit that term when you raped Kiira."

The vehemence in my tone made him whimper.

"On his feet," I commanded, stepping back. My guard hauled him upright. "Strip him."

Another raced forward, using a knife to shred his fine clothes from his body. Screams and pleas of mercy tore from his wife and daughter, but I paid them no attention as I turned to the nobility.

"Witness my wrath. Imprint it on your memory so that you may never attempt to rise against me."

With that, I dug the blade into Ollmund's skin, dragging it in one forty-five degree line, then another, until a large X covered his portly torso. Had I taken inspiration from Rokath? Absolutely. If it worked for him, it would work for me.

"Bring the whip," I ordered, palm up and waiting. A guard settled it in my hand a moment later. With predatory slowness, I rounded to his naked backside. I stared every head of house down, slow and unblinking.

Muscles tense, Ollmund attempted to smother his sobs. I raised the nine tails studded with metal, the air hissing past my ear.

And then, I struck with all my might.

He screamed, pitching forward. If it weren't for my guard holding him, he would have collapsed to the ground. I didn't hesitate to deliver another blow, then one after that. Blood welled as I tore up his backside, but satisfaction was still out of reach.

Many females turned away as a garnet puddle formed around us. Yet the males, with hard set jaws, watched on, knowing they'd be judged for it. The firelight reflected their rage back to me. Their defiance. Their malicious intent. Mixed among the fearful were a few *brave* souls who would receive personal visits from me over the coming days.

Ribs emerged from the flayed meat of Ollmund's back. The heat from the pyre rose to a new height, searing into my skin.

The crackling accompanied my ominous steps as I drew my dagger and rounded the pathetic male.

Tears and snot streamed down his face, and his head hung limply. I gave him a few slaps to stir him. "You are no male, and for that, you will have your cock and balls removed before I throw you onto the logs. Pray to the Weaver now to bring you back as a female so you aren't shamed with your utter lack."

Eyes wide, he started to plead with me again, but I reached down and *yanked* what the Weaver had not blessed him with in this life. A scream ripped from him, and I wasted no time in slicing both away. Blood spurted from the wound, but I kept hold of the offending organs, intending to use them as proof to my cousins that I was committed to our changes.

What would Kiira think when she received them? Would she realize then the lengths I would go to for her? Would she see me as her protector as she saw Rokath?

That was all I wanted from her now. For her to remember the way we'd laugh late into the night. The softness of her voice, the way she'd prop her feet on my lap while we drank decadent wine. How she'd lean into me as I settled her in my bed to sleep it off.

I wanted to return to the before of her resentment. Before she turned to Rokath for confirmation instead of me. Before she clung to Rapp, let him make her smile and chase away her pain.

She should have looked at me like that.

Damn the consequences the Fates would invoke for disallowing Ollmund to call upon his second favor. This was far more important.

"Burn him," I commanded my guard.

They dragged his now-limp body away, leaving the pool of his life behind. Without much care, they tossed him onto the pyre. His wife and daughter screamed again, lost to their hysteria. Orith sprinted past me, falling to her knees just out of range of the blaze.

His wife collapsed, and no one moved to help her, which pleased me greatly.

"Find me a box for these," I told one of the soldiers, lifting Ollmund's dick and balls. "And a wet towel."

"Yes, My Kral," he said, then hurried away. At the entrance to the ballroom, I kicked off my boots, not wanting to stain my floors with the offender's blood. By the time I reached my throne, servants appeared, boxing up the organs and cleaning me off. Once they finished, I lounged on my throne again.

"Who wants to go first?" I asked casually, like I hadn't just slaughtered one of their own and forced them to watch.

Several heads of houses hurried forward, dropping to one knee and resting their foreheads on their arms.

Exactly where they should be.

"Repeat after me," I ordered, pulling a slip of parchment from my pocket. I'd formed the oath carefully to ensure their loyalty was to me, rather than our house as a whole.

"I, the devoted head of my noble house, bow to the burgundy banner of House Vrak."

A handful of masculine voices echoed my words, slightly muffled by their positions.

"Before the sacred gazes of the Weaver, the Giver, and the Reaper, I kneel in unwavering fealty to the sovereign ruler of the Demon Realm. I sacrifice my blood to bind my magic, my body, my fate to the Kral."

Each male drew a dagger and cut deep into his palms, giving the stone their offering.

"To House Vrak, I pledge my sword. To the Kral, I pledge my eternal servitude."

They repeated all my words back to me flawlessly.

"May the thread of your loyalty to me be woven into the

tapestry of your life, unbreakable and enduring. May your gifts hold strong when I call upon you. May the Reaper's eye pass over you that you may follow me into an age of domination on this continent."

I let the words sink in, giving the crowd a quick scan. Then, I issued my command. "Rise and kiss the signet ring."

One by one they did, whispering further pledges to me as they touched the sacred gem. After they settled back in their places, another group rushed forward, and we repeated the process. No male, female, or child was exempt. The ceremony lasted long into the night, and by the time everyone had finished, many swayed on their feet.

Yet I had one more order for them all. One that I hoped would satisfy Kiira and win her affections back to me.

"All fallen will be paid double for their services, and none will be held against their will any longer. They are free to live their lives as they were before, should they so choose. A missive will be sent across the realm in the morning, along with stories from the High Priestess. Read them all and imprint this new order onto your minds. I will not stand for anything less than utter compliance. Am I clear?"

"Yes, My Kral," the voices affirmed, many bowing their heads in deference to me.

I didn't deign to dismiss them as I strode from the room. The door slammed behind me, and my guard fell into step as we wound through the palace, back to my chambers.

The nobles knelt. Bled. Affirmed their allegiance. To me.

And soon…so would Kiira.

45

R☠KATH

The Skala Mountains loomed nearer with every breath. When we'd passed through Lutsk, it wasn't merely deserted. The earth had been churned by the boots of hundreds of thousands of feet. The city had been scrubbed from the map entirely, like the Angels had erased what was left of the crumbling walls during their retreat.

Behind Assyria and me, what remained of our survivors from Fured marched, growing more grim the higher the peaks speared into the sky. The battle we'd faced weeks prior was nothing compared to what was to come.

"Someone is approaching," Assyria muttered, eyes narrowing on a speck of movement in the distance.

"Search," I commanded the hounds, and they leaped into action. Like black blurs, they streaked across the earth, hunting whomever Assyria had spotted in the distance. We were closing in on the northernmost ridges of the range, where one of the largest outposts along the wall that divided the continent waited.

The very same one where I'd fucked up on my first mission

as Vezető. Where I'd gotten most of our unit slaughtered. And for which my father and the Kral had punished us by forcing me to kill Thast. After speaking my truth to Assyria, the memory of him didn't dig a knife between my ribs quite as violently as before. But the guilt, the same, still lingered.

"It wasn't your fault, mate," Assyria murmured into my mind, her voice a balm to the burning. I hadn't realized I was projecting my thoughts down our bond. With a sigh, I unclenched my jaw and uncurled my fingers from around my stallion's reins.

"It was, but I appreciate your reassurance." Before she could argue further, Grem and Zeec let out a wild series of barks. We dug our heels into our horses' sides, and they galloped forward. After cresting a rocky hill, we halted, surveying the scene below.

Two males were on their knees with my loyal beasts circling them. Their dark hair and red eyes loosened my chest immediately.

"Heel," I commanded the dogs. They retreated to their place between our mounts.

"Halálhívó, Szélhámos," Banand and Zurronar greeted us, rising to their feet. Once there, they offered us both a closed-fisted salute. Banand cleared his throat, then flattened his hands behind his lower back. "Hadvezér Trol is in the pass just ahead. With so many soldiers, it was impossible to bunk in Kohszak. He sent us to guide your way."

I studied them intently, not saying anything. I waited for the flicker of magic, the hint that an Angel was creating an illusion. After all, the two of them had been in their custody for months. But when Zurronar shot Assyria a wink, I let my suspicions drop.

They were replaced by the desire to rip out his eye.

I shoved the urge into the dirt and finally acknowledged

what Banand had said. "Take us there, and give me a report while we go."

"Aye, Halálhívó," he affirmed.

I glanced over my shoulder to see how far behind the rest were. Kiira and Rapp were nearly upon us, the first of the wagons not far behind. I was so fucking glad Rapp had been able to ride this entire time. The additional pium he'd been taking every day had done wonders.

"We're going into the pass," Assyria shouted for me. When she faced forward again, she dipped her chin.

We'd been working better and better as a team too since she started training to impersonate me. With our bond, we were able to anticipate each other's movements. That had translated into orders too.

And I found myself savoring the support. To my utter surprise, not having to do everything on my own, having her to lean on, had done wonders for my overall attitude.

"Lead the way," I told Banand and Zurronar, and they pivoted back toward the mountains. Grem and Zeec wandered off, checking the area, while the two former prisoners of war took their place between Assyria and me.

"Did you receive the raven in time for the attack?" Zurronar questioned, a hint of hope in his tone. I knew him well enough to know he cared deeply for the army. It was one of the reasons he'd been promoted time and time again.

As I regarded him from above, the night that irrevocably changed the course of my life—and this war—rose to the front of my mind. How I'd killed his brother for protecting my mate. Not that I had known. And still, he hadn't been furious. He hadn't cursed my name. Instead, he'd remained at the front, continued to fight for the Demon cause, when he had every right to leave.

He possessed an honor that I did not.

Assyria replied for me. "The day after actually. We were mid-torture of a Myrza when a messenger came. The Halálhívó was quite annoyed at the interruption."

Zurronar snorted a laugh, but Banand's brows pinched.

"How many did you lose?" Banand ventured like a dagger was pressed to his throat and the wrong number would send it plunging into his skin.

"Too many, but not enough to make a serious dent. We still have plenty of power," I reassured him. The guilt he carried for his plague was etched into the lines of his face.

"Especially with the addition of the females," Assyria added, knocking her leg into his shoulder. He glanced up at her and offered a tense smile.

"How has that been going?" Zurronar asked her next. "I see you now have a helmet of your own to match the Halálhívó's."

She beamed, and the pride in her expression made my heart ache. Seeing her this happy, so in her element...it was everything.

"After the initiation ritual, the males started to integrate them of their own accord. Now they work closely together, like equals," she gushed. "I hope that they'll keep it up once we reunite with everyone. We really do have some powerful magic among the female soldiers. They'll be great assets to many units."

"We will ensure they are welcomed," Zurronar promised, but the way he shifted in his saddle gave me pause. I studied him further as Banand echoed his sentiment.

The path grew steeper as we entered the foothills of the Skala Mountains, and ahead, a canyon waited for us. This route was one I'd ridden countless times over my centuries of life. Once we rounded the first bend, a small pool would line the right hand side, the perfect place to refill a waterskin if needed.

After that, a tough incline challenged all riders, but the winding path beyond it was an easy enough ride to the barracks and outpost at Kohszak.

"What else?" I prodded them as we approached the water. There, two horses were tethered, and the males fetched their beasts and mounted them.

"We've done our best to support Hadvezér Trol as he spread us out along the northern part of the wall," Banand said, his gelding falling into step alongside my stallion. Assyria rode ahead alongside Zurronar. "We still have custody of two of the Angel females, and we managed to capture a few more who attempted to sneak into the camp."

"What of your magic?" I asked him.

He dropped his gaze, studying the leather reins in his hands. The path pitched upward suddenly, and he leaned into his horse's neck, helping him clear it. We did the same, their breaths labored by the time we reached the crest.

"Banand is...struggling with it." Zurronar turned in his saddle, his eyes first locking with mine and then drifting to his comrade. A muscle feathered in Banand's jaw.

"My guess is that it's more a mental block and less a physical one. The shame he felt after his rescue was apparent," Assyria slipped down our bond.

"Aye, that was my assumption as well."

"We'll discuss it later," I decided, wanting to change the subject. Speaking of it now would only further Banand's anguish, and I needed him to pull it together to aid us in winning the war. "What happened to the third female?"

"She stole a dagger from one of the guards and killed herself," Zurronar stated, his tone colder than the wind clawing through the canyon. An ember of something that looked a lot like rage smoldered in his maroon eyes.

Assyria sucked in a sharp breath. "Which one?"

"The one with the ocean eyes. She was always the nasty one." He lifted a shoulder and dropped it like her death meant nothing. And to him, why should it? The torture the Angels had inflicted on the two of them had been brutal. Horrific. Gut wrenching.

In truth, her suicide didn't affect our plans at all. She was the least powerful and therefore the least useful one. Not like the Angels thought any of them still lived.

A perusal glance over my shoulder revealed the rest of our traveling group ascending. Rapp and Kiira's horses were close, their heads dipped and quiet words passing between them. Beyond them, the last of the supply wagons appeared over the ridge. More males and females streamed behind them on foot. Parancsok Olet, along with all the Százados who brought up the rear, would ensure every soldier successfully arrived at the outpost.

"Hadvezér Trol can explain the rest when we reach him. The edge of the camp is just ahead," Banand said, pointing to a bend in the distance.

"Aye," I grumbled. We hadn't been gone long, and yet everything had changed in that time. Females—powerful in their own right—walked among seasoned warriors. Assyria had emerged as a force unto her own. Kiira had joined the army too, seemingly indefinitely, though she wouldn't participate in any real fighting.

And Xannirin?

Fates only knew what he was doing. I hadn't heard from him since he departed the military academy. A raven never appeared among the desert rocks, bearing an acknowledgement of my request.

At least the reinforcements should reinvigorate those who might still see the loss of the fifty thousand as an utter failure on my part—I hoped.

We needed to integrate them quickly with new units so they could spread stories of Assyria and me. Kiira had been right—once all of the academy was hooked on the mythos of us, belief had shifted quickly.

I hoped it would sway the rest of the realm too.

I glanced at my brave mate. The Fates had certainly deemed all the blood I spilled for them worthy if they'd given me such an incredible female to have by my side. There was plenty more to offer their thirsty soil. I'd gladly drench it so long as they kept her safe.

Too many times now, I'd almost lost her. First to the cobra in the Paks Desert. Second to the Angel's kidnapping. Third to an assassin. Fourth during the Battle of Fured.

The number wasn't nearly as high as the number of times I'd almost died myself. Yet each one was far, far too many for my liking.

I'd spent centuries preparing for war. For death. For glory. But nothing—fucking nothing—had prepared me for loving her. Nothing had prepared me for how fucking willing I was to burn the world down if it meant keeping her alive.

The first sounds of the camp reached my ears as we rounded the high cliffs dotted with towering pines and cloud trees. A few large cacti clung to the sides, absorbing whatever moisture dripped down from the few clouds that managed to cross the peaks of the Skala Mountains. Here, at least, the highest points were far lower than they were closer to Uzhhorod.

On the other side of the range, Eloi, the largest city in the northern part of the Angel Realm, loomed. From there, the Angels were poised to invade into the Demon Realm. For centuries, they'd launched their extermination attacks between here and the ocean from that base. That they'd returned yet again to that position made my jaw ache.

We'd commanded the city once. But with their numbers swelling, could we do it again?

The war camp unfurled before us, yet it was different than it had been on the open plains. Instead of a cluster of organized chaos, tents hugged the sides of the cliff face. Warriors ducked out of them, their expressions hard. Many faces were wan, and more than a few far too thin for my liking. Furs wrapped around shoulders to ward off the chill.

More scattered on either side as the canyon widened, bearing a sour note of displeasure. Fingers jerked in the direction of the females trailing behind us. Whispers echoed off the narrow walls. I noted them all.

Assyria, deep in conversation with Zurronar, paid them no heed.

Yet Grem and Zeec's hackles raised as they trotted along the thin thoroughfare.

The valley bloomed ahead of us, and even more soldiers appeared. These, however, greeted us with more enthusiasm, salutes and my honorific slicing through their otherwise busy day.

Like the spokes of a wheel, paths carved toward the barracks. Zurronar led us through the maze, single file as there wasn't enough room to ride abreast. My stallion's ears flicked in all directions as sounds bounced off the mountains. I stole a glance up toward the road that led to the wall, memories of that fateful day surfacing, just like every time I returned here.

Assyria subtly slowed her horse so the distance between us lessened. My attention cut to my mate. Her helmet gleamed, and the sun highlighted the little flecks of purple in her eyes. Ebony hair spilled down her back with a slight wave from sleeping in a braid. The black leather she wore made her look all the more formidable atop her mount.

"Our absence hasn't changed them, right?" A hint of worry slipped into her tone.

"I don't know, little imposter. We will have to see. And if they rebel again...well they would do well to remember the consequences from before."

She nodded and faced forward, thumb raking over the small garnet in her ring. We neared the only permanent building at last, and officers spilled out of its cool interior.

From the shadows, Trol appeared. His face was even more weathered than when we'd met in Ustlyak and he'd been covered in month's worth of dirt and sand. His lips twisted into a smile as we slowed to a stop in front of him, but the sentiment didn't reach the corners of his eyes. "Halálhívó, I am grateful for your quick return to the front."

I dismounted, handing Assyria my reins, and approached my second Hadvezér. Boots hit the ground behind me, and then Rapp joined us.

Trol let out a low chuckle. "Good to see you alive and well, Rapp. You're looking even better than before your injury."

Rapp grabbed Trol's arm and pulled him in for an embrace, clapping him on the back at the same time. "I'm glad to be feeling better too. Fured was certainly healing for me."

Trol looked beyond us to the line of wagons and new soldiers. "How many?"

"About ten thousand. The valley looks like it's full to the brim already," I commented, glancing around. Makeshift structures claimed every available inch of space. Some soldiers had to turn sideways to navigate the narrow slots between them.

"Aye, it is. We'll have to figure out where to put everyone, though I think once you hear the latest update it will solve our problem," Trol added, running a hand over his close-cropped hair.

"Let's talk, then." Our weeks by the sea had been a nice break, but now, it was time to focus again.

From the chaos, Assyria and Kiira appeared. The High Priestess strode with her shoulders square, not deigning to offer any of the males her attention.

Assyria too carried an air of importance as she came to a halt beside me. "Where do you want us?"

"You'll come with me," I told her. "Kiira, can you try to find a temporary place to settle everyone else?"

Trol swept into a low bow. After all, she was cousin to the Kral and the highest of nobility in addition to her position as spiritual leader for the realm. "High Priestess. It is an honor to have you among us. The operations managers in the first battalion should be able to help you for now."

"Thank you, Hadvezér Trol. The Fates shine their favor on you for your continued sacrifice and work in their names," Kiira replied, her tone warm and inviting. She was magic in her own right. "I'll bring a few of the females from the Deathveiled with me. It would be good for them to start speaking of their time at the academy."

"Aye," I told her.

Trol snapped his fingers at one of the Százados hanging in the periphery. "Take the High Priestess to the operations manager."

"Certainly. If you'll follow me, High Priestess," he said. With a small wave, she bid us goodbye, calling out Maariya, Izzenna, and Vokkia to join her.

"The Deathveiled?" Trol clarified when they were out of earshot.

"We have updates of our own," I told him. "With so much time apart, I'm sure we'll need hours to discuss everything that's occurred."

"I don't doubt it. The command room is ready and waiting

for you," Trol commented, spinning on his heel. Two Vezető jerked open the doors to the barracks, allowing us entrance.

Yet this was no homecoming—it was something far more dangerous. It was the ascension of dangerous new legends, lethal new leaders, and a warning for all who dared defy us.

The Demons were rising, and with it, the Angels would fall. But in the shadows of the mountains, our victory would not come without a sacrifice.

46

R☠KATH

In the command center, surrounded by haunting memories and critical stakes, we regrouped for war. The permanence of this place gripped me as I surveyed the familiar furniture. A heavy oaken table. Carved pine chairs. Decorative weapons pinned to the stone walls. A hearth with split logs stacked to the side.

The crackle of it assaulted my ears as Olet strode into the room, finally caught up from the rear, and greeted the Parancsok who had remained with Trol.

Assyria sipped from a metal mug and nibbled on a bit of goat cheese produced in the city that supported the outpost. A platter of fresh food awaited us should we want more. It was far better than the long-storing gruel we had to eat during our rapid trek here.

Trol went to a cabinet and pulled out a small box. Twined to it was a letter, the crosspoint bearing a burgundy wax seal. I accepted it from his outstretched hand, noting Xannirin's signet stamped into it.

"This came for you just yesterday, Halálhívó. A rider from the outpost closest to Uzhhorod passed it along personally."

My brows climbed my forehead. Xannirin had acted quickly. His silence had spoken volumes—or so I'd thought. Perhaps he wasn't as resistant to the changes, or the nobles had accepted them readily upon his return. Whatever the reason, I was grateful for his communication.

Assyria craned her neck to see what I held.

I tugged at the thin rope, breaking the seal. "Did he have any reports from riding the length of the wall?"

"That is one of the matters I wanted to discuss," Trol stated. The other officers shifted in their seats around the large table. Judging by the looks exchanged between them, they already knew.

Rapp's boots clicked against the stone as he came to stand beside me. He was well aware of my current feelings toward my cousin, our Kral.

Rokath,

Additional soldiers to help defend the realm have been sent to the outpost near Uzhhorod. Both male and female. A chunk of my personal guard accompanied them since they are untrained. I ordered them to begin instruction as soon as possible to ensure their lives aren't entirely wasted the moment the Angels attack.

Additionally, I have declared all fallen free from their forced servitude. Many volunteered to join the defense. You'll find them among the rest once you reach the wall. To further my commitment, rape is now an offense punishable by death via dismemberment.

Kiira's stories and the portrait of Assyria and you are quite compelling. I have already begun to distribute them with the aid of the priestesses.

I issue you one warning: should you try to move against me and claim my throne with your mate, you'll have a war of a different variety on your hands.

The box and note inside are for Kiira.

The Kral

I clenched my teeth, wanting to punch my cousin in his fucking face for daring to suggest I wanted to rule in his stead. Again. His arrogance was grating my nerves.

Rapp reached for the box, turning it over and examining it from every angle. "What do you think he'd possibly send Kiira?" he murmured, loud enough that only Assyria and I could hear.

"No clue. Open it and find out," I suggested on the off chance Xannirin had dared to play some trick.

With a shrug, he flicked off the latch and opened the lid. A moment later, he dropped it onto the table like it was a snake that had bitten him. He slammed the top shut before anyone could glimpse its contents.

I smacked his hands away and dragged it closer to me. Slower than he had, I eased it open.

A musky old tang assaulted my nostrils. Assyria's metal mug clattered against the table. The fire popped, the volume like an explosion in the utter silence.

Because staring back at me was blackened blood clinging to a shriveled dick and balls.

Shock gripped me, freezing every muscle in my body. Because there was no doubt who these had belonged to if this box was intended for Kiira.

Ollmund Varrir.

So Xannirin had killed him for what he did to our cousin.

"I was certainly not expecting that," I remarked, closing the lid and handing it to Rapp.

"Nor I," he growled, securing the latch. "I'll warn Kiira before I give it to her."

"Aye," I agreed, attention drifting to my mate, who slid her plate away. Nose scrunched, she slumped back, arms crossed over her stomach. The horror of her posture said she'd seen enough.

Clearing my throat, I redirected the conversation back to

battle plans. Rapp took his seat beside Trol, tucking the box away for later. "So, what did the rider have to say?"

Trol flattened his palms on the table and stared at the map carved into the middle. "Every outpost is still manned, currently."

"But?"

"But their numbers are dwindling with frequent raids from the Angels."

"All of them?" I clarified.

Trol nodded. "They all need reinforcements, and I sent the first wave out with the rider upon his departure. But I suspect they'll need more."

He paused for a moment, jerking on the collar of his jacket. The officers around the table held their breath. My shoulders tightened as I waited for what else he had to say.

"Speak freely," I insisted, but the grating in my tone contrasted the encouragement I wanted to deliver.

Trol swallowed, unable to meet my gaze. "I have no idea where the Angels have gone."

"What do you mean? How the fuck do you lose an army?" My voice didn't rise, but the chill in them silenced even the burning logs at my back. My fingers dug into the wood, turning my tattooed knuckles white.

Trol didn't answer right away. Assyria reached for me, peeling my hand off the table. I forced myself to release a breath through clenched teeth.

"Only a handful remain at their base over the wall. Once they reached the foothills, they took to the skies for their retreat. With the high sun, we couldn't see where they went."

Fuck.

The Myrza had proclaimed that one of their Seers had delivered a prophecy of a battle within the mountains. Clearly, they weren't simply regrouping to force us closer and seek out weak points in our defenses. They were spreading out to find the location of this final stand.

Technically, the wall was a neutral zone. Each side had outposts or small cities along its length, but set back into our respective territories. Since our rise to power, I'd ensured that the Demons had gained control of most of it, allowing our riders to pass freely without fear of running into a group of Angels attempting to patrol its tops.

My mind worked over this new information, weighing each outcome and possibility. I doubted they'd attempt to go south of Sivy and Uzhhorod, preferring to brave the peaks between the capitals in an attempt to bring about a swift end. The Skala Mountains rose to a crescendo at the end of Keleti, making travel through their peaks nearly impossible.

No, the foretold battle would occur in the north.

"If we don't have eyes on them, we need to do that, and quickly. I doubt they've left us without surveillance," I ground out around clenched teeth. "Which means they'll know of our arrival."

I paused, reaching for Assyria's hand. Despite the twisting in my gut, I knew what I was about to say was the right thing to do. "We'll spread along the length of the wall. My mate will assist us in fighting through this rough terrain."

Assyria lifted her chin and offered them all a devious smile. "I've learned quite a few tricks since our last meeting."

"Is that so?" Trol asked, a wry grin tugging at his war-hardened lips.

In seconds, she wore my face like a prophetic mask. Many of the officers started at the sudden duplicity of me. Rapp pressed his fist to his mouth to hide his amusement.

"But that's not all." From my shaved head, white hair fell, and my burgundy eyes turned aquamarine. Tattoos melted away, revealing the regal face of the Myrza. "I'll lure the zealots into my trap and we'll kill them all, save for one. They will return to their camp, spouting off nonsense about one of their own betraying them," she said in Demonic.

The unnerved expressions at seeing this Angel's face speaking our language, was understandable.

"What...are you?" one of the officers breathed, studying Assyria with rapt fascination.

"An Imposter. The Szélhámos." She returned to herself. "The female who is going to bring the Angel army to its knees."

A grin—vicious, feral, possessive—rose to my lips as I watched my mate. My equal. My Fate.

"We'll need to capture a few more Angel officers as well so we can perpetuate this story. Make them tear themselves apart from the inside," I furthered, detailing the hard-wrought design Rapp, Assyria, and I had discussed during our travels.

"It's a good plan," one of the Parancsok commented. "My units will be thrilled to join any missions you require of us."

"I'm glad you said that," I began. "Because with us, we have several thousand powerful magic wielders who just so happen to be female. They held their own against the Angels in the Battle of Fured, and I want to ensure the units here embrace them. Who will take them on, and who needs to be *reminded* that my word is law?"

Several commented that their males would accommodate, while others noted they still struggled with sections of their battalions. I made a mental note to visit them with Assyria as soon as possible.

After that, we ventured into logistics. How many units we'd send to each outpost both to the north and south of our current location. What weapons needed to go where. The number of healers, cooks, and clothiers to disperse. I moved markers across the map until I was satisfied with the placement of them all.

"Everyone remembers the fire signals, yes?" It had been nearly a decade since we'd had so many soldiers at the wall. At intervals along the way, massive basins waited to be lit. The communication was far faster than sending ravens, especially during times of strife.

"Red for imminent attack. Gold for requesting aid. Blue for sickness. Green for storms. White for diplomatic approach. Smoke for lost position," a different Parancsok listed off.

"And if we lose a guard tower or section, we must press forward on either side and retake it as quickly as possible," I reminded them.

They nodded their acknowledgement.

"Good. We'll spend the rest of the day integrating the new magic-wielding units into your battalions. Gauge their responses, and when we meet in the morning, we'll decide who to send where." My focus locked on the map of Keleti carved into the table and the stones dotting the length of the wall that divided the realms. "Remember we have the power. We have the positions. And we have us." I indicated my mate and me as I snapped my gaze to each of the officers in turn. "With our combined powers, we are unstoppable. Relay that to those who dissent."

Then, I straightened to my full height. Assyria too rose, uniting our front. "Dismissed."

Chairs scraped. Boots thudded. Murmurs drifted as the Parancsok coordinated their next tasks.

My two Hadvezér lingered. "What's in the box?" Trol asked when he was certain we wouldn't be overheard.

"The dick and balls of a coward," Rapp snarled. My gaze snapped to my Hadvezér. We hadn't discussed it with one another, but he knew. To see his reaction now, as violent as my own—perhaps even more so—was interesting.

Trol didn't even flinch. "Tell me how the integration actually went so we know what to prepare for here."

Assyria huffed a laugh and collapsed into her chair. "What we really need to prepare for is the males trying to seduce their new female compatriots. I swear, if I have to deal with another fight over one..."

Rapp chuckled, his dark mood dissipating. "We'll have a tough time with that here. Most of these males haven't been with a female for a year or longer."

"We need to ensure everyone remembers *why* sexual activities are discouraged in the war camp," I groused, pinching the bridge of my nose. "And that if it is non-consensual, the punishment is death, per a new decree from the Kral."

Assyria bolted upright, her earnest gaze trained on me. Tears welled in those gorgeous almond-shaped eyes. I brushed the backs of my knuckles across her cheek, capturing one as it fell. "The Kral has also seen to it that all fallen are released from their compulsory duty."

"Really?" she breathed.

"Written in his hand," I murmured, stroking her soft skin.

"So...he's listening?" she questioned, almost like she couldn't believe it. Fuck, I wasn't sure if I did either.

"If there are fallen among those stationed at the outpost closest to Uzhhorod, then yes."

A watery smile bloomed on her face, and something between a sob and a laugh choked out of her. "I did it."

"You did, little imposter." Wrapping my arms around her tiny frame, I pulled her in tight. A mosaic of emotion flooded our bond. I welcomed it, letting her pour everything into me.

A light tap sounded on the outer door, and Kiira appeared in the entry. "Is everything okay?" she asked, studying how I embraced Assyria.

My mate pulled away from me and beamed at my cousin. "More than alright. You should sit down."

Brows pinched, she rounded the table and dropped into a seat near Rapp. Trol cleared his throat and excused himself to attend to helping the Parancsok sort through the new arrivals.

He shut the door behind him, giving us privacy.

Rapp brought the box out from his lap and slid it to Kiira. "Fair warning, the contents are...gruesome."

She eyed it warily, attention bouncing between the three of us. "What is it?"

"A present from Xannirin," I stated. "There's also a note, though none of us spotted it in the split second we looked inside. If you want Rapp or me to extract it for you, we can."

Kiira's mouth thinned. Reaching for the box, she brought it closer. She hesitated for only a moment before flicking the latch. Then, with a sigh, she lifted the lid.

A small shriek fled her as she slammed it shut, much like Rapp had done. "Is that what I think it is?" she questioned, her voice shaky.

"Yes," Rapp replied, taking it from her. "Do you want the note?"

"Later," she said, her skin taking on a sickly sheen. "I need to go lie down. Assyria, do you need to as well?"

My mate jumped to her feet immediately. "Of course, it's been a long ride. Rokath, where can we sleep?"

"I'll show you the way and leave the dogs with you too. Rapp and I need to go help Trol. He's worked hard enough lately and deserves a break."

"That he does," Rapp agreed, rising without a single sway or pained expression.

Thankfully, the nicest rooms were only one passage away from the command center. Trol had secured one for himself, leaving the other three empty for us. I opened the door to the one typically used by the highest ranking officer in residence. It wasn't anything special compared to how we had been living at the military academy, but it was clean with an attached bathing chamber.

"We'll have your belongings sent up once we step out," I promised my cousin and my mate.

"Thanks," Assyria shot back, her arms around Kiira, who nodded weakly. "I'll let you know if we need anything else."

I brushed my lips against her temple, then left the females alone in my room. Rapp fiddled with the rings in his lip as we walked away. "Hold on a second. Left my dagger in the command center." He trotted off without waiting for a response.

I watched him go, suspicion curling in my gut as I noted the blade attached to his hip, as it always was. Yet I remained still. The chill of the winter mountains crept down my spine. He returned moments later, red-faced and teeth raking over his lip.

"Did you find it?" I asked casually as he strode past me.

"Yes." The word was short, clipped. I shook my head and let it go as we stepped into the sunshine.

We found Trol and slipped back into our normal army routines like we'd never been away at all. By the time dusk fell, I'd almost forgotten about Rapp's odd behavior and how severely the Kral felt threatened by my mating bond with Assyria.

Yet dread coiled around my ribs like an icy wire. The Angels hadn't merely retreated out of our realm into their own. They'd disappeared like locusts at the end of a plague, hidden away until their next attack.

And I had no fucking idea when that was coming.

47

ASSYRIA

A hush fell as I shut us in. Like even the air needed a moment to recover from Xannirin's "present." Rokath bled males before my eyes. Gifted me feathers and bones as tokens of his adoration.

Yet this was...different. Disgust curled in my stomach, hot and sour. Kiira's lower lip trembled, and she swayed on her feet. Stumbling toward the bed, the High Priestess collapsed onto it. A whimper shuddered in her chest, and she clutched at her heart like she could stop it from hurting her.

In two swift strides, I was there, settling beside her. Her locks spilled like ink onto the blankets. I gathered them gently, twisting them into a knot like I was binding her wound that refused to heal. "You're safe now. He's dead."

"I know," she whispered through a broken sob. "I—I wasn't ready. Not for that. Not like that."

Grem and Zeec hopped up to the mattress, tearing a creak from the bedframe. With a low whine, Grem nudged Kiira's hands, forcing her to put them in his fur. Zeec curled up beside me, his body warm against the chill.

"That makes sense. Feel what you need to feel," I told her,

drawing circles on her back as soft as the petals of a rose. Words I'd once ached to hear, but no one ever spoke. Thankfully for me, finding purpose in leadership, even while I'd been impersonating Vagach, had healed so much of my feeling voiceless.

Learning to fight had done the same for Kiira. Yet the feeling of being powerless, the memories of it, never truly faded completely. Panic gripped my throat as I felt hands around my waist, yanking me away from safety. The smell of blood flooded my nostrils. The stench of alcohol burned my throat. The moment Vagach had been about to rape me before I killed him surfaced, as piercing as it had been when I flashed back to the moment in front of Rokath. He'd grabbed me from behind, triggering the visceral reaction, but instead of hurting me, he'd pulled me back from the abyss. Told me to find him in the dark.

"Does it make you feel better that Xannirin did it?" I murmured, smoothing back her hair.

She shook her head, cries softening into hiccups. "I don't know that I want to read his note either."

"I can read it for you, if you want."

An exhale, shaky and slow, slipped out of her as she sat upright. With the back of her long sleeves, she dried her eyes. I went to the bathing chamber and returned with a cloth. She blew her nose into it before casting it aside like it carried too much. "No. I should. Just not today."

"Fair enough." I heeled out of my dirty boots. Kiira sat forward and yanked hers off. They plopped against the floor, joining mine in a pile. Then she flopped back, arms across her stomach and staring up at the ceiling. Grem rested his head there too, and Kiira absently stroked his fur.

I settled beside her, noting the whorls in the plaster over our heads. The bed itself wasn't terrible—a little firmer than what we'd slept on in Fured but infinitely better than the rock Rokath called a mattress in the war camp. After weeks of riding, it honestly felt good on my back. I shifted a little and let out a groan as my neck and shoulders started to relax. Zeec huffed against my hair as he made himself comfortable too.

Kiira snickered. "No one tells you how grueling riding all day is."

"No, they don't," I replied. "You'd think I'd be accustomed to it by now."

"You did have a few months break," Kiira pointed out.

"True." I paused for a moment, weighing my next words. "Do you want to talk about what happened any more?"

Kiira was silent for a long moment. I turned my head to look at her, watching the tears spill over her cheeks. "I think just sitting here would be nice."

"That I can do," I promised, reaching out and giving her hand a squeeze.

When I moved it away, she grabbed it again and held it. I offered her whatever comfort I could then, so fucking glad I could give her what I never received.

Solidarity. Understanding. Love.

The very things I'd once begged the Fates for. Reaching a hand to the skies to save me from the prison of Vagach's house. Gripping the earth like I could dig my way to my home and away from the torture of being married to him. Shrieking into a pillow as my family perished one by one.

And all they'd given me was their backs. Silence. Stillness.

Until now.

A tear carved down my cheek. Another coated the back of my throat in salt. I choked on them as savage, repressed emotions clawed up from the depths of my being.

Rokath appeared in my mind like a beacon in the dark. *"I'm so sorry you suffered, Assyria, and that I played a part in that during our initial encounters. I hope my devotion to you now shows you all the love you desire and more. I will spend every day proving that you are not just wanted. You are cherished."*

"It does," I told him, my voice weak. More hot tears swept from my eyes. *"Never stop."*

"Never," he swore. *"You're mine. To protect even if I must rip the world apart for you. To crave like I do my next breath. To possess until all you know is my name. In this life, in the next, and the one after, where I will find you bleeding and broken and burn whomever dared to make you feel that you are anything less than a fucking alter upon which to worship."*

His words rewound time and pieced the fractures of me back together. Overcome, all I could do was send warmth back through our bond before the tide dragged me out. Wave after wave crashed through me—of grief, of rage, of trauma. Kiira held my hand tighter, and together, we wept for everything we'd lost. Everything we'd had to suffer because of our sex.

"United, we are stronger," I murmured through a throat thick with emotion.

"We are," she whispered back.

"Xannirin freed the fallen," I rasped. "He made rape a crime punishable by death."

She turned over then, and I mirrored her. Her eyes were puffy and red, no doubt a reflection of my own. "He did?"

I nodded, another wash of tears dripping onto the bed. "Apparently, many volunteered to join those going to the wall."

A half-smile tugged up the corner of her mouth. "Who wouldn't? When the alternative is being forced to do something you don't want."

"That's what I've been saying all along," I laughed, the sound coarse and watery.

We hugged each other then, silent witnesses to the changes occurring because of our insistence. Because we were tired of being used, abused, and broken, all for the male's gains. When we separated, I dried my eyes. "Fuck, I really need to wash my face now."

Kiira laughed, pushing herself upright. "And your mouth with soap. You curse like the soldiers who have served for decades now."

I couldn't deny that. "At least once a day, I realize I sound exactly like Rokath. Barking orders, making thinly veiled threats, intimidating the soldiers."

Kiira followed me into the bathing chamber. A deep tub stood against one wall, while a basin and mirror greeted us straight ahead. Between the two was a chamber pot, thank the Fates. I'd had enough of latrines for my entire lifetime. I turned the taps and filled the washbasin so we could both wipe the grime and tear stains away.

"He's starting to sound like you too. Stopping to consider others' feelings on the matter," Kiira commented, finding another cloth to dry her face and tossing me one too.

"I guess that's the point of a mating bond, isn't it? Two souls becoming one."

"It brings out the best of both of you. Holds the rest of us to a higher standard. Shows the world what true devotion is. Makes us believe in sacred bonds." Kiira listed off a litany of other repercussions to our blessing.

My mind flashed to the portrait Kiira had insisted Rokath and I do before our departure. The copy I had in my bags. The moment stood so clearly in my mind, I didn't even need to look at it again to bring back the feelings that standing over the bloody battlefield, staring up at my mate, had evoked.

That drawing was supposed to spread the mythos of the two of us like wildfire. I sincerely hoped it did. It was so different, wanting to be seen, rather than trying to hide.

I squared my shoulders and looked at myself in the mirror.

The girl who once sought refuge among the garden plants, praying for her violent husband to pass her by, flickered behind my reflection. But I didn't look away. I saw her, acknowledged the part she played in my story. Thanked her for never giving up.

Because if she had, I wouldn't be standing here, on the precipice of winning a war, with my mate by my side.

You've got this, Assyria.

It was time for me to display the true fire that lay inside me. To bring the males of this army to their knees in veneration of my power.

But most importantly, it was time to make the Angels fear me too.

This time, I wouldn't just survive; I'd lead. With Kiira, with the former priestesses, with the fallen...we'd carve a new future in blood.

"Ready to take our rightful place as leaders during this war?" I asked the High Priestess, who had suffered as much as any of us for Xannirin's ambition. For the war waged against the Angels. For being the only female to stand against her two male cousins.

"I am," she replied, shaking her hair out. Then, she twisted it around her finger and secured it at the base of her neck with a leather strip. "May the Weaver open wide our path. May the Giver bless our magic so that it never fails us. May the Reaper turn her eye onto the Angels. May the Fates witness our rise and bolster our success."

Each prayer, struck like a war drum, reverberated in my bones. "May your thread hold strong, High Priestess."

Kiira's answering grin was as vicious as my own. "May your gift never fade, Szélhámos."

With disjointed groans, Grem and Zeec rose, shaking out their fur. Their nails clicked as they landed on the floor. Kiira and I pulled on our boots, and I secured my helmet again, before we slipped into the hall.

Shouts dragged us outside like a rope around our waists. This transition, yet again, would not be an easy one, but we'd already done it once, and we'd certainly be able to do it again.

They'd buried us before, thinking we were weak.

Not realizing they were planting fire-mouthed, thorny seeds.

And now, we'd bloom by their side in battle—sharp, devious, and wicked.

48

ASSYRIA

"I've been fighting in this army for ten years. Survived too many battles to count. All without a female 'watching my back' with her magic," a Vezető snarled down at me.

I crossed my arms over my chest. "You will speak to me with respect. I am the Szélhámos," I hissed. Kiira stood by my side, her posture similar to my own as we faced off with this group of detractors. Grem and Zeec flanked us, the latter raising his hackles at the offending male.

Rokath and Rapp were elsewhere, dealing with messes of their own. Apparently, in all our time away, many had forgotten my mate's departing decree. Factions had formed within battalions, those more welcoming of additional aid, while others, like this stupid male, were seasoned and hardened against the violence. They'd been in so long and so deep they couldn't see anything outside of swinging their blades.

He scoffed, a sharp, derisive sound that made me want to curl my lips back from my teeth and bite. "A leadership position you did not earn. You were merely given it because you fucked the Halálhívó."

Fury ravaged the last scrap of my patience. "That's it," I muttered under my breath. Vicious obsidian burst from my hands, swirling around us in a frenzied display of my power. One section lashed out and wrapped around the male's throat, lifting him off the ground. His feet flailed through the air. "I am the *mate* of the Halálhívó. And you've been serving long enough to know that his wrath is not something you want to incur. Not that I need him here to protect me. I am certainly capable of that on my own."

Twisting my left hand, I snaked more magic beneath his pants and wrapped them around his pathetic balls. His scarlet eyes bulged so hard I thought they might pop out of his head. In a desperate attempt to break my hold, he called upon his own power. But it was no match for mine.

For me.

I was their final reckoning. Should they fail to submit, they'd never get another chance to die at the hands of the Angels.

"Guard," I commanded the dogs. They leaped forward, backs bowed as they barked up at the Vezető.

A sarcastic laugh slipped out of me, and I turned my attention to those surrounding us. "If anyone else has anything to say, I'm more than happy to offer you similar treatment."

Hard eyes in weak-powered shades of red stared back at me. Jaws were held tight, as if many were attempting to restrain themselves from speaking. I threw the first offender away without a second thought, then yanked those few to me. They stumbled to their hands and knees, and Grem and Zeec circled them like they were nothing more than sheep, ensuring they wouldn't escape their pen. I went to the male in the middle and pressed my boot into his fingers.

He glared up at me. "Being his mate still doesn't mean you've earned our respect."

I put more weight into my foot. To his credit, he didn't flinch.

"Allow me to demonstrate *why* you should then." Inhaling deeply, I tugged on the threads of my magic and wielded my secondary power. In a split second, the Halálhívó himself stood before them. The crowd took a collective step back. With more bulk on my body, two of the male's fingers cracked, and a string of curses fled his lips.

I stepped away, having proven my point. Then, shadows swirled again, leaving the Myrza who attacked Fured standing before them.

Kiira snapped her fingers at the males. "Behold the Szélhámos and all the magic the Giver blessed her with. The Weaver crossed the Halálhívó's path with hers for a reason. It is time for you to profess your trust in their divine creations."

After our conversation the previous night, she looked far healthier. Divinity glowed from her as she owned her role as High Priestess. Command exuded from her like she alone decided who would receive the Fates' blessings. Maintaining her judgmental glare, she yanked a ceremonial dagger from her side, the hilt embedded with glittering diamonds. With a simple flick of her wrist, she proffered it to the gathered males. One brow raised, challenge carved into her posture, she dared them to deny her.

They shifted, looking at their companions as if they were waiting for someone else to make the first offering.

Fucking males.

"You," I pointed to one of the kneeling offenders. "Will you sacrifice your blood to the Fates? Thank them for keeping you alive only to defy their grand plans?"

Shakily, he sat back on his heels, staring at me with wide-eyed trepidation. Understandable since I was still wearing the form of the Angel. With a sigh, I let it go. Shoulders softened and tension bled from their frames.

"The Fates don't want obedience. They want devotion. They want willingly-given sacrifices. Do it now if you want the Reaper's eye to pass over you."

Begrudgingly, he pulled his own dagger from his hip. Glancing between Kiira and me, he sliced across his palm, then squeezed into a fist. A pattering of crimson dripped down his hand and onto the earth.

"Anyone else?" I groused, popping out a hip and narrowing my eyes on the gathered unit. More drew their blades and made similar, albeit small, offerings.

"The Fates will shine their favor upon you in the next battle. For they reward those who are faithful to the paths they weave," Kiira explained, each word slow and pronounced like they were fucking younglings.

I had to smother a snort.

At least she sounds convincing.

That encouraged a few more contributions, until everyone had at least let a few drops of blood hit the ground.

"Excellent. I shall inform the Halálhívó that your unit does not require additional discipline," I told them, my voice a mix of snark and sweetness.

Without deigning to wait for a response, I spun on my heel and prowled to the next pennant in the battalion. Kiira fell into an unhurried step beside me, her expression serene compared to my irritated one.

A series of snarls vibrated in Grem and Zeec's throats before they joined us in navigating the complex maze of the war camp. Trotting ahead, their tongues lolled, and their eyes glittered as if the whole encounter had been an exciting game for them.

"I think we convinced Szarvas squad," I reported to Rokath.

"Good. Who is left?" he asked. His directness was expected,

though I still wished he'd offered a little more sympathy after *another* squad had been such assholes. They made the Rokath I'd first met look innocent in comparison.

"Zolom," I replied. At least my mate allowed me to force them to see my value on my own, rather than threatening them on my behalf. This was the level of autonomy I'd always desired, and that Rokath was holding back the parts of him that wanted to shield me from the vitriol of these males spoke volumes.

"Good luck. Let me know if you need my assistance."

"Will do." I focused my attention on the tents looming ahead of us, dragging in a steadying breath. A smattering of caws drew my attention overhead, and I noted three crows high in the blue sky. Kiira's attention too was drawn there.

"The Fates," she murmured quietly.

"Something is about to happen," I replied, coming to a stop.

"Why do you say that?" She whirled, studying me with pointed intent.

"Because ever since Rokath's soldiers arrived in Stryi to conscript, three crows have appeared at every major turning point in my life."

We looked at each other for a long moment as Kiira processed that information. "Let's speak more about this later."

I nodded, and we continued onto the Zolom section. The Százados waited beneath the flag, an anxious look on his face. "Szélhámos," he greeted me with a salute. For Kiira, he swept into a bow. "High Priestess."

We acknowledged him in turn. "Where are they?" I asked.

"Just beyond those tents. But, Szélhámos, they are a bit agitated. There's one male in particular who is vehemently opposed and he has been stirring up the others all day," he said, unable to hide the nervousness in his tone.

"And you have been unable to bring your soldier to heel?" I asked.

"I've tried, I swear. He's just...always been a bit on the aggressive side. It serves him well in battle. Not so much in camp. There's a reason he's never been promoted," he explained. He picked at his nails for a moment before shaking his hands out and tucking them behind his back.

"Understood." I blew out a long breath, looking up to the cloudless sky.

Just one more idiotic soldier to deal with. He's nothing compared to me.

"Heel," I commanded the hounds, and they followed us deeper into this section.

It didn't take long until I heard the would-be orator in action. "...they're smaller, weaker, slower than us. And their magic? Come on, we all know that even if they have the same color eyes, or darker, they still can't wield like we can."

"Fucking asshole," I muttered under my breath.

"I was going to say righteous prick, but that works too," Kiira commented, her tone turning sour.

"Ready for this?" I asked her as we neared the tent from which the sound emerged.

"As I'll ever be." Then, she forcefully smacked the flap back, bursting into the room like she owned it. I entered with similar bravado, the dogs winging me.

The voices ceased immediately, and my attention locked on the male with eyes of a blood red shade standing at the head of them.

"Kneel," I ordered, lifting my voice and imbuing it with threat.

A few had the good sense to. Others, not so much.

"If it isn't the fake-fallen herself," he sneered. His hair was cropped short, nearly baring his scalp, though he boasted a thick beard. One side of his face was heavily scarred, along with one of his forearms, like he'd been too long in a fire before being yanked out.

But he didn't frighten me in the least.

I yanked my sleeves back, exposing the H carved into my wrists. "I see no F here, soldier."

"That's why I said fake," he spat. "What a flimsy story the Halálhívó told about you."

A malicious smile spread across my face. "I doubt you'd say that to him directly."

"I certainly would. He should hear what we really think rather than forcing his decrees on us, especially when the majority disagree!" he protested, shaking his fist in the air and looking around him like he was rousing his comrades into action.

I dove into the well of my magic again and pulled Rokath's form over mine. He didn't flinch, which pissed me off. "Speak the words again." My voice was all gravel and violence, exactly like Rokath's.

The male seemed unperturbed. "Your story about your supposed mate was as thin as the air in Uzhhorod. I can't believe he sacrificed fifty thousand of us to save you."

I gritted my teeth, trying to find it within me not to kill him.

Fuck, was there even a difference between Rokath and me anymore?

Releasing my magic, I returned to myself. "How many did you lose? Enough to hate those who survived? Those who would fight by your side?"

"We all lost thousands," he snapped. "This offer of more magic to protect us is horseshit. I see through the lies now."

I cocked my head, pressing my lips together to smother a smile. I failed intentionally. After all, I'd learned a thing or two from Rokath about the power of appearances. Might as well use my expressive face to my advantage since I didn't possess Rokath's ability to appear unaffected by everything around me.

"Do you?" I said, each word dripping condescension. "Or are you simply grieving and want someone else to blame?"

The male's face turned a bright shade of red. "What would you know about loss?"

"Plenty," I snarled, my patience a mere gossamer.

"The Weaver and Reaper had plans for them," Kiira cut in before it snapped entirely. "Just like the Fates have plans for all of us. The Halálhívó and Szélhámos took the time to burn each of their bodies to send them onto their next lives, where they will be blessed greatly for their sacrifices."

The male scoffed at that too. "Whatever you say, *High Priestess*, your magic is as useless here as hers." He indicated me with a jerk of his chin.

"Unfortunately, we might need your help," I sent down the bond, then sliced my focus back to the male. "If the next words out of your mouth are not an apology for your disrespect, I'll have you taken to the whipping post."

His lips curled back, revealing the extra sharpened teeth that males who'd served for decades liked to file. "I'd like to see you try." Then he spit a wad of saliva at my feet.

Kiira and I shared a long look. "Escort," I snapped at the hounds. They weren't the source of my anger, but I had no energy to put into tempering my tone when all of it had to be directed at maintaining order among these males.

Grem lunged for him, nipping at his heel. The asshole sidestepped into Zeec, swinging for my babies.

But before I could unleash my magic on the fucker for daring to touch my dogs, a heavy thud quaked the ground beneath our feet.

A second later, Rokath and Rapp burst inside, the former emanating fury hot enough to scorch the tent to ashes. His attention landed like a warhammer on the male standing at the front, facing off with us.

"Is there a problem?" he growled, the overt threat in his tone raising the hairs on the back of my neck.

The majority of gathered soldiers blanched and shrank back. Yet the blood-eyed male puffed up his chest like he was going to stand up to the Halálhívó. "I'm tired of your pretense. You get to fuck but the rest of us don't. You have all these rules, and yet you break them all."

Rokath took a menacing step forward, somehow growing even more massive at the outright challenge. "If you believe you could lead this army better," his voice was low and promised violence, "then fight me for it. To the death. No one has managed to kill me yet, so if you do, then you might have earned the position."

Only then did the male seem to lose some of his bravado. He swallowed hard, making his throat bob.

"Not so fearless now, are we?" I taunted, unable to help myself. Rokath cut his attention toward me in warning. I lifted a shoulder and dropped it in turn.

The male's glare hardened again. "Name the time and place."

"Now and in the barrack's yards. We will have an audience witness your demise and the consequences of threatening the stability of this army," Rokath bit out. Then, he sliced dagger-like glares over the rest of the gathered warriors. "I will fight any of you who wish to dispute the order. Step forward now if you wish to follow this idiot into the next life."

No one did.

"Go and tell your comrades where to gather," he gritted out, pointing to the exit. All hurried past us without needing further encouragement.

"Come on, dumbass," Rapp said, throwing two thick black

ropes around the blood-eyed male with a lazy flick of his wrist. Bound, with his magic locked down, Rapp marched him out of the tent. Kiira, Rokath, and I fell into step behind them. Rapp paraded him through the thoroughfares of the camp like a prized hog. The dogs trotted on either side, snapping at those who got too close.

By the time we reached the yard, the crowd was so thick Rokath and Rapp had to shout for them to part. Males and females pressed against the bars around it, and many spread up onto the hills for a better view. A few dared perch on the roof of the barracks too, while more hovered overhead, the occasional flap of their wings keeping them aloft.

I grinned up at Maariya, Izzenna, and Vokkia, who yanked their sleeves back and exposed their devious eye tattoos. The sight twisted my lips into a vicious grin. All around me, others did the same, a cry of Szélhámos tearing from their throats.

I shrugged off my jacket, bearing my tattoo and my brands for all to see. That only elicited more shouts of my name.

The gathered males stared at our arms, then at one another. This was the first time we confronted them with our solidified power. Showed them that we were our own unified front. That our rage had a place among theirs.

Rapp threw the male down in the center of the sand, releasing the binds with a wave of his hand. Kiira and I found spots at the edge of the yard, beneath the overhang of the barracks. Rokath stalked toward him, removing his helmet and the armor covering the top half of his body in an extra show. He handed the pieces to his Hadvezér.

The High Priestess didn't speak. She didn't need to. Her silence alone was a verdict to the faithful. Her stillness was essentially a death sentence for this male.

With predatory slowness, my mate drew his sword from its scabbard. The sheath he tossed to the side before flipping the blade that had already claimed countless lives. The garnet embedded in the eyes of the skull on the pommel glinted in the sun. The detractor scrambled to his feet, drawing his own weapon—a standard issue sword without the extra features that Rokath's had. It was flimsy, to use his own word against him, in comparison.

"There will be no breaks. No mercy. From the moment we start, the ending is only death," Rokath pronounced, loud enough for those close to hear. They relayed it back through the crowd.

Then, he raised the dark blade. With shaking hands, the offender did the same.

"On my mark," Rapp shouted out, nearly startling me. Somehow, during all of Rokath's posturing, he'd returned to our side.

I dragged my attention forward when he shouted, "Go!"

Rokath swung immediately, not waiting for his opponent to gather himself or attempt an opening. The clang of metal striking metal jarred my teeth. Kiira sucked in a sharp breath as Rokath pressed forward, shoving the male backward. He stumbled, half-scrambling to get away from the Halálhívó.

Grem's head nudged my thigh, and I twisted my fingers in his thick fur. Not that I thought Rokath would lose—there was no way. Honestly, I was afraid for the male facing imminent death. It was only a matter of if Rokath felt like playing with his food or making a quick meal of him.

It turned out to be the latter.

Rokath stalked him across the sand, and the male retreated, retreated, retreated, until he was pinned against the fence. Those who had been pressed against it jolted away. In an instant, Rokath had the asshole gripped by the throat and lifted off the ground like he weighed nothing more than a feather.

"I hope you see just how futile your challenge was," he

ground out, his teeth bared. His attention dragged over the crowd too, holding their gazes—terrified, angry, excited—as the male kicked nothing but air. His face turned the color of his eyes, then a lovely shade of purple. "Should any of you dare to question a direct order again, you will face a similar fate. Me."

Rokath squeezed harder, his thick fingers digging hard into the offender's neck.

"Should any of you disrespect the Szélhámos or the High Priestess, you will face their wrath as well."

Just as the male's chest stuttered, Rokath tossed him away like he was a scrap of moldy bread. His gaze locked on me and he gestured for me to approach. Shoving off the wall, I stood tall as the attention of the army fell over me. The male choked on the ground, his life prolonged only temporarily.

The scent of piss stung my nostrils as I came to a stop before him. Yet I didn't deign to give him my attention.

"While I would love nothing more than to torture him for insulting you, mate, I recognize that you making an example of him would elevate the level of respect the rest of them will give you. You have my blessing to do as you please."

My heart warmed at his consideration. I couldn't deny how much I loved when this primal, possessive side of him rose to the surface.

"Together. Let's show them we're united beyond the words we speak to them."

His burgundy eyes glinted with malice. Yanking the male up by the collar, he forced him to face me. I drew the dagger I used during the daily ritual sacrifice to the Fates and stalked forward.

"Weaver, Giver, Reaper, I draw blood in your name!" I shouted, letting the blade flash in the sunlight. "Reaper, curse this male who questions the holy weavings of you and your sisters."

The first slice was across his cheek, drawing a cascade of ruby to the surface of his skin. The male grimaced. "You were only able to do that because you're too weak to face me yourself. You need the Halálhívó to hold me in place."

Rokath's growl ruptured the air—feral, furious, final. The crowd surged back, away from the threat.

I laughed, low and laced with venom. "That was entirely the wrong thing to say."

A split-second later, Rokath threw him to the ground again, pressing a heavy boot into the male's chest. The male wheezed, ribs caving beneath the weight of Rokath's wrath. "You've insulted our chain of command enough. I will not give you further opportunity to fight because you've already lost. And as for the insult you offered the Szélhámos, well, I'll let her choose how she wants to end your life."

He jerked his head, giving me permission to act. Yet I already knew exactly how I wanted to kill him. With a devious smile on my lips, I dove into my well of magic, pulling the offender's form over mine.

Let them all watch him die by his own hand. Let them choke on the horror of it—the horror of what my rare power was truly capable of. Let them see the Fate that walked among them, alongside their Halálhívó.

Whispers broke out as I stalked forward again. The male's eyes widened as he stared up at his reflection. "It's a shame that you chose this route, really. You could have fucked sooner rather than later had you not."

He blinked as if he were trying to comprehend hearing his voice coming from somewhere other than his own mouth. Still holding my ceremonial dagger, I knelt, dragging the tip along his unmarred cheek until I reached the tip of his ear.

"Since you were unable to hear our commands..." I sliced, yanking his ear away from his head. Blood spurted from the wound, and he screamed. I tossed it aside and moved the blade to his eye.

"Since you were unable to see the value in the new order…"

"Wait, no!" he started, but I stabbed. I had to clench my teeth around the bile that rose in my throat. Violence had never been my first inclination—but this wasn't senseless abuse. It was power in its purest form. And I'd wield it however necessary to prove my fucking point.

I shuffled until my dagger hovered over his dick. "Since you were offended that my mate and I could couple and you could not…" I felt the cringe of every gathered male as I sank the blade to the hilt.

Blinded by pain, the male convulsed, limbs twitching toward the sky, then collapsed backward. I let my magic go and rose, holding my mate's gaze.

"Your orders, Szélhámos?"

"End him." The two words rolled off my tongue with such ease.

Rokath removed his boot and replaced it with the tip of his blade, right over the male's still-beating heart. "For the insults lodged toward the Szélhámos, my Fates-given equal." Then, he jammed his sword down.

We remained locked in that position, both bloody, desire thrumming down our bond, as the final bits of the male's life drifted away.

Silence reigned around us.

"Think we proved our point?" I spoke into his mind.

"I think so, little imposter." He broke our connection and glanced around us, lips curled back from his teeth.

"Are the consequences clear?" His tone was low, threatening, and made my core flutter.

Nods answered him as far as I could see.

"Good. You are all dismissed. Assimilate into your new units by the end of the day or face punishment," he barked, contempt darkening his tone.

Trol put two fingers in his mouth and whistled, drawing attention and issuing further commands. Rokath wiped his blade clean, then took mine and did the same. His hungry gaze raked over me, sending a shiver down my spine. *"After that display, I need to be inside you."*

"Please," I whimpered.

He glanced at Rapp. "Help Trol. I'll return later."

Rapp sniggered as Rokath and I passed him and entered the barracks. Then, loud enough that we could hear, he said to Kiira, "That was just foreplay for them. It's a good thing we'll be out here for a while."

A small giggle escaped me as the door swung shut behind us.

Rokath had ordered their obedience; I had demanded their devotion. Not only to me, but to every sacred, bleeding, rage-honed female who walked among them.

They would not soon forget what had transpired.

49

ASSYRIA

Rokath's fingers trembled against my skin as he stripped me—not with hesitation, but with desperate need sharpened by war. Here, with no knowledge of where the Angels were, every moment was danger. Every heartbeat could be our last. Every detractor could spell our death.

Leather fell away, leaving only my breasts and core covered. A shiver swept through me, and I bowed into him, seeking the heat of his skin. To remind me he was still here. Still breathing. Still with me.

His lips pressed into my neck, hot and wet. Sharp teeth trailed across my pulse point, eliciting a hiss. "You are my sacred fire. Born to wage war beside me. To live as a legend with me."

He nipped there, and I dug my hands into the sweaty, carved muscles of his torso. The dark ink flexed and bunched as he wrapped his arms around me and backed me into the wall, bumping into a dresser in the process. I didn't even feel the collision when all I could think about was Rokath's mouth on me. A low groan escaped him as I reached down and wrapped my hand around his thick length.

"I love when you defend me like that," I breathed, giving his hardness a firm stroke.

"I promised I'd always protect you, mate. That is what I intend to do. In the most violent way possible." One of his tattooed hands wrapped around my neck, applying just enough pressure to keep me pinned in place. Those riotous burgundy eyes lifted to meet mine, offering me his savage devotion.

My blood and our bond *thrummed* at the sight.

"It's been far too long since you chased me," I gasped around his hold.

"It has," he agreed. "Unfortunately, there's nowhere for us to go here." He crowded me until our bodies were entirely flush. Bracing his forearms on either side of my head, he leaned down and whispered in my ear. "But you can fight me. I'll wrangle you with my shadows. Force you into the position *I* want you to be in. Use your mouth before I ruin you over and over again with my cock. You'll be utterly at my mercy."

Heat bloomed between my thighs at the image he painted for me. "What are you waiting for, *Rokath*?" I landed the taunt like a well-placed strike. Darkness surged from my palms at the same time and collided with his torso.

My mate stumbled back, a wicked smirk rising to his lips. The sight of it sent ice skittering down my spine.

His magic swept from him like he commanded the night, veiling the room in obsidian. Heart hammering against my ribs, I shimmied to my right, keeping my steps light. The wisps undulated, and Rokath emerged from between them. I wasted no time ducking under him and out of his reach.

Once again, I disappeared. Yet so did he. Our room morphed into a void, disorienting me.

"My little imposter." Rokath's voice seemed to come from multiple directions at once. "You'll never escape me."

"Watch me," I quipped, the thrill of our play racing through my veins.

A thump sounded to my right, and I lunged left. Onyx smoke whispered in my ear. I called on my own power and flung it in all directions. Wood splintered, and he cursed. I smashed my lips together to smother the smile. Easing my way backward, I searched for the entry to the bathing chamber.

The stone gave way and I slipped around the corner, back hugging the cool surface.

Our bond tightened as he approached again, loving our game as much as us. Obsidian pooled in the entryway as I set a trap for my mate. The heady taste of power coated my tongue. While Rokath normally claimed the upper hand in our relationship, my control had improved significantly. And tricking him was far too fun to pass up.

Primal need scorched our connection. Two sniffs sliced through the thick black fog as if he were searching for my scent. "It's almost as if you wanted me to catch you so easily."

Yet as he took another step, I tightened my fist. His heavy boots snapped to the floor. A low, sinister laugh that raised the hairs on the back of my neck followed. "Is that the best you've got?"

In a blink, the void dissipated. Midday sun filtered through the windows behind me, momentarily blinding me. "I'm almost disappointed."

A smirk adorned his ruggedly handsome face. His eyes mapped our close proximity like it was a battlefield.

"Don't be." A similar grin pulled at my lips. I yanked on my magic like I was tugging a rug out from beneath a piece of furniture. He stumbled, shadows leaping from his hands to right himself, but I was already shimmying past him and into the bedchamber.

His footsteps pounded behind me. I whipped around, his

body a blur of ink. We crashed into the dresser a second later, splintering it to pieces. "So devious, little imposter. I fucking love it."

Our mouths met like a storm breaking open, all flashing teeth and thundering tongues. A metallic tang swept between us as I bit his lip. He groaned, the sound so masculine that wetness dripped from me. A second later, he was cupping there.

"This needs to go," he decided, ripping the fabric covering my center away with one strong motion. The bite from the fabric stung, only heightening my pleasure.

"This too," he added, shredding the bind around my breasts with the same ferocity.

Cold air ghosted over my nipples for only a moment before his hot mouth replaced it. A wanton cry caught in my throat. I dug my nails into his shoulders to steady myself against his onslaught. Broken wood scattered around us, and the last thing I wanted was to impale my foot.

As if he sensed the direction of my thoughts, Rokath hoisted me up his body and carried me to the desk. It sat haphazardly away from the wall, and I realized that was what I'd thrown him into before.

He didn't bother straightening it as he laid me out on the top like it was an altar and he was preparing to worship. Our mouths tangled again as he worked his belt loose. When his cock sprang free, it slapped hot against my thigh.

Rokath broke our kiss, leaving me breathless. Onyx thorns wrapped around his arms, and before I could react, they leaped forward and captured me in their hold. Like I was nothing more than a puppet, he spun me so I was on my back with my head hanging off the end of the desk.

Rokath rounded it, his dick bobbing with each step. His magic moved, shackling me in place. But ebony snaked over my skin, eliciting another cascade of pebbles. Up my inner thighs they swept, and involuntarily, I pressed them together. Rokath's power shoved them apart.

His burgundy eyes raked over me like he was a male starving. Fisting himself, he pumped once, twice, three times. My attention snagged on the arousal leaking from the tip and dropping on the floor. "Open wide. I'm going to ruin that smart mouth of yours."

I flattened my lips in defiance. Darkness flashed in his eyes, and my core clenched. More of his magic wrapped around my legs, squeezing tighter. "Is this the game you want to play?"

I nodded—a pure, unquestionable challenge. He'd have to earn my mouth. My body. My everything. Not because he commanded me, but because I *chose* to be his.

He'd win his opportunity to claim, and after, he'd fall to his knees in worship.

His hardness brushed against the seam of my lips. "Then let's play."

Shadow crept higher, higher, higher, until it vibrated a breath away from my slick heat. The gentle touch of it was driving me wild. I thrashed against the binds again, trying to relieve the ache building there.

Then, like Rokath himself were between them, the cold, black smoke caressed my clit. A gasp fled my lips before I could stop it, and Rokath leaped on his opening. The first thick inch of him pressed into my mouth. Then the second.

"Good girl," he praised, his magic continuing to ghost over my center.

A whimper slipped out as the tip hit the back of my throat. Yet this angle was better than others, and I didn't gag quite as hard as I normally did.

"That's it," Rokath growled, bracing his hands on either side of my head. "Take it all."

He thrust again, then dragged out to the crown before

repeating the motion. Our eyes locked on where we joined as he quickened his pace, using my mouth just as he'd promised. His power kept me coiled, offering a mix of featherlight brushes across my center and tight binds around my arms and legs.

I couldn't silence the sounds I made, which only seemed to spur him on. "I'm going to come in your mouth, and you're going to swallow all of me," he gritted out, his abs flexing. "Tap the table twice if you understand."

A tendril of his magic loosened, allowing me to do just that. His hips jerked harder, and he went deeper still. I dragged in a breath through my nose, growing dizzy from the lack of air. Then, he buried himself completely, and jets of hot cum spilled down my throat. "Fuck, Assyria," Rokath groaned, body trembling.

He withdrew, allowing me to swallow. Darkness dissipated, and I pushed upright. Holding his gaze, I licked my lips. His nostrils flared, and a muscle feathered in his jaw at the sight.

"Spread those pretty legs for me," he commanded.

Offering him a saccharine smile, I did just that.

"So. Fucking. Wet," he praised, eyes locked on my core. He stepped forward, his dick still engorged and hard. Planting a hand on either thigh, he opened me further. His thumbs swiped through my arousal. One he ground into my clit, rubbing a slow, torturous circle.

"Rokath," I mewled, bucking into his hand.

"Do you like that, little imposter?"

I nodded, eyes rolling back as he added a finger. "How about that?"

"Yes," I whimpered. "But I'd like another too."

"Would you?" he rasped. "I didn't hear much of a request in that statement."

"Please add another finger." My center pulsed around the one already inside me.

"Good," he praised, giving me what I asked for. It still wasn't enough.

I ground into his hand, chasing the pleasure my body was primed for. "I'm going to make you come around my fingers. You're going to gush over them so when I stroke my cock again, it will be completely soaked in you. But you're going to do it quietly, so the whole camp doesn't hear."

"Yes," I agreed immediately. He added a third finger, spreading me wider. A moan, recklessly loud, clawed up my throat.

"Those sounds you make are downright sinful, Assyria. There's a reason I don't want anyone else to hear them."

He circled my entrance, spreading me wider.

"You're so tight. I need to loosen you up again before you'll be able to take all of me." His fingers curled against that spot deep inside.

"Whatever it takes to make it fit. I just want it. Want you. Need you," I panted as he drove me closer and closer to the edge of ecstasy.

A low laugh rumbled from him. "So greedy. Do you need to be reminded how to ask nicely? It seems you've forgotten today."

He ceased all movement, and I made a noise of protest. "Please, Rokath. I need to be filled. *Claimed.*"

"That's better," he said. His fingers worked faster this time, his thumb drawing circles over my sensitive bud in a way that sent my walls clenching.

My head dipped back as I was lost to the pleasure he delivered. My hips moved of their own accord, and he spread my legs wider so he could work them deeper. "Oh, yes," I hissed as he hit the *perfect* spot.

"Come for me, Assyria." He flattened a hand over my mouth, bowing me across the desk. "Drench my fingers."

My center fluttered at the starved look in his eyes. I nodded against his hand. He dug the heel of his palm into my clit. "Only for me. Because you're *mine*." The way he uttered his possession of me was my undoing.

With a cry muffled by his hand, I *shattered*. "Rokath," I whimpered, though he couldn't hear me. He didn't stop, not even as I became so sensitive I backed away from him. Every drop of pleasure wrung from me was a victory to him.

With a growl, he released me, allowing me to heave in air. True to his word, he wrapped his wet hand around his dick and stroked. It shone in the light after only one swipe. Then, he yanked me to the edge of the desk, the hard wood digging into my lower back as he threw my legs up on his shoulders.

Planting a kiss on the inside of one ankle, he lined up with my entrance. "Since you were so good and coated me so well, I'll give you my cock."

When he pressed into me, it wasn't simply to fuck—it was a ritual, one only he knew how to perform.

"More. Harder," I begged. Then, I hurriedly added, "Please."

"That's more like it." The deeper he went, the more my body coiled tight. He was so fucking thick. Every nerve inside me was alight with pleasure—it was impossible not to be with how he stroked every single one of them.

"Fuck, the feel of you," he groaned. "How I want to worship your cunt every moment of every day. There are simply not enough hours to accommodate how long I want to spend inside you."

When he bottomed out, I sucked in a sharp breath. My hamstrings ached from the position, but it was the type of exquisite pain that heightened my pleasure. Rokath moved his hands to them and massaged, loosening the aching muscles for me. "I'm going to break this altar from how hard I'm going to fuck you."

"Do it," I shot back, my tone all breathy need.

He retreated, then slammed his hips into mine. The slap that echoed around the space clashed with the one after that, and the one after that, as he drove into me. One hand pressed into my lower belly, pinning me in place. The other wrapped around my neck.

"Tell me," he commanded, his tone making me grip him.

I knew exactly what he wanted to hear. "I love you, Rokath," I moaned as he circled his hips. The legs of the desk scraped over the ground as he slammed into me. "I belong only to you."

We jerked backward again, and stars exploded in my vision.

"You belong only to me."

This time, his thrust was accompanied by a low, animalistic rumble. His brows pinched. His mouth opened and he dragged in air. Sweat slicked his forehead and torso, dampening the backs of my legs as he pounded into me, harder, faster.

The edge of the desk smacked against the wall, and I gripped the sides of it in a desperate attempt to remain on it. Rokath yanked my arms overhead instead, pinning my wrists against the wood and allowing me full use of my lungs once again. "I command all your pleasure. It is by my will that you come."

I nodded, breath hitching as he bottomed out. My walls tightened with each pass, gripping him hard enough that he swore.

"Fuck, Assyria. You take me so well. Made for me," he managed to grit out. Pleasure engulfed our bond, drowning all other emotions save for one—love.

Our eyes locked. Rokath had me at his utter mercy. I clawed primal sounds from him simply because he was inside me.

It was a dichotomy of power.

It was amorous hate.

It was mollified violence.

It was agonizing pleasure.

All of it was the eclipse of us.

"Please, I need to come again," I pleaded, the desperation in my tone disregarded. "But I want you to come with me. At the same time."

We'd forever be a single soul in two bodies, but if our ecstasy exploded at the same time, we'd be as close to one as we could ever possibly be.

And I wanted nothing more than that in that moment. With everything we were risking, with everything that came next, I needed this with him.

With my mate.

"I'll fall apart without it."

Rokath nodded, agony in his eyes as he sensed that vast longing, that sharp fear rising within me. "Lose yourself in me. I'm not going anywhere."

He dragged himself over that deep spot inside, tearing a gasp from my throat.

"That's my good girl," he growled, hips slamming into mine. The force of it crashed the desk into the wall. He switched his grip from my wrists over my head to my hips, dragging me to the edge again.

"Now come for me."

He drove into me, so fast and so hard I had no other choice but to cry out. "Don't you *dare* stop."

"Bite your hand," he commanded, and I shoved my fist into my mouth, trying to stay quiet when I was so close to shattering.

Then, a crack sounded, and the ground rushed to meet us. Shadows burst from him just in time to cushion our fall, but he didn't stop fucking me for a second.

He knew I needed this. I knew he did too.

I barely registered that we were now on the rough-threaded

rug as my entire world became the place where Rokath and I joined. His cock throbbed inside me, and my walls offered the same rhythm. I whimpered again, brows pinching as the sparks of pleasure fanned into a full blown inferno.

"So. Close," Rokath gritted out, his fingers gripping me to the point of bruising.

The pained expression he wore, the ecstasy flooding our bond, and the sight of him giving me everything *fractured* me. With a cry, my orgasm ripped through me, burning up every thought, every worry, every reminder that we were fighting for something larger than ourselves beyond these walls.

I bit down so hard on my knuckles that I drew a hint of blood. Rokath's hardness pulsed inside me. He groaned—deep, feral, destroyed—and came. With a harsh jerk, he pulled out. My pussy ached at his absence. Hot cum gushed over my stomach.

Dizzy and pleasure-drunk, I lay beneath my mate. Salt slicked our skin, and air burned our lungs. Blinking, awareness returned to me. Something sharp dug into my shoulder. I tilted my head, registering the chaos and fractured furniture.

"Oops," I giggled, pressing the back of my palm into my mouth to stem the flow.

Rokath shook his head and shoved off the ground. His muscles flexed deliciously with the motion, and I wanted nothing more than for him to bury himself inside me again so I could claw at those carved peaks and valleys.

Instead, he reached down and hauled me upright. After a moment's consideration, he swept my legs out from under me and carried me into the bathing chamber. "Can't have you stepping on something and being out of commission for our next fight. Need you there."

The sentiment spread warmth from my scalp to my toes.

Rokath opened the taps for the tub. I slid down his sweat-soaked body and stepped into it. Despite the small size, he joined me, pulling me into his arms.

"I needed that," he admitted, brushing a kiss to the top of my head.

"I can't lose you." My voice cracked. Even after everything—the battles, the late nights spent reshaping the realm, the small moments between—that fear still had its claws buried deep. It didn't matter how powerful I had become in my own right. How I'd united my sex and forced the males to accept us. How the mythos of us had spread like a wildfire.

If Rokath died, I wouldn't merely grieve. My soul would be shattered into a thousand tiny shards. Each would rip up my chest and leave me breathless. I'd be broken, bleeding, and desperate to join him in the next life.

His heart hammered against my cheek, and I clung to it. Because it meant he was alive. Still here. Still with me.

Because the Angels were out there. Watching. Waiting. Plotting.

Who knew if or when we'd snatch a moment like this again.

All I knew was that if he fell, I would follow.

There was no him without me, or me without him.

50

R☠KATH

"The scouts have spotted Angels here, here, and here," Trol said, moving pieces of stone around the map on the table.

"Which means they're likely going to try to breach our holds in these outposts," I reasoned, tapping three spots between our current location and Uzhhorod. If they'd speared so far south already, they were moving quickly. Which meant we needed to as well. "And they were all clustered in those groups? Nothing more?"

"No," Rapp replied, tongue working over the rings in his lips as he studied the board with us. We'd sent everyone else away so we could focus on how to divide the battalions and ensure the survival of the Demon race. "I flew out with one of the scouts early this morning to see the closest group for myself. They seem like they're priming for a three pronged attack."

I opened my mouth to admonish him for pushing himself but he shot me a glare. "I am fine. My chest held up fine. Honestly I feel almost back to normal now. All the pium worked its magic."

"Good." A bit of tension bled from my chest. Because the

last thing I wanted was to throw Rapp into a battle on his own, unable to swing a sword, pull a bow, or fly through the air. His knowledge and skill in aerial battle was paramount now that we were among the jagged peaks.

The words I needed to say still sat heavy on my tongue. "We need to split up again."

Rapp and Trol picked their gazes up from the table. "Unfortunately, you're right," Rapp sighed, sinking into a chair. "I don't see any other way around it. Which means they're planning something."

"Since they were able to wipe out a large section when we split last time, Zahal Ishim must think he can have success with the maneuver again," I grumbled. He was a fucking horsefly that needed to be squashed before it could attempt to bite again.

"Aye," Trol affirmed. He dragged the marker that indicated his position to the closest one. "I'll take a smaller section here. With my magic, it will be easier to herd the Angels in a way that makes them easier to kill. You'll need larger forces closer to Uzhhorod."

He wasn't wrong. "We'll set some traps along the way. Help pick off the more powerful groups to aid you."

"Thank you," he replied, his focus still on the map. "With the females and other magic wielders from Fured spread evenly, that should help quell any protests about who goes where."

"I'll take the ones still harboring resentments with me. If they don't get on board with the plan, they can become my puppets on the battlefield," I groused, pinching the bridge of my nose. At least after our display, the males had quietened. The females, despite the dropping temperatures, strutted around with their sleeves rolled up, their devious eye tattoos on full display. On my way in, I'd even seen one of the Vezető sporting one.

Rapp snorted, shaking his head. "The peaks are highest and most dangerous near Uzhhorod. I'll take that section. If you don't mind, I'll also need more of the fliers."

"Take as many as you need," I told him. The three spots we were guessing the Angels would go to were spread at odd intervals along the wall, and unfortunately, Trol would be the farthest away again. But with the positions Rapp and I would hold, we'd be so fucking close to Sivy. Should we beat the Angels back, we'd be primed to take the city. Kiira's vision would come to pass. This would finally end, and I could enjoy the rest of my life with Assyria.

"What if they backtrack and try to take out Trol's position since he'll be the furthest from aid?" I threw out, wanting to check my logic.

"They could, but then they'd descend straight into the Paks Desert, and that path would not serve them to reach Uzhhorod," my Hadvezér commented. He paused, rubbing the back of his neck. "Unless they took the wall and marched south along it, to pin your groups."

"So we need to watch out for that to happen," I mused. "How many mated pairs do we have now?"

A wry grin spread across Trol's face. "You'll never believe what I'm about to say."

I raised a brow, glancing at Rapp. He sat up straighter, focus trained on the other Hadvezér.

"By all means, speak," I prodded. Whatever information he possessed, it was clearly important.

"We got about a dozen new pairs in the last few days." His words robbed me of air.

"You're joking," Rapp shot back. We shared a look like we couldn't decide if he was pulling a mean prank for us leaving him alone so often.

Trol shook his head, still sporting a smug expression. "I am grateful that I'm not. Ask the High Priestess. She'll tell you exactly what she told me—that it is a sign from the Fates that they want to ensure our victory."

I sat there, stunned to silence. All this time, these priestesses were serving beneath Kiira, and all these males beneath me. We'd always struggled to communicate over such large distances. And now that we'd brought the sexes together, one of our largest issues had been solved. Sure, the male pairs had been useful, but there were far fewer bonds granted by the Fates than male and female pairings.

Is this how the Angels were able to coordinate so easily?

I cursed myself for not thinking of this solution sooner. And Xannirin for suggesting we subjugate females in the first place. I knew why we'd shaped society the way we had—and this only confirmed to me that we were in fact walking the right path.

The ability to speak finally returned to me. "How many others know of this?"

Trol lifted a shoulder. "Those who were around perhaps. It's not quite the level of gossip like you and the Szélhámos were, from my understanding of what the new recruits have told me."

"We need to make it a bigger deal," I pronounced, my mind working on how to play into this to motivate the army. "As part of the new orders, they'll come to the stage so Kiira can bless them. We'll leave out the part of having to split them up and tell them that after."

My heart clenched at the thought of parting from Assyria, especially over the distance it would require. And so soon after their bonds snapped into place. But it was a necessary step. "They can have private rooms to themselves until we leave since it will be a...painful goodbye."

Almost involuntarily, I rubbed the spot where my magic rested. Rapp offered me a look of sympathy. I glared back.

"Who thought you'd find empathy somewhere inside you?" he teased, thumbing his lip.

"I never found it because I don't have it," I groused. Trol barked a laugh. "Not you too."

"You have changed for the better, Rokath." Trol dropped into his seat, and with a grumble, I sat too. From the edge of the table, he pulled a pitcher of water brimming with pium leaves and poured us all drinks. Not quite the alcohol we would have shared if we were anywhere else, but the symbolism was there nonetheless.

Raising his mug, he said, "Assyria is your perfect match. It's been an honor seeing the changes in her from our first meeting to now. You are truly blessed by the Giver."

I clinked the rim of the metal cup against his. "I am indeed."

Rapp added his to the mix. "It took you long enough to get there. But seeing the two of you work together now...it is something to behold."

My chest ached for an entirely different reason as I took a long drink. With the miracle leaves, it was refreshing, invigorating, and aided in breathing at such high altitudes. Not to mention when ground and mixed into a potion, it aided all Demon's innate healing abilities. It was why Rapp still lived.

I'd never been more grateful for a plant.

"So it's settled then. Rapp will take the southernmost position with a group of fliers. I'll take the middle with the largest force on the ground, including all those who silently oppose the changes. Trol will take the northernmost position with enough halves of mated pairs to ensure messages get to both of us if he needs help."

I glanced between the two, who both nodded their agreement.

"Then we'd better start adjusting and preparing to leave.

With the Angels this close to the wall and Uzhhorod, we can't spare any more days."

✵✵✵✵✵

Snowdrops dotted Assyria's ebony braid as she finished readying herself for the ceremony. I sat on our bed, drinking in the sight of my mate.

Mate.

The word struck me like a punch to the gut. After everything I'd done, everything I'd been through, the Fates had still seen to weave me my perfect match.

And she was so much more than that. She was my reason for fighting, the reason I slept at night. She was the haven I returned to time and time again when the weight of my duty dragged me down. The way she had blossomed into the Szél-hámos brought me to my knees, ready to worship at her fabled feet.

I craved her every touch, every smile, every spark of fire in her eyes. Even her sharp tongue with those defiant words that ignited a savage blaze in my blood.

She was not a weapon. She was the war itself. A force that should be feared and revered in equal measure. And I would be the male at her side to cut down any who thought otherwise.

So when she faced me, cheeks flushed with excitement, wispy strands of ebony framing her high cheekbones, I was rooted in place. Awestruck that she was mine—in this moment, in all the moments to come.

"What?" she asked, her head tilting to the side.

I wanted to speak, but my lips wouldn't move. She approached, the sway of her hips tugging on the strings of my sanity. Somehow, I managed to capture her waist and bring her body flush against mine.

"I don't tell you nearly enough how blessed I am to have you," I rasped, running my nose along her neck and inhaling her scent. Roses and berries filled my nostrils—a smell I'd willingly drown in, so long as I died knowing it was my mate.

She let out a soft sigh, draping her arms over my shoulders. "You could have broken me. Instead, you helped me bloom."

My throat thickened. "I was awful to you. At first."

She pulled back and cupped my face. "And you have more than atoned for that."

Grasping the back of her head, I pulled her into me. Our mouths met with the passion of a wildfire. Our tongues with the ferocity of a battle. Our wills with a heady mix of love and hate.

Breathless, I broke our kiss. Assyria's lips were redder than her eyes, swollen from how I'd claimed them. "We'd better go or we'll be late."

She offered me an unguarded smile dripping with adoration. "I can't believe so many mate bonds snapped into place."

"Nor I, little imposter." Rising, I adjusted myself. A small laugh escaped Assyria. Threading my fingers through hers, we exited our room. Grem and Zeec trotted on either side of us, tails wagging.

Hushed voices reached us the moment we stepped into the valley. The army—both sexes mingling—had already gathered, their leathers gleaming and collars flipped up. Among them, many of the people of Kohszak stood. Their sturdy wool cloaks hugged their bodies as the wind swept between the peaks. Assyria's teeth chattered as a shiver wracked her frame.

"We'll be warmer among the crowd," I told her.

"You lead the way. I can't see over everyone," she replied, stepping behind me. Together, we worked through the throng toward a nearby hillside where Kiira, Rapp, and Trol already waited, along with the newly-mated pairs.

Excited whispers reached my ears as we passed group after group of soldiers. The myth of Assyria and I's bond had spread faster than a mountain blizzard. At least here, with those under my command, we were succeeding in driving much-needed change.

Discordant caws sliced the air as we ascended the hill. Our gazes jerked to the cloudy sky, where three black dots stood in stark contrast to the grey. Assyria sucked in a sharp breath. Kiira too lifted her head, mouth parting and silent words passing her lips.

We joined the High Priestess in surveying the gathered as the birds drifted out of sight. A mosaic of red reflected back from the sea of faces. My attention sliced to the pairs kneeling on a makeshift platform below us. Dug into the hillside, upheld by the magic of a handful of former priestesses, the dozen were visible to all.

Kiira's black dress billowed as another breeze swept through the valley. She waited until the wind died before lifting her arms wide and high. "Come now and bear witness to the divine weavings of the Fates."

A hush fell over the army.

"The three have brought us more blessings with the bonds between these brave soldiers," she began, sweeping toward the mates. "By their holy will, they are shaping our lives, our victory, that we may rise unified in our new order."

Rounding them, she came to stand beside Assyria and me. My mate straightened her spine. "If it weren't for the path they wove for the Halálhívó and the Szélhámos, these pairs would have never met. Their threads would not have become one. Their lives would have been like drinking from an empty glass."

She approached the crowd again, letting her words linger in the air.

"But now, they are full."

More than a few mates glanced at once another, small smiles tugging at their lips.

"Let us pray," she whispered, dropping her head to her chest. Like a wave, the gathered knelt.

"Weaver, who entwines soul to soul with threads unseen, bless these bonds you have spun. Let their steps fall in perfect harmony. Let the colors of their tapestry blend. May the path before them be unbroken, even in war."

Muttered affirmations to the Weaver abounded. I grasped Assyria's hand again. "Blessed by the Weaver."

Kiira intoned again. "Giver, grant them magic not just to wield in battle, but to sustain each other in weariness. Let their power rise in tandem, their union a force that sings your name in every breath and blow. By their combined might, may they bring majesty to your name."

The soldiers and townspeople prostrated themselves. So too did the mated pairs.

"Reaper, let your eye pass over them, for they walk the path you have permitted. Should they falter, let them rise together. And if death comes, let it come to both, for what you have bound shall not be easily undone."

Assyria's fingers tightened in mine. Kiira looked to the cloudy sky like she could peer through their heavy gray and beg the Fates to let them all live. With how close the two were, there was no doubt my mate had confessed to my cousin her fears about my survival. Our survival. Simply because we loved one another.

Releasing a shuddering breath, I rose to my full height. Our bond hummed with bliss, rather than contention. Like a beast with a mind of its own, it had fought us both, forced us together, and we'd faced our reckoning because of it.

Now, it needed to do no such thing.

Kiira lifted each couple one by one, offering them further blessings. The rest of us watched on.

"Bound by the Weaver, sanctified by the Giver, protected by the Reaper, go now as two who are one, and let the world tremble at what love has wrought."

Kiira's final words sent a chill straight to my core. Assyria looked up at me, those dark lashes fanning against her cheeks.

"Always mine, little imposter."

"Always yours."

As the army dispersed, I knew, deep down, that our love would send tremors through the Angels in the coming days. For our departure was imminent. I only hoped that empowering Assyria, aiding her in impersonating high ranking officers, wouldn't result in her death.

Because if she perished, I'd follow. Leave the whole army to burn to ashes. There was no point in saving the Demons if I couldn't have my mate with me after.

51

ROKATH

Wisps of white magic flitted through the alpine trees ahead as we crept toward the Angel scouting party. The group prepared their encampment for the night, erecting tents, lighting fires, and cooking meat. Swirls of black shrouded us, hiding any movement that might garner attention.

A twig snapped. My closed fist flew into the air. The soldiers behind me halted. I didn't dare breathe as I listened for the next telltale step. From between two trunks, a figure emerged, not even a stone's throw away from me. Blue eyes scanned the dark forest.

All that kept us hidden from him was a wall of our magic.

"Everything okay?" Assyria appeared in my mind.

"Movement ahead. Hold your position," I shot back, my entire focus on the approaching male.

The muscles in my legs burned from holding this crouched stance. Yet we couldn't move without alerting him to our presence.

A bush rustled. The Angel swept off to my left, searching for the source of the sound. My fingers flexed, preparing to grab the hilt of my blade and free it from my back.

But from the clearing, a female called out for him.

With one last look into the abyss, he returned to the safety —temporary as it may be—of his unit.

Air fled my lungs. I glanced over my shoulder, noting the position of my half of the Deathveiled.

Assyria had taken the others in a long loop around the outside so we could ambush them from multiple directions.

"On my mark," I said down the bond.

A flicker of unease swept from Assyria before our connection muted. My heart lashed against my ribs before I reminded myself it was merely from her magic and not because an Angel had taken her.

This was the first time she'd impersonate the Myrza we'd slaughtered in Fured. This was the test that our plan might work. Executing it flawlessly was essential. One fuck up, and we'd have to scrap everything and start over.

It was for that reason we'd only spoken Angelic the past week.

A loud rustling drew the attention of the unit. Their heads whipped in Assyria's direction. Breath lodged in my throat. Like a white wraith, the Myrza—Assyria—appeared in the night. The flickering of the fire cast her in a haunting relief. Blood and grime caked the white armor, making her appear as if she'd been traveling for weeks.

"Report," she barked with authority in Angelic. A startled few shot up from their seats, greeting her with the traditional words praising the fucking Goddess.

"We thought you were dead," one of the males spluttered. "The Zahal said the Halálhívó arrived in the mountains weeks ago with new reinforcements."

"The Zahal was mistaken. A few of us escaped once we realized we were going to be overpowered in Fured. We managed to survive long enough to return to our home and out of those cursed lands," she replied coolly. Her accent was slightly off from his, but I doubted anyone would notice. Her words were also carefully chosen and practiced, because we needed at least one survivor to run back to the larger group and spread the word that one of their own was betraying them.

"Then where are they?" a female pressed, scanning the area.

"They're safe." She stepped closer to the fire, holding her hands over it as if she were trying to warm them. Winter in the mountains was bitter, and snow draped over rocks and tree branches like lattices of lace.

"Safe where?" the same female asked. The disbelief and suspicion in her cerulean eyes was evident, even from this distance.

"Let's go," I ordered under my breath. Dropping my magic, I rose to my full height and unsheathed my sword. Despite my best effort, the scrape of the edge against the scabbard still shredded the night. Down the line, the remainder of the Deathveiled did the same.

"In the Demon army," Assyria replied, drawing a weapon of her own and swinging it through the flames. The tip nicked the female's throat, and blood sprayed from the wound. She slapped a hand over it like that would save her.

Screams ripped the still air as we charged forward, our heavy steps ringing a death knell. Assyria grabbed a male with lapis eyes and held a knife to his neck while we slaughtered the rest. He struggled against her hold, managing to wrench himself free.

She cursed in Demonic and lunged for him. Shadow shot out of my palms and wrapped around him, dragging him to his knees. Assyria regained control of him again.

I approached, rivulets of crimson Angel blood dripping with

each strike of my foot against the earth. "Where are the rest of you?" I growled at the male in Angelic.

His mouth sealed tight. Defiance blazed in his eyes even as they locked on my soaked sword. I turned my attention—very intentionally—to Assyria. "Well played, Myrza. You'll have a place in the new order once we slaughter Stadiel and Iaoth."

The male's eyes went wide. "Traitor!" he screamed in Angelic, thrashing against my binds. "How dare you betray the Goddess for these animals?"

I released him, and Assyria shoved him to the ground. The male clutched the cut beneath his jaw. We needed him alive after all. "Because I know we will lose to them after seeing their power in Fured. Better to survive than to live for a Goddess who is not protecting us," she explained. A flit of horror crossed her face as she mixed up the words for live and die.

A chill colder than the ice dug into the boulders swept down my spine. In the heat of the moment, Demonic curses could be overlooked. But with his entire focus trained on her, that one wrong word could upend our plans.

Anxiety flooded our bond. Assyria's thumb pressed into her forefinger, searching for a ring that wasn't there.

I kept my gaze firmly on the male, gauging his reaction. My hand twitched, ready to slaughter him if he caught Assyria's mistake.

The male at our feet didn't seem to notice—thank the Reaper. His face twisted into abhorrence as he started up at the visage of his former officer.

"Run and tell the others to meet here if they wish to survive the rest of this war," I growled in the common tongue, tearing his ire to me. He shrank away as I leaned ever so slightly forward. The raw, helpless fear in his eyes was delicious and everything I'd been missing these past months.

Assyria kicked him in the ribs with the side of her boot. "Now!"

He wasted no further time scrambling to his feet and bolting through the trees. The soldiers behind us let out sinister laughs as we watched him race away until his white hair was no longer visible in the dark.

"What do we do now?" Uzadaan, a ruby-eyed male who had known Assyria from the beginning of her journey, asked. After his performance with her in the initiation ceremony and learning his magic allowed him to freeze blood and thereby render a person unable to move, I permitted him to join her guard. He very much understood the consequences of harm befalling my mate.

He'd protected her well during the Battle of Fured too.

"Leave the bodies. They'll likely return knowing that we didn't burn them. But first, we leave a message." I found an Angel with a flayed-open stomach and dug my fingers in. They squelched as I pulled them free, coated in his blood.

I went to one of the rocks and cleared it of snow and ice. The Angels wanted a Goddess? I'd give them one in Assyria.

I painted my message in steaming garnet.

JOIN OR DIE

"Loot the camp and let's get going. It's fucking cold and we have a long march back to the wall."

The firelight flickered over the dark art, one line dripping into another as I smeared it in all three languages to ensure I was *entirely* clear.

When I finished, I found the Deathveiled rummaging through bags. A few knocked over tents and caused general mayhem with wicked grins on their faces. Assyria drifted to my side, still wearing her stolen skin. Her brows were pinched, and her hand hovered over her stomach like she was going to be sick.

Unfortunately, she'd have to maintain her magic until we were safely beyond the wall again. A scout spotting the transition would ruin our plans, and now they knew the Myrza was about, they'd be everywhere searching for him and the supposed survivors.

"You did well," I praised her, resisting the urge to reach for her. Any affection on my end would indicate something amiss too.

"I fucked up," she stated. "Twice."

"He didn't notice," I tried to reassure her, but she shook her head.

"I have to do better." A muscle feathered in her jaw. "There is no other option."

"You will. I'll make sure of it." That seemed to ease some of her lingering frustration.

"What will you do if a group of Angels returns here, actually wanting to join us?" she asked, changing the subject.

I snorted. "They won't. One Myrza isn't enough." Not that I truly thought any would. They'd rather die than be captured by us. Who would willingly surrender to our control?

The soldiers stuffed their packs, hefting them onto their shoulders. One by one, they trudged into the trees. I couldn't help but glance over my shoulder as we followed, almost expecting another dozen Angels to emerge from the darkness.

Silence, save for the crunch of snow and twigs beneath our boots, reigned as we returned to the wall. An icy breeze rustled the branches overhead, dusting us in a fine white powder. I brushed my shoulders off, not wanting my armor to rust. Assyria shivered, and instinct roared to wrap her in my arms, to offer her what heat I could.

"We'll be back soon," I reassured her. After almost losing her in the battle, I'd become even more attuned to her needs. The slightest shift in her down our connection snapped my focus to

her. The next time our bond went mute, I'd know the instant it happened.

Because I wasn't naive enough to think that another occurrence was impossible.

She nodded, eyes trained downward. A male beside me cursed as he tripped on a hidden rock. This was why we'd taken so long to approach. Silence was our shield. Yet our return trip didn't need to be as surreptitious. Flickering flames atop the wall greeted us half an hour later. A yell went out, signaling our return.

Those at the top threw down ropes for Assyria to climb, while the rest of the Deathveiled called upon their wings to carry them to the top. Unfortunately, my mate hadn't quite figured out how to use the fake white wings of the Angels to propel herself. I was more concerned with her learning the language since we had other methods of transport.

I followed behind her in solidarity. When we reached the top, Trol, Rapp, and Kiira were waiting.

"How did it go?" Rapp questioned the moment my boots struck the stone.

"We'll see the reaction once we find the next group," I told him, heading toward the guardhouse. A fire burned in the hearth, chasing the chill from my skin. I stood beside it, soaking the heat into my bones. Assyria dropped her magic, shaking out her limbs like she was trying to rid herself of the lingering effects of impersonating our enemy. With a groan, she collapsed at my feet like one of the hounds. Skittering echoed down the stairs, and then Grem and Zeec bounded forward, barking a greeting.

"Oh, yes, come here," Assyria cooed, dragging Zeec to the floor and curling around him like his fur was the key warming her body.

I rolled my eyes. "It wasn't *that* cold."

"Speak for yourself," she shot back, her voice muffled. Grem lay on her feet so she was nearly smothered by black fur.

Kiira joined her on the ground, and they had their own conversation while I turned my attention to Trol and Rapp.

"We'll leave at first light–" Assyria made a noise of protest, but I ignored her. "We'll leave at first light, Trol. Are you sure you're alright with the numbers you'll have?"

"Aye. We'll have enough to manage whatever the Angels deem is necessary to throw at us," he replied. "A forward scout returned while you were gone. There's another exploratory group half a day ahead."

"Good. We'll give them the same treatment as here," I announced. "What of the larger force's position?"

"A day's ride down into the valley. I think the closer groups are testing for weaknesses," he ventured, rubbing the back of his neck.

That made sense. "Try to pick them off however you can. And whatever happens, holding the wall is of the utmost importance."

"Yes, Halálhívó."

I offered him my arm, and he grasped it. "We'll try to get a few hours of rest before our departure."

"Sleep well," he told us, then disappeared the way Grem and Zeec had come to one of the chambers on a higher level. The soldiers were in the barracks just below the wall, with the ones who would continue on camped outside them.

"Come on," I said to Assyria, who had straightened and was petting the greedy hounds.

"Ugh," she protested as she rose to her feet. "I hope they put out the thick fur blankets."

Our tent had been cold the past few nights, I'd give her that. *"All the more reason to be close to one another if they didn't."*

"You'd like that, wouldn't you? Your dick pressed against my ass?"

"I'd like it to be more than pressed against it."

"If you two are quite finished, I'd actually like to sleep," Rapp interrupted us.

I shot him a glare. "Fine. Go," I groused, sweeping my hand out.

He wasted no time bursting through the far door, Kiira right behind him. The latent heat of the guard tower clung to me, but the stark cold outside slapped it off the moment we stepped outside. Calling on our black, membranous wings, we leaped off the edge of the wall and metered our descent to the camp below. With a thud, we landed in front of our tents.

"Goodnight," Assyria bid Kiira and Rapp, tugging on my arm and leading me into our space before I could say anything to either of them.

"Eager tonight, are we?" I rumbled, gripping her waist.

"Tired," she replied, unfastening her fur jacket. I tied the flaps closed behind us, noting the bag of rocks at the foot of the bed. Hovering a hand over them, I found them still warm. Assyria stripped to nothing but her underclothes. She held out her hand. "I need a shirt."

"You know where to find them," I told her as I began unbuckling my armor.

"So I can take whichever one I want?" she asked, cocking her head to the side.

Grumbling about her under my breath, I fetched her one that hadn't been washed yet and tossed it her way. She shimmied it over her head, the hem kissing the tops of her knees. Then, she climbed into bed and huddled under the blankets.

The last of my armor secured, I stripped out of my sweaty fighting clothes and rinsed the blood from my hands. By the time I crawled into bed beside her, Assyria's eyes were closed and her breathing was soft and even. With a sigh, I kissed her forehead, then blew out the candle on the bedside table.

Curling around her, I buried my nose in her hair. Yet as exhausted as I was, I couldn't sleep. My mind raced over a thousand outcomes.

Through them all, one word remained. Repeated like it was the only word a raven could caw.

Sacrifice.

52

ASSYRIA

The next outpost coiled into the mountainside like a snake ready to strike. Wooden buildings hugged the slope, with the premier seemingly carved from the stone itself. High turrets jutted into the air, providing a view to the wall.

My heart twisted at the sight because it meant one thing: Kiira and Rapp would leave us. The High Priestess and I rode beside each other, a few paces behind Rokath and his Hadvezér. Grem and Zeec barked and bounded forward, icy flakes clinging to their long fur as they buried themselves in the snow. More sprayed as they leaped and bounded through it, snapping at the air.

Kiira and I shared a laugh at their antics. At least someone was happy to be here.

"I'm going to miss you so much," I told her, sorrow sliding between my ribs.

Kiira swayed in her saddle for a moment before responding. "Me too. But we'll be reunited soon." Somehow, she didn't sound convinced.

Worry twisted my gut. "Your vision says so."

She nodded, eyes still trained ahead as if she were searching for something. "Nothing has changed. I haven't seen anything else since then, so it is still set in stone. Of course, if I have a new one, I'll let you know immediately."

Rokath and Rapp steered their horses downhill, and we followed, leaning back and letting our horses pick their footing. The hounds were nowhere to be found, but a trail in the thick power told me which way they'd gone.

"I still can't believe so many mates were waiting for each other," I commented once we straightened out again.

"Truly a blessing from the Fates. Much like your bond. The populace craves more of the two of you, according to Xannirin's latest raven. I'll have to write about your latest exploits before we go."

Heat scorched my cheeks. As much as I'd become the face of this revolution to the army, something about millions of others knowing so much about my life felt foreign, like a splinter wedged beneath my skin.

"The whole army seems to believe in it now too." My attention drifted behind me. The Deathveiled rode closest to us, and Zurronar shot me a wink. Banand was in the prisoner's wagon some distance back. The two were basically inseparable, which was understandable given everything they'd endured together.

It mirrored what Kiira and I had forged in Fured, which made the coming goodbye ache like a broken bone.

The clouds parted overhead, making the snow on the trees glitter. More powder slid off the roof of the buildings as a group of males emerged. Rapp and Rokath were nearly to the center of the outpost already. The soldiers fell to one knee and rested their foreheads on their arms in veneration.

"Halálhívó, we've prepared space for you and the rest of those joining us. The second accommodation downhill is also in working order," the leader explained. I noted his rank as Vezető, though he wore red armor instead of the typical leather—one of Xannirin's guards.

So it was true, the Kral had sent the aid he promised.

"At ease, soldiers," Rokath rumbled. He and Rapp slid from their horses, and the guards rose.

Kiira and I came to a stop behind them. With easy grace, we dismounted. Another male approached, taking our reins and leading our horses away.

"If you'd like, I can give you a tour. We've spent a few weeks renovating it, since it wasn't in the best shape when we arrived," the Vezető explained.

"Lead the way," Rokath instructed with a sweep of his hand.

As we stepped inside, I glanced over my shoulder, finding the wagons and soldiers spilling into the valley. Harnessed horses dragged massive tree limbs through the snow, clearing space for supplies and tents. The Parancsok leaped into action, directing the movement like puppeteers.

"How long has it been since you were here, Halálhívó?" the male asked as we stamped our boots on a mat in the center of what appeared to be a weapons storeroom.

"Decades," he replied.

Much like where we'd stayed near Kohszak, the majority of the building was rows of bunks stacked three high and communal washrooms. The changes, he noted, were that each floor was now designated by sex rather than by unit. The first level was for the females, and the bathing chamber had been cleaned so thoroughly it gleamed as sunlight spilled over the stone. "We built additional chamber pots here for privacy."

Kiira and I shared a look. Whether it was this Vezető's idea or Xannirin's, it mattered not. The females were being shown they mattered.

"That was very thoughtful. We thank you," Kiira praised,

her tone all warm honey. The male blushed and averted his gaze. I resisted the urge to snort. She had that effect on people.

"If you'll follow me, I'll take you to your accommodations."

Up three flights of stairs, we found ourselves on a floor with several rooms hugging each wall. They all had doors that closed and locked. At the end was a meeting space, complete with map, albeit a worn and disused one, and a small planning table.

"The dining hall has been moved to the first floor, adjacent to the weapons storage, where there's more room to host everyone," he finished.

"Ensure lunch is served soon," Rokath instructed, tugging on the tips of his gloves as he surveyed the space.

"Yes, sir," he replied, scurrying away and leaving the four of us alone.

"So this is home now?" I asked, striding toward the windows. The view was striking, with the valley spreading out below. The second building, I noted, was some distance away. Groups were already striding in and out of it, unloading the wagons. Banand and Zurronar were helping the group of captive Angels from one of them.

My eyes narrowed on the former as he held the hands of the turquoise-eyed female, Araquiel, as she leaped to the ground. Their gazes met for the briefest of moments before Araquiel ripped them apart. Banand's expression was pained before he smoothed it away. He'd already admitted to having some affection toward her, but this looked different...

Grem and Zeec burst from between some wagons, tongues lolling and tails wagging. They circled the Angels, teeth flashing as they yipped. Some of the prisoners paid them no mind. Others shrank back.

Our bond tightened as Rokath approached. My body hummed from his presence, and I took a step closer to him. His attention drifted down to the Demons working below us. "We need more Angels for you to impersonate."

Along the way, we'd picked up a handful of Bassi—the Angel equivalent of a Vezető. But it wasn't enough to sway a swath, not like it had been when I'd used the form of the Myrza. According to the new captives, word of his betrayal had spread like a plague. Furious officers spent hours planning his demise before he could wreak further damage on morale and belief. The irony nearly made me laugh.

"We need to speak with Banand too," I insisted, clocking the way his hand hovered near Araquiel's lower back as he escorted her inside.

"Why?" Rokath murmured, bracing his forearm on the window and following my attention to the pair.

I hated that I understood the leverage of love. Of affection. Hated that I was considering using it. But if it meant that my friends would survive—the Demon race would survive—I'd use it. War was a game. The weak played it safe and clean. What I had to say could fall off the edge of the blade in one of two ways—glory or treason. I hoped it wouldn't be the latter. "His affections for Araquiel seem to have deepened these past months. I wonder if we can turn her to our advantage."

A growl vibrated deep in Rokath's chest. "Now you're really starting to think like a leader."

I preened under that praise. "He and Zurronar have been helpful since they joined the raids with us too."

"Aye, they have," Rokath agreed. "After our meal and offering, we'll grab them and bring them here."

"What for?" Rapp asked, joining us in surveying the scene. Kiira was nowhere to be found.

Rokath gestured to where the two were corralling the Angels inside the barracks. "See if they can convince our prisoners to assist us."

A wide grin split Rapp's face. "That's brilliant, Rokath."

"It was all Assyria," he told his Hadvezér. Pride etched his expression as his regard settled over me.

Rapp raised a brow, the studs above them catching in the midday light. "I'm impressed." Then, he backhanded Rokath in the stomach. "I told you she was smart and would be useful to us all along."

Rokath grumbled something under his breath, eliciting a bark of laughter from Rapp.

"Are you ever going to promote them?" I questioned, gesturing to Banand and Zurronar. Both had powerful magic, and after all, we were missing several Parancsok after the massive loss when Rokath chose me over his soldiers.

"I don't see why not. Now is as good of a time as any," Rapp shrugged, leaning his shoulder against the polished glass.

"Technically, we replaced them when we thought they were both dead. So they were officers before. Though Zurronar was only a Vezető," Rokath pointed out.

"We have plenty of empty slots to fill," Rapp countered. "Just because they aren't now doesn't mean they can't be placed where they should be. From Trol's accounts, both stepped up the moment they were well enough to do so after their rescue."

My mate was silent for a long moment. His brows pinched ever so slightly, his mind working over all the possibilities and probabilities. "We'll offer them a chance to earn new titles after we speak with them. See if they want the challenge."

I rolled my eyes. Rokath very much believed in proving value, and if either could turn the Angels to our side, they certainly would have earned their title of Parancsok.

"I need a nap before lunch. Too many early mornings after too many late nights." Rapp yawned, the motion nearly unhinging his jaw.

A weariness tugged at me too. "I can't object to that. Besides, if we're going to go out again tonight," I looked at my mate, nodded in confirmation, "then I definitely need some sleep to replenish my magic."

"Let's go then. They'll fetch us when it's time to eat," Rokath said. When he pivoted to exit the room he commented, "I see Kiira is already a step ahead of us."

Rapp chuckled as we reentered the small officer's floor. "Aye. She knows we'll have a long ride ahead of us the day after tomorrow."

Rokath halted, his boots squeaking against the newly-cleaned floor. My breath caught in my chest.

"She's going with you?" His tone was far more measured than I thought him capable with the riot of emotions burning up our bond.

Rapp realized the error of his words a moment later. Kiira hadn't wanted him to say anything to Rokath until the moment they were about to leave. True to my word, I hadn't revealed a whisper of their budding relationship to my mate. Though Kiira hadn't exactly been forthcoming either, so I couldn't comment on anything more than their shared affections.

"What, you don't think I'm capable of protecting her?" Rapp said, a hint of challenge in his tone that contrasted his neutral posture.

"After what happened to her?" Rokath ground out. "The only one who can protect her is me." His nails dug into his palms.

Rapp scoffed. "And yet, you weren't the one who ripped Ollmund Varrir's balls off."

Rokath took a menacing step toward his Hadvezér. "Neither were you."

Rapp's eyes flashed, and his lips curled back from his teeth.

I darted between the two, placing my hand on my mate.

"We're all tired. Let's talk about this later?" I tightened my grip to get his attention, and he tore it to me.

"Fine," he said through gritted teeth. Glaring up at him, I shoved him in the direction of the largest room, leaving Rapp standing in the middle of the hall. I hoped he'd go to a different room than the one Kiira had snuck into. Their being alone in the same room would only further my mate's discontent.

I shut the door behind us and locked it as an added deterrent. Rokath's jaw ticked, and his movements jerked as he stripped out of his armor. The moment his chest was bare, I shoved my finger into it. "You are an asshole. Kiira does not need to be coddled just because some spineless noble took from her what she did not want to give. You never treated me any differently because of it, so don't do that to her."

Rokath caught my wrist and tugged me into his embrace. With his other hand, he threaded his fingers through the hair at the nape of my neck. Pinned in place, he forced me to look deep into his eyes. "I will protect the people I love. No matter the cost."

"That includes Rapp," I pointed out.

He looked away, nostrils flaring.

"He will protect her too. They spend all their time together. He wrote to her more frequently than you did while we were marching to Lutsk. I think you can trust him not to let anything happen to her." The last words slipped out as little more than a whisper as I sensed him starting to calm.

"I know," he said, blowing out a long breath. "I just feel so guilty. I've spent so much time away, fighting. I had no idea so much was crumbling between Xannirin, Kiira, and me. Yet I was the only one who could safeguard us. Still am, really."

He walked us to the bed. The mattress sank beneath his bulk. I climbed into his lap, straddling his hips, and walked my fingers to his temples. A small groan escaped him as I massaged the tight muscles there.

"You have me to support you now. You're not fighting alone."

"Out of the three of us, only my magic serves a purpose on the battlefield," he murmured. "So it was always my responsibility to fight."

"You've given so much. To everyone. Whether they see it or not." I moved lower, finding the tension in his jaw.

"What matters is that you see me, mate." Our eyes locked, and all barriers between us fell, leaving only one raw emotion burning between us—love.

"I do. I see you, Rokath." Cupping his face, I pressed my lips to his. "Now hold me while we sleep. Because I also know that is what helps you rest more than anything else."

He offered me a rare smile. "My insomnia is no match for you, little imposter. Much like everything else, you fight it with fire and leave ashes in your wake."

"Don't forget that," I teased as I wriggled off him and stripped out of my clothes. When we were both bare, he flung back the rough blankets. We curled together beneath them. I didn't merely want to sleep beside him. I wanted to sear the shape of his body into my memory. Sink to darkness together, where we both belonged.

Where we both could drop our masks and just *be*.

53

R☠KATH

Assyria's half-finished throne stared at me as I sank onto the floor of the weapons storage. Rapp settled across from me, meeting my gaze for the briefest of moments before turning his focus to the pile of feathers and bone. Assyria perched on a workbench, her long hair unbound, sleep still clinging to her eyes. Yet dark glee brightened them as I twisted the legs about, deciding what needed additions next.

"This one is too short. Better to save it for the back," Rapp commented, examining an arm bone from one of our more recent attacks.

"Aye," I agreed, plucking it from him and placing it among a different pile. The adhesive was nearly ready—a mix of sap, boiled hooves, and raw sugar that became clear when dried, leaving the bones perfectly white and ready to intimidate any Angels who foolishly requested a meeting with me.

Let them kneel before the chair built from their fallen and know it was primal devotion that laid the first bone. I couldn't wait for the first time the Zahal crawled out of his hive, begging for a reprieve from our next assault. The fury that would twist his face as he beheld my mate and me lounging atop the remnants of his soldiers. Another Myrza skull would certainly polish off Assyria's throne, though it wouldn't be nearly as satisfying as the one from the female Ishim had loved adorning one side of mine.

"What's that smell?" Zurronar asked, his nose wrinkling as he entered the space. Even with the doors flung wide, the sour scent of the adhesive was pungent. Banand offered us salutes, and Zurronar hastily mimicked him.

"At ease," I told them, dipping the flat stick into the mix and giving it one last stir. Rapp held the first section upright, twine keeping the bones exactly how I wanted them.

"I have a challenge for you. Take a seat."

Assyria scooted over to give them room along the far wall. Zurronar shot her a wink, and she made a face at him in return. Gritting my teeth against the overprotective beast, I dug the stick into the canister and slathered the first scoop across the bottom. The thick goop dripped onto the threadbare cloth beneath our knees, immediately beginning to harden. Rapp lifted the section ever so slightly off the ground to ensure it didn't permanently stick.

"You can begin," I told Assyria down our mental connection.

"How has your relationship with Araquiel developed over the past few months since you've been back in the Demon camp?" Assyria asked Banand, straight to the point. I kept an eye on his reaction.

Something flashed across his face, though he managed to smooth it away quickly. "She is our captive, and understandably, she's unhappy about the situation."

"Would more freedom make her happy?" I questioned. Another thick layer of adhesive went over the middle, and carefully, I removed the twine there.

"I think it would," he ventured, his words slow and measured. "I'm assuming there's a price for it?"

I paused my work and looked straight at him. "You've been on our last few raids. What do you think the price is?"

His fingers drummed against his biceps. "You want her to help us."

Zurronar shifted his weight, crossing one leg over the other. His attention flickered to Banand before he pointedly studied my work.

"She might run off with them if we bring her on a mission like that straight from being shackled," I replied. "As you said, she is unhappy being a prisoner of war. Which is where you come in."

Rapp tested the bottom and middle sections of the bones to ensure they were dry enough that removing the top bits of twine wouldn't send the whole thing falling apart. With a tug, he freed them. I scooped more adhesive and painted it across.

Silence reigned until I stuck the stick back in the container.

"What can I do?" Banand ventured, his tone tipping into eagerness.

Assyria twisted her ring around her finger as she regarded him. "You know her best. What would make her switch allegiance?"

Zurronar let out a sigh, running his hands over his long hair and straightening the leather strap holding it atop his head. "Tell them, Banand."

The adhesive dripped straight onto the cloth as my hand paused midair. Rapp whipped his head over his shoulder, staring at the pair too.

Banand's face was nearly as red as his eyes as he glared at Zurronar. "I don't know what you're talking about."

"Don't start this again," Zurronar shot back. His body tensed, like he was preparing to fight his friend.

The two remained in a faceoff, the room at a complete

standstill, until three caws rent the air, and three black crows sailed by the open doors.

Assyria sucked in a sharp breath.

"Whatever you are about to say, it is important," she whispered. Then she tore her attention to me. "Kiira said the caws and crows are the Fates at work. They might be the crossroads where her visions could change."

Fuck.

But it all made perfect sense. All the times I'd heard crows since Assyria came into my life roared back—when she was bitten by the snake, when I rode out to meet the Angels to trade for her life, when Blaeze returned to us, during my conversation with Kiira and Xannirin, before the blessing of the mates...

"Tell them," Zurronar urged again. "Or better yet, show them."

"Show us what?" I growled, my tone leaving no room for argument. I surged to my feet, the throne forgotten. Rapp, thankfully, kept it upright, though his knuckles were as white as the structure he gripped.

Banand glanced among us all, muscle ticking in his jaw. Fingers clenched and unclenched. "There was a time," he whispered, but his voice was like a whistling blade through the pregnant silence. "Where I prayed for anything else. For a way out of what the Fates had given me. When we were imprisoned, I'd begged the Weaver for a new path. This wasn't what I meant."

A haunted expression claimed Zurronar's face before he shook it off.

Then, with lips curled back from his teeth, Banand whipped around and yanked his tunic overhead.

Assyria gasped, her hands slapping over her mouth. Bones clattered like a judgmental echo of the dead.

Because between his shoulder blades was a perfect black circle.

Exactly the same as the one between Assyria's. Between mine.

"Araquiel is your mate?" I questioned because I had to be absolutely fucking sure.

He shrugged his tunic on and fell into the wall like offering the truth hadn't gutted him. He seared Zurronar with another hateful look. "She is." The tension in his voice was even more evident than the tension in his posture.

"Fuck, Kiira needs to hear this," Rapp croaked. He leaped to his feet and jogged to the stairs. I couldn't agree more, even if I was still pissed she was leaving with him. And that he was the one fetching her.

Never had I heard of such a pairing in all our histories.

"Why didn't you say anything before?" I snarled, heat licking up my spine. "Are you still loyal to the Demons, Banand?"

"For this reason," he snapped back, anger yanking him to his feet. All formal pretense vanished. "Of course I'm fucking loyal to the Demons. I suffered for months, protecting our people. You wouldn't have trusted me if I'd told you when you rescued us. Besides, I've fought it since the moment it happened."

I whirled on Zurronar. "You kept this hidden too. Who else knew?"

"Just me. None of the others who were with us the day it happened survived, I swear," he said, raising his hands in surrender. "It was months after the plague began. She was new to the unit that was charged with guarding us. She ensured no one ever saw the mark on him either when they stripped him. It would have been just as dangerous for Araquiel to be discovered too."

I took a threatening step forward, but Assyria pinned me with a glare. "He has a point. But," she paused, turning her wrath on the two, "I saw Araquiel without clothes when I was trying to become her. She bore no mark."

Banand hung his head, unable to meet her gaze. "Did you put shackles on her yourself?"

"No," I ground out, heat gripping my neck and shoulders. "Why?"

"She's an incredibly powerful Sensor. If you didn't put them on yourselves, she probably used her magic to trick whomever thought they did. Then kept influencing everyone to ensure they still thought she had them on," Banand explained, his shoulders slumping inward

I didn't think. Just lunged like a venomous snake. I gripped him by the throat and shoved him backward. Metal clattered from the collision. "All this time, you left us exposed? Left the camp at risk?"

"I put some on the moment I realized she wasn't actually wearing anything!" he protested, his complexion deepening into a midnight purple. "That is reason enough to give me the benefit of the doubt, is it not?"

Shadows slammed into the crook of my arm, forcing me to release him. I ripped my attention to my mate, whose magic licked up my torso and clamped like a collar. Tight. Possessive. Deadly.

"So whose side is she on then?" Her interrogation was sharper than the blades scattered around us.

"I don't know. Not exactly the Angels. Not exactly ours. Obviously, the Angels want to exterminate us, which would mean me included. There are no exceptions in their plans," he coughed, clutching the workbench for support.

I forced myself to put space between me and the two near-traitors so I didn't fucking kill them.

Rapp and Kiira burst into the weapons storage, my cousin's eyes wide and lips parted. "Is it true? You have an Angel mate? And three crows flew by?" Her brows creased as she studied the scene before her. Assyria surrendered her bind around me.

"Yes," Banand hissed, jerking his shirt up high enough to flash the High Priestess his mate mark.

She approached, tracing it with her finger. "Fates..." she whispered, her eyes growing distant. I studied her for any sign that a vision might be overtaking her. I wouldn't let her collapse and injure herself against the hard floor. Rapp seemed to have the same thought, because he eased closer. "There hasn't been an Angel-Demon pairing in at least two thousand years. Their offspring was the first Seer..."

Rapp swore under his breath.

"I thought there had never been one?" I bit out.

She shook her head. "Our grandfather never allowed the writings to be made public, but I still retain copies in my library at Varbad Temple. The insight in them was important to my magic."

"So that's what kicked off the Age of Prophecy?" I clarified. It was a subject I hadn't paid much attention to, preferring to study texts of war and battle since it was more important for my role in society.

She nodded, twisting her unbound locks around her finger and securing them at the base of her neck. "That Age is still ongoing, alongside the Age of War. One of those books foretells the end of both, though the words are vague enough that I've never been able to make sense of them, save for that there is an end."

"Do they happen together?" Assyria prodded, leaning forward.

"No." Kiira stepped away from Banand at last. "Where is your mate?"

"With the other prisoners at the moment," he grumbled, his tone more bitter than many of the potions brewed by the healers.

"Which is where she will stay until you can convincingly promise us that she will not betray us to the Angels," I growled, crossing my arms. "Can she listen to us right now?"

"No," Banand snapped. "We both keep our mental barriers firmly in place. Not to mention I think in Demonic and she thinks in Angelic. Neither of us exactly want this. We both have a lot to hide from one another."

He met each of our gazes in turn, his eye contact strong and steady as if he were imploring us to see his truth.

"Unfortunately, the Halálhívó is right. But this was what we were going to challenge you with to earn your place as a Parancsok. Both of you," Rapp sighed, rubbing the back of his neck.

"We can do it," Zurronar promised after a moment's consideration. "We've treated them far better than they treated us, at least. Our actions alone should tell them we're not the animals they think we are."

"Tell no one of your bond," I warned Banand.

"Trust me, I won't." His jaw was set hard, and his focus drifted to the floor. Assyria's shoulders softened, along with her expression. And fuck if I didn't feel bad for him too, just a little bit. I'd gone insane those first months with Assyria, fighting myself over the primal need to protect her, to possess her, to claim her.

Banand had suffered tremendously. First, being forced to create a plague to wipe out his brethren. Then, a mating bond with his sworn enemy snapping into place.

"Will you make an oath to the Reaper?" I challenged him.

"Anything," he swore, finally lifting his gaze. The desperation in his eyes hit me like a blow. He wanted to be believed, to be trusted. The guilt he had initially carried made much more sense now. And why he was struggling to use his magic.

I drew a dagger from my hip and returned to the piles of bones I'd prepared for Assyria's throne. Banand did the same and stood across from me. Without hesitating, I cut deep into my palm and let the garnet droplets splatter over the white.

"You will obey mine and the Szélhámos's command, and all those we appoint to speak in our name," I began.

Banand sliced deeper, spilling more of his blood over the Angel remnants. To his credit, he didn't even flinch or give them a second thought. "I swear upon my life, the life of my mate, that I will not speak of my bond outside of this circle of knowledge. I take full responsibility for her actions, and should either of us betray the Demon cause, let the Reaper's eye fall over us."

I held out my hand, and he clasped it. I squeezed harder and sent more ruby splattering from both of us. What better way to seal this oath than into my mate's throne?

"May the Reaper curse you should you break this oath."

He knelt, resting his forehead on his bent arm. "Halálhívó, my sword has always been and will always be yours. The Szélhámos's too. For I proclaimed her as such, she will always have my devotion."

I jerked my head, and Assyria hopped down from her position atop a workbench and joined me. He lifted his gaze and planted it firmly on my mate. "Allow me to remain part of your guard, Szélhámos, and I swear I will give my life for yours should the time come."

"Convince Araquiel to join us, and you shall keep your spot," she told him. The command in her voice, the confidence in her posture, the curl of her lips made my dick harden.

"Aye, Szélhámos. You have my word." With that, he rose. "If you'll give me leave, I'd like to speak with her now."

I looked past him and leveled a heavy gaze on Zurronar.

"Your fate is tied to theirs. Take the High Priestess with you. If you want the title of Parancsok, your next actions will make or break our decision on the matter."

"Yes, sir," he said, shoving to his feet and giving us a salute.

"Dismissed," I grumbled, since we were back to formalities now. Kiira dipped her chin to me, affirming she knew what to do. She'd be the best to observe this, given how in tune she was with the Fates.

The three of them swept into the chilly afternoon sun, leaving Assyria, Rapp, and me alone. I pinched the bridge of my nose and let out a long breath. "Fuck I was not expecting that."

"Nor I," Rapp grumbled, easing to the ground beside the half-finished group of bones we'd been working on. I joined him a moment later, cursing again when I realized the adhesive had hardened completely.

"I can warm it again," Assyria offered, reaching for the bucket. I handed it to her, noting the tension around her mouth and eyes. Clearly this news had unnerved us all.

"We'll figure it out, little imposter. There is nothing to fear," I reassured her as she walked away.

She dropped the container in front of the hearth, spinning it in a steady circle so the heat of the flames licked against the edges. Without looking at me, she replied, *"I'm not afraid. Just...I don't know. What if we've already killed a hundred pairs like Banand and Araquiel before they ever knew the other existed?"*

Her throat worked like she was raking it across the coals. *"How can we continue down this path of complete extermination, knowing the bonds can cross races? Why do we have to slaughter an entire people because of their beliefs?"*

"With the Angels, it's always been kill or be killed."

"But what if it doesn't have to be anymore? The myth of us is spreading...and our campaign to make the Angels think one of their

own is betraying them is too. We could do more to end the war than just killing."

She wasn't wrong, but the Angel's beliefs were so entrenched, I wasn't sure what she was suggesting would be at all possible.

"We tried diplomacy for a long time. So long as Koron Stadiel and Korona Iaoth sit atop the Angel's throne, this is our only option."

A wave of dejected sadness swept down our bond. She sighed, hefting the adhesive and returning it to us. The stench overpowered my nostrils immediately. *"Then we will continue until they are dead."*

She settled on the floor, bracing her head on her folded hands. Slumped inward, she watched Rapp and I work with quiet intensity. Yet her mind was a riot of emotion, and her thoughts leaked down our bond. I wanted nothing more than to comfort her, to reassure her, that everything would be okay.

But I couldn't promise that.

This was war.

So the three of us remained silent, save for coordinating the final pieces of Assyria's throne, late into the night, when we gathered our gear and departed on our next mission.

54

ASSYRIA

A chill crept into my awareness, and without thinking, I shifted closer to Rokath, seeking his warmth. Yet when I reached the spot he should have been, nothing brushed my fingers. Cracking open an eye, I realized his muscled form was missing from our bed. The barest hint of moonlight slipped through the curtain covering our window. I sat upright, a shiver wracking my frame as my skin was exposed to the cold air.

I glanced toward the bathing chamber door, finding it open and the room beyond empty.

Where has he gone?

Tapping into the magic of our bond, I sought him out. A faint thread tugged me upward, and I craned my neck, realizing he must have gone outside. I dressed, grabbing my gloves on the way out of the door. I closed it quietly behind me, not wanting to disturb the other officers in the hall. On silent feet, I made my way to the exterior stairs that led from this floor straight to the ground. The night guard nodded to me and opened the door to outside. Yet instead of taking them down, I called upon my wings and sailed higher.

Air froze in my lungs as I beheld my mate. The white of the stars and moon bathed him in a glow, sharply contrasted with the black of the night on his other side. His severe features were cast in haunting relief—the tear in his ear, the heavy set of his brow, the slight crook in his nose. Gingerly, I lowered myself to the roof beside him.

He didn't look away from whatever held his attention in the distance.

"Can't sleep?" I asked, banishing my wings. Pulling on my gloves, I settled beside him so our shoulders touched.

"Not tonight," he murmured. "Not when I have so many questions and so few answers."

"What's bothering you?" I wrapped myself around his arm.

With a sigh, he leaned into me too. "Rapp, Kiira, Banand, Araquiel, Xannirin…"

"I see my name is absent from that list," I teased, hoping to lighten his mood.

He merely grunted in response. "For once."

"Rapp and Kiira will make it safely to their outpost. And she didn't have another vision before they left, so that's a good sign. Nor have we heard that she's had another," I reminded him. The mates that had been separated struggled, but they knew they served a higher cause. That didn't stop my heart from aching for the female who sobbed in my arms after half a day with that third of our army gone.

When I'd offered to let her yell at some of the males who saw her as weak for doing so, she perked up. Warmth spread through my limbs at the memory. The priestesses-turned-warriors were vicious in their own right, and more than one had dressed down their male counterparts in a way that left me entirely impressed.

"I know," he finally replied. "I've just never been good at drowning out the voices once they start screaming."

"Is there anything I can do to help tonight?" All was still, and even the wind didn't blow through the trees, relieving them of their powdery burdens.

"Just sit with me," he said, an ache in his voice I wanted to grasp and soothe.

I scooted closer so more of my body pressed into his. Freeing his arm, he draped it around me instead and brushed his lips over my temple. I wrapped my arms around his waist, snuggling deeper into his warmth.

A small smile tugged at my lips. How odd it was to show each other such unrestrained affection when we'd been at each other's throats over the smallest infraction during the summer.

A realization dawned on me then. "Is tonight the new year?"

"Aye," Rokath confirmed. The moon hung fat and heavy in the sky, seeming so much closer with how high we were in the mountains that snatched for the stars like they were a delicious treat.

"Why aren't we celebrating then?" I asked him.

"With everything that's happened recently, I forgot until I looked at the clock when I couldn't sleep," he admitted.

"What did you do last year?" The new year was always a source of joy in the Demon Realm. In Stryi, the whole village took a week off of work, gathering in the square for revelry. Dancers, fire breathers, elaborate displays, and charms were abundant. It was one of the few times I left the estate while married to Vagach, simply because he headed many of the ceremonies we held during that time to venerate the Fates. Yet I'd always been kept away from the crowds, perched like an ornament far above them. Exactly how Vagach had liked me to be.

"We were trying to maintain what ground we could as the plague swept through," Rokath deadpanned.

Guilt gnawed at my gut. Of course, they had been. I'd been

grieving the loss of my family and hadn't even left the manor, despite how Vagach had attempted to coerce me into attending. After I collapsed on the lawn, unable to carry myself forward, he'd sent me back inside.

"This year will be better," I pronounced, hoping that the Fates would hear me and make it so.

"I already made my wish," Rokath mumbled.

I craned my neck to look up at him, finding his burgundy eyes swirling with a mix of emotion. "Are you going to tell me what it was?"

"No," he said, looking forward again. "You wouldn't understand."

I scoffed and squeezed his ribs as punishment. "Why tell me you made one then?"

"For that reaction right there." He met my gaze once again. This time, his expression was full of smug amusement.

I rolled my eyes. "Well I haven't chosen mine yet."

Rokath released his hold on me. Spine protesting, I straightened. "Go ahead and do it now. Then we'll tell each other."

"Okay but no spying in my mind." I wagged my finger at him, then rolled out my shoulders and faced the moon.

But as I sat there, sifting through all my desires, I found it difficult to discern which I wanted to come true the most.

The end of the war, yes, but what if wishing for that caused us to lose?

Continuing progress with solidifying the female's place in the army? That seemed too weak even though it was a mighty goal.

That Rokath and I's love would never end? Yet that was already true, simply because we were fated, woven, planned to be together for now and in all the lives to come.

There were a dozen things I could wish for others. But for

the new year, we were supposed to be selfish. Supposed to set ourselves up for the next four seasons.

Glory wasn't important. Infamy bloomed like a Bordova rose in the summer. But what did I crave in the quiet of the night? When I let myself believe anything was possible?

Freedom.

The word emerged like a fabled sea monster from the depths of the abyss. Yet it was what I'd always truly wanted. I had some now, far more than ever before. But I wasn't rid of the shackles that held me back.

The trauma of my marriage to Vagach. The oppression of our society and how it had silenced me. The fear of my magic being discovered and what would happen to me once it was. More and more layers of all the ways I'd had to hide, had to survive, had to protect my heart from loss after loss.

Even now, I held back with many I wanted closer simply because I didn't want that acute ache to tatter my soul even more. Death was the reality of war, after all.

Rokath had suffered too, but his was different than mine. He's always been free. Powerful. Esteemed. *Feared.*

I stared at the heavens, tugging on the stars as if I could command the Fates to look down upon me. And then, I spoke to our deities.

"Weaver, Giver, Reaper, I wish for freedom to embrace my power without limits. To continue to find the strength to survive, even to thrive, as I claim the destiny woven for me. To not harden against the horrors to come, even though the losses will be difficult. May this year bring further healing, love, and the courage to reclaim everything that was taken from me."

Closing my eyes, I allowed the feeling to fill me to the brim. When I was close to exploding with it, I let it go, sending it out into the world and hoping it would return to me.

"This was mine," Rokath spoke into my mind, letting the memory of the moment flood me.

"Weaver, Giver, Reaper, give me the strength and wisdom to protect those I love. Ensure no further harm comes to the mate you blessed me with. Let victory and peace come to our realm at last."

His emotions consumed me too—the vastness of his devotion, the terror of my potential absence, the craving for peace. I *understood* everything he desired. Because more than anything, I wanted him to live beyond the war too, so that we could carve a slice of serenity far away from conflict and strife.

I crawled into his lap, and he enveloped me. A spicy, masculine scent called me home. His muscles flexed as he dragged me closer, nearly robbing me of air. "You're my reason for fighting, Assyria. You're the reason I begged the Fates for the end." He spoke the words like a haunted, desperate prayer.

"This will be our year." I grabbed his forearms and squeezed, gently rocking in his hold.

He planted a kiss on the side of my neck. "Let's go back to bed. I'm ready to sleep now." His hot breath ghosted across my ear, and his hardness grew and dug into my backside.

"Only after you beg for my forgiveness for listening in on my thoughts when I told you not to," I breathed, nails digging into his skin.

A soft laugh huffed against my shoulder. "That is not how this works." In one smooth motion, Rokath lifted us off the ground and threw me over his shoulder.

A giggle escaped me as I smacked his back. "Put me down!"

"Never. I'll never let you go, little imposter." Wings sprouted, and with gentle ease he flew us to the base of the building. At the doors to the weapons storage, two soldiers jolted into pristine posture, startled by our sudden appearance.

"At ease," Rokath told them. "And get lost."

"Yes, sir," they said, saluting us before racing away. I shot them a devious smile as he flung one of the doors open and then set me on my feet inside. With more force than necessary, he slammed it closed.

The barest of fires flickered in the hearth, but it was more than enough to witness the dark expression on my mate's face. With a hungry, predatory gaze, he devoured every inch of me. I took a step back as he approached, kept going as his pace quickened. My knees buckled, and then I was sitting.

A glance behind me told me it was the chair Rokath had built for me.

Rokath braced his hands on the arms, towering over me with a wicked glint in his eye. "Once these clothes are off you, I'm going to start our new year off right. Between your thighs. On this throne. When the war is over, you will sit beside me and accept their surrender with the ultimate fuck you right in their faces."

My breath hitched as my center wept.

Rokath's bone chair, like mine, was meant to intimidate. Meant to break the Angels before they even knelt. But tonight, we'd imbue mine with a different kind of power.

"Now start unlacing that top so I can worship the damning body the Fates gave you."

He shoved off, taking the heat of him away. Instead of obeying, I uttered two words that always yanked on his animalistic instincts.

"Make me."

His nostrils flared, along with divine dark desire down our bond. Then, his lips curved into a sinful smirk. "Oh, little imposter, I will."

Ice shattered through my veins as his magic swept out of him like an inferno, binding me to the throne of bones. He twisted his fingers, directing tendrils to tug at the laces while others slipped beneath my clothes and caressed my bare skin.

Another wrapped around my throat, cutting off the tiniest sip of air.

Strands brushed against my core. A whimper escaped me at the kiss of them between my thighs.

"Do you want to bow to my will now?" he crooned, curling his fingers into his palm. His magic did the same against my center.

"Never," I swore, knowing I was pushing his limits. But the fire that sparked inside me, filling my core to the brim, told me it was more than worth it. I loved nothing more than this battle with him.

He came closer, crouching so his knees were level with mine. I stared into those riotous burgundy eyes, the swirl of challenge and domination in them making me *drip*. "You said I should beg for your forgiveness for spying on you. I think you should beg for my forgiveness for disobeying a direct order."

Planting a hand on either one of my legs, he spread them wider. His shadows pooled around my core, continuing to stroke there. The ache was madness, yet I could do nothing to stop it. He was giving me just enough to fan the flames of my desire without dousing them completely.

"And what order was that?" I panted.

"Removing your clothes." His words were all raspy gravel. "Now beg and then do as you are told."

I rolled my lips together, planning on a final protest, when his magic ceased moving altogether. "Please." The word slipped out before I could stop it. He was far too skilled in melting me with his commands and caresses.

"Please, what?"

"Please forgive me for not listening the first time," I whimpered, straining against his hold. The shadows shackling my hands loosened. I wasted no time grasping the edges of the laces they'd begun to undo. In moments, my jacket hung loose, revealing my bare breasts.

Rokath let out a low, masculine groan. "Didn't dress fully, little imposter?"

"Around you, it's nearly impossible to keep all my clothes on," I quipped, lips curving into a smile.

More of his power drifted away, and he reached for my shoulders, sliding the fabric off me and tossing it to the side. Without waiting, he cupped them, then brought one of my hard nipples to his mouth. Sucking harshly, he tore a cry from my lips.

"Quietly, tonight. This moment is just for us, Assyria."

"Yes," I told him, gritting my teeth as he did the same on the other side. A low hiss swept through them instead, and a rumble of approval vibrated in his chest. While he worked over my breasts, I undid the laces at the top of my pants.

Barely releasing me, he lifted me off the seat and yanked them clean off my legs, leaving me completely naked. Kneeling between my thighs, he stared at my glistening center like it was a holy fountain.

"Always so fucking wet for me," he ground out, hands moving to part my thighs. He dug into the muscles there, kneading and pulling a low groan from me. "Tell me, Assyria. What makes your pretty pussy weep the most?"

"When you say things like that," I rasped as his face drifted closer. "When you use your shadows to bend me to your will." His hot breath ghosted across my core before he planted a kiss so, so high on my inner thigh. "When we fight first. With words or physically."

His tongue swept out along the seam of my leg, so close and so fucking far from where I wanted him to be. I removed my hands from the chair and dug my nails into the tattoos on the back of his scalp, trying to direct him to put his lips on me.

He resisted me, huffing a laugh against my center. "Your challenge gets me so fucking hard." In one smooth motion, he rose, and my hands fell to the thick length of him straining against his pants. "Keep stroking me."

I did, staring up at him as he worked over the buttons of his shirt and tossed it aside, revealing the torso sculpted from the craggy Skala Mountains. The muscles in his abdomen flexed, drawing my attention to the delicious V that pointed straight to where I touched him. His cock throbbed against my hand, and I reached for the ties of his pants, giving them a tug.

"Take out my cock, little imposter," he murmured, his burgundy eyes igniting with dark hunger.

I didn't hesitate to obey. When it sprang free, my mouth watered at the sight. His dick pulsed—glistening, flushed, swollen—with the promise of the pleasure it would deliver. I leaned back, easing my legs open and letting the firelight glint off of the slickness between them.

Rokath shucked off his boots, baring himself to me. Wrapping a strong hand around his thick cock, he stroked up and down, up and down, as he venerated the vision beneath him. I had to bite my lip to stifle a groan at the sight.

"So. Fucking. Gorgeous. I don't even need you to touch yourself to ensure my dick will fit in that perfect cunt. You're slick enough already."

"Then get inside me," I pleaded, the heat of his gaze more than enough to wind me tight enough to snap.

"Ask nicely," he shot back, making my core clench.

Popping out my lower lip and batting my lashes, I did. "Please, master. I want you to fill me."

"Fuck," he groaned, his eyes closing. More arousal dripped from the crown. "You have no idea what that does to me."

The primal desire sweeping down our bond afforded me a hint of understanding. That need expanded as he stepped closer. A log cracked and popped in the fire, but it didn't shatter our moment. It was merely background noise, melting away with the rest of the world as he knelt and yanked me to the edge of the seat.

At this angle, his hardness was the perfect height to enter me.

"Eyes on me," he commanded, and I dug my nails into his shoulders to steady myself as I held his gaze.

Then, he pushed inside me. Slowly. Excruciatingly. To the point I wasn't above calling him master again simply so he'd give me all of his thick length.

"Rokath," I breathed, his name like a plea and a prayer.

"Assyria," he returned, his tone like honed worship. He reached up, brushing the back of his knuckles across my cheek. "My perfect fucking mate."

He seated himself to the hilt, and my arms trembled from holding myself so still. One hand slid to my lower back, while the other went to the leather tying my braid. He tugged it, letting my dark hair cascade free with a few shakes of his fingers through it. "That's better. I love seeing it unbound while I fuck you."

The ends tickled my skin, eliciting a small gasp. Rokath moved again, dragging himself out to the tip. A shudder wracked my frame as he slid all the way in again. He repeated the motion, collapsing my entire world to the place where we joined, the slow glide of him inside me, and the savage devotion in his eyes.

"My protector," I intoned as he withdrew.

"My Halálhívó," I whimpered as he bottomed out.

"My mate," I breathed as he arched my back, sinking even deeper inside me.

"Mine," I whispered as I looped my arms behind his neck and dragged myself closer.

Our lips met in a passionate kiss, all tongue and slow movement, savoring each other like we had an eternity. Lost in the embrace like adventurers out at sea, his thrusts maintained a steady rhythm, rolling with the tide of our pleasure.

The way his arms tightened around me, holding me like I was a precious weapon, coupled with the utter adoration sweeping down our bond, had pleasure building to a pyre inside me. Arousal drenched my thighs, and my breath came in ragged, battling for space in the moments our lips didn't join.

He broke our kiss and pressed his forehead to mine, forcing me to look deep into his eyes. "This year, you are all mine. You will belong to no one else. It is the first year of the rest of our lives."

"Yes," I agreed, arching into him, wanting to feel him against every nerve inside me. His cock throbbed, only serving to increase the tension coiling in my core. "You'll finish this throne for me. We'll win this war. Then, we'll return to Stryi so you can show me exactly how no one else should ever have had me."

A wicked groan reverberated against his ribs. "Nothing gets me harder than when you talk like that."

To prove his point, he speared into me with breath-stealing force. I felt him along every inch of my center. "Except for maybe when you direct that fire my way."

Gripping me to him, he stood and flipped us so I straddled him on the throne. "Ride me like you're claiming your vengeance. Make a fucking mess all over the bones of those who dared lay a hand on you."

My pussy constricted around him, eliciting another primal sound from his throat.

"Just like that. Let your cunt squeeze out every last drop from me."

I worked my hips, sliding along his length, dragging my clit over his cut abdominals to give myself the extra friction I needed. Rokath's biceps flexed as he guided me up and down. Despite the cold, sweat dripped down my spine.

With each pass, my core tightened, until I was mere moments away from shattering. Pants mingled with whimpers, but I smothered them with teeth digging into my bottom lip.

After all, this moment was for us. To align with what was to come. To become one, as we were always meant to be.

"I love you," I gasped out as the remnants of my breath fled. Then, ecstasy blazed through my veins. My spine arched. My core fluttered. Stars danced in my vision like we were still outside on the roof. Rokath didn't stop dragging me up and down, even as my arms and legs gave out from the force of my orgasm.

He gritted his teeth, our eyes still locked. "Fuck, I love you, Assyria. I never thought I'd be capable of it. But I'm finding, with you, I can do anything." His dick throbbed, sending a final spark of pleasure through me. A whimper clawed up my throat as he pulled out, settling me on his thighs while he squirted his cum all over his stomach and the chair beneath us.

It had barely stopped before he tugged me against his chest, smoothing my hair and whispering words of adoration and praise. My eyes were heavy, and I let them close as I listened to the steady beat of his heart.

Before I knew it, I was back in our bed with him curled around me. The soft dawn whispered through our window, bleeding light over our bodies. It was the first day of the year— but the last before war demanded its toll.

55

ASSYRIA

A gust of wind rustled the branches of the evergreens overhead, like the trees were whispering warnings. I prowled forward, using the sound to mask my footsteps. Flake after flake of snow dusted across my cheeks, and I clenched my teeth to avoid chattering them. Around me, the Deathveiled slipped forward, hugging the thick trunks and easing over large rocks. The scrub in this section made navigating the terrain difficult, and many snaked their shadows through the tangles to hold them wide enough to pass through without creating a clamor.

This was the farthest we'd ventured from the outpost for a raid, and with clouds cloaking the moon, we had the advantage. Though it was a risk to be so close to the Angel's camp with so few of us. On my one side, Uzadaan and Zurronar held close, tasked by Rokath with protecting me at all costs, while he led part of the unit from a different direction.

"We're almost there," my mate spoke down our mental connection.

I held up my fist, and everyone with me halted. I crept closer to Uzadaan and Zurronar, lowering my voice. "We wait for Rokath's signal to enter the camp. Then we find the Padisa."

"Banand swore Araquiel wasn't lying about where she'd be. I'm not worried," Zurronar whispered.

"She's a Sensor," I reiterated, my stomach churning anyway. Araquiel had given up the name and location of a top Padisa with direct ties to Zahal Ishim. The plan was to capture her and bring her with us to the outpost. One, so that I could impersonate her in the future. Second, so that Rokath could anger the Angel's leader further and force a meeting. The psychological warfare we'd been waging already had a vise-like grip over our enemies and sowed chaos like they were seeds during the harvest.

"But he opened up their mental connection and searched her mind," Zurronar protested. Out of everyone involved in this situation, he seemed to be the one who was most okay with it happening.

"You don't think the Halálhívó knows everything that goes on in my mind, right?" I snapped. "Now quiet, we need to listen for the signal."

With a grumble, the three of us faced forward, creeping toward a large bush and peering through it. A twig snapped behind us, and I whipped my head around, heart stilling when I saw it was only Izzenna, the ruby-eyed Nightmare creator, and not a group of Angels that had snuck up on us.

"Sorry," she mouthed. Beside her, Vokkia, the cherry-eyed Destructor, picked her way forward more carefully. Maariya had continued on with Rapp and Kiira to the outpost closest to Uzhhorod.

I was grateful the two had chosen to remain with me. They closed in quickly, joining our huddle. The five of us tucked close, trying to remain unnoticed.

Firelight flickered in the distance, and only a few Angels wandered the fringes at the late hour. Much like when we'd rescued Banand and Zurronar, we were going to cause a distraction, diverting everyone away from the true target.

Minutes passed, and heat dripped down my spine. My legs trembled from the effort of holding our position.

Where the fuck is Rokath?

The thought had no sooner crossed my mind before the first shout sliced through the stillness. I counted to thirty, each number enunciated, hoping that the volume would rise. When a large, armed group raced by, I knew it was time.

Dipping my eyes closed, I dove into my magic well, bringing the twister of onyx over my frame and becoming the Myrza. In seconds, I was taller, broader, and male. "Let's go," I ordered in Demonic. At least now, most of the unit was accustomed to the language coming out of his mouth.

We stalked forward, scanning the area for sentries. Since I'd supposedly switched sides, I crafted brown leather armor, which helped me blend in, versus the pristine white boasted by the Angels.

No one remained to cover these woods. Quickening our pace, we penetrated the camp, steering for the rear portion where the Padisa would supposedly oversee all of her section. Finding the striped tent was easy when it was surrounded by fire and pressed against a rocky outcropping.

Smart, so no one could sneak up from behind. Foolish, because she'd be easier to pin and drag back with us.

We ducked into an alley, only to collide with a group of five Angels. Half-dressed, weapons in hand, they looked like they'd been roused from sleep and were on their way to Rokath's diversion. Uzadaan and Zurronar sprang into action, flinging their arms forward and pinching their fingers together. All five froze in place, their blood unmoving. Izzenna and Vokkia lunged past the males, bronze blades slicing across their throats. They eased each body to the ground without a sound.

We hushed along, the flames flickering as we closed in on the Padisa's location. Hurried Angelic burst from behind the flaps. I tried to count how many voices there were, but with the frantic tones and people talking over one another, it was difficult.

"At least four," I muttered under my breath.

Once again, Uzadaan and Zurronar called upon their magic. Ebony strands of power snaked beneath the fabric, seeking out those inside. I held my breath. If the Angels noticed the encroaching darkness, we'd never capture the Padisa.

"They're frozen," Uzadaan announced.

My chest loosened. We couldn't kill them all without laying eyes on them first.

The two moved in tandem, pulling open the entrance while maintaining their holds. Izzenna, Vokkia, and I hurried inside, the females shoving the bodies around while I stalked toward the officer and drew my sword.

With a huff, Uzadaan and Zurronar released their magic before they accidentally killed someone from lack of blood flow.

"You're coming with me," I told her in Angelic, grabbing her arm and hauling her forward.

She thrashed, and I tightened my grip. My sword swept to her stomach as an added incentive. The Padisa went still, a hand resting at her side while the other remained on my wrist. "So the rumors are true."

"They are," I stated simply. The females slit the throats of those still watching, while Zurronar gutted one, leaving him partially alive. At least long enough to report what we'd done.

As I marched her forward again, she twisted, and pain

burned in my arm. "Fuck!" I swore in Demonic without thinking. But that wasn't my worst mistake. No, it was the silver dagger biting into my arm.

Panic ravaged my ribs. Pain seared my skin. My form flickered, the pale color of the Myrza replaced with the dark tan of my body.

With a shriek, I released the Padisa. Dropping the hilt, I yanked out the weapon and shucked it across the tent.

My magic quivered. I blinked in and out of height as she bolted. Uzadaan tackled her, crashing to the ground and skidding with his momentum.

"What's wrong? Are you okay?" Rokath shot down our bond.

"Fine," I ground back. The wound was manageable and not life threatening. "Someone kill him," I snapped, pointing to the one we'd intentionally left alive. "Can't have him telling everyone the Myrza isn't actually alive."

Vokkia slaughtered him without hesitation.

That one hit of silver had gulped a solid portion of my well. Anxiety spiked as I struggled to create the form over myself again. "We need to make more of a scene now," I instructed, my mind working at a sprint, fueled by the fear I couldn't wield my magic. That I was powerless in the midst of our enemies. "Gag her first so she can't say anything. Oh and check her back for a mate mark."

Uzadaan and Zurronar held her arms while Izzenna ripped her tunic open, finding the skin bare, but a few hidden sheaths. Izzenna snatched them all from the Angel.

"You will fucking die for this," the Padisa hissed at everyone. Her lapis eyes glittered with hatred.

"No, that will be you," I bit out. "Unless you join our cause. But that's a discussion for later. Let's go."

The males hauled her upright, using a torn bit of her tunic

as a gag. She writhed, a muffled scream shredding her throat. Her long white hair tangled in a thrash of limbs. "Can I knock her out?" Uzadaan threw over his shoulder in Demonic.

"Once we get into the woods." Chaos clawed through the camp, and somewhere, a fire spit smoke into the night. Any who passed by us were either killed or left clinging to life.

"We're almost out," I relayed to Rokath.

I received a grunt in response. Once the shadowed trees enveloped us again, I gave the males permission to silence the Padisa. Uzadaan threw her over his shoulder and marched on, focused on his task while I scanned our rear with Izzenna and Vokkia, ensuring no one was following us.

"Quickly now," I encouraged, seeing no flashes of white. We had an agreed upon rendezvous point, and I wanted to reach it before Rokath's group simply because my magic was already waning.

Sweat beaded my brow as I pressed on. Legs burned from the uphill climb. Air scraped down my throat like shattered glass.

"Szélhámos, are you alright?" Izzenna asked me, slowing her pace.

"Fine," I panted out. But I was quickly realizing that I was not, in fact, fine. Dizziness overtook me, and I stumbled, rocks slicing into my palm.

At least I was making an offering to the Fates for a successful mission where no one died.

Izzenna and Vokkia caught my arms and hauled me up the remainder of the hill. "Maybe you should let your magic go now? So you don't burn out?" Izzenna suggested, helping me sit on a rock. With a well as deep as mine, that was nearly impossible, but I didn't have the energy to correct her.

The males had paused, and Zurronar's face was pale as he examined me.

"Let it go," he murmured, giving my shoulder a reassuring squeeze. "We've got you."

I did, mostly because I thought I was going to be sick. Zurronar grabbed my shoulder, sucking in a sharp breath. "We need to get you back immediately."

"Why?" I asked, but then bile rose. Gagging, I turned to the side, retching over a bed of moss. Vokkia rubbed soothing circles on my back until I came up for air again.

I wiped my mouth with the back of my hand, blinking through blurred vision. Rokath burst through the treeline, blood-slicked, with death in his eyes.

Behind him, the Deathveiled tore through the underbrush. All of them. I breathed another sigh of relief.

"What the fuck?" he growled, racing to my side. He bared his sharp teeth at Uzadaan and Zurronar. "Who let this happen." It was less of a question and more of a demand for information that would certainly end in one of their deaths.

"Mine," I wheezed, my chest growing tight. I clutched it, and then, Rokath noticed the dark blood on my own.

"The Padisa stabbed her. The blade must have been coated in a poison. It's what they injected me with shortly before you saved me," Zurronar explained, hovering close like he would save me.

He was an honorable male, just like his brother.

A snarl tore from Rokath's throat, and he whipped back to the camp. Fury took form in my mate. The rage that poured down our bond nearly ripped it apart. The savage beneath the surface exploded, burning me from the inside.

There was no mercy. No diplomacy. Only lust for blood.

"I should end every last life in their camp now."

"Maybe save mine first?" I suggested, the world spinning around me. I tried to stand, to get his attention, but I pitched to the side.

A roar—Rokath's?—shattered the night. My vision tunneled to a pinprick. I wasn't afraid of the dark. But I was afraid of leaving my mate behind without me.

Shadow. Silence. Surrender.

Nothing but a void.

56

R☠KATH

Assyria's eyes rolled to the back of her head, body collapsing inward. Leaping forward, I caught her inches from the ground. Her frame, so small in my arms, felt like a dying ember. The weight of her limp body twisted a knife between my ribs. Terror blistered my blood, black and thick like pitch.

Why did this female continue to take poison and venom like it was nothing? When I fucking saved her life again, I was going to shake the foolishness out of her. After I fucked her so hard that she knew nothing other than my name.

"Get everyone back safely and you'll have earned your rank," I snapped at Zurronar. Without waiting for a response, I yanked my membranous black wings into existence. Air resisted me as I speared through it, clipping the treetops and begging the wind at my back to aid my desperate flight.

"*You will not die on me,*" I growled down our bond. She was unconscious, but even in that state she would fucking hear me and she would fucking obey for once in her life.

I refused to believe otherwise.

A cough rattled her chest, and I clutched her to me, trying to keep her warm. Crystals solidified on my metal armor, the cold and the altitude lacing a deadly combination.

Faster, Rokath, faster.

I flew like fury made flesh, my only focus on what lay ahead. Everything behind me didn't matter. Only Assyria's breath. Her pulse. Her sharp tongue that shredded me to ribbons.

Flapping my wings, I clawed for every bit of distance. The embers dotting the outpost crackled into full blown flames. Assyria trembled as death licked her skin.

I slowed my pace, preparing to land. My feet thudded against the roof of the second building where the healers were located. Pounded a staccato rhythm as I neared the edge and leaped to the exterior landing. With my heavy boot, I banged on the door. A female—still dressed in wool sleeping attire—appeared in the crack. Her eyes went wide as she beheld us.

"Halálhívó!" she exclaimed, throwing it wide and allowing us entrance. She shouted for assistance while directing me to place Assyria on a table. "What happened?"

The former priestess yanked bottles from shelves, instruments from drawers, and gathered clean cloths onto a tray.

Hooking my fingers beneath the metal, I eased Assyria's helmet over her head. She needed an antidote, or more, and the slim cutout down the center of the metal wasn't enough to reach her mouth.

Flakes of half-digested food clung to the edges. I'd clean it later, once I knew she would live. "The Angels stabbed her with some sort of poison-coated weapon. A soldier we rescued initially came in with the same ailment."

The doorway filled with a line of bodies. One of the healers that had been there when we'd brought Zurronar home shimmied through the crowd and studied my mate. He offered rapid-fire instruction to the others, then conversed with the female who had awoken first.

I forced myself to take a step back and let them work. The bond shrieked at me for daring to put space between my mate and me while she was injured, weak, vulnerable. I gritted my teeth, fingers biting into the metal I'd had crafted for her.

Zurronar had recovered quickly, unlike Rapp, and the sooner they could give her an antidote or whatever the fuck, the sooner I could take her to bed and hold her.

That didn't stop my feral pacing or the sharp attention I paid to their movements.

Someone tipped a vial into her mouth—pium, from the green color of it. I nearly laughed. It was probably unnecessary, but she was my mate, and they weren't going to let her die. They were going to throw everything at this to save her.

Minutes that felt like hours passed before her lashes fluttered over her cheekbones. With a gasp, she bolted upright, those devious burgundy eyes seeking me out. A few healers sighed. Others slumped against the nearest object. Probably because now they knew they'd all live.

"Assyria," I breathed, snatching her to me. The snake binding my chest slithered away, leaving room for air to expand my lungs.

She let out a hacking snicker.

"This is not funny," I snapped at her. "You do not get to laugh when I almost lost you."

That only served to amuse her more. "Yes it is and yes I do."

"You almost died. *Again.*" The violence in my tone had everyone else in the room taking a healthy step back.

"The Fates enjoy fucking with me. I've escaped death more times than I can count now," she giggled. I pressed the back of my palm to her forehead, finding it sweaty and feverish.

"She's delirious," I pronounced. "She needs her temperature down."

"We know, Halálhívó. If you'll allow us to keep working," the female healer said, wringing her hands.

"I'll stay right here," I informed her. She nodded and then gestured for the rest to join her.

"I'm not delirious," Assyria protested. I gripped her shoulders as they cleaned the wound on her arm, which, thankfully, wasn't too deep. She hissed as they poured pure alcohol on it. She whimpered as they dug a needle into her skin to stitch it closed.

"This is so much worse than when you branded me," she pouted. A few pairs of eyes flicked in our direction.

"Keep fucking working," I snarled back. They wisely refocused on their tasks. With a fire going, salt slicked my skin and dripped down my temples. I risked a moment of releasing Assyria to yank my helmet off my head. It joined my mate's at my feet.

Tension eased from postures around me.

Good to know its intended effect works on them too.

Assyria sagged into me as the healer tied off her stitches. The crease of pain in her brow was absent, and those bow shaped lips were slightly parted. Fatigue washed down our bond.

Once her arm was wrapped in a white bandage, the female healer declared there was nothing more they could do and that her fever would break sometime in the night.

"You'll come check on her first thing," I commanded, my tone leaving no room for argument.

"Certainly, Halálhívó," she promised. And with that, plus a few potions, I departed, Assyria in my arms. By the time we landed at the primary building, the rest of the Deathveiled had returned.

"Oh, thank the Fates," Zurronar swore when he saw Assyria

was still alive. Her other protectors seemed equally relieved, especially the two females.

"Without her, I don't know that we would have been able to stay," Izzenna murmured, looking at her like she was a fallen Fate.

"You would have. She's not the only reason these changes are happening," I replied, my brows pinching. These females were useful, and they'd proven themselves worthy of the challenge over and over again.

Vokkia eyed me with a hint of suspicion. "Before her, we were only useful as priestesses or mothers. Because she fought for us, she gave us another purpose. She is our symbol of hope."

Had Assyria been conscious, she would have burst into tears. This was what she had always wanted—maybe not to be so venerated, but for the females to feel free. For once, I welcomed that emotion for her. Allowed myself to feel the pride in what we had built together.

I cleared my throat. "Good work tonight. Rest up and tomorrow we'll see what kind of damage we caused."

Wicked grins split many of their faces.

"What do you want me to do with her?" Uzadaan asked, hefting the Padisa higher on his shoulder. Thankfully, she was still unconscious.

"Secure her in a cell away from the rest. Don't want them giving her any ideas," I said. I'd deal with her in the morning. At least Araquiel had spoken true, despite the fact Assyria was currently injured and feverish.

"Yes, sir," he replied, taking to the air and sailing downhill.

Zurronar, Izzenna, and Vokkia lingered for a moment longer, their concern for my mate etched into their expressions. "She'll be alright," I told them. Like I didn't need that reassurance for my fucking self.

"Yes, Halálhívó," Vokkia murmured, ducking her head. She

linked arms with Izzenna and the two strode down the stairs to the bottom level where their bunks waited.

Zurronar shifted from foot to foot.

"Yes, soldier?" Irritation nipped at my nerves. All I wanted was for Assyria to rest, and these delays were not helping that.

"I wanted to apologize, Halálhívó. I should have protected her better. I didn't see the Padisa's dagger until it was too late. I understand if you don't want to offer me the title of Parancsok now."

A tumultuous mix of rage and regret tumbled in my gut.

His brother had died protecting my mate. Here he was, despite that, ready to give his life for her too. But more than that, a glimmer of my younger self reflected back at me. The guilt. The self-loathing. The what ifs.

"You have earned it, Zurronar. Now rest. We'll speak tomorrow."

He nodded, offering me a firm salute, and sailed off after Uzadaan.

I dragged in a breath, the chill searing my throat. Then, I shoved open the door and entered the officer's floor. It was emptier without Rapp and Kiira here.

Shaking thoughts of my best friend and my cousin off, I settled my obstinate mate into our bed. A small noise of protest slipped out of her as I retreated. But she sighed and scooted into her pillow. I went to the attached bathing chamber and cleansed myself of blood. When I rejoined her, she was curled on her side, breathing even. Her skin didn't burn as I lifted the blankets and settled them over us.

She stirred and flipped to face me. "You saved me. My hero." Her tone was light, teasing, and made me grit my teeth.

"I told you during our first meeting, little imposter, that I am no hero. I am decidedly the villain."

She snorted and walked her fingers up my chest. The pale wrap flitted in the edges of my vision.

"Did you not ensure the Padisa was unarmed?" I gritted out, snatching her arm.

She huffed, blowing hair out of her face with the same breath. "It was late at night. She didn't appear to have any weapons."

"Assumptions kill," I admonished. "You have to disarm someone before you grab them. Otherwise, one wrong move and this will happen *again*."

Her brows pinched. "Can you not right now? My head hurts."

"No." I pulled her flush against me, her breath hitching. "It is my duty to ensure you are capable of surviving when I am not by your side. I cannot lose you. Now tell me what you will do the next time you are capturing an Angel."

"I'll remove all their weapons and pierce them with bronze so they can't use their magic too," she sighed, forehead dropping.

I released her arm at last. "Good girl. We'll train it more specifically tomorrow."

With a groan, she flipped over and pressed her back into me. "Fine. Now fuck off so I can sleep. My head is killing me."

I pressed my lips to her soft temple, inhaling her garden-like scent. She'd lived through another tenuous mission. But how many more times would the Fates allow it? How many more times could I allow her to wander away from me?

Guilt clawed at my stomach at the thought. I'd empowered her all this time, but I was weak—so fucking weak—when it came to her. So I draped myself around her like I could fasten her to my side. Because when we woke, I wasn't sure I could let her go.

57

R🕱KATH

The black army pennant whipped from the apex the guard towers flanking me. Atop the wall, we stood, gazing down on the hillside below. Ice, like long veins, dug into the rocks. A lone Angel female approached on horseback, her white hair pulled tight against her head. Beside me, Assyria shifted forward, much fucking better after almost dying yet again. At our backs, the Deathveiled and officers were poised, ready to strike should more of her comrades decide to spring a surprise attack on us even after waving the green flag.

I wouldn't put it past them simply because I'd do the same.

Two days had passed since our latest raid. It had taken one to extract all the information we needed from the Padisa. Much to my pleasure, she'd revealed Zaph was among the group facing us. It was almost comical how quickly she'd given that morsel away. He was such a fucking parasite that even most of the Angel officers didn't like him.

I couldn't wait to slaughter him. To pick off his wings one by one. To rip his bones from within his flesh and add his skull to Assyria's throne—the final piece to complete it. It was no less than he deserved for hurting my mate.

The Angel slowed her mount, craning her neck up, up, up the high wall. Her throat bobbed as she beheld the contingent of Demons waiting for her. With shaking hands, she reached into her cloak and produced a note. Holding it high in the air and turning it about, she announced, "Zahal Ishim wishes for you to read this, Halálhívó!"

Her voice was high and thin, and her eyes bounced around as if she were worried we'd jump down from above and drink her blood. Which, knowing what lies the Angels spread about us, was probably what she believed.

With a jerk of my chin, I directed Izzenna to fetch the paper for me. Black wings unfurled from her back, and she launched into the air, gliding in a lazy circle to the base of the wall.

The white mare neighed and retreated as she landed. Ignoring the beast, Izzenna reached for the note. The Angel female handed it to her by the tips of her fingers like she carried a lethal disease that would kill her simply from breathing the same air.

Izzenna wasted no time dusting her with dirt and returning to the wall. Landing in front of Assyria and me, she dropped into a kneeling stance and held out the parchment.

My blood thrummed with heady anticipation as I unfolded the note. Assyria edged closer and peered at it with me.

Fuck you, Halálhívó. How dare you take another from me? This time, there will be no mercy for your mate. We will string her up and bleed her dry like the animal she is. Then, we'll make a great show of sacrificing her to the Goddess.

Tomorrow at high sun, meet on the wall. I want to see these Angels who have supposedly switched to supporting the Demons. Who have abandoned their faith and chosen to support your false idols. The figments of your imaginations.

As you know, the punishment for such actions in the Angel Realm is quartering, and the Koron and Korona wish to make an example of them. I have something you will want in return.

Zahal Ishim

I snorted and shook my head. We'd meet here, as he requested, but there was nothing he could trade me for our prisoners—mostly because they were all dead or close to it. But he didn't know that, not yet. Assyria had been doing a damn good job of playing the part.

Each poisonous word revealed how thoroughly I'd rattled him. How I'd carved the perfect opportunity to create further disruption in their ranks. To plant dark seeds of doubt in the minds of those who accompanied him.

His desperation was blood in the water, and I was a predator who scented each drop of it. Let him wear the mask of dominance if it made him feel in control.

Because we both knew the truth.

He never stood a chance against me.

I stepped forward, my attention settling heavily over the Angel messenger. "Tell Ishim he will have his meeting tomorrow."

She nodded, then yanked on the reins and steered her horse back the way she'd come.

☠☠☠☠☠☠

THE ANGELS SQUINTED AS I THREW OPEN THE DOORS TO THE ROOM where we'd been holding them. Banand shot Araquiel a sharp look before approaching me. "What did the Zahal say?"

"He wants to meet tomorrow," I announced. Then, I stared his mate down. "Bring the prisoner to the main building. We need to talk."

"What about me?" the Padisa hissed, stomping to the edge of her cell and gripping the bars. Blood caked one side of her face, though it was more healed than it had been the previous evening.

"Have you decided to switch sides?" My question was sharp, direct, and piercing.

She bared her teeth in response. "Never. Ishim will come for me and I won't disappoint him by doing that to survive."

I grunted and turned away from her. "Let's go," I told Banand, then stalked into the valley. Everyone else was already in the primary building, waiting for us. Assyria had offered to fetch them with me, but I wanted to speak to the pair alone.

The late afternoon sun flitted through the sparse trees, warming what little skin showed through my heavy clothes. With the new year upon us, the seasons would change soon, though in the high peaks of the Skala Mountains, that came far later than in Uzhhorod or any of the other cities in the Demon Realm.

Araquiel blinked rapidly as the light hit her turquoise eyes. Banand kept his hand on her upper arm, despite her attempt to jerk it out of his hold. The tension between them was thick enough to slice with a sword. She stumbled, and the tender way he kept her from falling, the way they glared at one another after, struck me like a blow. It reminded me so much of Assyria and I when we'd first been forced together.

"Halálhívó," Araquiel greeted me coolly when they came to a stop in front of me.

I glanced around us to ensure we were alone. No one seemed to want to be outside, even though the sun was shining.

"Have you coupled?" I demanded, not bothering with niceties.

"My body is not yours to command," she snarled, embers sparking behind her eyes. "It is no business of yours."

"It is when the two of you are living in my camp," I snapped back. "It is when both of you pose a risk, and your bond even more so."

I shifted my focus to Banand. "I remember how the bond screamed at me to claim my mate. It was an incessant, unrelenting beast. It took tremendous self control to resist it, and I know the challenge was far more difficult for me than it was for the Szélhámos. So have you?"

A muscle feathered in his jaw. "No."

My brows climbed my forehead. Months had passed since their bond snapped into place. I'd barely held out a week.

"I do not trust him," Araquiel hissed, the mask she'd worn since her capture slipping.

"Nor I her. But this fucking bond..." Banand planted a fist in the center of his chest, and I understood his meaning without him having to explain further. "I can't stay away. She never has been able to either."

She yanked her arm out of his grasp and crossed her shackled wrists. "These haven't exactly been conducive either."

"Nor was being in a cage," he shot back. The heat between them was scorching. Banand leaned in, ever so slightly, like he wanted to capture her mouth to force her to close her furious, blazing eyes.

"What would it take?" The conversation was devolving, and I needed an answer before it fractured entirely.

Their attention sliced to me. But it was Araquiel who spoke. "What do you mean?"

My nostrils flared as I exhaled. "What would it take for you to fuck?" I snapped, my patience wearing thin. "For you to let him take you, and for you to take her?"

Banand ground his teeth. Araquiel stabbed him with a hateful glare. Both spoke at once, but I held up a hand, silencing them. "Ishim has requested a meeting for tomorrow. He wants to see the traitors for himself so he can tell the

Koron and Korona all about it. Maybe even return to Sivy with a few."

I let the information hang in the air like an executioner's blade. The mates paled. For the first time, Araquiel's animosity bled away, replaced by unfiltered terror.

"Unless you can figure out a way forward, where Araquiel can comfortably insert herself on the Demon side, she'll go with them."

Banand's face turned a dark shade of red and he lunged for me. But I was prepared, having been challenged over my mate as well, and I caught his arm and twisted it behind his back. Holding him close to my chest, I looked over his shoulder at Araquiel. Her face was a light shade of green, like she was going to heave up the contents of her stomach.

"Threats are no way to make me believe you aren't an animal," she said, but her voice was weak. The barest hint of clinking metal reached my ears.

"Do you truly believe that?" I asked her. Banand snarled and jerked in my hold, so I wrapped an arm around his throat, cutting off the blood to his brain.

She watched him slip from consciousness with horror in her eyes. I wouldn't kill him—it was all a test for the two of them. One both were currently failing.

A scream caught in her throat, and she clutched it like it was her air scraping to be let in.

"Stop! Please!" She surged forward like something sacred was ripping from her chest. She leaped toward her mate like she could snatch him from me and ferry him to safety.

But she was no match for my might.

"Answer my question," I commanded.

"No! I don't! Have not I given you information enough?" she burst out, her grammar in the common tongue crumbling.

Immediately, I loosened my hold on Banand, who fell to his

hands and knees, gasping for air. Araquiel went to his side, brushing his hair out of his face and checking on him with unexpectedly tender care.

I crouched down, still more massive than both of them. "So what will it take?" My voice was low, deadly, dangerous. "Alcohol? Lust? The threat of death? Will it take watching each other die before you admit what's already been done?"

Banand sat back on his heels and grasped Araquiel's hand. He held her gaze, deep enough that I almost felt like an intruder in their intimate moment. In a way, I was, because I'd caused it, forcing their hand rather than waiting on them to work it out.

"You're already mated. The bond is unraveling you, piece by piece. Shredding your sanity. And when the next battle comes, you can bleed together or bleed alone."

Banand's throat worked like he was swallowing glass. "This is not easy. I never saw myself in this position. Everything I thought I knew was thrown into question. But this is happening for a reason."

Araquiel nodded, rolling her lips like she was trying to hold back a sob. "My people would execute me for this bond alone. They'd call me cursed. It is the gravest sin to lie with a Demon," she admitted. She looked at her mate like he was a puzzle her Goddess needed her to solve. "I don't know. How do I walk away from everything I've ever been taught and choose you?"

"Together. You move forward together." I straightened to my full height. "And you move forward under the Demon banner. Because we will not kill you, Araquiel. Not if you and Banand accept the blessing of your bond. Would your people offer him the same kindness?"

A tear spilled over and tracked down her cheek as she shook her head. "But what about after? If you win?"

"*When* we win, you will have a home on this continent. Believe it or not, our goal was never complete extermination," I told her. Banand nodded in confirmation. "If we needed to stamp out every Angel to ensure our survival, we'd do that. If we could cut off the head of the snake and everyone else would fall in line, then we'd do that. You can make the latter a possibility."

Banand helped her to her feet. To my surprise—and his—she went straight into his arms. With her wrists bound, she couldn't wrap him in an embrace, but burying herself into his chest was as close as she could get. Her mate, on the other hand, broke, clutching her to him like she was the most precious thing in the world.

As he fucking should.

I massaged my temples, a headache pounding behind my eyes. "Whenever you are ready to accept the full force of your bond, you can remove her shackles. After that, she doesn't need them any longer."

"Thank you," he replied, his voice thick with emotion.

"Take one of the rooms on the upper floor after our meeting. I'll ensure no one else bothers you. Then tomorrow," I paused, waiting for Araquiel to look at me. She did, her eyes rimmed with red. "You will stand by us. You will show Ishim and whomever else he brings with him that we treat our prisoners far better than they treat ours. You will fucking lie and go along with everything I say, true or not. Am I clear?"

"Yes, Halálhívó," she affirmed. Stepping away from Banand, she awkwardly offered me a Demon-style salute.

"Good. I'll see you in the meeting room in ten minutes. If you do not show up in that time, I will send out a search party for both of you. You will not come back from that alive." With the threat still hanging in the air, I spun on my heel and made the remaining trek to the primary building. I didn't feel the least bit guilty as I ascended the stairs, coming face to face with my mate.

"Do you think they will?" she asked, her voice lilting and full of hope.

Devious little thing, spying through our bond.

"There's nothing like the threat of death to make you realize what really matters." I grabbed her waist and tugged her to me. We both knew the reality of that all too well. I planted a kiss on her forehead, then looped my arm over her shoulders and steered her toward the command room.

"I hope so. I like Araquiel. She reminds me of me before I let myself love you. They could be good together if they'd just allow it to happen," she sighed, leaning into me.

Similar words, spoken by Rapp, rang in my head. It had been days since we'd had word from him or Trol, and when we were finished here, I planned to find the separated mates and request updates on both fronts. I'd inform them of Ishim's location and our planned meeting atop the wall.

Settling in a chair, we waited, along with Zurronar, Olet, and the other Parancsok under my command for the bonded to appear. Banand would elevate himself to the fourth position as soon as he'd claimed Araquiel.

Because there was no doubt in my mind that the moment their bodies joined, there would be no going back. They'd both be irrevocably changed, much like Assyria and I had been. Except for Araquiel, there was no return to her people. Perhaps not even her Goddess. Only forward, into a war that might chew them up and spit them out anyway.

58

R🕱KATH

White gleamed as the sun parted the clouds. My throne of bones clanked against the hard stone of the wall. I flared my nostrils, trying not to snap at the males arranging it. "Scoot it back a foot," I managed to instruct without vitriol. Despite the nip of fading winter, sweat slicked my skin. Yet I didn't dare remove my armor, not when the Angels could burst through the treeline at any moment.

Appearances were everything, as I learned so many centuries ago. My armor, the chair constructed from fallen Angels, the still-living ones standing on our side, would only serve to infuriate Ishim.

Especially when he found a second one with wispy vanes forever crystallized in a thick lacquer. All that was missing from my mate's matching seat was a skull for the second armrest.

A group of four females carried it forward, the light catching the feathers and making them glitter like diamonds. Their care far exceeded their counterparts. But with the way the former priestesses worshipped the ground Assyria walked on, it wasn't surprising.

With reverence, they placed it beside mine. One even used

her sleeve to buff out a bit of dirt. Satisfied with the placement, I dismissed the group to their respective positions.

The space between the two guard towers was a flurry of activity. Those with the most powerful eye colors framed the thrones, preparing for the Angel contingent's arrival.

Araquiel and Banand emerged from the depths of one building, and many gave the Angel pointed side-eyes. Yet they knew better than to comment on her presence. The reason they'd been selected wasn't only for their magic—it was also because they knew the stakes of this meeting. They'd hide their disdain before the zealous arrived.

After all, we had to show the Angels we were better than them. Now, with females among the army, even Angels— though Araquiel was the only one currently convinced—they couldn't claim moral superiority any longer.

They'd still try.

The Padisa, chained up in one of the guard towers, had refused to break and join us. She was our pawn in the elaborate game Zahal Ishim and I played. Araquiel, in a show of loyalty, had cut out the Angel officer's tongue to ensure she couldn't speak during the meeting once she was dragged out.

All the pieces were falling into place. Yet dread still twisted my gut.

For our pretense to succeed, Assyria had to impersonate the dead Myrza. Therefore, someone else had to pretend to be my mate. Izzenna had volunteered, and given she was the only Deathveiled that mildly resembled my mate, we agreed.

The helmet I'd commissioned for Assyria was too small for her, which was a massive blow. Now, we had to pray that they didn't fully remember the details of my mate's visage.

Izzenna sauntered up a moment later. She looked *almost* right—but just enough wrong to make my skin itch. Heavy kohl applied around her lashes, long hair unbound and styled in a wild way, and lips dyed a bright red with berries picked from nearby bushes, her carefully chosen facade was all a distraction from her eyes that were slightly off from the infamous burgundy shade.

My nails bit into my palm as she settled onto Assyria's chair. "Like this?" she asked me.

"That's fine," I told her, keeping my tone even when I really wanted to tell her to get the fuck off of it. "Just let me do the talking. Sit there and glare but don't make direct eye contact with anyone."

"Yes, sir," she said, all military formality.

Olet broke through the throng, his long strides carrying him to my side. "A green flag has been spotted on the Angel's side."

Bringing my fingers to my lips, I let out a sharp whistle. Everyone ceased their movements and faced me.

"The time has come," I growled, my tone threaded with the promise of violence. A hush blanketed the Demons as they readied themselves for the confrontation. Females flicked their hair back. Males rested hands on their weapons.

Grem and Zeec trotted toward me, their lips pulled back from their razor sharp teeth and tails wagging. They tasted the tension in the air like it was their favorite treat.

After commanding them to settle at the feet of the thrones, I risked a glance at the second guard tower, where Assyria, disguised as the Myrza, waited. No windows or slits in stone allowed me to peer into the room where she sat. The bond reassured me that she was there all the same, though our connection was muted, like every time she became an Imposter.

As much as I loathed even an ounce of disconnect from her, I was glad she was already in form and ready to go. A few of the Deathveiled guarded her as an added measure, should the Angels try to sneak in from the other side.

A horn blew, once, twice, three times, the sound pretentious and scraping at my nerves. Too many times had that noise irritated me. Caused me to lose blood and bodies and sanity.

I stalked to the far side of the wall, glaring down at the approaching Angel party. Ishim rode at the head, his dapple gray horse tossing his mane. The metal decor dripping from his reins tinkled. I rolled my eyes at the ostentatious display.

Behind him, the group fanned into a V, spreading through the sparse trees. More emerged behind them, and I made a quick count of their numbers—forty total. Among them, I noted was Korona Iaoth's brother, Vaeron.

My nails dug into my palm.

The male had the power to speak a single word and command all those within earshot to do what he bid. Like other mind magics, the only way to combat it was to plug ears with shadow or have something bite into flesh to ground oneself in reality.

I didn't want Assyria anywhere near him. Under my breath, I relayed an order to prepare for what Vaeron might do. That he was present now had concern twisting my gut. His sister used him like her personal pet. Rather than assisting Ishim—where his magic would have been most useful—he gallivanted around the Angel Realm. They didn't call him the Issaraeth, Mind-breaker, for nothing.

Then, I returned my attention to the swarm of insects.

"You requested a meeting," I tossed down, keeping my tone bored.

The Zahal leaped from his mount, boots thudding against the earth. In three long strides, he was staring up at me. The long plumage at the front of his helm dipped with the motion. Like me, he'd come dressed to make appearances, though his polished silver attire left nothing to be feared, unlike the horns of wicked ebony that curled from the black skull over my face.

He said nothing, just offered me a hateful glare, as more of his companions dismounted and joined him in looking up at us like the Gods we were. I quite liked seeing them beneath me—where they were supposed to be.

"You may approach," I announced before he could speak again. Spinning on my heel, I stomped toward my seat.

A cold calm settled over me as the whispering of feathers filled the air. I glanced up, finding the sun at its zenith. The shadows they cast were minimal as they landed in front of us, those charged with protecting their leader making a quick assessment of our positions.

Ishim's focus immediately landed on my throne of bones, then sliced to the one beside it. A muscle jumped in his jaw, visible in the space beneath his helm since it provided no protection whatsoever.

Idiot.

But then, a slow, sinister smile spread across his face. "Halálhívó, you have been busy indeed."

He snapped twice, and a female emerged from behind Vaeron, carrying a rolled slip of parchment. Kneeling, she handed it to the Zahal. As she returned to her spot, the Korona's brother tracked her every movement, like he was on the precipice of leaping forward to ensure she didn't run. The heat in his expression reminded me so much of how I'd first looked at Assyria.

The female's shoulders were tense beneath her white armor. Silver hair knotted high on her head disguised nothing as she skirted Vaeron, bumping into other soldiers rather than arcing closer to him.

Interesting.

Ishim made a show of unfurling the paper, drawing my attention back to him. He turned it about and glanced between the two bone chairs.

A laugh—more forced than genuine—barked out of him. I

wished he'd get on with whatever the fuck he was trying to pull.

"Oh this is good. Divine, even." His attention returned to me as he let the paper snap shut. He handed it to Vaeron, who tucked it into his breastplate without a second glance, like he had no need to read the script his sister's menagerie had written. "You see, Halálhívó, our Seers have predicted this moment exactly. This meeting. The second chair made of the bones of our people. You animals are so predictable."

"So?" I drawled, sinking onto my throne and gripping the skulls at the front. Even in death, his female assisted me in rattling him.

His ice blue eyes flashed with righteous anger before he smoothed his expression again. A deranged grin rose as he crossed his arms. "So, that means the rest of what the Goddess showed her will also come true."

Unease curdled in my veins, but I forced myself to focus on maintaining my cool, derisive demeanor. My hold on the skulls tightened until I feared they'd crack beneath my palm. "Whatever you think, Ishim. We know how your predictions have gone in the past."

He lifted a single brow. "Quite well, if I remember all the times we ambushed you correctly."

I gritted my teeth to contain the words that wanted to bite out. Counting to ten, I willed myself to calm before addressing the Angel's leader again. "What do you want, Ishim? Other than to retrieve those who you deem traitors?"

I motioned for the males guarding the door to the tower to open it. All the Angels' attention slipped there as Assyria—impersonating the Myrza—emerged, dragging the tongueless Padisa with her. A dark hood covered her head, and bronze shackled her wrists.

When they stopped between us, Assyria yanked it off,

revealing the bruised and broken Angel officer. A gag wedged between her lips, and blood dripped from the corners of her mouth.

Ishim paled. The male he'd sent to Fured to kill our more powerful stood before him, wearing leather Demon armor. Holding one of his own hostage.

"So what do you have to exchange for her?" I prompted. His eyes cut back to me, albeit with much struggle.

"Someone you'd love to carve up again," he purred like a cat pleased with the mouse it had caught for its master. Then, he shouted over his shoulder, "Bring him."

Moments later, Zaph, escorted by two others, flew over the wall. His hands, bound in chains much like the Padisa, prevented him from using his magic. The males threw him at my feet, and Zaph looked up at me with even more hate than Ishim.

I laughed—a cold, cruel, *violent* sound that shattered the serene expressions on the Angel's faces. "So you finally see how useless he is too?"

Assyria slid into my mind a moment later. *"Are you going to trade for him?"*

We hadn't planned on taking any offer, given how much of everything we were faking. The only real person we could trade was the Padisa, who hadn't really betrayed or converted, despite our attempts to do so. Ishim might still want her regardless.

I nudged the parasite with the toe of my boot to cover my attention diverting to my mental conversation with my mate. *"What do you think we should do?"*

"If they'll take the Padisa, then yes. I'm more than ready to claim our vengeance and add his bones to your throne."

"As am I. Let's see what other cards Ishim thinks he has to play." I resisted the urge to smile at her feral, dark tone.

Izzenna, playing the part of Assyria, snorted and shook her head, sneering at the male curled at our feet. Wisely, she covered her face like she was attempting to disguise her laughter as his attention drifted her way.

Ishim's expression darkened. "Sacrifices must be made for the greater good."

Three caws sliced the air. My eyes drifted upward, catching the black feathers of the crows before they dipped around a guard tower.

Fuck.

"And that is?" I pressed, worry knotting my gut. The Fates were watching this moment. Testing us. Testing me. One step down the wrong path, and Kiira's prophecy could change yet again.

I needed to know what Ishim had planned. Needed him to fucking say it rather than forcing me to guess. My strategic mind could have crafted a dozen possibilities, but feigning ignorance had served me in gathering intelligence in the past.

"Extermination of your race. The time has come to slaughter you all, once and for all. Our most powerful Seer," he gestured to a female standing a few paces behind Vaeron, "has been blessed by the Goddess with the exact way in which it will happen. It starts with you handing over the traitors."

The Seer's lips quirked with knowing.

"Why would you tell me that?" I cocked my head to the side, studying him. "If that is truly how our end begins, why would I give them to you?"

"Do you actually believe me?" Ishim taunted, his sinister grin growing.

I didn't, not for a second.

"So I have placed an option at your feet, Halálhívó. One that you know will affect whether you win or lose. But you don't know the truth, and you won't know if you chose correctly until you are about to meet the Reaper, the pretend Goddess who your filth thinks takes your soul onto the next world."

Hot tension clawed across my neck and shoulders. A clever game, yet one I was determined not to lose. Not when there was so much at stake.

"Take the Padisa, then, if you care about her so much," I ground out.

Assyria threw her forward with the same roughness they'd offered Zaph. He attempted to sit upright, offering his Zahal a look of indignation, but failed. Grem shuffled forward, lips curling back from his teeth mere inches from the inept male's face.

"I want the others," Ishim snapped, widening his stance and trying to take up more room like he was the one in charge here.

Assyria chuckled and shook her head. "I'm not going with you."

"Nor am I," Araquiel pronounced. I angled my head over my shoulder to look at her, impressed that she'd spoken up without being called to do so.

Wisely, Banand kept his attention firmly forward. But if anyone was paying close enough attention, they'd see what I did—the way his muscles were coiled tight, his hand hovering mere inches from her body like he'd pull her out of harm's way before throwing himself into it to save her.

"Shivk," Ishim spat the word for traitor in Angelic at both of them. Continuing in their language, he pressed, "Why do you turn your backs on the Goddess? On the Koron who elevated you? On your noble houses?"

"Because I will live," Araquiel shot back. Their fresh coupling had unleashed her fire, for which I was grateful.

"And the Halálhívó is merciful to those who aid him,"

Assyria added. "It's why I've been entering our camps and trying to convince the others to join us. It's why so many have."

"Finhya," he swore, his gaze narrowed. "You never would have given up so easily. The male I knew would have killed himself to honor the Goddess rather than change sides."

Whispers abounded between the Angels as Assyria and Ishim spit venom at each other.

Before the animosity we'd brewed shattered with one wrong word from Assyria's mouth, I rose from my throne, drawing everyone's attention. "If we could return to the matter at hand," I intoned in the common tongue. "Will you take the Padisa alone? Because I will not force them to go with you, knowing they'd be going to their deaths. Not when they've changed their allegiance. They're too valuable for me to willingly relinquish."

Ishim dragged his attention back to me. The Seer's focus was razor sharp on me too. I pinned her with a hateful glare.

"We'll make the trade." He gritted out each word like it was physically painful for him.

Victory warmed my veins and hardened my cock. Zaph shouted against his own gag, while the Padisa cried tears of joy. Dark satisfaction swept down Assyria and I's bond.

Ishim snapped his fingers, and the two males who had hauled Zaph gathered the Padisa in their arms. Zurronar and Uzadaan swept forward and dragged Zaph away from the rest of the Angels, lest they attempt to grab him and run too.

"It was a pleasure as always, Ishim," I growled, using his given name rather than his title.

Instead of anger flashing in his eyes, triumph shone.

So this was what he'd predicted happening...

Ice slithered down my spine. Kiira's visions were always stronger and I trusted her over whatever this icy-eyed female saw. Still, I'd convey every detail to her, Rapp, and Trol when we debriefed later.

"I'll enjoy killing you," Ishim replied, grinning, as he flapped his white feather wings. Around him, his companions did the same, keeping their faces to us as they descended back to their mounts and ground support. Only Vaeron lingered, gaze searing into me, as if he weighed judgement like his Goddess.

Then, he turned and followed the rest of the Angels.

I stalked to the edge of the wall, finger digging into the balustrade. Assyria and the Parancsok joined me. Together, we looked down upon the overexcited Angels as they gathered their horses and disappeared into the trees.

"That went better than I expected," Assyria muttered under her breath. "Especially after the caws."

"Aye," I said, a sick, sour feeling clawing in my gut.

Another crossroads had shoved into our path. Darkness loomed down each one, foreboding and ominous. If Kiira's guess that the three crows were a symbol for moments where we'd be able to change the outcome of the war, I wasn't sure if I'd chosen the right direction.

"How long until that poison works?" Banand asked as the last flits of white vanished.

"Maybe another hour?" Zurronar guessed, a dark chuckle rumbling in his chest. "By the time they return to their camp, she'll be closing in on death and there isn't anything they'll be able to do about it."

"You've earned your title as Parancsok now, Banand," I announced, turning away and finding the male who'd ambushed me and started the fucking war in the first place.

"Your first responsibility will be to clean all this up and ensure they aren't circling back for an attack." I took a step toward Zaph, whose eyes widened in fear. "The Szélhámos and I have other business to attend to."

Let the Angels hunt visions of their victory. Assyria and I would carve ours in blood.

59

ASSYRIA

Metal clanked as Rokath dragged Zaph into a dark, dank cell. His thrashing limbs, his unrelenting fear, his utter helplessness, coiled dark desire low in my belly. Once, he'd had me in a similar, vulnerable state.

I'd lived beyond it.

He would not.

The promise of violence rolling off Rokath was a heady wine, an intoxicating rose, a decadent dessert.

I'd thought we'd have to capture Zaph on the battlefield and give him a quick death. This was far, far better.

The heavy metal door slammed shut behind us, ringing finality into our ears. A window, cut high in the damp stone, offered the barest hint of light.

"Find a lantern," Rokath instructed me, his focus still entirely on the male who had caused us so much pain. Gripping the chains in the center, he tossed Zaph against the far wall.

Teeth dug into my lower lip, I grasped the metal and stuck a lit match inside it. The embers grew until they cast haunting shadows around the room, an omen of what was to come.

Rokath peeled his helmet over his head, his eyes never

leaving Zaph. The moment it was off his head, he gripped it by a horn and stalked forward. Zaph shoved his feet into the ground in a futile attempt to put space between him and my mate.

Removing my own, I savored the delicious fear radiating from the Angel. A nearby table offered the perfect perch to witness Rokath's torture. What he would do simply because someone dared harm me.

I hopped onto it, setting my armor to the side.

My mate leaned close, his face mere inches from Zaph's. Lips curling back from teeth, he growled, "No one touches my mate and lives. Not only that, but they die slow, excruciatingly painful deaths. I needed a skull to finish her throne. Yours will do."

The stench of urine assaulted my senses, and I wrinkled my nose. "It's really pathetic. All his bravado to piss himself at the penultimate moment?"

Rokath let out a dark chuckle. "It truly is. But he's never been more than an annoying pest. It's time to squash him."

Obsidian ecstasy heated my veins.

Rokath's hand snapped out and closed around his throat. With the barest bit of strength, he lifted Zaph and threw him onto a table in the middle of the room. A crack sounded as his back hit the wood. I felt more sorry for the furniture that had to take Rokath's abuse.

Perhaps I should have felt shame. After all, I'd been beaten. I knew the fear that accompanied each oncoming strike.

Yet I couldn't find it within me. My soul had turned to pitch long before this moment. Possibly even before I accidentally killed Vagach.

Rokath bore witness to it and did not retreat. Instead, he dragged me deeper into the abyss with him.

Flattening his palms over Zaph's chest, Rokath pinned him in place. Then, his burgundy eyes dragged to mine. "I'm about to show you, mate, just how much I love you. Everything I'd do to protect you. Everything I'd do to avenge the wrongs done to you."

My tongue danced over my lips before I offered him a devious smile. "Maybe you'll win me over for more than one day based on your demonstration."

"To earn that, I will ensure the show is one that pleases you greatly," he growled, the double meaning in his tone clear. That only served to dampen my thighs.

Rokath grabbed Zaph's hands and yanked them overhead. Fishing a chain from beneath the table, he secured them in place before rounding it and doing the same with his feet. Still gagged, his cries were muffled along with his thrashes against the binds.

With more care than he'd shown Zaph, Rokath placed his helmet and chest plate beside my own. Threading his fingers through my hair, he knocked my legs open and settled between them. His gaze drifted to my lips. The moment hung, air frozen between us.

His mouth collided with mine, bruising, demanding, *aching*. Teeth and tongue battled, only twisting the tension on our bond. Excitement thrummed in my veins, and I gripped his tunic, calling my magic to the surface of my skin.

Onyx smoke shoved my mate away. "Don't forget these," I said, leaping from my position and finding the silver stakes I'd stored in sheaths on my thighs. The very same ones Zaph had used to pin Rokath in place.

I wanted them on me should we ever cross paths with the offender. It was fitting they accompanied our vengeance. They'd found their place in Zaph's death ritual long ago.

The metal clicked as I dropped them into Rokath's hands. "Get to it."

His eyes turned to molten ebony. "With pleasure."

Our mouths seared one final time before he stepped away, leaving me breathless. Every strike of his foot against stone imbued his frame with power. To me, Rokath was more than a male. More than the leader of the Demon army. More than the Halálhívó.

He was death made flesh. The solemn assurance of savagery. The final midnight of life.

Even the Reaper should tremble beneath his wrath.

Zaph's eyes bulged as Rokath grabbed a thick-headed hammer. I seated myself again, tucking my legs beneath me like we were lounging rather than torturing.

The Angel clenched his hands. My laugh—wicked and hair-raising—reverberated in the room. "That won't save you."

Rokath shoved the sharp silver tip between Zaph's fingers. His body jerked against the binds.

A heartbeat passed, then another, as Rokath prolonged the moment. Without warning, he swung. Zaph's hands flew open as the first stake lodged itself between his bones. The second clawed a tear down his cheek.

It was a glorious sight.

Rokath's destruction didn't end. He didn't allot a second for the Angel to adjust to his new decorations. From a sheath at his hip, he drew a bronze dagger. The tip dragged down Zaph's middle, only deep enough to strip open his tunic. Tufts of white hair appeared, heaving against the musky air. His fearful focus never left the sharp point slicing open the fabric covering his entire frame, until he was bare before us.

"How fitting that I carved an H into his forehead the first time he defied me, and I'll carve your entire honorific into his chest before I kill him?" Rokath murmured, pressing the blade to the skin above his waistband.

"It's entirely fitting," I told him, my tone breathy.

A scream shredded his throat as Rokath carved a jagged S.

In the dim light, the A he'd allowed me to cut into his wrists danced. Like the H he'd put into me.

Our mutual claim on one another. The symbol of how we'd looked into one another's souls and found a mirror. His fractured edges slotted perfectly with mine.

Zaph though? He wouldn't have time to scar. No, before this day was finished, he'd be broken beyond repair. Our vengeance would be complete. All that would remain was burning Sivy to the ground.

Rokath stepped back and admired his handiwork. "Would you like a turn?"

"I much prefer to watch your violence," I purred, my thighs growing slicker with each slice of his blade. Our bond hummed with wicked desire.

"Good. I didn't really feel like sharing." He proceeded to carve the E. Another muffled cry surged from Zaph at the same time a laugh bubbled from me. Rokath finished carving my honorific with jagged lines, arrogating the entire expanse of the Angel's torso.

"Don't forget, he wanted to rape me," I reminded Rokath. Fury, white hot and violent, blistered from within him.

"That will be the last thing I take from him," Rokath snarled. Tears leaked out of Zaph's eyes. "But he dared touch you in the first place, and that demands penance."

From a smattering of rusting devices, he picked up an axe. Flipping it in his hand, he tested the weight. It hissed through the air before embedding itself in the wood, a hair's breadth from Zaph's wrists. The sobs that wracked him sent a cascade of crimson down his ribs.

A smile curved up the corners of my mouth as Rokath pulled it free and raised it again. His miss had been entirely intentional.

How many times would he swing before he finally removed the offending limbs?

I received the answer to my question moments later.

Three in total.

Blood gushed from the stumps, but before Zaph could yank his arms to his body, Rokath pinned them each with a dagger through the forearm. The thick vein that would have had him bleeding out all over the table throbbed against it, unpunctured.

"You are nothing compared to me," Rokath snarled, leaning his face close to the Angel's. Lips curling back from his severely pointed teeth, rage burning in his eyes, body vibrating with coiled restraint, my mate had never been more intimidating than in that moment.

And I'd never wanted him more.

"I should have killed you rather than carving up your face and letting you live. You've bothered me far too long." The low, deliberate way he spoke raised the hairs on my arms.

Zaph whimpered, squeezing his eyes shut. Rokath's hands snapped out and forced them open again. "Do you know what happens to insects who bite and linger?"

He gave the barest shake of his head.

"They get swatted." Rokath reared back and delivered a resounding blow to his face. Blood sprayed as Zaph's head whipped to the side. A tooth clattered to the wood beside his shoulder.

Rokath grabbed his jaw and forced his face forward again. Another dagger, pulled from the myriad of places he always kept them on his person, removed his eyelids. I twisted my mother's ring around my finger as he opened up Zaph's lower legs and ripped out the bones of his shins.

Each time, my mate knelt at my feet and proffered them to me, like I was the Kralovna and he was presenting me with royal gifts. I accepted them time and time again, until I had a nice pile at my side.

Zaph was barely conscious by the time Rokath was finished. He gave him a few slaps to the face to rouse him. Head lolling, he looked up at the male he'd attempted to best time and time again. Unsurprisingly, he'd fallen short.

No one compared to my mate.

It was like trying to defy one the Fates themselves.

"The time for the finale has come. You're going to enjoy it," Rokath sneered at Zaph. Then, he tilted his head over his shoulder, meeting my gaze as he spoke his next words. "You are mine, Assyria. No male will ever touch you again."

A bronze dagger flashed in the low light, and then, the metallic scent of fresh blood filled the air again as Rokath sliced Zaph's dick and balls from his groin.

Those lidless eyes went glassy and lifeless a moment later.

Rokath's hands shook, but not from fear. The carnal need to destroy burned in him. Engulfed our bond. Scorched my veins.

"Rokath," I whispered, my voice like a boom in the silence.

Yet the thread of his control continued to fray. He was a hound whose bloodlust had overtaken all reason. The only thing he wanted was *more*.

"Rokath," I snapped, trying to draw his attention. "You killed him. You avenged me. Avenged us."

Awareness returned to my mate in slow blinks. His peace was a fragile, tenuous thing. The beast beneath the surface, the one that harbored vast rage, unrelenting fury, was poised to strike again. My voice was his only tether to sanity.

"You didn't slaughter him for vengeance alone. You did it for undying love."

He plopped the offending organs on Zaph's carved-up stomach. Chest heaving, he whirled on me. In two strides, he knocked my knees apart again. Garnet dusted his face, coated his hands, and yet, when his gaze crashed into mine, only aching, arduous adoration remained.

The riot of burgundy captivated me like nothing else ever had. Those orbs called to me, the same as the male who owned them. Every line of ink on his powerful frame was indescribable devotion. One no crown, no vow could command.

Only love. Only me.

Because both of us were grown from seeds of hate. Somehow in that unforgiving garden, we'd bloomed with sharp thorns. My mate wielded his on the battlefield, protecting us all. I wove mine into my words, into my undying will to free the females of the realm.

Together, we were devious ruin, wicked victory.

Together, we were unstoppable.

"Have I won you over today?" he murmured darkly, his tone like rocks rolling down the side of the mountains that surrounded us.

The heat pooling between my thighs offered a resounding yes.

"Not only for today. But always." I reached out and ran my nails through his beard. "Thank you."

Those two words shattered the glass behind which he imprisoned his self-control. He captured my waist, pressing his sweat-soaked body against mine. His grip was with the ferocity of a male starved. He claimed my mouth with hot passion. I kissed him back, nipping his lower lip with my teeth, twisting my tongue with his, inhaling the spicy, masculine scent of him.

"Take me here," I begged him down our mental connection. Breaking apart from him, even for a second, would destroy me.

Shadows exploded from his hands, weaving beneath our clothes and ripping them from our bodies. Before my ass hit the wood again, Rokath dragged me to the edge of it. In one powerful thrust, he seated himself to the hilt.

The thick, hard length of him touched every nerve inside me. Our bodies one, we moved together. Eyes locked, we became a singular being. Minds wide open, the place where I began and Rokath ended disappeared.

The world around us was no more.

All time, all words, all of everything disappeared until it was only he and I.

One infinite loop.

One perfect circle.

One endless moment.

He slid against that spot deep inside me, eased by how thoroughly I soaked his cock. My lashes fluttered against my cheekbones before a wordless nudge had me opening my eyes.

My mate loved to see the pleasure he delivered me.

Our breaths became a single tide, rising and retreating with each relentless thrust. My mouth popped open as he buried himself to the hilt. Ragged air dragged against my lungs, the sound matched by his own jagged breathing.

The tattoos decorating the hard muscles of his torso danced as we did, the blooming roses digging into the skulls nestled between them. I gripped his shoulders, trying to find a semblance of balance as his thrusts grew more forceful. Blood-soaked bones scattered as the table smacked against the wall. The sound was nothing more than a distant echo of what no longer existed.

"Mine."

"Yours."

His arms caged me against his body. The heavy pound of his heart matched the pace of my own. I flattened my palm over his chest, desperate to feel the full force of the organ that beat only for me.

Rokath shifted his grip to mirror my position. Dark, smoky shadows leaked from beneath our palms. Ghosting across our skin, they wrapped us in a veiled shroud. Hiding us from what lay beyond. Disavowing any intrusion on this divine moment.

The two magics tangled, undulating together like they were meant to be a singular entity.

Rokath groaned, long, low, deep, *primal*, as my core clenched over his cock. *"Come for me, mate. Shatter into a thousand tiny shards only I can piece back together."*

My breath stuttered as ecstasy flooded my veins. I was so, so close.

"Show me how much you appreciate me killing him. The way I tortured him for you."

I gripped him harder, arching my back into him. *"The way you protected me."*

"I will always *protect you, mate. You are the most precious thing in all the worlds to me. Nothing can ever replace you. You are the only person who understands me. The only person who sees me. The only person I want to see me. I do not have to hide from you. I am in constant awe of you and the powerful leader you have blossomed into being."*

Tears welled in my eyes. Carved a love-guided path down my cheeks.

"You and I are anything but ordinary. Together? We're legendary. Infinite. They'll speak of us long after we have moved onto new worlds together."

Our hearts pounded into the scars we'd carved into one another's wrists, the constant reminder of who we were and who we belonged to.

"I love you, Rokath."

He throbbed inside me, dragging me closer to the edge of bliss.

"I love you, Assyria."

The vehemence to his profession fractured me into a thousand shimmering splinters. A whimper tore from my lips as my orgasm blazed through me. Rokath's hand slipped from my heart to the back of my head. He pulled my forehead against his, forcing me to focus only on him. "My mate. My perfect mate."

His hips worked faster, harder, lifting me from the table with the force of his thrusts. My pleasure tumbled on and on, and I was utterly lost to it, lost in the burgundy swirls of his eyes.

"Made perfectly for me," he rasped, movements becoming jerky. "Made just for me."

"All yours," I whimpered. Ecstasy crackled under my skin.

"All mine," he growled, spearing deep inside me. I cried out, sensitive from how hard I'd shattered. But he only gripped me harder, muscles trembling as he spilled himself deep inside me. His groan—low, longing—made me want to come again.

The inky strands around us ceased their frantic swirl as we relinquished our stolen moment. Covered in sweat and blood that didn't belong to us. Joined in the very threads of our beings.

Rokath captured my mouth in a bruising kiss. I fell into it, drowning in bliss. My center ached as he removed himself from me. My breath hitched as his fingers replaced his cock. "Sorry, I couldn't pull out." With a swipe through my center, he flung out combined arousal away. "Let's get back to our room, and I'll wash you."

My body was boneless, limp, and utterly wrung out from the intensity of my orgasm. All I could do was nod. He brushed a kiss to my salty forehead, then handed me my clothes. I tugged them on, each movement a protest when sleep begged me to surrender to it.

"Do you want to walk?" he asked me, studying me with a smug, masculine smirk.

"I will forgo my independence this once if you can fly me," I sighed, my legs trembling as I put weight on them.

He snorted, then threw me over his shoulder like a sack of grain. "Hey!" I protested, smacking his back. He grabbed our discarded armor, completely ignoring me as he walked us back through the dungeon, leaving Zaph's body to rot.

The males on guard startled at the sight of us. A possessive growl vibrated in Rokath's throat, and they quickly averted their gazes.

The moment we emerged into the late afternoon sun, his mighty wings sprung from his back. Not wanting to die, I shuffled around so I clung to his torso like a child. And then we were airborne, soaring toward the top of the primary building.

I let him carry me all the way to our room, into the bathing chamber, and strip me again, savoring the feeling of utter surrender, utter trust, in my mate.

One day, they'd sing of us. Our victory. Our love. They'd worship us like the Fates themselves.

As they should. Because we were transcendent.

60

R☠KATH

Night had consumed the outpost, but war didn't wait for the rise of dawn. For days, the preparation had not stopped. The Angels' belief that the next battle would be the last gave them a cockiness we could exploit. Which was why the Parancsok, Assyria, and I were gathered around the map table, planning our next advance.

The door slammed open, drawing all our attention at once. One of the mates from the pairs that had been split up panted there, her hair wild and unkempt. "Hadvezér Trol is under attack," she burst out, not bothering with salutes and honorifics. The frightened look in her eyes, like her other half might perish at any moment, told me it wasn't good.

"Shit," I swore, snatching for my sword.

Before I could even buckle the scabbard over my back, another male raced up, his countenance similar to that of his fellow messenger. "Hadvezér Rapp reports a mass of Angels approaching over the ridgeline," he blurted in a rush.

The final word hadn't ceased ringing in my ears before a horn blasted through the night. The length of the call signaled that our enemies had been spotted closing in on our location.

Fucking Fates.

A vise constricted my chest. Ishim had coordinated a three-pronged attack. This was why he thought he'd win. The battle in the mountains wasn't a singular location.

It was everywhere we were, all at once.

Which meant no aid could come should we fall.

Assyria whipped her head up, eyes clashing with mine. Embers burned in them. There was no way I'd be able to convince her to remain behind. In this room. Out of harm's way.

The Parancsok leaped to their feet. My mind sharpened like a blade. Years of arduous honing culminated in this moment. I called on the cold, calculating calm that aided me in countless victories.

If I panicked now, my mate would surely die.

"They think this battle will bring them victory over us," I growled, attention cutting to Olet, then Zurronar and Banand, and finally the other officers. "But it will not. The High Priestess saw us in the streets of Sivy. Let's beat them back to their homes in the trees. And when we arrive, we'll burn them alive inside."

The energy in the room crackled with tension. I turned to the messengers. "Light the fires along the walls. Tell your mates to relay that our position is also under attack. The Hadvezér are to hold their positions at all cost."

"Yes, sir," they both said, eyes going vacant as they communicated with their counterparts.

"How can we help, sir?" Zurronar asked, rolling his shoulders back. Dressed in armor already, prepared to fight on a moment's notice, he was every bit the officer he had previously been.

"Rouse your units. Get to the wall as quickly as possible. It must not fall," I commanded him and the rest.

"Aye, Halálhívó," they said in unison. They bolted from the

room, their feet pounding a heavy rhythm through the halls and down the stairs.

Assyria remained, grinning up at me like she was winning a game of kazat. "Where do you want me?"

The thought of her on the battlefield stabbed a poisoned blade into my belly. After her near-death, I couldn't send her out there.

But I had to. It was what she wanted. The world needed to see her fight.

A war waged inside me, ripping me to shreds.

I'd spent months training my mate. Working with her to sharpen her magic into a weapon all its own. The females believed in her. Fuck, the males did too. Scarcely a dissenter remained after her continued success on stealth missions to infiltrate the Angel's camp.

And she had the Deathveiled to guard her too. None of them —especially not the former priestesses—would let her fall. They'd give their lives for her.

As would I.

"This time, with me. The terrain is too uncertain and we'll do better together."

She stepped closer, flattening her palms on my chest. "We're always better together."

"Fetch Grem and Zeec and strap them into their harnesses. Then meet me outside," I instructed her, reaching down and brushing the backs of my knuckles across her cheek.

The heat of her skin seared me as much as the ferocity in her gaze. She truly was a force unto herself.

Assyria leaned into my touch as if she too sensed the gravity of this moment. I wanted to linger in the space of that breath, where she was safe and I was with her. Our bond thrummed with nervous tension, neither of us voicing the fears that laced the backs of our minds.

Three attacks on three fronts. Three chances for the Demons to overpower the Angels and push down through the Skala Mountains to Sivy like Kiira had seen.

Three opportunities for the ice blue eyed Seer's vision to come true.

I gritted my teeth against the thought.

I was no mere soldier. I was a curse whispered into existence by the Fates. The blade that tread the earth in their name. The Angels feared my coming. And this night, I would remind them who the fuck I was.

The Halálhívó.

The Fates' chosen with the power to call upon the dead.

Noise rose like a black tide, devouring the silence of the night. The outpost throbbed with the pulse of the awakening battle. With the anticipation of the clash of blades. Of black and white streaking through the sky until only one side remained to wield their power.

I drank my mate in like a dying man reaching for a final sip of water—agonized by the knowledge I may never taste her again.

She was the finest scale. No other liquid could compare. I yanked her close, memorizing the shape of her body and how it pressed against mine. The fire in her devious eyes and how they cradled my heart in their depths.

I cupped the back of Assyria's head. Tangled my fingers in the silky strands of her hair. Pressed my lips to the curves of hers. Tasted roses on her tongue.

Savored her. Fed my craving. Cherished this last moment of peace.

Ours wasn't a connection of lust; it was of reckoning.

She broke away first, and my entire being rebelled. I nearly snarled at her to keep going. I needed this. I needed *her*.

"Go," she whispered. The word was frayed, like even she

knew this was no ordinary skirmish. The Reaper's eye was drifting straight to us. And that might have been the final kiss granted to us by the Weaver.

I could only fall to my knees and beg the Giver for our magic to hold strong.

A flicker of worry broke through the otherwise steady flame behind her eyes. "I'll be right behind you."

An ache bloomed between my ribs. I forced air into lungs that wanted to collapse. The bond shrieked with the primal instinct to *protect*. "Five minutes. Then I'm coming to find you."

I backed toward the door, but my gaze never left her. I carved this vision of her into the darkest parts of my mind. Because in the heat of battle, when my muscles burned, when my body begged for a reprieve, I needed to remember why I still swung my sword.

"Because you'll always be able to find me. Even if I try to run." Her words, no louder than a whisper, echoed like a final vow. A hidden plea.

"Don't forget that, mate," I said, my voice a low, gravelly threat. "You are mine whether you want to be or not anymore."

"I'd never want to be anything else."

I tattooed her words on my heart as I turned toward the end of a war.

61

ASSYRIA

I was alone, and yet noise engulfed me as our soldiers prepared for battle. The ache of Rokath's absence lingered in my bones, planting itself beside the knowledge that the fight to come would be fraught with danger.

The peaks were far more challenging to navigate than the fields outside Fured. My hands trembled as I braided back my hair. Many, so fucking many, would die this night. The battle at the academy had shattered me. I hadn't lost anyone since.

Would seeing members of the Deathveiled fall in front of me render me unable to breathe? Unable to continue to swing a sword?

I'd only grown closer to them. And they *would* die for me.

Tears seared my eyes and throat. I let one fall. Just one. Because I'd chosen this. Chosen to fight for the females to be freed.

And they chose to fight with me.

I secured the end of my hair with a leather strap. With a sniff, I rolled my shoulders back and dried my face.

We could fucking do this. We'd been training for months.

Kiira had seen us stalking the streets of Sivy. I refused to believe we'd perish among these mountains.

We would fucking win.

Resolve hardened, I stalked toward our room where Grem and Zeec were snoozing after a hard day of chasing balls. When I opened the door, though, they were already on their feet, tails wagging. Grem yipped and spun in a circle as if the ominous energy fed him rather than filled him with dread.

Zeec followed me to the trunk that held their harnesses. His nose nudged my leg as if he were telling me to hurry up. Grem stuck his head in the moment I cracked it open, snuffing sounds echoing through the space. I shoved them both back, a small, breathy laugh escaping me. Their antics eased some of the tightness in my ribs.

"Stand," I instructed both of them. They backstepped and stared up at me, tongues panting out of their mouths. One by one, I wrapped the hardened leather around them, securing the buckles and ensuring they were protected. There was no way I'd risk losing either of them again. When we'd found Zeec bleeding on the ground, so close to death, after Rokath sacrificed his battalions for me, I'd been terrified.

Fingers scratched the soft black fur behind their ears. I cooed words of love and praise. Wrapped myself around each of their necks for good measure. Zeec licked up the side of my face. My nose wrinkled, and I swiped his slobber off.

"Save that for after," I chided as I found the rest of my own armor and weapons. With night fallen, I'd need an extra layer. My jacket waited on the back of a chair, and I shrugged into it, grabbing a few extra daggers and sliding them into hidden slots. Thankfully, my gloves were tucked into another pocket. The supple material was flexible enough for me to wield magic and grasp for blades. Numb hands would not serve me.

I looked up, straight into the mirror. The sight robbed me of air.

Reflected back at me was the *Szélhámos*—burgundy eyes shining with determination, mouth set in a firm line, hair pulled back and revealing sharp brows. The cascade of ebony down my back was contained in a thick plait. The high neck of my jacket provided extra protection but also gave me an even more commanding air.

No bruises decorated my face. No cuts from harsh slaps marred my tan skin. My innate healing abilities weren't kicking in to mend sore ribs.

I was no longer the victim of abuse I had been at the hands of Vagach.

No, when I looked at myself in the mirror, all I saw was the leader I had become. The leader I was always meant to be. The female who would weave a new path forward for the Demons. Who was *already* doing so.

"I am the fucking Szélhámos." Speaking my own honorific aloud imbued me with strength. "No male's hands will mark me again. No Fate can define my path. I am my own salvation."

All semblance of nerves and doubt slipped away as I stepped into the power I'd always possessed and only recently learned to wield.

"I brought the Demon Realm to its knees. Now, I will do the same for the Angels. These fanatics will fear my wrath."

The rose-covered helmet settled over my brow, sealing my identity. Darkness engulfed my eyes as I inhaled a deep breath and surrendered to the pull of it. The heady presence that had grown stronger in my time with Rokath. The one he'd encouraged me to embrace in all ways. After all, he was so deep into the black that the night feared him and his mighty power. He was the master of death, the blade of the Reaper, and the executioner of the Fates' will.

As was I.

"Let's go," I told the dogs. In three swift strides, I flung the door open. They hugged my heels as we wound our way through the hall and onto the stairs outside.

The air kissed my cheeks, and the nip in it made me immensely grateful I'd grabbed gloves. Excitement slipped from Grem in Zeec in excited barks, yet they didn't break my command and dare sprint ahead. Beneath us, males and females raced in all directions, strapping into protective metal armor if they were of a higher rank, reinforcing their arms and legs with plates if they were not. Brown leather blended in with the surrounding trees, while black wings blended into the night as group after group soared overhead to the wall that divided the Angel and Demon Realms.

At the rear of the building, I found Rokath shouting orders.

I halted, breath catching in my throat.

There he stood—ferocious in his command, violent in his protection, death wrapped in flesh and bone.

I understood then, the sacrifice he'd made. Why he'd shut out all emotion to become the executioner of night itself. Why he'd resisted our bond at first.

Horns of wicked ebony speared from the skull-shaped helmet, black as the void between stars. Beneath it was the face I'd come to love with an aching, savage ferocity. The face I'd burn the world to protect.

He'd simply gotten there before me.

As if he sensed my presence on the fringes of his awareness, he tilted his head—slow, deliberate, calm—and through the dart slits of his helm, a flash of burgundy met mine. "Come, mate."

The words hummed in my bones, in the center of my chest where our bond rested. I obeyed, not because he commanded, but because this was where I belonged. Grem and Zeec followed, framing the two of us as I settled at his side.

Before us, the Deathveiled gathered, falling into precise formation. At the front, Zurronar and Uzadaan stood, hands folded behind the smalls of their backs. Just beyond, Izzenna and Vokkia waited, their chins high and shoulders set. The dozen others held similar postures, all ready to whet their blades in Angel blood.

Then, to my utter shock, Banand and Araquiel emerged from the chaos, hand in hand. They circled around the group and knelt at our feet. Dyed burgundy leather hugged the lean muscle Banand sported, while Araquiel had donned a dark brown. Her fog-colored hair whispered over her shoulders as she tilted her head up, first meeting my eyes, then Rokath's.

"Halálhívó, I wish to join the fight. I know your trust in me is still tenuous, and I wish to prove myself to you this night. All I ask is that anyone I manage to subdue is taken prisoner and given the same generosity you have shown me," she spoke in the common tongue.

I couldn't stop my eyebrows from shooting up my forehead. With Rokath's helmet firmly in place, his expression was unreadable. Yet his mind whirled, too fast for me to keep up with, as he considered all the possibilities.

His attention sliced to Banand. "Should she betray us, her life is forfeit and you will take it," he growled in Demonic. My gut twisted. No one else here—save for Zurronar—knew of their mating bond. Many would be with us to witness how they interacted. Rokath had backed him into a corner, with accountability and stakes of the highest regard.

If Araquiel betrayed us, the rest would be watching for him to kill her. It was a test for both of them, and one I sincerely hoped they would not face.

The Demon blessed with the ability to create plagues lifted

his head, his expression determined. "I swear to you, Halálhívó, she will not leave my side. I will end it swiftly, if I must." His throat worked, and a war of emotions played out on his face in painful twists.

My tattered heart squeezed with sympathy, but I understood why Rokath had spoken the command. And as a team, I wanted to show we were united on this.

I cleared my throat and spoke to Araquiel in the common tongue. "For too long, females in the Demon Realm were subjugated to the will of the males." My focus drifted beyond, meeting the eyes of every warrior elevated to battle alongside me. "We had nothing outside of our fathers or husbands who controlled our lives."

Muscles feathered in the jaws of the former priestesses, many of whom had joined the faithful to escape the path I'd been placed upon with my marriage to Vagach.

"Now, we have a chance to change that for the better. For our entire realm and sex." Araquiel held my gaze as I returned it to her. "Fuck that up for us with your betrayal, and I will kill you myself."

Her turquoise eyes remained locked with mine for a long moment, silent understanding passing between us.

"You have my word. For whatever it means to you," she finally spoke.

"Rise and fight," Rokath commanded, his voice as sharp as the sword on his back. They did, falling into the rear of the group. No one offered Araquiel a disdainful glare or shifted away from her.

Pride bloomed in my chest. Perhaps we were changing more than the perception of females in the Demon Realm. Minds and hearts were opening like Bordova roses in the summer, and who was to say that they couldn't blossom into full acceptance?

The hopeful thought dashed away as Rokath gave the order

to move out. Onyx strands reached for Grem and Zeec, snaking around their bodies and lifting them off the ground.

Stepping away from Rokath, I gave us both space to unfurl our wings so we could fly to the wall. Our unit did the same, and we rose as one, both dogs howling and paws swiping through empty air as my mate carried them along with us.

Crimson fires dotted each gaping basin, stretching as far as I could see in either direction and disappearing over ridgelines in the distance. Males and females bearing bows lined up at the lip of the far side, arrows notched and ready to fire when the officer called for it. I spotted Olet at the closest guard tower, counting out soldiers and weapons. Females raced by him, carrying buckets of bolts between them.

Rokath angled us toward him, and we landed in quick succession in the only open space. Olet offered Rokath and me a quick salute before launching into an update on the Angel's position. But his words were cut short by another blast of the horn. Our attention ripped down, and whispers of white appeared among the treeline.

Ice shattered through my veins as the Angels raced into the clearing. Thousands of them, many still stuck among the thick boughs, boasted furious, hateful, *determined* expressions. More rose from over the treetops, bringing with them a pure white light that lit up the night.

Stars winked out, unable to compete with the power of the Angel's display.

Time slowed to a crawl as flashes of my mother, my father, and my sweet, sweet sister twisted my clamoring heart. Then Olrus and Izgath surged from the depths. The priestesses I'd barely gotten to know. All the people I loved who had died. Who I would meet in another world should we fail tonight.

Terror seized every muscle in my body. But I refused to

fucking yield. Not now, not ever, to them. I'd show my people who and what we fought for.

"Prepare yourselves!" Rokath boomed, the depth of his voice reverberating along the stone. From his back, he drew his sword. The garnets embedded in the eyes of the skull on the pommel glinted in the light.

I yanked my own blades free, knees bending slightly as I prepared to face our enemy. Shouts threaded through the tension for the archers to prepare their first volley.

Almost instinctively, I sent a prayer to the three deities who had put me on the path that led to this moment—where my destiny would be realized, where all our fates had converged across Keleti.

Weaver, Giver, Reaper, hear me. Grant Rokath and I life after this. One more breath together. One more kiss. I will bleed the world dry for you. Feed your earth every drop of my blood if I must. So long as in the end, I have him.

A collective roar rose from the Demons, raising the hairs on the back of my neck with its ferocity.

And then, arrows flew.

62

R●KATH

Angels plummeted from the skies like white streaks. Bolts jutted from broken wings. Blood streaked their pale uniforms. Branches snapped beneath their fall. Cries of alarm fractured the air, then silenced with satisfying crunches.

"Again!" I bellowed, and the archers notched and aimed. But the airborne Angels were faster with their bows drawn and at the ready. Arrows, like an oncoming storm, sailed toward us.

A shield of black shrouded the wall, saving us from the worst of the damage. Two bolts sank into the males at the front, one in the thigh, the other in a shoulder. Both pulled them free, though the one with the latter stepped out of line, a female from the second snatching his place.

A swell rose to our left, and Olet raced away to manage that section. "Fire at will," I commanded the archers. To the Deathveiled, I said, "Use your shadows to cover them. When the Angels reach the base of the wall, we attack."

"Yes, sir!" they replied, spreading out behind the third line. Beside me, Assyria's magic unfurled from her fingertips, poised to spear into the skies and protect our soldiers.

"

Her focus remained on the Angels approaching from below, gauging their distance as much as I was. "I need to be everyone," she murmured, her brows pinching as she thought. "Me one moment, you another, the Myrza after that. Each form has its advantages."

Arrows rained down again, barely visible until they were close enough to strike. Without hesitation, her shadows burst outward, creating a thick veil that left no one vulnerable. Not a single strike found purchase. When the clattering ceased, she dropped it, allowing the projectiles to fall all around us. Those at the rear scooped them up and shoved them into quivers for reuse.

The first line fired back, felling another dozen Angels from the sky. Too late, they saw the ones diverging from the right. Projectiles sank into the males at the front. Many collapsed backward, hands clasped over wounded necks.

The first dead.

I glanced at Assyria, worried for her reaction. Her jaw was set hard, but she didn't crack. Didn't crumble. Merely bore witness to their sacrifice. Accepted it as part of their path.

More soldiers filled the empty space. Hands reached to pile the deceased out the way, where they could be burned later or wielded by me.

The Angels on the ground closed in, and the archers fired down, halting their advance for the briefest of moments.

It was time.

"Cover us."

"Yes, sir," the Vezető in charge responded without breaking his focus.

"Let's go," I shouted at the Deathveiled. Zurronar and Banand spun on their squads, barking instructions. Their Százados relayed further information over the wall, where most of the ground forces waited.

Beside me, Assyria's magic swirled around her form, until I stood shoulder to shoulder with myself. My magic snaked out and wrapped around her waist. I collected Grem and Zeec in my web, then eased us off the stone. Bringing my fingers to my lips, I let out a sharp whistle, signaling our advance.

Like a swarm of red and black, our army rose. Wings buffeted the air. Shadow crawled through the night, battling with the Angel's light for space in the skies. We dove toward the ground, covered by the power of thousands atop the wall.

Dozens of squads landed on either side of us in the clearing. On one side, Olet's battalion charged forward. On the other, two Parancsok combined forces, sending their soldiers clamoring over rocks to cut off any opportunity to take the wall.

The scrape of swords removed from sheaths, the whoosh of glaives slicing through the air, the clink of throwing daggers being stacked, all of it formed an all too familiar harmony.

"Prepare yourselves!" I shouted, digging my heel into the dirt. Beside me, Assyria did the same, drawing a sword that was more appropriate for her normal size. But she wouldn't impersonate me for long. Just enough to sow chaos into the rabid, fast-approaching Angels.

"Cease shadow!" came my next command. All Demon magic dissipated, bathing the clearing in light. Confusion flickered in blue eyes, and paces slowed, especially in the groups directly facing us.

"Now!" I roared, and as one, the Demon army raced forward, polearms taking the first swipes at our attackers.

Blood spilled for the Fates a moment later. The clash of bronze and silver rang through the clearing next. Cries of the dying followed, and I chased them, adrenaline flowing in my veins. Beside me, Assyria pounded the earth, churning it as she skidded to a stop and sidestepped a blow. Zeec bounded forward, protecting Assyria's flank. I sank my blade into the neck of the first pathetic Angel to challenge me. The next died without so much as a scream.

A boom sounded to my left, and the dirt exploded, sending a group flying backward. Retaliation came in the form of the illusion of a dozen more sailing overhead. Yet it was a pathetic attempt at best, and I ignored it in favor of cutting down a female headed for Assyria.

She whipped around, and a smirk curved my lips. "You're welcome."

Her eyes glittered with amusement through the slits in my helmet. "I'll never believe that you don't know how to joke," she quipped. Then, she swung her blade out, catching a male passing by in the side. It was an impressive move for her only having seen him in her periphery.

"Don't tire yourself out," I cautioned, stepping closer so we battled side by side. "It will be a long night yet."

A group of Angels fell to their knees in front of us, clawing at their eyes. We leaped through the shimmer, cutting all of them down. Izzenna appeared from Assyria's right, wiping sweat from her brow. With another twist of her hands, she created a new nightmare. We stomped them out of existence.

Assyria released my form with her next breath, the height and bulk unnecessary as the Deathveiled worked magic and weapons together to carve a gouge into the Angel's line. Yet for every dozen we cut down, two dozen more came to take their place.

The scent of iron thickened the air. The leakage of corpses soaked the dirt. And still, we fought.

Movement above caught my eye, and I snapped a hand out, barely managing to yank Assyria out of the way of a falling Angel. His glassy, lifeless navy eyes stared up at the light slowly petering out overhead.

She stumbled into me, and I savored the feeling of steadying her. My grip tightened of its own accord. I was a possessive beast, especially with her here on the battlefield. My pulse pounded in my ears, and hers beat against my armor.

With her safe in my arms, I snatched an opportunity to assess our surroundings. In every direction, Angels and Demons battled for the cleared space in front of the wall. The left flank was holding strong, but the right was faltering. Angels pressed inward like they were flexing the bend of a bow, and the soldiers struggled to straighten out.

"We need to head that way." I spun her so she saw what I did.

"Then let's go," she replied, determination threaded in her tone. I forced myself to release her.

"With me!" she shouted at the others. I cursed as she took off at a sprint, leaving me behind. Izzenna and Vokkia raced after her, leaping over the bodies they'd helped slaughter and whooping from the thrill.

Zeec bounded alongside my mate, and I whistled at Grem to follow, rage and fear a tumult in my chest. The rest of the males chased after us, Uzadaan swinging a massive hammer at an Angel who tried to take advantage of our change in direction.

Blood pooled under broken wings—feathered and membranous alike.

Another group burst through the trees, cutting off my line of sight to my mate. Fury flared, and I swung a powerful arc toward the center. The Angel soldiers leaped out of the way, then two lunged for me at once. A blast of shadow sent one stumbling. Grem leaped, teeth bared, and closed them around the male's throat. The second I sliced from dick to sternum.

Zurronar froze three more of them, allowing another female to stab each between the ribs as she raced by, following the Szélhámos who had given her the ability to stand on the battlefield in the first place. The devotion these former priestesses showed my mate warmed my cold heart.

The threat cleared, I finally reunited with her—and not a moment too soon. An Angel female leaped for her, and their weapons collided. Assyria's teeth gritted in determination. A small explosion rocked the ground at their feet, but Assyria bent her knees and absorbed the blow. Vokkia leaped in and finished her off.

"Thank you," Assyria panted. Then, she saw me approach, and relief unpinched her brows.

"Do not run off without me again," I growled, my tone leaving no room for argument. Yet pride—at her merciless kills, at her unyielding effort, at how far she's come since our bond snapped into place—heated me from the inside out.

She shot me a saccharine grin. "Make me."

My nostrils flared as my cock twitched. "Now is not the time for your games."

"Come on, Halálhívó. We both know we love nothing more than this banter." Lust flooded our bond as she stepped closer. "And fucking after we get bloody."

A low groan vibrated against my ribs. I grabbed her arm and yanked her close. "I will fuck you on the streets of Sivy after this for your continued disobedience and use of that smart mouth."

"Do it," she purred, batting her long lashes against her cheeks. "But for now, we have a battle to win."

Dark satisfaction curled through me at the devious look in her eyes. My blood sang for her. For the slaughter. For what would come after. "Aye, we do."

I released her, and she flipped the hilt of her sword around her wrist. Zurronar's squads had held the line while we stole a moment amid the bloodshed. He and Banand worked in tandem to dent the Angel's forces as the Deathveiled regrouped.

Araquiel moved between them, many of her kin screaming obscenities in her face as she jabbed a glaive into their midst.

I watched for a moment, wondering if she'd falter. If doubt would cross her stoic expression. If she'd turn that weapon on her mate and the Demons around her.

She didn't, even as a tear carved down her cheek, mixing with her sweat.

An oncoming attack ripped my attention away. Metal clashed in my ears, and I disarmed the male in three vicious movements. I fell into the steady rhythm of strike, parry, kill, command. Grem and Zeec worked diligently to take down Angels alongside us, ensuring my mate was fully protected. The Deathveiled thrived, working in perfect unison.

Until the trees shivered like one of the Fates had dropped among them. My blade stilled mid-air. The females closed ranks around Assyria.

From the shadowed abyss of the trunks, a figure emerged.

And grinned like a silver blade gleaming in the dark.

63

ASSYRIA

Zahal Ishim's low, poisonous laugh scraped against my nerves. Light coiled around him as though he'd stolen it from the heavens. In the darkness, he radiated an ethereal glow. But there was nothing holy in the rapture on his face.

White twisted around two struggling forms, and the air in my throat constricted.

The Zahal's magic shoved Banand to his knees. Onyx strands battled for control, but they slipped through his fingers like smoke in the wind. Like whatever power Ishim wielded transcendent even that of a plague-creating Demon.

Araquiel stood at Ishim's side, eyes like polished glass. Her hands were clasped before her, luminous white binding her wrists into a parody of prayer. A puppet knelt at her Zahal's altar.

A low growl rumbled in Rokath's chest. Zurronar skidded to a stop beside us, his maroon eyes wide.

"We didn't betray you!" Banand shouted in Demonic before more magic shoved into his mouth and silenced him. Tears leaked down Araquiel's face. Yet she didn't blink, didn't move.

Banand thrashed against the blinding strands, a scream shredding his throat. The sound was so feral, so helpless, that my own bond twisted in agony. A male watching his mate weep through the prison of her own body. And his magic was unable to free her.

Another male—a Myrza by the looks of his armor—stepped forward, silver blade gleaming with wicked delight as the Zahal's magic reflected off the polished surface.

"An abomination," Ishim began, his nose upturned as he looked between the mates. "This type of filth cannot be allowed to live."

How did he know?

"Ishim isn't just a zealot like the rest of the Angels. He's a parasite. His power of the Hive seizes control of living minds and has them act like his own personal puppets. He must have sensed their bond and invaded Araquiel's mind to capture them," Rokath growled into my mind.

That was infinitely more fucked up than Rokath calling upon the dead. He was no better than the males of the Demon Realm who stripped their wives and daughters of autonomy. At least we could fight back.

Araquiel could do...nothing.

"You'd kill them both for a blessing from our deities?" I shouted before I could smother the words, rage rising like a firestorm, directed at this self-righteous male. Lust for his blood coiled in my veins. He needed to fucking die before he snatched the will from another living being.

"This is no blessing," he shot back. "And your allowing them to live after discovering it is further indication as to why you animals must be eradicated from this earth."

The Myrza raised his blade overhead, preparing to slice into Banand. Without hesitation, I blasted obsidian spears in their direction in a desperate attempt to knock Banand out of the way of the swinging blade.

Time fractured. The world thinned into singular strands.

Araquiel's mouth opened in a silent scream, whatever hold Ishim had over her shattering beneath the might of their mating bond. Darkness scorched through the night. Banand's eyes squeezed shut. Ishim grinned with malice. Rokath leaped between the Angel's leader and me.

Everyone froze.

Uzadaan and Zurronar stepped forward, the only two of the group who could move. No heartbeats passed as they raced to Banand and Araquiel. Uzadaan knocked the would-be executioner's blade aside as he tackled him.

Zurronar bolted for Araquiel, earth churning beneath each stride. He reached for her—Fates, so fucking close.

Then, the corner of Ishim's mouth twitched. Grew into a smile made to slaughter.

Fear flashed among the maroon of Zurronar's eyes. His magic had faltered, failing him at the penultimate moment.

He twisted mid-stride, but the silver blade was already there. In one swift strike, Ishim buried a dagger between his ribs.

A choked gasp slipped from Zurronar. He stumbled, colliding with Araquiel, his momentum unstoppable. They fell together—their fates entwined, helpless in the grip of the Hive's will. A blur of limbs and blood, swallowed by the void beyond.

A scream tore through me, nearly as violent as the roar that ripped from Banand's throat.

But that wasn't the worst sight before us.

64

R☠KATH

Uzadaan stabbed the Myrza and whirled into a crouch to face the Zahal. Flashes of white from deep below highlighted each bare branch in stark relief. A bronze vise crushed my chest.

We'd made a terrible mistake.

In that moment of frozenness, others had been given time to creep forward, under control of Ishim's Hive.

The surge of glassy-eyed puppets broke the treeline. Quaked the earth beneath my feet. I yanked Assyria behind me, forcing her out of Ishim's line of sight.

"Do not be afraid. Hold your ground. Protect yourself at all costs. You are the most precious life here."

My pulse pounded like a war drum in my chest as I calculated how many dead were around us. How many I could Call to shield her. To shield all of us.

I counted how many precious seconds we had to live.

The number for both was far too few.

But I would not let her die. The world bent to *my* will.

I dropped to a single knee.

Curled my furious fingers into my palm.

Cocked my fist.

And *slammed*.

A shockwave of ebony shadow clawed across the hillside, knocking our attackers back for a single, precious moment.

All around us, corpses rose. Sweat beaded my brow as I pushed my magic farther and farther afield, gathering whomever I could to serve me.

The roar of the fight was lost on me as I called, begged, *pleaded*, with the dead to assist us. With shaking legs, I shoved to my feet, head still dipped down as I dug into my mighty power.

"Reaper, I wield in your name."

I spoke the words aloud as I brought my arms out in front of me, pointing directly at Ishim.

The ground trembled as the bodies surged on the wave of my fury.

"Let your eye wander here."

I snapped my gaze forward, locking with the ice blue eyes of the Angel's Zahal.

"Giver, bless me with the power to slaughter the remainder of these insects."

Screams rose to a crescendo around me. Vague awareness of the Deathveiled fighting the ring of Angels around us slipped away. My sole focus was on the male calling more and more Angels to his Hive. Because he wouldn't deign to enter the minds of the Demons, and that was his fatal mistake.

Our staredown continued as the living and dead fought in massive stacked rings.

"Weaver, let the Demon threads hold strong."

I took a menacing step forward, dipping to pick up my blade at the same time. Ishim drew his, both our attention split between each other and the Gods-blessed power we wielded.

He swung first. Sparks scattered from the force of our collision. I shoved him with all my might, muscles trembling with exertion. I had the uphill advantage, and yet he hardly stumbled. His movements were crisp, his breath unbroken, fresh as if he'd awoken only an hour before. And I had led from the fall of night, side by side with my soldiers since the first warning shattered our planning.

Coward.

Heel dug into the dirt, he launched under my blade, aiming for my legs. I leaped at the last second, reaching for a low hanging branch. With one hand, I swung myself behind him, spinning the moment my feet struck the earth. But Ishim's lithe frame made him faster than me, and he was already poised to strike.

A wall of obsidian was all that kept his blade from grazing my armor. With a growl, I pressed forward, hoping to make him stumble going uphill. Flashes of white dotted the edges of my vision as more and more of his soldiers worked their way through the trees to the height of the battle.

They gave us a wide berth as we fought like feral beasts. Dozens of my corpses were falling permanently, either unable to use their limbs any longer or because my well was drying up like water in the Paks Desert.

Ishim sidestepped, leveling out with me. Behind me, I knew, was a smooth outcropping. There, slaughtering him would be easier. I let him back me there, laying my careful, precarious trap. The earth gave way to rock beneath my boot.

Only a few more steps...

My heel hooked on something in the dark, and my world tilted on its axis.

Ishim seized the opportunity and leaped forward, blade spearing straight to my middle. I crashed to the ground, unforgiving metal slamming into my spine. Agony speared my upper thigh as the tip of the Zahal's blade dug between the plates of my armor. I snatched the sharp edges with my gloved palms, silver biting through the fabric there too. But the pain was ashes beneath the fire of my will to protect Assyria. I'd endured far worse and had the scars to prove it.

Blood cascaded from my hand as I wrenched his sword free and threw it into the darkness. The luminosity cast by the Angels flying overhead was dimmed here, rocks and thick-needled pine trees blocking it out.

Ishim drew a dagger by the tip, arm poised and ready to throw. There were only a few places it could penetrate my armor, but I knew from past experience he had good aim. And in this position, with me on the ground and him standing over me, the space between my helmet and my chest plate was exposed.

Smoky gray unfurled from my frame and then stuttered out entirely, my magic waning from contact with silver.

Fuck.

How could I have stumbled at the penultimate moment? Ishim wouldn't hesitate to slaughter Assyria once he was done with me. Image after image of him torturing her flashed through my mind. He wouldn't hold back. Not after all the times I'd tormented him, taking the females he loved from him.

I swallowed, hard, as the white of his form gleamed. He took a long, confident step forward, passing through a stream of light that managed to flit through the branches. Like he knew he had me pinned like a wounded animal, and he was preparing to deliver the killing blow.

He cannot end me. He cannot have my mate.

I gritted my teeth and prepared to defend myself, injured leg aching as I attempted to rise from the cold ground.

"I love you, little imposter. In this life and all the rest."

I had to tell her one last time. Because I might never be able to again.

Fury and fear twisted our bond tight. An all too familiar scream ripped through the night, and my stomach plummeted. Ishim's attention ripped toward the main battle as another feminine one sounded—but that one did not belong to mate.

"Assyria!" I shouted down our bond.

Shadows ripped through the slashes of white overhead. A small, dark silhouette flew through the night a heartbeat later, slamming into Ishim. The two skidded along the length of rock. Daggers clattered. Bronze flashed as Ishim's attacker stabbed. Silver followed. An agonized shriek shredded me to pieces. Over and over they tumbled, battling for leverage, as they careened toward the edge of the cliff.

"No!" I roared, lunging for them. I slammed against the ground, denting my armor and punching the breath from my lungs. My hands scrambled for purchase around a pair of boots.

But the leather was slick with crimson. My palms even more so.

And my mate fell.

Swallowed whole by the abyss beneath me.

In the mountains, the drops were long. A pulse of pain dug into our bond before ebbing.

For a moment, all I could do was lie there. Numb. detached. Disbelieving that after everything, fucking *everything*, the Reaper had taken her from me.

One tear slipped out. Then another. By the third, I was no longer the Halálhívó, the most feared Demon in all of Keleti. I was a shattered husk of a male, begging his Fates to weave any other path.

"Assyria," I croaked, her name a desperate, broken plea.

I didn't want to live in a world without her. Without my little imposter. The female who had so ungraciously upended my life, threatening to kill me from our very first interaction.

My world narrowed to the end of that ledge. The sweet

relief it promised me. The chance to see her again in my next life.

Yet, through my addled power, a flicker snatched my attention. The faintest of tugs had me dragging myself forward, peering into the void. Overhead, Angel magic flashed, illuminating two burgundy eyes.

And one bloody arm barely hanging on the rim of a jutting rock beneath me.

"Can you fucking help?" my mate shot up at me.

The next tear that slipped out carved relief into my cheek.

"Can you fly?" I shouted.

"He sliced me with silver as we went down, I don't know that I can call on my wings," she said, brows pinching as she desperately held my gaze.

That protective beast inside me roared to life.

I will not let her fall to her death.

Gritting my teeth, I yanked on all the magic remaining in my well and pulled my black, membranous wings into existence. In seconds, I sailed over the ledge, dropping straight to my mate. When I captured her waist in my arms, I'd never been more grateful to feel the curves of her body pressed against mine.

Sweat slicked my skin as I flew us upward, the magic of our mate bond the only thing keeping me going. The rock cracked from the force of our landing. We tumbled to the ground, and with the last of my strength, I hauled Assyria on top of me so she wouldn't be crushed beneath my bulk.

Breath heaved in and out of my lungs from the force of my exertion. Yet I couldn't tear my gaze away from Assyria.

Stained with crimson, coated in dark dirt, and with eyes of devious burgundy shining down at me, I couldn't decide if I wanted to kiss her or spank her.

"What the fuck is wrong with you?" I berated her through a chest still constricted by a vise.

"I saved your life. You're welcome," she shot back, grinning with wild abandon. "Oh, and I killed another Myrza too. She was planning on doing what I did, but to you."

Rage battled with relief inside me as I crushed her against me. My heart thudded so hard against my armor, I was certain it would beat right out of the metal casing. "Do not do that again."

I could almost feel her eyes rolling. "Let go of your magic now before you exhaust yourself. The wall is holding and the space between the stone and the trees is clear."

I had the moment I leaped for her, because she was the most precious thing in this entire world and I'd rather burn out every last drop on saving her.

"Then we need to press on," I told her. "We're not in Sivy yet, and there are still more Angels standing between our current position and the capital."

Releasing the tension in my arms, I allowed her out of my hold, though I hated every inch of space between us.

She let out a small laugh as she ran a hand over the new dents in the black metal on my chest. "You're going to hate this when you see it in the light."

I sighed and shook my head. "Where did you leave the rest?"

"Up there," she jerked her head in the direction of the wall. "Figured you'd want to regroup before advancing."

She wasn't wrong.

With a groan, I pressed to my feet, swaying slightly as I put weight on my injured leg. But the wound wasn't deep, and enough time had passed that the silver's effects were wearing off.

"Come, let's find the others." I slipped my hand around hers and hobbled off the cliffs—before any more crazy ideas sprouted in her mind. She tucked close to my side, letting me lean into her for support.

Bodies littered the ground as we trudged uphill, my lungs and legs burning from the exertion of the last few hours. When we emerged into the clearing, I found most of the Deathveiled huddled together, Olet among them.

And, to my utter surprise, Banand and Araquiel.

"Halálhívó," they greeted me in unison. Every single one dropped to a knee and rested their foreheads on their arms before rising.

"I've never seen you wield so many at once before," Olet said, awe lining his tone. Then his attention fell to the garnet dripping down my leg. He reached into a pocket of his fighting jacket and pulled out a vial of green.

All I could do was gaze upon my bold, beautiful mate, even as I gulped down the pium. "Well, I've never had someone to protect like this before."

She grinned up at me, though sorrow glistened in her eyes. And our bond told me exactly where it originated.

"Who did we lose?" I asked, attention flitting among the group to see if I could figure for myself. "Where is Zurronar?"

Araquiel dipped her gaze briefly, clearing her throat. "I lost him in our roll. I couldn't find him." Her voice was thick and heavy. Banand closed his eyes, tipping his head toward the sky. The two had been through horrors too awful to speak together. Even before that, they'd been inseparable.

To lose Zurronar now, after I'd promoted him again, after he'd continued to fight in the army, carrying his untarnished honor, was a massive blow.

Araquiel hugged his side, and yet he still didn't lower himself to this moment with us. Grief on the battlefield was a risk, and one he knew all too well. Death was inevitable, as much as we loathed losing the ones we loved.

Assyria sniffed, wiping at her eyes. I squeezed her hand, letting her know I was there. I wanted her to feel. Wanted Banand to feel. And all the rest too.

But the war wasn't won yet.

"We lost a few thousand. Lots of archers, fewer ground soldiers," Olet reported. "Though the Angel casualties were far higher."

I scanned the area, noting the sheer number of white haired bodies face-down in the soaked earth.

"We need to move out. We can beat them back to Sivy if we move quickly. Send a group of able-bodied to fetch horses, wagons, and other supplies. The rest need to reform and follow us immediately. The night is long, and we have an advantage in the dark."

"Yes, sir." Olet saluted me, then turned on his heel and jogged up the hill. Wings sprouted from his back, and he swept toward the wall, sounding off orders.

Banand and Araquiel turned to us, and the latter cleared her throat. "Thank you. For saving us. My life, my blade, my magic, are yours to command." Araquiel knelt, her head resting on her arm. Love and pride shone in Banand's eyes as he looked at his mate. Yet beneath it was a profound sadness.

"Go with Parancsok Olet. Assist him however he needs. Your service was and is commendable," I said. He could at least find the space to feel for a few moments, saving face with the rest of the soldiers, if he returned to his quarters.

Banand grasped his mate's arm and helped her to her feet. Wings unfurled behind them—black membrane and white feather brushing. "We'll rejoin you soon." And then, they leaped into the skies, hand in hand. I couldn't blame them. They'd almost lost each other after finally accepting their bond.

The rest of the group remained, awaiting my next command.

Units from all directions converged, and once a large enough force had gathered, I spoke. "You all fought well tonight, but the battle is far from over. Press our advantage. Conquer what should be ours. Protect our race from those zealots. Százados, reform your ranks and continue your march."

The officers organized their squads, working with quick precision. The Deathveiled lingered, sitting on the ground, catching their breath, cleaning off their blades. I noted that other than Zurronar, we'd only lost one other, and none of the females. Grem and Zeec flopped on their sides, tongues wet with red and lolling. Feral grins pulled their muzzles back like they'd reveled in their slaughter.

I removed my helmet, letting the winter night air cool my overheated form. Exhaustion tugged at my limbs, and the shadows in my chest were scarcely more than a gray whisper. Clouds moved in overhead, and then, fat flakes fell from the sky. They nearly sizzled as they hit my bare scalp.

"Let's hurry it up!" I shouted. We needed to move out before we lost too much of their trail to the oncoming storm. My breath frosted in front of me, indicating just how quickly the temperature was dropping.

Thankfully, they did. Even Banand and Araquiel managed to rejoin us, noting that Olet would oversee the supplies moving forward and didn't require extra assistance.

I brought my fingers to my lips and whistled. As one, the mass of bodies began to move, Assyria and I at the front. But when we reached the rocks where we'd defeated Ishim, I tugged her to the side. It would provide us with a view down into the valley below, and with her keen eyes, she could help me spot any lingering danger.

Grem and Zeec trotted to the edge, scanning for themselves. Curiosity had me peering down to see if I could find the body of the Angel army's leader. The drop was steep and long. There was no way he could have survived a fall of that magnitude.

But I had to be sure.

The Zahal's broken form crumpled over a group of severe boulders. Garnet leaked from the hole caved into his head, and a sharp point protruded from his ribs.

Assyria drifted to my side, helmet tucked under her arm, wispy hairs at her brow plastered to her forehead, and looked down at him too.

"Funny. I've now killed two males that ended up looking like this after."

My attention sliced to her. I raised a brow in question.

She shrugged, a small smile curving her lips. "I caved Vagach's head in with a meat mallet after I stabbed him in the ribs. Then I buried him in a deep hole. Just dropped him in there without a care. Basically, he looked exactly like that." She gestured toward Ishim's form below.

A wicked laugh burst from me before I could stop it. I shook my head at my mate. I shouldn't have expected anything different from her.

Draping an arm over her shoulders, I tugged her into my side. Salt mingled with a rosy garden as I buried my nose in her hair and inhaled deeply. Our bond hummed with contentment —the kind that came with unwavering devotion on both sides.

The last of the Angels' white light faded overhead as they retreated further down the mountain. Boots crunched over the fallen leaves and branches as the Demon army marched on.

Yet in the darkness, Assyria and I burned brighter.

Hate? That was where we'd begun. Somewhere in the vehement abhorrence, we'd found vast adoration in those wounds buried deep inside us. They'd called to one other, healed bit by bit by our bond. Until a love, so dark, so tempting, so infinite, remained.

"I love you, Assyria. My perfect mate," I murmured.

With a soft sigh, she leaned into me, wrapping her arms around my waist. "I love you, Rokath. My forever protector."

We stood together in the hush, the mountain a silent witness to all we had lost, all we had gained. Her pulse thrummed with mine, steady and even, when both had raced at the thought of either being permanently stilled.

A moment passed before she spoke again.

"Thank you for living."

<h1 style="text-align:center">65</h1>

<h1 style="text-align:center">ASSYRIA</h1>

"Thank you for living," I said again, my voice wavering on the words. Because everyone I had loved had died. But not him. Never him.

Even though he'd come so close that very night.

He hummed, looking down at me, burgundy eyes burning with dark devotion. Rokath's thumb stroked my hip, the hard beat of his heart the only sound I wanted to hear amid the dark.

"What will you do?" I asked, studying the lines of his face. The powerful shoulders that held the weight of the realm. The lips that had whispered of his enduring love for me.

His brows dipped together, tugging on the snake fangs that inked his temples. "What do you mean?"

"When it's all over? When peace reigns?"

A gasp slipped out of me when he gripped my hips and spun me to face him. His hands cupped my rear, pinning me against his hard body.

"Little imposter, I will build you the grandest of gardens. Somewhere where only you and I exist. I'll claim the earth there, like I claimed you. A sanctuary carved from stone and

710

soil, brimming with the beauty you embody. It will flourish and bloom as you help lead us into our future."

Tears pricked my eyes and the back of my nose.

"Together, we'll kneel among the plants, tending to them with the same love and care you have shown me, and the rest of this army, all these months. We'll teach Grem and Zeec to dig too, so that they have purpose in their new lives."

I pressed my mouth into a thin line to smother a sob. I'd told him—only once—that I'd dreamed of a fated mate who would hold me as his equal and join me in my passions.

He remembered.

Rokath caught my bottom lip with his thumb, as if coaxing my feelings free. "I'm not sure who or what I'll be when we're not fighting the Angels." His lips brushed against mine, the spicy scent of him filling my nostrils. "But I do know that I'll be your mate. Your protector. And you?"

He smiled—a genuine twist of his lips, rarer than any precious stone. The sharp flash of his teeth rolled a shiver down my spine. The molten heat of his gaze didn't merely brand me. It was a claim, a possession, against all who sought to take me from him.

"You'll continue to change our society for the better. You won't let us settle. Won't let us slide back into the inequality. Now, more than ever, the world needs you to lead. And I will be by your side, clearing the path for all those who dare to doubt the mighty Szélhámos."

Salt dripped down my cheeks as I beheld the male I'd first hated, then loved with reckless abandon. Who I craved with shameless desire. Whose reverence left me breathless.

Because he was right. He *saw* me.

I was no longer the abused wife of a sycophantic Kormánzó.

I had eyes of devious burgundy. Magic that allowed me to become an Imposter.

I was the change. The symbol. The power.

"I am the Szélhámos," I breathed, my honorific speaking into existence the riot of emotion inside me.

"Yes, you are." His voice was tumbling ebony. "My perfect mate. My equal in fire and fury. And always," his mouth closed over mine for the briefest of moments. "Always mine."

Rokath devoured me with the obsession of a male possessed. His craving insatiable as his tongue slid against mine. A growl vibrated in his chest as he yanked me flush, fingers digging into my hips with beautiful brutality.

I welcomed it. Breathed him in. Drank him down.

Because he was right—the path to pure peace was not one beneath the sun. It would be clawed through darkness. With Demon society in upheaval, with the battles still to come, with the Angels still determined to exterminate us, the end would not be easy.

But despite all that, Rokath and I had defied death. We'd lived through what had killed so many. And someday, long after the war had been laid to rest, the world would know our names. Not as rulers of realms, but as mates made for war and peace.

Rokath lifted me, and I wrapped my legs around his waist as he walked us into the dark overhang, away from prying eyes and pounding boots. Ink spilled out of him to further hide us from view as he lay me back against the rock. Still our lips did not part, even as he removed his bloodsoaked armor and mine.

The chilled air dusted my skin in pebbles, but the heat of my mate soon banished them. With a groan, he slid inside me, and that perfect ache between my thighs bloomed from his thick length.

Our eyes locked. Our breaths synced. Each thrust brought me closer to the edge of ecstasy.

We needed no words, not when our bond conveyed every emotion, every thought, every burst of pleasure.

"Rokath," I breathed, my head tipping back as he hit that spot deep inside me. His teeth raked over my pulse point, and I dug my nails into his back, clutching the male who would never leave me. "My perfect mate."

Approval rumbled in his chest. He fucked me harder, little stones digging into my flesh, bringing the bite of pain I needed with my pleasure. His cock thickened inside me. My center pulsed around him.

And then, beneath a frosted canopy, we came together— shadow-cloaked, battle-worn, and *alive*. In the ashes of what we'd flamed, in the breath between battles, we did the most dangerous thing two people could do in the midst of war.

We chose to love.

💀💀💀💀💀

You didn't think I'd give you all the answers to An Age of War and Prophecy at the end of this book, did you?

The war is far from over. The lies run deeper than you can imagine. And the ones who waited on the fringes in the Death-caller Duet?

Some of them are already sharpening their knives.

Power never disappears; it *rearranges*.

Loyalties will fracture. Blood will spill.

The truth?

The end will ruin someone. Maybe more than one...

So step carefully into **And So The Breaking Begins.**

The betrayals are just getting started.

The first chapter waits for you on the next page.

And So The Breaking Begins is out now!

If you enjoyed Horns of Wicked Ebony, please consider rating or reviewing on Amazon, Goodreads, BookBub, or any other platform you prefer to use! Your support means everything, and taking a few moments of your time to let others know how much you liked the book is appreciated.

Not ready to say goodbye yet?
Grab your bonus epilogue here.

Signed Special Editions, Merch, & Audiobooks:
www.laceylehotzky.com

Where to connect with Lacey:
Instagram - @laceylehotzkyauthor
TikTok - @laceylehotzkyauthor
Discord - Lacey's Insidious Blooms
Facebook - Lacey's Insidious Blooms
Goodreads - Lacey Lehotzky
Amazon - Lacey Lehotzky
Pinterest - Lacey Lehotzky

SYLAIRA

The first time I Saw my fated mate, I was only one hundred and eleven. Too young for my power to have taken root. Far too young to have my heart shattered into a thousand pieces with the knowledge that if he ever found me, he'd rob me of everything I dared love.

Unlike most Angels, his hair was an iron gray. His brows, so serious, with one jagged scar, were a dark contrast to the glacial hue of the orbs beneath them. I knew not who he was, only that his gaze pierced my defenses and choked me of air.

I'd returned to reality screaming into the darkness.

I never wanted to meet him.

Whoever he was.

Sight was supposed to be the holiest blessing from the Goddess. I thought it was a curse.

And my fated mate?

He'd only finalize the doom that our deity had started upon blessing me with irises in an icy shade of blue—the most powerful color among the Angels.

"Sylaira," Heraphia hissed, drawing me out of the haze of anger and back to reality.

I started, hand slipping and nearly cutting myself with the sharp scrub brush. The skillet I'd been cleaning had a deep gouge from the force of my actions. "Sorry," I murmured, dropping both into the washbasin. Water sloshed, frothing the soap bubbles and wafting citrus into the air. I turned to face my oldest friend, shoulders slumping inward—only to find aquamarine eyes wide with fright and scouring mine.

My heart leaped into my throat. "What's happened?"

Heraphia swallowed, a hand hovering over her heart. "I think we need to move."

I took a tentative step forward, the dishes forgotten. "Have you had a vision?"

Like me, Heraphia was *blessed* with Sight. Her eye color was only a shade weaker than my own, which made her—both of us —a great prize for the rulers of the Angels. For decades, we'd hidden from the crown. The Koron and Korona wanted the Seers to wield like weapons of war.

I wanted no part in their violence. In their bloodshed. They called the loss of life Goddess-sanctioned, but it was ritualized slaughter. The mere thought of all the broken bodies I'd Seen brought bile up from my stomach. I'd spent my life among the Elessarum, and I'd do whatever it took to ensure my hands remained unstained by ruby.

Except See.

Which was why I consumed virelthorn like it was the air I needed to breathe.

"Yes," she whispered, her voice shivering despite the heat of the summer. Heraphia didn't take the herb to suppress her visions. Three times now, a flash of the future had come a day before hunters for the Korona. Three times now, she'd saved us from being snatched from our beds in the middle of the night.

"When?" I pressed, dread drowning my veins. We'd only just settled in here. But the bounty for reporting members of our peaceful group had doubled since the Demons invaded the Angel's sovereign territory the previous winter. The army had beaten them back, but the current peace was tenuous at best. It was only a matter of time before the two realms, positioned on either side of the Skala Mountains, clashed again.

It had been ten brutal years, to say the least.

She shook her head. "I don't know. It happened so quickly. Maybe it was nothing…" Heraphia trailed off, her teeth sinking into her lower lip as she gazed out the window behind me.

I grasped her hands and gave them a reassuring squeeze. "If you think we should go, then we will go. What did Zuriel say?"

She sighed. "He isn't back yet. That's why I came straight to you."

I glanced behind me at the stack of unwashed dishes. "Okay, here's the plan. Alert the others. I'll finish up here. We'll be packed and ready by the time he returns."

Our group of peace-lovers was scarcely more than twenty these days. Two years ago, an Elessarum stronghold had been raided, during which my parents had been slain. After the massive loss of life, we'd kept to smaller numbers, hoping to remain unnoticed among the myriad of merchants coming and going.

Zuriel, having been born to one of the noble houses of the Angel Realm, carried a regal air that was unmistakable. Perhaps he'd been spotted in the village and someone had alerted the local hunters, which had triggered his wife's latest vision.

Whatever the case, if she sensed it was time to move on, it was time to move on.

"Do you need me to pack your bags?" Heraphia asked, dropping my hands and stepping back.

"If you can." I offered her a sad half-smile. "There shouldn't be much to put away. Haven't had much time to unpack."

Anguish twisted her lips. "I know. I'm sorry."

"Hey, hey, it's not your fault. You are always protecting us," I said, yanking her into a warm embrace. I rubbed my hands over her back, trying to soothe the ache of having to move on so soon. We relied on her to keep us safe, a fact that made me feel guilty more often than not. But I couldn't bring myself to come off the herb and allow myself to fall into the horrors in my head.

"You're right," she hiccuped, and I released her. She dashed her cheeks with the backs of her wrists. "Okay, I'll go now. No time to waste."

"Go in peace," I told her.

"Always in peace," she replied. Then, she disappeared from the kitchen and into the long hall that led to the other rooms in the estate we'd rented.

Tears pricked my eyes the moment her skirt swished out of view. I held my breath for another ten seconds, stomping back toward the washbasin, and tried to stem the flow of salt so I could see what I was doing as I yanked another plate from the dirty pile.

But it was no use.

A sob choked out of me.

I was tired. So fucking tired. Of running. Of never having a place to call home. Of always looking over my shoulder. Of fearing a missed dose of virelthorn. Of the encroaching darkness that came with a vision.

Bitterness bloomed on my tongue. I stuck it in the side of my cheek and tried to ground myself.

Movement out the window caught my eye. A horse galloped toward the house, dirt flying beneath its hooves. The lake that curved against the road glittered in the midmorning sun, a gilding over the panic in the rider's expression.

The plate I'd been holding shattered, the crack ripping my gaze away from my best friend's husband and snapping it back to what my hands were doing. In my bones, I knew there was no time.

"Heraphia!" I yelled, backing away from the window. My fingers flew to the pockets of my skirts, searching for those precious bottles of virelthorn. I yanked one free, finding it half empty.

Fuck. We hadn't been here long enough for me to harvest more. But I had a few spares in my bag...

Spinning on my heel, I raced into the hall, nearly colliding with my friend.

"What is it?" Hair had come loose from her long, pearlescent braid in the minutes we'd been separated, a testament to the terror she'd masked before.

"They're coming," I gasped out, spotting my pack in her grip. I snatched it without apology. We'd done this often enough that niceties were not expected, not when every second mattered in escaping a fate worse than death.

She shouldered past me as I dug into my belongings. My hand closed around the cool glass vials, only offering me a modicum of relief. Without care for propriety, I ripped my skirt off and shoved it inside. The tights beneath were far more conducive to sprinting.

Chaos crescendoed in the halls as Heraphia shouted a warning and pleaded with everyone to hurry. I ducked and dodged members of the Elessarum as I wove toward the front door. Flinging it open, I found Zuriel a breath from busting it down.

"The hunters are coming," he gasped out, chest heaving. "Where is Heraphia?"

"Here!" she called out, emerging into the sun. She tossed Zuriel's pack to him. He caught it with a loud smack and slung it over his shoulders in one smooth motion.

"We can't wait for the others. We have to go. Now." His

normally measured, calm voice was anything but. "Korona Iaoth sent her best forces after us."

"You don't mean..." I trailed off, unable to finish the thought.

"That her brother is among them?" Zuriel gritted out, grabbing our arms and tugging us along toward the nearest copse of trees. "The Issaraeth is here, and if he uses his Command power, we'll all be his hostages before high sun."

Heraphia gasped, clutching her forehead like she could prevent him from breaking her mind and bending it to his will with a single, forceful word.

The Issaraeth was the most feared of all the Elessarum hunters. *He* was responsible for the death of my parents during the stronghold's raid. Or so I'd been told. I'd never so much as glimpsed him, which counted me among the lucky ones.

His presence dug a chill into the marrow of my bones.

"We have to warn the others!" I protested, digging my heels in.

Zuriel dragged me a few paces, churning up soft earth, before he halted and gave my arm a vicious jerk. "Do you want to be forced to See until you die, Sylaira? If they capture you and Heraphia, you'll never escape."

"But they'll suffer too!" I ground out, yanking my arm out of his hold. Most of them had irises in weaker shades of blue, and the lone Illusionist couldn't conceal them on her own.

"They have to take their chances," he shot back, a muscle jumping in his jaw like it too was impatient to flee. "Both of your visions are too powerful. Too frequent. I won't let that happen to my wife. Or you."

Heraphia bolted, her feet a frantic beat against the grass. Her pack bounced against her back, overfull. Just like me, her skirts were gone, aiding her escape. "Come on!"

Guilt gnawed at my gut. Zuriel was right. If I wanted to

maintain my freedom—what little I had—we needed to go. Now.

Black horses surged through the thick trunks of the forest. White frothed against their bits, their riders leaning low in the saddles. Bridles gleamed with polished gems and silver adornments.

Tingles spread from my scalp to the tips of my toes.

Zuriel hadn't been lying. The royal hunters were here.

A fleeing couple cried out, light magic exploding from them in an attempt to shield themselves against the oncoming group.

One horse reared, his scream echoing through the clearing. His rider gripped his long, black mane, mouth set into a firm, furious line.

My hand flew to my throat. My vision tunneled into a single pinprick, focused solely on the male I'd seen far too many times—but only ever in the torturous throes of my power.

Iron-gray hair. Scarred brow. Eyes colder than a glacier.

I couldn't breathe.

I couldn't coerce my feet into unsticking from the ground. Horror had pierced my toes to the soft grass beneath my feet.

No. No. No. Please no. It can't be him...

The lake shimmered beside him. But to me, it was a mirror shattering. A thousand shards of my fate. Glittering. Falling. Too late to catch.

After all this time, I finally knew who my mate was.

The male who haunted countless visions. Who drove me to drug my mind into silence.

The male the Goddess cursed to be mine.

The Issaraeth.

And so the breaking began.

Order And So The Breaking Begins now

AUTHOR'S NOTE

One of my main goals in writing this duet was to explore the way belief—personal, political, and religious—shapes entire societies. Propaganda is merely a story told with enough conviction and emotion that it becomes truth. It can create massive change—both divine and detrimental.

"For those who stubbornly seek freedom, there can be no more urgent task than to come to understand the mechanisms and practices of indoctrination." —Noam Chomsky

Assyria desperately seeks both truth and freedom. And Rokath, the fierce warlord, cracks his carefully crafted facade and confronts long-buried truths that have haunted him.

Along the way, the Deathcaller Duet became more than an exploration of belief. It evolved into an excavation of identity, legacy, rage, and reclamation.

In its soul, it's a story of two people who fought their way toward a future they weren't supposed to have but claimed it anyway.

Assyria and Rokath are warriors, yes, but not only on battle-fields. They clawed their way out of trauma—hers born of systemic oppression, his from violent bloodlines—and still, they found a way to love. To let that love hunt vengeance. To let it become healing.

Rokath chose to make space for Assyria's rise. Assyria chose to trust that Rokath wouldn't turn away when she grew thorned and wild. They chose each other, over and over. Even when it hurt.

Through them, I found new pieces of myself.

Assyria taught me that rage can be righteous. That grief is love's echo. That softness is not surrender. That it's okay to let someone hold you when you're breaking.

Rokath reminded me that devotion can be fierce and undying, and that when someone offers to protect you—not to control, not to cage, but protect—you can let them.

This story is for anyone who has ever been trapped against their will, choked on silence, or told they were too much. It's for those who bled to break free.

I hope one day you find someone whose love is raw, sacred, and unquestionable.

The war isn't over. But I promise you this: Rokath and Assyria find peace. Their story continues, and you'll see them again woven into the threads of future stories in An Age of War and Prophecy.

Until then, be the devious eyes who see through the lies. Let them call you wicked for it.

Acknowledgments

First and foremost, thank YOU for continuing Rokath and Assyria's story. I've loved nothing more than reading comments on my socials from people who were absolutely feral for Horns of Wicked Ebony after the ending of Eyes of Devious Burgundy. I hope this ripped your heart out, made you throw your book, and giggle and squeal the whole way through.

To my betas and editors—Courtney, Sierra, Thea, Kristina, Kat—thank you for your thoughtful feedback and helping me bring home their story. I couldn't do this without you guys!

To my ARC readers & bookish creators—thank you for continuing to share about Eyes of Devious Burgundy and screaming about Horns of Wicked Ebony up to release day! Word of mouth recommendations are still the best exposure for books, especially as an indie author. I appreciate you!

To Amarah and Sam—You guys are my lifeline. Our sprints got me through the toughest chapters. Thank you for telling me how to spell things. Thank you for all the laughs. Thank you for helping me shape this story into the epic masterpiece I wanted it to be.

To my author friends and group chats—S7, WBF, HL, Logan, Emily, Nicole, Briar, Rachel, Lauren, Ella, and so many others, I love being coworkers with you. Thanks for all the helpful advice and support when times get tough.

To friends & friends that are like family—thank you for all the patience and support as I navigate this new chapter of my life, being a full time author! I'll try to leave the house more and stop working earlier... maybe.

To Beholden Book Covers—not only are you an amazing artist, but I am so lucky to call you my friend. I love our voice notes and that our brains are in sync on designs. Horns is your best one yet.

To Harry Osborn & Ryan Montigny—thank you for the amazing helmet designs for the cover. You brought my vision to life perfectly!

And finally to my fated mate—Andrew, our lives this past year have been rough, but there's no one I would rather struggle with than you. Thank you for always protecting us. Thank you for holding space for me while I cried over this story. Thank you for always believing in me. Thank you for helping me bloom.

About the Author

Lacey Lehotzky is an international bestselling author, photographer, and Brazilian Jiu Jitsu enthusiast. She is most often found with her nose in a book when she isn't training to be a fighter like her main characters. Lacey has her best ideas while traveling, where she finds inspiration for people and places in her books. She especially loves exploring the darker side of life, writing characters with deep flaws and even deeper trauma while ripping her reader's hearts out and leaving them begging for more.